The Abyss line of cutting-edge psychological horror is committed to publishing the best, most innovative works of dark fiction available. ABYSS is horror unlike anything you've ever read before. It's not about haunted houses or evil children or ancient Indian burial grounds. We've all read those books, and we all know their plots by heart.

ABYSS is for the seeker of truth, no matter how disturbing or twisted it may be. It's about people, and the darkness we all carry within us. ABYSS is the new horror from the dark frontier. And in that place, where we come face-to-face with terror, what we find is ourselves.

"Thank you for introducing me to the remarkable line of novels currently being issued under Dell's Abyss imprint. I have given a great many blurbs over the last twelve years or so, but this one marks two first: first *unsolicited* blurb (*I* called *you*) and the first time I have blurbed a whole *line* of books. In terms of quality, production, and plain old story-telling reliability (that's the bottom line, isn't it?), Dell's new line is amazingly satisfying . . . a rare and wonderful bargain for readers. I hope to be looking into the Abyss for a long time to come."

—Stephen King

TURN THE PAGE FOR MORE QUOTES

OASIS AND *DARK ADVENT*

"YOU'LL BE PLENTY ABSORBED . . . Hodge once again plays by the rules—but with a frightening catch. His characters breathe and his prose is chilling and crisp."
—*West Coast Review of Books*

"FINE DEGREES OF NUANCE AND SHADING . . . Hodge's knack is in invoking sympathy for his characters. He draws on a talented mix of humor and suspense to entertain. It makes for compelling style. His writing races ahead . . . carrying the reader along."
—*Deathrealm*

"HODGE KEEPS THE READER'S INTEREST. . . . He writes well, he is adept at both atmosphere and action, and his sense of story is good."
—*Fangoria*

"NEVER PREDICTABLE, NEVER BORING, AND NOT AT ALL EASY TO PUT DOWN . . . a fresh style that makes for a very enjoyable and often surprising read."
—*New Blood*

"HIS VOICE IS STRAIGHTFORWARD AND DOWN-TO-EARTH, HIS STORIES ARE ABOUT REAL PEOPLE, HIS WRITING IS HONEST . . . HIS MANY READERS CAN EXPECT TO HEAR MUCH MORE FROM HIM IN THE FUTURE."
—*The Horror Show*

DEATH GRIP

BRIAN HODGE

A DELL BOOK

Published by
Dell Publishing
a division of
Bantam Doubleday Dell Publishing Group, Inc.
666 Fifth Avenue
New York, New York 10103

ISBN: 0-440-21112-3

Printed in the United States of America

Published simultaneously in Canada

June 1992

10 9 8 7 6 5 4 3 2 1

OPM

For two friends, one old, one new,
one here and one departed:
Gerald Mayo,
pilot of the airwaves;
and
Ray Rexer,
July 29, 1953–April 27, 1991.
No man is an island . . .
but a few are peninsulas.

ACKNOWLEDGMENTS

Man, this page just gets longer every time out. To the following people, many of whom answered some of the weirdest questions imaginable, go heartfelt thanks:

My agent Lori Perkins and editor Jeanne Cavelos, for being such skilled, astute, dependable, and pleasant partners to deal with.

For electronic media insights: Tom and Jerry, Weasel, Ebes, and Brett Blume, personnel past and present of WMIX-AM/FM; Ron Hamburg, Robert E. Carter, and Earl Flanigan of WSIL-TV.

For medical information and other ooky tidbits about our bodies and minds: Jeff Hamilton, R.N. C.E.N.; Keith Backes, R.T.; Dave Griffith, R.P.T.; Susan Coady, R.P.T.; Anita Bauer, O.T.R./L; Joe Wilks, R.Ph.; and Charlie Hughey.

For photography pointers, Dan Ober; for oil refinery info, Caroline Quinn. And major undying gratitude to Dick Sanders for the Macintosh loaner while waiting for Apple to catch up with demand.

Ah, might as well throw in the music of Skinny Puppy, Nine Inch Nails, and Fields of the Nephilim, for fueling inspiration and imagery during the hard parts.

And thanks and love to the usual circle for sanity of one form or another: Mum and Dad, Dolly, Clark, Beth, Wayne, Yvonne, Jeff, Joan, and Bill. Buy me a beer, and you too can end up on this page next time!

When we peruse the first histories of all nations, we are apt to imagine ourselves transported into some new world; where the whole frame of nature is disjointed, and every element performs its operations in a different manner, from what it does at present. Battles, revolutions, pestilence, famine and death, are never the effect of those natural causes, which we experience. Prodigies, omens, oracles, judgments, quite obscure the few natural events that are intermingled with them.

—David Hume

Men think epilepsy divine, merely because they do not understand it. But if they called everything divine which they do not understand, why, there would be no end of divine things.

—Hippocrates

Friday, November 22, 1963/Chicago

In the years to come, nearly everyone who had struggled through childhood would remember exactly where they were, what they were doing, when they first heard the news. Carmine would, no question. He had, just minutes before, rolled his cab curbside for the first of the day's two most memorable fares.

Midafternoon, and the remaining hours of his shift could be measured in miles. Miles without end, these traffic-choked streets that had become his lot in life. The drizzle was a royal pain, too, slickening the pavement and making quick stops a frantic guessing game as to whether he'd slide into someone's back end. Or whether someone would do the same to him. Temperature in the sixties, humidity steaming his windows, and some days you just could not win.

All roads led home, eventually, though home was rarely more inviting; home, den of ear-splitting noise on Chicago's south side, domestic bedlam of four rooms in a third-floor walkup, hot and cold running cockroaches, and these days filled to capacity and beyond. Carmine Costelli. His wife, much too tired for love these days, even if privacy had been more than a dead dream. His wife's corpulent *mamma mia*, screeching harridan intent on becoming as broad as she was tall. And the brood of kids who shat their pants at every available opportunity and were becoming furniture climbers of near Everestial skill. Home sweet home.

But there was the bright side. America, hotbed of dreams and opportunity. His grandparents had crossed the Atlantic in steerage to get here. Kingdoms of gold could stand on foundations of sweat, or so Carmine had been told, and he figured his sweat was as good as anyone's. The man in the White House made him feel that way, assurances, some grand and glorious new road just around the corner. And if not that one, then perhaps the next.

Dreams of a better tomorrow. You could lose yourself in them sometimes. Never want to come back.

He picked up the old guy on Michigan Avenue, this slight, tautly smiling fellow hailing him from the curb. Dapper, in a seedy sort of way. No topcoat against the drizzling rain, only a dark pinstripe suit, old but well-kept. A silver watch chain looped against his vest, visible when a gusty wind flapped at his jacket. Pink scalp gleamed like a dome rising from the monk's fringe of white hair. A closely trimmed beard of the same color, threaded with nicotine stains.

Carmine would always remember his eyes the most. Eyes of a fallen saint, martyr without a cause.

The old man ducked his head while entering the cab, mouth twisting into a pained grimace to reveal teeth as stained as his beard. He settled comfortably into the back, slammed the door like a man in a hurry.

"See those men back there?" He pointed out the back window.

Carmine looked, said he did. Two of them, suits and long topcoats —none too cheap, visible quality even at thirty yards—and they were coming along in a hurry.

"Lose them for me? Please?"

With a lurch and a squeak of rubber, Carmine was back in the thick of it all. Meter activated with one fell swoop of his arm. He laughed softly, shaking his head in disbelief.

"You're kidding, right? Six years I been driving, not once does anybody *ever* ask me to lose a tail."

No answer, so Carmine shut up. Leave the old guy to his own problems or his own fantasies, whichever. After another few moments, Carmine heard what sounded like the rattle of pills from a plastic bottle. He angled his head to peek into the rearview, timeless cabbie tradition. Some of the things you saw were not to be believed. Nothing much this time, only the old man popping his hand to his mouth. The pills went down dry, harsh.

He had the regular radio tuned to WBBM, volume low so it didn't override the dispatch. There flickered a momentary compulsion to up its volume, but he didn't. After another moment, his new fare was humming. Catchy, vaguely familiar. Something classical, Carmine thought, but he could pin it down no closer.

"What's that you're humming?" Curiosity had gotten the better of him. Bad habit. You really should leave people alone if they don't look like talkers.

"Beethoven. *Ninth Symphony.* 'Ode to Joy.'" A wry, twisted little smile. No joy there, more like irony. "I appreciate a good joke now and then."

Carmine frowned. Something wrong with this man.

"I decided today," the fellow continued, "that it's time for me to retire from what is very probably the worst job in the world. You'd think I'd be happier about that. Wouldn't you?"

Carmine shrugged behind the wheel. Flicked a glance into the mirror, beyond the backseat this time. Any sign of the two alleged pursuers? Not really. More cabs, always more cabs, but none careening after them.

"I don't know," Carmine finally said. "You do something long enough, you miss it, you know? I got these kids, every time I turn around, one of them's dropped a big smelly load in his drawers. But when they grow out of that, what you want to bet I miss that, kind of." Shaking his head again, smiling. "Do something long enough, it becomes a part of you."

"Amen," the old man's voice sad, distant. Utterly lonely.

"So what was it you did all these years?"

"It was . . . a form of public relations in the medical field. I suppose that's the easiest way of saying it. I've kept on the move a lot." He withdrew his pills from a jacket pocket, regarded them a long moment before putting them back. A dreadful sigh, gazing dead-on into Carmine's mirrored eyes. "I . . . have done . . . some of the most ghastly things you can imagine."

Carmine studied him in the mirror a moment. This guy putting him on? No, he didn't think so. No. Those eyes, too serious, too hungry for something. Empathy, maybe. Or absolution. Bless me, driver, for I have sinned. Taxi hacks were probably third in line for such honors, right behind priests and bartenders.

"Never too late to change," Carmine said.

"For you, maybe." He leaned back then, sullen and silent, seemingly content to stare out the windows. And eat his pills like popcorn.

Carmine was starting to wish this ride was over. He sensed no danger from the fossil in his backseat, but every now and then, rare moments, a perceived threat was actually preferable to the all-out *strangeness* some people exuded. An attempted robbery could be dealt with, one way or another. All cards were on the table at times like that. But folks like this guy? They were worse, in a way. They lingered. They crawled beneath your skin and burrowed into memory, in that place to which you consign things you hope to forget and know you won't.

Carmine didn't even know where the guy wanted to go. Just driving aimlessly so far, taking corners at random. Maybe he should at least ask.

The radio, WBBM, soft and low. Loud enough, though. Some announcer, breaking through with a CBS News special bulletin.

And for Carmine, it may as well have been the end of the known world, and a lot left unexplored. *The man was dead.* That trailblazer on the horizon, that symbol of an entire nation's dreams. John F. Kennedy, dead of an assassin's bullet in Dallas.

Carmine stared past the windshield, stunned into something worse than silence. All of downtown Chicago and the entire world receding away, like lines converging into a vanishing point. The cab was driving itself. Somewhere out in the void, the sound of rolling tires and automobile horns and the tide of humanity. These masses who had sacrificed their brightest and best down in Dallas and didn't even know it yet.

The next thing he knew, tears were on his cheeks.

"Shot him dead. Huh. I'll be damned." The old man clucked his tongue, shook his head. "Now aren't some people wasteful."

Carmine blinked, the vast numbness inside making way just far enough for righteous bile. *How can you take this so calm? You got no idea what's happened, is that it?*

It was almost as if the old man had read his thoughts. "You know, in the overall scheme of events, this doesn't matter much. One man. It won't matter. No matter how great he was, or what he stood for. Because . . . if you only knew what else goes on in this world that hardly another soul knows about." He grimaced, shook his head. "But you're young. Maybe you'll learn that in time."

Carmine's knuckles were white against the steering wheel, tight enough to wring out old sweat. He was looking for a lifeline in this worst of all possible moments, something, anything. And all he had was the bleak philosophy spouted by this heartless old bastard too twisted by his own problems to care about anything else. No more. No more of *this*, at all. Get rid of him and that would be the first step in the right direction. He glided toward the curb, saw someone else needing a ride, hailing him with an umbrella. A young couple. More parasites, deaf and blind, wanting something from him. Closer . . . The woman was pregnant, the man had his arm on her shoulder.

All right. Perspective. For them he would stop. But first things first. . . .

"I want you out of my cab!" And damn the meter.

Tires squelching against the curb, the fat yellow taxi ground to a halt before the waiting couple. One moment of panic in the old man's eyes—the premature stop?—and then a look of hurried resignation. He reached into the pinstripe jacket to withdraw a thick envelope. Tossed it into the front, and it landed beside Carmine with a weighty thump.

"I'm not a bad sort, not really," and now he was very nearly grandfatherly. Patriarch of stoic misery. "I'm just a great deal unluckier than most. And sometimes . . .

"Sometimes I hate them for it."

He yanked the back door open, smiled at the expectant young couple. Looking as if the pregnant woman, in her bulging coat and dripping scarf, were the most delightful sight he had ever set eyes upon.

"Congratulations," pumping the hand of the father, who managed to look both proud and bewildered. "When's the due date?"

"In two more weeks," said the mother-to-be.

While the old man nodded, glancing at traffic behind them, inside the cab Carmine was checking the envelope. Unsure as to what sort of nonsense he would find inside. But even John Fitzgerald Kennedy's shattered skull faded from thought when he saw the stack of currency. Large denominations, lots of bills. Unbelievable. Just *unbelievable*.

Later, when thrice counted to account for nervously botching the job, the sum would total over six thousand dollars. Some tip.

Luck of the draw. You lose some, you win some.

"Allow me," the old man was saying to the father, releasing his hand and reaching for the woman's. "Chivalry is not *quite* dead in this day and age. Though rare is my opportunity to help a pretty young thing into a car."

The father managed a helpless shrug. Who would be so callous as to deny this dapper little old man such a simple pleasure? Quite the gentleman, he took her hand, holding the back of her upper arm in case she slipped. Her face, tired and faintly puffy, lit up when she smiled, flattered to no end. A fleeting, mischievous glance at her husband, marital semaphore, as if to say, *See? You could learn something from this man.*

The old fellow leaned in after her, doting, making sure she was comfortable, treating her as he might a daughter rather than a stranger whose name he would never know.

His hand lingered atop hers for another moment. And for the slightest instant, Carmine could see that she suddenly feared that intimate touch, in some small way, and she drained of color.

The old man, now straightening, watching the father get in. Smiling wide-eyed in what looked like nothing so much as relief, as if this day of gray drizzle and national tragedy were the sunniest in memory. A patented Chicago gust drove darts of rain into his face, cycloned through what remained of his hair.

The mother, looking at her hand, mesmerized, slowly flexing her fingers . . .

"You take good care of that baby." A tender curmudgeon's warning, given for all the right reasons. "He'll be a fine one, I bet."

The father perked up in his seat, just in time to see the door slam in his face. *"He?"* the father said, but the old man was merely peering in through the glass, waving good-bye with waggling fingers as the taxi pulled away. And then, that final glimpse of him, standing at curbside, attention quickly drawn by the sudden arrival of another cab. Turning crisply, starting to run into the flow of foot traffic. A man who wished nothing so much as to simply lose himself. Carmine had seen that look plenty of times.

But, running *from* something . . . or *to* it?

And who really cared, anyway?

It was another block before Carmine could touch base with the real world again. He swiveled his head back, topical conversation, had they heard already, had they heard the news from Dallas? No, no they hadn't, dear lord, how *awful.* And then, from the mother, a sound with which he was already so very well acquainted. *She was going into labor.* No false alarm, this one, he knew from the tone. This was the real thing. It came clear up from her toes.

Some wild day, was all he could numbly say to himself. Maps unfurling in his head, plotting mental routes. Northwestern Memorial would be the closest hospital. *Some kind of wild day.*

Stranger in a strange land, yes, the old man was all that and more. Albert Meerschaum was relatively new to Chicago; this Near North Side neighborhood was foreign and familiar in the same glance. The streets and their unfamiliar names, the buildings and businesses that were much the same as anywhere else he had wandered in the city. That comforting sprawl of metropolitan anonymity.

The clatter of footsteps on wet pavement behind him. Just wouldn't let him rest, would they? Ever. The fear, the awe . . . These were abundant. Compassion? This was something else entirely. He gave them something to chase; he moved swiftly for his age.

I never asked for that thing. Never asked at all. Bastards just never could seem to get that through their heads.

He could at least give them a ferocious surprise, that much he *could* do now. Now that the burden on body and soul had been lifted. A curious feeling, the elation and the sorrow. So very bittersweet.

Urban familiarity. He slipped through the stream of afternoon walkers like a man on the most final of missions, and knew what to do when he saw the El sign. Grinning over his shoulder at the two men quickstepping behind him, he ducked between a pair of people wearing slick wet raincoats, and up the stairs he went. The handrail felt wonderfully chilly beneath his palm. Albert was feeling things in a long unfamiliar way, a new being. An *ordinary* being.

Up the stairs, feet sure of purpose. Even from here he could feel the rumble of an approaching elevated train. One of the delights of the city, always that next train coming along.

They followed, of course. They always followed.

He joined the others on the platform, wind in his face, gentle rain in his eyes. Saw the nose of the coming train, a block away and ratcheting along the tracks, sure as death and taxes. Its perverse beauty was not unappreciated. Albert gently nudged his way forward through the gathering crowd, as if eager to be the first to board. With a bitter grin he noticed that he had kept his hands stuffed into his pockets while wriggling through the crowd. Old habit, ingrained over the decades. Such were the hardest of all to die.

The train, coming, platform trembling underfoot . . .

Tweedledee and Tweedledum had pressed in close behind him. He knew it without looking, felt them there, their passage through the crowd.

"Come on, Albert, please. Don't be this way. If you need to talk, we've got all the time in the world." This from the stouter of the two, the American.

He found it easier to ignore them now. Secrets bred smugness.

"Albert." This one more stern, exasperated, the tall Brit. Gavin. "You're behaving like a loon. This helps no one, you know."

Albert sighed. Of the two of them, he had liked Gavin more. Gavin the pragmatist, Gavin the realist. Gavin, who was upfront and didn't wheedle about like that other mealy-mouth. Give me a man who speaks the truth, any day. Even if his concept of truth is distorted.

Albert turned, pulled a hand from his pocket. They flinched, and it was not a gratifying thing to see. Even if it meant they did not suspect him of having left everything behind in that taxi. He reached into his jacket pocket and produced the small bottle of morphine tablets.

"A present for you, Gavin," and he pressed it into the young man's hand. Grimly smiled while watching the sudden realization spread across that long British face.

As fitting a final utterance as any.

The train, roaring toward the platform . . .

Albert jumped. Retirement day, indeed.

There was little to see, nothing to hear. A life, there, then gone. The train hid all. Down below, through the steel beams and girders, there would be the red drizzle. But up on the platform, little beyond the rippling horror of an aghast crowd. It took something like this to punch through their facades. Something like this, or news from Dallas.

They eased away, these last two who had known Albert Meerschaum by name. Numb tread toward the far back of the platform while the others up front craned their necks for a glimpse of carnage. Something to tell at the family dinner table.

"Oh bloody hell," Gavin murmured, gazing out toward the street from which Albert had come. All those people, all that traffic. *Taxis.*

He saw one pass by, identical to hundreds. Thousands, perhaps. He followed it into the distance, until its roof was but one more panel of metal among a hundred others.

"Oh bloody hell."

I
Consecration

We need heretics, not because of their teaching, but because they stimulate us . . . in our search for truth and for a proper understanding of everything in the world.

—Peter Lombard

1

"You want to avoid trouble? I'll tell you how to avoid trouble," said the man in the booth. "Leave that dial tuned to KGRM—the *only* radio station in St. Louis registered by the FCC as a lethal weapon." Then, to prove the point, he dipped into the wellspring of classics, 1973, Alice Cooper's "No More Mister Nice Guy."

The man in the booth was also sounding more than a little stuffy today. Must be one tough virus indeed making the rounds; Peter Hargrove's normally smooth tenor sounded funneled through a sock. Paul watched through a four-by-six-foot window—aquarium for deejays—and he could sympathize. Riding the airwaves when your head felt like a rotten melon was no fun.

Paul Handler leaned against the corridor wall to wait out the hiatus, one foot unconsciously keeping time with the music. Peter noticed him from inside the booth, gave a good morning salute, then throttled his own nose with an anguished grimace. He was then joined on-air by the station's program director, David Blane, he of diminutive stature, whose Sominex voice had earned him the nickname of Captain Quaalude. David held the dead-of-night shift until Peter took over at six A.M., then hung around until midmorning. A few moments of on-air banter, and then it came time for holy ritual. Stump The Captain.

The routine never varied, only the questions. David Blane, walking encyclopedia of arcane musicana, taunting Peter Hargrove into asking some obscure question. A case of import beer was eternally on the line. Captain Quaalude would feign stumbles and stammers over a tape of some local band doing a jangling rave-up rendition of the theme from *Jeopardy*. Out would pop the answer, and Peter Hargrove would take his lumps with heroic stoicism. Five mornings per week, two-plus years this had been going on, and the Captain had not been stumped once. Peter vowed an inferiority complex was due to set in any day.

KGRM, 92.5 on the FM dial, had been Paul's secondary home for the past seven months. His favorite so far in a career that was but seven years old, a veteran's span in deejay terms. He had been a defector from a larger St. Louis station, where he'd been the junior inmate in a three-man Morning Madhouse team, nearly a year of hurling quips and barbs, spinning generally heavy discs, and racking up respectable ratings. Then a format change, the great scourge of the radio industry, reared its ugly head. A move calculated to make the station better appeal to a more upscale, slightly older, more affluent target audience. St. Louis Urban Professionals. The jocks called them slurpies.

Loss of soul was always sad. The station's powerhouse sound degenerated into 100,000 watts of milk toast, and Paul abandoned ship, coaxing a sizable portion of his audience with him to KGRM. The rebel station, one of the last outlaw frontiers for music and personalities beyond the fringe. At last. He was home.

The move had entailed a shift out of St. Louis proper into the Central West End adjacent suburb of University City, so named for nearby institutions of higher learning. Easygoing blend of residential, commercial, and campus areas, an arty tidal pool beside the larger urban sea of St. Louis. The nonconformist could always find a niche here. Paul liked it so much he moved to an apartment within walking distance of the station. Spending just as much time there as ever, KGRM, top floor of a limestone office building, a paradox of tasteful decor, pastel walls, sedate hanging planters, and high-intensity music.

Stump The Captain, predictably, ended with Peter's ritual humiliation. David Blane, a bounce to his step, vacated the booth and gave Paul a high five. A silent swinging door deposited Paul inside the eight-by-ten haven. It was crammed with hardware and music, with little excess room. Peter had cued up a bizarre offering from Alien Sex Fiend titled "Now I'm Feeling Zombified" in honor of his head cold.

"You sound awful today." Paul pinched his nostrils shut to imitate Peter. "There go the Arbitrons."

Peter tugged off his padded headphones, slid down the booth speakers' volume. He wearily shook his head and pitched a plastic bottle of nasal spray into the trash.

"I miss the old days," he said. "Payola. A record rep drops off some new album he wants you to play, and there's a packet of cocaine inside. We never sounded like we had colds then."

Paul nodded, sympathetic to the cause. "Compact discs killed everything."

Peter leaned back into the swivel seat before the mike. Tight fit. First-time station visitors looked at him, thought no way, this could *not* be the source of that tenor voice. Peter stood well over six feet, with generous helpings of both fat and muscle. Black beard and bushy eyebrows, Rasputin reincarnated as a disc jockey.

He busied himself loading the next tune while Paul flipped through new arrivals of promo albums, UPS delivery. A generally democratic system, they would all be voted on by station air staff as keepers or trade-ins at the used music stores in the area. When the Alien Sex Fiend faded out, Peter replaced his headphones and back-announced the song while waving Paul closer.

"Wicked Uncle Pete knows when to send out for help, you've got to give me that much credit," he said into the mike. "With me now is Lethal Rock Radio's cleanest-living soul, the lovely and talented Paul Handler."

"Lovely and talented, who could argue there? But that cleanest-living thing, you know, that's still under scrutiny."

"A few minutes ago, I see him walk in, I realize now here's a man who just might be able to drive those summer cold demons right out of my skull."

Paul cocked his head, an uncertain grin. *Whaaat?*

Peter rolled his hand, go with it, go with it. "Always a groundbreaker, always innovative, KGRM is proud to bring St. Louis another radio first: an actual laying on of hands done live over the air."

Paul, consummate professional, shifted directly into improvisational mode. He leaned in closer and stuck one hand on the front of Peter's head. When he spoke, his voice came out as dry and analytical as if he were describing a putt at a golf tournament.

"Yes, I'm in position now, and my hands *are* in place. I might add at this point that Mister Hargrove could benefit from a new shampoo."

Peter rolled his eyes and scowled. Fearsome.

"Yessss, brotherrr," Paul suddenly crooned in a nasal parody of every southern evangelist who had ever pounded a fundamentalist pulpit. "Do ya believe I have the POWER to expel that EEEVIL summer cold demon out of your skull?"

"Oh yes, I do!" Peter cried, hands aflutter.

"Dew ya BELIEEEVE, I said!"

"I do! I do!" Enraptured, Peter clutched his heart and rolled his eyes in full socket perimeter.

"Then FEEL the power of ray-diooo! I say, FEEEEL the power!"

"I can feel it, brother, I can feel it!"

The adrenaline charge was flowing now, the high of working directly before that unseen audience, tens of thousands, treading the tightrope with neither script nor safety net.

"Stick yer hands inside that control board and FEEL the power of ray-dio. It'll shock yer ass across the station, yes indeed!" Under his hand, Peter quivered in spasms, face turning a lusty tomato red as he held in an explosive laugh. "Then by the power vested in me by the FCC, I hereby command that FIFTY THOUSAND WATTS come down from our tower and CLEANSE this poor suffering wreck of humanity. Out, demon, OUT!"

Peter swiveled in his chair and charged the microphone. He threw his head back, *aaahed* once, twice, then blasted the mike with a fake sneeze, all the buildup and blowout of a hurricane.

"Hallelujah!" Peter cried, and launched the next song. AC/DC's "Highway to Hell." Fuck 'em if they can't take a joke.

Peter unslung his headphones again as Paul stumbled back to the wall and slid to the floor. The laughter was too much, just too much. Catharsis. Paul's shoulder sent the trash can spinning across the floor, inspiring further hilarity at the spewed paper and soda cans, and his legs wavered in the air.

"We got to take that on the road, bud. We—"

Peter clammed up in a hurry. The normally silent swivel door burst inward, put them face to face with a man who looked as if he might once have been a pear that sprouted arms and legs. Then gone into management. Vince Atkins, station manager, in all his glory. They called him Popeye; the laugh was the same, the build was antithesis. His cheeks flamed with anger, or the exertion of having walked from his office. Perhaps both.

"Do you have any idea," his voice low, deadly, and Paul immediately knew visitors were in the wings preventing a more vivid display of temper, "that I'm trying to do business with some people out there who just might start pouring a shitpot of advertising dollars into this station? Some people from a Catholic hospital? And that one of them is a *nun*? I do *not* need a couple of witch doctors at this particular moment." Glaring, Vince opened his mouth once, twice, most likely trying to think of something else and finding nothing severe enough. Finally, the anticlimax: "Get out of the floor, Paul." He straightened jacket and tie and was gone.

Paul and his fellow shaman indulged in one more round of snickers, then he righted the waste can and finally himself.

"Well. Maybe it *was* a little blasphemous." Paul looked skyward, mouthed the word *sorry*.

"Fuck it. If Popeye thought it would raise revenue, he'd have us in here doing animal sacrifices and drinking goat's blood."

Peter wound out his shift with a slab of industrial paranoia from Nine Inch Nails, then announcing, "And I'm out of here like prunes through a nursing home." He surrendered the booth to Paul, while the news director commandeered the next few minutes of airtime from a separate booth. Paul used the lull to get set up: select a couple of opening songs, check the commercial log and locate their tape cartridges. From a wall shelf he grabbed his two indispensable totems: coffee mug with its logo of five interlocking rings and legend USA OLYMPIC MONGOLIAN CLUSTER FUCK TEAM, and a stuffed koala given to him by a college girlfriend when he'd graduated eight years ago.

Receptionist Sherry Thomason brought in the communal coffee pot so he could gas up, and jokes abounded as to how brown Popeye's nose got whenever potential clients visited. Sherry, blue and yellow sundress, dark hair in a French braid. Only a year or so out of high school; kiddie porn. All the male station jocks bemoaned the fact, and felt as protective of her as a younger sister who had blossomed too early. A switchboard light winked, and she left to take the call at her own desk.

Two minutes to eleven and counting. Paul blew on his coffee, sipped. Through the window looking in from the corridor he saw Popeye and his three VIPs. Another moment, and Peter came through the other way, probably having just vacated the bathroom. Vince introduced him around, all smiles and putrid phony charm, his public relations persona all the more obvious since Paul could not hear them through the glass. One of the visitors, a guy who

looked to be in his midthirties, around Peter's age, said something
to him. Peter nodded, said something back, a nod and a shrug. Body
language betrayed the entire exchange, Paul would have bet on it.

"You don't look the way you sound," this was what the guy had
said, surely. "That's not the way I had you pictured."

Most of them heard it, or variations, a lot. And after a while you
got to thinking that some of those loyal listeners would rather take
the dust and clay of the earth and make you over in their own
image. Public property, why not?

None of them looked the way they sounded, to Paul's eye and
ear. Peter's was the most glaring discrepancy between voice and
visage. David Blane looked like an undersize sculptor in a fine arts
high school and droned like a hypnotist. With a mop of blond hair
and a pristine tan, Lorraine Savage—Paul's afternoon successor—
looked as if she would be more at home waxing a surfboard on a
SoCal beach, while her street-smart air voice was as far removed
from expected Valley Girl diction as you could get.

And Paul Handler, lord of midday? He had always been happy
with the sound of his voice. Clear, vibrant, neither too high nor too
low. He was fully aware of a tendency to come off at times like a bit
of a smartass; blame late nights with David Letterman for that one.

Yet he could never settle on what looks his voice alone conjured
forth. Wasted time, the instances spent before the bathroom mirror
puzzling it over. A not unpleasant face stared back, but neither was
it arresting. Merely average. Oval, beneath thick eyebrows and dark
brown hair kept a little shaggier than what career counselors would
advise, with warm brown eyes he felt were his main salvation. An
average build and average height topped off the entire nondescript
ensemble.

News director Russell St. James wrapped up his allotted time,
fired his finger at Paul through a shared window. Passing the torch,
time to saddle up and ride the airwaves. Paul punched up his first
cartridge to unleash the sonic montage that served as his usual
opening. Light baroque strings evoking a PBS fine arts snoozefest,
rudely interrupted by a needle plowing across the surface of a
record into a screaming Hendrix guitar slide. Then a rapid-fire
mishmash of "The William Tell Overture," reverberated Porky Pig
stuttering, and a snippet of the demon-possessed Regan's voice
from *The Exorcist*.

"*Lock up your children and hide your sheep!*" he warned those
unseen thousands. "I'm Paul Handler, and I'm in your face for the

next four hours, right here at KGRM, FM ninety-two-point-five, Lethal Rock Radio, where music and madness collide. For all I know, they aren't even insured."

He sat like a jet pilot in the swivel seat, flying by the proverbial seat of his pants. Soundboard before him, cartridge machine and CD players above it on a rack, turntables at his right. Commercial log open before him, and most prominently, the ever-important microphone. He checked a tiny chalkboard on the wall, got the day's number.

"We're into day number five-hundred-sixty-eight of our all-Madonna-free marathon, and today's burning social question is this: Do *you* think anybody ever got horny on *Gilligan's Island*? And bear in mind that a fat guy in a skipper's hat who lives with a skinny guy and calls him 'little buddy' may not always be what he appears. So what do you think? Phone lines are open and operators are standing by."

First song, he brought it to life, boosted the volume, tugged his headphones off, spun one complete circle in the chair. Saluted Peter, who leaned in the doorway with a triumphant smile.

"Guess what."

Paul, palms up, arms wide. Ready for anything. "What?"

"I'll give you a hint." Peter straightened to his full height. Made a grand show of clamping his lips together and breathing unhindered gusts through flaring nostrils. He sounded like a bull preparing to charge. "No more stuffhead. I do believe you cured me."

Paul grinned. Nice gag. Pete had probably cloistered himself in the bathroom, steamed himself open with the shower running full blast hot.

"What do you say we keep this our secret, okay?" Paul cued vinyl on turntable one. "Next thing you know, this gets out and Popeye'll be in here, begging me to fix his long-rumored impotence. I'll lay hands on only so much, you know."

Peter stepped in, bent over to plant a loud smack atop the crown of Paul's head. "Does this mean my hemorrhoids are out of the question?"

Paul wrinkled his nose in disgust. "Don't get greedy."

Moments later, alone again, himself and the music, always the music. Paul looked at his hands. As unassuming and nondescript as the rest of him. Wondering. What *if* . . . ? Really.

Naaah.

2

 It was one of the great cosmic wrongs of the twentieth century. Somehow—*somehow*—Amanda had ended up facedown at the bottom of the stairs. As to how it could have happened, Donny Dawson hadn't the slightest idea.

This isn't real, a puny sentiment indeed. Denial, flimsy last bastion of defense. *This can NOT be happening*.

Then he was shooting down the stairway after her, utterly the concerned husband, two and three steps at a time. Scant seconds, but in that span, a hundred dark thoughts clamored for attention. The concept *dead* at their forefront.

The house, as well as the compound of nearby buildings, had been built five years ago. A three-story anachronism from the Georgian Court period, Ionic columns gracing its front. A paean to tasteful elegance, each of its nearly forty rooms was a study in sheer romantic overindulgence. It sat on the western fringe of the compound like the Big House on a plantation of the antebellum South, a plantation where saving souls was the order of the day rather than raising cotton. Amanda had been at home here like no place she had ever been.

On the way down the stairs, everything leading up to her calamitous dive replayed in Donny's mind. Rising tone of voices as they left their second-floor bedroom. Her insistent, "I'm tired of living out lies! I don't think it's right anymore!" His angry demand, keep your voice down, don't raise it to me that way. Her first tread onto that grand ballroom stairway, his grip on her upper arm.

Her tearful twist, to be rid of his touch.

To the bottom, then, express-style. Incredibly endless slow motion trek of flailing arms and unbelieving eyes, too shocked for accusation, too helpless for fear. Finally, worst of all by far, the horrid crack her head had made when it struck the banister.

Donny knelt beside her in numb futility, eyes roving, for once finding himself left entirely to his own fragile devices. The feeling was ghastly, simply ghastly. He rolled her over, gently, gently, recoiling at the rivulets of blood tracing the left side of her face from temple to jawline. And limp, so limp, a rag doll whose stitches were but frayed threads. Donny's hand shook as he reached for her face and felt the faint warmth of her breath. Thank God.

"Mandy. Mandy? Honey, open your eyes."

He thumbed her eyelids back, found her staring straight ahead at everything, at nothing. No reactive shrinkage of her pupils to light, just a glassy, dull stare. A moment later, he realized that her pupils were of vastly different sizes. The right had dilated into a tiny black button. He released her eyelids, and they slid closed.

Now, at last, the final insult to injury: the stench of her newly loosened bladder and bowels. Dear God, what dignity in this?

"Mandy. Mandy, I'm sorry. I'm *sorry*."

Begging and pleading, beseeching and cajoling, none of it had the slightest effect. Donny's voice trailed away, and she did not care. He quit nervously massaging her hands, and she took no notice.

But there was another way. Maybe. If he was lucky. *Again.*

And so, as he knelt beside his rag-doll wife, clasping one limp hand between his, Donny Dawson began to pray more fervently than he had prayed in years. Asking God above to hear this prayer of a humble servant, a servant who had at least once upon a time been blessed with the power to heal. Asking God above, please, please, let it happen again, once more make this humble servant the channel for the healing touch, give him the power to bring back this stricken child of Heaven.

Breath coming quicker by the moment, sweat dotting his forehead, Donny felt strangely cold. Ah, but of course . . . No stage lights this time, no tele-voyeurism of four rolling cameras. And no crush of people packed into an auditorium, looking at him, expecting a miracle. Neither drama, nor theatrics. Just the two of them.

Because this time it was personal. *And for real.*

Donny held her head in his hands, fingers spread wide to cradle it, touch as much of her as possible. Seeking vital contact as tears brimmed his eyes.

"Open your eyes, Amanda. *Open your eyes.* God, let it be done!"

Continuing to kneel, to cradle, to stare into the undead face. While she knew nothing of his concern, his efforts, the blood gouting from his own soul. The bottom fell out of his stomach, took him with it.

"Let. It. Be. *Done!*"

Except . . .

It wasn't.

Numb and blank. *Abandoned.* Stupefyingly so. Donny rose, turned. Paced, thought, paced some more. Not unlike an expectant father, please tell me my baby's all right. He gazed across the Persian rug in the entry hall and into the parlor, eyes fixing on a table, the item resting atop it. Behold, the telephone. Help is just a phone call away.

And yet. This was not a simple matter of placing the call, waiting for the paramedics to take it from there. Roll in with lights blazing, sirens wailing. Such a public spectacle would not do at all. For the paramedics would know precisely where they were going. And the subsequent check-in at Hillcrest Hospital in Oklahoma City would mean names. *Amanda Dawson,* they would write. *Next of kin?* And he would have to answer. *Donny Dawson?* they would say. *Why, the Donny Dawson? Donny Dawson the faith healer? But why are you . . . ?*

Only a few days, and it would be a matter of public knowledge and national record. The wire services would pounce on it like dogs after a particularly tasty bone, and *Time* and *Newsweek* would laugh it up, while supermarket tabloids would splash it across their lurid covers, sentencing him to doing time with the most tasteless stories conceivable, because gullible minds want to know. He could already see the headlines.

Forget Oral Roberts and his claims of celestial blackmail. Forget Jim and Tammy Bakker, their entire holy rolling soap opera. Forget the carnal dalliances of Jimmy Swaggart. Old news, all of it. Now there's *fresh* sacrificial meat on the televangelism altar, and his name's Dawson. Everybody grab a piece, there's plenty to go around.

Donny gave it a thorough mental once-over, deciding that when the going gets truly tough, you bring in a second valued opinion. He covered the distance to the phone, punching in the number for the chapel across the compound, where one of the secretaries answered.

"I need to speak to Gabe." Quell those tremors in his voice, he *never* sounded this way. Eternities passed before Gabe was located. Donny didn't ask what he had been doing, didn't care. Whatever it was, Gabe had no qualms about dropping it and heading for the Dawson house. Good. Oh, good good good.

There in eight minutes. After stepping in through the front door without knocking, he gripped the knob and stared. The sight took some getting used to. Dying sunlight prismed through the beveled glass of the door.

"Donny?" he said. "Is she . . . ?"

"She's alive. But Gabe, I . . . I—" His theatrical voice failed him once more. He stood by her, arms outstretched as if to show nailprints in the palms, wounds of future media crucifixion.

He needed to say no more, for Gabe seemed to comprehend everything, the obvious and the implied, in a single glance. Gabriel Matthews, right-hand man, priceless appendage. He was only thirty-two, but Donny considered him to have the acute instincts and business acumen of a man older by two decades or more.

The silence was more than Donny could bear. "I don't know what happened, one second we were talking, all we were doing was talking, and then . . . then—"

"Donny. Shhh. Just let me think a minute."

Gabe quietly shut the door, moved forward. Not a tall man by any means, but compact, solid without being bulky. His sandy hair was full in front, trimmed close on the sides, the back. He had a wide mouth and his lips were often clamped tight. His deep-set eyes were generally serious, and this was appropriate: The saving of souls could be a serious business.

"What are we going to do?" Donny slumped onto the bottom step, elbows on knees and head in hands. Shell shock. "*What* are we going to *do*?"

Gabe reached down to clasp Donny's hand, soul-shake style. Power and strength. "Get hold of yourself. *Think.* I'll call Irv Preston. You provide him with enough tax writeoffs, he'll be good for a favor even if he didn't have the Hippocratic Oath weighing on his conscience. We'll let him take care of Mandy, decide what she needs. And I promise you, I'll make certain he understands the need for discretion."

Donny perked up, the light of a glorious new dawn beaming into his head. "That's a good idea. . . ."

"As for now, you've got a show to tape."

Donny uttered a startled little chuckle, slowly shook his head. Hands starting to quake anew. "*Oh* no. I can't go over there *now*, I can't tape a show, not this evening, I—"

Gabe's wide mouth, now a pacifying smile. "Think a minute, okay? You've got nearly three thousand people coming into the chapel. If you want to delay things, fine, we'll make some kind of announcement about equipment problems, and they'll be happy to sit there all night if that's what it takes. But if you send them home, there's all that revenue lost. There's credibility that goes with it. There's unnecessary attention called to the ministry. And in the end, you've still got a show to tape sometime." Gabe waited for the bulk of this to settle in, slow going. "It's up to you, of course, but there's not a lot you can do for Mandy as a basket case. Don't you think she'd want you to carry on tonight?"

I'm tired of living out lies!

Donny watched his hands knead one another. Hands of clay. Feet to match? He refused to believe that. "I suppose she would."

"Then there's nothing more for you to do here. Mandy will be fine, I'll see to that. And you? You go see to your show. That's where you belong right now. Where you're needed."

Donny nodded, telegraphed a quick prayer, mandatory strength. He let his legs carry him through the house, drifting, while vaguely aware of Gabe's voice on the phone, quiet, urgent, diplomatic. Donny followed his legs out of the house and across the back porch, the double-seat swing and minor jungle of potted greenery. Farther beyond sprawled the English country garden, and at its far edge, in their pen, a pair of Irish setters yapped happily at him. Adam and Eve. Donny mounted a modified golf cart that whisked him along a tarmac path leading away from the house, the protective seclusion of its surrounding oaks. Soon he was puttering through the compound, more open and airy, the trees younger and more spindly. Green velvet lawns rolled among a scattering of buildings that resembled a miniature brown brick college campus: main office building and production studios, dormitories for some of the ministry's workers and wards, and at the far edge, the chapel. Just past the chapel, the parking lot appeared filled near to capacity. A steady tide of people channeled toward the main entrance in the chapel's north end, some in wheelchairs, some hobbling along on crutches. Just as they would leave.

Donny parked his cart on the south side, entering through the rear to find himself thick in the usual backstage hive of preshow bustle. Before stopping by for makeup, he sought out the stage manager and director, had them delay kickoff by a half hour. Blame it on whatever's convenient, equipment malfunction if that's convenient enough, but don't plan on getting off the ground until seven-thirty, at the earliest. There were no questions. They followed orders like buck privates in the presence of a general.

Seclusion, then, the low-ceilinged maze having led him to his dressing room. Donny relished the time alone, away, the familiarity of weekly ritual. Compose thyself. And bring this terrible night into perspective.

I couldn't hack it. Not when it was real.

God's will, he offered in rebuttal. *It's just God's will. I've done it before. I'll do it again, surely, when the time is right.*

Sure, sure, that other voice, redolent of skepticism. *Do we care to place any bets on this?*

Do not put the Lord thy God to a foolish test, and that shut the skeptic up for the time being.

Later, when the stage lights came up and the music swelled and the choir sang and the theatrics held sway over all, Donny Dawson knew he was precisely where he belonged. Momentary fears surfaced—who would take Amanda's place on the hidden FM transmitter, its receiver a tiny hair-concealed plug in his left ear? But Gabe was back, taking over as proficiently as if the job had been his all along.

They would make it through the night, he knew this now. For he was on display before the lost and the searching, his stage the focal point of an auditorium whose rows of seats stretched before him in immense wedges, the aisles between like the spokes of some huge wheel. The machine of his own creation. And Donny, epicenter of attention, tall and fit and resplendent in his white suit and toting his oversize Bible. His golden-brown hair swept back from his forehead, his chin strong and assured. Eyes radiant with promises of a better life everlasting. Making it through the night, all of them.

You could take that to the bank.

3

Lorraine's eyes lit up while she was on the air, as distinct as throwing a switch. She could come in, batteries dead from an already-tiring day or lack of sleep the night before. Then turn her loose in the booth and regeneration was automatic. Those so green eyes, glowing with film noir neon. There is something immensely endearing about such an expression on the face of someone who so passionately loves what she's doing.

Paul wondered—not for the first time since his arrival here back in the winter—if she looked this way while making love.

The poor timing was classic: Lorraine Savage had been a nine-month newlywed when Paul first defected to KGRM. He had come to St. Louis after a stint at a station in Indianapolis; if only he had sought employment at KGRM first, instead of waiting a year. He could then have had three months to subtly get her to reconsider her choice of spouse.

She retained her own surname for air continuity, which he took as meager hope. Paul had met the guy a couple times, briefly, at station functions she had coerced him into attending. Craig Sheppard, nice yuppie name for a yuppie kind of guy, corporate holdover from the greedy eighties. Complete with BMW and button-down collars and a University of Hitler Youth haircut. An overdrive personality fueled by a high-octane ego. Craig Sheppard, here to take the world on his own terms. Paul couldn't stand him, and only occasionally felt guilty about it.

Friends. He'd tried friends first, keeping his feelings confined to that level and no deeper. Losing battle. Surrender had come in February, some concert at a venue called the American Theater, not yet three months after his arrival at KGRM. The station had sent a delegation to a concert by the Indigo Girls, whom Paul revered, and the Ellen James Society, about whom he had heard nothing, and of whom he had left a committed fan.

A magic holy night, femme-folk, femme-rock, absolutely no artificial concessions to commercialism, and Greenpeace in the lobby. Seating was dinner-theater style, and six of them from the station sat clustered around a tiny table, far more intimate than standard arena seating. Paul sat beside Lorraine, absorbing everything. Her throaty laugh. The animation of her hands. Soft loose curls corkscrewing past her shoulders as he wondered if the streaked blond was natural.

Opening set, the Ellen James Society, and Lorraine was the only other one at their table who had caught the reference to John Irving's *The World According to Garp*. The two of them sat watching some lone dancer down front, when all of a sudden Lorraine nudged him, leaned in, deadpan, and said, "Wouldn't it be funny if she was into stage-diving, instead?" And the image leveled him, one lone stage-diver, arcing off toward the audience with no one to catch her, splatting to the floor. Again and again and again. It was so cruel he couldn't help but laugh.

Friends? Surrender. Just admit it, he was smitten. But not to act on it, curbing that passion, content to worship from afar.

Present tense. Lorraine kicked off a commercial-free half-hour and shut down the microphone.

"Any reprisals from that little faith healing service you guys did yesterday?" She grinned crookedly, twirling a lock of hair around one finger. "Warn me next time, okay? I was listening in the hammock in the backyard, and I fell out. You almost broke my wrist."

He reached for it, kissed it with healing chivalry. "No foreseeable reruns. Popeye was less than thrilled." He explained the circumstances. "He came through that door ready to explode."

"Yuck. The biggest blast since the *Hindenburg*."

Paul shook his head, so sorry, some people just don't get it. "I don't think he really understands what he's supposed to do here, you know? Rock and roll is *supposed* to be offensive, it's the nature of the beast."

"He's the original hypocrite, didn't I warn you? The man's soul could fit in a thimble."

On and on, management-bashing, the deejay's favorite contact sport.

Paul watched her set things up for more tunes, smooth ballet from cart machine to turntables to CD players to racks of albums. Poetry, sweet and carnal. Then, with her back to him, she bent at the waist to rummage in the cabinet beneath the turntables, where some CDs were stored. That view, inverted heart-shaped denim perfection. Fifteen years ago, surfing through puberty, such a sight would have sent him scurrying shamefaced to the nearest toilet to drop to his knees and conjure fantasies so intense they *hurt*. Now? He tried not to ogle. He really tried. But in some ways, the male of the species was *always* stuck at fourteen.

"Peter Hargrove," her voice a sudden growl, "I hate you when you do this to me!"

Paul watched as she straightened, bringing with her an ashtray, clear glass muddied with nicotine grime. She stared into the jumble of butts with profound disgust. Was there any antismoker so venomous as an ex-smoker?

"He does this on purpose, you know." Her eyes narrowed to slits, as if nothing would give her greater pleasure than concocting a tasty ashtray stew and serving it to a helplessly quadraplegic Peter Hargrove. "About once a week, he hides this where he knows I'll find it. It's just like when he holds those unlit cigarettes under my nose before he smokes them."

"He's just a zealot is all." Paul Handler, attorney for the defense.

"And *you*. You're just as guilty as *he* is." Those green eyes were luminous now. "You've got four hours to find these things and get rid of them before I show up."

Paul, sappy grin and all, went backwalking across the booth, Lorraine advancing like some vengeful temptress. She held the ashtray before her, and he formed a cross with two fingers to ward her off. But she was invincible. Pressed him against the wall, close contact in five or six exquisitely stimulated spots while she lifted the ashtray into dumping position, say aaah, and had him beg for clemency.

A golden moment, shattered when he looked toward the booth's door and saw they were being watched.

"Such professionalism," and it was spoken with a bemused smirk. Clifford Frankl, one of the sales staff. Or sales geeks, the current term of vogue when they were in absentia. He joined them, and the ashtray was unceremoniously emptied into the waste can. Paul, wistful, watched the gray ashes sift downward while Clifford spoke his business.

He had just sold a remote broadcast for the following Tuesday at University City's newest business, a record store called The House of Wax, on Delmar Street. Popeye's boy wonder, that was Clifford, the sales geek who always made his quotas and usually smelled as if he had just eaten his way through a truckload of Certs. Clifford had sold the store owner on the idea of pairing up KGRM wildmen Paul Handler and Peter Hargrove for two hours of live-on-location on-air mayhem. Paul said fine, dandy, and Cliff sprinted for his desk phone to call Peter at home. Leaving as one happy sales geek indeed.

"I'm jealous," Lorraine pouted. "You guys get all the glory. Nobody ever asks for me."

Paul smiled, hugged her, and patted her on the back. "Show more cleavage," and they both laughed when she pulled away to slug him on the arm.

Plenty of affection between them, Paul had no qualms with that, in fact it had been very quick in coming months ago. Little kindnesses, warm moments, and small intimate touches . . . but never intimate enough. He knew there could never be passion, had resigned himself to that dismal fact, never those animal strivings for blissful union, turning breath desperate and voices hoarse. And this was worse, really, than complete rejection. For the regret was endless, perpetually renewed, always there.

Sunday morning, two days later.

Paul was just working his way into some strange dream about riding a horse when the noise came, rhythmic pounding that the dream incorporated as thunder. His grasp was tenuous, the dream scattering into gossamer filaments as he swam to awakening. He opened his eyes, focused on the bedroom ceiling.

Too bright, too early. The clock radio near his head blinked nine-thirty-six. Good morning, Mister Sun. Piss off and die.

The infernal pounding at his door persisted, and Paul grumbled himself out of bed. He navigated the stagnant sea of dirty socks and underwear on his bedroom floor, then covered the narrow hallway to the living room. During the night his shorts had twisted themselves to one side; fixing this was priority one of the new day. He kicked aside a stray section of yesterday's *Post-Dispatch*, and it tented beside a table laden with books and tapes and the odd beer bottle or two. At the far end of his sofa, on a table of their own in a leaker aquarium they called home, lived a pair of gerbils christened Calvin and Hobbes. They peered at him, four bright black eyes, then scurried behind their wheel, as if fleeing a carnivorous giant intent on breakfast and none too picky.

Paul opened the door in midpound, confronted a smiling Peter Hargrove with arms full of good tidings.

"Rise and shine! Ready for company?" Peter set his sacks on the floor, plucked out a Pete's Wicked Ale—he claimed the brand was named after him—and twisted off the cap as if wringing the neck of a chicken. He offered it to his host.

Paul declined, sagging against the doorjamb and scrubbing sleep from his eyes. "When you said we should get together today, I kind of thought you meant, like, noon or after."

"You midday jocks are such pussies." Peter retrieved his sacks and aimed for the kitchen. Keep a schedule like his, and this was the biological clock's equivalent of early afternoon.

Paul shut the door, then collapsed into his couch, a plush old secondhand monstrosity that did everything but hug you. Sinking into its cool depths, he listened to Peter rearranging the contents of his refrigerator. Bottles clinked endlessly.

"If you woke up Mrs. DeWitt and got her all cranky," Paul croaked, "I'll kill you. Not kidding."

"Relax. I'll sit on her."

Good enough. Janet DeWitt was a fifty-something widow who lived directly below lucky lucky Paul. She gave nearly everybody in the building grief about too much noise, real or imagined, but Paul, by simple virtue of logistics, caught the biggest portion. One of the kinder building rumors about her he had heard was that her husband must have died in self-defense.

"Hey," Peter called. "You got this package of cream cheese in here that expired last December. Want me to pitch it?"

"Naaah. Leave it. That's my science project."

It must have been a deejay occupational hazard. You're single, you still live like a college student years after the diploma. Only the married jocks were grownups. And the divorced ones, like Peter? They were the worst of all.

He returned to the living room, toting his ale and a bag of pork rinds and the orange juice pitcher. Paul accepted the latter with both hands, like a child with an oversize mug, and swigged directly from the spout.

"Breakfast of champions." Peter settled into a plaid recliner that no one reclined in because it tilted back unevenly, felt like the next stop would be the floor. He fed himself an enormous pork rind; the crunch might have leveled a lesser building.

Paul propped both bare feet onto his coffee table, a shellacked piece of stained pine balanced on a pair of orange crates. The gentle breezes wafting in through his third-floor windows were warm and comforting, to be cherished. It was late June, and soon the temperature would only be shooting upward toward misery. St. Louis summer humidity was infamous.

They stared at each other, orange juice to ale, sleepyhead to the guy with crumbs in his beard. Peter smiled. "Are we having fun yet?" and Paul responded with a thumbs-up.

"How long ago was it you were married?" Paul then asked.

Quick mental calculations. "We got married twelve years ago. We split, mmm, five years ago."

Paul nodded. "The seven-year itch."

"Shit. Tell me about it," and Paul could hear the regret, very very faint, 20/20 hindsight masked with bravado or indifference. Equally phony. Peter generally spoke of marriage in only the most disparaging of terms, listen to Wicked Uncle Pete and save yourself a world of hurt. As if it would take a cattle prod to get him back up the aisle. All bluster, Paul sensed. All bluff. He was as frightened of pain as anyone. Maybe more so; he was already presensitized, knew extremes of pain on a first-name basis.

"Answer me this: When did you talk the least about her? At work."

Peter stroked his beard. "When it got shitty, I guess. I don't know why. That was just the way I was."

"Don't you think that's the way most people are? Or, say, one extreme or the other? They don't say a thing, or they talk *too* much, like they're trying to convince themselves everything's great, everything's great."

"I suppose. Yeah, you're probably right."

Paul nodded, wiggled out of his slump to set both feet on the floor.

"Lorraine?" Peter asked. "Is that what this is about?"

"Just wondering. Just curious," and indeed, he was, staring into his pitcher to contemplate the marvels of Minute Maid and life in general. How things had fared in the Sheppard/Savage household in their first several months was before his time, and it wasn't something he wanted to go around asking about. Not proper, not proper at all. But since he had found a home at KGRM, since he and Lorraine had forged a genuine friendship, the amount of information she had volunteered about married life wouldn't even fill a Post-it note. Which, in retrospect, seemed a bit odd. Silence could carry more implications about the state of affairs than innuendo.

"So ask her," Peter finally said. "Just sit her down and point-blank ask her how things are going. Easy enough. She wouldn't mind, hell, she likes you better than any of the rest of us, I think."

Paul, shaking his head, "No, no, I couldn't do that. I'm not out to cause any trouble, really, I'm not."

"Might work, you never can tell." Peter leaned back and poured down a big sullen gulp of ale, smacked his lips once and held them tight. Staring straight ahead. "That's how my ex ended up with the guy she married after me."

"Oh," Paul's voice soft, tiny, surprised. "I didn't know. I'm sorry."

Peter, nodding, yeah, yeah, everybody's got their story, the one that got away, here's how I fiddled while Rome burned. Silence on the home front, while outside, in the city, some distant church bell rang clear and hollow, a wafting memory of smaller towns, more innocent days. Innocence lost. Ten o'clock and all's hell.

"My my my," Peter said, "what an absolutely cheery morning *this* is turning out to be."

Paul felt like a weasel. Drag the man down, way to go, dredge up the worst time of his life. He perked up, change of subject: "Cartoons. We need cartoons."

"Now you're talking. Is Elmer Fudd on? I'd kill for some Elmer Fudd."

Paul got up and went for the TV, clicked it on. An older model, not yet having given up the ghost, its video lagged behind audio while the tube warmed up.

". . . and while she's gone, she wanted me to let you know that she's thinking about each and every one of you." Some as-yet-faceless voice on the TV, emerging from the great gray unknown. "She keeps you in her prayers night and day, and I know Amanda would welcome yours as well. Both for success in her missions, *and* her safe return."

"That's not Elmer Fudd!" Peter rattled his cellophane bag in annoyance. "I know what the man sounds like, and that's not him."

The picture rippled into being, and Paul saw a man standing before a large pulpit, surrounded by lilies, other greenery. A tall fellow, wearing a white suit, Pat Boone syndrome, his handsomely chiseled face earnest and imploring. Lush purple curtains comprised a partial backdrop, apart from a choir, and across the curtains draped a gold banner that read ARM OF THE APOSTLE.

"Okay, get that clown off the air, I know who that is."

Paul's hand lingered on the knob, trigger pressure. An overhead tracking shot caught an audience in an auditorium, colorful sea of smiling people amid fields of golden carpet, with tall thin rectangles of stained glass set along ivory walls.

"Who is he?" Paul said. "I don't recognize this one."

"Never heard of Donny Dawson?" Peter shrugged when Paul said the name drew a blank. "One of those faith healer bozos, shouts a lot and throws people's crutches across the stage, that kind of crap. Give him a few more years and he'll be as bad as Oral Roberts, claiming he's raised people from the dead. What a crock."

"You don't think there's anything to it?" Paul flipped the dial until he found gold, Daffy Duck. Surely Elmer would follow.

"Hell no. Come on, you've never seen those guys in action? All that ranting and raving? It's just a big show. Like pro wrestling, except for holy rollers. Aw Paul, don't tell me you actually think these guys are for real."

He had returned to the contemplative solace of the sofa. "I'm not saying that none of it is faked. I just think it's a mistake to lump everybody into one category. Maybe there's somebody genuine among the crooks, you never know."

"Well it's sure not him." Peter rolled his eyes, turned the first ale into one dead soldier. "I knew that Methodist upbringing didn't leave you unscarred." His voice sounded condescending, a veiled invitation to drop the whole thing. Punctuated by a return trip to the fridge.

And who's to say, Paul thought, *that I didn't actually cast the summer cold demons out of your head?* He couldn't decide if he was half joking or three-quarters serious.

Paul watched the cartoon as an exploding cigar effectively stripped away all of Daffy's feathers, leaving him this nubby little plucked thing, fuming with indignation. By next scene all his feathers were back in place. Nothing short of amazing.

That magic of television. The one world where anything could happen.

And given time, probably will.

4

The lies didn't taste nearly as bad in Donny Dawson's mouth as he had feared.

All well and good. It looked as if he and Gabriel Matthews and a tiny supporting cast were actually going to pull this off, this elaborate charade. The microcosm making up their world at the Oklahoma City compound and over the airwaves was being spoon-fed vast amounts of not-quite-truths regarding the whereabouts of Amanda Dawson, and they would happily swallow every last morsel.

All had, of course, begun frightfully enough. As Donny was on his way to the chapel after her fall, Doctor Irv Preston had been summoned, leaving the last of his day's already-behind-schedule patients double-parked in his waiting room. A quick on-site examination lent voice to his fears, cerebral hemorrhage, brought on by a sharp blow to the head. Result: arterial bleeding and cerebral edema, swelling of the brain.

Preston had disinfected the gash in her scalp, then covered it with steri-strips, thin pieces of tape to close it until suturing. He had run his hands over her to check for broken bones, and found none. But it wasn't going to be enough, his voice was grave on this matter. Hospitalization was essential. Amanda was comatose.

Preston had taken her in himself, registering her under a false identity. She would not be staying long, perhaps a week, long enough to get proper emergency care. A CAT scan confirmed Preston's suspicions of edema, lots of intracranial pressure needing relief. Amanda was started on an intravenous regimen of Manitol. With a bit of luck, over the coming week her swelling would abate with the ease of slowly letting air out of a balloon.

After this, she would be moved back home, to a bedroom outfitted for her very special needs, tended to by a private nursing staff of three, each holding down an eight-hour shift. And paid extraordinarily well, for silence as well as expertise. Preston would take care of securing the nurses, highly skilled and tight of mouth, all three.

Gabe had briefed Donny on it all during a break in the taping of the show that first terrible night, the two of them in his dressing room, door locked, conspirators in seclusion.

"It's not going to be enough," Donny had said. Hands trembling until he laced his fingers so tight they appeared bleached. "We'll have to account for her disappearance."

"I know, I've thought of that." Gabe massaged the bridge of his nose and poured ice water for them both. "I think I know a way around it."

Donny was all ears and clammy sweat.

"Since this is a coma, we're talking about a wholly indefinite period of time. It could just be a matter of days before she comes out of it. Or it could take a lot longer. Irv told me you just can't predict it, ever. Since we can't predict it, we can't plan time frames around it."

Donny's eyes closed. This was getting worse all the time, lie upon lie upon lie. "So what do we tell everyone?"

"That she's on a missionary trip, indefinite length of time. I think El Salvador would be good. No small need for Christian people there, and it certainly has its share of violence and turmoil. Tomorrow I can talk to Carmen in the photo lab. She's got a good stock file of pictures she shot there last year. Now, we'll have to let her in on this, so this is up to you. Do you trust her?"

Donny nodded, reflex action. Gabe's idea, let him do what he thinks best. "She's good people."

"Fine. She's talented enough to superimpose negatives of Mandy onto some Salvadoran backgrounds. That way we can show Mandy at work, Mandy waving to everyone at home and in the audience. It will add a lot of credibility to the story."

Gabe drained off his water, poured another glass. Ice cubes tinkled, brittle as cold bones. "And if worse comes to worst . . . if

Mandy doesn't . . . make it . . . we're covered. She'll have been martyred."

Gabe. Oh, but couldn't he be the cold-blooded one about things when the situation truly called for it. The proverbial double-edged sword, the one thing Donny truly admired about him yet. at the same time feared. *Martyred.* Lovely choice of words, such a gulf lying between the generic form, *killed,* and this window-dressed alternative. And wouldn't the love offerings come pouring in if the word *martyred* were to hit the airwaves?

My wife. My love. And dear lord, we're discussing her the same as we'd discuss a stock portfolio.

Yet she would understand, wouldn't she? They had labored side by side for more than fifteen years, same goals in mind and visualizing that same pot of gold at rainbow's end. Two peas in an evangelical pod, in no way would she wish to endanger that. And now that, by sour chance, circumstances had indeed arisen that could prick up the ears of media jackals, set their jaws slavering for another man of the cloth to rend to bits, Amanda would not want to make their task any easier. A rock, a saint.

I'm tired of living out lies.

Hated phrase, it wouldn't leave him alone for long, its recall frequent and punctual. Had to have been Satan talking to her, through her, confusing her. The master deceiver. He wasn't the cute, pointy-tailed little red sprite with the goatee and trident of popular imagination. His wardrobe was limitless; the lie, the doubt, the fear, the unbelief, the loss of faith.

Yes. Amanda would want it handled this way.

All of which had transpired Thursday. It was now Sunday, and the intervening days had served only to harden the conviction that they had acted properly. Brains and prudent judgment had prevailed.

Following the compound-only morning worship service, Sunday afternoons were generally quiet in the Dawson household and throughout the grounds. Day of rest, sorely needed. The only thing he could hear as he sat in his living room was the steady pendulum tick of the grandfather clock, catercorner across the room from the sofa. Along the same wall, multipane windows gave a wide western view, a panorama of trees. In the corner directly across from him sat a six-foot Sony with projection screen. A window to some parallel universe where all was polished, perfect, preplanned. This afternoon he found the room conducive to thought, contemplation of what genuinely mattered in life.

Doing the right thing was not one of life's trivialities, because it didn't always mean making the most obvious choice. Or the easiest. And at times, when values clashed, the accompanying strife could turn your heart into a battleground.

Was it right to conduct holy worship with vaudevillian pomp and flair, complete with sleight-of-hand and trickery and implanted suggestions of near-hypnotic power? Indeed it was, for there were plenty of people out there who needed precisely that. Craving something to bring them closer to the Almighty, hungering for that which they could see and touch and hear. And which they could replay a thousand times over on their VCR if so inclined, only $29.95 per tape, specify VHS or Beta format. And if he could provide a sagging spirit with an uplifting jump start, so much the better.

Donny Dawson, celestial cheerleader.

And the money? The house? The Cadillacs? Nothing wrong with these at all, so long as your heart was in the right place, truly appreciative of the just rewards for doing the right thing. And for every liberal secular humanist who piped up to accuse this humble servant of bilking his followers for whatever he could, all you had was one more termite working in vain at the foundations of Heaven. Let him chew on eternity in Hell.

He liked that, liked the sound of it. Have to write that one down.

"Knock knock," soft voice from the living room doorway. Gabe joined him, the relaxed Gabe for a change, the at-ease Gabe. An Izod shirt and tan slacks with creases sharp enough to slice underbrush, this was as relaxed as Gabe ever seemed to get. He held a manila envelope in one hand.

"Have you talked to Irv yet today?" Gabe asked.

Donny nodded. "The swelling's gone down some more. He's tentatively planning on discharging her on Thursday."

Gabe sat in a plump chair angled off one end of the sofa. Shook Donny's knee with a firm hand. "And how's her husband?"

The eternal question, the challenge writ in heartbreak. Devoid of easy answers. "I miss her, Gabe. I feel so incomplete. I have been cut in half."

Gabe, respectful as ever, deference given as needed. He would be in and out, with no wasted time. "Just a quick briefing for you. I have the initial pictures Carmen worked up in the darkroom. I think you'll like these."

Donny opened the manila envelope, flipped through the short stack of eight-by-ten glossies, black and white. Amanda in El Salvador, a trip that never was. He was duly impressed. Carmen was a genuine wizard of negatives and enlargers and Kodak paper. For the briefest of moments, even he could believe the lies. Amanda, there she was, full of life and renewed vitality. Properly lovely, black hair swept back from her ears, the only thing preventing her from looking indecently alluring being her widening hips and her saintly eyes. Amanda, standing in the doorway of a ramshackle dwelling. Clutching a microphone and singing her heart out beside a rudimentary pulpit. Others, equally good. He could very nearly believe she was there.

"They're excellent," he said, handing them back.

Gabe nodded, yes, yes, knew you'd be satisfied, and when he left, Donny couldn't quite decide if he'd sent Gabe away, or if the man had stepped out of his own volition. He had that effect sometimes, that subtle manipulation of perception. Amusing, under some circumstances, unsettling under others. But Gabe's heart was in the right place, and this, above all, was the most important consideration. Gabe abused no power, craved no personal glory.

I don't know what I'd do without him.

Yet his function and proficiency could extend only so far. For the seat of command was still the loneliest place to be.

5

The House of Wax was founded on one simple credo: The music lover should feel as if death had set in and Heaven had been attained. Paul, music lover to the end, felt blissfully at home as soon as he set foot past the door. This place was not to be believed, a three-level candystore, and he was the kid with the biggest sweet tooth around. New, cutouts, used, imports, all in mass quantities and prime condition. Walls covered with posters of everyone from Arthur Fiedler to Frank Zappa. His bank account was going to be taking a beating, sure as death and taxes. Might as well cut to the chase, start endorsing his paychecks over.

Tuesday brought the remote broadcast for the official House of Wax grand opening. Equipment in place, most outdoors on the sidewalk facing Delmar Street. The weather, warm and sunny, was more than agreeable enough for a miniature street party out front. The neighborhood cried out for such things, like St. Louis's own version of Greenwich Village. They called this drag the Loop, shops and sojourns where you could thumb your nose at conventionality. Get your hair cut as unique as you wished, or dine Jamaican while some other cuisine is flavor-of-the-month. See art films at the Tivoli, and afterward debate their meanings at a coffeehouse. Find a thrift shop hat, black of course, and wear it to Blueberry Hill, lovingly jumbled hybrid of bar, restaurant, and oldies rock and roll museum. And above all, think for yourself.

Street party, hah. Try that in the provincial stuffiness of a suburb like Ladue.

A station engineer had set up an antenna linking them with KGRM, connected by coax cable to their portable transmitter, which in turn fed into a PA mixer and speakers inside the store and out. KGRM itself was picked up by a home receiver patched into the PA. A two-way communication system rode piggyback on the transmitter so they could speak with Lorraine in the booth as privately as a phone line. Dutifully, Peter masking-taped cords, precious safeguard, for inevitable klutzes were always looking to trip them from their jacks.

Sales geek Clifford Frankl introduced them to store owner Danny Schalter, whose glossy black ponytail hung to center back. He was a benign Mephistopheles with a wicked moustache and goatee to match, and the biggest, most soulful eyes Paul had ever seen. The man had brains, as well, for he had chosen the date of his grand opening with a strategist's eye. Late June, the crowd that consumes music like popcorn newly out of school with wallets and purses filled with the first weeks' wages from summer jobs. They had turned out in force, browsing through the labyrinth of bins, gathering before the store in righteous celebration.

"When's the first break?" Danny asked, beseiged at the counter.

"A few more minutes. We'll go into it at four o'clock, straight up," Paul said. "Is it okay with you if we kick things off out front?"

Danny said sure, sure, whatever works. Paul watched him bag a stack of tapes. Crinkly plastic, with the store logo and the words HOUSE OF WAX SAX. Cute.

Paul wandered outside, feeling those preremote jitters in his stomach. Silly, but he always got them. Speaking to the masses was one thing from the insular solitude of the booth, quite another when you were on public display. Blend into things, get their feeling, immerse.

The mood out front was festive, the gathering perhaps forty strong. U2 was tearing from the speakers, and several were dancing to hypersonic guitar, impassioned vocals. Peter watched, impenetrable behind dark shades and facial hair, taking his post beside the equipment to guard it from thieves, klutzes, other assorted evildoers.

"Check her out," Peter said, and nodded with his chin. Some chubby girl dancing energetically fifteen feet away, great hair and the world's tightest jeans. "A cross between Tina Turner and the Goodyear blimp, right?"

Paul frowned. "You're a cruel bastard."

Peter was all protested innocence. "Hey, I didn't say I didn't like her." He stroked his beard, a white slave trader watching the arrival of a new ship from the Orient. "She's bouncy. I like bouncy. She looks *fun.*"

Paul watched for another few moments, then decided, as long as they were being complete sexist pigs, he would much rather rest his gaze on Tina Goodyear's dancing partner. A willowy sylph in Chic designers and a loose pink tank top. Dark blond hair spilled down around her face and shoulders in a manner almost lewd; early Bardot.

Wonderful. The combined ages of these two likely wouldn't far surpass Peter's alone. Their fathers were probably cops, too. If living like a college student was occupational hazard number one, then this was a close second—too much contact with early bloomers. Statutory city. Prudent judgment, if you please.

And it was time to check in with the station. Paul donned headphones and keyed the two-way link with the booth. So long as her studio mike wasn't open, his incoming signal would arrive through the soundboard speaker used for cueing album tracks before play, a kind of long-distance intercom.

He panted heavy breath into his microphone, then whispered, "Oooo, first thing I'm gonna do, I'm gonna bite off all your buttons . . ."

"Sexual harassment, you perverts are all alike," Lorraine fired back through the headphones. Then a breathy sigh of disappointment; so close to his ears, the express lane directly to his libido. "All talk and no action."

And here it was again, that flirtation, no holds barred, nothing's shocking. So upfront it was almost casual. This could not, *could not,* last, he reasoned. Either wane, or progress, but running it into habitual routine seemed unlikely.

And which of these would be the more frightening?

"Everything shaping up there okay?" Lorraine asked.

"Not a hitch. You ready to be upstaged for two hours?"

That laugh, defiant acceptance of the gauntlet of challenge. "In your ear."

Contact was broken, and he and Peter killed off the remaining minutes doing crowd circulation, weeding out likely prospects to put on the air and sing the radiant praises of The House of Wax. Most were more than willing, hungry for their shot at fame, the Andy Warhol fifteen minutes. Cliff and Danny Schalter joined them, and the zero hour drew nigh.

"Hey, listen up, special treat for you now," Lorraine's voice clear and strong, backed by one-hundred-watt speakers and stereo separation. "The roving Peter and Paul show is on the loose again. We let the guys out of their cages and sent them over to The House of Wax on Delmar, here in U City. Property values will never be the same, I'm *sure*. Peter Hargrove . . . Paul Handler . . . the air is yours!"

Peter cut the station volume to nil and booted up their mike levels in the same motion—no feedback *here*—and Paul charged in with his frequent war cry: *"Lock up your children and hide your sheep!"* The throng reacted with a mighty roar. They had just hit the ground running.

Keep it loose, keep it hip, keep it hyper. For the next five minutes, they lived and breathed and sweated for The House of Wax, greatest thing since sliced bread and free enterprise. Then they turned it back over to Lorraine, and music once again wailed through like an air-raid siren. Rockers, boppers, plugging into it and the dancing was fresh, renewed, energized.

During the next break, Peter held the mike for several of the crowd, their preselected few, the unrehearsed cavalcade of rocker-in-the-street impressions of the store. Tina Goodyear and her friend —Stacy Donnelly, as she gave her name—made enthusiastic spokespersons. Once they had punted back to Lorraine and Paul was coiling his microphone cord out of harm's way, Stacy wandered up and smiled at him. Eyes, large and wide-spaced, a shade of blue the color of heartbreak. He could have puddled onto the sidewalk. Give me strength.

"So *you're* Paul Handler?" she said, and Peter gave him a discreet wink and a nudge. Scum.

He nodded. "Ah, yes. For better or for worse."

"Wow. I mean, you look exactly like I had you pictured."

A career first. Paul felt like a Greek god. This lass was bucking for the just-conceived office of Sweetheart of KGRM. She seemed to hang close after the festivities moved indoors. Could it be, his first KGRM groupie? Anonymous phone titillation didn't count. If only she weren't so achingly young. No fair.

The next two breaks were conducted from inside the store, air-conditioned comfort, drawing names for prize giveaways. Danny Schalter glowed, happy man in his element. Paul found himself, in the lulls of his own duties, watching Danny from across the store. Wondering about him, who he was inside. This place was so obviously a dream come true for him, and as such, sacrifices had surely been made somewhere along the line. What had he given up along the way to create this triumphal afternoon?

Paul never really thought much of sacrificial terms until moments like this. Disc jockey, his dream? Yes, humble though it may have been, that was it. Likely he'd never be wealthy, but his needs were simple enough anyway. No great sacrifice there. A love and a relationship to call his very own? That's it, twist the knife a little deeper. Seven-year career divided up among five midwestern cities, somehow there had not been a lot of time or opportunity for roots and interpersonal solidarity. Town to town, up and down the dial, the *WKRP In Cincinnati* credo. Wonderful. And now here he was, Paul Handler, living a cliché according to the dictates of late 1970s television.

Dirty price, but somebody had to pay it.

The fifth break was scheduled for five o'clock. Peter and Paul carried their mikes back outside, found the crowd had grown by perhaps half again. This was actually getting impressive.

"Clear your calendars, okay?" Cliff, guarding the sound equipment in their absence. "Danny's saying he might like to do something like this once a month, at least through the fall."

Peter wiggled his shades up and down. "Kickbacks in the form of free albums for Peter and Paul, you say?"

"Hey, you're a hit, I can work on that," and no doubt dreams of lucrative commissions were dancing in his head—

—as Lorraine back-announced the last three songs she had played.

—as Stacy Donnelly sipped from a can of Diet Pepsi.

—as the sound of tires striping hot asphalt during sudden takeoff slashed through the air.

—as Tina Goodyear mopped glistening sweat from between her ample breasts.

—as Peter caught Lorraine's segue into their break.

—and as Paul abruptly looked to the east and shouted the forbidden word *shit* live on the air.

His attention had been pulled to the other end of the block by the double-thud of tires mounting concrete over a curb. It might have been funny, that first sight, Buster Keaton slapstick with sound. Young man down the block with knees pumping in a furious gallop, neither grace nor form, only speed inspired by threat of death. And it was enough. His mouth was open wide, but there was no sound, the silent voice of frozen dread. He abruptly disappeared into a recessed shop doorway, like a vaudeville comedian yanked offstage by an enormous shepherd's crook. While the car behind him stayed its course, straight and true.

Big tan junker, grimed with dust, a solid gas-guzzler from a by-gone era, held together by scabs of rust. It was bearing down on the crowd, *driving down the center of the sidewalk*, grillwork looming like the broken grin of a skull. And herein lay the seed of guilt, that everyone's attention was focused on the two minor media celebrities to such an extent that no one else even knew it was coming.

But given the locomotive impact of surprise on Paul's face, Peter's a moment later, they knew. *They knew.* Something wrong, terribly terribly wrong. Those with quicker presence of mind spun to check their backsides.

Stampede, chaos and pandemonium. People bailing toward the street, running to press themselves flat against storefronts, sprinting away along the sidewalk. Paul dropped his microphone, and a hysterical wail of feedback razored the air. He grabbed the two nearest pairs of shoulders and hoped for the best and hustled them toward the building. Peter chugged across the sidewalk—Paul had never seen him move so swiftly, nor even considered he could—and scooped up two more, tumbling with them off the curb between two parked cars.

But it wasn't enough. With nearly seventy people knotted onto a city sidewalk, it could never be enough. Too many people, too few shelters. Compounded by shock, rabbit-in-headlight paralysis.

Paul heard Lorraine's voice, urgent over the speakers, *What's going on*, then heard the horrid thud of grillwork colliding with a yielding body. Saw a kid go pinwheeling up the car's windshield and over the roof to tumble down behind. The same sound, a reprise, and this time a girl hit the sidewalk with the force of a sledgehammer. The sound yet again, and someone else followed the same trajectory as the first boy.

Madness, complete and surreal. And the screaming, yes, plenty of that to go around. From victims and near-misses and witnesses on all sides. *That sound*, flesh and bone and steel, please God make it stop, and the excruciatingly lovely Stacy Donnelly was airborne, shooting star, bursting through a plate-glass window into The House of Wax, disappearing into the crystal blizzard.

Paul himself was screaming, an involuntary reaction yanked from heart and soul, and he lost track of how many more sickly thuds imprinted on eardrums and memory. The car swerved nearer to him and his two terrified wards, cutting closer with frightening deliberation, like a shark cruising near enough for a diver to reach out and touch its smooth hide.

The driver turned to gaze into Paul's face as he passed, a severed moment that spoke volumes on the bizarre eloquence of madness. No rational thought, but on some instinctual level Paul wanted to see rabid foam, wanted cunning and savagery and manifestations of all things abhorrent. They would mean nothing, but would at least seem expected. But they were not to be found, not on *this* passing face, plain and calm and set with purpose, with only the tiniest of smiles to indicate that some grim pleasure was to be had from all this.

The car passed, finally, to bound off the curb onto the cross street, hooking left and disappearing from sight, from sound, from reality.

There settled an eerie moment during which nothing and no one seemed to move, and Paul knew that neither water nor tears could soon wash away the grief and vague guilt these moments had heaped upon their heads. He looked at young faces grown ancient, heard a peculiar sobbing, timeless, heard too many places all over the globe. Beirut, Northern Ireland, El Salvador, wherever loss comes too quickly, violent and irrevocable. U City? Welcome to the world.

Danny Schalter came bursting from his front door, and he was weeping. It was a ghastly thing to see, the death of the dream. The rape of the golden moment, stripping it down to lead. He was the trigger.

As those who were able began to sort through the wreckage, to pick up the pieces.

6

The House of Wax tragedy was but a few hours old, and already the talk of the town. The media were abuzz, while fact and speculation and misinformed gossip blazed like wildfires. It was the last thing Paul wanted any part of, whether as participant or passive listener. Too close, he was too close, and much more proximity in the next few hours was going to tear his soul into shreds.

Tonight it could only be Tappers, there was no other choice. Tappers Pub, a favored U City hideaway often frequented by the KGRM staff. There were flashier bars, trashier bars, trendier bars, but all roads eventually led back to Tappers, as real and comforting as a log fire on a cold winter's day. They descended on this place with a knowledge that bordered on telepathic: None of them need be alone tonight.

Paul and Peter and Clifford were later arrivals, having spent nearly three hours as guests of the police, giving their statements. Paul had been the only one to get a solid look at the driver and had flipped through mug files in a futile attempt to hang a name onto that face. And then, just as suddenly, Paul was escorted into an entirely new set of circumstances, his first lineup; point that finger of accusation. They told him nothing, only that a suspect had been brought in, and there was never a doubt but that they had the right guy.

There was no triumph in this, *Number four, he's the one, yes, officer, I'm sure of it.* Only an incredible sadness, a total incomprehension as to why this had to have happened in the first place. He couldn't even look at the plain-faced, stoop-shouldered man, now with his gaze cast down toward his own shoes, and hate him for what he had done. Strongest, Paul supposed, was simply a bone-deep wish to turn back time. He felt far too old. . . .

And felt little better when they got to Tappers, but here, at least, were friendly faces, familiar surroundings. A haven of brick and ancient mellow wood, and in a touch of bohemia, paintings by area artists hung on the walls. He and Peter and Cliff scooted a second table adjacent to that of the earlier arrivals, Lorraine and David Blane and receptionist Sherry Thomason. Nods of greeting bobbed around the table, and for a long moment, no one said anything. Paul broke the ice, finally, told them the wacko was in custody.

"This is probably a ghoulish question," said Captain Quaalude, "but what was the final casualty report?" He was rumpled, unshaven, hair in tufts. Probably hadn't thought to shower after awakening to the news of what had happened.

Peter fielded this one. "Three dead. Eight in the hospital, five of those in serious condition."

Among them, the once-lovely Stacy Donnelly, and every time Paul thought of her, lying inside the store and littered with shards of glass, he wanted to curl into a fetal ball and shake. Seventeen years old. Her leg, her hip, twisted at angles nature never intended. Feeling somehow responsible, *Would she have still been there if it wasn't for me, if it wasn't for whoever she thought I was because she hears my voice every day?*

"Who do you think this nutcase was?" Sherry asked, and Paul couldn't answer.

"Do we have any enemies?" David said.

Cliff shrugged. "Maybe somebody's got a grudge against Danny Schalter."

"Yeah, and maybe there's just a lot of sick fucking people in the world." Peter, with no little irritation. "What do you say we give it a rest for fifteen minutes, okay?"

Sound advice. They sat beneath lights gone dim, in the gentle wash from a cane blade ceiling fan. Behind the brass-railed bar, Tequila Mike had tuned the TV for baseball, Cardinals versus Mets, airing from New York. In one corner, a couple of borderline yuppettes were locked into a game of darts. And best, crossing over to their tables, an angel of mercy in a peasant's blouse.

"Jackie." Paul smiled, and by now his head was slumped down atop crossed arms on the table.

"I'm so sorry," she said. "So very sorry."

Jackie planted herself behind Paul to administer a brief neckrub, and he groaned. She had the firmest hands. She supplied every beverage need with a smile, took no unnecessary bullshit, and wore her philosophy of business on a button pinned over her left breast: TIP ME OR DIE OF THIRST. He could fall asleep in moments, a pleasant cocoon of background babble and Jackie's hands. Damn, all the good ones were married.

"Get you guys your usual?" she said, and affirmatives were given, sooner the better, and she left, patting Peter's head and tweaking Cliff's nose.

"She likes you best," Peter said. "Barmaid's pet, that's what you are." He fumbled in his pockets for a pack of Salems. When he glanced up at Lorraine, beside him, a faint hint of Wicked Uncle Pete resurfaced in his eyes. An oddly welcome sight, any diversion welcome. He wiggled the unlit cigarette beneath Lorraine's nose before she could scoot away.

"Oh, just give me the damn thing." She snatched it from his hand, lit it from the tip of the one David was smoking. Inhaled, shut her eyes, exhaled a wispy cloud. She opened her eyes and hit Paul with a guilty little smile. "Just this one. For medicinal purposes only."

Jackie was soon back with the usuals, and set down a pitcher of Bass ale for Peter and Paul, along with two frosted mugs. Gin for Clifford. The liver abuse started immediately, trying to drown sorrows that had learned to swim.

"KGRM." Peter's voice was loud, declamatory, edgy. "Lethal Rock Radio. Shit. I don't think I can ever say that again."

David nodded, drained his long-neck Coors and traded it in for a fresh one. Jackie was in for combat pay tonight. "I suggest we reconsider the merits of that particular slogan. I'll talk to Popeye about retiring all our Lethal station IDs."

"Too bad," Sherry said. "I really loved those."

Peter tipped his mug in a bitter salute. "End of an era, kiddies."

That was the problem with anything you could define as an era, Paul decided. It never lasted. Decline and fall, same old sad story. Gone in a haze of smoking rubber, exhaust, and burning oil.

He grew hungry, remembered he had not eaten since breakfast. The suggestion was put forth for food, and three platters of Mighty

Macho Nachos were ordered. They arrived looking like steaming slices from someone's lawn, deluged with enough shredded lettuce to choke a lawn mower. Tequila Mike brought them himself. Special occasion.

"Three Mexican garbage pails, on the house tonight. I figure you could use *some* good news." Good old Tequila Mike, so named because no one could match him in a guave worm eating contest. Rock-solid friend to loyal patrons, and for the occasional Olympian hangover you might complain of, he could whip up a Bloody Mary to reanimate the dead.

News director Russell St. James was the last to arrive. He settled at the head of the tables, promptly scalded his tongue on melted cheese, nacho napalm. Tall guy who denied his receding hairline, preferring instead to call it an advancing forehead. What fuzzy hair remained left him looking like Art Garfunkel, circa late seventies. He'd never make the jump to TV news.

"Did you get anything out of the police before you left?" Lorraine asked.

"A little." He nodded, rolled his eyes, as if having heard too much of the wrong thing. "I know this one guy at the main station, he'll usually slip me stuff off the record. They're not releasing the guy's name or background, not yet, but he did give me the gist of what the guy told them when they asked why he took a car through the crowd."

"Why?" Paul said. As if any excuse was going to make sense.

"Said God told him to do it." Russ sat staring into the table, chewing on the inside of one cheek. Objectivity was gone this time, the news too close to home. "He said he was listening to the broadcast, and then God came on and told him to take care of it. So . . . he did."

The revelation was met with the expected silence, the same uneasy greeting of any lunatic raving about mad divine sanction. Had the events today not been so horribly tragic, this might have almost been funny. Paul could hear the jokes now: God? Wonder what kind of Arbitrons *He* pulls? Wonder what the FCC will have to say about this?

God, infinite patience and love aside, must get awfully tired of all the crazies lining up to claim His partnership.

And so they drank, and numbed themselves from the inside out. A miniature city of bottles and glasses grew over the tabletop, roadmapped by sticky rings, foliated by stray lettuce and guacamole. Cliff excused himself and began to chat up the two dart players. The tournament soon became a threesome, and Paul wished him silent luck. Diversions were needed, tonight of all nights.

"Funniest thing I ever saw in my life involved that guy," Peter said, kicking back to watch Cliff try to get laid. And on went the story, KGRM legend that Peter had promised to tell Paul someday. The time had come, the night of nights. Two years ago, according to Peter, Cliff had been working on a new stranger for hours, never had seen her in Tappers before. Buying her drink after drink while she sat at the bar in perfect poise and regal control. At last, he moved in for the kill, nuzzling close, telling her how much he loved her hair. Suave, charming, and as debonair as Cary Grant. *If you like it that much,* she'd told him, *go ahead and take it.* To which she whipped off what proved to be a wig and showed him a bare head, sparse wispy fuzz. Chemo.

Paul laughed and it was obligatory, but Peter never noticed, and this was as Paul wanted it. Chemo and its ravages, yes, he knew what they were like, and he would never find them funny . . .

The night grew late, later, and their ranks dwindled. Sherry the first to leave, Captain Quaalude next, vowing he had just enough time to grab a little coffee and sobriety before starting the graveyard shift. Clifford vanished into the night with the taller of the two dart-slingers. Peter and Russ vacated at the same time, bemoaning how morning was going to come too early for them both.

And then there were two.

Paul and Lorraine sat across from each other, relying heavily on elbows. Time-lapse photography throughout the night would have marked the passing of the hours by their gradually slumping closer to the tabletop.

She checked the clock behind the bar, groaned. A quarter to one. She peered down into her drink. Over the night she had consumed an orchard of fuzzy navels.

"You want me to call Craig, so he can come get you?"

She shook her head, held up a hand, traffic cop stop. "He wouldn't answer. He's in San Francisco. Bizzzzzness."

"How about a cab?"

She looked up, ignoring the offer. "Bet you if I went over to that phone over there and checked our answering machine, I'd find out he didn't call me tonight, either. Come on. Bet me?"

"No," he said quietly. He leaned back in his chair, tried to mentally tally up the scattered change and bills, Jackie's well-earned tips. Surrender was quick. Sadly, simple addition was now on a par with differential calculus. And wasn't tonight just the night for misery and self-pity, anyway? Tequila Mike really needed a better selection of jukebox blues.

Lorraine's fingertip traced wet circles around the rim of her glass. "Who are you serious about these days? Are you still seeing what's-her-name, the one that writes the movie reviews?"

"Joanie." He shook his head. "It didn't work out. I suppose the clinical term for my condition is 'between relationships.' But I prefer layman's language."

"Which is?"

"My love life's in the dumper."

She giggled, wearily pushed her mass of hair back from her forehead and giggled more when it fell forward again into her drink. It seemed very funny to Paul at the time, too.

"Well don't you sweat it, Paul." Her voice lurched and dragged in spots, despite a heroic fight for clarity. "Here's what you do. Need a pen? Never mind, I'll remember. Before you get serious, make sure you're compatible. Take a whole bunch of *Cosmo* tests or something."

His shoulders wiggled in silent laughter. *Would we be having this conversation if our kidneys weren't floating? Probably not.* He had no idea what to say, was grateful when she went on.

"You know what pisses me off the most? Craig doesn't even want to take my career seriously. Like, like it's not as important as his, or it's just a phase I'll grow out of. Okay! Okay! Maybe he does make about three times what I do. But you never see *me* coming through that door at night all stressed out."

Paul was nodding, yes, yes, but inside, *I really don't think I want to hear all this.*

"And bedtime. Huh!" She tossed her hands up, let them clunk to the table. "His idea of foreplay anymore is to yell, 'Get ready.' "

They both broke up laughing, sudden gallows humor, and Paul was finding it very necessary to laugh. Self-defense. If allowed to brood too long, he would surely picture the two of them in the conjugal bed, Lorraine's mounting frustration as she tried to elicit a more protracted sexual response, the give and take of carnal raptures. He didn't need those images. For if he saw them with too much clarity, he just might have to apply his fist to the nearest wall and work things out.

"So what if KGRM isn't at the top of the heap?" she said. "I've worked hard to be taken seriously in this town, do quality work. I think it's paying off, too. You know, when I first got into radio, it seemed like most GMs and program directors wanted me to come off like some no-brain sex object." Lips pouted, eyebrows arched, she dropped her voice into sultry breathiness. "Hi, this is Lorraine *Savage*. And I'll be *up* with you all night *long*, right here on WORG, Orgasm Rock Radio." She shelved the act with abrupt disdain, and shook her head.

"Well *I* like it," and he pressed a glass of melting ice to his face and hissed, venting steam.

"Oh you pervert." She made as if to swat him on the arm, squeezed it instead. "And you know the hell of it? I think if Popeye had his way, that's exactly what I'd be doing at KGRM. Lucky for me David's smarter than that."

"Popeye's not the most enlightened GM I've seen, no."

"Tell me about it. The man's a pig in a three-piece suit. Have you seen the way he looks at Sherry sometimes? He does everything but sniff her chair when she leaves a room."

The red flare of anger was righteous, sudden. Protective instincts resurfacing, us against them, downtrodden versus management. In this case, compounded by their receptionist's extreme youth. For years he had been cast in such a role, the big brother. Friend, confessor, confidant; these he had been to young women ever since high school. He used to feel flattered, then a so-called friend had told him it just meant they considered him no threat, and after that he wasn't sure quite what to think.

Take things for what they're worth, he figured. They are what they are.

"I'm going home," he said.

He killed off the last of the Bass ale. Definitely time to retire the mug. He tried and mostly failed to stifle the Mount Krakatoa of belches, and Lorraine keeled over in laughter, shoulder to tabletop, as he rose.

"And with *that*, madam," cloaking himself in the tattered shreds of his dignity, "I think I shall bid you good night."

"Wait, wait, wait. I should leave too." She wriggled out of her seat, wavered with arms extended for high-wire balance. "Whoa. Steady. I think I should've left with Sherry."

Paul gripped her forearm, the blind leading the blind. His own internal gyroscope had taken quite a beating, as well. They bade fond farewells to Jackie and Tequila Mike, then left Tappers behind. Sidewalk on a summer night. The air had cooled to pleasant, fresh and head-clearing after hours of smoke and enclosure. Headlights and neon played havoc with their eyes for a few moments.

They were not alone, the sidewalks were still well-cruised. Barhoppers in transit, insomniacs out for coffee or a slice of late-night pizza. The Loop, alive with the midnight musings of poets and troubadours. Here there was desperate romance, and solace, and hope, and dawn was very far away.

He walked Lorraine to her car, found half a block away in a nose-to-bumper string of vehicles. She drove one of those old abominations that Volkswagen had christened The Thing. She dug into her purse for the keys.

And then her shoulders slumped, deflated, and she looked up into his eyes. Profoundly miserable all of a sudden, as if the prospect of her empty house were the last thing on earth she wanted to face.

"I don't want to go home, Paul. I think I'd sooner sleep in the gutter tonight. Can . . . can I borrow your couch or something?"

It was the last thing he had expected, packing a heavyweight wallop. Roll with the punches, he was loose enough. "Sure, sure. You probably shouldn't even be driving, anyway."

They abandoned her car and kept going, Paul doing most of the navigating. Prolonged exposure to the night air seemed to benefit their legwork, practice makes perfect. Two sots who pass in the night. He wondered what upwardly mobile Craig would have to say if he saw her now. Probably wouldn't find much humor in the situation, and this infused Paul with a wonderfully exhilarating rush of one-upmanship, however short-lived it might be. *We got you this time, Craig.*

"You are one nice man. You know that?"

He felt the flush of low-grade embarrassment creeping into his cheeks. "Right. Saint Paul."

"Seriously!" She gestured emphatically with her hands. The lethargic wind-down that had been overtaking her in Tappers was being driven out by renewed energy. "Everybody says that."

Paul grunted. "Peter says I'm too nice for my own good."

"Peter Hargrove is a Viking who was unlucky enough to have been born a thousand years too late." Lorraine leaned into him, resting her head on his shoulder a moment. "*I* respect you."

"Good for you. That's *one*."

"I'll bet anything you're not from a city originally. Are you? You have this kind of, oh, small-town compassion about you. Am I right? Bet you anything, bet you a pitcher at Tappers. Where were you born and raised?"

"Chicago."

"Oh, you *smartass!*" she wailed, wounded. "I feel so stupid now, thank you *so* much."

"You want me to rub your nose in it some more?" He cackled and ground his palms together, Torquemada at the Inquisition. "I was born in the back of a taxi. My mom went into labor a couple of weeks early, really sudden. The cabbie couldn't even make it to the nearest hospital on time. It happened the day Kennedy was shot."

"No kidding? Cause and effect, you think? Did the news shock her that much?"

"More like coincidence, I'm sure."

She was clearly impressed, the most interesting birth story she'd heard, she said. "Do you get back to visit your family much?"

He shook his head, and right, here's where memories became treacherous. "I haven't been to Chicago in years. My dad died when I was twelve. Cancer. Mom, I don't know. She just wasn't ever really the same after that. When I first left for college, she moved to Ohio, to be close to her sister. She works as a checker in a convenience store. She's . . . not all there anymore."

"I'm sorry, Paul." Lorraine was nearly whispering. "I didn't mean to stir up bad memories."

Bad memories, such gentle understatement. The threshold to puberty was a double-barrel blast of *atrocious* memories. Watching Dad drop pound after pound, shriveling into himself a piece at a time. Lines cutting into his face while he fought the good fight, even as he radiated the stench of rotting from within. And watching Mom shrink into herself, as well, a psychological counterpoint to the way Dad had died. And young Paul himself, suffering in silence most of the time, unable to shake the creeping sense of being somehow to blame, all this was his fault, and he had only to figure out why.

He remembered the diagnosis, *cancer,* and what a horrifying awakening that had been, the first true sign of weakness in this man who had once been immortal, who had stood taller and firmer than the Colossus of Rhodes. *It's my fault.*

Intellectually, even at such a tender age, he knew better. He understood death. Pets had died. Relatives had died. As had classmates and neighbors and strangers with familiar names. But in the best of all possible worlds, fathers should be spared. At least until their sons and daughters were grown, until they had balanced grandchildren on their knees. Only then, one day, could they be allowed to go to the grave, secure in knowing that a legacy did indeed exist, that they had not fretted and toiled for nothing. Unfinished business was the worst loose end of all.

And guilt belonged in the past. But this was not the best of all possible worlds. Even so, sometimes you still get lucky, and someone, somewhere, offers a small gesture of support to make it bearable.

Like when Lorraine reached down to hold his hand. The cool press of interlocking fingers, he let it happen, relished it.

They had the giggles again by the time Paul figured out which key to use to access his building. The night could no longer swallow their voices after they entered through a rear doorway. The hall seemed to amplify them at once, hugely so. Massive audio shock.

"*Shhhhhhh!*" Paul raised a finger to his lips, spluttered laughter again. If he looked her in the eye at this precise moment, he knew he wouldn't get off the floor for a half hour. "We have to be quiet so we don't wake the wicked witch of the second floor."

"Who?"

"Mrs. DeWitt." Once they had reached the staircase, he peered dramatically upward, holding her back, here there be dragons. Coast clear. "You *don't* want to meet her."

"Is she really that bad?"

"Remember that scary old bitch in *Throw Momma from the Train?*" he asked, and she said she did. "Well, this could be her younger sister."

They hauled themselves upward, hand over hand along the banister, Lorraine softly chanting, "Wake the wicked witch, we wake the wicked witch." Paul trembled with suppressed laughter and demanded silent stealth, but she would have none of it. She dropped her voice into Elmer Fudd, his little chugging laughter, "We wake the wicked witch, you wascally wabbit." He couldn't stand this, his seams were bursting, and finally they slogged through his doorway, awash in silly drunken hilarity, moments that seem funniest after midnight, and the later the better.

Paul hit the lights, then the stereo. A cut from Pink Floyd's *Dark Side of the Moon* was drifting from KGRM. Captain Quaalude's Classics. He was probably tracking albums tonight, fewer chances to screw up before total sobriety set in. Paul collapsed into his couch's embrace while Lorraine set off on an expedition into the kitchen, yanked open the fridge door. Clinked every single bottle and jar inside.

"Hey! Cream cheese!" A squeal of delight. "I love cream cheese! Do you have any bagels? Please say you have bagels!"

"No, I don't, and don't open that. It's toxic waste by now."

He listened to her muttered disappointment as she continued to redecorate his fridge. Then, silence. Could be trouble. A moment later, Lorraine shuffled in across the well-worn carpet with a carton of blueberry yogurt. She nibbled a spoonful, grinned at him. With her hair in her face, blouse only half-tucked into her jeans, and posture abysmal, Lorraine looked disheveled and frowzy. And absolutely adorable.

"I found yogurt." She held up the refilled spoon to prove it. "Can I have some?" He said no, and she chose to ignore it and shuffled past, leaning over to peer at his pets within their glass walls. She smiled and waved to them.

"What cute little hamsters," and she then squeaked in an apparent attempt to establish communication, I know just how you feel in there. They remained aloof. "What are their names?"

"Calvin and Hobbes. And they're not hamsters, they're gerbils."

"What's the difference?"

"Gerbils take longer in a crock pot."

She whirled, eyes wide with horror. "Oh Paul Handler, you're the sickest human being in the entire world. And you deserve punishment."

Lorraine bounded onto the sofa, and he bounced alongside her, and she set the yogurt container on the coffee table. The spoon she retained, and the sizeable blob of yogurt it held. Clasping the end of the handle, fingertips only, she drew the business end back like a catapult and sighted in. Steady . . .

Paul sat erect, chin thrust defiantly. "Lorraine . . ."

Aim . . .

"Don't you dare, don't you *dare*—"

Fire! The yogurt splatted onto his right cheek like a creamy bird dropping. Lorraine tried to compose herself, prim and perfectly innocent, but the giggles got the best of her all over again. Giggles turned to shrieks when he hooked his fingers onto her ribs, he knew *those* were ticklish, the chink in the armor. Paul was laughing as hard as she when they both thudded to the floor, rolling and rebounding in a horizontal clinch as she kicked weakly and whooped and gasped for breath. She squirmed like an eel and they ricocheted off an orange crate, she begging *No no no stop stop*, and he insisting *You've gone too far this time*, and she vowing *I take it back, I'm sorry, I'll be good.*

The next thing he knew her face was pressed against his and she flicked out her tongue, licking the offending yogurt from his cheek, her hands tickling him in retaliation, and their lips brushed accidentally—or *was* it, really?—and then their mouths made a second dive for each other and this time lingered. Tight, so tight, so fervent.

The rolling, the struggling, these dwindled, ceased. The music pulsed on, murky saxophone wringing melodies of desperate futile melancholy. Lorraine lay still beneath him, cradling him with parted legs, muscles taut and straining. He propped himself onto elbows to better gaze down at her, her wide startled eyes. Her breath was coming in sudden little hitches; he could feel it beneath him, the quick rise and fall, could feel its sweet peach scent upon his throat. Her parted lips were trembling. *Trembling.* He had never thought he could make a woman tremble.

"Paul?" Quietly, timidly. "What's happening here?"

"I don't know." An honest whisper. "Do you mind it?"

Eyes wider still, a tiny shake of her head. Voice now a hush. "No."

He stayed put, secure in that pelvic cradle, motionless. Balanced atop some judgmental fence from which he could tumble down one side or the other. Oh, so many things to consider in mere seconds, the decision not just a matter of simple lust, never that, not with her. He thought of marriage, how he still believed in its sanctity. How he could truly love her if she would allow that. How Craig hurt her in ways he probably wasn't even aware of, Craig, this night over the hills and far away while she was here of her own free will.

He wanted this so badly, more than just one night, but if one night was all that it was, then it would have to do. Things are what they are.

He felt that peculiar delicious fear of shared vulnerability, allowing another to risk the dive within your soul. To turn back from this brink now would be so very difficult, so very painful.

The decision was made, had been made all along, and if only dawn might never come.

7

 The morning sun was brutal even through his bedroom curtains. Paul turned away in a witless attempt at escape, and as it burned away sleep, along came recollection. The past twenty-four hours, the tragedy and the ecstasy, all leading up to this rather agreeable feeling of not waking up alone.

Complete thoughts, finally, present situation.

Number one: *I have beer farts.*

Number two: *How can I discreetly deal with this?*

He glanced at Lorraine, who slept in a childlike curl with the sheet in loose folds up to her shoulders. He bent forward to lightly kiss the exposed shoulder, and she rewarded him with a happy murmur of sleep, sweet dreams. He could easily grow accustomed to beginning his days with that sound.

Suffering the jet lag of new morn sobriety, he tiptoed into the bathroom and shut the door, alone with his traitor digestive system. Selfish thing that it was, caring not a bit that a lovely young woman had shared bed, body, and soul with him, and he wished to avoid offending her. An old clawfoot tub hunkered across the room, tattooed with stains that defied all known cleansers, and he ran water to mask his noise. Master of diversion.

Lorraine awoke when he crept back into bed, and she groaned, stretched with the sinewy grace of a cat. She played racquetball, and he could tell it; he was pleasantly sore in places he had forgotten he could be. The sheet pulled away to waist level, and her breasts were pale against the gold of her tan. She relaxed, licking dry lips to moisten them.

He was a little dry himself. Ironic, this proclivity of people to pair off and go home to exchange bodily fluids after having drunk enough to dehydrate themselves. So bad that Gatorade became an aphrodisiac.

"Hi," he said. A light opener for the day, easygoing, not at all indicative of having just broken Commandments Seven and Ten.

"Hi yourself." Lazy little smile, which—for some reason—didn't seem quite enough. He wanted more. Cartwheels would do.

Married. Oh yeah. Shit.

"You don't have a maid, by any chance, do you?"

He swept his arm to show off the room's floor, one giant underwear and sock drawer. "I gave her the year off."

"Rats. No room service."

"I could fill in. You should see me in a frilly apron and heels." He scooted up to sit, molding a pillow between back and headboard. The clock radio read 8:52.

Paul watched her for a moment, increasingly uneasy over what he saw. Her hand, performing the utterly useless task of smoothing out sheet wrinkles. Her eye contact, fleeting at best. He felt the first fearful quivers in his belly, high and nervous.

A treasure trove of things he wanted to say had accumulated over the night. That he could love her, deeply. What would happen when Craig returned home, and what of the more distant future? Countless variations and repetitions of each, none of which seemed remotely appropriate at the moment. Overstepping his bounds, perhaps? Where did the boundaries even lie anymore?

"How do you feel this morning?" An open-ended question.

"Pretty decent." She leaned into the sun's rays, soaking them in as if to recharge. "I thought I'd be more hung over."

It wasn't what he'd meant, but that's what you get for open-ended questions. Last night had changed everything, and he was burning to know to what degree. Because some genuinely wonderful magic had been conjured up in the living room and bedroom just hours ago. For better or for worse, magic changes things. No stagnation allowed in the Magic Kingdom.

"Are you happy?"

She didn't turn around, not yet, still faced the filtered sunbeams. It took several seconds, but she finally nodded. It didn't matter how long it took, seconds or an hour, the effect was still the same: It hurt like hell. *She'd had to think about it first.* And no matter how much the rational left side of the brain told him that this wasn't the easiest thing in the world for her, either, the intuitive right would have no part of it. Emotion flexed muscles the size of Schwarzenegger's; logic was built like Pee-wee Herman.

"Are you scared?"

She turned, at last, sunlight firing a golden forge through that glorious touseled hair. Her eyes huge, nakedly vulnerable, allowing neither lie nor rationalization to escape. He knew the answer before she nodded again.

"Are you sorry?"

That did it.

Lorraine shut her eyes and scooted closer, let the sun melt her into his waiting arms, and he rested his cheek atop her head. Her hair still smelled faintly of smoke from Tappers.

"No. I'm not sorry. And right now, I don't know if that's okay, or if I should be. Because that means . . . that means there's a lot in my life that I have to get sorted out, before . . ."

I really don't want to hear this.

". . . before I go making any important decisions."

He shut his eyes, tried to soak in every last nuance of the moment. The physical closeness; the deepened emotional bonds, however tenuous they might turn out to be. Odds were, he was quickly realizing, that this scenario was a one-shot, unlikely to repeat soon, if ever. So he became a sponge, absorbing whatever he could, preserving it, whole and perfect, so it could later be pulled out and cherished like an heirloom. So he could assure himself that, yes, they had happened, if only for one lovely, shining night.

Better that by far than turning it into something tawdry. Furious bathroom copulations during the newscast between their airshifts. Skulking about in dark bars and restaurants, entering theaters after the show had already started, and even then worrying who might see them, who might talk. He could not live like that, love like that. And could play no part in forcing her to do likewise.

Believing that she could simply have turned her back on her current life and walked straight into his? Delusional thinking. A rationalization. But honest, so very painfully honest.

Lorraine pulled back, ran fingertips along the sides of his face in sweet caress. Kissed him. No obligatory kiss, this one, meant to serve as some emotional pacifier, but wholly genuine.

"I'm sorry, Paul," her eyes begging for a depth of understanding she seemed to fear she could not reasonably expect. "Plus . . . we've been talking about maybe having a baby."

Insult to injury, salt in the wounds. Babies meant that major-league commitment was still in the cards. He felt sicker than ever, the hot squirm of regret. A child, just what her husband needed. *Her husband*, don't say his name and he becomes less real, right? A child, someone to follow in his Gucci footsteps. What, me, bitter?

Another fierce hug, another futile try at making time stand still and bottling the essence of the moment. Then she was up and off the bed. As he took in the sight of her before all would be forever-more hidden in clothes, it was a classic case of the unattainable goal looking infinitely more desirable.

Was anything worse than unrequited love? But of course. The genuine, two-way real thing roadblocked by prior commitment.

Lorraine gathered her clothes from the living-room floor, carried them to his bedroom doorway. Could she borrow his shower, and he gave her his blessing, even proved it by fetching a fresh wash-cloth and towels from the narrow linen closet.

The water surged on, causing a brief shuddering of pipes and walls—bathquake. When he heard the metallic clitter of the shower curtain circling the rod, he wandered to his kitchen wall phone and dialed KGRM's request line. Talking to Peter, please please take my airshift too, I can't handle things today, and maybe you could make up some bullshit excuse for Popeye while you're at it. Good old Pete, not so wicked after all. Remembering who had been the final two left last night, he quickly and accurately fit the puzzle together. No problem, he said.

They signed off, and Paul stepped into a pair of gym shorts doing double duty as an oven mitt these days. A few minutes later, Lorraine poked her head from the bathroom, wisps of humid steam accompanying her in ephemeral wreaths.

"Do you have any deodorant I can borrow?"

Paul retrieved it from his bedroom dresser, handed it over as she half-hid herself in the doorway, towel knotted between her breasts. Not so uninhibited today, are we, and he caught himself. No spite, not toward her.

"Thanks." She inspected the label, her hair a wet blond curtain. "Old Spice. Great. I'll smell like a sailor all day."

"Probably get the urge to pee standing up."

It was like that for the duration, trading quips and quirks with an almost desperate need to do so. As if it would shield them from dwelling on the previous night and its implications. Keep a nice safe lid on the hidden longings and the regrets and the suppressed urge to grab each other and reprise last night's magic and this time try for bona fide wizardry. It was either that, or make each other laugh. Emotional Tupperware; seals the humor in, keeps the passion out.

At last came the dreaded moment after which nothing would truly be the same, and life would have to go on as before, if only in appearance. She had to leave, and he did not argue. Arguments led to irretrievable remarks and loss of dignity. No thanks. They faced each other at the door, stricken with a sudden loss for words. Having to suffice with a stiff, awkward hug during which he could smell his shampoo in her hair, and a mumbled, *See you later, okay? Okay.*

The door latched after her with the final slam of a bank vault whose riches would remain forever locked within, eternally in the dark, to collect only rust. He listened to her fading footsteps until he couldn't.

Now, at last, honesty with self. No more fronts to put on, nor stiff upper lips to exhibit. Slowly backing from the threshold. There came no moment of fist-through-wall fury, no cyclone of destructive energy. Only the sad regret, glacial in its chill, if only, if only, the Ice Age of the heart.

He retreated to the sofa in miserable defeat, with KGRM on low for company, a much-needed friend. He drew knees to chest while turning his back on the room, the world, sinking into a profound quagmire of pain. Self-pity was allowed within your own four walls, here comes the bitter flood. He wept. He wept.

But along about three o'clock, he knew that perhaps he might survive after all. While dashed hopes may have run deep, they had been short-lived, less than twenty-four hours old. Their roots could have gone far deeper. Perhaps he might get over things one step at a time, so long as he could still stand.

After all, Lorraine was managing.

"I want to get serious here, before going any further," she said over the air, to an entire city and beyond. "You've heard it before, I know, from everybody who's been on the air since yesterday afternoon. We're all shocked and saddened by what happened at The House of Wax. There's no way we can expect to understand why something like that happens, but it touches us all, one way or another.

"So let's all lean on one another a little harder, okay? Try to be patient with each other, and remember what's important in life.

And if we screw up now and then, and if we say or do the wrong thing at the wrong time, let's not forget to say we're sorry for whatever pain *we* might have caused. We owe each other that much, at the very least. Don't we?"

Paul turned over to face his apartment, his world, for the first time in hours, and she played her first song of the day:

Vintage Fleetwood Mac, "You Make Loving Fun."

He needed a walk. In the worst way. Lorraine's opening remarks —that first crusted scab of healing—were but an hour old, and he needed a walk. One more minute of staring at these walls would render him in need of a straitjacket.

He slipped into some exquisitely faded and comfortable Levi jeans and one of those white muscle shirts emblazoned with red and black Japanese emblems. Rock and roll. He took his car southeast a couple miles, into Forest Park. He abandoned the car on one of the winding drives near the zoo, former stomping ground of Marlin Perkins. Took off on foot, following a meandering eastern path.

He kicked around shaded bowers, watched people of infinite variety, all ages. Walking dogs, or jogging, or hurling Frisbees back and forth. Living their own private lives, so separate from his own, and he wished them well. He bought a chili Polish and a liter of Pepsi, breakfast of chumps, and strolled along.

At the eastern border of the park, Kingshighway was nearly jammed to capacity with rush hour traffic. He stared across it, beyond, at the huge health complex. At, in particular, Barnes Hospital. Long catatonic moments in contemplation, eyes never leaving its walls and windows, acknowledging the subconscious drive that had no doubt led him here. He felt summer sun, summer wind, but experienced them almost secondhand. He was that far inside himself.

He had already checked: He knew who was here. Knew *why* he was here. Deep down, he knew.

What I did the other day with Peter, and he felt a little silly even voicing this to himself, *could that have been real?*

It had nagged and nibbled at him ever since last week. Time now to put it to the acid test. He took life in hands and found a spot to cross Kingshighway and headed on into Barnes. A whim. On a dare with self. Obligation.

Inside was a labyrinth of corridors that might even have befuddled the Minotaur, but he found his way up to Stacy Donnelly's room with few wrong turns. Destiny.

She lay on the far side of a semiprivate room, one of hundreds of such sterile quarters in this place of life and death. He passed an unknown girl sleeping in the first bed, was then facing what had become of the lovely woman-child he had met yesterday. She lay on her back, swaddled in bandages on her limbs, around her head. A few ugly lines of stitches crosshatched across swollen bruises, so purple, so black. Her right leg was sheathed in a cast molded from hip to toes. A smaller one covered her left forearm. IV lines plugged into her arms, and she was mercifully asleep. Just as well. The only thing of any possible enjoyment here were the flowers, and they were plentiful.

His arrival woke a woman propped into a chair in the opposite corner. Blond hair cut nearly identical to Stacy's, and fuller hips. He had no doubt but that this was her mother. Too aware of that timeless competition, the mother who fears the loss of youth, the daughter who embodies emergent vitality and sexuality. The love-hate so strong between them, the agony and the rapture.

She blinked at him in brief puzzlement; probably thought him younger, given these clothes. "Are you one of Stacy's friends?" Her voice was fuzzy from sleep, poor sleep at that. "I don't recognize . . ."

Paul shook his head, barely spoke above a whisper. Hospitals and museums and libraries, do not disturb. "No. I just met her yesterday. At the broadcast. I was . . ." Oh go on, say it, don't be a wuss. "I was one of the deejays there."

She let out a pent-up breath, regarding him with newly awakened eyes that frosted over even as they sharpened. He could easily guess the label she now applied. He was no longer an individual. Now he was someone connected in an official capacity with the tragedy. Fodder for hatred and litigation.

Yeah, Mrs. Donnelly, I guess in a way it's my fault that your daughter's in here. So if you want to blame me for it, okay, go ahead, but please don't say it out loud. Not today.

"How is she?" he asked.

"She's been better," and her voice could hold every bit as much frost as her eyes.

"Is she going to be okay?"

"Yes. But good as new? They don't know yet. She was a dancer. A very good dancer. She wanted to make a career out of ballet. *Do*

*you have any idea what compound fractures can do to a dancer's
leg?"*

He bit his lip. Steady. "I'm sorry, Mrs. Donnelly. I just wanted to
see her for a minute, and then I'll go. I promise."

"Yes, I wish you would."

Venom in his ears, Paul tried to shut her out for several moments.
With her eyes of ice and voice to match, she was too much of a
distraction. Yet she was also a catalyst, these psychic accusations
bringing him into closer contact with the deepest parts of himself,
the parts that hurt because Stacy hurt. The brotherly love he knew
he should feel for anyone in this situation.

He stood along the right side of Stacy's bed, and it seemed almost predestined that her right arm was little harmed. That the cast
was on her left. Her good hand lay by her side, atop the sheet, two
scant inches from the low stainless-steel retaining rail.

Letting his own hand creep forward, upward, Paul reached between the rails. The angle was so discreet, he didn't think Mrs.
Donnelly could see him doing so. He loosely clasped Stacy's small,
cold hand, recalling what had at the time been one more crazed
inspiration to entertain the listeners of KGRM. Last Thursday
morning. Laying hands on the terminally stuffy Peter Hargrove,
casting out the demons of summer colds. For laughs.

Peter's voice, newly clear: *I do believe you cured me.*

He had thought at the time that Peter had steamed himself open
with the heat of a full-blast shower. Except there had been no
relapse, no return of congestion, no more sneezing. Ever.

This was insane, it couldn't work, he couldn't just hold her hand
and expect her to get better. But he waited a moment, watching
carefully . . .

And was absolutely right. Nothing happened.

Damn it. Deep breath, hold, release. Well, now wait a minute. Of
course results weren't going to be forthcoming if he stood there and
didn't even expect them.

After all, even though last Thursday's ceremony had been strictly
for amusement, a certain part of him had nevertheless taken it seriously. Not out of any hope of succeeding, but simply because he
had thrown himself heart and soul into the moment. Playing the
part. Feeling it. Doing it. Method radio.

So let's play it again. For real.

With the focus of a surgical laser and the broad pattern of a
shotgun, Paul gripped Stacy's hand a little harder. As if by doing so

he might reach back through time and yank her from the tan car's path, to safety. He pictured his failure to do so, mentally retracing her arc through the window at The House of Wax. Summoned up the prone, twisted image of her lying amid the glass wreckage.

And now, *now*, he could feel her sorrow of dreams ruined, her dancer's leg pierced with nails of bone. His own sorrow at having let it happen.

Paul knew virtually nothing of her, little beyond her energy, her beauty, her spirit. Her love of life that had been apparent to anyone with an ounce of perception. This much he knew. He knew her name. He knew her pain. Apparently these were enough.

The empathy was astounding. He could feel the subtle energy coursing between them, generated from some emotional turbine he had never known he possessed. Cranking tentatively at first, as if its parts were corroded from disuse, then more freely, oiled by the misery of having had secret dreams of his own dashed to pieces this morning. He could feel that turbine spin, whipping their separate agonies into a single pure blend. All flowing into him, because for now, he was by far the stronger of the two, and he would help her shoulder this immense burden. Carry it the first mile because she needed it, the second because he wanted to.

Paul felt no extra heat radiating from his touch; her hand remained cool. No matter. Whatever he felt was working on the inside, where it counted. Bone cells regenerating, knitting together into a pillar of strength on which she could once again stand, leap, pirouette. Leukocytes massing into inner fires to burn out the infections. The adrenal surge of healing, a steady erosion-in-reverse working its way up through the layers: striated muscle, lower dermis, fat, collagen, corium, epidermis. Lacerations sealed and paled under their stitches and bandages to become ghosts of their former selves. Her sleeping mind shifted suddenly into the REM state, to gift her with a wondrous dream of benevolence personified, reaching down to touch her.

He seemed to instinctively know when it had been enough, and slid his hand out of hers.

It no longer mattered that Mrs. Donnelly still looked daggers at him, that his resting heart rate had soared to more than a hundred beats per minute. For he was jubilant within, soaring and weightless and free, *I did it I actually did it*, and exactly how or why seemed far less important than the simple fact of its being. He had controlled it, made it work at will.

And she had slept through the whole thing. Not that he had expected her to pop up and crack open the casts like the eggshell of a newly hatched bird. Too melodramatic, he didn't want that. Better this way, quiet and unobtrusive. For he had not turned back the clock and made as if yesterday had never occurred, he had only repaired the damages. She would remember, and she would hurt, with soreness and stiffness to work through, and strength to regain. But he had bought her the chance to do so without the accompanying heartbreak of a less-than-complete recovery at the end of that road.

"Sleep well," he whispered, then bade a quiet good evening to Mrs. Donnelly and returned to the hall.

A jaunty stride down the corridor, so far removed from the trepidation with which he had arrived, past nurses and patients and visitors alike. Infused with energy, enthusiasm, big stunned grin breaking across his face, oh, tonight he would rejoice. Tonight he would howl in celebration as old as time.

But not yet. Not yet. This night of glad tidings had just begun, and there were seven other kids out there who deserved a visit.

He would not disappoint.

So. The path of civilized men who tilled the soil to reap its bounty, who built monuments toward the skies, had led to this.

The scribe watched the procession wind through Uruk's dusty streets, above it all, standing just past the doorway to the temple of Inanna. City guardian, goddess of fertility, goddess of love. *She*, who had in the Days Before Men decided that her city would be the greatest center of culture in all of Sumer, in all the civilized world. *She*, who had brought them splendor, glories beyond counting.

Yet other divinities lived, gods and goddesses, some of whom were hungrier. Unsatisfied with fearful worship and appeasement in spirit, they wanted more. The scribe had fiercely hoped that Inanna would intercede on Uruk's behalf, make her objections known to the priests and priestesses who had decreed the fate of the four wretches now wheeled through the streets.

But neither dream nor whisper, neither omen nor divination. Nothing. She kept a silent tongue. Very well, then.

He was Annemardu, chief scribe of the temple of Inanna, overseer of all scribes who recorded temple business. Inscribing hymns and letters, accounting for the holdings and transactions of grain, livestock, land, more. In centuries past, such need had driven the Sumerians—the black-headed people—to develop a system of permanent record-keeping, the invention of the written word. Cuneiform, wedge-shaped characters etched by a carved reed stylus onto tablets of clay.

Of its lasting significance, Annemardu had but the vaguest of notions. A practical solution to a problem, that's all it was. Just like the round wooden wheels devised so that donkeys and oxen could more easily pull grain carts. Just like the fields that once were arid desert, here in the Land Between the Rivers; they were now irrigated with a complex system of canals and dams, water drawn from the natural levees built by yearly flooding of the Tigris and Euphrates rivers.

Man, he knew, was seen as inherently no more unique a being than the beasts of burden who helped the farmers till their fields beyond the city walls. No more noble than the feared lions stalking the reed marshes. Certainly man could not be the most feared creature that walked the earth. As a young man, years past, Annemardu had seen a bone unearthed from clay in the marshes. Trembled at its size, the single bone longer than his entire body, and his imagination reeled in fear as to the size of the being these remains had come from.

What walked this land before we did? he had wondered at the time, and since, had never stopped.

But of man—of themselves—there was no sense of awe. Yet on contemplative nights in his house, head swimming from the effects of the barley beer he bought in the city bazaar, Annemardu ventured to speculate if perhaps they were wrong. What other animal *could* wonder what walked the earth before it? Even if it did, what other beast could give voice to the musings? And even if those animal bleats were understood by its fellows, then what beast could write them down? Something to consider.

Man, merely a higher form of animal? Perhaps. But an animal with audacity like no other.

Perhaps the inherent greatness separating man from lesser beasts, while good, was fraught with its own kind of perils. Great accomplishments could only be born of great passions, and great passions sometimes went astray to become great injustices. To live together, to work together, to divide the labors of daily life—these gave them all, from aristocrat to commoner to slave, a power unlike any other race of men. And with power comes pride.

Annemardu watched as the procession turned a corner, headed for the main gates in the city walls.

Uruk, for you, this day I weep.

The complex of temples—for Inanna, for An, for others—stood taller than any building in the city. The crown of Uruk, it was, vast tier-stepped structures called ziggurats, built from mud-brick in imitation of mountains. From the upper terrace, a temple worker could survey any and all of Uruk he or she pleased. Houses and public buildings, each built from the same bricks as the temples. This sea of mankind, the same hue as the desert, was interrupted by patches of greenery, landscaped public parks. Here and there were markets and bazaars, where merchants and traders sold meat and fish and produce, and goods made by local artisans or craftspeople from other Sumerian city-states, and even exotica from far-off lands. Linking all were gridded streets, and enclosing all were the walls of Uruk, straight and solid, as if the desert itself had risen up. These great walls and their nine hundred towers had been built the previous century by Gilgamesh, king of legend, hero among men, a god upon death. Beyond the walls, to east and south and north lay the fields and canals, suckling from the Euphrates. To the west lay the desert, dull brown wasteland without end. Here dwelled the *utukku*, demons of human suffering.

Summer midday sun from a cloudless sky, the city baked as surely as an oven. Tempers grew hotter on such days. Perhaps, as well, their minds dwindled in the heat like sun-scorched plants.

The procession below numbered at least two thousand. All on foot, but for the four condemned innocents. In the lead was the *lugal*, the king. Following him was his near-equal in the city's eyes, the high priestess of the temple of Inanna. Following them were temple slaves, women who played instruments to soothe the tempers of the gods. And behind them . . .

Each condemned man stood tied into his own chariot, drawn by a donkey, with wrists lashed to either side to root him where he stood. Submissive now, the finest and strongest slaves of the temple, naked before the world and the gods. And escorted by ranks of Uruk's soldiers, whose copper helmets gleamed with a blinding sun.

It could never be said that the temple was unwilling to sacrifice less than its best.

The gaze of one, sadly resigned to fate, traveled up and back toward the temple he had served so very proudly, locking across the distance with Annemardu. Scribe. Master. Friend.

"Eannatum," he murmured. "I wish you a better lot in the netherworld." Slim hopes, in all likelihood, but one could always wish.

The gates were opened. And with reverence, with fear, with hallowed purpose, the procession moved into the world beyond walls.

Later. The sun had traveled farther toward the desert, still high, ignorant of mercy. So far, since the trek beyond the walls, the day had been uneventful.

Annemardu concluded his daily accounting and hobbled from his chambers. His left leg had been shorter than the other since birth, not so badly that he couldn't walk, but he had never been a man who moved with authority. Once, when the world was less civilized, a deformed child such as he would have been put to death, a burden instead of a family asset. But in his lifetime, the only real stigma he felt was his inability to serve under the generals as a younger man. A heavy enough shame in those days, but younger men's pride is easily wounded. Older men may be slower, but they know more of importance. And as a man of learning, Annemardu had more than earned his right to walk as proudly as any man with two good legs. Scribe; keeper of myth and fable, proverb and law. The man or woman who wrote was a creature of awe, eagerly sought by the people to aid their business. In a scribe's head lived the eight hundred symbols of the cuneiform vocabulary, and it guaranteed high regard.

He descended the ziggurat's flights of steps, his youngers affording him ample room whenever he met them on their way up. Annemardu wore the traditional garb of male temple scribes, kilt of sheepskin, upper body bare. His flabby torso was burnished bronze, and his teats sagged like an old woman's.

He felt it in the streets, that veiled fear. Apprehension. The eternal question, *Are we truly doing right?* They spoke little, the masses, and it was far more than just the heat.

At the city walls, Annemardu ascended the stairs. Slow going. From the top he could view the land with a soldier's eye. West, gazing across harsh baking plains, boundary between civilization and chaos. He paced around the top of the wall, wide enough for a chariot to circle the city, then stopped along a northwest stretch. Ascended more stairs into the tower, so that he might better peer down.

He was not alone. Sartuk, one of the priests who served Inanna. His head and beard shaved, the bare skull beaded with sweat. Away from the temple, at so crucial a time in Uruk's tempestuous history, he would have left a gypsum votive statue at the altar as a stand-in for himself. Busy worshippers often did, in this world where gods demanded constant prayer. The statuettes praying in their stead, graven eyes huge in awe of the *dingir* whose favor was sought.

"They live, still?"

"Still." Sartuk motioned him to step nearer the edge, see for himself.

Annemardu leaned against the ledge, peered down along the outer wall. There, off to one side—the four sacrificial offerings. Upright, tied by wrist and ankle with tanned hide to copper bands affixed earlier to the wall. Their bodies gleamed with sweat, and they bent at the knee under the weight of the sun. Periodically, a soldier trekked past the gates to give them water. Even this high, one could still hear the occasional mournful groan. Eannatum among them . . .

Eannatum, the young bearded man who had for years fetched his clay, shaped it for writing, smoothed it for the reed. He had always done so with great cheer, his only regret in life being his inability to attend the *edubba* for schooling in the scribal art, in math and science. That irked him more than his impoverished father selling him into slavery as a boy.

Annemardu felt like the worst of traitors now. He drew back from the ledge, sighed. You came to love others, you could sometimes not help but hate the *dingir* for what they demanded of mortals.

"It was their request, you know this," Sartuk said.

Annemardu had never been good at wiping his feelings from his face. "You have no friends among that lot. One slave as good as the next."

Sartuk bowed his head a moment, then raised. Placed a hand on Annemardu's shoulder. "Slave or freeman, priest or not, we love our gods first. Without them, we would not be. And if they choose to take from us, we and all we build are theirs to be taken."

Annemardu shut his eyes, no outward arguments. *Yes, we belong to the gods,* with this he had no qualm. *But what of those who speak for the gods? Can they always be believed? Can they always be trusted to pull themselves apart from their own vanity and speak the truth?*

This was as important now as any occasion he could recall. Times were fierce as summer sun. For this farming season, the Euphrates was frightfully low. Less water, less irrigation for the fields, less food. Already the effects of famine could be felt rippling across Sumer. Disease came next, fevers and other plagues birthing from the bodies of the weak and the dead. Hostilities were rarely quiet, but had now erupted with renewed fury over water rights across the land, with the city-states of Ur, Eridu, Lagash, Nippur, others. And, as always, with the marauding wildmen from the eastern hills, the Elamites, who had much less than the Sumerians, and meant to take what they could.

Sumer knew the stink of death this season like none other.

And so the priestess had prayed, had dreamed dreams and read the entrails of a butchered ox. And knew what was required.

Uruk need not unduly fear; Inanna had not forsaken them, or worse, turned against them. Nor had An or Enlil or Enki or Ninkhursag, the four creators. Lesser gods were deviling them, petty and jealous sky gods who had, in the Days Before Men, fallen to the underworld to lord over plagues and famines, wars and death and destruction. They could be cruel, indeed, but could nevertheless show kindness. Nergal, for one, was also a god of healing.

They were not unreasonable. They could be bargained with. A sacrifice for each, to restore and maintain the balance. And to give them their due.

Naturally.

And wasn't it just the way of things, Annemardu reasoned: When you acknowledge something with a name, you thereby create something to appease.

Hours later, when the moment of transition had come. Night for day, in a moment that was neither. A lowered sun, a sky and a desert as deeply red as a battlefield. Annemardu could easily imagine the creation of Man occurring on such a twilight as this, Man, who had been fashioned from clay and the blood of a slaughtered god. Half lowly, half divine.

Sartuk saw it first, perking up at a hint of distant noise. Annemardu joined him at the ledge and they watched it gather. . . .

A spot on the western horizon, darker than the coming night, boiling across the desert and blotting out a portion of the setting sun. And heading their way, of that there was no doubt.

"They come," Sartuk whispered, face in frightened rapture.

Annemardu's throat tightened, dried. Fists clutching the ledge so tightly that grit worked beneath his nails. And he stared. The storm-that-was-not-a-storm marched across the desert at a terrible speed.

Surely nothing could live in its path. Serpent would wither, scorpion would roast.

It bore down upon them without signs of slowing, a cloud of driven dust and wind and rage. Feeling its approach was like standing before an oven.

"What have we summoned?" Annemardu could scarcely find his voice.

"*Pazuzu!*" Sartuk screamed, and reeled back from the furnace onslaught.

Pazuzu, lord of the searing north wind. The name alone inspired pristine fear. The city wall was assaulted as never before, by past winds or army or foe unknown. Even Gilgamesh may never have intended them to withstand so formidable an attack. Gusts of hot sand lapped over the wall, and the roar of fiery wind was like that of a lion.

Annemardu steadied himself at tower's edge, bracing with thick stocky legs, one shielding arm crooked round his face. He may never have been a swift runner, but he could stand, oh, he could stand firm. This he would not allow himself to miss, learned and rational man staring into the maw of the unknowable. He glanced back, found he was alone in his resolve. Sartuk was sprawled back onto the platform, paralyzed with fright, his tunic bunched around his waist. Coward.

The darkness poured in across the desert, much as the tail traveling behind the lights that sometimes arced across night skies. Thickening behind the wind of Pazuzu, gathering in a black knot. Annemardu squinted against wind and sand, felt grit collect in his eyes, nose, mouth. He stared into the heart of the maelstrom, no, no, you will hold no secrets from me, I promise you that, or I promise I will die. . . .

It moved within; it squirmed. *It lived.* It lusted.

And what of Eannatum? Dear young man, if the gods were merciful, he and his fellows would have been taken in that first terrible instant. Surely. No one below could have survived.

And yet . . .

They moved.

Annemardu clung to the ledge, staring straight down through the cloud, and when would this end? To watch a loved one suffer was to feel the bile of helplessness. And to feel helpless was to know the true might of the gods. . . .

While wind and heat and sand slowly scoured the flesh from

their bones and filled their mouths with silent screams. No enemy army could be more cruel than this. Choking on powdery dust, Annemardu reeled back from the wall. No longer able to stare into its face; if this was what the gods were like, let him be godless.

A tremendous cacophony had arisen from within the heart of Uruk. Priests and priestesses exhorting temple slave musicians, come, come—come play for the gods so that they will be pleased with us, that our offerings will be enough. The din arose, the dissonant clamor of harp and lyre and pan pipe, the frantic striking of drum and tambourine. To mortal ears it grated; to chthonic gods it may well have been music. For it spoke so very eloquently of the terror of men and women.

Pazuzu roared. Paving the way . . .

Beyond the walls they gathered, these gods no less mighty for their fallen state. And they waited, unable to hold still. He could chart their progress around the city walls, a churning dustcloud in their wake, boiling into the red sky of dusk. South, then east, then north and west and finally south again to where they had begun. Again. *Again.* Around, around, this was impossible, *nothing could move with such speed.* Around yet again, whipping along the perimeter of the city, a hike that took an able-bodied man the better part of half a day to complete. While each circuit of the gods took scarcely a minute.

Annemardu fell to his knees, seeing this sight of terrifying majesty as no one else in Uruk was able. Poised between earth and sky, oh puny man, who was he to sit in his temple quarters and ponder the wisdom of the gods, thinking he could stare into their saturnine faces and remain in control? Surely no man on earth had beheld such a sight as this, and lived. He sobbed in sheer awe of its spectacle.

Walls trembled. Earth rumbled. The blood of the sky deepened toward black . . .

On this longest of Uruk's nights.

Morning, too long in coming, never a more welcome sight.

An eerie calm had settled over Uruk for the past hours. Morning brought few of its usual noises; the city, man and animal alike, seemed to hold its breath. Dust settled wherever breezes carried it, and lingered in the air, a yellow-brown haze to filter the rising sun.

While it had been calm for hours, no one dared venture beyond the walls before daybreak. Desert night held too many ill secrets.

Annemardu had joined the masses gathering on the boulevard before the city gates. Hot, exhausted from a night of little sleep. Filthy from head to toe, skin raw from heat and stinging sand. He combed his beard with fingers, fairly amazed at just how much dirt it could hold.

Daybreak. Lots of talk here at the gates, very little action taken. It seemed prudent to wait for the *lugal* and the high priestess. Only when they came, quiet and solemn, were the gates opened. And out streamed the curious, the faithful, the brave.

Annemardu hobbled at the forefront, resolute, following the lead of priestess and king as they moved along the outer wall. See what had become of the offerings. Hundreds of feet tramped behind, raising a dustcloud, small by last night's standards.

They halted. Stared. Those toward the back who could not see surged around front.

Annemardu had been expecting little, if anything. Perhaps a jumble of dry bones, heaped along the wall where wind and sand had pushed them. Skull here, rib cage there, half-buried. The rest, flesh and blood and muscle and spirit, consumed. Or maybe a small scrap of hide, tanned like leather.

But this? *This?* This he had not expected in his wildest imaginings.

I saw them die, with my own two eyes I watched them die.

And yet . . .

They lived.

I saw Pazuzu tear them open.

Four of them, temple slaves in a former life. Had their eyes ever been so wide, so staring? Had they ever beheld such wonders as last night? Had they even dreamed such things existed?

Surely not.

But had I waited . . . I might have seen . . . the rest.

Just what might that have been? The filling of body with new spirit. The restoration. But he would never know. Maybe the gods knew best after all, for they had not taken selfishly and left those behind to mourn.

He lives and breathes, still.

The authority of the dumbfounded king was forgotten, and Annemardu smiled broadly and stumped forward toward the slave who had been more like a son. Eannatum stared, as if any moment he might scream, or burst into tears. Did he even know who he was anymore? Annemardu would tell him, gladly, as much as he needed to know. Man's memory, sometimes such a frail thing.

Eannatum sobbed, dropped to his knees before his one-time master. Clutching tight to the uneven legs with the desperation of a lost child. Annemardu reached down to pat his head, brush the matted hair.

Then fell beside him with a scream.

His leg, *his leg*. He could feel flesh and bone straining beneath his kilt, and while there was no pain, incomprehension was far more terrifying. He was no longer a boy; his bones had ceased to grow some thirty years before.

And when it was finished—while murmur and comment rippled through the crowd behind him—Annemardu stood. Trembling. Atop two good legs like any man of dignity, and so very little in this world did he understand anymore.

Eannatum backed away, naked and cowering, staring at his own hands. Their eyes met, and his understood no better than did Annemardu's.

"What magic is *this*?" asked the *lugal*. Flanking him, soldiers stood at the ready, short spears thrust before them. Annemardu had never seen a soldier look any more bewildered as to friend or foe.

Eannatum, now the center of attention, was joined by the other three, clustering about him as if they were only just beginning to comprehend the night. Its gifts, its curses.

"Nergal?" Annemardu whispered to his slave, remembering. Lord of plague, lord of healing.

The night of wind and storm had loosened more than flesh and spirit. The base of Uruk's wall was littered with bricks, fallen whole, crumbled into halves. The high priestess, still regal in elaborate braids, one shoulder bared by her robes, walked to the wall. Stooped. Retrieved half a shattered brick . . .

And hurled it at Eannatum. It struck his chest, sent him staggering backward. He reached forward in confused plea, but dozens of others had been quick to follow the priestess's lead. The morning sky rained brick, and the four naked slaves scrambled for safer ground, covering heads with folded arms.

Annemardu's heart broke, he wanted only to give aid, give comfort, give thanks. He was about to cry out in objection. A respected man, they would listen to him. But one look into the face of the *lugal* was enough to seize his tongue.

"They have no more life with us." The *lugal* at least spoke kindly to him. Was there sorrow in his eyes? Yes. Yes. "They can no longer live as citizens of Uruk. They are no longer ours. They belong to something else now."

Annemardu bowed his head while crowd became mob, and mob gave chase. As the fallen bricks were cleared away, to be put to new use. . . .

Driving the unwanted into the welcoming arms of the desert.

His temple chambers offered little comfort that day, after he was cleaned and dressed in fresh clothing. Annemardu sat quiet and still at his worktable, staring into the blank face of a wet square of clay.

Other men may have been out and about the city, traveling anywhere a restored leg might take them. For that, there would be ample time later. The next day, and the next. For now? His heart had always been closest to the pursuit of learning and the preservation of knowledge. Such a man he would be until he died.

Upon his wall, a small tablet of clay, worked with the reed, then pressed there while still wet. The dry heat had leached its moisture over time, until now it was a part of the wall. Across its face was written a proverb that had always given him inspiration: *A scribe whose hand moves as fast as the mouth, that's a scribe for you.*

But what of a scribe whose hand moves as fast as the human spirit? What of him? What sort of mark may he leave on future generations?

He thought of the four brave young men who had faced the night alone. And the lesser gods they had no choice but to serve. Oh, what a man of tiny mind he was, thinking the night had been their ordeal. When the ordeal was just beginning.

Annemardu touched stylus to clay, and began to write.

Their legacy would be heard in time—in the voice of the scorching windstorm, in the rustle of breezes through the reed marshes when wind stirred soft as memories . . .

Alas, Babylon.

II
Martyrs, Sinners, Saints

But what greater temptation than to appear a missionary, a prophet, an ambassador from heaven? Who would not encounter many dangers and difficulties, in order to attain so sublime a character? . . . Who ever scruples to make use of pious frauds, in support of so holy and meritorious a cause?

—David Hume

8

 Amanda was back home, where she belonged, and this was easily the most nervous Donny had been about her mere presence since their wedding night. Sixteen years ago, and she had been a great deal more lively then than now.

Returning under cover of darkness, near midnight on the final Thursday of June, in an ambulance from a private firm hired for the occasion. The job had been doled out through nepotism; the driver was a nephew of Doctor Irv Preston. Keep things in the family, they tend to stay quieter. Not that a couple of well-placed tips didn't smooth matters along, hush hush.

The ambulance had come quietly down South Squire Road out of central Oklahoma City, turning into the parking lot by the chapel. A brief pause at the far end of the lot for electronic clearance at a gate, then they were allowed onto the private drive leading to the house. A tunnellike gauntlet of trees, then a looped cul-de-sac, and they stopped before the Dawson home's doors. Preston and his nephew unloaded Amanda, strapped her into a gurney, and brought her up the walk. Donny took over for Preston then—the least he could do —and they eased her up to the third floor. The midnight-to-eight nurse was waiting, ready to help get Amanda settled into what had once been a guest room.

Such a contrast in decor. The Queen Anne dressing table and flowing drapes over the multipane windows, these ties to the everyday remained. The four-poster canopy bed was gone in favor of a hospital model; like a child's puzzle, which of these does not belong? The clinical additions abounded: The stand for Mandy's IVs. Boxes of Ensure and Sustical, bags of complete balanced nutrition in an ultrapuréed blend. The IV bags of potassium chloride solution to replace the electrolytes she was losing. A floor receptacle for her urinary output. And all manner of other odds and ends to make her life, such as it was, easier.

The daily routine was as settled as it was boring. Feeding would be handled through her clear plastic nasogastric tube, kept around eighteen hundred calories per day, with each so-called meal followed by water. She would undergo the usual range-of-motion exercises to combat muscle atrophy. The nurses would turn her side to side every four hours to discourage bedsores, and should one dare show the beginning of its ulcerous face, inflatable O-rings were at the ready to slap over it. She urinated through a Foley catheter, unaware, and her bowel movements were cleaned up like a baby's. No cares, no worries, no responsibilities.

While the midnight nurse quietly went about making the final connections Amanda needed to sustain life, Preston placed a fatherly arm around Donny's shoulders. Stout old guy, with half-gone hair and a walrus moustache and bifocals. He sometimes resembled a doc from some western frontier town, forever inspiring confidence, trust, loyalty. Unless you were with the IRS.

Preston steered Donny into the hallway, back the same way they had come. The nephew remained a few paces behind.

"Talk to her a lot," he was saying. "I doubt she'll show any signs of hearing you, but do it anyway. She'll hear you, and something may very well get through, and mean something to her. Okay?"

Donny nodded, yes, yes, anything.

Preston smiled. "A few years back, I treated this five-year-old kid who'd gotten banged up in a car wreck. He was in a coma for two weeks. His mom and big sister would talk to him, and I'll be damned if they didn't actually get responses out of him. He'd squeeze their fingers to answer when they told him to. Sometimes he'd nod his head to questions. They'd ask him if he wanted an ice pop, and he'd nod, and they'd ask if he wanted orange, 'cause that was his favorite flavor, and yeah, he'd nod again. And he'd suck on those things like a baby with a bottle. They'd read him stories and fairy tales and comic books. The kid had no memory of it when he came out, but nobody can ever convince me that that mother and that sister didn't help bring the little guy out of it."

"Do you think I might get any response like that out of Mandy?" Anything would be better than her stone wall of silence, and he'd only been around her, what, fifteen minutes since her fall? Day in, day out, it would be maddening.

"There's always a chance. If you do, terrific." Treading from third floor to second now. "But if you don't, don't be discouraged. It's not the rule, it's the exception. And bear in mind that she'll probably rise and fall, so to speak, during the duration. She'll be in there at different levels."

They had come to the final length of the staircase. The big one, the guilty one, here where it all began. . . .

"She might remember something she hears while she's under, though. Not necessarily right away. It would seem like a dream. You know how you'll dream and not recall it right away, but later on in the day, a word, a thought, something, will trigger the memory? It's the same principle."

They reached the bottom of the stairs, Preston leading his own way to the door. "Let me know of anything you might get out of her. I'll be by once or twice a week, more if something changes. Now, if you have any problems with the nurses, you let me know. I wouldn't expect any, not from these ladies, but I realize how, well —*delicate* this situation is."

There it was, wasn't it? Understated, but undeniably there, the conflict in ethics. A man of medicine not only condoning, but aiding and abetting a fraudulent healer. A man of God who saw to it that *thou shalt not steal* was overlooked, at least in the case of charitable contributions the man of medicine showed in his ledgers. One hand washing the other, I won't tell if you won't.

God understood, surely. These days, big government and big business just made getting along so much more complicated than they had to be. It was their own fault. And God understood.

Once they had reached the door, Gabe stepped from the parlor, where he had been keeping a patient vigil. Donny leaned in to give Preston a hug, lingering a moment while the doctor slapped him good-naturedly on the back.

"If you need anything at all, just call," Preston said. "Anytime."

"Thanks for everything, Irv. God bless."

"You too. And especially Mandy."

Donny locked the door behind Preston and his nephew, leaned his head against the translucent glass. Heard the ambulance roll away, and oh, didn't the days of trial lay ahead *now*?

"You need anything?" Gabe asked. Still in his workday suit. Might as well leave it on and sleep over and begin fresh at nine the next morning. What commitment, this man had no life of his own. No friends apart from the ministry, no woman in his life, no family anymore. Just career and God. It couldn't be healthy for him, but Donny wasn't about to say anything, not now, not when Gabe was needed more than ever. Have to remember to talk to him about that someday, get a life.

"Just pray with me, Gabe," and they knelt at the foot of the stairs. Taking turns going to the Lord in a petition for mercy and healing and bestowment of strength in these needful hours. Fifteen minutes of tag-team prayer, after which Donny arose, and if he wasn't on fire, at least hopes were rekindled. He decided to sit up with Mandy for a while and sent Gabe back to the parlor, to the waiting book he had tabled, spine up.

The long climb up the stairs, this time alone. Into Mandy's room. The night nurse was Alice Ward, and having met her patient's every need for the moment, she could only watch and wait for something else to come up. A homely woman in her midfifties, she kept to a chair beside the bed, clock steadily ticking on a table to let her know when Mandy would require turning again, like a steak on a grill, and she thumbed through an antiques magazine.

"I know you just came on duty," Donny said, "but why don't you take a break. I'd like to be alone with my wife awhile. You understand."

As he wished. The magazine went with her to the door. "Would it be all right if I go to the kitchen to fix some coffee? First night and all, I'm not used to these hours yet."

Donny told her to help herself, coffee in the pantry, machine on the counter, can't miss them, make it strong. She left with no noise, seemingly no breeze of departure. Where did they learn to walk like that? You couldn't teach that in class, could you? Maybe it was innate, a sign of their calling.

He had met the three nurses earlier in the week, handpicked by Preston and submitted for Donny's approval. Although why he would object when Irv wouldn't, he didn't know. Courtesy, Donny supposed, and this he appreciated. All had been given the nod.

Each was a single woman, to avoid the need to account for the particulars of her shift to a curious husband. There was Alice Ward, a widow, and despite her bulldog countenance she was easily the most mannered and cultured of the three. Probably the most dependable, which was why she had been offered the graveyard shift.

Alice was relieved by Edie Carson in the mornings, who stayed until four in the afternoon. Never married, no boyfriend, according to Irv. Just a quiet little mousey thing who would never raise a second glance, getting through life with as few bumps and obstructions as possible. Noble and sad.

The last was Sally Pruett, tall leggy blond, rounding out the schedule from four to midnight. No intentions to marry, said Irv. Lots of relationships but none very close. Keep this Jezebel at a distance; there would be no reenactments of Jim Bakker's PTL scandal, real or alleged, originating under *this* roof.

Three nurses, all skilled, more than capable enough for the present situation. For Amanda did not look to present much of a challenge. She lay beneath a single sheet, slightly curled onto her right side, facing him. The once-lustrous perky hair now hung limply from her skull. Hands and face looked pale, the skin nearly transparent and waxen, and she was dotted with sweat. Dark circles ringed her eyes.

He scooted the nurse's chair so he could get as close to Mandy as possible, without actually climbing into the same bed. It wasn't enough. He could climb into her head and even that wouldn't do the job, for he feared he would find himself utterly alone in there. Frantic cries to rouse her going unanswered, echoing through her inner darkness like lonely drops of water plinking in some subterranean cavern.

They had not had children yet. Often discussed, but something he had always felt would be better postponed, the time never right. For whatever reasons, multitudes, the ministry never quite able to spare the attentions a child would require. He had never been any gladder of it than now. To be subjecting children to the sudden absence of Mom would have added a whole new dimension of hell to this entire ordeal.

Donny took her hand, leaned over, kissed those lips so very gently. Warm, but unresponsive. A prone statue, sculpted from flesh instead of stone, and if he could have breathed more life into it, he would have slaved over her for as long as it took.

"I miss you, Mandy," a whisper into her ear, half covered with limp hair. He uncovered it the rest of the way, silly attempt to allow the words better access. "God alone knows how much I miss you. A man couldn't have asked for any better a partner than you."

I'm tired of living out lies, and damn that memory anyway.

"Hon, can you hear me? If you can hear me, squeeze my hand."

Waiting. Waiting. In case it took the words abnormally long to register, for the synapses to fire and make sense of them. A minute, two, three. He could have waited all night, but she wasn't going to squeeze. Here he was, knocking at the house of someone who could not make it to the door. That didn't mean he still couldn't stand at the threshold and call in. Hoping.

"I tried, Mandy. I really tried *so hard* to help you. But it just wouldn't come." Donny wrapped his other hand around hers, swallowing it between his palms, trying not to choke on his own words, a performance first. "It just. Wouldn't. Come."

And there she lay, silent testimonial to his own inadequacies. He could probably live with just about anything fate or God or Satan threw at him, except for the loss of her respect. Too much. And so, he could never let her forget. . . .

"But Mandy, honey, you can't deny that it happened that once, that I really did it, that I brought that boy back from the brink of death." A hesitant smile through tears threatening to break free and cascade upon her bed. Anointed tears. "Do you remember those days? Fine days? Sometimes I think those were the best days we ever knew. You remember, don't you? Sure you do. Squeeze my hand if you remember. . . ."

Fine days indeed. Exhilarating, in their own rudimentary way, the fulfillment coming from putting themselves wholly in the hands of God and letting Him guide where He wished. For the time being, He'd seen fit to leave them as poor as churchmice.

August 1980. An election year, the Carter presidency on its last leg as it headed toward the first Tuesday in November. If you believed the polls, the outlook was bleak. But in the south, as Donny and Amanda thumped the evangelical trail, hope sprang eternal. With a washed-up actor running for president on the Republican ticket, the south would rise again. Count on it.

Donny Dawson, traveling preacher, self-ordained. He was twenty-seven that August, Amanda his junior by four years. They took meals with hospitable congregations and, in between, took brief day jobs to keep them solvent. Haircut money was saved by adopting extremes. Hers she wore bound, nearly to the waist. His was in a crew cut, because that took longest of all to grow out. They didn't even have enough cash to get swindled, and it was just about the holiest, most romantic life they could conceive of. This was simple perfection.

Their chariot was a 1966 Ford Falcon, once white but now a rolling shrine of dust and great splats of mud. It carried them through small towns in Georgia and Alabama and Louisiana and Mississippi, these towns the same everywhere, except for different names across peeling-paint water towers standing against trackless skies. These towns with the same people working the fields, or strolling to the market with half a dozen of the same kids in tow, or sitting half-hidden at twilight behind screened porches, guarding secrets the world had no right to share. These towns of burning sidewalks, buckled and cracked from the passage of too many seasons, and overhung with the lazily bobbing branches of weeping willows. The highways and byways between them all were encroached upon by kudzu vines, here forever, creeping up with no less a goal than total conquest of land and town.

As Donny was discovering while he and his bride pushed from revival to revival, these same proud people had the same thirst for the Word of God. Same needs of assurance of an eternity far better than the lot they had drawn here on Earth.

In the Mississippi Delta, they would roll across the rural landscape, Amanda staring out the windows at ramshackle hovels, black children, white children, the same haunting stares from each while parents broke their backs in the fields. Amanda would gaze at them with tears barely held in check, sadly shaking her head, completely forgetting that in most cases, the people she saw probably had more in worldly goods than did she and Donny.

It was the compassion, above all else, that had bound him to her. She kept him mindful of others, their needs; rich or poor, they were all needy in a way.

Northwestern Alabama, the sawdust trail having led them to a pair of rural hamlets called Courtland and Valdosta. A paper mill kicked a lot of paychecks into the area, but life remained much the same as it had always been; one step forward, two steps back.

A chuckholed succession of back country roads led them to a dingy clapboard building with a sign that read SALVATION CHURCH OF THE PENTECOST. An oft-patched, open-sided tent had been erected on the lawn before the church, in a clearing surrounded by trees. The tent was crammed with rows of rickety folding chairs, full of some of the singingest, shoutingest people he had ever seen. Some decked out in rural Sunday finest, clothes old and ill-fitting but clean, and others wearing work clothes that had seen hard mileage all the way. Faces ran with sweat, and the occasional breeze only dropped things down from stifling to merely sultry.

Amanda took over on the piano, hauled outside earlier, and pounded away with reeling abandon. Seasons of humidity had detuned its strings into a honky-tonk warble. Hymns and songs of celebration churned out rapid-fire, a clarion call for the believers. Foot-stomping and arm-waving, beholders of visions and speakers in tongues, they waited for the words of Donny Dawson.

Magic was in the air, all right.

And another sound, as well, the rumbling blat of an ancient tractor from up the hard-packed dirt road. Donny heard it well before it came into view, shambling mechanical dinosaur held together with baling wire and fervent prayers. The driver, little more than a silhouette against the fields and woodland beyond, was waving from afar.

Donny nudged Salvation Church's regular preacher, Sonny Millgrove, who bounced his bulk and clapped huge hands with the sound of cured hams butting heads. The two of them stood off to one side of the podium while another man led the singing.

"What's the story down there?" Donny leaned in and asked.

Reverend Sonny grinned, dimples cratering his fat cheeks, pausing in midclap. "Oh, that'n's a simple boy, he is. Simple in the *haid*." He tapped his own skull to illustrate the point. "Jimmy McPherson. Loves to steal his daddy's tractor and gets a bailt whupped on his backside ever time. Never never learns."

Donny alternated between watching Amanda at the piano and watching the tractor as it neared. Clouds of dust churned from the monstrous wheels, billowing out behind in a brown wake. Over the top of the upright piano, Mandy eyed him, grinned, wound down the song. Throwing it into a minor key and tossing out blues runs. That was another thing he loved, that imp within her; ninety-five percent angel but the rest pure mischief.

The congregation was primed, on their feet with hands lifted to the skies. The intensity of their hunger was palpable, as heady as their scent of sweat and starch and sweet cologne. Donny was at the pulpit and leaning toward them, a man on righteous fire. Asking a simple question about their faith, what it meant to them all, was it a lamp unto their feet and a light unto their path, or was it just some spiritual fire insurance policy on which they grudgingly kept up the payments?

The Pentecostals were shouting, no, no, lamp unto our feet, a universal declaration, and Donny knew it would be several moments before he could continue. It wasn't just the uproar of the crowd. The tractor was nearly adjacent to them, its exhaust as noisily distracting as a machine gun.

He turned once more to see the driver. Simple Jimmy McPherson, perhaps fifteen, a big ugly kid with a lantern jaw, a chunky belly and narrow shoulders, and carrot-red hair topping off the whole ridiculous ensemble. If the Good Lord was merciful, this lad would never see a mirror. Jimmy stood up behind the wheel and hooted and waved his arms, a spastic parody of their own actions from moments ago, or a sincere attempt to become one of the gang. From his unbridled enthusiasm, it was impossible to tell which.

His enjoyment was so immense that he neglected one of the basic rules for the operation of farm machinery: *Steer it.* The small, close-set front wheels suddenly dipped into a vast crumbling chuckhole, wrenching the tractor down and to the right with an impact that joggled the boy like a loose egg in a carton. The tractor quickly gained a mind all its own, bearing hard for the roadside ditch. The front wheels sank in, twisting sideways and plowing up ditch-dirt while the huge back tires barreled on full speed ahead. Gravity did the rest. With a grind and a roar, the tractor overturned, clearing the ditch and crashing at the edge of the church lawn.

Directly atop Jimmy McPherson, who howled like a car-struck dog.

One shocked, silent moment, and then the entire crowd was galvanized, streaming from chairs. Already on his feet and at the end of the tent nearest the road, Donny reached him first. He knelt, he gently cradled the boy's trembling head. Jimmy was free only from the chest up, blood already bubbling from the corners of his gasping mouth.

Salvation Church suffered no shortage of large, able-bodied men. They circled the tractor and heave-hoed the thing upright, peeling it up and off the boy. Donny took one look at the damage and wanted to be ill. Jimmy would die, and soon; in parts these remote, his chances were nil. If this were a dog, someone would already be going for a gun, and in that first horrified instant Donny found himself wishing, *Die, oh just please die, you poor kid, save yourself the misery and just let go.*

Both legs were broken, bent at the knees. The left shin was bent as well, as if newly received of an extra joint. His torso had caved in, a crimson meat platter from which two naked, jagged-tipped ribs protruded by an inch or more. Jimmy wheezed red mist when he tried to cry out, the blood speckling Donny's hands, clothing, face. Jimmy, broken frightshow caricature of himself.

From behind, Amanda's hands dug heedlessly into Donny's shoulders. She coughed back a cry, and he felt tears plinking onto his sunburned neck. *Baptism of ineffectuality, here am I, man of God and completely useless, words of comfort just aren't enough, all I can do is wish this boy dead. Not enough, it's not enough.*

Jimmy shivered, cold, so cold. One arm raised painfully upward, that last plea for help, even the simple of mind need to know they are not alone at the end. Donny knew he had nothing to lose by cradling the dying boy in his own arms.

"Dear Lord, we need a miracle here!" Donny cried out, eyes aimed upward. "This boy won't make it another minute without Your help, so please, *please,* show us Your power! Because we've got nothing we can do for him! Show us a miracle!"

Ask and ye shall receive.

Jimmy thrashed his head, moaning, and Donny nearly dropped the shattered body when he felt the abrupt blast of warmth. Asking was one thing. Getting an immediate answer, like a gumball out of a penny machine, was something else.

Before a circling crowd of onlookers, who began to ooh and aah as if watching an impressive fireworks display, the massive injuries began to self-correct. Legs straightening, snapping into place with the ease of puzzle pieces coming together. Fragments of a shattered hipbone regrouping, then solidifying. Denuded ribs withdrawing like claws into a cat's paw, the mashed chest reinflating as Jimmy's breath returned to an unhindered flow.

Just as Donny's own breath clutched in his throat, *I can't believe I'm SEEING this!*

He ripped the boy's flimsy shirt the rest of the way open, used it to scrub away the slick of blood, finding only unbroken flesh beneath. Not even so much as scar tissue. He ran a hand down along the left leg, now straight and strong and whole.

In complete and utter awe, numbly pulling his hands back as if they were someone else's, *I'm not sure what just happened here, but thank You. Thank You.*

Before the hushed ring of spectators, Jimmy sat up. Five minutes later, he worried only about what his daddy would do to him for overturning the tractor. And shortly after that, every last soul at the

Salvation Church of the Pentecost hung on to Donny Dawson's every word as if it were the last sermon they might ever hear.

A cheap motel that evening, on the outskirts of nearby Decatur. Offers for the night's shelter had been plentiful, and all had been politely declined. Time for reflection was sorely needed, and as much as he loved these people, he knew they would begin turning up in droves just as soon as it was decided where he would lay his head. Better an anonymous motel, then, and for once they could easily afford it. The love offering had been especially generous.

Donny and Amanda, at dusk, made the most awe-inspiring love of their marriage thus far, and she trembled in his arms afterward. Both so wet, so sweaty, so drained. She curled beside him on sheets neither wanted to see in strong daylight, her hand resting on his chest.

Softly, "I was so proud of you this afternoon."

He shook his head in the netherlight. "It couldn't have been me that did that, that was—"

"I know that. Silly. But it was you that called on it. You brought it down. Donny . . . the kind of *faith* that took."

But did I, really? Did I? Lying beside her, trying to piece it all back together, every moment, every fragment. Like trying to assemble sand. Could a process even be qualified?

"What did it feel like? Did it feel divine?"

His shoulders stiffened, relaxed. He stumbled through an answer that felt wholly inadequate, yes, it did, if you consider divine as kneeling in the presence of something that dwarfs you, but it had happened so suddenly. And hadn't he, afterward, been vaguely disappointed that there had been no celestial lights, no heavenly sanction? Not that he would tell her this; she had led such a sheltered life compared with him, had known only Arkansas before they had met and married. Life was more cut-and-dried for Amanda. Things either were, or they were not.

She rubbed his chest with her fingers, magic hands that could coax a piano to jumping life. And his own hands? What magic did they bear these days? The mind reeled, the soul ignited.

"My man," Amanda murmuring into the hollow of his throat, "chosen for a holy mission."

He smiled at the ceiling. *Maybe I am.* It had, after all, happened. No one could argue that point.

Mandy planted a kiss firmly on his lips, ran the tip of her tongue along his cheek to his ear. "Don't ever turn your back on that mission," a soft seductive whisper. "You saw how those people needed that boost today. . . ."

. . . And Donny rose from his sleeping wife's side, her hand still held loosely in his. He once more kissed the warm, dry lips that never knew he was there. A mouth that once had brought delights to both body and spirit.

Please come back to me. Whenever you can.

He left the bedroom, inner sanctum to remain forever secret from the outside world, even most of those on the inside. Nurse Ward waited silently in the hall. He never even knew she was there.

I've lost so much. And it started a long, long time before I ever lost her.

He met Gabe downstairs, ready to tell him to go on home, sleep, feel free to make it a half-day tomorrow by coming in at noon. He never got the chance. Business first.

"Five minutes, Donny. And then I'll get out of your hair, I promise." Three fingers went up rigid. "Scout's honor."

"You were never a Scout," Donny, grinning on his way into the parlor.

"I never had the chance." Gabe shook his head after sitting, scrubbed his hand through his hair, a long long day. "Look. I know this is lousy timing to hit you with a suggestion like I'm about to. But then, there's never going to be a really good time. So I'm just going to come out with this.

"What I'm wondering is, if it might not be a good idea to get you away from here for a while. Take your work on the road and do a series of revivals and rallies."

"Gabe, I can't just—"

One palm out, stop. "Just hear me out, okay? And sleep on it, I'm not talking about hitting the road tomorrow. But listen, Donny? I really think this would be the best thing for you. Therapeutic work value, look at it that way. If you stay here with Mandy in her condition, that's going to gnaw at you like nothing else could. Because all this is going to be going on right under your nose, and there's not a thing you can do about it. If you get away for a while, you'll at least remove that distraction. Plus, it won't hurt to divert attention away from the ministry grounds."

"But what about Amanda, if you think for one second I'm going to abandon her now, when she needs me most . . ."

Gabe spread his hands wide. "She'll be under expert care, you've seen to that already. If there's any change at all in her condition, we can have you back here in hours, at the very most." Gabe's voice lowered. "Irv explained it all before. It usually takes a coma patient hours, or days, to fully come out of it. The signs will be there, the nurses will know. You'll be right there when she comes out of it."

On it went, far longer than the allotted five minutes, and for every objection Donny could think up, Gabe was right there with a rebuttal that made far more sense. You had to respect the man who put so much thought into an informal proposal. To an even greater extent, you had to respect the man who knew which buttons of yours to push to get his own way, and decided to leave them alone.

And what of duty, doing the right thing? Gabe might well have asked. But didn't. No need, though, the matter was weighing heavily enough already ever since he'd left Mandy's side.

Don't ever turn your back on that mission, good advice from the finest lady he had ever known. He had promised her he would never do that, even if the mission came ahead of family needs. Long-term good outweighed short-lived desires, and for the man faithful to his mission, the final scales would put everything into balance. You win some, and you win some.

A return to roots. Which sometimes meant a return to something lost too long ago, too far away.

He didn't need to sleep on it to know it was exactly what was needed after all.

Good idea, Gabe.

It was pushing two in the morning when Gabe got home. Bone weary, while every fiber in his being cried out with a shout of victory. He'd actually pulled it off, and it hadn't been nearly as tricky as he had feared it might.

He lived barely three miles from Dawson Ministries, small apartment for one in the back lot of a larger private household. They were fine landlords, not in the least bit nosy, and he was the perfect tenant, barely a noise from his place, in fact, not even at home all that often. The pure white walls were fine, the polished wood floors were a delight. Very little furniture, no excess. Here, life was contemplative, spartan.

Monastic.

Gabe hit the TV when he walked in, nearly always tuned to CNN, no different tonight. See what's new in the world at large. He shed tie and jacket, popped a kettle of water onto the stove; herbal tea would hit the spot, soothe him for sleep. He shelved the book he had been reading at Donny's; Stephen Hawking, *A Brief History of Time.* How many times through it did this make, one or two shy of a dozen? Couldn't agree with everything the man had to say, but ye gods, what audacity to try and come up with a single unifying theory for *everything.* You had to admire a goal that grandiose, and if Gabe could do half for the field of metaphysics that Hawking had done for less abstract sciences, he could die a completely fulfilled man.

How many others could say that, even dream about it? Not Donny, that was for sure. Poor misled sap, the man was his own worst enemy. Crook with a bleeding conscience.

Gabe watched CNN until the kettle whistled, steeped a bag in his favorite mug until the scent of tea was strong and heady. Down with the TV volume, and he grabbed the phone. Checked the clock. In Scotland it was just after eight in the morning, six hours ahead of U.S. Central Time.

The phone, ringing, then answered half a world away in the Scottish Highlands. Loch Nevis, the most beautiful spot he had seen in the entire world, and certainly the most secure little world-within-the-world he had ever known. Two years residence, and he would as soon die there as anywhere. With luck, with luck.

The switchboard operator answered, thick with Gaelic crust.

"This is Gabriel Matthews, June code six-fifty-two-liquidity." Cringing, he hated these silly codes, could never say them with a straight face, let's play spy versus spy. Why did they even bother? They ran voiceprint ID checks at the other end anyway. Discipline, probably. "I need to speak with Gavin."

"Urgent? He's about to leave for golf, y'bastard."

Gabe, smiling, "He'll kiss you for the interruption."

Mutters and curses, dwindling away while the phone went on hold. Minute, two, three, then Gavin Bainbridge himself:

"Gabe? Make me proud."

"Yes, sir," spoken with all the confidence of one who has trained a lifetime for the high jump, and cleared the bar with inches to spare. "He went for it. Donny wants the tour."

An audible sigh of relief, heard across the Atlantic. "That's the second best news I've heard since 1963."

9

St. Francis Medical Center was a five-story, 320-bed acute care facility west of University City, in the suburb of Olivette. Trim, tan and gray masonry, it looked like a hybrid between public school and minimum security prison, between which Paul, in more juvenile days, had seen little difference. No shame in fessing up, he'd been a typical teenage idiot.

St. Francis was owned and operated by an order of nuns. Over forty MDs on staff, plus over three hundred nurses, and scores more in support capacities: laboratory, physical therapy, radiology, dietetics, housekeeping, others. It also utilized a thriving system of volunteer workers, and this was what had whetted Paul's interest.

Weeks before, those first few days of July—a week after the healing of Stacy Donnelly and the others—the realization had come. He had a newfound ability of profound implications, use or lose it maybe, and better to put it to well-thought-out use, at that. The House of Wax aftermath was only the beginning.

Which had caused a media stir all its own, every bit the equal of the original tragedy. After leaving Stacy's bedside, Paul had called KGRM, caught Lorraine just minutes away from signing off for the evening. He had her rummage about Sherry's desk and Popeye's office until a list of accident victims surfaced. The station had planned on sending flowers to each hospital room; that Popeye, a touch of genuine sympathy, you just never knew. Paul had bummed an ink pen from a desk nurse and jotted down names, hospitals, room numbers.

Some, like Stacy, were at Barnes. A couple were just along Kingshighway at Jewish Hospital. Another southeast across the city at Alexian Brothers. So, on that same Wednesday evening and the next afternoon, Paul had made more visits, deejay crawling out of hiding to check his listeners. Shaking hands, touching shoulders, patting forearms, a couple of hugs. Expressing his personal sorrow to those awake to hear it, maintaining a short bedside vigil for those who were not.

But always leaving them in better shape than he had found them. His only regret the three beyond his help, he could not raise those who now could only be mourned.

The coincidences took a few days to be noted. Different hospitals, different doctors, too little communication. Still, time made the links unavoidable, a proliferation of trauma center gossip, doctors and nurses forced into astonished wonder by the progress of their patients. Broken bones had rejoined, severe lacerations had been sealed, internal injuries healed. With incredible speed. This had no precedent whatsoever.

The media got inevitable wind of it, every kid injured in front of The House of Wax getting an exceedingly early discharge and a clean bill of health. Doctors scratched their heads and refused to commit to any definitive explanation, while more than a few people tossed the word *miracle* around like a newsworthy football. All of which Paul found pleasantly amusing, as if he had been wondrously transported back to grade school, king of mischief, and could once again watch the payoff of the grandest of practical jokes while basking in the luxury of complete anonymity.

"Check it out," he told Calvin and Hobbes during Channel Two's *Ten O'Clock News*. He saluted the disinterested gerbils with a half-full ale. "We made the tube again."

Paul no longer worried over being connected with it, the very last development he would want. Immediately after the healings, apprehension had been knee-jerk quick. Some keen-minded reporter, hottest thing in a newsroom since Woodward and Bernstein, would somehow sniff him out as the common link between every miracle patient. Just as quickly, though, calm reason had quelled that fear. His visits had attracted little attention at the time—of interest only to the serious KGRM fan—and he had not always found conscious people to realize he'd been there at all. Regardless, assuming someone *did* manage to place him in every room, what then? Even the trashiest of tabloids wouldn't go far enough out on a limb to guess the truth.

The Channel Two news story wound toward a wrap, the photogenic face of Stacy Donnelly replaced with a tracking shot of her leaping across the burnished floor of a dance studio. Human interest postscript, here's how she lives happily ever after, and Paul toasted the TV with his ale.

Case closed, now what next, what encore for this minion of miracles? The day was far off indeed when he could feel remotely justified in hanging it up and feeling the smug satisfaction of a task well done. Assuming such a day ever came at all.

It would likely be at least as long before he so much as understood what had singled him out for this, *Why me, HOW me?* The obvious explanation pointed toward something divine. Certainly those he had healed and their families were leaning in that direction. Barnes Hospital and the others were without a doubt fine institutions in the science of medicine, but not a one made claims of same-day service for someone rolled in on the critical list. And the odds of each kid independently possessing some uncannily fast regenerative ability, well, those were too astronomical to calculate.

So. Eliminate chance, eliminate the inevitable skeptic's claim that the whole episode was an elaborate publicity hoax, and only one reasonable alternative remained. Divine intervention. Paul was comfortable with that. Perhaps all part of some greater whole, a lesson to be learned. For himself, for now. Perhaps for others later on.

The lesson learned thus far was that no greater task existed on earth than to help others, no expectations of reciprocation. Too bad more of such high-visibility preachers didn't approach the concepts of God and the hereafter from that angle. He'd always had major problems with those who took the usual route, the afterlife as some sort of celestial country club, and pulpit ravings as to how we first and foremost should feel inherent guilt over being human to begin with. As if we had another choice. This from the same fellows who, away from the camera eye, gleefully submitted to their own human urges with secretaries and bargain-boulevard hookers.

Magic hands, where to take them next. The answer came a couple days later while skimming the *Post-Dispatch* in David Blane's office. He spotted a feature on a woman named Candace Oliger, the director of volunteers at St. Francis Medical Center, and the success of her program. He paid a visit to St. Francis and volunteered his services, and promptly had his enthusiasm hosed down a bit upon learning he would have to undergo the standard classroom training required of all volunteers. Two weeks' worth. So much for instant gratification.

Training consisted of learning the layout of the hospital, for starters, then an overview of the departments, and from then on it was mostly commonsense psychology and practice on dealing with patients. Smiles and optimism are good, running for the nearest door at a chronic malodorous whiff is bad.

He passed indoctrination with flying colors and got to choose his assignment from a number of options. Working in the gift shop, or patients being discharged. Delivering flowers and mail and so on to individual rooms. Running staff errands. Escorting patients between departments. More.

He opted for patient deliveries, maximum contact with as many sick ones as he could get his hands on. And when Candace Oliger asked what kind of shift he preferred, and how frequent, he told her to put him down for afternoons on Monday, Wednesday, and Friday. Say, four to six.

She blinked rapidly while making notes, we have a live one here; definitely a heavy schedule as volunteers went. But there was only so much radio he could throw himself into, and these were days when he hungered for more, some kind of fulfillment beyond the airwaves. Lay that one at the tanned feet of a beach-blonde named Lorraine.

No bitterness, still, yet after a while it seemed as though bitterness might have been preferable, because then at least the feelings would be strong. Instead, day after day, all was chatty and amiable and completely surface level, vapid exchanges of formulaic friendship. Nothing was true and deep anymore, as if some huge barrier had been unspokenly declared, a line of death. We cross it, we talk of tumbling into bed that night, and we die. Let us instead dwell on weather, and music, and the wisdom of *TV Guide*.

For Lorraine's sake, maybe it was safer that way, with fewer dangers of recurrent behavior. Maladroit philosophy, you won't drown if you don't get your mouth wet. But he was alone and selfish, yes, proclaim it to the world, some occasional reminiscing now and again would be agreeable. A little mutual reassurance that it had been grand, it had been glorious, it had been soothing balm on a night of too much pain.

But it was her choice, takes two to have a conversation, and whenever she wished to come to terms with the fact that, yes, she had breathed her ecstasy into the mouth of another, he would be there to listen. Meanwhile, life awaits.

And so there he was, on a Monday afternoon, pacing through the softly gliding electric-eye doors of St. Francis. Ready for his maiden voyage through its halls, and he touched, and he held, such harmonic empathy from these exchanges of flesh to flesh, making brief open books of these lives he had no right to peruse unless he could improve them. . . .

Room 217

This man named Ted Brandmeier, who at forty-three took greatest pride in that he felt as fit as he did at twenty, and whose weekend fast-pitch hardball game had ended with a trip to St. Francis. An inept slide into home plate had turned tendons, ligaments, and muscles into shredded cabbage. So much for attacking life with the gusto of a domestic beer commercial, here in this brewery town.

This is how it starts, getting old. You start falling apart, piece by piece, and that was the engine of the scariest train of thought Ted had ridden in quite some time.

No disappointment when the mail arrived, several stiff envelopes, plenty of cards. More than half bore the delicacy of feminine handwriting, and he couldn't wait to get into those.

The mail had been brought by some guy, irritatingly young. Energetic in jeans and a knit pullover, and yet you couldn't hate him for his youth when he seemed so damned concerned about your welfare. Not out of apparent obligation, but a genuine desire to hear the answer. And when he swung his hand in for a quick soul shake, sure, you could begrudge him a little, but respect him too.

Hell of a firm grip . . .

Room 269

This man named Arnie Dubrinski, addicted to television, to food, not necessarily in that order, and the body within was fast approaching shutdown.

The doctors had given him a word-picture to chew on. Picture the inside of a pipe running with a regulated liquid flow, its walls closing steadily in with the accumulation of residual filth until the pressure reached the danger zone: Arnie's circulatory system. The man himself, a three-hundred-pound cholesterol dumping ground, a prime candidate for balloon angioplasty to open up the clogged arteries around his heart.

Comfortably lethargic in his bed, multiple chins bunched atop his upper chest as he dropped off to sleep during a cartoon rerun, and someone entered. Someone with a build a fraction of Arnie's, pausing at bedside, setting down a solitary envelope bearing his sister's return address, the only one who bothered returning his prodigious flow of letters.

Arnie huffed in his sleep as the figure rested one hand on his marshmallow-soft shoulder, and a little bit of Arnie began to melt inside. Like a marshmallow over the flame. Merely what did not belong, draining from arterial walls, running like candle tallow into his bloodstream to be voided with the rest of his wastes, and his great heart had not known such rest in years. . . .

Room 332

This woman named Julie Hyde, keeper of monthly ritual. A few days after the end of her period, with husband off at work and kids at play, she would seclude herself in the bedroom. Topless, reclining on the unmade bed, and, palm to nipple, working a slow circular path around each breast.

The dreaded paydirt had been struck this month, the mysterious lump. Followed by the whirlwind of consultory fear: gynecologist, mammogram, then ultrasound, and finally the grim recommendation to see an oncologist, specialist in tumors. Every rung up the ladder had decreased the odds that she was merely the butt of a physiological prank involving a simple fibrous cyst.

This morning, the biopsy, the surgeon removing a bit of the lump for diagnostic purposes. A thousand prayers offered, a thousand novenas recited, a thousand candles lit. And the resounding thoughts of amputation, mandatory deformity, of being somehow horribly diminished. She thought she had advanced well beyond the notion of basing femininity on the biological endowments of her chest. Not so, apparently, now that theory had been supplanted by reality.

He set a bouquet of carnations and roses on her bedside table, this unexpected visitor, even paused to spruce them up. Then told her good-bye, as if sensing by intuition or eye contact that, no, not in the mood for conversation at this moment. A simple good-bye, then a pat on the wrist—the sheer presumptuousness! Then she reconsidered; she had been on the receiving end of enough cheap low-grade feels to know he wasn't trying to cop one. No. He was just being kind before moving along. Familiar voice, too, though she couldn't seem to place it.

Julie Hyde, a good news/bad news proposition lying ahead of her. A finding of malignancy in the biopsy mass, with its accompanying reaction of tears and anguish and cries to Heaven, why, why? Followed by the answer to prayers, her doctors unable to find a single trace of cancerous cells so prevalent in the newly healed biopsy incision.

Eviction. . . .

And the maiden voyage sailed on, the memories always there with every room Paul entered. The nightmare photo album of recollections made more intense by time. Good times forgotten because by the end, there were none, only the bad remained. Here's Dad sprouting his tubes and wires, here's Dad lying in the ravaged wasteland of his own flesh, here's Dad trying so gamely to leave his only son with proverbs and paternal wisdom enough to last a lifetime. His most lasting legacy being the thick miasma of decay and the misery of cannibalizing himself from within.

And, oh, all the things Paul knew he would miss about the man, of course they were there in living color, but all the things he never thought he would yearn for were there too. *I want to be yelled at for curfew. I want to be grounded and sulk for half a week, I want to be manfully teased about that girl sitting two aisles across in homeroom at school. Just once more, just once more. I want to be pulled from playtime to help with one of your endless chores around the house, and I never hated them as much as I let on, because you were there then, YOU WERE THERE, and damn you, DAMN YOU NOW YOU'RE NOT. . . .*

And I so much want to know what you would think of me now.

But neither pain nor tears nor the death of Dad shall stay this carrier from his appointed rounds.

10

Morning sun, glaring even before breakfast. Beneath it, Donny Dawson paced steady laps in his pool until his arms felt ready to fall off. A faith healer without arms, aye, now here was rich laughter. It was nearly as funny as a faith healer without faith.

His pool was a fifty-foot baby blue rectangular oasis from the cares and concerns of everyday life in general, and more specifically, running the ministry that bore his name. Both of which could bear down with horrific pressure if you let them. He lost himself here, the water, the deck of dark blue and tan tile. Swim, bask in the sight and scent of the walk-through gardens, and the most jaded of hearts had to soften. The sickest of souls had to heal.

Wednesday, the final day of July, the last full day to be spent at home for nearly two months. Tomorrow *The Arm of the Apostle* show would be hitting the road in full force, three buses' worth. Donny and Gabe, singers and musicians, camera crew and technical staff, ushers and assistants to handle the collection of crusade offerings and herding the carefully selected infirmed near the front. One big happy rolling family, with one goal uppermost in mind: Save those souls and let them feel the blessings that come through giving.

Most of the trip's itinerary had been planned from Gabe's desk, Donny's own input merely occasional. Gabe had engineered the countless little details with stunning proficiency. Renting the auditoriums, contacting affiliate churches for publicity, setting up advertising and mass-mailed invitations, making hotel reservations. It was a formidable list, and Gabe had proved himself Donny Dawson Ministries' most valuable player.

The route had them leaving Oklahoma City and dropping south into Dallas for tomorrow night, to tape the kickoff for Sunday's broadcast. Then east to Shreveport, Louisiana; Jimmy Swaggart country. Onward, eastward through the southern states until they could boomerang west. After Nashville, they would travel north to Louisville, Kentucky, then Evansville, Indiana, then St. Louis, and work their way back to Oklahoma City.

Just so many pushpins on a mental map, though, as Donny knifed through the water. Six laps, end to end, rest. Six more, rest. Six again. The world focused sharp and narrow each time he slid forth, bubbles and turbulence and foam.

He had thought of calling Gabe, trying to catch him before he left home, tell him to bring his trunks, join in for a quick morning swim. Might do him wonders. Donny hadn't bothered, though, it would do no good. So far as Donny knew, during the five years Gabe had been in his employ, he hadn't so much as dipped a single toe into the pool. Fear of water? This was possible, given what Donny had learned of his teenage years. But Donny had baptized Gabe himself, and it hadn't seemed a problem then, so who knew? Perhaps he was overly modest about exhibiting his body, even with trunks. Gabe did seem very private in that regard, certainly no sin, always buttoned up in those crisp clothes, like armor. Such modesty, a rare virtue.

Not everything could be pieced together from the routine background check Donny had run on *everyone* he allowed to get very close. You do not entrust a ministry of this magnitude to strangers with potentially harmful secrets or hidden agendas. Hence his periodic reliance on an Oklahoma City private detective agency, specialists in discretion and contemporary personal archaeology. Digging up the dirt and peeking under the rugs.

Five years ago, when Gabe first crossed his path at a rally, he had checked out fine. A bit beyond the routine, but nothing too abnormal. Orphaned at age four, a ward of the state of Michigan. Respectable grades in high school and college, although there *was* that incident with the drowned girl when he was seventeen. Clearly her own fault, though the repercussions probably still lingered. The trail dead-ended a month after college, for two years, the last thing to turn up being a one-way flight to Glasgow, Scotland. Not to worry, though, lots of American college students knock about Great Britain and Europe after graduation, although two years seemed unduly long. He *had* had the money, though, insurance from his parents that had collected a pretty penny in interest. The trail picked up again in 1984 after the two-year sabbatical, back from Scotland, and Gabe had gone to work at a Chicago brokerage firm. A fast-track reputation was quickly earned, an utterly nerveless trader willing to take risks that truly separated the pros from the pikers. Two years, Gabe had held that job. His emotional breakdown was inevitable, in retrospect, for Donny had the omniscience of an angel. Gabe Matthews in college: business major, philosophy minor. Anyone could see that the two separate halves making up his whole would someday clash.

After swimming, Donny toweled himself off, slipped into a light cotton robe that hit him at the knees, kicked his feet into thongs. Thus girded, he returned to the house. Several days' accumulation of dirty dishes in the kitchen sink. Housework had fallen well below par since the dismissal of the maids. They were a regrettable casualty in this, but it would not do to have them dusting off Mandy like a piece of furniture. He bypassed the sink without a second glance, bypassed the second floor entirely.

Third floor. His morning vigil with Amanda had become as automatic as his first cup of coffee.

Edie Carson, the day nurse, was reading some fluttery romance novel when he came in, and she quickly marked her place, set the book aside. After a month of duty, the nurses still seemed to feel that pang of guilt when he came in and found them reading, as if they were wasting his time and money. He should ease their worries, have no fear, ladies, we both know Mandy doesn't require much more than routine maintenance. But there was something very powerful in that wielding of guilt; it elevated him, let them know who was truly in charge. You didn't waste a thing like that.

She asked him how swimming was this morning. Pleasant conversation, meaningless. You couldn't see these nurses every day and not get acquainted, at least marginally. Best to keep things superficial, though. They had no business knowing more.

Edie stood, ready to head down for the break that came this time every day, and grabbed her own coffee mug. She smoothed her skirt. White uniforms were pointless, given the nature of this job, and could only draw unwanted attention.

"Before you go, Edie, I want to ask a big favor from you."

"Oh. Yes sir?" Standing at attention, her usual glance up from below, peering shyly past the bangs of her short hair.

"You know I'll be leaving tomorrow for our crusade tour. But I still want to be able to speak to Mandy every day. Before you leave this afternoon, I'll leave you a Sony Walkman and a pair of headphones and some tapes I've made. I want you to make sure she hears a tape every morning, on a rotational basis. Would you do that for me?"

"Of course I would," almost astonished he might have doubts.

Donny paused, hand on the door. "I, uh . . . I suppose you think that might be silly."

Shaking her head, "No, no, not at all." Tentative smile. "I think it's a very sweet thing to do for her. I think it's very loving, and I think it couldn't do anything but help."

And when she left, he knew she had been the proper one to entrust with this responsibility. Edie Carson was as quietly reliable as anyone he had ever met. Call it a hunch, but meek, mousey Edie probably had little else in her life, and thereby drew all her satisfaction from career. Humanitarian pursuits.

Donny settled into the chair by Amanda's bed. Looking any better today? No, of course not, same story every morning, the hope struggling to remain alive.

It was not enough that she remain forever sleeping, so far beyond his reach. It wasn't enough that she not respond to his voice, his touch. No. There was more. He got to watch her age perform a race of gold medal stamina. Got to watch it surge from behind, catch up with her, surpass her.

She had dropped some weight in the month-plus she'd been comatose. The precoma five-foot-five Mandy had weighed a trim 120. She was down to 106 now, and Irv said she would level off around eighty-five to ninety, in time. Her skin, translucent and pale and sweat-sheened, looked drawn, wasted. Dark circles still ringed her eyes, and whenever he thumbed back her eyelids, the pupils remained fixed in that same unequal dilation from the fall. Her feet and ankles were puffy with fluid retention. Her right foot had been propped up with a dense foam device designed to fight foot-drop, wherein the top of the foot on the afflicted side levels out with the shin.

Irv Preston had tried to prepare him for it all. Comas are unpleasant, comas are unsettling. Their victims do not look like their usual robust selves taking a long nap. Forewarned is forearmed, Irv had said.

Sure. As if he truly knew what it felt like to watch your wife deteriorate day by day into a breathing corpse. As if Irv could begin to empathize with the eloquent pain. Irv knew clinical facts, barely understood the wretched grief, dear God, spare me this ceaseless waiting, waiting, waiting.

And as he had done for a month of mornings preceding this one, Donny linked his hands with hers, speaking softly into her ear, telling her he was with her, asking her to remember. Begging her to remember . . .

The best days they had ever known.

The reputation of a man whom an entire congregation—even in the Alabama outback—has seen heal a retarded boy of mortal injuries begins to precede him in certain quarters. The man is a certified draw, of monetary offerings as well as spectators.

There are drawbacks to this, as well as obvious advantages. For one, the spectators arrive at revivals with preordained expectations. History is expected to repeat itself. They want a miracle, they want it *now,* and they hate disappointment. So what are you supposed to do?

You give them what they come for, what makes them happy.

Donny could have penned a how-to manual on the subject. How to develop a multimillion-dollar business from the early days of abject poverty, when its sole assets were a battered car and a few clothes and dreams and precious little else. . . .

You keep moving, church to church and town to town, aided by local believers to arrange your next destinations at sister churches nearby. You praise them for their hospitality. You raise their roof with rhetoric, then bring them down with accusations of just what lowly sinners they are, and then promise to lift them up again.

You pump them for offerings, passing the collection plate as soon as they are primed to fever pitch generosity. Dig deep, now, and *feel* the love generated by all that giving.

And, of course, you heal them.

Not to worry, though, should it turn out that the day by an Alabama roadside was a mysteriously unexplainable one-shot fluke. Never mind that at all, for your corona of holiness is already in place. Your meal ticket is punched.

Instead, you master a few tricks of the trade. Confronted with a cancer patient? Sleight of hand with concealed stage blood and some organs from a chicken—*"Does* this *look like it belongs in a human body? Praise God, NO, it doesn't!"*—and it appears as if you have reached right in and plucked their tumor out. Meet up with a chronic alcoholic seeking release? You give him a sip of your self-styled holy wine, actually Hi-C fruit drink with a wang of fermentation, and you bless him and admonish him to sin no more. You're brought someone suffering everything from arthritis to asthma, tired of prescription medicine? You deal with her only after a lengthy session of singing and chanting, shouting and swaying, until all have achieved an emotionally charged state not unlike brainwashing. And by the time you lay hands upon her, she will believe herself cured of anything.

Prepare to be amazed, by all means, for a great many people will actually walk out of your services feeling better than when they arrived. The placebo effect: They believe? They remain convinced of your claim of a hundred percent cure rate? They don't wish to be left out in the cold? Then of course they shall feel better. Whether you have been the push to get them over a psychosomatic ailment, or have stimulated the brain to secrete pain-killing endorphins, or have simply convinced them they are far better off for having met you—it doesn't really matter. All that matters are the results of the moment.

And, naturally, the collection's bottom line tally.

But what happens if the cancer still rages, if the alcoholic lapses into his old ways, if arthritis and asthma flare up with redoubled fury? How do you deal with this without losing face? Simple; *It's not your fault.* After all, "faith healing" consists of two halves. And when faith isn't sufficient on their part, surely you cannot be expected to bring about a successful healing. Better they know this now, through the reminder of illness, than to forever burn able-bodied in the fires of Hell.

And how they will love and respect and idolize you for bringing this to their attention. For you, truly, are a saint among men.

On the other hand, how do you deal with God? Should you feel even the faintest unease over invoking His name as a routine component in deceptions beyond counting? Never. Because you cling to an old adage heard since childhood:

The Lord helps those who help themselves, which isn't even in the Bible, but ought to be.

And to the words of Jesus Christ Himself, according to the Gospels: *He who is not against us is for us.*

So. You go forth and speak to larger crowds, increasing numbers of followers. You widen your spectrum of crowd-pleasing tricks by putting your wife on a secret microphone to transmit to your hair-concealed earplug on shortwave frequency 37.15. megahertz. She feeds you information gleaned by staffers before the show, circulating with questionnaires, but to the faithful it looks as if facts are coming to you from divine origins. And you convince the barely-able-to-walk, the barely-able-to-see, that the final remnants of these faculties have never been more acute than when they are standing before you. You slip in a few healthy ringers to feign illness now and then. Oh, your tricks are legion.

You must, however, ignore those hopefuls who show up in an undeniably irreparable state, left without alternatives by medical science. Those who look to you as the court of last resort, who enviously watch the miracles and wonder why they are so lowly as to never be called forward for the touch of your blessed hands. And who leave in tears.

You don't even think of them. Don't meet their eyes, for now and again one might convey such misery that a hole is ripped through your righteous facade and will leave you feeling like the parasitic swindler you actually are. Keep your distance, dealing with *them* only through the buffer zone of your mailroom ministry, sending them personalized computer-generated form letters to let them know you pray for them by name and need, and wouldn't they like to plant a seed of faith with Donny Dawson Ministries? No amount too small, because you feel in your heart that A MIRACLE COULD BE ON ITS WAY!

You cultivate that vital mailing list with a gardener's care. Keeping in frequent touch, at least every other week, and hiring a staff to tend all those names like flocks of sheep, whose wool is green. And comes in denominations of ten, twenty, fifty, one hundred.

And so you amass your bank accounts, and hire a comptroller to manage all that tax-free income, and similarly delegate responsibilities to other specialists. You hit the airwaves and buy TV time to syndicate a show taped in the sanctuary you have built. You rent studio time with local stations to do your editing until you can afford to build your own facilities. And then you can reach more people in a week than during a lifetime of stops on the sawdust trail. Because there's an entire nationwide market for you, disillusioned by local churches, or too feeble to attend, or who simply prefer their religion packaged in the same manner as the rest of their entertainment.

Should you gain the attention of detractors—and you will, you will—you need do no more than accuse them of being pawns of Lucifer, seeking to undermine the kingdom.

And you also have the good sense to hire a young, ruthless commodities broker who comes to you for guidance in remorse over a short career filled with cold-blooded dealings that have left lesser opponents on the skids. He doesn't have to be named Gabriel Matthews, but it helps. You counsel him, dry his tears of emotional collapse, inform him he is loved as a brother, and loved by God as a wayward child. Seize this opportunity to convince him he should remain at your side, learning the ways of the righteous while serving your needs. Everybody wins.

Then you can coast. Bask in the earthly world you have created, lit by the light of the heaven you have sold to those willing to pay for it. The fruits of your labor, tangible proof that God is good, and rewards those who do His work.

Even though you have long since forgotten what His work is all about.

But don't forget to pray that the person closest to you throughout the entire climb up the ladder, your lovely wife, does not experience a change of heart over the methods you have chosen to adopt. That she doesn't examine her heart and conclude that she has been deluding herself into acting as an accomplice to shearing the flocks.

You want to avoid that at all costs. For if it happens . . .

All hell can break loose.

And sitting there at her sleeping side, he remembered it all. The best of times, the worst of times.

I'll quit this someday, Mandy, I promise. Maybe I've bent a few commandments, but I'll go straighter. I—I'll open a soup kitchen, and a homeless shelter, and—and you'll see.

But not now, now's not a good time.

Someday.

11

Dreamtime, visceral and surreal, and Paul watched it unfold with wide-eyed wonder. The horse, large and pale, grazing in a nondescript field of pure pastoral serenity, while a friendly sun shone from a sky bluer than a baby's eyes. Postcard perfect, until the horse went suddenly wild, electric stark panic one would associate only with a burning barn. Bucking, straining, like an unbroken bronco exploding from a rodeo stall. Until it could do no more than sag its drooping head before splayed front legs, its muzzle dripping foam.

The hide in the center of its back began to tent upward, sharp thrusts, as if pushed by a secondary pair of grossly malformed clavicles. The flesh itself was torn asunder, parted by a brutal human fist punching through into daylight, the arm next, and a second arm.

Sky darkened, midday dusk, bruised and swollen clouds rolling in to obliterate the blue, and the world dimmed into a never-ending palette of grays as the rider was born.

Hands braced on the lips of the massive wound while scarlet ribbons streamed down the beast's heaving sides. Flex, push, the rider hauled himself out the hard way, head and shoulders and torso and legs yearning to breathe free of their makeshift womb. Until he could straddle the horse while it bellowed equine mortality into a mounting wall of wind sweeping the plains.

Anonymous, this rider, cloaked in a caul of tattered remnants from his steed and fierce black boots. Stretching, luxurious freedom at last, as he twisted one fist into the mane, then reached back into the red meat crater saddling him to retrieve one last item. A long rod of some sort, glimmering wetly, topped with a short crosspiece.

A simple click, and six-inch stilettos came switchblading back from the heavy bootheels. One flex of his legs sent them digging into the horse's wasted ribs, no mundane spurs for *this* apparition. Gale force winds and a dead bolt forward, horse and rider barreling past a backdrop of savage clouds, across fields swelling with a sweet symphony of screams too loud to be human, too terrified to be anything else, and he raised his rod on high, readying to sweep it down with the force of a headsman's ax—

As Paul awoke with a spasm, never quite so glad to see the simple, mundane ceiling of his bedroom.

A groan, rolling over on twisted covers, *Where did* that *come from?* He shook his head to shoo away those final grotesqueries, and when he did so, up came a wracking surge of nausea. He doubled into himself, fetal-style, shutting his eyes tight.

Maybe it was the late Saturday night pizza and beer he'd had with Peter Hargrove ten hours prior. Thick crust, extra everything, and maybe a little ptomaine around the edges, hmmm?

He tried to wait it out, but the misery had staying power. When he sat up on the edge of the bed, a headache waiting in the wings slammed into place, starting at the top of his spine and traveling upward, opening like a Chinese fan between left and right hemispheres.

This was some serious heavy-duty hurt.

Paul scrambled hands-and-knees into the bathroom, barely got to the bowl in time before losing everything in his stomach. It was the most wretched sick-up experience of his life, and he thought crazily of prophecy. Just this week he and Peter had introduced a new character to their lineup of bogus radio voices, the world's most seasick mariner, Captain Horatio Chunkblower. This was the real thing, one great tidal wave of malaise.

The porcelain, a cool, smooth friend. He weathered out the worst of it, and when movement brought tolerable misery, he looked at his hands. Pressed them to the sides of his head, why not, what could it hurt to try? He moved one down over his stomach. What rotten luck. Physician, heal thyself? Not this time. Contact with self apparently led to nothing more than a giant short circuit.

Everybody lucking out on the receiving end except poor old Paul, oh, wasn't *that* fair?

He dry-heaved once more and deemed himself finished, then flushed and stood tall enough to wash his face at the sink. He raised the rest of the way, staring at his rumpled unshaven reflection. Pale skin, darkly circled eyes, wet spikes of hair clumping up from his forehead, water beading like heavy sweat.

"Oh, now *there's* a handsome devil," he mouthed off at the mirror. "Sid Vicious, after death."

He shuffled into the kitchen for a can of 7-Up. His dad had sworn by the stuff when the one-two punch of cancer and chemo had left him nauseous, and his mom had given him plenty whenever stomach flu had gotten the best of him as a child. No flu bug this time, though, he felt sure of it, and he hadn't had nearly enough to drink last night to boil up so virulent a hangover.

Maybe he'd been pushing it too hard at the hospital, he wondered on his way to the sofa. Two weeks of steady healing, as covert as an industrial spy. He had kept no running tally of how many he'd touched, a silly adherence to a rule similar to Peter Hargrove's prime drinking regulation: Counters don't drink and drinkers don't count. A certain hardcore wisdom there.

Healers don't count. But maybe they should.

After two weeks, surely it had to have been over a hundred patients whose burdens he had helped to shoulder. Perhaps in doing so, he was making them his own.

But no, that was ludicrous, you couldn't catch injuries, or noncontagious conditions such as arteriosclerosis and sickle-cell anemia. You could wallow in their tissues, and it wouldn't do a thing.

Give it all of Sunday to subside, and see how he felt by next morning. Already, with twenty minutes between himself and awakening, he was either feeling better or learning how to tough it out. As for the time being, it might not hurt to check up on how the pros handled it.

He tuned in to Donny Dawson's *Arm of the Apostle Hour*, which by nine-thirty was half over. A warm breeze, sticky with early August humidity, washed through the apartment, and Paul sank into the sofa, ah, blessed solace.

Dawson wasn't in his home pulpit, Paul caught this right away. A similar ARM OF THE APOSTLE banner hung in the background, and someone had made an attempt with greenery and so forth to replicate the Oklahoma City church. But home turf it was not.

"There are a lot of people out there, detractors, you know who I'm talking about, who'll try to make you feel ashamed of your earthly rewards," Donny was saying, and some in the as-yet-unseen audience murmured assent. "I think they mean well, I honestly believe they do. But that's the trickiest kind of guile the devil lays out for us: Making otherwise well-meaning people bring us down for something there's no sin in. *That's* Satan's oldest trick, *divide and conquer, am I right?*"

A thunderstorm of amens rose.

Donny was nodding, and he paused a moment to mop his brow with a silk handkerchief. When he smiled at the audience, the tape cut to another camera, and Paul could see a great many more gathered than would fit into the home church. With its large main floor and two balconies, the place looked to be a civic auditorium of some sort.

"Divide and conquer. One of the oldest military strategies in the book. So why shouldn't the devil get his mileage out of it as well? To set the community of the righteous at one another's throats over an issue like . . . money." Away went the hankie. "But friends, I'll tell you this, you'll never convince *me* that God doesn't believe in running a successful business. There's too much biblical evidence to the contrary. How about when Jesus took the five loaves and two fishes—a single boy's lunch—and multiplied them to feed over five thousand? Now *that's* one respectable profit margin!"

Choruses of amens, more than a little delighted laughter.

Is this guy ever smooth, Paul thought. *But is he for real?*

This he pondered throughout the rest of the show, whose final quarter was devoted to healing. What he'd been waiting for all along, a fascination of watching wheelchair-bound people stand upright, apparently for the first time in years. Of watching Dawson cup his hand over someone's eyes, should they suffer from cataracts, and then hearing them count aloud, oh so excitedly, how many fingers Donny was holding up. Of watching Donny know, with no prompting, their names and ailments and addresses and even the names of their doctors.

But was he for real?

Paul watched as the tape broke away to someone giving a tearful testimonial as to how surely Donny Dawson knew Jesus better than anyone else around. And maybe he did, who knew? Paul felt caught in the middle of skepticism over Dawson's ilk as a whole, all the negative press they had slagged over the years, and firsthand knowledge that healing could in fact be genuine. Stranger things in Heaven and earth, Horatio, *et cetera*.

Okay. For now, give him the benefit of the doubt.

As lively hymns played under the closing credits, Paul shut off the TV and returned to the sofa. Lying there to wait out the lingering discomforts of head and belly.

While, quite unbeknownst to him, subtle, permanent changes worked themselves within his body.

Dog day afternoon, when August heat clips tempers short and sets them alight like fuses. Registration day at Wayne Johnston Elementary School in West St. Louis County provided a perfect exhibition.

A sublimely typical brick and masonry building, its front walk was lined with a melting pot of angry parents and concerned citizens and that peculiar breed of busybody with more curiosity than brains. Lots of placards and picket signs in this group, along with shouted protests and invectives, a scenario of ironic throwback to war protests recent and distant, Persian Gulf and Vietnam, when they were righteous and full of brotherhood and love of fellow humanity.

Any way the wind blows.

A lone pair—not counting the two uniformed cops flanking them —paced up the front walk, eyes aimed only at the school doors. The woman was Carole Manion, he knew this from the papers, and her son was Chad, eight years old and a veteran of more humiliation than anyone should experience in a lifetime.

Chad Manion, hemophiliac, blood transfusions going back years. And now here he was, like Hester Prynne of Nathaniel Hawthorne's novel, condemned to wearing a scarlet A. Hers had been literal, *adulteress,* and while his was figurative it was no less stigmatic. Chad Manion, the latest AIDS poster child and cause célèbre on a seesaw of skewed values.

The last thing in the world mattering to the populace was that Chad had not developed AIDS Related Complex—not yet, at least —but merely had the virus. Dormant. The word was enough, AIDS, touch of death, and that was all they needed to know.

A long, hot summer had come to a frothy head, lawyers and mediators squaring off, the school board and ACLU in head-to-head combat, all to simply win Chad permission to attend public school again. Rather than sequestering him off in some airless little cubicle away from other children, circa 1920s tubercular care.

Victory had gone to the Manions, but permission meant only that they had the law on their side. No judge on earth could mandate acceptance and understanding and sympathy as a part of the decision.

By the sidewalk near the school doors, beneath a cloudless sky and a flag, stars and bars in flight, Paul watched this solemn processional. The boy was small for his age, with enormous eyes under uneven bangs, and he grasped his mom's hand and stuck very close to her side.

Mama's boy, some would jab, but could you blame him? The only person in the world left for him to trust. The paper had catalogued ample family tribulation. Chad's father hadn't been around for years, while relatives found excuses to keep their distance, nothing personal. Neighbors and parents of classmates had put on such shows of support as pitching bricks through Carole's car windshield and slashing its tires, and spray-painting graffiti on their house. And the phone calls, anonymous and ceaseless and brutal, heedless of hour, and despite a switch to an unlisted number, it still somehow got out. According to the paper, Chad often lugged around a male Cabbage Patch Kid named Elliott and called it his best friend, only friend.

Those who claimed that AIDS was God's wrath upon homosexuals obviously were not seeing the full picture. Nothing like the tunnel vision of the self-righteous, and Paul wished they could all be brought here.

Following the lapse earlier this month, he had never felt better in his life. He was primed. Watching the Manions, he felt the baseball in his hand, idly spun it in his fingers. And eavesdropped on whatever conversations went on around him, more intimate than the tiresome shouting. Those who traded ignorance and superstition and dread back and forth with a dark glee.

"—don't understand why they don't just lock him up—"

"—heard he spits at people so he can take as many with him as he can—"

"—and he's always bleeding out his little hind end—"

A bottomless pit, no limit to the wit and wisdom of these sages. A plethora of paranoia. Only a matter of time, then, before someone directed a comment his way.

"*You* don't look old enough to have a kid coming here." This from some plump fellow, mid-thirtyish and round-faced and peering at Paul through thick glasses. His sanctimonious little lips were pursed in concentration. Mister Priss. "Do you have a brother or sister coming here?"

"No." Paul glanced up at the picket sign the man carried, DISEASES DON'T HAVE CIVIL RIGHTS, very clever, think of that all by yourself? "I thought I'd come down here for a look at just how far some pea-brained assholes would really carry something."

Mister Priss nodded, happy to find an ally. "Boy, you got that right. Those Manions are going way too far."

One beat, two beats, dramatic effect only, but after years on the radio, Paul had it down perfect. One more glance at the sign, then straight-on at this goofy butterball.

"I wasn't talking about the Manions."

Mister Priss blinked, sputtered something that kept tripping over his indignantly quivering lips. He shook his head in astonished disgust and, tossing nervous glances back over his shoulder, scurried off for the shelter of kindred souls.

Gotcha.

Chad and his mother and their escorts were some twenty feet from the school doors when Paul stepped onto the sidewalk. He was extremely conscious of body language, trying to convey as little threat and as much relaxation as he could. One cop's hand dropped to his nightstick, at the ready, and Carole Manion braked to a halt, child at her side, and Paul was more afraid of her eyes than any nightstick. Tough, oh *man*, had she gotten tough, and the cop was warning him aside, polite but no bullshit allowed here.

Chad was scared to death, huge petrified eyes, and Paul wished for a quick close-up, run *that* sight up the flagpole and see who goes home with his tail between his legs, shame on you all.

"I don't want to stop you or anything, I just wanted to wish you good luck." Paul squatted, closer to Chad's level. No one can pose much of a menace with elbows on knees. "And I wanted to give you a present."

The baseball in his hand had been a brainstorm he had gotten after reading that Chad was an enormous Cardinals fan. He'd had KGRM newsman Russell St. James exercise a couple contacts he knew within the Cardinals organization, and obtain a baseball with a very special signature.

Paul held the ball toward Chad, perched in fingertips, the autograph visible. Undecided, Chad glanced up at his mom, what do you think? Though still wary, she had softened considerably, and nodded.

Chad took the baseball. Cupped it in his hands, looked up with amazement. "Wow. Ozzie Smith?"

"You don't already have one, do you?"

He wiggled his head back and forth. "Nuh uh," turning the ball over and over, as if to convince himself beyond doubt that it was real.

The cops didn't know what to make of it. Carole Manion wasn't faring much better. And the welcoming committee was looking at Paul as if he were some alien life-form, more loathsomely reptilian than human. He rather liked that look on their faces. For in no way did he wish to be one of them.

He only wished he could pass his hands over the lot of them, and remove all the fear, all the misunderstanding, so Chad could get on with the usual Tom Sawyer/Huck Finn business of growing up in Missouri. But not everything could be changed here today.

Maybe the Manions could move somewhere else, their names and faces unknown, where midnight phone calls would not disturb their sleep. And where total anonymity was a blessing that would make them even with everyone else. It was Chad's best chance, perhaps his only one, and this they would have to figure out for themselves.

"That baseball will cost you a hug." Paul nodded as if he could never take no for an answer. "You look like maybe you could use one."

Chad, ever so tentatively, nodded too.

So Paul collected his due, letting it linger a good long moment. Because he wanted to make extra sure about this one.

12

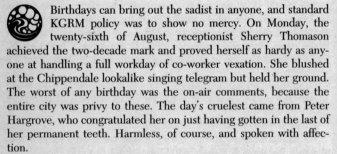Birthdays can bring out the sadist in anyone, and standard KGRM policy was to show no mercy. On Monday, the twenty-sixth of August, receptionist Sherry Thomason achieved the two-decade mark and proved herself as hardy as anyone at handling a full workday of co-worker vexation. She blushed at the Chippendale lookalike singing telegram but held her ground. The worst of any birthday was the on-air comments, because the entire city was privy to these. The day's cruelest came from Peter Hargrove, who congratulated her on just having gotten in the last of her permanent teeth. Harmless, of course, and spoken with affection.

It wasn't until noon that the day took its turn for the worse, and Paul was in the booth when it came. Fresh into his shift and finishing up with five back-to-back tunes and doing a passable Clint Eastwood/Dirty Harry voice, "Did I play six songs, or only five . . . ?" He punched up a commercial and was loading the CD when he noticed Sherry in the doorway.

"What am I going to do, Paul?" Spoken with all the plaintive hopelessness of a child summoned to the principal's office.

"About what?"

"Lunch." She leaned into the doorjamb, tugging at the twist of braided hair coiled over one shoulder. "Popeye says he wants to take me to lunch for my birthday."

"He's finally found a cause worthy enough to stick a crowbar into his wallet. You should feel flattered."

Her small nostrils flared. "I'm serious, I *don't* want this. Would *you* want to spend an hour across the table from that man?"

"Popeye in full feeding frenzy, you have a point."

"What am I going to do, I can't flat-out refuse him."

"Okay, okay, give me a minute to think." Paul frowned, performing control board tasks by second nature, hands guided by instinct. Then he slumped back into the chair. "Have you told him you have other plans?"

She rolled her eyes. "I can think of something like that on my own, thank you. He wanted to know what they were, if they could be changed."

The man's audacity continued to amaze, the pushy bastard. "What'd you tell him?"

"The phone rang, and it was for him. He took it in his office, and I guess he's still there. I don't know what to tell him when he comes out. Because I *don't* have other plans made."

"So let's dig you up a lunch date," Paul said, and she nodded eagerly. "How about a chaperone? Tell Popeye he can come along if he wants to and hope he backs out. You save face, and even if he tags along, you can stick him for the extra meal. You can't lose."

"You're a genius." She bounced over, a peck on the cheek. "Not Cliff, though. That would be worse than Popeye alone."

He pointed out the door. "Go hide in the john for a few minutes, I'll see if I can find you a prior engagement. And you'll owe me, I *will* collect on this someday."

He went forth a minute later, the CD programmed to cover his absence for a song or two. The deities of fate and interoffice politics must have been smiling down benevolently. The sales geek bullpen held out the most hope, and his second attempt was game for the idea, sales manager Nikki Crandall saying she would act as the third wheel. Popeye got word of these other plans moments later, a close call, and while it turned him grumpy, it didn't stop him from making it a threesome.

It was one-thirty when Paul caught the lowdown on the results, Sherry back in the doorway, a wraith with hollow eyes. No more simple discomfort, what am I going to do, not this time. This time she was near tears but wouldn't let herself go, hanging tough. She spoke clearly, half intimidated, half enraged.

The ruse had begun with promising success. Popeye insisted on

driving, and while his Bossman vanity plates were rather ostenta-
tious, after all, it *was* his gas and parking fees. Riding shotgun,
Sherry turned back to Nikki and the two of them maintained a
spirited conversation on anything Popeye might find exclusionary.
Dresses. Makeup. Diet colas. The new *Cosmo* and *Vanity Fair*.
Popeye didn't stand a chance.

He took them to the Fedora Cafe inside Union Station, and everything fell apart within five minutes, when they ran into an account of Nikki's. She had just tried Nikki at the office not ten
minutes before, and had to talk to her before a flight to Boston in
two hours. She would even go so far as to have Nikki's lunch ca-
tered in and pay for a cab ride back to KGRM.

She couldn't refuse. And Popeye, ever the businessman with his
eye on black ink in the ledgers, looked downright ecstatic.

Before you could say sexual harassment, it was just the two of
them. A discreet table, the clink of silver on china, the ghosts of
murmured conversations drifting past. And the unbridled leer
of Vince Atkins's eyes as he told her what a shame it was that they'd
not done this sooner, that they hadn't gotten to know each other
very well during her year at KGRM. He dangled the possibility of
what he termed a substantially lucrative raise. He waxed sensitive
and philosophical about the perils of a young woman without a
college degree who, heaven forbid, should find herself jobless and
with a poor recommendation from her first and only full-time employer.

Because, in Vince's words, "I've got a very special position in
mind for you. And if you're a smart young lady, like I think you are,
you'll assume it," after which he eyed her over the top of his vodka
martini. He mentioned a predilection for homemade videotapes,
and over the glass, encircled by his cigarlike fingers, his eyes gave
mere hints of further indignities. She had sat there, agonizingly
queasy, but curiously numb, as well, thinking, *It's my birthday and
I really don't need this, how could a job I love so much go so wrong?*

"The whole thing was just one big sick scheme to get me away
and proposition me," she said. Sherry had wandered over to the
album racks and was running one salmon-colored nail along the
spines.

"What did you tell him?"

"Nothing, yet." She hugged her arms around her chest, a retroactive shield against Popeye's leer. "Not that I would even *consider*
doing anything with him. I don't even get coffee for him."

Paul sat up, pleasantly surprised in this strange moment. "And you do for me?"

A quick smile, a tight shrug. "Don't let it go to your head, I can stop anytime without notice."

The booth felt supremely odd, Sherry's refuge, last place in the station she felt comfortable, an Alamo of sexual politics. And here he was again, Paul Handler, brother confessor playing the platonic soundboard again. It was no burden. The sight of her fanned all the right flames within him, and he could feel a hot pulsing in his cheeks and hands that longed for release, to raze Vince Atkins into a mound of ashes.

"How about nailing him on sexual harassment charges?"

Sherry violently shook her head. "Oh, he was a clever son of a bitch about this, I'll give him that. No witnesses, so it's just my word against his. And he didn't say one thing that was overtly a pass. It was all double-meanings, and that—that filthy *look* he was giving me. He'd claim I was just misunderstanding everything he was saying. Paul, I couldn't prove a thing."

She talked, she fumed, she tried to get some of it out of her system. Until she had been in the booth as long as she figured she could get away with, then began the last mile back to her desk, her final comment being that she did *not* want to have to leave KGRM.

Nothing he could do in the meantime, so Paul let it simmer, back burner, throwing himself into the remainder of his shift with a vengeance. Until the matter could be pulled off again, in full boil.

Crossroads. How to handle this? As with his dual function at the hospital, moral support alone seemed woefully inadequate, not when he was capable of more. Not to act would be far worse than being incapable. Yet he didn't wish to overstep his bounds. Sherry was bright, she was no pushover, she needed no Lancelot to come riding to her rescue.

Hell with it. Something like this was anybody's ball to play. While Vince Atkins may have been their boss, he was no Caligula with absolute power and authority. If he needed a reminder, so be it. Paul was comfortable being the one.

Strange. In the past several weeks, he had experienced a steady decline in regard for all those people who, for whatever personal cowardice, slinked away from the line of fire, applied thumb to rectum, and waited in the shadows until trouble blew over. Sure it was a cranky outlook, but he could live with that. He would wade in where fools feared to tread.

Even so, he chided himself for suspected brain damage on the trip to Popeye's office. Might as well just stroll on in, plunk his scrotum onto the man's desk, and hand over a mallet. It would at least eliminate the suspense of waiting to see how much of a ballbuster Vince would be.

"You sounded excellent today, Paul, excellent." Vince was all smiles, fed and fat and happy and no doubt unspooling a mental stag film starring the young lady out front. He leaned back in his chair, an oversize leather throne on casters. The entire office, with dark paneling and brass and cut-glass liquor bottles displayed with snifters, was a crafted womb of power.

Popeye leaned forward, elbows on desk, offered Paul one of the two chairs before his desk.

"No thanks, I'll stand." A trick of dominance; the chairs sat lower than did Popeye's, putting you at the automatic disadvantage of having to look up to him. "It won't take long."

A tiny flickering frown. "Suit yourself." Smoothly shifting into response, eyes straying across his desktop and finding a book, *A Passion for Excellence*, that had to be reshelved. He remained standing, still maintaining a frozen smile.

Oh go on, nobody lives forever. . . .

"Since you seem to be into understatements today," Paul said, "I'll put this in the same kind of terms. A lot of people around here would be upset if you suddenly let Sherry go."

Popeye's smile began to crack around the edges, and he tried to salvage it with a show of benign ignorance. "I beg your pardon? Why would I do that?"

"I don't know," Paul wheedled, two could play this game. "Because, say, you two are mismatched and she's the one with enough brains to know it?"

This one torpedoed the smile off Vince's face. His blood pressure must have been on the rise, for so was his color. Red.

"How I conduct myself around my employees *away* from work— and no one here is paid for their lunch hour, by the way—is no concern of yours." Strained through clenched teeth. "I suggest *you* haul ass out that door and not bother yourself with what goes on in the off-hours. Understand?"

"All I want to understand is that you'll just let Sherry do her job. Without worrying about what she has to do—in the *off*-hours—to keep it."

Popeye breathed heavily through his nostrils, a bull ready to charge. "Do you like *your* job, Paul? Because nobody is indispensable around here. *Nobody.* Do you understand *that*?"

Paul felt a peculiar relaxation wash over him, the eye of the hurricane. When it came down to the bottom line, this was the worst the man could do: terminate his status as KGRM midday man. Paul doubted he would have any trouble catching on somewhere else before long. Hell, industry wisdom maintained that you haven't truly worked in radio until you've been canned once.

"I think my job's just peachy. One or two things around here I might change, but . . ." He left it at that. Understatement.

"Well, if you like your job, and *if* you would like to have it tomorrow, I suggest you find your way to the production booth and start cutting the commercials you have to do." Florid-faced and leaning across the desk to uphold that vital dominance, Vince emphatically pecked his finger into Paul's chest. "I think you've got more than enough in there t—"

Paul fired his own hand up to catch Popeye's in midpeck, before he even realized it. He clenched tight and held firm, not budging as Vince's eyes bulged, all rage and loathing. And surprise? Yes. That too, and how gratifying that was.

You fat bastard, guys like you don't even belong in the same species with the rest of us.

He longed to say it, ooh, and how, but while convinced that Vince's threat was bluff and bluster, he saw no sense in taking the extra chance. Besides, there was a certain power in limiting your words to as few as needed. It kept others guessing.

Paul released his hand, turned, and vacated the office. While Popeye didn't say a word.

Point made. And taken. In spades.

Vince Atkins left the KGRM offices at close to six that evening and had, in nearly three hours and by conservative estimate, urinated six times. Heavily, big long satisfying pisses that felt like he was draining away the weight of a bowling ball. Didn't seem right, not at all. A fever, maybe?

Not to worry, he came from sturdy stock, and he wasn't even thinking about it while leaving the building. Mind on a pitcher of martinis, oh, that would taste better than good, that would taste glorious. And wouldn't hurt toward slaking that powerful thirst he could feel coming on . . .

* * *

. . . for within his body, a shift was occurring on microscopic levels, dextrose and sodium and potassium leaching into his bloodstream, emptying into his bladder, voided, flushed into the sewers. Electrolytes fleeing like rats from a sinking ship. The entire process sped along by the world's most common diuretic, alcohol, and the floodgates had just opened. . . .

Twenty hours, give or take, and Paul grinned at the change in Sherry's mood. Yesterday afternoon had been trauma. Today, and likely to stay, was malevolent glee. She meant business, and Paul never wanted to get on her bad side. Women were just sneakier when pushed, that's all there was to it. Heritage, he supposed. Shortchanged in upper body strength, might as well compensate in covert operations. Paul could respect that.

"I had a talk with Lorraine last night," she said.

He was juggling a CD and an album and commercial carts with precarious dexterity, and paid her more than all the attention he could spare. This should be good.

"She gave me something to nail Popeye if he ever tries anything like yesterday again. I almost hope he does." She grinned. Had she been male, and a silent movie villain, she would by now be twirling the tips of a handlebar moustache.

"An elephant gun?" He peered toward her purse.

Sherry opened it and withdrew a small tape recorder, wired with a small remote microphone. "Lorraine said she had to use this once herself. I can hide this in my purse and have the mike near the top, and take it straight to a lawyer."

Headphones cockeyed on his skull, Paul swiveled the chair around and shot her a victorious thumbs-up. She smiled and went through some brief pantomime, and he wasn't sure, but it looked like a scissored castration. Ouch.

"Any more subtle advances out of him this morning?"

She shook her head. "He's barely said two words to me today. Maybe your talk scared him off. And if it did, thank you. And even if it didn't, thank you anyway, for trying."

He mumbled something, no thanks required, and realized he wasn't handling appreciation very well. Probably because he had been doing a lot lately for which thanks would be given if only the recipient knew whom to thank. Which was fine, really, no attention was the way he preferred it. He had gotten used to the secrecy rather quickly.

"But you've got to admit," Sherry said, "it would be fun to sue his fat pants off," and they laughed. "Anyway, I don't think he's feeling good today. He only comes out of his office to refill his coffee mug. But at the water fountain, isn't that weird? Just since eight o'clock, I bet he's gone to the fountain a dozen times."

Speculation was rife with comic possibilities. In anyone else, it would sound like a bizarre new fad diet, but Popeye? By the next day, it was obvious that dieting was the last thing he was up to, the polar opposite. Universal KGRM assessment was just how awful the man looked. Truly awful. Spectacularly awful.

Merely fat before, he was now positively bloated. Peter said the sight reminded him of Elvis in his last days, who sweated his way across the stage in a miserably grotesque parody of himself. Russell St. James predicted that, despite obvious evidence that something was awry, he would be too proud and stubborn to consult a doctor anytime soon.

And Sherry reported that he had switched from a coffee mug to a large plastic pitcher, economy by volume, yet those trips to the fountain were even more frequent than the day before. . . .

Within his body, a state which would have sent alarms clanging through the head of someone more sensible, less stubborn, oh, this horrid thirst which had no end.

But the body can metabolize only so much water at a time, and Vince had gone into overflow, having saturated his cells, then his bloodstream. Now the incoming water and newly released glucose— from his body's breakdown of fatty adipose tissue in a desperate bid for energy—had no place to go but between his tissue cells. Fluid steadily damming up within his lungs, around his heart.

Diluted, his blood thinned such that its pressure had dropped to a level dangerous even for a man who was fit and trim, let alone carrying so much extra poundage. Decreased lung capacity allowed the buildup of carbon dioxide acid in his bloodstream, as he grew shorter and shorter of breath, but the thirst, THE THIRST, it just would not go away. . . .

Thursday, near the end of a horrendous week, and Vince Atkins sat wheezing behind his desk, all he could do to manage upright posture. Tired, so tired, and weaker than a month-old teabag. The past couple nights' sleep had been a joke, no more than a single hour of unbroken slumber at a stretch. Countless times awakening to the bitter darkness of his bedroom, groaning at the realization it had been mere minutes since the last time he had checked his clock. Sometimes it was the diarrhea that woke him, building up with sufficient force to shoot out like a cannon; other times, the parched landscape of his mouth and throat.

It was not bad enough that he drained seven pitchers of water at his bedside last night, and unmeasured more at the sink. He was also piddling and soiling the bed like an incontinent child, awakening to find the sheets soaked and stained and cold. No dignity in this at all, this knew no boundaries, and he never wanted to get old, lose that bodily control for good.

Vince braced head in hands, there, more pain. Like heavy needles through his brain, jab one in long and slow, then twist, twirling gray matter into swirls like a fork in pasta. He coughed, an anemic rumble as he labored for breath, and even the lights were painful today.

With spastic hands, Vince grasped his pitcher, brought it sloshing to his lips. Clamped his mouth down and tilted it back. The relief was minor, temporary, and more than a little water cascaded down cheeks and chin, soaked his shirt collar, which in itself was giving him fits. Too tight, as were his shirt cuffs and slacks and shoes. Even the waistband of his underwear had become a length of razor wire threatening to slice his belly.

For the dozenth time, maybe more, reaching for the phone, letting his hand fall short, *I'll beat this on my own, won't find me whining to a doctor about being thirsty, for fuck's sake.*

His hand.

It looked like a rubber glove filled taut with water.

Slowly, slowly, he poked at the flesh on the back of his wrist, and stared in horrified fascination as the puckered dimple *stayed* there, like an indentation pressed into bread dough. What the hell? Pillsbury Doughboy.

He attacked the pitcher again, alcoholic fervor toward the day's first bottle, and lapped at the rim to catch every last drop. He gurgled and set it down, not enough, never enough.

Vince's in-basket had become, since Tuesday morning, a logjam of paperwork. Endless paper tide, where to even start, and now it was Thursday, and what the hell was he doing here in the first place . . . ?

Empty. Pitcher was empty. That would never do.

How many had he downed today? Fifteen? Twenty? The normally shiny top of his desk was covered with dried water rings, side to side, front to back. A mineral quarry.

Empty. Already? Time for a refill, immediately.

He shoved himself to his feet, heave ho, swirling gray mist in the room. He wavered until it cleared, gasping, then scooped up his pitcher and lurched for the door. A dinosaur plodding through the offices, ignoring the stares of alarm from the staff, and then Cliff Frankl in his face, where's that contract I turned in for signature on Monday, I need it before August billings are compiled, and Vince became W. C. Fields, go away boy, you bother me, and he still managed to lose the water fountain twice.

He found it, then decided to bypass it entirely. Far too slow, he needed some *real* water pressure, and made tracks for the bathroom. Should anyone be inside, especially that son of a bitch Paul, then they would automatically be dubbed earth's lowest life-form, subject to immediate squashing.

The john was as empty as his pitcher, and he was puffing like a steam engine, and slumped against the wall to catch his wind. Those lights, fluorescent lights, ground zero nuclear blast, squint, and he shut his eyes altogether when he saw the sweaty, bloated thing he had become. That brief glimpse in the mirror had shown him a blimp made flesh, wearing a damp, rumpled suit inadequate to even close around him. Set into an otherwise shiny face, his eyes looked dark and sunken—and dead.

He cast aside the pitcher, as inadequate as his suit.

Fumbling with buttons and zippers, wrestling the hateful strait-jacket clothing from his bulk, no time to waste, and he really should call a stupid doctor, soon as he was through here. He lumbered into the shower, twisting the knob for maximum output and the cold spray was a shock to his body. Furthest thing from his mind, though, it mingled with the sour sweat greasing him from head to foot. He adjusted the nozzle from spray to jet . . .

Cold, soothing water . . .

Finest of nectars to minister to the raw ravages of his throat . . .

By standing on tiptoe, Herculean effort, Vince hauled himself up by the stall frame and clamped his mouth around the nozzle. Bit so hard his teeth grated on metal, and he swallowed, and he inhaled, and even though his filled-to-capacity belly rejected it and sent the water surging back up his throat, even though he gagged on the fluid jetting into his lungs, he tried to gorge even more, sometimes you just can't get enough of a good thing.

It hit him like a pile driver, the left side of his chest, then paralysis in his left arm, and Vince Atkins was dead on his feet of congestive heart failure.

His body came bursting out the open door of the stall, timber, and struck the floor with a tremendous thud that sent a geyser of regurgitated water arcing across the room to splash the opposite wall.

And there he lay until someone on the outside noticed the water seeping beneath the door.

13

Gabe Matthews loved taxi drivers, was in love with the whole idea. Perfect capsulized examples of sterile encounters in a world where people were afraid to even touch one another, never can tell what diseases are waiting to be caught. But cabbies, they were friends in otherwise friendless lands, whisking you where you wanted, no questions asked. They could even point you in the proper direction for things they could not do. All it took was the application of the proper solvent.

Gabe had long known how the game worked.

In chemistry, water is the universal solvent. In the world of human passions, it's money. Cash dissolves willpower and morals, loosens tongues and unfetters inhibitions.

Tonight, just one more demonstration. The driver who had picked him up in front of Nashville's Holiday Inn Crowne Plaza proved an eager study, willing and able to earn a quick and painless hundred. Two phone calls, that's all it took, and then they were rolling on pavement that steamed from evening rain. Saturday night, final night of August.

The Arm of the Apostle tour had rolled into town hours before, a night of freedom before the scheduled Sunday night rally. They had checked into the Crowne Plaza—the Hyatt, once upon a time on previous visits, but so goes the world—around four, then rode the glass capsule elevators to the ninth floor, where a wing of rooms awaited.

Donny had roamed, restless as a lion, and shortly thereafter disappeared into his room to unpack. Then he emerged and simply stood at the retaining wall near the elevators. The hotel's floor plan was square-shaped, the tower built around an open central core, twenty-five stories of free-fall shaft. Spy down upon the lobby, upon greenery and chairs and love seats, all so tiny so far below. To jump would be easy, immortalized in hotel legend.

Gabe had been watching through the hair's breadth he had opened his door.

Donny had gazed down for minutes, alas poor Yorick, then disappeared into his room for good. He had already announced intentions to dine via room service tonight. A far cry from the old days, an odd nostalgic twinge, when Donny and Amanda would hire limos to take them and several select guests to dine in the finest of four-star restaurants. Champagne at a hundred bucks per softly popping cork.

Gone, those days, maybe for good, and if there was pity on Gabe's part for Donny and the loss of his glory days, there was also an admiration for the newfound asceticism, get back to those roots. If indeed room service and a TV could be called austere.

The taxi was steadily approaching Nashville's southern fringes, the last sign he had noticed reading HILLSBORO PIKE. Night was falling like an angry cloud, and the clockwork sweep of the windshield wipers kept perfect time with his heart.

So in tune tonight, so alive.

Gabe was as casual as he got tonight, pressed cotton slacks and a dark blue polo shirt, a light jacket to ward off the rain. Running his hand down through the open V of his shirt, his fingers closed on a thin gold chain he constantly wore. Rarely visible, usually walled behind closed collars and ties. Donny had the mistaken impression that it bore a crucifix.

Naive, but understandable; a harmless deception.

Gabe's nimble fingers teased it out, letting it hang outside his shirt for a moment. A gold-plated razor blade. Two edges, double your pleasure, double your fun.

Their month of touring, with another three weeks left to go, had been an unqualified success. The nightly offerings were usually grossing, depending on the sizes of the venue, city, and crowd, somewhere between forty and fifty thousand, mostly in small bills. Gabe himself supervised a staff of four who counted and sorted and parceled it in one of the auditorium's back rooms. He also walked it by suitcase to a safe aboard the motor coach Donny rode in, a task for which he occasionally helped himself to an allowance. This was not stealing, this was appropriation of funds.

The camera crew was filming each night, and every Wednesday a courier jetted back to Oklahoma City with the week's film, to review it and select the best night. Which was then edited in the studios for regular Sunday syndication.

Donny had been in peak form most nights in the pulpit, cresting the audience like twelve-foot breakers. Apart from the pulpit, though, he had been as introspective as Gabe had seen him over the five years. Yes, knowing your wife lay at home in a coma could dim anyone's enthusiasm, but it didn't end there. He fully expected —or hoped, anyway—to pull that healing rabbit out of the hat again. This poor man, why couldn't he just face reality? Probably because he had such a limited view of reality to begin with, but that was hardly his fault.

Poor poor man, expecting to find something out here on the road. Not even once considering that something might find him, instead.

The driver's attention was fully on the rain-slick road, but Gabe didn't care if the man saw him. After all, suspicions had to have been aroused by tonight's special request. So. He hooked one finger in the neck of his shirt, tugged it aside to expose the ridge of his collarbone. Took the gold blade in his other hand, and pressed one keen edge perpendicular to the bone. Notched it hard, rocking it back and forth as he shut his eyes and felt the warm trickle down his upper chest.

Sweet bliss, dark rapture of pain, *please take me higher oh please make me purer*, mere prelude to a night of miracles.

The taxi took him to an address which meant nothing, only that what he wanted, needed, was on the inside of that house. Discreet seclusion, as he had fully expected, English Tudor set far back from the winding treelined road. More trees, dripping with an afternoon and evening of rain, shielded it from streetside eyes seeking to pry beyond the iron fencing. The taxi idled between two brick pillars while the driver chatted to an intercom, and a moment later a gate parted, divine access.

"Can you make it back here in three hours?" Gabe teased the driver with a brief flash of another fifty-dollar bill.

"Your chariot shall await, my man." Grinning as Gabe nodded and exited the taxi, watching for a moment as the cab turned around and rolled back to the street.

And the driver flicked a head-shaking glance into his rearview. "Ya fucking freak," he said.

The mistress of the house was named Belinda, which was all she said he needed to know, mistress being the operative word. Mistress Belinda, dominatrix extraordinaire, specialist in bondage, pain, humiliation, and punishment, any and all available upon request. Rates of three hundred dollars per hour. A bit steep, perhaps, even by the standards of high-class call-girl operations, but when dealing in the rough trade, it is quickly learned that quality and discretion cost money.

Belinda cut a tall figure of feminine muscularity. Skin as smooth and pale as marble, in vivid contrast to the network of black leather crisscrossing her torso and playing peekaboo with her breasts and pubic mound. Fingerless gloves crawled up to her elbows, and four-inch spike heel pumps set her towering. A studded collar circled her throat, and her hair was cropped close, slicked back from her forehead. Scarlet lips, ebony fingernails, and unfathomably deep eyes, gray as smoke.

She would do nicely. *She* meant business.

"So what are we into tonight?" Her voice, hard as cinders.

Gabe grew aware of the erection raging behind his zipper, no use fighting it. *Just take a little off the tip*, perfect reply to this barbershop kind of question, but he held it back.

"You've been a naughty, naughty boy today," half statement, half inquiry.

"An absolute shit," Gabe said. "So why don't you just lay off with the questions and assume the worst, and we should get along fine."

The ruby lips pursed a moment as she appraised him in a glance, then blew a light kiss. "I *do* so admire forthrightness."

Once financial transactions were out of the way, a carnal distraction from more spiritual implications at hand, she led him through the house. Tasteful and arty, contemporary, giving no hints as to the occupational leanings of its owner. She probably played the role of neighbor well, and he admired that immensely, he could identify, and just how hard was it for her to maintain that pretense of normality?

Especially given the contrast of her—what? Office? Rec room? Workshop?

Dungeon.

Cellar level, walls of brick and black mortar. An iron chandelier descended from center ceiling, throwing both light and shadow over all the toys scattered throughout the room. The rack of assorted whips. A display case of enormous dildoes that bristled like porcupines. An iron chair with leather restraints and an anal spike. A bed with similar restraints. The room's centerpiece, an enormous X of rough-hewn wood. Daggers and chains and metallic orifices and a potpourri of full-head leather and vinyl masks with zippers, and so much more.

A De Sade Disneyland with nothing but E-ticket rides, it took the breath away, and here he would peel away the taints of the world, of life and career and the confusion of deception. He would be himself, the true Gabriel on the quest for purity and purging, and Belinda was suddenly beside him, grasping his jaw with one hand, leaning close enough to rip his ear off with her teeth.

"You *will* strip for me," and she smeared a vicious kiss onto his mouth, a harsh thrust of her tongue. Degradation, the kiss of a whore, no telling where that mouth had been, and he drank it in, he deserved it, and if she demanded, he would drink of the musky nectar between her thighs.

Strip; it was not an option, and Gabe readily complied.

For several moments, Belinda stood before him for an altogether new appraisal, the wicked arch of her eyebrows suggesting that even she was impressed. Not by biological endowments, but by the alterations on his torso as a whole.

Gabe's flesh was a topographic shrine to masochism, a mosaic landscape of scar tissue. Thin and wide, horizontal and diagonal and vertical, etching him from pubis to shoulders. Scarcely any area greater than two square inches left untouched.

Belinda regained composure, nodded approvingly. "Yes. Oh yes. I know exactly where to begin with you."

She seized a fistful of ridged and rippled skin on his shoulder, pulled him over to the wooden X. Pressed face-first against it, Gabe extended his arms and legs along the crosspieces and let her strap him on by wrists and ankles. She stood behind him with a whip fresh from the rack, and from the swish of the air as she tested it, he knew the lashes were multiple. So much the better. So much more efficient, and he wanted it all.

Another second passed, and the lighting mutated from clean white to glowing red, and when the first lash of the whip came striping across his back, Gabe cackled and grinned and dug his fingers into the well-gouged wood, the bite of splinters.

He looked back, saw not her face but a face from half his life ago, and it was right and proper. He was prepared.

"Oh yes, you've been an absolute hellion," a groan from scarlet mists behind him, punctuated by the crack of the second of what would be many strokes from the whip. Leather lashes biting with rawhide teeth, bringing exquisite agony, tearing away the worldly Gabe and stripping him to the raw, the elemental.

For to truly live, and see, one had to suffer.

Belinda was breathing hoarsely now, salt droplets of her sweat stinging the tenderized flesh of his back, and she began to scream the most vile, most humiliating curses she could think of, music to his ears. His hips ground against wood, and he gasped and left behind a sticky smear, so glad to get *that* out of the way, and the most uplifting thing he could think of was that this night of gleeful torment had barely begun.

14

Who was it with that old proverb, the Chinese? *Be careful what you wish for, because you just might get it.* Had they ever known what they were talking about. It was one of those philosophical questions to which Tappers Pub lent itself quite well.

"I still can't believe he's dead." Paul's hands were doing duty around a frosted mug of Bass ale. "Four days now, and it has *not* sunk in."

Peter nodded, his sole partner on this sultry afternoon of spirits and shelter. "We all thought Popeye was an asshole, and that was justified, but man—I never would've wished going out like that on anyone."

The autopsy revealed that Vince Atkins had been stricken with a sudden and severe electrolyte imbalance that had led him to consume staggering quantities of water to satisfy a thirst he perceived as unsatisfiable. In effect, the exact opposite of dehydration had occurred. The man had *over*hydrated himself, and the only thing that had prevented him from drowning within his own tissues was his heart's inability to handle the strain. An extremely rare phenomenon, though not unheard of.

Popeye, cast adrift on an eternal sea of his own gluttony. Somehow this reeked of a terrible poetic justice.

He was little more than a bad memory by now. As he had been divorced for several years, with no family in St. Louis, his mother had had the body shipped back west for burial in his hometown of Columbia. Certainly within driving distance, but not one of the KGRM staff really wanted to make a trip for today's funeral. Lousy timing for a funeral anyway, Labor Day.

"I didn't really want him to *die,* when it came down to it," and Peter tugged thoughtfully at his beard. "I just wished he'd disappear for good, vanish."

"Retroactive abortion," Paul said.

"Exactly."

They had a booth this time, kicked back and lazy and none too talkative. Let the noise from the other revelers take the place of their own conversation. Being Labor Day, most of the city was at rest, nobody working but us retail clerks and bartenders and deejays. Tappers was far more crowded than usual at four in the afternoon, everyone with just enough elbow room to keep from getting irritable, and who were these transient strangers, anyway? Didn't they have their own bars? Their voices competed with KGRM coming over the sound system, and the TV behind the bar played a silent rerun of *The Munsters.* Do-it-yourself dialogue, if you were so inclined. Few were. Others checked out new paintings on the walls. Paul's favorite was an ancient Roman king with a southern black man singing to animals, titled *Romulus and Uncle Remus.*

Peter looked back from the TV. "I hope we get somebody halfway decent to replace him."

"Yeah. Hopefully the barrel they scraped him from the bottom of has been pitched." Speaking ill of the dead, yes, it was, but regardless of life or death, it was how they all had felt. Paul saw no need to sugarcoat now.

KGRM was one of thirteen stations across the country owned by a minor air mogul headquartered in New Jersey who made it to St. Louis for a day every four to six weeks. They would have a new manager within a couple weeks, he had promised, already having sent out feelers for a new GM by the time the medical examiner's scalpel sliced an enormous Y-incision into Popeye's torso and received a gusher of water in reward. Until then, David Blane and sales manager Nikki Crandall could share figurehead responsibilities.

Bass ale, percolating straight to Paul's brain, he'd had nothing to eat since breakfast. But keep those pitchers coming, for he had nothing to do and no place to be until airtime late the next morning. Strange, to have a Monday afternoon free.

This was the first day since beginning volunteer work at St. Francis that he had called in to say he couldn't make it. On Friday, twenty-four hours after Popeye's aquatic demise, he had felt surreal, moving through hospital corridors and rooms as if they were mined. One stray thought nagging with the persistence of a piranha at an open wound: *What happens if I meet somebody here I really can't stand?*

Popeye's autopsy had revealed that his condition had to have snowballed over three or four days, and this was verified by the KGRM staff. From late Monday on, the same day he and Paul had locked horns, Vince Atkins just had not been seen without a mug or pitcher of water. Paul knew, in retrospect, that he hadn't so much as lifted a finger to help the poor slob. He had gone about his business, feeling rather smug about getting Popeye to back down, letting him stew in his own juices. Until they had killed him.

So what happens if I meet somebody I can't stand? Would I even be able to heal them?

Surprisingly enough, in six weeks of hospital work, the issue had not arisen. Yes, there had been many patients about whom he had felt ambivalent, though none he had actively disliked. But somebody would show up, surely. Every doctor, nurse, and tech had favorite horror stories about a rogue's gallery of insufferably wretched patients, and it was only a matter of time before he had his own.

And so the question remained, would he be able to do the job if his heart wasn't really in it? And how many shared burdens could that same heart withstand before deciding enough was enough, and sealing itself off like a king's ransom? Not that he was ready to give it up this soon, but the need for rest and relaxation had come up far sooner than anticipated.

And *that* was scary.

He had heard it said before, if you can heal people, you've suddenly found yourself with a new full-time job, and this was profound truth. You could not turn it on and off like a light, or hang it up like a lab smock at the end of your shift. You carried it with you everywhere, a part of you forever watching for someplace else it might be needed. And as distressing as the constant awareness of how many hurting people lived out there, even worse was having to bypass so many he truly longed to help, and knew he could not.

Because stopping a stranger to rework a malformed limb or absorb mongolism would have blown his cloak of anonymity. Thrust him into a public spotlight that would drain him as surely as a slit jugular.

So. Vacation time. Rest, relaxation, perhaps reevaluation.

He and Peter played darts, sometimes against each other, sometimes against challengers. They ordered food, one-third-pound burgers with the works. They scrutinized Lorraine's on-air performance, rating her ad-libs with scores scrawled onto napkins with felt markers. And near seven-thirty, Peter hung up his mug for the night and went home.

Paul sat scanning the bar for familiar faces, found no one he really wanted to talk to, not tonight. Instead, found himself increasingly disconcerted by the amount of smoke this boom crowd had brought with it. He paid a final visit to Tequila Mike and got a quart of ale for the walk home.

When he hit the sidewalk, he squinted against the last of the day's sunlight. Not even dark yet, and here he was with a full-tilt buzz on. Quite the hedonist, and it was only Monday. He toasted, here's to the American work ethic, and set off for home.

Not so unbearably warm now, he could almost believe in the coming of autumn again.

A pleasant trip home, strangely light on his feet, and his gently buoyed spirits ducked underwater only when he set foot through the back door of his building and wobbled a moment. And realized he was face to face with the scourge of fun-loving neighbors one and all, Janet DeWitt, wicked witch of the second floor.

She was heading for the dumpster to appease it with a plastic bag, maybe a sacrificial offering after prayers for a date, and the thought brought a wet snort of laughter. It was out before he could stop it, and she glared. This was unseemly.

"It's behavior like yours that gives younger people a bad name," spoken with cryogenic charm. Her nose was stuck in the air, all the better down which to regard people, and her lips were pressed together lockjaw tight. Lint-brown hair topped a severe figure, all bones and angles.

"Good evening to you too." Ale sloshed in Paul's bottle and belly alike.

"If people could only see themselves when they drink, they might think twice about doing it, that's my guess." Probably a closet tippler on the sly. Her type seemed to breed hypocrisy like the plague.

"The only thing that would make me think twice is right now I'm seeing two of you. Do you know how *scary* that is?" Those sputtering, half-drowned spirits had bobbed up again with gleeful resurgence. It was everything he had wanted to say to her but, for the sake of peace, had not. Erosion of restraint, courtesy of Bass ale, and he blurted ahead. "Tell me something. I've wondered about this ever since I've lived here. Do you lie awake at nights, just thinking up things to bitch about the next day?"

Her face registering affront upon affront, "Why you little bastard, if you weren't so drunk—"

"Winston Churchill said it best, 'Yes, I'm drunk, I'm very drunk. And you, madam, are ugly. But *I* shall be sober in the morning.'" Oh, such eloquence, and he pushed past her for the stairway. Game, set, and match.

She screeched, she crowed, she called him names, she threatened to kick his sorry ass. And proved herself all the more pathetic. It all seemed so very clear now, just some lonely, self-repressed witch. He was at the stairs with his sorry ass still intact, apt to stay that way, and over his shoulder she would not give up, but he could afford to laugh it off.

"Well you just better keep quiet up there tonight, or I'll have the landlord *and* the police on you, they'll kick you out and *I'll* be the one laughing." Yeah, right, and she paused only long enough to reload on breath. "With any luck you'll just pass right on out tonight, that's what I'm hoping for. Not like that night a few weeks ago when you brought home that drunken slut with you."

Boom. There it went, all the joy of besting her, rising above her —gone in an instant. For while drinking can deaden memories recent and distant, sometimes it can corrode the defenses and let the pain come seeping through like acid.

And the very last thing he could tolerate was hearing Lorraine dismissed as a drunken slut, anything but that. No fair.

When he turned at the foot of the stairs, slowly, he was faced with the awful sight of Mrs. DeWitt realizing she had sunk the verbal knife into a vital artery. Her face was that of a cat stripping the feathers, then the flesh, from a crippled bird while its wings still feebly beat. Emotional blood, he was dying here, and it became her fount of renewal. The advantage hers.

"You didn't think I could hear you that night, upstairs? You and that tramp kept me awake for hours."

Oh you cruel, cruel bitch, the only thing Paul could think, coming up from someplace fathoms deep in his soul, and with it came the hate, black and so surprisingly powerful.

Mrs. DeWitt made a grand show of sudden surprise, oh *here's* an interesting thought. "Come to think of it, that was the *only* time I've heard those noises. What happened, I wonder? Did she leave you for someone else?"

Much more of this and the drunken tears would spill, but he couldn't bring himself to retreat. Unthinkable; defeat here would only bring more salvos of abuse in the near future.

Of course she had further points to make, a fistful of daggers to sink, and she stepped up into his face. Shaking a finger, here's what I think of *this,* and Paul knew hate was the purest emotion on earth, nothing could distract it, and you sure couldn't say that about love, could you? He wanted only to buy time, mount a counteroffensive. He met her halfway, lashed out to grab that shaking hand, holding tight and squeezing harder than necessary, let this bitch *know* he was mightily pissed now.

Janet DeWitt's eyes went wide, and Paul fixated on her angular frame, almost visualizing her skeleton as he imagined the numerous broken bones he had healed since the first night beside Stacy Donnelly's bed. . . .

And Mrs. DeWitt dropped her garbage bag and her left arm went suddenly rigid, yanked upward, marionette style. She looked at it, surprise, and within seconds it was obvious she felt more than alarm at an unexpected muscle spasm. *Pain,* lots of it.

Paul dropped her right hand, backing onto the first stair, but it was too late, no stopping this. She choked out a soft cry as her arm, locked at the elbow, began to tremble. Then a leg. Tension, all was tension, irresistible forces and immovable objects, and she staggered backward, eyes huge as she regarded Paul with fear and loathing.

Tension—and breaking point. Upper arm compacting into itself with a crack as sharp as a rifle shot, and she shrieked, a jagged shank of bone spearing through skin and blouse, blood splashing the wall beside her. Leg following suit, two compound fractures punching through flesh, and her leg folded inward at a truly impossible angle, the impact swatting her to the floor.

Paul could only watch, frozen in temporary paralysis, *this is not for mortal eyes, I only touched her, ALL I DID WAS TOUCH HER!*

Mrs. DeWitt jittering on the floor, and another splintering crack, thick and wet, a crimson bloom on her right elbow. The sound again, one foot kicking askew, a thrown shoe slamming into the wall, *ALL I DID WAS* TOUCH *HER*, and the hallway had become terribly claustrophobic, alive with the shatter of bones.

At last, her head whipped around, *crack*, and though she lay on her back, her dimming eyes stared into the floor.

Silence, and she moved no more.

"I only touched her," Paul whispered, and regarded his hands. No different from before, no clues as to what had just been channeled through them. Five-fingered enemies, they were, with ghastly secrets all their own, and oh, to be rid of them.

Before any curious neighbors might step out to see what had caused such commotion, Paul ran upstairs, didn't even breathe until he was safely past his apartment door.

Meager comfort. For he was beginning to fear that enemies found their best hiding places on the inside.

15

He missed the old days. Mike Lancer remembered them well, a few years ago before the great holy conversion to computer, when the editorial department clacked with typewriters. Now, everywhere, video display terminals, a harvest of Apples, humming with quiet little lies. The typewriters had been a welcome distraction from the air conditioner, on its last leg since something like Reagan's first term in office. Hearing the thing labor, you were reminded of just how poorly it worked, and given September heat in southern Florida, Mike would just as soon hear the typewriters. A service call? Get real, the publishers of *The National Vanguard* protected money like an elite corps of bodyguards.

For perhaps the twentieth time since the morning mail, he pulled out a glossy flyer from the stacks of paperwork on his desk. Stared at a picture of a woman in the midst of a group of poorly dressed Hispanics.

Something wasn't right here, but damned if he could figure out what it was. Well, sure, the lady had married a crook, but this one went beyond old grudges, some new wrinkle. Amanda Dawson, looking like the white bread queen of the Salvadoran jungle, offered no hints. Only that sweet, sweet smile.

Mike sighed, tossed the Dawson Ministries newsletter aside, took a long swig at the sweaty bottle of Jolt near his elbow. Double the sugar and caffeine of mere mortal colas. Three bottles a day helped provide the minimum daily requirements in two of the seven basic food groups à la Lancer: sugar, fat, starch, grease, caffeine, nicotine, and alcohol. Accept no substitutes.

Mike Lancer was a thirty-four-year old medical miracle. Joyfully abusing everything from brain cells and liver, to soles of bare feet on hot asphalt, errantly tempting fate with a nightclub full of social diseases, tanning himself to perfection under the Florida sun, and his health was better than an iron-pumping nun's. The *Vanguard* mandated yearly checkups for health insurance purposes, and the doctors hated him. He flaunted defiance of everything they stood for.

And did it with a smile. His longish face twinkled when he smiled, appeared almost somber when he did not. But life was fine.

Oh yes, there had been that crisis of career goals a few years ago, waking up after a decade of decadence to realize that, no, he would never rise to Woodward and Bernstein levels, would likely never rise above working for newspapers bought impulsively in the checkout lines of supermarkets. Go ahead, laugh it off, I fucked up in the game of Life. Legions of people would not let themselves laugh, which still left him several squares ahead.

The National Vanguard was one of seven leading tabloids in the country, five of its competitors published within jogging distance here in what was sometimes called Tabloid Valley in southern Palm Beach County. Down the coast in Boca Raton were the *National Enquirer* and the *Weekly World News*. Up the coast in Lantana were three more. The *Vanguard* sat plunk in the middle in Delray Beach. And its lurid covers, between which lurked mondo bizarro stories of UFOs and plastic surgeons to the stars and Elvis reincarnate, looked just the same as the rest. They had merit.

And he was a pro, could churn out the oddball article with the best of them, but *damn* that clingy desire to write just one piece of genuine worth. It kept him strangely vigilant in a job where vigilance was not required.

Take the latest newsletter from Dawson Ministries. Fluffy trashcan fodder, usually, but not today, though he could not say precisely why.

Dawson and his dubious brethren cut from the same self-styled holy cloth had been an object of fascination for years. Even more so when their ranks proved as vulnerable to worldly foibles as the most secular of organizations. Such joy watching the tumble of the PTL empire, the political burial of Pat Robertson, the carnal revelations about Jimmy Swaggart. These guys were a never-ending source of entertainment, who needed afternoon soaps?

Mike had seen to it that, under a false name, he was on the mailing lists of some two dozen of these self-styled demigods. A dollar or two donation in each case, and a semiliterate letter listing a few nonexistent prayer needs, and he was assured of a monthly deluge of half-baked theological interpretations—sometimes equally semiliterate—and financial pleas coming to *The Vanguard*'s post office box.

He would sift through it all, hypocrisy was fascinating at any level. There was no level to which some of these people would not stoop if it meant tapping into more dollars. And—be honest, now—he would dearly love to be somehow instrumental in seeing that one more of them took a dizzying fall.

His sister Allison had instilled *that* desire. Rest her soul.

He retrieved the Dawson piece again. Let the current story in progress—a quasi-interview with some teenage nymphette who had filed a paternity suit against a soap opera stud—gather more electronic dust. Mike scanned the newsletter . . . inspirational testimonials from Dawson's flock, more inspiration from the man himself, pictures and case histories of so-called "healed apostles." The real goods, though, were in a black and red shadow box, an update on Amanda Dawson's incursion into foreign missions. The body copy was supposedly a letter excerpt:

> The Lord is indeed being glorified through works in His spirit even in the midst of a nation torn with a civil war. DAILY we are seeing souls won to Him! And with your continued help, we might even see an end to fighting here in the jungles and cities of El Salvador. All it takes is prayer, and of course it does indeed take dollars to keep us here and keep us working. So please help us, and please do the very best you can, as the Lord loveth a cheerful giver. I love you and pray for ALL of you daily.
>
> —Amanda

Dawson and his wife bringing about a peaceful settlement between the rightist government and the leftist guerrillas, aah, give us all a break.

Time to call in an expert opinion. Mike vacated his desk, weaving through the gauntlet of others whose fingers clicked those quiet keyboards. A tiled stairway with well-worn traction strips took him down into production. Cooler down here, lucky shits. He passed the tilted paste-up slabs and continued into the photo department. Old Kodak paper boxes were stacked onto nearly every available flat surface, and file cabinets bulged. The darkrooms were empty and a lone tech hunched over a worktable. A heavy acrid chemical smell shared the air with Mozart. The *Serenata notturna in D major,* party on, dude. Ramon played that stuff all the time.

"Ramon," Mike said to his back. "Got a minute?"

"Always." Ramon straightened, and the overhead lights gleamed from a single gold earring, left lobe, heterosexual and proud of it. Mike saw that he was cropping the excess from a print of Joan Collins, snapped by an alert photographer the day before at Miami International. Big deal, but the hausfraus ate it up. "What is it?"

Mike unfolded the newsletter with a snap, tapped Amanda's picture. "Take a look at this. Is this real?"

Ramon was the resident king of photo manipulation. You wanted to see Vanna White strolling Sunset Boulevard with a yeti, he was the man for the job. He took the flyer and spread it atop his cutting board, then swung his flexible lamp around for better lighting. Bent lower and frowned.

"Fine-looking lady. My guess is you don't think she belongs in there with the rest of the beaners. Tell me I'm wrong."

"What do you think?"

Ramon straightened and waggled narrow eyebrows and cracked his knuckles. Heavy drama. He snatched a magnifying glass and flipped the lens into place. "Let the doctor examine." Back to his hunch, lens at work. "Hmmm. No Mackey line that I can see, so if it's a fake, it wasn't a simple paste-up job."

"Mackey line?"

"Yeah." Ramon was still poring over every detail, lecturing by rote. "No matter how well you cut something from one picture and position it onto another, it still jumps out at you. Like a three-dee movie. So you sand the edges down on the back to bring them in to the same level, but I can always tell. And I don't think this mother was a paste job." Frowning into his lens, tongue absently working the inside of his cheek. "Could've blended it. Taken two negatives and done test strips. Exposed the background onto a print except for her exact shape, then covered the ground and exposed her negative into the hole. All one print then. And if that's what this one is— it's one fine piece of work. 'Cause *I* sure can't see anything around her edges that gives it away."

"So you can't tell if it's fake or not." Five more minutes, and he'd be back at that dreadfully boring paternity suit story, please find something.

"Hold your water, Mikey, I'm not through. I was just looking for the obvious." His head popped up a moment, weaving to Mozart, a few seconds of shut-eyed bliss. "Let's see how good this job *really* is."

Time passed. Minutes ticked. Life-forms evolved and became extinct, all while Ramon made little grunts to himself. Potential giveaways being shot down in flames. Then:

"Oh, Luuuucy!" Impeccable Ricky Ricardo, he would only do it for a select few. "You gotta lotta essplaining to do!"

Mike leaned over his shoulder, eager, "What? What?"

"We got us a winner." Ramon grinned like a man who had just discovered a lost civilization. "Check the lighting. Somebody got a little careless here."

Another quick scan did no good. "I can't place it."

"The nasal shadows." Ramon took his X-acto knife and used its blade for a pointer. "I'm guessing this outdoor scene was shot early morning or late afternoon. The shadow of everybody's nose is going off toward their left cheeks." Beneath the lens, the blade looked as wicked as a broadsword, and indicated the shadows of a couple of the more prominent noses. Then Ramon switched to Amanda's face. "She was taken with an overhead light source. The shadow's directly under her nose. Hmm. Looks like a little teeny Hitler moustache."

Mike snatched up the newsletter and tossed an arm around Ramon's shoulder, a hug as quick as it was clumsy, a thousand thanks. On the way back up to editorial, Mike took the stairs two at a time. If Dawson was faking his wife's presence in El Salvador, he had to have a good reason. Or dire *need*. It just didn't feel right to be another unique grab for cash, why bother with all that trouble? All he had to do was send out a mass-mailing, here's a cause God has revealed I should undertake, or here's some new ministerial calamity with a choke-hold on our finances. Please help. And if he was as bold as Oral Roberts, he could throw in the stipulation of a heavenly death sentence if not enough dollars were raised.

Missions in El Salvador? That would be the day. But it left one more pressing question: Where *was* Amanda Dawson actually spending her time these days?

It took a quarter-hour of verbal wrangling, but Mike finally convinced the celebrities editor that something was brewing in the ranks of Donny Dawson Ministries. And that the public appetite in seeing fallen idols of his nature wasn't even close to being sated. And should *The National Vanguard* be first to break it wide open . . .

Well. His editor could figure that one out for herself. She reluctantly signed a voucher to get him some operating cash.

Five minutes after that, a tousle-haired Mike Lancer banged down his phone after a quick conversation with his travel agent. Out of this office at last. He killed off the remainder of the now-warm Jolt and scratched on a memo pad, *Friday 9/6, 10:10am TWA 745 to OK City Donny, your ass is mine!!!*

16

Heat often strives its hardest on late summer days, and for Paul those days had melted into an indistinct mass. Let that sleep schedule get seriously thrown out of whack, doing away with the buffer zone between the days, and insanity finds it easier to squeeze between the cracks.

He remembered the police from Monday night, going door to door, eventually to his own. Routine questioning of all building residents regarding the death of neighbor Janet DeWitt. He had been deeply into his private beer stock by then, far drunker than upon arrival. The only way to dull the senses, numb the touch. He had slurred and wavered, quite the sorry spectacle of dignity lost, and no doubt the police had mistaken his cheesy pallor as one more alcoholic side-effect.

In Paul's account of his evening, he adhered to truth until the point of actually stepping into the building. Then a replay of how he *wished* the evening had gone: A few reprimands from Mrs. DeWitt about his condition (in case neighbors had overheard), then stumbling up the stairs, across his threshold, and tuning in to catch some videos on MTV—see it on over there?—then promptly zoning out on the sofa. He had seen nothing, heard nothing.

Did they believe him? Apparently so. After all, though disheveled, he was free of bloodstains. There was also the raw power involved in what had killed Mrs. DeWitt. With all those broken bones, she looked to have been bulldozed by a locomotive. Had she been found in the street rather than in her building, hit-and-run would have been anyone's first guess. Obviously, it had taken someone with enormous strength to do that kind of damage. Paul, who by generous estimate didn't even look to reach 160, was not even in the ballpark . . .

And had little reason to worry about accusations. The autopsy contributed even more confusion. Death by massive trauma, the kicker being a broken neck, this much was obvious. However, her injuries were too great to have been sustained during a theorized fall down the stairs. No contusions were present that would indicate she had been beaten with a blunt instrument, and no bruises as evidence anyone had so much as laid an unkind hand upon her.

So far as the medical examiner could tell, the poor woman—with nearly half the bones in her body broken—had undergone the compound fracture equivalent of spontaneous human combustion. File this one under UNEXPLAINED, because no one had a clue. . . .

Except for one, and he had his hands full keeping the reins on runaway sanity, a continuous mental replay of every indelible contortion and snap of bone. Here, watch it, again, *watch it*, dream awake and see just how ghastly a process can be invoked by a mere touch. See what your hands have wrought?

Until, like self-fulfilling prophecy, Paul actually did pass out on the sofa. No balm, this, no quiet slumber, no soothing rest for the sick of heart and spirit. For the old nightmare was waiting, welcome back, and it held him with arms of dread. . . .

The same pastorally serene field gone gray, same horse and vivid birth of its rider from a back-borne womb, and the retrieval of the strange-looking rod.

Gale force winds and a dead bolt forward, horse and rider barreling past a backdrop of savage clouds, across fields swelling with a sweet symphony of screams too loud to be human, too terrified to be anything else, and he raised his rod on high, readying to sweep it down with the force of a headsman's ax.

The horse plunged heedlessly into a field of corn, row upon row swaying in the winds, as the rider hacked a broad swath down their center. Cornstalks, tall and healthy, a staple of diet and life itself, ears plump in their husks, *slash*, watch them fall by the scores to be trampled under mouldering hooves. The rider's advance knew neither fatigue nor mercy, seasons of wither, back and forth, end to end, swing and fall, until the field was reduced to little more than stubble.

And the litter, everywhere, a newly devastated field that could have been the entire world. The fallen husks had peeled back to reveal, no, not kernels and cobs, but human bodies, bleeding in their fetal curls.

The rider dismounted, grand master of the dark harvest. His black boots grinding the fallen into yielding earth, a careless and unceremonious burial. While behind him, his steed's purpose had apparently been filled, and it collapsed into a twitching heap, leaking twin streams. Blood from back, foam from muzzle.

The rod, instrument of decimation, see it, finally, identify, and may merciful God in Heaven help me now. A long staff topped with small wings, twin snakes intertwining up its length: the caduceus, ancient symbol of the science of medicine.

The healer, used to bring death to the masses, and when the rider stripped away the caul of tissue obscuring his face, Paul wasn't even surprised to see his own face staring back.

He greeted Tuesday morning from a repository of empty bottles, in clothes reeking of rancid sweat. MTV droning in never-ending rapid jumpcuts, held in check at the mental periphery. Sightless, he stared at everything, nothing. Dust motes drifting through shafts of sunlight, changing course when caressed by air currents too small to be felt. Victims of fate and circumstance, subject to whims they could not see, powers they could not fight.

Limbo. We are the dust of the earth.

He ignored the ringing of the phone late in the morning. It could ring until the wall caved in, that would be dandy. Later still, he let the knocking persist at his door. A familiar thud, a familiar voice he recognized as preceding his own on the air, back when life was good and sane and normal. He was getting skilled at this game, ignoring the door as it shuddered in its frame, the rattle of the knob, grateful he had at least had the foresight to lock it hours before.

At last, the intruder must have conceded defeat, gone away.

I only touched her, and how many times had he told himself this? *Just like I only touched Popeye.*

But the two of them were dead, and how. The connection had come somewhere in the predawn hours, a recollection of flaring tempers accompanying hands-on contact. Denial was now a moot point. But he at least had an answer to the question that had plagued him right up until last evening at Tappers.

What happens if I meet somebody I can't stand? Simple. I can wipe them right out. Because not only can I heal disease and injuries . . .

I can inflict *them.*

His hands were more than five-fingered enemies, as he had regarded them last night. Lethal weapons, in and of themselves, and just what in hell was *happening*?

Flukes, that's all they were, the optimist tried to reason, even while the realist pissed in his face. Flukes, two freak incidents stacked up against uncounted healings, legitimate and pure. Flukes brought on by extremes of anger and pain, the wrong person in the wrong mood at the absolute wrong time.

Options were frightfully scarce. He could shut himself up within these walls, cloistered from the world while paying bills by remote control. And when his meager savings ran dry, panhandle the streets in the thickest pair of gloves he could find.

What to do, he pondered this while the calendar bought itself more days of obsolescence. The phone continued to ring, and the knocking continued at his door. And Paul, sitting in the hallway floor, willed the caller to hang up, the intruder to go away. Biting his lip at the sound of the voice on the other side of the door, Peter twice, once Lorraine, and he buried his face into crossed arms and clenched shut his eyes, trying not to think of how she had looked, how she had felt, how she had tasted.

The TV, soundtrack to remembrances of Popeye, drippy and bloated, and Mrs. DeWitt, the amazing human pincushion. He drank everything of potency, with power to dilute the mind, and found it somehow obscene that, despite it all, physically he felt better than he ever had in his life.

Mentally, well, another story. Somewhere in the gulf of time his skull had become an iron skillet, his blood hot grease, his brain raw eggs. Listen to them sizzle, listen to them pop, and just where the hell could he go from here?

Go on like before? Head on straight and hands to himself whenever the interpersonal started to heat up? He had to live with it no matter what. It would not be easy, anything but that, yet it was the only chance for redemption he knew. You can't drown if you don't get your mouth wet; you can't kill if you keep your hands safely tucked away.

It took three days to figure *that* out? Thursday night, still in the same clothes and smelling as ripe as a gym locker. He found the phone, dialed the KGRM request line, took a deep breath when David Blane answered. The voice that launched a thousand naps.

And Paul told him not to worry, he was safe, he was well, he would be there later on in the morning.

Sincerity must have been his strong point, and he had never realized it before. Three days of AWOL behavior was inexcusable, but he found it surprisingly easy to get away with. Lies, or convolutions of the truth, whichever. He told them that he had witnessed something, had been devastatingly upset, and that the police had asked him not to talk about it. Lawyers too; he threw that in as an afterthought. Co-workers were curious, but of course, yet they did not press.

Fine. Put it behind him, and settling into the booth again felt as comfortable as slipping his hand into a well-worn glove. Here was his one true lifeline, and he threw himself into it headfirst. His opening barrage, then the day's burning question, "Can you play air guitar in a vacuum?" The air swallowed him whole. Genuine commercials, then a decoy he had made recently—Motley Cruex, guaranteed to soothe groupie-induced jock itch. On to the news unfit to print: Mud-wrestling at the Vatican to determine a new pope, a new film starring Clint Eastwood and Patrick Swayze, *Dirty Harry Dancing*.

The first hour of his shift became two, became three, home stretch now, he was surfing the airwaves in glory. The request line blinked, and he answered.

Just when did it begin, this creeping sense of the awry? The phone call began so typically, "Could you play—", and then the coughing, how could *anyone* live with a cough like that? So harsh, so wracking, lungs filling with phlegm like water into a glass. He held the phone away from his ear, listened to it continue, *stop please stop that*, and was he to blame? Hadn't some minuscule detail of the caller's voice sounded like Popeye, and triggered immediate bad associations?

Oh fuck, did I do that to him?

Paul's voice, the voice of the city's alternative underbelly, Lethal Rock Radio. Oh, such a voice, fifty thousand watts behind it, giving it the power to reach out and touch someone, and wasn't his voice an extension of himself?

I'M KILLING YOU!

The song he had played minutes before came to an end, dead air, a hiss of static pulsing from the speakers, listen closely now, and you can hear what lives in the white noise . . . whispered voices, murmurs of conspiracy—

set them free, Paul, set them all free
in the hands it's in the hands
the hands
they feed on you, Paul, they all feed on you
set them free, they hate it here
they hate you, Paul, they all hate you
hate them just once with your hands, your hands

The scratch of turntable needle stuck in the album's runoff matrix, around, around, the noise becoming the rhythmic sweep of a reaper's scythe, and watch them fall by the scores.

He let the phone clatter onto the control board, lurching to his feet while the chair tipped onto the floor, and he whirled, the walls of the booth closing in. The sound of nails driven from above, and the booth had become a coffin. Seal in this killer, this heretic, bury him alive.

The microphone aimed at him, reaching across the booth, a new kind of spear—

touch them, Paul, the voice can roar
the voice can kill
rotted meat, you can smell it
smell them, Paul, kill and eat

He bellowed, wrapping arms around head, and charged the door of the booth, couldn't stay here, and he burst through with explosive fury, free at last.

The hallway felt wonderfully cool and open. He stumbled to the wall, slid along several feet, the only way to remain upright, and yes, they were around him now, co-workers coming to investigate dead air. Their voices swirled, look how pale he is, ad nauseum, and Paul finally slid down to the floor.

Catch you on the flipside.

"So what's the deal, Paul? It's not like you to wig out during the middle of a shift. It's not like you to wig out at all, up until this week."

Had the Captain spoken? Yes. Yes, he had. Paul tried to focus, at least long enough to maintain conversation. Lying on David Blane's office couch, staring at the ceiling, it was all too easy to lapse into a world of disjointed fragments. Fragments felt safer. You don't care for one, just float off toward the next.

A smorgasbord of realities, *focus* . . .

"As far as I'm concerned," David said, "you walking off the air won't be mentioned again. But, man—you can lose your license for pulling something like that."

True enough. FCC regulations, no laughing matter. Some bureaucrats just can't take a joke.

"I don't know what to tell you, Dave. I just don't know." He combed mental files, let's start under PARANOIA, looking for excuses, what's another lie among friends? "Maybe I just wasn't ready to come back to work after all. That phone call, I just started hearing things, I—I freaked."

"And scared that guy half to death, I hear, dropping the phone and screaming like that." Behind his desk, David sighed, rumpled and with the slept-in hair of a wildman. Red eyes, sleep interrupted by Sherry's worried phone call. To a person working normal hours, this was like getting yanked from bed at two in the morning. "And you can't tell me anything about what's going on with you? I mean, I know you had a neighbor that got killed, does that have anything to do with this?"

Mayday, mayday, "Don't press, Dave, please?"

He shuffled papers in frustration, straightened a stack of CDs. Drummed fingers on desk. "I caught the first hour of your shift. You were sounding great. You know, I can say for a fact that if you keep your head on straight, you'll go a lot farther than KGRM. The way you were sounding today, you could kick some major ass in markets a lot bigger than St. Louis. But if you start getting a rep as a flake, man, you can kiss it good-bye, and that's the honest truth."

This is going nowhere, Paul thought. David's intentions were noble, but he had no idea what was going on beneath the surface. *For that matter, am I any better off?*

"Do you want some vacation time? Another week or so?"

"It wouldn't hurt."

"No, it wouldn't. I haven't announced this yet, so you're the first to hear it, but we're getting a new GM next week. You'll make a lousy first impression if you pull another zinger like today. So consider yourself on vacation until"—he checked a desk calendar—"until a week from Monday. September sixteenth. Think you can show up like your old self then?"

"I'll give it a try." And what humiliation, treated like a tantrum-prone child.

Captain Quaalude gave a worn-out smile. "All right, then. Now we're getting somewhere." Shaking his head. "Shit, man. Deejays. I'm not used to acting like a station manager." He stood at his desk. "Hang loose a couple minutes. The vacation schedule's still in Popeye's office. I better make sure this won't conflict with anyone else's."

Several moments later, Paul swung up on the couch. Both feet on the floor, one giant step for mankind. He looked at a table, the day's *Post-Dispatch* in loose sections. Any diversion was welcome. Main news? Too heavy. Comics? Not in the mood. Ah, Section F, "Calendar," a guide to upcoming events. Who's up to what, when, where, and how much it costs to watch. Perfect for the man on vacation, too much time and blood on his hands.

He browsed. Club and movie listings. Art exhibits, seminars, and singles minglers. Plenty of ads. Fly with us, eat here, your perfect getaway weekend. And whoa, what's this?

An upcoming revival crusade featuring TV evangelist Donny Dawson, Tuesday evening at six-thirty at Cervantes Convention Center. Miracles of restoration of body and spirit performed right before your eyes, promise.

Well. So much for one night of vacation. Only ten to go.

17

If patience really was a virtue, he figured he was eligible for sainthood. Saint Mike, indeed, patron of muckrakers. It was Monday, his fourth day in Oklahoma, and Mike Lancer had packed in over a week's worth of boredom. At least the woodland was a pleasant change of scenery from Florida sand and palms, if sadly lacking in bikinis.

After arriving late Friday morning, Mike had rented a car, then checked into a motel and unpacked. Reviewed his Dawson file and local maps while sprawled atop the bed with a meatball hoagie. The only place he knew to begin digging was the Dawson complex on the southern outskirts of the city. Fingers crossed. For if he crapped out there, then his editor could very well demand his backside, served up with a helping of humility.

Dawson's little world appeared much the same in person as in the ministry literature. Junior college or minimum security prison, take your pick. He cruised through the vast parking lot just off South Squire Road, surprisingly well used on a weekday morning. Then he realized, these cars probably belonged to the slave-wage mailroom employees. Dawson's ilk found a fertile supply of such workers in society's lower strata. Low on intelligence and imagination, and slow to question ethics and tactics. Beyond the lot stood the assortment of buildings, tan brick against a blue sky, interconnected by treelined walks. Far beyond, what had to have been the Dawson home was scarcely visible through the trees. Accessed by its own private drive branching off from the lot, but a formidable gate kept it blocked.

Of course he had to get back there. Some way. Just a peek.

Two choices: He could park here among the rest and stroll back as nonchalantly as possible—which was risky, for while security appeared lax, that didn't mean it was nonexistent. Or he could stash the rental nearby and trek a backway path through the woodland. A greater inconvenience, but until he had a better lay of the land, it was no doubt the safer option.

Mike backtracked, left the car a half-mile up the road in the dusty lot of a cut-rate carpet and tile outlet. Compact binoculars around his neck, he ducked into the woods and blazed a steady trail to what he hoped would be a hidden vantage point from which to observe Dawson's home.

The word *fiasco* quickly came to mind. He was used to beaches, palms, hot tarmac. Not underbrush and vines, creepers and treachery hidden beneath leaves. Once he stepped on an angled branch, sent it springing up like a booby trap to rap him in the crotch. His resulting oath sent birds into flight; just peachy, behold the new Davy Crockett.

Onward, until he was within twenty-some feet of the bordering treeline. Snarls of undergrowth between the trees offered ample hiding space, and for a time he merely watched the front. A lone car was parked on the drive's cul-de-sac, a small, older model Chevy. Gray, sensible, no frills.

After a glance through the binoculars, he jotted down the license number, then prowled to catch a view of the back of the house. He froze; someone was tending to a pair of Irish setters inside a large pen. Dirty coveralls, an iron-gray buzz cut—the man was probably a groundskeeper. He trudged away minutes later.

Nothing of note until four o'clock, when another car came wheeling back. Flashy red Mazda, and when the driver stepped out, Mike was rapt, oh *man*, so good to know blondes of this caliber were not exclusive to Florida and southern California. She let herself into the house with her own key—interesting—and a few minutes later the Chevy's owner emerged, puttered away. She was an unassuming little thing, all the more by contrast. Short dark hair, a manner of movement that was more scurry than walk.

Mike waited until dark, until hunger and boredom drove him back out. He retraced his path, a paragon of care; wrench his ankle in a hole, and he might not be found for years. A skeleton in white drawstring slacks and pastel yellow shirt and leather Top-Siders, no socks. Quite the attire for the budding woodsman.

He drove for hamburgers, catnapped in the car for a couple hours, then cruised back to resume his vigil at ten-thirty. At midnight the earlier routine repeated: New car, driver with house key, and the blonde departed in her Mazda. These looked for all the world like shift changes, the new arrival some sturdy old woman, her car a heavy sedan. As well, the one light burning on the third floor never winked out.

Some quick math; the blonde had been there for eight hours, would this one stay until eight in the morning? He bet she would, and headed for his motel, shower and shuteye. Back after dawn, dressed more sensibly for tramping through the woods, and fortified with a bit of food and coffee and a wad of toilet paper. The midnight car had not moved, and in the daylight he pegged it as an Olds Delta 88.

At eight o'clock that Saturday morning, paydirt was struck. The wallflower arrived in her drab Chevy Nova, and the apparent cycle began all over again. After that, the pattern was easy to establish. Three women, eight-hour shifts. Donny was on tour, Amanda supposedly in El Salvador, and no one else was coming or going besides the three mystery ladies.

Short-term goal: Find out who they were, for which he would have to wait until Monday morning. He spent the duration sitting tight, making sure there were no deviations from the schedule he had plotted, no additional players. Neat and clean in both respects.

Early Monday, Mike phoned a contact and sometimes poker and drinking buddy who held a secure, boring job with the Florida Department of Motor Vehicles. Always good for a favor. Mike read off the license numbers, then waited on hold while the guy accessed computer networks, dug out routine information on the owners. Mike jotted down the results in a self-styled shorthand that would stultify even an army codes expert.

Staring at the notes—and the plot thickens—he grinned ear to ear. Three names, three addresses. Unrelated women, apparently, unmarried. And all three registered nurses, hot dog, a common denominator. Plainclothes nurses, now *this* was interesting.

Mike kicked back on his bed, poured a snort of George Dickel Sour Mash into a plastic bathroom glass. Morning, yeah, but what the hell, celebration was in order. For he was willing to lay down serious cash betting what those nurses were up to.

And who their patient was.

Monday afternoon, four o'clock, a stakeout of a different sort on South Squire Road. He sat behind the wheel of his rental, engine idling, in the lot of the carpet and tile dealer. Sweaty bottle of Jolt notched between his thighs.

As expected, Edie Carson soon came piloting her Nova past his position, heading north for the city, and Mike slid out in leisurely pursuit. No confrontations today, strictly reconnaissance, get more of a handle on this woman.

Wisdom suggested focusing attention on one nurse and one alone, and try to breach her wall of security, if possible. The decision as to which to choose had not taken long.

He had right off dispensed with Alice Ward, the midnight to morning nurse, she of juggernaut bosom and bulldog face. She looked like a brick wall, which left him to choose between the younger two nurses, judging solely by their appearance. Stereotypes, a risky proposition in any undertaking.

Sally Pruett, who smoldered even through binoculars and flaunted that flashy car? Or Edie Carson, as colorless and indistinguishable as her Nova? He was leaning toward the latter, assembling a mental profile of a girl who, years before, endured high school and college with a painful shyness and dreamed of clandestine dates with football captains and wrote poetry inside secret notebooks. Who devoured Harlequin romances by the bushel and turned to nursing half out of a desire to act as Florence Nightingale to someone who, when healed, would fall madly in love with her out of gratitude.

A cruel and sticky business, this formulation of life stories through binoculars. But the world prized beauty above most else, doling its favors accordingly. A world of haves and have-nots, with the former granted far more concessions than the latter.

He need look no further than his own family for evidence. Mike had gotten the looks, without a doubt. Sister Allison, a year older, had merely been warmup; sweet as honey, right up to the very end, but as plain as a slice of dry toast. Every step of the way, Mike had been the favored child. By teachers, relatives, and neighbors, and, in subtle ways they probably weren't even aware of, by their parents.

What he wouldn't give to have a chance to make up for it now. He'd trade anything but his soul for that.

So. Edie Carson it was.

He tailed the Nova, hanging safely back, then edging closer the more traffic picked up. Her first stop was a stucco building with movie posters in the windows, splashy roof sign reading SILVER SCREEN VIDEO. Mike sat idling, watched her take in a stack of three tapes, to emerge minutes later with two more. Observation number one, she liked her VCR.

Her next stop was a deli, then home to her apartment, and the perfect solution came to mind moments later. He careened to the nearest telephone booth, used his credit card to place another call to a Miami TV station. It was booted through the hierarchy until he caught up with a production engineer he hoped so desperately would still be there. They slung the bull back and forth with the familiarity of veteran sleaze mongers, and Mike got down to business.

"I need a favor, a biggie," Mike said. "Could you dub me a video of all the rough footage for those features on faith healers you ran last spring? It doesn't have to be smooth, or in any particular order. And if you want, you can drop all the evangelist footage except for the Dawson stuff."

"You gonna have something you can turn us on to?" and Mike told him he might. "No problem. You want it in VHS or Beta?"

Mike winced, he didn't even know which her machine was. Go with VHS, though. If she was in the habit of frequent rentals, Beta would substantially cramp her style.

"One more thing," Mike said. "Could you overnight that to me— like tonight?"

A sigh of martyrdom, all the way from Miami. "Yeah, yeah. But you better come through with something good."

Mike read off his motel's address from a matchbook pocketed earlier, then fired up a cigarette. Nicotine celebration.

Nothing like closing in for the kill.

The package was dropped off in the middle of Tuesday afternoon, and there was Mike, rested, two balanced meals in one day, a first. He had shaved, showered, Visined the roadmaps from his eyes. Clean clothes—tan slacks and white shirt; socks, even, he really was going all-out for this.

Shortly before four, he resumed his stakeout and waited for the familiar gray Nova to putter by. Safer than waiting in her home parking lot, given Murphy's Law probability that today she would radically alter her routine.

But no, old habits die hard, and he tailed her with no surprises in the equation. Home was an apartment in a complex of sixty or so, buildings of sheetrock and brick and rustic woodtrim. Each dwelling with its own little balcony, large enough for a barbecue grill or a chaise longue, never both.

He gave her thirty minutes to settle in, freshen up. When time was up, he gave one last glance into his rearview, brushed his hair into place with fingertips. A silent snarl to check for embarrassing food particles, then a test smile, perfect working order, who could resist that face? Then he pictured Edie Carson slamming a door in it, and the smile drooped.

Tape in hand, Mike left his car, do or die.

Strategy had been a point of great deliberation the last couple of days. He had decided against running a snowjob, feigning personal interest in hopes of delving into her professional life. It couldn't be rushed, but moreover, it was downright cruel, and if it blew up in his face, he would have no more chances.

Sincerity, then, appealing to Edie's concerns for humanity. Admittedly, though, without the tape, he would have been at a loss for an icebreaker.

Second floor, thumbing the doorbell. Noting a change of light in the peephole as she checked him out, and the door opened.

Edie Carson stood in her doorway, hand on the knob. She wore jeans, an oversize T-shirt, hair pulled back into a stub of a ponytail. Face all eyes, wary innocence.

"Miss Carson?" he said, and she nodded. "Hi, my name's Mike Lancer." He loosed the smile, the warm one, not its flirtatious cousin. "I'm a reporter from a Florida-based newspaper, and I was wondering if I might talk to you for a few minutes."

Wariness deepening, "About what?"

And here it was, make or break: "Your current employer."

"I have to go now." Averting her eyes and setting the door into motion; she would make a terrible liar.

Mike's free hand shot out, stopped the door. Thin ice, he was definitely waltzing on thin ice here. "Please. You don't have to say a word if you don't want to. But if you could do just one thing for me—"

"I don't even *know* you!"

"If you could just watch what's on this videotape." He held it up, took his other hand from the door. "I'll even sit outside the whole time. But if you'd take a few minutes to watch it, maybe you'll change your mind. For what it's worth, though, it's no secret. I know you're working for Donny Dawson."

Standing in her doorway, Edie's face was that of a child, hesitating atop a sliding board; could she trust someone to catch her at the bottom? He offered the tape again.

"I guess . . . I can at least watch it," and she accepted. Then met his gaze on even terms. "But you're not coming inside."

He stepped back from her threshold, lifting his hands, you're the boss. "I'll wait on the steps."

She hurriedly shut the door; two clicks, knob lock and deadbolt, then the chain, and he grinned. Wandered along the concrete landing and took a seat on the top stair. A cigarette made the waiting easier, turned into two. Hot winds taunted him, carrying gusts of music from open windows. Country and Wagnerian opera. Smoke from grilling steaks drifted past, and now, more than ever, he longed for home. His roots, however humble, were at least his own. Looking to rip open other lives in an unfamiliar state, too far from home, who could live like that for long?

Mike wished he could watch Edie's face for her reactions to the tape. Yes, the video was rough, it lacked the polish of editing and the cohesion of studio anchor introductions. But it also contained material never seen in the finished product of a weeklong series of nightly features. Some of which was the most damning of all.

He had watched his own copy to know it by heart:

There are the false starts, the out-takes as the on-location reporter fumbles words and flubs lines and, in one joking moment, wags his microphone in phallic symbolism.

Behind him, in one shot, the plaza before a Miami auditorium, aswarm with people of all ages and backgrounds, and the reporter informs the camera that all have come to see evangelist Donny Dawson.

Another shot: Amanda Dawson speaking inside the lobby to a stooped old woman with a cane. Wizened as a prune, but unexpectedly spry as she hands Amanda a beige notecard which she has just filled out.

"One common tactic used by faith healers is to have assistants acquire personal data from their followers before the show," says the reporter. "They will then use various methods of memory recall during the service to give the appearance of being given knowledge by divine means."

The camera tracks as he approaches the woman Amanda Dawson has just left, and tries to engage her in conversation. She eyes him with suspicion, then undisguised hostility when he asks what sort of information she provided on the card. Despite the evidence on tape, she denies it all, no, no, there is no card.

"Why, you're not true believers!" she cries. "I shouldn't be talking to you. Get thee behind me, Satan!"

Another shot, the reporter seated in a modest living room, open and breezy, numerous green plants, and he speaks with a diminutive man with white hair and hawk's eyes. A superimposed caption identifies him as a spokesman for a group known as the South Florida Humanist League.

"Some people maintain that while the faith healers are not actually healing," the reporter says, "they should be left alone to conduct what are essentially little morality plays. What's the harm in what they're doing?"

"The harm is," says the white-haired man, "that not only are they deceiving people outright with so-called divine cures, they're also killing people. They're convincing these people that they don't need to take their medication, and don't need to seek or continue medical treatment for serious health problems. They're saying that so long as you sufficiently believe in their nonsensical laying on of hands, everything will be fine and dandy. Well, it's not fine and it's not dandy —because a lot of people are dying from it. Or at the very least, living in misery they could otherwise be avoiding."

Another shot: Outside the Dawson rally, preshow. Young mother, poorly dressed, pushing her wheelchair-bound daughter toward the entrance of the auditorium. The child can't be much more than six or seven; beneath a thin quilt, her legs are obviously twisted from birth defect, accident, illness. Yet their eyes are brighter than freshly minted coins, full of anticipation.

Again, the camera tracks as he approaches, and their eyes shine even brighter with the expectation of seeing themselves on TV. They make willing subjects, sacrificial offerings on the altar of private misery made public.

"And why are you here today?" the reporter says.

"We came because Donny Dawson wrote us and told us a miracle is coming our way," Mom explains. "We just know he can heal Kathy and make her normal. He really knows what God's will is!"

And their excitement is bolstered all the more the closer they get to the entrance.

Another shot, still outside, post-rally, people in mass departure. Including the same mother and daughter interviewed earlier. The child is still confined to her wheelchair, and the only difference from before is that now they head in the opposite direction. And the addition of a great many tears.

"These two never even got close to Donny Dawson today," he says, their sorry plight depicted in the background. "Although our cameras were not allowed inside the actual rally, I did see that ushers escorted them to a dark, secluded little alcove for the entirety of the program—along with several others with obvious health problems. None of them were ever called forward. None of them received the slightest attention from either Dawson or his staff—except when it came time to collect the offering."

The camera tracks relentlessly as the reporter approaches them once more, a span of just over four hours, yet filled with a lifetime of humiliation and shattered hopes and perhaps the realization that Donny Dawson Ministries has just played out a grand joke at their expense.

As soon as she is aware of the crew's approach, the little girl hides her face—red-eyed and smeared with snot—by tugging up her quilt, fumbling it over her head. The revealed legs, poking from a threadbare dress, are every bit as wasted as conjecture might imagine. Her mother, equally overcome, averts her eyes, pushes the wheelchair with renewed determination, shoulders hitching with minor spasms.

And in the plaza before the auditorium, surrounded by hundreds who apparently believe they have witnessed miracles, the reporter stops ten feet from his quarry. And lets them pass. He turns to face the camera, mouth compressing into a downturned crescent as he makes a slashing movement across his throat. Does it again, and he looks too old, too tired.

"I can't do it," *his voice a hoarse whisper.* "Shut it off. I can't do that to them—"

Cut to the static of blank tape.

Scrape the underbelly, and you will eventually see more than you want, Mike knew this all too well.

So he sat, smoked another cigarette, and when he heard Edie Carson disengage her locks, he didn't turn around right away. He waited until she stepped from her doorway, came closer. And when he turned, finally, he saw that she did not carry the tape to shove back at him.

I'm in, but the victory was hollow. Smash someone's illusion, and just how good could you feel? "So what do you think?"

Edie frowned, blinking, keep those eyes dry. She folded her arms over the shapeless T-shirt and sighed. "I didn't know—know he was . . ." And she trailed away. "What do you *want* from me?"

"I just want to know what's going on at Dawson's home. Why three private nurses are showing up around the clock, seven days a week. Why a guy who says he heals the sick needs you three there in the first place."

Her face screwed up with deliberation, oh, such pained eyes. What a delight, she had a wonderfully expressive face. And what horror to realize the pain it took to bring it out.

"He's a very nice man," she said. "I mean—it's so obvious that he loves his wife very much."

Amanda, huh? He hadn't even been the first to bring her up. Mike flicked the dead butt of his cigarette down the length of the stairway, watched it land on the sidewalk below.

"He's also getting rich on other people's money claiming to do things he can't do. You saw that much on the tape. It's not just some harmless little fantasy everyone's indulging in." A thin smile, full of irony. "As a nurse, don't you find that just a little reprehensible?"

Edie dropped her gaze to the concrete deck. "If all that's going on, then why doesn't the government or somebody step in and do something about it?"

"Politics, mostly. A lot of pinheads out there, all they're interested in is covering their asses and keeping their jobs and offending as few people as possible. Not a one of them wants the public image of being some evil crusader trying to shut down a preacher. Never mind that he'd be doing a public service, maybe even saving a few lives. The fundamentalist types would turn him into hamburger. And they swing a *lot* of votes at election time."

She nodded, leaning against the rustic railing of one-by-sixes. Through the open door of her apartment came strains of local TV news.

"What paper did you say you're with? You didn't, did you."

The urge for another cigarette. "I'm with *The National Vanguard.*"

Edie rolled her eyes, looked as if she were stopping herself just short of laughter; bitter laughter, at that. "Why even bother talking to me? You'll just print what you want anyway."

Perhaps it should have stung, but it didn't. Not when she had probably assumed he had come from someplace of the caliber of *The New York Times* or *The Washington Post.* The tabloids, no comparison, journalism's red-headed bastard children.

"No. No, I won't, I want it to be the truth, all of it. I think in this case the truth is plenty." His eyes firmly on hers, he was surprising even himself, never recalling any more commitment to a pursuit than in this moment.

"And nothing's in it for you, right?" Her new skill, sarcasm.

"Satisfaction, mainly. What I really want is to create a little more public awareness. Look at what the *Enquirer* did to Gary Hart's presidential campaign. They were the ones who first broke the pictures of him with Donna Rice. Nobody remembers it was a tabloid that did it, they just remember the facts. What I want is to make people take the same kind of notice of Donny Dawson. He's never produced one legitimate healing he can prove. And last year his income was almost thirty million, tax free. You know where a lot of that comes from? A lot of it comes from old women living on Gravy Train so they can send him their pension checks. *That's* what Donny Dawson's about."

Oh, just shut up; he didn't know where it all had come from. Neither planned nor rehearsed, just a few facts absorbed through research, spilling forth like blood from a wound.

Edie studied him for a long moment, his face, eyes. This woman on the timid and insubstantial side, with such a sharp appraisal it left little doubt that underestimating her was a mistake. A solid core lined that exterior. No surprise, really, it would be a prerequisite to deal daily with the sick.

"This really matters to you, doesn't it?" She made her first step toward meeting him halfway.

Mike nodded. Sure, why not, let her have it all: "I had a sister. Allison. She was a year older. And she was—I don't know. Put it this way, I haven't known very many truly kind people in my life, but she was at the top of the list." He lit up again. Hands shaking? Surely not, a trick of the eye. "She was a diabetic. And very spiritual, always wanting to improve that part of herself. She was trusting to a fault, too. She went to this faith healer's service a couple years ago. I wish I could tell you it was Donny Dawson, but it wasn't, so I don't suppose it matters who. Anyway. He told the entire mob of them they were healed, and all these people came running up to pitch their medicine onto the stage, to show their faith, like, hey, we don't need these anymore. And Allison was right up there with them, and tossed her insulin onto the scrap heap."

Edie's expressive eyes, clouding. She knew the next part.

"She died a few days later. Alone. Just her and her blind faith in something that never should've touched her in the first place."

There was more, but it was trivial, and so he sat, and smoked, and stared at his knees. He couldn't remember the last time he had told this story, if ever, and there was no cleansing. You don't put the senseless deaths behind you, the needless ones; they tag along forever, like demented little dogs. You live with them; die with them, when your turn comes. The best you can hope for is that the tale might once in a while fall on sensitive ears.

The aroma of grilled steaks, hot winds, cool air leaking from her open door. And Edie Carson, coming to sit beside him. Did he even care anymore? Yes, somewhere deep inside, he still did, and she looked to the sky forever.

His curling smoke kept wafting into her face, and he snubbed the cigarette out. Seemed the courteous thing to do.

"If I let you know what's going on, can you *guarantee* me that I'll remain totally anonymous?"

Mike nodded, promised.

"And if you're not busy tomorrow—I can even show you."

18

Paul was a concert veteran; dozens, maybe hundreds. See them all, you eventually see all kinds of audiences. Tuesday night, the tenth of September, at Cervantes Convention Center, was little different, and that was a surprise.

He had been expecting Donny Dawson's Arm of the Apostle rally to feel something like a regular church service, scaled up several times. But no, the crowd was here to pay adoration to the man, here to cheer his words, curry his favor, applaud his miracles. Here to witness a spectacle to remember and cherish, and think back upon with pride, saying, "Yes, I was there. I *saw* him."

They had sung hymns, had clapped and cheered, had openly wept with splendor in their eyes. And Paul, nine rows back, could feel that sweeping tide of emotion tugging him, despite wanting to maintain an open mind. Easier said than done, once you were here and submerged into the experience. Like trying to walk against an ocean current, surrender, just go with the flow.

They were in the Center's main hall, the floor covered with ranks of folding chairs. Dawson conducted his service from a stage built up from the floor, accessed by tiered steps on both sides. Near front and center stood a modest pulpit, but he spent little time behind it. Purple backdrops ran the length of the stage, festooned with the gold ARM OF THE APOSTLE banner. Low plants squatted on either side of the stage, mingling with PA speaker cabinets. Near the back sat a

miked piano that had been given a real workout earlier and a synthesizer that, via the PA, rumbled like a cathedral organ.

After a soloist had soothed them all with her sweetest of voices,
Donny had taken over. Trademark white suit, pacing every inch of
stage he could get to, dramatically trailing a microphone cord and
milking it with every bit as much skill as Roger Daltrey at the peak
of The Who. Maybe better. Daltrey could send a crowd of fifty
thousand to its feet, packing around the stage. But Paul had yet to
see a rocker reduce his throng to tears of rapture. The Beatles
didn't count.

Man, is this guy ever good, Paul thought, for while the effect
came through on TV, the airwaves still diluted it. No way could four
cameramen seize that palpable energy generated between Dawson
and his crowd, back and forth in a kinetic frenzy that knew no
downslide. The crowd had become a psychic generator, and Dawson the spark plug.

And to wonder what it felt like being up there, oh, just incredible. Paul thought back to the winter, newly arrived at KGRM, when
the station had promoted a concert at a club called Mississippi
Nights, at Laclede's Landing down on the riverfront. David Blane
had suggested Paul introduce the act—some new guitar wizard who
called himself Nick Paganini—and make the preshow announcements. A PR move, primarily, to disassociate him from his former
station and ingrain him into audience heads as a newborn KGRM
personality. Paul had happily done so, and while roadies performed
last-minute rites and waitresses worked the capacity crowd of one
thousand, he took the stage. Lights died, and there he was, burning
in the center of a spotlight, hyping the crowd and they were eating
every word. As much as he loved being on the air and knowing the
unseen were tuned in, this was better. The give and take was immediate, and only the sensory dead could miss it.

And it wasn't even him they had paid to see. How much greater
the high to stand before the throng and know *you're* the draw.

The sermon had gone on for over an hour, full of the *amens* and
hallelujahs Dawson called for, and he played them like a master.
Then a squad of ushers worked the crowd with large plastic buckets, passing them along the rows for an offering, and Paul watched a
staggering amount of cash empty from wallets and pockets and
purses. He threw in a twenty before he even realized it was leaving
his hand, but at least he did not feel like an outsider. Something to

belong to, the hive. Not only cash was coughed up, but prewritten checks and jewelry and the odd gold coin or two.

At last, though, time for the miracles.

"Oh, I tell you," Donny thundered from his perch at the lip of the stage, one arm raised to Heaven. "I feel a *lot* of love here in St. Louis tonight. A lot of love of the spirit! And the devil hates that, yes he does! Tell you what I'd like you to do out there. I want you to turn to your neighbor, and I want you to say, 'God loves you and I love you too,' and then I want you to *hug* your neighbor. Because when you've got a friend in the Lord, you've got a friend for life. Amen! Hug a neighbor and hurt the devil!"

Galvanized into action, devil-stompers one and all, whirling one to another. Paul felt somebody latch happily onto his arm and spin him into hers. A stout woman, solid as a fireplug with rouge and lipstick, brassy hair piled atop her head.

"God loves you and I love you too!" she spluttered, her smile a red crescent moon, and she crushed him with a hug that displaced her mammoth breasts to either side.

Paul wheezed out the same, then stumbled from her arms into the subdued embrace of a girl of perhaps nineteen, who shyly looked askance and blushed, and this was all exceedingly weird. Here they were, holy strangers, no need to brave rejection. Donny says it's okay. The ritual embrace, the litany of love on command, and then Donny took charge again.

"You know why I had you do that? Do you know? Because I wanted you to get to know those around you a little better. Because if this group of fine people here tonight becomes anything, I want it to become the most gracious crowd it can be. Because I know, *I know*, that some of you out there are hurting." His voice had suddenly shed the earlier glee, growing somber. "Amen to that one, right?"

Pin-drop silence, vast and enormous, with a few scattered *amens* rippling in response.

"Some of you out there are suffering. And the devil rejoices in that, my friends, he claps his hands and twitches his pointy little tail at every ache and pain to enter your body. So if you see that your neighbor is in pain, have a little more sympathy. And have a little more faith. Faith that . . . DOCTOR JESUS IS GOING TO BE DOING SOME HEALING HERE TONIGHT, HALLELUJAH!"

The response was massive, human thunder, the answer to "play ball" heard at the World Series. Cheers of hope and triumph as the synthesizer unleashed a whirlwind of musical celebration. Poised between crowd and musicians, Donny Dawson lifted his face to the heavens, the microphone to his lips.

"There's a Leonard Dixon here tonight, isn't there?" he asked, and from somewhere behind Paul came a screechy affirmative. Slight commotion as the man worked his way toward the aisle, and spattered applause from those around him. "Come on down front, Leonard, let us all see what you look like."

A stringy old fellow with an ear-to-ear grin, he looked to have lived a hard old life of toil. Blue mechanic's shirt with oval namepatch. Down front, a pair of burly ushers came from one side and followed him up the stairs, and they halted before Donny.

"Leonard Dixon," Donny mused, cocking his head to the sky beyond the rafters. "Four-sixteen Chesapeake Avenue, Maryland Heights? This *is* your address, isn't it?"

Leonard gaped, astonished, and could only nod.

"Good heavens, man, can't you see what those cigarettes are doing to your insides?"

Leonard hung his head in shame, and Donny thrust the microphone before his face. "I—I've tried to quit smoking," the man stammered. "The doctor, he tells me—"

"That's Doctor Storment, isn't it? Of course it is. Leonard, God's already told me your problems. You've got lung cancer, don't you now, Leonard?" Donny's voice, that of a disappointed father.

With hangdog shame, Leonard nodded.

"Well Leonard, Doctor Jesus is here tonight and he's here to let you walk home a changed man. You may have brought your ills on yourself, but leave it up to Jesus and He'll take them away." That voice, now a sunrise of optimism. "Sounds like a pretty good deal to *me,* Leonard! How's that sound to *you?*"

Face streaked with tears, the man nodded, burbling words the mike did not pick up, then he clasped his knotty hands together.

"Well amen, now we're *getting* somewhere!" and Donny leaned in to plant his free hand in the center of Leonard's chest, fingers splayed. "LET'S BURN IT OUT RIGHT NOW!" a shout, then a shove, "AND IT'S DONE! HALLELUJAH!"

Leonard's knees buckled and the crowd went berserk as he fell backward into the waiting arms of the two hefty ushers. He quaked, then got back on his own two feet to perform an impromptu jig of sheer elation. Tears streamed from behind black plastic glasses, and he left the stage to strut back down the aisle, into the welcoming embrace of family and brand-new friends.

He was the happiest man Paul had ever seen, something had truly *happened* to him up there, and by then it was time for the next, and the next . . .

And Paul wondered: Would the man in white call him up as well? He had filled out a card upon arrival, printing name and address; one more mailing list awaiting him, he figured. But another line asked if he had any special prayer concerns, and he had written, *I feel like my soul is coming apart.* No exaggeration after a three-day weekend spent in contemplation of life and death and their place in his hands. Heady stuff, leading nowhere, like chasing your tail.

All he wanted was a little counseling from the one man he knew of who might understand the turmoil in his life. Didn't seem too much to ask for, certainly not with bosses drowning themselves and neighbors turning inside-out at his touch.

touch

Donny had gone through an entire front row of people confined to wheelchairs, ultimately hopping into one and letting its former occupant push him back to the steps. He mounted the stage, sweat dripping from his brow, and let them all know he was just getting warmed up, plenty more work to be done, amen. . . .

"Who is Paul?" Donny barked into the mike. "Paul Handler? Where is he . . . ? Ah, there you are!"

He was on his feet and wading for the aisle, the response smooth and automatic, as if command had bypassed brain, gone straight to legs. The rows of folding chairs had gotten very cockeyed by now, and he could feel the gaze of hundreds, thousands, their acceptance of him as a fellow struggler in the ocean of life, lucky enough to have been thrown a line.

Striding down the aisle, lighter than air, *Can't believe I'm doing this,* trying his best to harness whatever mechanism had been turned loose within him. He had to stand out, make himself worthy of Dawson's post-rally time, because obviously the man could not meet with everyone seeking a private audience.

Earlier in the day, Paul had contemplated electricity. How it could kill if absorbed in a sufficient jolt. Or merely catch your attention, a harmless static charge. Couldn't he liken his own new-found abilities to electricity? Sometimes flowing out, sometimes in. Sometimes helping, others harming. Were that the case, surely it could be restricted to a benign spark, oh please.

Paul felt the eyes, the camera lenses upon him. The presence of a flesh-and-blood man who had heretofore been confined to the netherworld of TV. A man who smiled down, welcoming him to the world of the saved . . .

And Paul began to mount the steps.

He loved St. Louis and they loved him, and Donny Dawson was in peak form to prove it. This audience had him feeling as though they were his home flock and he their pastor. Money buckets brimming, the healed collapsing left and right in fits of ecstasy, into the arms of Ricky and Robby. The two catchers kept them from cracking skulls on the stage. Bad business.

"Next one, this one looks good," Gabe's voice in his ear, the tiny receiver. "Name's Paul Handler."

"Who is Paul?" Donny barked into his microphone. "Paul Handler? Where is he?" Donny scanned the crowd with his practiced eye. "There, ten rows back or so. "Ah, there you are!"

"This is his prayer need," Gabe said, and Donny cocked his head, tuning in to Heaven's wavelengths, " 'I feel like my soul is coming apart.' That's it."

"Come on up here, Paul, you're among friends tonight," said Donny, and wouldn't *this* be a simple one. Not a single physical symptom to worry about.

The man was moving down the aisle, bordered by applauding spectators, and what a surprise when he drew near. Younger than expected, perhaps mid- to late twenties. A fractured soul sounded more like the ailment of an old soul, but it takes all kinds.

He wore gray slacks, a pastel blue shirt with narrow tie, a bit out of keeping with the mild shag of his hair. At any rate, a nice visual change from the elderly and frail who had comprised the bulk of tonight's callouts.

"Paul, I can feel your pain all the way over here," Donny said as the fellow ascended the stairs. Held out a welcoming arm, drew him closer. "I can sense a troubled spirit as easily as I can a leaky faucet, because the happiness that's rightfully yours is just draining away bit by bit, isn't it, Paul?"

The young man nodded, face a study in worried fascination, of bearing the weight of worlds upon his shoulders. No divine inspiration was needed to discern that something was eating this fellow from the inside out.

"Well Doctor Jesus is a specialist in the spirit as well as the body,

I'm happy to tell you. He's a general practitioner with a specialty in every field, and He's reaching down to you right this very instant. . . ."

On and on, hoping to coax a burst of joy from this Paul Handler. Unlikely that Ricky and Robby would be needed for this one, no paroxysm of self-induced elation and collapse, he was still so somber; now come on Paul, you can do better than this—

And then, most unexpected, the young man leaned forward, eyes sharpening, and his voice barely audible, "I have to meet with you after the service."

Now *this* wasn't a part of the script. Not to worry about it being heard, Donny had always had the foresight to use a unidirectional microphone, and it was pointed at his own mouth. But this kid's agenda could be problematic. Keep it moving.

"I want you to take hold of my hand, Paul. I want you to take hold of this hand and feel the strength of the Lord flowing back into you and renewing the spirit inside you," and all was well again, for the young man obeyed, and Donny slid his hand into Paul's smooth grip . . .

Felt him squeeze briefly . . .

And the unexpected grew by leaps and bounds. This was like shaking hands with a live wire, a split-second flash of light inside his eyes, *inside them,* and it felt as if every pound of flesh and blood and bone had been freed of gravity. Overcome, swamped with a sense of well-being that was anything but, coming out of nowhere like this it could only be terrifying—

And with no one back there to catch *him,* Donny Dawson fell smack on his ass.

Glancing with stupefaction into Paul Handler's gently smiling face—*He knows what he's doing!*—Donny found that face almost ancient in terms of self-awareness. Yet childlike in its sense of accomplishment. No mean-spirited delight, this; and more—relief?

Donny had felt nothing quite like this since a long-ago day in Alabama.

The professional showman within took over—mayday, mayday—instincts surfacing, he'd better bounce back and cover for this colossal blunder. The longer he stayed down on the stage, the heavier his foolscap would become.

"I tell you, *I'm* feeling the hand of the Lord at work tonight!" He bounded to his feet, forced a little laughter. "Sometimes He's got to reach right down and cuff you on the back of the head to get your attention, can you give me a hallelujah?"

The catchers were hustling the fellow offstage, and thankfully he was putting up no fuss. Just smooth things over, let the nervous laughter and applause trickle through the crowd, no problem, folks, minor unforeseen turn of events, but life goes on.

Donny slapped his tongue on automatic for the next couple of minutes, then let the song leader take over the proceedings. He went behind the backdrop to gulp ice water, kept asking himself just *what* in the name of merciful Heaven could have happened out there? The implications were too enormous to fathom all at once. True, he had been hoping—expecting—to find something on this tour, but nothing could have prepared him for the wallop of Paul Handler's touch. This, from a young man who had looked so deceptively ordinary.

Gabe maneuvered back to find Donny minutes later. He was spending the healing segments locked into a private room while manning the transmitter to Donny's earpiece and watching the rally on a closed-circuit monitor. Mandy's former province.

"Donny?" Gabe's features were pinched into a mask of concern. "Are you okay?"

Donny loosened his tie, gulped more water, while on the other side of the stage and backdrop, the crowd was in the midst of a rousing rendition of "When the Saints Go Marching In."

"What happened to you out there?"

Donny, shaking his head, "I'm not sure. I—I grabbed his hand, and it—it felt like I'd been shocked. But it didn't hurt. Just the opposite. Gabe—it was incredible. He did it on purpose for some reason, he knew *exactly* what he was doing, you couldn't see his eyes, but I could, *I could see it in his eyes.*"

Gabe frowned, cautious. "But why? What was he after?"

"He said he wanted to see me after the crusade. And Gabe? I think that would be a good idea. Do you remember what he looks like, where he was sitting?"

"Yes. I do. Ninth row."

"Good. Good. I don't want him to walk out of here tonight without knowing where to find us later. All right?"

And Gabe, ever the obedient servant, nodded.

The only way Paul had figured he would ever see the inside of a suite at the Hyatt on Market Street was by invitation. Maybe he was adding prophecy to his list of talents, for here was where his private audience with Donny Dawson would be granted. One media personality to another.

Fourth floor, definitely upscale, and he rapped the suite door with his knuckles. It was answered by the same guy who had winnowed him out of the audience back at the rally, a rather humorless sort, with razor-styled hair and a widely grim mouth.

Sanctum sanctorum; Paul entered the suite. The place looked bigger than his entire apartment, not bad, but oh what a bitch to clean. Across an acre of carpet, sitting ankle-over-knee at one end of the sofa, was Dawson himself. No different from before, still in his suit, though perhaps a bit more tired. He stood in greeting.

"I'm glad you came, Paul," very cool, cordial. No offer of a customary handshake; perhaps one surprise a night was enough. He gestured toward the fellow near the door. "You two have already met, though not formally, I suppose. This is my aide, Gabriel Matthews."

No hesitation of a handshake here, Gabriel's grip was hard and confident, and whatever it was he did, Paul bet he was quite good at it. A compact man, with quick, precise movements, no wasted motion. And little excess warmth. A stalking panther came to mind.

"Sit, please, sit." So odd to hear Donny speaking one on one, no impassioned vocal theatrics. While they planted themselves on the sofa, Gabriel clicked off the TV and some unknown black and white movie vanished, and then he sat before a glass-topped table to pore over a stack of papers.

"I don't mind telling you, you certainly caught my attention tonight." Donny smiled, steepled his fingers. "You must have had a very compelling reason for doing that."

Paul was fidgeting at his end of the sofa, comfort elusive. He finally decided it wasn't the furniture's fault.

"Something's been going on in my life," he said, "and I can't talk to just anybody about it. You're the only one I know of that might help." Deep breath, hold, release. Might as well jump in with both feet. "I can do the same thing you can do. I can heal people."

Media veterans know how to roll with the punches, keep the unexpected from getting the best of them. Takes one to know one, for while nobody else may have noticed, Paul saw it: He had clearly taken Donny by surprise. The rapid blinking gave him away.

"You know, Paul, I've come across, mmm, two dozen people who have told me the same thing and they couldn't prove it." The skepticism was understandable, though not wholehearted. He had, after all, brushed against something that sent him to the floor.

"*I* can, if you want. If you had somebody who was sick, or hurt, or . . ." And how ghoulish this must have sounded, asking for someone in pain as if placing a deli order. Just to prove a point.

Gabriel looked up. "If he needs a chance to prove himself, maybe we owe it to him." He clearly had found the conversation more interesting than his reports. "I assure you, it'll never get past this room."

Donny pursed his lips in thought. "What do you have in mind?"

"Just a little something. Excuse me for a second," leaving the table, disappearing into a short hallway. Tinkering noises next, sounded like a bathroom, and Gabriel returned with something in hand. "You don't mind if I borrow this, do you?"

A twin-track razor was in Gabriel's fingers, and Donny's eyes widened. "Gabe? You don't need to—"

Smiling, shaking his head, "It's the only way to be sure. It'll just be a minor wound." He touched a finger to his lips, hush. "Really. I don't mind."

The intensity and commitment of these people could sometimes be a little creepy, and Paul watched in queasy silence as Gabe placed the razor's pivoting head across a fingertip. A hiss of drawn breath, *slice*, the twin blades cutting horizontal. For a moment, nothing, pale parallel wounds, then bright blood welled up, and he set the razor aside. Drip, drip.

"I don't think anyone could deny that's a proper cut." Gabe leaned in, showed his bleeding finger for Donny's approval, then moved before Paul. Waiting, expectant, "It's up to you."

The gauntlet of challenge, sure, two could play this game. The familiar tautness within, the flush through nerves and blood, and he reached for Gabe's finger, felt the slippery warmth.

It took less than a second.

Drawing his hand away, Gabe wiped the blood clear of the cut, found there *was* no more cut. The skin was unmarred by so much as a hairbreadth of scar. He stood, staring at his finger, oblivious as Donny leaned in agape.

"That was too simple," and Paul wanted to laugh, giddy relief, he'd been asked to perform on demand like a circus freak and he hadn't choked. Tables turned momentarily, and he in charge, to Gabe, "But please, you don't have to give me anything worse."

Gabe, still staring, bloody finger healed and whole, Gabe the statue, Gabe the stunned. Ten seconds, fifteen, and his mouth moved silently, and when he finally looked up, the belief was there. Oh yes. Total. He excused himself, stepped toward the bathroom again, wash up. Quiet. So reverentially quiet.

"How long," Donny finally said, "have you been able to do this?"

"Since early summer," and with the barriers down, Paul plunged into the unabridged version. The House of Wax and Stacy Donnelly, then the others, progressing from there. Gabe was back, and Paul had a most attentive pair of listeners who did not interrupt. Strangers, the both of them, and not even remotely close to the types he considered friends—these ramrod, suited types were aliens—but damn it, they listened. They believed. And moreover, they cared.

"So what is your problem with this?" Donny asked. "What you've described so far is an absolute blessing."

An urge to laugh in the preacher's face, let's twist the old adage, shall we? *This* silver cloud has a very dark lining.

"I've had . . . accidents. Things have gone wrong, somehow, when I've been upset." He wanted to stall, to window dress the gruesome truth, but there was no way to pretty it up. "I think it can go both ways. I can inflict sickness and injuries in the same way, and—*and I can't handle the thought of doing that to people.*"

There, out in the open, for better or for worse. If he peered into Donny's eyes and saw profound disgust, revulsion, he would understand. These were to be expected. Perversions were largely a matter of taste, but some were universal. But—but no, Paul saw nothing of rejection. Care and concern, the very things he had longed for, and never mind the earlier misgivings, the fear of this man being a fraud. A fraud he was not. No fraud could heal so sick a soul with a glance of acceptance, and Paul knew he had made the right choice after all in coming here.

I feel like my soul is coming apart . . .
But not anymore.

Donny could scarcely believe his ears, let alone what his eyes had shown him to be true. Here on his doorstep, circumstance had dropped a foundling seeking guidance. And *such* a foundling.

The Lord indeed works in mysterious ways.

Self-control, more important now than ever, he had to keep a lid on the excitement he felt bubbling up within. Because Paul Handler was not looking for an attaboy and pats on the back, he was seeking a sympathetic friend who could help him sort out the confusion. And what had he just said about inflicting illness . . . ? So very difficult to concentrate right now . . .

Because here was the real thing. Almost immediately he was pouncing on the obvious ramifications, *I have to win his trust, I just have to. I could always have used him for the ministry, but he might be the one to bring Mandy back. Mandy.*

Donny strolled over to the suite's bar, asked Gabe if perhaps they could have a little privacy, had to ask again to get Gabe out of some persistent vegetative state. What was with him, anyway? The rational efficacy, overwhelmed by the irrational? Could be. Donny poured a pair of 7-Ups on ice, returned to find Paul hunched forward onto the sofa, chin on fists. Self-contained.

"Tell me something. What you just demonstrated," and Donny nodded in the vanished Gabe's direction. "Is it always dependable? Or does it come and go?"

Paul straightened. "It's always worked, as far as I know. I can't think of any time when it wasn't there. I could feel it."

"Incredible, just incredible." There was no need to feign awe, this was certain. Donny studied him; Paul wasn't much older than Donny himself had been that day in Alabama. So raw, so vulnerable, in need of a confidant. A little soul-sharing could flow both ways. "Works every time. I admire that in you, Paul. Because it means you've actually got a better batting average than I have."

Surprise became mutual.

"It's true. I can't always count on it one hundred percent. Usually I can, I'm sure you've seen that on my show, as well as tonight. But sometimes? Sometimes I run across someone who defies my best efforts. Who knows the reasons why?" Amazing, how easily the pseudo-truths slid from his lips. But surely there could be no harm in a few fibs when a far greater good was to be served.

"I want to show you something, a piece of my past." Donny slipped momentarily into a bedroom, brought back a Bible he explained had been his as a teenager. Dog-eared and worn, not the impressive tome he carried onstage. He pulled an equally worn snapshot from the back. "This was taken eleven years ago. That day was a turning point in my life."

Paul studied the picture, a younger Donny Dawson with his arm around some raw-boned kid with eyes of idiot bliss. The kid was grinning like a loon as they stood before a clapboard building. Mundane in the extreme—except for the clotted gore spread across the boy's chest. Nobody could smile with that much blood on them, could they?

"The preacher of the church behind us took that and mailed it to me. Not fifteen minutes before, the boy you see there was pinned under a tractor when it tipped over. His rib cage? Crushed. I was preaching at a tent revival when it happened right in front of us, and not a one of us knew what to do for him. So I prayed. I lifted my voice to Heaven and I asked for help harder than I'd ever asked for anything."

"And it worked?"

"Right before our eyes. His wounds healed—in seconds. And I knew right then where *my* path was to lead." Donny took the picture again, stared back into such long-ago days. Better days? In a way. Everything had seemed so clear then, black and white. Too much gray in life and the world these days. "But ever since then, I'll be honest, there have been times when I just couldn't restore a body to health. But I'm sure the Lord has a good reason for holding it back, do you see what I'm saying?"

Paul nodded, and surely it was by divine prompting that Donny was managing to push all the right buttons tonight.

"Just as there must be a good reason for the troubles you've had. Maybe God's trying to tell you something, did you ever think of that?"

Paul cocked his head, clearly the first time he had considered this. "I never really looked at it that way, no."

"How many times have you had your accidents?"

"Twice."

"And were they good people? Tell the truth, now. The real character of these people. Was it good and kind and God-fearing?"

A rueful shake of Paul's head, reluctant. "No. No, they weren't."

"I had a feeling as much. And you say these happened when you were upset?"

"That's right."

"There you have it, I think." Diagnosis complete. "Life's upsets come along when our life itself is out of order. What you're being told is that your present life is not what it should be. Think hard now, haven't you been feeling that way lately?"

Paul bowed his head, and Donny had seen it all before. The sinner come face to face with the calamity of days near and far, the accrual of transgressions come due with a vengeance. God alone knew what sins he was remembering, from lust to pride to adultery to having other gods before the one true. Never a pretty sight. He stood convicted, yes, but not alone.

"I've had some problems," Paul finally admitted.

"I know you have, it's obvious enough." Donny stood, pacing to the window. Market Street traffic, never still, and he let the curtain drop. "I really do believe you should think about making some major changes in your life. Something that will help you accommodate your gifts a little more . . . harmoniously."

"Like what?"

"Right here and now, I can tell you're a man of character. You're a man of compassion and concern, and I know you want to do the right thing." On went the persuasive smile, so helpful when soliciting extra contributions. "I'm offering you the chance to come work with me. In an environment that will keep you free of the stress that's twisting your gift into something wicked."

Paul, wide-eyed, "Just pack it all in here at home and drop everything?"

"Well, yes, it would mean moving to Oklahoma City," *I can't push him, can't force him too far too fast,* "but Paul, home is where people truly love you and accept who and what you are."

"I don't know about this," slowly shaking his head. "I mean, everything I ever worked for is here now."

"But are they works that are going to *last*? Our works are going to undergo a trial by fire come Judgment Day, the Bible makes that plain. Are your works going to last? Or will they burn up?" An abrupt snap of his fingers. "I'm giving you the chance to use your gifts in a way that'll do the most good for the most people. At a starting salary of, say, twenty-five thousand dollars a year? Plus rent-free living quarters, if you want. The choice is yours, of course. But when the Lord comes knocking, *you* have to be the one to open up. He never forces the door, Paul."

This would take time to sink in, of that Donny was painfully aware. No immediate answers, much as he wanted one, to know that Mandy's days in her coma were numbered. If he could have throttled cooperation out of Paul, well, that would be worth a try, but the decision had to be his own. Or at least appear so to him.

So there they left it, a standing invitation that could be accepted at any time. Donny jotted down the tour's remaining itinerary, plus his home phone and the day he would once again be there. At Mandy's side.

And when Paul left, the future was so close, Donny could taste it, could have laughed with glee and torn his hair out in the same moment.

So close, yet so far away.

Caught between two worlds, now this was indeed the worst of dilemmas. Two worlds, and alone in both, entirely. The inner Gabe, submerged for years beneath subterfuge; the outer Gabe, still vital to maintain the image of Dawson loyalty and professionalism.

The role had been played so long, though, tough to say where *it* ended and the true Gabe began. You steep yourself in something for five years, an entire life lived under pretense, wouldn't some of it seep in by osmosis? When do the fibers of two separate lives intertwine? And how great the pain when they are newly torn apart?

I dislike the hypocrisy he stands for, and Gabe shut his eyes in self-examination, *but I* will *miss Donny when this is ended.*

Hyatt lobby bathroom, public access, where cleanliness was more than hygienic, it was a fiscal consideration. Pants around ankles, he sat in one of the stalls. Focus, he badly needed to get focused. Too many thoughts careening about, it was like trying to listen to a roomful of screaming children and make sense of each one.

From a jacket pocket he pulled a small clamp, spring-taut metal, and pressed it open. Reached down and snugged part of his scrotum into it, release, and oh the pain the pain, shuddering, *I have to be worthy of this,* a quick spasm and it was over, he was right again. Deep breath, and his head began to clear. He stood, pulled underwear up, tucked his burdened genitals within, then up with his pants.

Focus. He could function again, on all levels.

In the world of Dawson Ministries, a minor kink had arisen tonight. Disaster from Donny's viewpoint, bringing him down less than an hour after Paul Handler's departure: Their unit director, who supervised the camera crew and couriered each week's film to Oklahoma City for editing the Sunday show, had been taken from the convention hall to a hospital. Emergency appendectomy.

Another potential ministry embarrassment, but Gabe had soothed Donny, not to worry. On the off-chance that it did go public, they could release a disclaimer saying it had happened when Donny was simply unavailable.

Regarding Sunday's show, Gabe himself could take a red-eye flight out of Lambert Airport back to Oklahoma. While any peon could baby-sit the film to the studios, Gabe was the only other one fully trusted by Donny to put the show together properly. See? No problem, you can sleep after all, Donny.

So much for the latest drama within the world of Dawson Ministries.

But there was that other world, wasn't there?

The hidden world of The Quorum.

And this was what had set his imagination soaring and soul aflame. Everything he had worked for, everything he had been trained for, everything he considered himself beneath the layers until what was true and fundamental was reached—it had all been validated this night.

We found him. After twenty-eight years we found him.

And when he placed that transatlantic call from a lobby pay phone, the call answered at just after six in the morning Scotland time in the western Highlands, that estate by the loch—Gavin's shout of joy made all the years of sacrifice worthwhile. It was the call Gavin had always been hoping would rouse him from sleep. The call Gabe had hoped he would be the one worthy enough to make.

Little scapegoat lost.

Who now was found.

Amen, and goodnight.

19

 It was the best omelette he'd ever eaten, quite possibly the finest use of eggs Mike Lancer had encountered anywhere, period. Edie Carson was just one surprise after another.

The previous afternoon, enough trust had been achieved so that she invited him to stop by for breakfast before the grimmer task of exposing Amanda Dawson to the world. Mike thought it was the least he could do to provide. After rousing himself from bed at an unholy six-fifteen and showering, he left the motel, then grabbed breakfast at a convenience store on the way to Edie's. A box of Hostess Ding-Dongs and a couple bottles of Jolt, the true power breakfast, screw Wheaties, guaranteed to keep you chugging for hours. Edie had been horrified.

Yeah, well. Omelettes with cheese and ham and all kinds of chopped vegetables were pretty good too. Coffee, strong and black, he couldn't complain. Even her kitchen was nice and bright, clean, except she had a thing for those stupid cutesy country decor geese. Nobody's perfect.

"Now isn't this better?" Edie said across the tiny table.

"It's digestible," deadpan, then a grin, my compliments to the chef.

She frowned across the kitchen to her counter, at his own culinary offering, obsolete. "How can you *eat* that stuff first thing in the morning?" Nurse Edie, nutrition on her mind.

"It took years of intensive training."

A mock shudder. "I pity the doctor who does your autopsy."

"I'm immortal." Very matter of fact. "I've got so many additives and preservatives in me, I figure I'm good until at least the twenty-third century."

"Be careful, you'll wind up in your own newspaper." A smug smile. "The world's only human being with a shelf life."

She had a real nurturing streak in her, it was obvious in the way she'd set him down at the table, whipped those eggs into a froth with a wire whisk. Like it was second nature, and he some soup-kitchen derelict. She probably brought in stray kittens and puppies, fed them, found them homes. He glanced around for a little feeding bowl; eureka, around the corner from the stove.

"Did you always want to be a nurse?"

She nodded emphatically. "In my neighborhood? When I was a kid? Whenever somebody scraped their knee or something, I was in heaven. I had the toy stethoscope, and bandages, and bottles of sugar pills—I had it all." Edie cocked her head. "What about you? Nobody wants to grow up and write for *The National Vanguard*."

"Baseball player, that was my big goal. When I was a kid, my dad used to run me all across the state on weekends, and we'd see all the teams down in Florida for spring training. I thought, hey, that's the life for me."

"So what happened?"

Mike shrugged. "A little thing called mediocrity. I was barely good enough for second-string college, let alone the pros." He was laughing to himself, laughing *at* himself; had done it so long, it no longer bothered him. "Luckily I had a talent for embellishing on the truth."

The change on her face was night from day. "I need to ask you a serious question."

"Sure."

"Today? Amanda Dawson? What kind of approach are you going to take with it once you get back to your office?"

"I'm not sure I follow."

"I mean—is it going to be all hype and flash and scandal? You know. Like you're gloating over all the dirt you've dug up on these people?" Her eyes, so fretful, so concerned.

"It's not up to me." As honest an answer as he could give. "But personally, I just want to play it straight."

"And what will it be in there with? I got to wondering this last night. I mean—will she be in there with a bunch of pictures of freaks and murder victims and things like that?"

He couldn't help but laugh. "You haven't read a tabloid lately, have you?"

"I look at the headlines in the grocery store. Doesn't everybody?"

"You don't see much of the hard-boiled approach anymore. That was the old days, when the buyers were mostly men, getting them in tobacco shops and newsstands." Finally, a topic about which he could wax authoritative. "Ever since they started selling through supermarkets, the buyers got to be mostly middle-aged white Anglo-Saxon women, and nobody wanted to gross them out. So the contents shifted. Celebrities, psychics, diets, all that garbage."

Edie was grinning. "You don't take it very seriously, do you?"

"I don't take much of anything seriously. Just a few." He shook his head. "At the *Vanguard*, we have this mental profile of our typical reader. Somebody even hung a name on her, we call her Aunt Hester. And the old broad's our yardstick for what gets printed. Would Aunt Hester like this? Would Aunt Hester be really offended by that?" He finished his coffee, set down the mug. "You can't take anything seriously when it's geared around some make-believe old lady who sounds like she was named after a milk cow."

Time to leave. They piled dishes into the sink; she grabbed her purse, he grabbed his camera, and that was that. Odd seating arrangements down at her Nova, Edie insisting he ride in back, all the easier to hide later on. Morning drive time, the commuters of Oklahoma City; it felt as if he were being chauffeured in the lowliest of limos.

Mike had been half expecting to find her ready to back out of it this morning, second thoughts about showing him the truth behind the Dawson facade. But she was resolute, no hesitation, and this was admirable. It took true courage, even with anonymity as a part of the bargain. Hence the camera, a 35mm Nikon, ASA400 film with Amanda's name on it. One picture is worth a thousand signed affidavits.

How very weird. Sixteen hours ago, they had been strangers, Edie known to him only through voyeurism. And now she was an ally willing to stick her neck out for him and potentially drape it across the chopping block. How very rare.

Mike had lost track of how many women he had known carnally. A plundering Viking who sheathed his sword at every available opportunity, with time for neither conscience nor afterthought. Dancers and models, other reporters and television anchorwomen, stenographers and pediatricians and lawyers and so on, and he had generally humped a swath up and down the eastern Florida coast-line. Not a one of them could he count on for the quiet reliability of Edie Carson. And somehow, he didn't think it was their fault.

You get what you pay for. He had opened himself up this time as he rarely had before, out of necessity, an objective to be accom-plished. And rather liked the results; a few vulnerabilities weren't such anathema after all.

Edie. He studied her profile from across the backseat. He had written her off too soon. She was very cute, in her own way, you just had to wait for it. Invest a little in her to bring it out and see it for yourself. Once there, unmistakable, and he would not be at all surprised to learn it ran soul deep.

"You better duck down now, we're almost there," she said. They were already on South Squire Road.

Mike squirmed into the floorboard. Between his height and the Nova's negligible width, this was no fun at all. He tugged a light blanket over himself, all the better to disappear under. Edie reached back with one arm and did some rearranging.

"There you go," she said. "You look just like dirty laundry." A wicked giggle. "Kind of appropriate, don't you think?"

He grumbled. Everybody's a comedian. This abuse had to be worth a Pulitzer.

As good as blind, he tried to gauge their progress by sound, by movement. Off South Squire onto the compound grounds, the main lot. Dawson's drive, and a pause at the gates. She retrieved a digi-tally encoded card from the glove compartment, used it to punch in and open the gates, then put the card back. On down the private drive, forever, then cutting a tight circle to the left. Stop. She killed the engine.

"Sit tight," her voice soft. "See you in a few minutes."

He listened, eyes closed, sensory deprivation in stuffy darkness. Every sound took on added significance, Edie's fading footsteps toward the house, her entrance, then nothing but the mundane ambience of a suburban morning. Florida never sounded this bor-ing, did it? Maybe it did.

He didn't move until he heard the slower footsteps of Alice Ward, fresh off the midnight shift. He counted off two minutes after her engine ground to life and she rolled away, then pronounced the coast clear. He shucked his wrapper and rose up slowly, and something rolled off him to thump on the floor beside him, *What the hell?*

He sighed. One of those annoying fabric softener teddy bears. Dirty laundry indeed. How dare she.

Mike left the car with the Nikon slung around his neck, the morning air newly cool and fresh. He was halfway to Dawson's front door before realizing he was hunched over, oh my, aren't we being sneaky? This was like revisiting his teenage years, infested with hormones and creeping toward a girlfriend's house after dark.

He lurked in the doorway another minute or so before it swung open and Edie hurriedly motioned him inside.

"Are you sure your parents are asleep?" He couldn't resist.

"Just don't break anything," ooh, severe reprimand.

While Edie relocked the door behind him, Mike took it all in, this foyer that went beyond elegance. If it fell, the chandelier alone would kill him. Bury him with the Persian rug as his shroud. Parlor to the left, TV den to the right, complete with one of those six-foot screen monstrosities. This was obscene. And just when he'd been thinking his own Florida dwelling wasn't such a pit after all, thanks a lot, Donny.

Edie pointed to the bottom of the stairway, wide as a loading-dock ramp. "That's where Doctor Preston says she fell."

He inspected, ran a hand over the heavy dark banister. Solid, it could really do a number on anyone's skull. If Amanda had begun her fall from the very top, it was a wonder she'd survived at all.

"Just *look* at this place!" He could hold it in no longer. "Aunt Hester would shit."

"Come on," Edie, tugging at his sleeve. "I don't like leaving her alone."

Mike allowed himself to be pulled along like a child reluctant to leave a toy store window, then fumbled with the camera and snapped a few shots of the stairway. The roll of film was thirty-six negatives strong, with another in his pocket, so might as well go for some variety.

The day could be a gold mine, prowling for a feel for the Dawsons' private life. Would Amanda's closet hold fifteen hundred pairs of shoes, à la Imelda Marcos? Would the bathroom fixtures be plated in gold, as had those of Jim and Tammy Faye Bakker? He would have eight hours to find out and soak it all up until running to hide in the Nova before the next shift change.

Third floor, a hallway of guest quarters, then stop.

"This is her room." Edie's voice had dropped to a reverent hush, a voice worthy of a sepulcher.

Mike followed her inside, paused several feet from the bed. One hand toying absently with the Nikon hanging against his belly. He could only stare, frozen, thinking of contrasts.

Amanda Dawson was a mere fraction of the vibrant woman he had become accustomed to seeing in the ministry literature. A shattered fragment, a wasted specter, curled onto her right side and facing him. Her face, once so pretty in a guardedly sensual manner, had somehow gone tight and slack at the same time. Deathly pale, and damp. Her fingers were brittle sticks. Permeating the room was the underlying odor of bowels voided time and time and time again.

Sleeping Beauty expectations, dead on arrival.

"This—this isn't what I thought she . . . would be like."

Edie nodded. "It takes some getting used to."

Mike couldn't take his eyes off her, this motionless woman, fascinating in the same perverse way as are the grossly obese, the malformed. To stare is rude, but so very human. Except in this instance, he could stare until his eyes glazed over, and she would never know.

And Edie dealt with her, this living dead, eight hours a day, no days off, one on one, solitary confinement. And to think he had pegged her as having the insides of a marshmallow, what a serious error in judgment. She deserved some kind of humanitarian award, all three of them did.

Sudden second thoughts, his own—surprise. What kind of sleazeball takes advantage of someone so completely helpless? Amanda Dawson had already been reduced as a human being. Now he was ready to mark her down even lower, into a commodity. A spectacle for mass-marketing and distribution to a public that could never consume enough.

Oh hell, why this attack of scruples, anyway?

"Mike?" Edie's hand, from behind, on his shoulder. He could swear she had just read his mind. "Remember what you're here for. Remember what you want to accomplish with this."

He nodded without looking back. Yeah, right, there *was* that, wasn't there? Dirty pool, sure—but if Dawson was disgraced in the public eye, then maybe the world could be a little safer for all of the Allison Lancers out there. All those who were still left.

He lifted the Nikon, opened its aperture for more light. Chose his beginning vantage point and started to click away. One angle, then another, and another, and it got easier with every snap of the shutter.

Plenty of natural lighting, no need for a flash. The window, overlooking the cul-de-sac on which Edie had parked, gave a northern exposure; Ramon had once told him that north light was the best light.

Still life through a Nikon viewfinder. He must have clicked off fifteen shots by the time the warped humor began to surface, purely in reflex defense against the ghoulish nature of the situation. Mike Lancer, photographer to the living dead, *Work with me, baby, beautiful, work with me, let's have some drool now.*

Gallows humor, repugnant. Laugh or scream.

Scream. He very nearly did when he heard it from off to the side, a single soft word: "Oh."

Bad trouble, he knew it even before his eye left the viewfinder. The voice had come from the doorway. And it had been male.

"Mister—ah, Mister Matthews," Edie stammered, and his heart had gone into a sickly flutter. Weak in the knees. It was the most brutally awkward moment of his life, of that there was no doubt. And this to a man who had experienced several awkward moments, cuckolded husbands and boyfriends coming home to find him astride the very last place they would want him.

Mister Matthews, Edie had said, and Mike performed a mental scramble. Matthews, Matthews, all the evangelists and their staffs were lumping together, no distinction among them, and then he had it, coming up a winner. Gabriel Matthews, Donny Dawson's right-hand man. Seldom photographed, though Mike had never concerned himself with that. Perhaps he should have, and oh shit, didn't all this paint just the *loveliest* of pictures?

"Oh no," Gabriel whispered, voice and eyes equally barren, shocked by this sight, and Mike didn't know who was more blown away at seeing the other. Wide grim mouth, trembling a moment, then a taut line. He gulped air, then suddenly yanked his collar open as he sagged a moment in the doorway. A gold chain around his neck, disco Gabe. He stared at Edie. "I'm disappointed in you. I really am."

Edie's head hung at a shameful half-mast, and then she rolled her gaze back to Mike, full of queasy dread.

"And *you*," Gabe said to him. "I don't even know who you are. You don't belong here."

Terribly mesmerizing in a sick way, watching him straighten in the doorway, swallow thickly, then curl his hand toward his face, nails, *fingernails and what's this?* He struck himself just above the right cheekbone, mouth wide in a silent scream, then a high warbling *ahh ahh ahh*, trembling, slowly dragging his nails downward, four ragged furrows opening red red red red, shaking so hard spittle flew from his open mouth, and worst of all he never blinked once.

While Amanda slept on.

Composed, all at once, implosively so, and he folded his hands tightly together. "Are either of you familiar with the Book of Matthew, chapter twenty-four? And the story of the unfaithful servant?"

The Book of Matthew, was he speaking of the Bible or himself? And Gabe, eternally patient, waited for an answer, got none. The silence excruciating, and Mike could not move. Mind games, he was playing mind games with them—

"I didn't think so. Donny taught me this." The unblinking eyes began to leak tears. "Fascinating passage, verses forty-five to fifty-one, this is the kind of loyalty he expected of me. Let me recite the pertinent parts for you." He cleared his throat, stared them down the entire time. " 'Who, then, is a wise and faithful servant? He is the one whom the master has placed in charge of the other servants to give them their bread at the proper time.' " A hurried, quavering recitation, no inflections, one run-on sentence. " 'How happy is that servant if his master finds him doing this when he comes home. But if he is a bad servant, he will tell himself that his master will not return for a long time, and he will begin to beat his fellow servants and eat and drink with drunkards. Then that servant's master shall one day return when the servant does not expect him and at an hour he does not know.' "

A pause, Gabe looking close to hyperventilation, the blood on his cheek like war paint, and for a second his eyes rolled back, white in the sockets, and he let his jacket drop to the floor.

" '*And the master will cut him into pieces.*' "

Mike could barely register seeing him move, it was that fast.

"I'M SORRY I'M SORRY!" he screamed, Gabriel Matthews, a coiled spring suddenly released of tension, and the nearest target was Edie. He went twisting around her, locking her head in the crook of his arm, the hand clamping atop her skull while his other hand seized her by the chin, and he executed a smooth, graceful pirouette of horrid speed. Huge wet crunch, oh dear lord save us, and Edie was suddenly staring back at Mike with eyes bulging and chin draping over her shoulder toward her spine, and then Gabe released her and she was crumbling to the floor with no control, no grace, no life.

Gabe was coming, target number two, and he had snatched up a bedpan, the unlikeliest of bludgeons but it would do the job. Mike knew he could never fight his way past this madman, nor slip around him. Edie, sorry, so sorry, but false heroics would get him killed and no one would be left to tell the tale.

Mike launched himself around and back toward the multipane windows, almost jubilant that the gauzy drapes had been pulled aside, and he crossed arms before face and shut his eyes and hoped for the best and let his forearms lead the way.

And the world was shattering glass and crystalline shards and open space of free fall, and he was granted eternity to ponder his body, so heavy, denser than lead, than iron, and every snapshot frame of the green grass below coming close closer closest—

Impact, and again he heard the now-familiar snap of bone, can't mistake that one, and his left leg imploded into a white quasar of agony, and he felt that he had been yanked to a stop as if on the end of a tether. The dangling camera whipped down into his middle with the force of a club to drive the breath from his lungs, and he gladly would have gagged if only he'd had the wind. The rest of him collided with the lawn a split second after his leg, and he went rolling through a rainstorm of glass and broken bits of wood.

Alive, though, somehow still alive after three stories of dead drop, and he realized the trip might not have had such a jolly ending had he landed on the asphalt ahead.

Edie's car.

He was at the bottom of a sea of trees and mansion, ocean floor rippling with grass, and he began to swim for the car, his life raft, every movement requiring the exertion of ten. Lungs wouldn't work, leg wouldn't work, they were wreckage holding him back, and as he struggled across the lawn, he knew what it meant to drown in air.

Yet somehow his fingers closed on the handle of the passenger door, and it opened, so inviting. Pulling with both arms, pushing with his good leg, three limbs in frenzied spasms, he flopped into the Nova. Could have wept for joy when he saw her keys still in the ignition, of course, who was going to steal her car back here?

Mike had regained just enough wind to scream himself into place behind the wheel when he heard the front door of Dawson's house burst open. He wrenched the key home, not even daring to check how close Gabriel Matthews was, he did not need this in his life at the moment, well, okay, just a peek—

Oh shit!

A truly frightful apparition, wild eyes, either righteously holy or blankly malevolent, and Gabe was reaching for the door handle when the engine caught. Mike slammed the Nova's transmission into D and stomped the gas pedal to the floor and heard fingernails raking metal as the car lurched into motion.

Sixty feet up the drive, Mike glanced into the mirror, fearing the worst—Gabriel Matthews perched on the trunk like a vulture, ready to eat through glass and metal and then the driver. But no, all he was doing was standing in the middle of the cul-de-sac. Little boy lost, who has just missed the bus.

Mike laughed, the most hysterical sound he had ever heard.

He dug the digital card out of the glove compartment for the exit, and by the time he hit South Squire Road, he was crying. And sweating great drops of blood from his forehead; he checked the mirror, discovered that his plunge through the window had opened up a sizeable gash leading into the hairline.

Car weaving, bring it under control, better, better, and he slumped against the door. One puréed blend of aches and pains and gross miscalculations—and yes, sudden grief—and he poured every ounce of available concentration into keeping the car under control.

And so he drove, and he wept, and he bled, and he swore . . .

Smart enough to know the ordeal was just beginning.

20

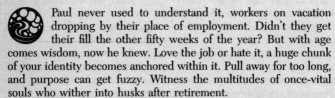 Paul never used to understand it, workers on vacation dropping by their place of employment. Didn't they get their fill the other fifty weeks of the year? But with age comes wisdom, now he knew. Love the job or hate it, a huge chunk of your identity becomes anchored within it. Pull away for too long, and purpose can get fuzzy. Witness the multitudes of once-vital souls who wither into husks after retirement.

But just in case anyone asked, he was covered. Had a good excuse.

It was the afternoon following his head-spinning meeting with Donny Dawson, and as soon as he stepped off the elevator and into KGRM's lobby, Sherry did a double-take behind the reception desk.

"You! *You're* not supposed to be here." What a sight she was for eyes that had seen too much. He hadn't realized how much he had come to enjoy seeing her around ten-thirty every morning. "You should be lying in the sun and trying new drinks and watching too much TV. That's how people on vacation behave."

"I can only take so much of that." He looked around, outer office, inner offices, yup, same old place. Then he fessed up, he had to retrieve his Walkman from the booth, and she said that was acceptable.

Paul had been taking a lot of walks the past days, a benign form of social contact. Seclude himself from humanity for too long, and his head would melt, it really would. It was bad enough that career largely entailed sitting alone in a room, but to spend an entire vacation that way was unthinkable. Hence his daily walks, and he immensely looked forward to them—actual face-to-face encounters with people!—and if he thought about it too much, the whole situation was going to strike him as very pathetic. Some year he was going to make a poor excuse for an old man.

He would stroll about and visit record stores, or Forest Park, or pit-stop at Tappers for a round or two. Sometimes he would find himself walking past churches, their sanctuaries quiet and reposed, and if they were unlocked he would wander in to pray for his soul and those of whomever he came in contact with. Denomination did not matter, he bowed to the spiritual wisdom of the Japanese: All paths lead to the peak of Mount Fuji.

Therapeutic, these walks, yet mildly incomplete. He missed his portable music.

"Has the new GM started yet?" he asked.

"David says tomorrow. Keep your fingers crossed for us."

Paul twined right index and middle fingers, held them up, went on his way. In the booth, Lorraine was newly into her shift, and for a moment he watched through the window. Omniscient, a secret, and the ache remained. Watching her go about daily life, no idea he was there, until finally it began to seem voyeuristic. He made sure the mike was shut down before rapping on the window and entering.

"Hey stranger," she smiled at him.

The booth speakers were alive with a bittersweet tapestry. Solo David Gilmour, apart from Pink Floyd, something called "Short and Sweet." Had she, on some fundamental level, known he was on his way, and cued up this most poignant of soundtracks? Women's intuition, here's some more salt for those wounds.

"I'm disappointed," he said, trying for levity. "The place hasn't fallen apart without me."

She shook her head, Lorraine in the midst of deejay ballet, scribbling in the commercial log and loading three carts. "We're getting by, but it's not the same. The old Hargrove-Handler-Savage triple threat really suffers the loss."

Captain Quaalude had been filling the midday shift with one of the more promising part-timers. A genuine talent, but he needed more seasoning, more self-assurance. Though who among us does not?

Paul leaned against the wall across from her, glanced over his shoulder to see a travesty. Someone had replaced a Sisters of Mercy promo poster with one of Erasure. At last, indisputable evidence, six days gone and all was *not* well. Upon his return he would retaliate with Jane's Addiction, take *that*, you swine.

"You didn't see Craig downstairs anywhere, did you?"

That name, such an annoyance. "No. Was I supposed to?"

"Stupid me, know what I did?" Lorraine tossed hands up in helpless surrender. "I was doing some production last night, for these spots starting later today. I was running late and I felt brain dead and I was supposed to meet Craig downstairs for a late dinner. So I thought I'd take them home to type up the labels. And I left the damn carts in his car, can you believe that?"

"What, he's running them by?"

She nodded. "Yeah. They should already be here by now. Look at my hand, I'm getting nervous." Steady as a rock. "This is your fault, you know. You've thrown us all out of whack."

Paul laughed, took the blame stoicly, but inside the bile churned. Dinner and favors and no harsh words about her husband, my oh my, didn't it sound like the picture of domestic bliss?

Knock it off, the knee-jerk response to his own self-pity. If they were happy again, more power to them. He wondered if they were still trying to get her pregnant, as she had confided after that drunken night of splendor. Maybe they would manage to pull it through the fire after all. And wouldn't it be the height of irony if Paul's sole night with her had been the one thing to cause her to reevaluate the marriage, renew her commitment? *Was I that bad in bed? Oh knock it off already.* Were that the case, he supposed he had done some good in her life, in a roundabout manner. Paul Handler, emotional tampon. Plug those temporary leaks, then cast him aside. *And cut this self-pity shit right now!*

"So are you . . . doing okay, and all?" Clearly unconvinced she should have asked, and what was she referring to, anyway? So many interpretations.

"Good days and bad ones." Sounded good, yet divulged little.

She wasn't asking merely to be polite, he could see that in those green eyes, the deep-seated ache. An ache that deepened his own, for he longed to know what caused hers—*Was it me?*—yet he dared not ask. Too many calluses layered over the night they had shared to risk touching her soul in the same way ever again, or allowing her to touch his. Replay the day-after devastation? Never.

Irony, he appreciated irony? Here it was: There lived an entire world population out there he was increasingly apprehensive about touching, for fear of the consequences. And in here, the one person he at one time might have felt like confiding this in was equally off-limits. The emotional counterpart.

Live with it. Just start building the walls inside and quit when the hurt is no longer visible. But keep bricks and mortar handy, you never know when you'll need to build anew.

"Paul? I know you haven't told anyone what's going on with you. I mean, I've never seen David so frustrated over anything, but he respects you enough not to push it. But . . ." She rolled her eyes. "I'm screwing this all up." She took a deep breath, her fingers twitching; he knew she wanted a cigarette. "I guess what I want you to know is, if you need to talk, I'm still here. I haven't gone anywhere."

To talk with her, the therapeutic value of a month of walks. Miles, marathons. His mouth ticked into a wry, one-sided smile.

"Paul, I don't like this any more than you do." Close to tears, the most she had shown of herself in weeks. "I don't like being shut out —not by one of my best friends in the world."

I can't stay here, trying to smile while going for the booth shelves and his Walkman. Lorraine watched with moist eyes, and if he let them, they would soak right through those walls. Mortar and trowels to their battle stations, just in case.

"We really screwed it up, didn't we?" she whispered.

He nodded.

"But don't you tell me I'm not your friend anymore, don't you fucking dare, if you told me that, I'd . . ." She trailed away, wiping a hand across her forehead. Deflating in her chair.

"We'll always be friends," he said, "no matter what," and it sounded so final, but maybe that was proper. "Just remember that, and we'll be okay."

She said she would, and he said he was glad, and then that supremely painful moment when he felt terribly compelled to hug her, and knew she felt the same. But they didn't. Leave those arms at our sides, it's safer this way, it's sterile. Perhaps what he had said a moment earlier had sounded so final because it truly was, and deep inside he was leaning toward accepting Donny Dawson's offer. More than a job, it meant a complete change of scenery and environment. An overwhelming idea at first, not because of moving —for a deejay, moving became a way of life, eased by the familiarity of the booth—but because of the total change in life itself. But look at current realities, and the idea had definite merit.

I can't stay here, he had thought. It had applied to far more than the here and now. He could finally admit that.

KGRM. This place had quickly become a museum of painful memories. Popeye's office, the shower stall, Lorraine in the flesh, the request line. All staring him in the face, singularly, sometimes in teams, oh what fun.

Paul let them filter in and out of memory, testing their strengths, while backtracking through the offices and waiting for the elevator. Good-bye to Sherry, then a downturned red arrow winked on with the ping of a bell. The doors slid open, and he rode the cab five floors down to the lobby. The doors opened—

And Paul found himself staring at someone who looked as if he had just stepped off the cover of *GQ.* University of Hitler Youth haircut and Pepsodent smile and all that went with them, Craig Sheppard, yes, he knew the guy was coming, but this was still the last person on earth he needed to see at the moment.

"Well hello there. It's been a while," said this picture-perfect trendoid.

Paul stumbled out similar pleasantries, not even aware of half of what he was saying—deejays can do that with ease—and he watched Craig brush a forelock of hair into place. One flip of a practiced hand, so smooth, *How could I ever compete with this guy? He even smells perfect.* Bastard.

Craig held up a fistful of cartridges. "Lorraine's getting stressed out, I think." With a wink. "She never used to forget anything like this before."

Paul looked him over, the lightweight gray suit and watch fob looping from a vest pocket—probably wasn't even attached to a fucking watch—and the even tan across his face. How completely, annoyingly *healthy* this man looked. Such a precarious state of balance these days, health, you could be whole one minute, ravaged by disease the next. It happens.

These guys with their Vic Tanny memberships and designer sweats and salads for lunch with Perrier, twist of lemon please, they really took their own immortality for granted. And wouldn't it be a blast to smear that smug complacency off the face of one of them, *just one?*

Paul could feel it uncoiling inside, the steepening of blood pressure, the quickening of pulse. The adrenaline charge as he remembered how hate was the purest emotion. His fingers itching, itching. And was the thought of Craig Sheppard and Lorraine Savage in conjugal ecstasy upsetting, especially when played over and over for a calculated effect? Wasn't that distressing? Why, it virtually drove spikes into the soul, a carnal crucifixion.

"She told me she was expecting those any minute," Paul said. Personable, nice guy, Mister Congeniality all the way . . .

So Craig would never know what hit him.

Nobody would ever suspect, *nobody*. The best forensics team in the world could not trace a massive coronary or a cerebral hemorrhage back as a murder weapon; the idea would never even cross their rational minds. And no telling what kind of exotic damage he could cook up when he really set his mind to it.

"Thanks for holding the elevator," Craig, so confident. "Good seeing you again."

How many people got this chance, to right a cosmic wrong, so that the *proper* sequence of events could then take place? Damn few, which was just fine, because it cut down on the competition.

Craig reached forward to shake like the professional gentleman he was, and Paul reached out to meet him halfway, smiling the whole time, *No one will ever have to know*, their hands scant inches apart and closing—

WHAT THE HELL AM I DOING, I'M NOT GOD!

His head cleared, and there it was, rationalizations aside, the ugly truth: murder. Whether premeditated or a crime of passion, he would be just as guilty. And Craig just as dead. Had he actually been naive enough to believe that Lorraine would rejoice? And assuming for the moment she did, and fled into Paul's arms, and they embarked on that happy road to forever—what of the first time they argued? Could he hold it back? Or would he let it go ripping through her just so he could get his way?

Such a turnaround from the guy who had walked the halls of St. Francis Medical Center a few weeks ago. How the mighty have fallen.

His fingers brushed Craig's before he could jerk his hand back. Craig hissed a quick breath, lost his composure for the moment, something very wrong here that did not fit within his narrow frame of reference. As Paul beat a hasty retreat across the lobby, sneakers slapping the floor, Craig stood stupidly in the elevator doorway and sucked on a dark burst of watery blisters that had suddenly sprouted on his fingers. An uncomprehending gaze, Paul to hand to

Paul again, and the elevator doors slid closed and staggered him, then rebounded.

Paul sprinted across the lobby, heedless of the building's midafternoon comers and goers, not even remotely caring what they thought of him, because all he wanted was to make it to the bathroom so he could blow nervous chow in private.

Too many ugly things to deal with as of late, the ugliest of all lurking somewhere just beyond the mirror. It was a confusing new world whose only certainty was whose itinerary he would be looking up as soon as he could make it home. And whom he would be calling.

21

Mike Lancer had thought he understood pain before. What arrogance, he'd had no idea, *no* idea.

He killed her. He fucking killed her. Walked right in and killed her. I don't believe this. He killed her.

The thought was repetitive, all-consuming. Motel room mantra, spoken over whiskey and throbbing bones. Murky by now, but earlier, thoughts had come through with screaming clarity. Once he had gotten safely distant from the Dawson compound and begun to assimilate what had happened right before him, the pain in his leg had honed every thought to a razor's edge. And had helped him decide how to handle a situation that had blown up in his face.

Fact: Gabriel Matthews was a very dangerous man, give the reporter bonus points for darkly humorous understatement. Yet despite his actions, Mike didn't think him a madman, at least not in any traditional sense. Self-mutilation aside, Gabe's actions had been brutally efficient, and there had to be a good reason for that. Granted, Amanda Dawson's exposure would be a tremendous embarrassment, but not the end of the world. Donny was a slick guy; forewarned, there would be time to concoct a cover story before the news broke. And the reasonable initial approach to take would be to offer money for both pictures and silence. In all likelihood, Dawson Ministries—or at least Gabriel Matthews—had something else going on with considerably higher stakes than the routine shearing of the flock.

Fact: Regardless of his methods and self-ordained status, Donny Dawson *was* a minister, in fairly high standing within the Oklahoma City community. And Mike simply a third-rate reporter, out of town at that, from a sleazy newspaper. No doubt a brutally efficient guy like Matthews would have Edie's body stashed and the mess cleaned up with ample haste. By the time Mike could file a report with the police, the evidence would be gone, and then whose word would be believed? Surely not the scandal-monger's. Or if Matthews was *really* clever and equally bold, he might even figure out some way to pin Edie's murder on Mike.

Suspected fact: Getting his leg treated in Oklahoma City might be the riskiest thing he could do. Emergency rooms kept records. Name, address, Social Security number; indelible footprints leading to Florida, for which he had no way to backtrack and wipe out. As it stood, Gabe Matthews had no way of knowing who he was, where he had come from. Should an emergency room enter the picture, it could be his death warrant. It was safe to say that Matthews and Dawson had ties to the medical community; they had gotten Amanda her necessary short-term care and kept it quiet. No doubt they could easily manage some discreet checking into who might have shown up on Wednesday, September eleventh with a broken leg or similar injuries that could have been sustained during a fall.

On his own. Gritting his teeth against the pain, Mike had driven back to Edie's and switched cars, taking care not to appear too obvious as he wiped down everything he had touched—get rid of those fingerprints—and swabbed the blood from his forehead. In his rental, he had driven until he found a pharmacy with a drive-up window, and bought a pair of aluminum crutches and the biggest bottle of Motrin in stock. By now, his leg, lower half twisted into a cockeyed hook, was swollen nearly double and throbbing like a bastard. Check the mirror; he was ashen and sweating like a drug addict in withdrawal. Next stop a liquor store, also with a drive-up, where he restocked on George Dickel Sour Mash. Last trip was to a hardware store in a shopping plaza—no drive-ups here. After an excruciating twenty minutes, he spotted a promising-looking punker walking past the car. Black clothes and Magic Marker tattoos. Mike paid him twenty dollars to go in and buy him a length of rope, easy money, no questions asked.

He returned to the motel, trying grimly to juggle everything at once, and to call his walk a hobble was charitable. He nearly fell face-first into the floor once he got the door open. He dropped everything and dragged himself to the phone and called the airport. He could catch a departure to Miami, layover in Atlanta, at eight-fifty that night.

It would do. He wasn't going dancing. Only one detail of note to take care of in the meantime. First, had to work up that nerve, deaden those feelings, and he began his own prescription. An afternoon of Doctor Lancer's faithful bottled elixir.

Later. Mike eyed his digital travel clock, twenty-five past four. Much more of the sour mash, and time would become too abstract a concept, which meant it was probably time to take care of business.

Curtains drawn, lights dim, this brutal afternoon of total self-reliance. The TV yammered too loud, some aged western, John Wayne and lots of gunplay, all of it hazy from too much pain, just enough whiskey. Got everything?

Ah. The rope.

"Shit," he moaned, and popped more Motrin, solid food to go with the sour mash. Do it, just do it.

Mike scooted down from the bed into the floor. Crabbing back and forth, he uncoiled the rope and ran one end toward the bed's headboard, looping it around one leg and bringing it back. He fumbled out a functional noose and brought it back to where he sat by the bed's foot. Scooted back nearly to the wall and braced his good right leg against the end of the bed. Plenty of rope to spare.

He finally turned his attention to the remnants of his left leg. The best for last. Amazing, he could sit here and stare at the surreal thing as if it were someone else's. The foot angled to the right and his shin bent in the middle like a secondary knee that buckled inward. It had swollen to stretch painfully against his grass-stained pantleg, and this would be a hell of a lot easier if bell bottoms were still in fashion. Knee to ankle, like one monstrous sausage, and he didn't want to see the flesh beneath the fabric, a sickly pastiche of bruisework.

Leave it all alone? He was drunk enough to live with that idea for now. But no, man of the world, he had a plane to catch, and couldn't travel with a leg *this* badly misaligned.

He fed the noose over his foot, tightened it around his ankle, none too snug, none too loose. Brought a pillow down from the bed, popped one corner into his mouth and bit hard. He looked at the TV; John Wayne would have bitten a bullet. When in a pinch, improvise. And pillows muffle more noise any day.

Mike leaned back into the floor, flexing his right leg against the bed, testing for solid footing. A couple of light practice tugs on the rope, the gentle pull on the noose a preview of more painful things to come.

His entire body broke out into one thick sheen of greasy sweat, son of a *bitch* what had gotten into him thinking he could do this on his own, and he snatched up the bottle and downed one last shot in case the pain killed him, and he wrapped the rope around his hands and ground his teeth into the pillow and *yanked* the rope back as if he were the last holdout on a losing tug-of-war team.

Biting into the cheap foam pillow, shrieking through clenched teeth, oh fuck oh fuck it hurt it HURT, and his leg erupted hot and thick and molten, and twisted straight with a meaty crackle, and every tendon and ligament and muscle fiber and chip of bone and screaming nerve went on full-alert overload, and the backwash of nausea swept him under, arms losing all strength while the gray haze dimmed his eyes, and he twisted his head around just in time to vomit a rancid puddle over his shoulder, and then he collapsed, flat. Empty.

Drifting, timeless netherworld of tortured sleep, no rest from the waking world. Sickly mingling of life and dreams, the stink of whiskey and bile. Carpet soaking undigested pills, and brown water stains on the ceiling, some new breed of map. Take me there, no hell on earth could be worse than this.

One hour, two, and the world again, Oklahoma City back in hard focus, John Wayne having given way to . . . somebody. He sat up —it was tolerable—and released his foot from the noose. He could write this up in an article, true-life fuckup detective, and no one would ever believe him.

Truth is stranger than tabloids.

The survival instinct was strong, and if it was not a case of grace under pressure, he still got by. Mike caught his flight on time, stinking drunk, clothes looking ready for Goodwill. Lurching about on crutches, praying he wouldn't fall. He hobbled into Miami International near two in the morning, little the worse for the additional wear, but plenty bad enough.

Finally, the hospital. X rays showed he had broken both bones in his lower leg and had cracked four ribs to boot, no wonder it hurt to breathe. He received a cast from midfoot to a few inches above the knee, barely escaping the need for steel pins imbedded into bone and emerging through the cast for traction purposes. They put him on IV antibiotics and pumped him with Demerol 100 every three to four hours for the next four days, days that coagulated into a blur.

When he finally came out of it, pain medication downgraded to Tylenol with codeine and anticipating discharge in a few days, he knew something was different. Proof positive, the nurses on his floor were as safe as in their mothers' homes. Not a single pass, not one hearty ploy for extra sympathy, let's see where this sponge bath leads, shall we? He was old.

And inside, something quite apart from bones had been broken.

I killed her. I really killed her. Just as much me as him, because I dragged her into it.

Mike's first evening at home, in an apartment utterly devoid of any discernible style of decor. Unless Late Post-College classified as an art form. The furniture was mostly rattan, with several posters on the walls, a few cheap prints. Homegrown shelves of brick and pine. Be it ever so jumbled, there's no place like home.

His dining room was merely an extension of the living room, and he sat at the table. Leg stuck off to one side like some new piece of furniture. George Dickel before him, on the rocks tonight. Class. Company coming.

Earlier in the day, prior to discharge—and pickup by a some-times girlfriend—Mike had phoned the offices of the *Vanguard* and hooked up with Ramon down in the photo labs.

"Still keeping in touch with your brother?" he had asked.

"Which one?"

"The one your mama still cries about."

Ramon, laughing softly, "That still doesn't narrow it much."

Cuban immigrants, Ramon's family, Marielitos from the early eighties. They had done decently for themselves, only one true black sheep. Ramon's older brother Julio took the honors, dirty job but someone's got to do it. Which was not to say he wasn't making more money than the rest of them put together.

"Julio, right?" Ramon had said. Chuckling. "What you need, Mikey? The pain pills you been getting aren't enough?"

More complicated than that, Mike had explained, then told him what he wanted. Julio's friends, associates, these guys were no one to screw with on any level. Lots of ties to South American high-profit cash crops, inventors of the Colombian necktie: slash the throat and pull the tongue out to hang from the wound in grotesque sartorial parody. The mere thought of indebting himself to Julio gave him the jitters.

But then, so did Gabriel Matthews.

Ramon had told him to sit tight while he checked. He'd called back an hour ago, good news, but Mike hadn't worried. Ramon was stand-up. He gave you his word, you could bank on him keeping it.

Mike's dining table had perhaps one square foot of open space left. The rest was covered with a computer and phone modem, plus stacks of papers and partial articles and recent issues of the *Vanguard*. His editor had put him on sick time, reluctantly, and he would be spending another couple weeks minimum here doing the stir-crazy routine, but at least he could manage a little work in the meantime. Mostly cranking out stories, usually embellished, based on oddities coming over the AP wire. Regarding the Dawson excursion, Mike had blatantly lied. Something brewing there, most likely, he had told his editor, but he had met with a mugging before he could close on it. She wasn't stupid, and he didn't think she believed him, but he stuck with it. He'd had enough time flatbacking in the hospital to build the yarn to its tiniest detail. Publishing the truth was no good; his byline could red-flag him for further retaliatory, possibly fatal, abuse. Anonymity wasn't courageous, but it *was* safe.

The table also held all his private files on Dawson Ministries, on top all the pieces of literature in which Gabriel Matthews was mentioned or pictured. Not even half a dozen. Bastard definitely kept a low profile. Like a shark cruising below the surface. Present, and deadly, but unseen until too late.

The doorbell rang, and Mike swung himself up to his foot-and-crutches configuration. Made sure he was balanced properly and crossed the apartment in a series of movements that still seemed alien, insectile. It required the patience of Job and the dexterity of the Flying Wallendas.

Ramon's face was spread wide in the peephole. Mike undid all three locks and opened up, and Ramon shut the door after himself. Army surplus pants and a Day-Glo orange T-shirt and a tiny emerald in his ear; looked as if he had come straight from work. Except for that heavy paper bag in his hand, the source of real interest.

"You look better than you did a week ago," Ramon said on the way to the table. "I give you that much, at least. I guess."

"Up yours. I look great."

"Oh. Yeah. Yeah. I see it now." Very exaggerated. He set the bag onto the table with a solid clunk, then helped Mike get situated into his chair again. "You're a lucky guy, Mikey, you still got your health." Ramon fetched himself a glass, poured two fingers of sour mash. "How much longer you got to spend in that thing?"

Mike rapped his cast. "Another five weeks or so."

Ramon shook his head, profound sympathy. "Puts a definite cramp in your style. Maybe you should take yourself to a ski lodge, see what kind of action you can score there. Ski bunnies, they're used to things like that."

Mike snorted. "How would you know? You've never been north of Pensacola."

Ramon drew up proud and scholarly, overly so. "I *read* it in the *Vanguard.*"

Mike smiled crookedly. "Yeah. Anyway. I think maybe I'm due for a break as it is. I think I'm developing a resistance to penicillin."

"You'll live longer." Ramon nodded, drained his glass and set it aside. Opened the sack. Out came a cloth-wrapped bundle. "Show and tell time."

He unwrapped an oilskin cloth to reveal an automatic pistol. It looked a little like the old army-issue .45's, but less clunky, more streamlined. More lethal. Nickel plated. Along with it came an extra clip and two boxes of cartridges.

"Okay look, this is not my field, okay? I'm just delivering. I can tell you what my brother told me." Ramon looked almost apologetic. "This is a Smith and Wesson ten-millimeter. It's the model the FBI issues agents now, more stopping power. They had it developed after that shootout down in Miami a few years ago, time those two psychos took out five agents. You shoot something with this mother, it's gonna go down and stay there. Serial number? It's gone, okay? It's unregistered, untraceable." He shoved the whole bundle across to Mike. "Never let it be said my brother stocks inferior merchandise."

Mike hefted the thing. Heavy. Probably recoiled like a monster, too. "Thanks for doing this for me. I owe you a big one."

"How about an explanation and we call it even?" When Ramon got no answer, he pressed on. "I mean, you take off to snoop out some TV preacher, I figure the worst is, you come back with a handful of tracts and a bunch of eye makeup on your shirts. But no, you come back looking like you been stomped by the Hell's Angels and wanting to buy a gun on the sly. So what's going on?"

Mike stared across the table. "I don't know. Honest truth. I really don't know."

Ramon nodded, hit his glass with another finger of whiskey. "Okay, fair enough. But level with me this much, you didn't get hit by any mugger while you were there. I don't buy that, and nobody else does much either."

"This is just between us? Goes no further?"

Ramon nodded, yeah yeah yeah.

Mike shrugged, here goes nothing. "I got banged up diving out a third-story window. I'm lucky it wasn't any worse than this."

"Wasn't just a jealous husband this time, was it?" Ramon looked able to laugh, but wouldn't let himself.

Mike, staring into space, the recent past, ghosts of guilt. "No. Not even close." He pointed to a blurry background picture of Gabe in one mailer. "This fuckhead. He killed a girl right in front of me. Bare hands, two seconds, that's all it took. And then he started coming for me. What, I'm gonna see if hitting him with my camera works? I did the best I could."

Ramon eased out a pent-up breath, shook his head. "Just you watch your step with these people, Mikey. I'm serious. And if you need anything else, you let me know. Okay?"

"How much for the gun?"

Ramon waved it off. "It's a freebie. Compliments of my brother. He was asking me who it was for, and why, all that, I had to tell him what I knew so far. He said you could have it for nothing 'cause he can't stand those TV preachers like Donny Dawson. Said they treat God like they're selling used cars, and he hates that. You believe that, man? This guy, he sells toot and rock and ice to kids in school-yards, and somebody like Dawson offends the hell out of him. Funny world, huh?"

"Yep." He lifted the gun again, acquainting himself with its balance. Five or six weeks in the cast, he and this piece had plenty of time to become friends. "I'm laughing more every day."

Summer 1193/England

It had been five days' ride north to Huntingdon, and the horses
traveled it well. The steeds of knights were bred for power worthy
of their riders.

Baron Walter of Kent had taken along three of his finest who
remained from the recent Jerusalem journey. Gaunt and hollow-
cheeked upon their return earlier this year, but alive, a luxury no
longer afforded many of those who had sailed east with them. Famine and disease had taken more lives than warring, but for those
who endured was the singular honor of returning with their red
cross—first worn on the breast of their tunics while traveling east—
now worn on their backs.

They were iron men. They were *cruciati*, the cross-bearers.

They were the crusaders.

They arrived at Widdershaw Abbey in the afternoon, met on the
road, just past the gates, by one of the monks. Others toiled the
fields adjacent to the monastery, these Benedictines doing what
they saw as God's work here in the midst of seclusion, their lives
full of constant prayer, constant work. Robes of black.

Walter and his escorts dismounted while the guest-master was
fetched to lead the other men to their lodgings. And he gazed upon
these formidable gray stone buildings with their gables and arched
windows. Holy ground, maintained by a brotherhood of humility

that had forsaken the rest of the world. He thought he must look quite the peacock among these black robes. His bright blue tunic, chest emblazoned with his family's crest of sword and cross, leopard and star.

With only a monk now for an escort, he entered the abbey. His second visit here in three months. Perhaps this time answers would finally be forthcoming.

Beneath vaulted ceilings, he waited. Save his king, there were few men for whom he would consent to the indignity of awaiting arrival. A man of God was an exception, a reluctant one at that, but this time he waited with a feeling close to fear. A trained warrior could always master fear in the face of any enemy—Walter had looked upon a veritable sea of Moslems and not blinked—but in these days of peace, he could no longer be certain of the faces he should stand against.

Abbot Baldwin did not keep him waiting long. A small man with hair like iron, he walked with the same authority as a nobleman. Obviously accustomed to obedience from all who lived here.

"Even in summer," Walter said, "these places are too chilled for me."

"We never notice. Such is the blessing of hard work."

"Your missive said a monk of yours could understand some of the writings I brought."

Abbot Baldwin nodded once. "Brother Maynard. He's quite old now. The records show he came here in 1152, after returning from the Holy Land. He was a prisoner of the heathen for a time."

"And I can see him?"

"Come. He is in the cloister now," and the abbot led the way.

A few years ago, before leaving for Palestine, Walter had not easily understood a place such as Widdershaw, the men who lived past its gate. A monastery in general, well, yes, *that* he could. Each man was born to serve God in his own way, whether by taking up cross and sword to serve as Christ's earthly warrior, or by devoting oneself to daily prayer and hymns and selfless charity.

But Widdershaw was different; most monks here had once been men of the other breed, soldiers who had pledged themselves to the code of chivalry. Years ago, Walter could not comprehend it. After living a life of battle and tournaments, the indulgence of fine foods and wine, the pleasures of women—why suddenly turn and deny all these joys? Exchanging them for ceaseless toil and endless regimens of petty discipline? Such a man seemed less a man than one born to the Church, or so Walter had believed then.

But he had aged these past few years. He now understood. He had glimpsed Hell.

And had quite possibly brought a piece of it home with him.

Abbot Baldwin led him out a side doorway of the abbey, to the separate building of the cloister. Far more austere than the sanctuary, its rooms given to studies by the younger brothers and their teachers, while older monks hunched at writing tables, painstakingly copying Scripture and other manuscripts. The nearest, Walter saw, was illuminating one page in a vast book, using a brilliant blue ink tinted with crushed lapis lazuli. The brother's work was as beautiful as any art in any cathedral in which Walter had ever set foot.

"Brother Maynard," the abbot called.

Old he was, indeed. A crusader of some forty years past, and he would not have been a novice knight even then. Stooped now, his face a mass of taut wrinkles, hair of white wisps, his blue eyes faded by a desert sun and time. But his hands, from the robe's sleeves— strong and steady. Hands well-used, and of talent.

Abbot Baldwin introduced them, and Maynard gazed into Walter's face with a knowingness that made him feel as if all his secrets were bared. Every stroke of his sword, cleaving life from another's body.

"Not long returned from the Holy Land, are you, sir," he said. "Even through the beard, I still see the bones of your face."

"My appetites are not what they once were," Walter said, and it was true enough. He sometimes had little stomach for eating when memories were strong, and questions stronger.

The abbot suggested they retire to a smaller room where the relics were kept, where Maynard had labored over them to unlock their messages. When they were alone, the brother looked to him once more.

"I dare say I have been as curious to meet with you, as you must be to meet with me," and then Maynard collapsed onto a rude stool, shaking his head over the writings. "God's mercy upon you, what manner of people did you take these from?"

Walter looked at them, arranged on the stout table. Clay tablets, baked by the sun into brown brick, inscribed with a most peculiar form of writing. Carved stone, black diorite, with a distinctly different writing. A few works of art, mosaics of shell and stone and metal. Brought here three months ago on Walter's last trip.

"Brother Maynard," the abbot said sharply. "Your Christian duty is not to act as inquisitor to a servant of the king."

The monk looked pained but held his tongue. Benedictine Rule, obedience. He pointed to the hardened clay, inscribed by some hand with unreadable wedge-shaped marks.

"This language is unknown to me," he said, then pointed to the stones. "But these are writ in Old Persian. I learned it from a Moslem scholar before being ransomed from their captivity."

In his faded blue eyes was an unspoken thought, just between crusaders. This stern abbot who preached the spilling of heathen blood would never understand, for he had never been there. And Walter knew this old monk had come to learn the same thing he had: *The Moslems—they were not the God-hating dogs we were told they were. Noble pagans, at worst. Sons of the same God, at best.*

It had been an uncomfortable revelation.

"These stones tell of a yearly ceremony enacted by the people of a Babylonian city, in the land between two rivers," Maynard went on. "The ceremony was to honor a bargain the people of an earlier great civilization had struck with spirits they feared. This bargain gave homes of flesh to the spirits, and spared their land from the worst of famine, and pestilence, and war, and death."

"What earlier civilization?" the abbot said. "We know of none who lived there before the Babylonians. Could this be Egypt?"

"It speaks of two great rivers, not one. As for the land itself, it does not say. But its people called themselves 'the black-headed people.'" Maynard reverently touched a finger to one of the clay tablets. "I dare say these would hold more answers, but could I read them."

"What of the ceremony?" Walter asked.

"Once a year, with summer at its worst, they would select four men and ritually drive them from the city into the desert to spend a night. And give thanks to their gods for sparing them."

Walter looked at one of the mosaics, which now made sense. A long panel inlaid with carved shell and lapis lazuli, carnelian and gold. It depicted four naked men, each tied to his own chariot, drawn by donkey and escorted by helmeted men with spears. Could these be representative of the very first?

"Driving them into the desert each year," said Walter, "this sounds akin to early Hebrew law, when the priest would drive a goat into the desert for the atonement of their sins."

Maynard nodded sagely. "But did not the Babylonians come to live before Hebrew law and its ritual of the scapegoat?"

"I will not hear of this!" cried the abbot. "Brother Maynard, you come close to speaking heresy."

He admonished further, then dismissed the monk, with downcast eyes, back to his duties. Maynard obeyed, meek as a lamb, and Walter thought it pathetic—this man of elite birth, an honored warrior of Christ, talked to like a churlish child. His life so changed that he would accept it without so much as a blow in return to defend his honor.

And Walter found it strange, what things these priests would tolerate, what things they would not. Love and mercy, they preached incessantly. A century ago they had frowned upon tournaments and their violence, which trained young knights in the ways of war. They had frowned upon the feuds and battles between English and French, decried these knights of Christendom, slaying one another for the sake of an earthly kingdom, saying it caused rejoicing in Hell. Then Pope Urban II had preached a new war in the east, to recover the Holy Land and the Holy Sepulchre from infidels, and all at once to make war was sanctified. How much better for these selfsame knights to die in waves of their own blood, drawn by infidels, on behalf of a celestial kingdom and in defense of the Catholic faith.

This the priests could accept. When mere words could cause them to tremble with rage.

Abbot Baldwin wished to continue outside, led him to another exit and into the garth, a courtyard surrounded on all sides by the cloister. And here they stood, grass underfoot again. Sun overhead, that same sun that had blazed him in the east. It knew more mercy here.

Walter had seen horrors that went beyond the fortunes of war. After the fall of Acre two years ago, surrender terms dragged on, and King Richard—named the Lion-Hearted by his troubadors—had ordered the slaughter of twenty-seven hundred Moslem prisoners he could not feed. And Walter had taken part, as was his duty, but he could find no glory in this. Beheading men bound by ropes, where was anything resembling their code of honor in *that*? It had not stopped there. The Moslems, knowing the plunder of a conquered city was imminent, would often swallow what treasure they could. The knights of Christendom knew it too, and Walter saw them hack the Moslems' entrails open in search of gold. Saw them burn the bodies and sift the ashes in case more had escaped their attention.

A century ago, the Holy Father in Rome had assured the salvation of any warrior who battled east for the sake of the Church. Had promised absolution of all sins committed while there.

But how could God pardon such wanton greed as *that*?

He wanted to ask the abbot. But did not bother.

Abbot Baldwin had, three months past, heard the circumstances by which Walter had come in possession of the relics, but asked to hear them again. Of renewed significance, with Maynard's labors.

So Walter repeated the tale, how the knights, under King Richard, had fought south after the fall of Acre. Coastal cities along the Great Sea, falling to the crusaders as they fought their way to the Judean hills, for the ultimate prize of Jerusalem.

In Joppa, Walter and others had stopped to cast Moslem relics from a church, to restore it to its rightful God. These saviors had taken time to explore, and a passage was found to lead underground, beneath the church. Stairs of cut stone.

And there they had been found. The inscribed stones, the ancient artwork. And four who dwelled there. Three women, one man. Saracens, all. With eyes that looked old enough to have gazed upon Adam himself.

Walter had been well back in the line of warriors, and remembered that long, long moment in which Christian and Moslem had stared at one another. The surprise of both sides. Now, thinking back, perhaps mercy would have been granted had the knights not been so new to Palestine. Those who had been living here had in many places come to a kind of peaceful coexistence with the Moslems, a tolerance that shocked newcomer warriors.

Still, the Moslems had been first to move. Three women, one man, falling upon the soldiers in this cramped chamber lit only by torches. *Unarmed,* seeming only to wish to touch the bare faces and hands of the nearest soldiers, who cried out as it happened, who struck with weapons even as they screamed, and Walter remembered wondering what could be happening to them. These soldiers showing mortal terror, as if their very souls were in peril despite the promise of a Pope some hundred years before, and one screamed of spirits. As these four Moslems were quickly put to the sword, they no longer fought . . .

And they even appeared gladdened.

In spite of themselves, it soon became apparent that these normal men at arms had been granted the ability to become workers of miracles. Frightening miracles, at that, by the mere touch of hands. The touch of one bringing death. The touch of another blighting a tree with withering rot, never to grow again. The touch of yet another inciting others to fury and berserker rage . . .

While that of the fourth could act one of two ways. Illness and injury could be inflicted, yes, but these could also be healed—and as Walter watched him place his hands upon wound and skin rot, to restore them whole, he had wondered if this curse was completely evil? Could there not be good at its heart, even though it looked to be pure witchery?

The poor men were well terrified even of themselves and were quick to be shunned by the others.

"What of these men now?" asked Abbot Baldwin.

"They made willing prisoners, they fought not when we put them under rope. I brought them back on my ship. And they are yet my prisoners, in the hold in my castle." Walter hung his head, remembering the treatment these men, now outcasts in their own land, had endured under his guard. "They will not die. I had them put to the sword, and no wound was mortal. I had them bound and cast into a river, as we might try a witch with the ordeal by water. Their bodies were accepted by the water, and while they sank to the bottom and we left them there—*these men would not drown.* And if we try to put them to the torch, the flame only burns the clothing from their bodies, and leaves even their hair unscorched."

"And what of holy sacraments?" the abbot said. "Do these have effect on them?"

"They take of communion daily, they long to save their souls." Walter looked to the ground, the sky. Birds in flight, circling overhead; they reminded him of the eaters of carrion in that far land. And what a bounty holy war had given them. "I cannot hold them for much longer, Abbot. Their presence alone is frightening enough to my own garrison. My knights may soon find reason to seek another lord, despite their pledges of ost. I've heard grumblings enough."

Baldwin pressed fingertips together, his lips pursed, his brow furrowed. Thinking, weighing matters of church and state. While from the abbey's short tower sounded the tolling of the bell. Day's work was done. While duty continued.

"Time for vespers," the abbot said.

"Come morning, when I take leave, I would like to leave with an answer. What do I *do* with them?"

Baldwin held up one finger, silence. "This is no decision for one such as I, this is more the decision of a king."

"We have no king, and you know it." Richard the Lion-Hearted was still captive; his officer of the crown was having trouble enough just trying to raise the ransom. Walter looked with scorn down upon the cleric. "This is no decision for a nobleman, either. I have done what I do best—and it failed."

The abbot sighed, and clearly he wished he were elsewhere. Presiding over the routine in his safe little world. "Then allow me the time to send a missive to Rome. If this is to become the responsibility of the Church, then the decision should be papal. Now, please? It *is* time for vespers."

He was gone in moments, leaving Walter beneath the sky, surrounded by cloister. Alone, to contemplate the peculiar fortunes of holy war. A better thinker these days than the man who had first assumed lordship of his barony a decade past. He had done little thinking then, had more taste for shows of strength.

Before sailing from Marseilles for the Holy Land, he had been with King Richard's entourage in Tours. There the monarch had been given the traditional pilgrim's staff for the journey. He had leaned on it—and it had broken. A bad omen.

And rightfully so. The triumphs of Acre and Arsuf and other cities had been but fleeting. There had been illness. Starvation. A decimated, demoralized army was all that remained to witness a fortified Jerusalem, beyond their capabilities. In Acre, Richard had had the brashness to tear down an Austrian banner raised by Archduke Leopold, then cast it publicly into the latrines; last December Leopold had captured him on his return home and turned him over to the Holy Roman Emperor for ransoming.

Such plagues of ill fortune did not stir much faith that God willed their cause after all. And now this most frightful of ancient legacies had come home with them.

A three-year truce had been negotiated with the Saracens, allowing free passage for those on pilgrimage. But he feared the world of Islam would never truly trust Christendom again, not after what had been done to the captives at Acre. The Moslems seemed to have long memories—and perhaps with what their world had finally freed itself of, if Brother Maynard were to be believed, their laughter would now be loudest of all.

Such legacies to leave. In the name of God.

He got his answers in the autumn of that year.

True to his word, Abbot Baldwin of Widdershaw Abbey penned a letter to Celestine III, dispatched to Rome by messengers who then waited for a reply. Baldwin then sent them from Huntingdon down to Kent with papal instructions.

Let the prisoners go. But with conditions.

Baron Walter pored over the documents again the night after their arrival. Colder nights now, longer, while the coming winter lay ahead like a wolf pack. Supper eaten, the chamberlain preparing his bed, he often spent evenings in the great hall of the castle, sitting in a vast chair before a blazing fire. Warmth was drawn where it could be found, and how he had once longed for England's chill when the desert sun threatened to bake him to his bones. His daughter Caroline played in a corner, watched by her nursemaid.

Daughters of gentle birth were generally sent away to be brought up in the home of another nobleman, or in a convent, but Walter found he had no heart for that. Caroline was in her fourth year, and damn custom if it meant parting with all he had left of his wife. Death had taken her while giving this child life, and while for a time he had thought to hate his daughter for that, there was too much of her mother in her face for hatred.

Even if his Nicolette *had* been lost before bearing him a son and heir. He could marry again, father sons. In time. But this new wife, whoever she might be, would be coming to his home under a sore disadvantage. A lover's heart never forgot its sorrow for the woman once truly loved.

The documents, papal dispensations . . .

The aged pontiff's position was that the Church could tolerate no living challengers to its history and tenets. Nor would it acknowledge demands, real or imagined, made by lesser spirits in the Holy Land. Enough pagan schisms and sects had arisen around heretics, without adding what these four creatures, however Christian their birth or mission to Palestine, might do.

Therefore, if they could not be killed, then they were to be released. Separately, one man at a time, and driven each in a different direction, so that they did not unite again. They were to be kept ignorant of all relics pertaining to the origins of their predecessors.

And in the case that there *were* some spiritual balance to be maintained—perhaps it would be right and proper to see that it was indeed kept. Not, of course, that the Church officially condoned such paganism. Matters such as this were best kept hidden from public knowledge.

To insure such secrecy and to oversee the pontiff's latter directives over the course of time, Walter of Kent and the Abbot Baldwin of Widdershaw Abbey were charged with the task of founding a new order. While in the elitist tradition of crusading orders already founded—the Knights Templars and the Hospitallers, the Knights of St. John—they would be *cruciati* of another type, who would follow these four scapegoats, so named after their animal predecessors under ancient Hebrew law, and observe them from near and far. Who by papal approval were to take whatever action was needed to accomplish their directives, and would never let their true work be known to those outside the order.

In this endeavor, at least, knight and churchman were truly brothers. The Knights of the Order of The Quorum.

Such was the last Celestine III, this Servant of Servants, would ever deign to speak on the subject.

He wishes us to be mercenaries in our own land, Walter thought. *Even against our own people, if it comes to that.*

The responsibility was an awesome one. Best entrusted to a man of iron. And if it had fallen to him by his decision to tread a stone stairway beneath a profaned church, then so be it.

Abbot Baldwin had consented to letting Brother Maynard write a complete record of what the carved black stones had to say. The history, and warnings passed along by oral tradition, supposedly revealed to a priestess of those who called themselves the blackheaded people. The embodiment of their deity of war was to be kept from the land's rulers if disaster were to be avoided. The embodiment of their deity of famine was to be kept from their own harvest. The embodiment of their deity of pestilence was to be kept from a barren woman . . .

And Walter crushed shut his eyes, wondering if his wife might not still be with him had she been barren. Yet . . . had she been, and thereby unable to bear him sons, would he have loved her all the same? When nights felt this long, he knew he would have.

Death made war on all things.

For a time he considered casting everything, letters and manuscripts alike, into the fireplace. Let them burn, let these dreadful secrets turn to smoke while he washed his hands clean of the whole affair.

But in cowardice there was no honor, whose code had determined his life before he was even born.

For honor, too, was forged in iron.

III
Children of an Ill-Chosen God

*Ambition and unscrupulousness have waxed
so powerful, that religion is thought to consist, not so much in respecting the writings
of the Holy Ghost, as in defending human
commentaries.*

—Baruch Spinoza

22

Saying good-bye to St. Louis hadn't been nearly as tough as Paul anticipated. Immersed in the whirlwind of preparations for sudden departure, he found it easy to overlook all that this town had meant to him. His best airshift times yet, his largest audiences, his favorite co-workers. The flowering of his confidence and skills into peak form.

For every high, a low, however. All had been circumvented by the worst days of his life. Human nature was often merciful, allowing memories of the best of times and the forgetting of the pain; nostalgia was the greatest polish of all. But not this time, not for him. He had gone too far.

After narrowly pulling back from allowing—or directing—a taste of mortality to go ripping into Craig Sheppard, Paul had sprinted home to consult Donny Dawson's itinerary. Hours and many phone calls later, that evening he had managed to catch the man at his entourage's hotel in Kansas City. They would be there two days before hopping west to Topeka on Friday. If Paul was serious about joining him, why didn't he spend the next couple of days wrapping up whatever business needed attention in St. Louis, then catch up with them in Topeka? On, say, Saturday?

It sounded fine, perfect. The way things were degenerating on the home front, he could no longer trust himself. Not that he was foolish enough to believe he could run from the wild talent that had taken him over inside; it would always be there, following as surely as a shadow. But at least he could run from the circumstances that brought out the worst in him, and run *to* something that might set him on a higher level of self-understanding. For whoever, or whatever, wherever in the cosmos, had seen fit to dump this on him, had shown less-than-perfect wisdom by withholding the psychic owner's manual.

Sanctuary, ready and waiting. All that remained was to sever the ties to the past, a life he still lived but could no longer lead.

He called KGRM and quietly resigned to David Blane, who did not push, who did not even sound surprised. A simple matter, really, without fanfare. Normally, when someone left, it was cause for as much of the KGRM staff as could attend to make a pilgrimage to Tappers or Blueberry Hill and send the departee into his future with a hangover worthy of the occasion. But there would be none of that this time, at Paul's request, the less said the better, just forget I was ever born.

He sold his furniture and the appliances that would not be needed in Oklahoma City. Gathered the rest of his belongings into garment bags and suitcases and cardboard boxes. Instructed the post office to hold his mail until notification as to where to forward it. He closed out his bank account and canceled his apartment lease, thereby forfeiting the remainder of September's rent and his damage deposit; bloodsuckers. He called St. Francis Medical Center, told them his temporary leave of absence from the volunteer program was to become permanent.

And on and on they fell, the dominoes representing life as he knew it.

Oddly enough, the one that caused the most sentimental regret was getting rid of Calvin and Hobbes. Gerbils, silly pets anyway, but he had grown attached, wanted them to have a good home. In the dead of night, when Captain Quaalude rode the airwaves, Paul let himself into the station, quietly leaving the gerbils—plus aquarium, food, and extra cedar-shaving bedding—beneath Sherry Thomason's reception desk. A note explained this bequest, and just so she wouldn't worry too much about his frame of mind, that his humor was as warped as ever, he told her it was the next best thing to a do-it-yourself chinchilla ranch.

He got phone calls from most of the station staff, all of whom expressed varying degrees of perplexity over this sudden departure, these even stranger plans for his immediate future. But all wished him well. Early Friday afternoon, Peter Hargrove toted over a case of ale and the two of them got quietly hammered together, one last time. Paul expected lectures, mind games, pleas to reconsider, and he got all of them, though in neither the quantity nor the vehemence for which he had braced. And when Peter left, taking the few remaining ales with him like surviving comrades, he and Paul hugged fiercely—first time they had ever done so, never like this, as if they were sad brothers separated by a war. Wicked Uncle Pete wasn't such a badass after all.

Conspicuous by her absence, though, was Lorraine. She never called, never dropped by, and quite possibly this was for the best. Final partings grow too messy when guilt lurks beneath their surface. Best to leave her behind to her own life and his past, recalling as their last encounter that plaintive reaffirmation of friendship, when he had known what lay ahead and she had not. It was not perfect, far from it, but he could live with it. It was, at least, dignified, and damn that adult thirst for dignity anyway.

Saturday, finally, the fourteenth, and Paul had managed a remarkably effective amputation from St. Louis, he and this city of gateways no longer a part of each other. He left for Topeka at nine o'clock, a faint cool in the September morning air. Virginal foretaste of autumn, that season of change, of turning away. That season for seeking shelter.

The city fell behind him and I-70 unrolled westward, and KGRM played his farewell from St. Louis. Pink Floyd in an eerie, brooding mood, bidding him welcome, welcome to the machine.

"I'll leave it up to you, Paul. Would you prefer to sit back and observe for a while? Or would you like to jump right in your first night?"

So far as Paul could tell, Donny wasn't leaning one way or the other, was just barely concealing his excitement at having him there in the first place. With all due modesty, this was understandable. Wasn't every day Donny got to team up with someone of equivalent talent, and guide it toward the fulfillment of its potential. He had made Paul's status apparent from the very beginning. There was to be no *Mister Dawson* between them, ever, as was the case with so many of the employees. It was to be *Donny*, always, first-name basis flowing both ways.

"I've already seen how the revival runs," Paul said. "I'd just as soon start earning my keep right off the bat."

Donny smiled, nodded his approval, patted him companionably on the shoulder.

Two hours remained before showtime, and the civic center buzzed with the same sort of activity that preceded all those untallied concerts Paul had attended. The technical crew checking and double-checking cords, cables, connections. The synth player stepping through various organ and brass and string patches in the Korg's memory bank. The pianist limbering up his fingers with scales and arpeggios. The piano's pickup mike was run through a digital delay, doubling the signal and detuning it fractionally so that it could sound like an old-time, honky-tonk upright. The vocal soloist was onstage doing a soundcheck for her own satisfaction; Laurel Pryce, Donny said her name was, stepping out from the choir for the featured spot ever since Amanda had gone to El Salvador. Paul remembered her performance from St. Louis, had to acknowledge he would remember *anyone* looking like her. Behind her, the ARM OF THE APOSTLE banner was being hung across the purple backdrop, until it draped just so. The last of the folding chairs were being eyeballed and straightened into precise rows, lacking only their audience.

All for the man in white, and the salvation he brought to anyone who would but take his hand. *And mine too, now, and just how did it happen this fast?* Paul and Donny were seated in the middle of the auditorium, and he tried to picture all these seats filled. A heady rush, nothing at all like the apprehension of a radio booth. Here you saw their eyes. Their needs.

"We need to have some subtlety in the way you work the crowd tonight. Or more specifically, the people I'll be calling out." Donny gave a smile Paul had seen a hundred times before. "Because, unless I'm way off base, you really would rather remain in the background. Am I right on that?"

Nodding, "Pretty much. I never really was the type to step into spotlights."

"That's a very Christian attitude." Donny grinned. "You *are* a rare one. And I count myself blessed for that, I hope you know. How about we head up to the stage for a minute?"

Donny led the way down one of the main aisles, then veered around stage left at floor level to disappear behind the entire vast platform. A few more folding chairs had been set up back here, grouped around a small TV monitor.

"This is where Ricky and Robby—they're two of my ushers—

spend the first part of the rally. Oh, they'll pitch in for other things as needed, especially if we're running short someplace else, but when it comes time for the healings and the blessings, that's when they come out front."

"So you want me to stay back here with them?"

"I think that would be easiest. Then, when you hear that we'll be starting to minister to the people, you come on out around to the front." Donny took the lead again, up the tiered steps, along the stage to center back. "You'll need to keep somewhere along here, and watch the crowd so you can tell where each one is coming from. I'd like you to be there to greet them by the time they reach the top of the stairs, and you can bring them on over to center stage. Comfort them, reassure them. A lot of them may be nervous, even frightened. I wouldn't know what to tell you any more specifically than that, because each one is going to be a bit different from the last. But I think . . . that you know the one thing to do in each case—don't you?"

Paul nodded. He stood beneath lights and ceiling girders, dwarfed by the enormity of this place. Yet feeling that he had never had greater purpose. He knew exactly what to do. Looking out over the regiments of empty seats, so much potential out there for pain and desperation, loss and searching. So much expectation . . .

Bless me, Donny, for I am here.

Midshow, exhaustion competing with heightened anticipation.

The drive from St. Louis to Topeka had taken nearly six and a half hours, and upon arrival, there had been the matter of chasing down the Dawson entourage. Paul had managed precious little sleep the night before, tossing and turning with the frightened excitement of new beginnings. Night had been eternal, while morning had come far too soon.

He could sleep now, *now*, of all the inopportune times. Wrung out in his folding chair and best suit, the crush of noise from the stage and beyond a most peculiar lullaby. The music and Donny's voice of thunder and the exultant throng he commanded, all became a whirlpool of singular magic, womblike as it enveloped. The purple background rippled, subtly hypnotic, and Paul's chin played tag with his chest. Head drifting down, down, a stolen moment, then snapping up again, no problem, just resting my eyes.

At least he was not alone, no need to fear sleeping through his cue. Ricky and Robby, an odd pair. They spoke little, which seemed in keeping with their burly size, yet the phrase *strong silent types* did not comfortably fit this line of work. They looked too refined, with that immaculately cropped hair and those tailored suits, and in all honesty, the only thing to distinguish one from the other was that Ricky had a moustache.

Will I look just like them after a year of this? It was a concern.

How strange to think that a mere four nights ago these two had been escorting him offstage. Briskly, firmly, no time wasted. He had made his boss look bad. Odd situation. Sprout five o'clock shadows on these two and stick them in jeans and muscle shirts, and they would make a fine pair of tavern bouncers.

Come to think of it, now that he had time to really take in his environment and new co-workers, a *lot* of Donny's staff looked like these two. Ricky and Robby were just the blow-up versions, the rest scaled down, scurrying about with their offering buckets and their questionnaires. Well-groomed, well-dressed, cheerful and unobtrusive smiles, eyes wide and happy. And vacuous? No, now that was cruel. The men wore, for the most part, dark suits. The women wore longish skirts and blouses whose buttons would never see more than the very top one unfastened for public display.

One big happy conservative family.

There were a couple exceptions. Laurel Pryce, for one. Female vocal soloist. Paul had roused to attention during her songs, watching attentively on the small backstage closed-circuit monitor. Tall, blond hair set off by a blue dress, no shortage of athletic sensuality here.

Then there was Gabe Matthews; he alone seemed to possess much sense of business instinct. Opportunities seized and opponents mastered, kind of startling until you got used to it. But in this ocean of calm complacency, Gabe was a refreshing change of pace.

All of which led to the inevitable sense of doubt: *What am I doing here? I don't know these people. I haven't belonged to a church since I was a kid. I don't even know that I believe all the same things they do, all the fundamentalist dogma.*

Now wasn't the time for this, and he tried to usher it from his head. First-time jitters, he had just undertaken a major life change and had barely stopped to breathe. He was forgetting the first time he had taken the air in a professional capacity—college amateur radio didn't count—at a small Indiana station. So nervous he'd first had to void his stomach into the toilet.

What was he doing here? Trying to make a difference, the safest way he knew to go about it, and the internal pep talk could not have come at a better time. . . .

"BECAUSE I'VE GOT THE FEELING—AND I'VE GOT IT ON GOOD AUTHORITY—THAT DOCTOR JESUS IS GOING TO BE DOING SOME HEALING HERE TONIGHT, AMEN!"

Donny's voice rolled over the crowd and invoked its roar of approval. Paul was standing automatically, stretching muscles from the hours spent seated and confined to self, then following Ricky and Robby, and this was it, his moment to shine. Shine, while keeping that light to himself, between him and Donny and the lucky souls who would never know what precisely had touched them. Now was the time to deny self and live for others, to put love for strangers to the test.

He felt the external Paul Handler withdraw, shrinking willingly, even gratefully, from the glare of stage lights and the waving arms. He swam away on a hot molten sea of light, leaving behind the elemental core that functioned not on rationality but on intuition and feelings and empathy. It was this Paul who smiled confidently at Donny, so much larger-than-life in his white suit and theatrical sweat. It was this Paul who took his place of duty near the back center of the stage, who waited until Donny plucked a name from midair as if planted by some celestial cue card, and then Paul went striding across the stage to help the first callout. An elderly woman who had to be guided by a friend because she could not see well enough on her own, oh those cataracts . . .

Paul took her by one sticklike arm, her thin flesh loose and pale and wrinkled as parchment, and he was concentrating, staring for a moment into the milky transluscence of her eyes. The empathy was there in abundance and she had become an open book. Her terror of failure as clear as a sour smell. This was the Supreme Court of healing she was dealing with, her avenue of last resort, for she was more than apprehensive about having the cataracts removed by surgery, she was dead-set against, because what did doctors know anyway, the butchers?

Like a slate wiped free of chalk, a whitewashed wall, Paul felt no taint of the anger he hoped to have left behind in St. Louis. A state of purity had been reached, the price a severance from the past, but well worth it, he could accede this in all honesty. And he could flow from himself to the old woman without her even catching on— blindsiding her, as it were—for all he was to her was hired help, certainly not the man with the touch of Heaven in his fingertips. He could let it run full circuit back into himself without so much as a thank-you expected in return. . . .

Because that wasn't a part of the bargain.

By the time he got her safely delivered to Donny and those blessed hands, the woman's emotions were in such a peak of rapture that she collapsed at his touch, into the waiting arms of Ricky and Robby, and the veil had been lifted from her eyes.

Glory, glory.

A subterfuge? Perhaps. Little white lies, intended only for the benefit of those who need not worry, who need only to rejoice in restoration. Cheering crowd and hot lights and thunderstorm of music aside, Paul knew that he was surely doing what was right and good and proper.

So bring on the next, and the next. And keep them coming.

23

Topeka on a late Saturday night, and Gabe's hotel room was lit only by the bluish glow of the television. Mood lighting with a touch of the unearthly, this seemed appropriate. The late late show, some black and white movie, plotless and pointless, so far as Gabe could tell. He paid no attention. He'd been unable to find CNN, had left it on this channel in mild despair.

He was shirtless, propped up on the still-made bed against its pillows, absently toying with the razor blade around his neck. Tap the keen edge, gently now, appreciate its power. He traced one finger along his collarbones. Running out of fresh skin to cut there, the little vertical scars lined parallel, end to end on both bones, like the hash marks of some ancient army veteran.

The moment was ripe for a cut, just a little one to get him through the night, but sometimes discretion was the better part of honor. Leave it alone, company was coming, very *important* company. It would not be good form to open the door while still bleeding.

Gabe let the blade dangle against his chest, and instead went for another totem, resting on the nightstand. The truest link to his parents he owned.

A rearview mirror, early 1960s Ford vintage, glass smashed into a thousand fragments but miraculously still in the frame. He had been only four when it got this way, and did not recall the day at all, knew of it only by secondhand stories and a yellowed clipping from the newspaper of some small Michigan town. They said his father had been holding this in his cold hand, when the wreckage was cleared away. Dad, trying to beat the train at an intersection without barricades, Mom probably scolding him in that moment; Gabe thought he remembered her frequent criticisms of Dad's driving. But what did he know, really? Can four-year-old orphans trust the accuracy of their memories? Those fragile glimpses into a life that was less substantial than a dream, snippets, probably one for every fragment of mirror glass.

Gabe held it, stared into its depths, *Dad, did you see yourself die?* He could hate the man in such moments, this man he barely remembered and who had condemned him to a childhood and an adolescence in a state home. Look at that fractured image, try to find the youngster behind those adult eyes. No wonder he had never been adopted. He had never been a cuddly child.

But he *had* grown up extraordinarily self-reliant. Could a lesser man have so efficiently dealt with the situation he had encountered this past Wednesday at Donny's house? Unlikely.

Edie Carson, formerly trusted nurse, allowing some mystery man to shoot photos of Amanda. Only blind luck—Gabe's having to courier the film to the studio—had prevented this scheme from reaching its intended conclusion. Whatever that had been; motives were foggy, and the man *had* gotten away with his camera, and Edie certainly was not talking.

Gabe had been unable to trace the man down, but it was not for lack of trying. He had tapdanced a verbal routine with local emergency rooms—surely the fellow could not have plunged three stories and escaped unscathed, not the way he'd landed—but Gabe had come up empty-handed. Whoever the man was, he had not sought local medical attention, and thereby had failed to finger himself.

Dealing with Edie's body had been the worst problem. An impromptu burial was out of the question. Too many hours of daylight left, and not enough time in his day as it was. The temporary solution was not long in coming, though.

He twisted her head back around so it faced front again, then temporarily hid her in a closet. Went home to his apartment to retrieve a large trunk lately used only for junk storage. He brought it back empty to Donny's and stuffed Edie inside, a tight fit, folding her one way and another until he could shut the lid and padlock it.

He had wanted to shed tears but would not allow it, what was done was done. Tears would serve no purpose.

Next he carted the trunk over to the cafeteria that served the mailroom employees and the dorms. Edie's final stop—for the time being—was the walk-in refrigerator, a back corner, little re-arranging required. He boldly left a sign taped to it, PROPERTY OF GABRIEL MATTHEWS. DO NOT DISTURB, and felt confident none of the kitchen peons would bother with it.

Rank had its privileges. A man with the run of this place could get away with murder.

Of course, she could not stay there indefinitely. Rigor mortis would run its cycle and depart, but he could not prevent her even-tual decay. For now, though, time to spare, worry about it when he had more time.

Back at the house, Gabe had phoned a glazier to arrange a quick repair on the window the photographer had broken in his haste. Amanda had to be dealt with, temporarily ferried to another bed-room with all her health care items, and most of her smell had aired away by the time the glazier arrived.

Gabe had also placed an indignant call to Doctor Irv Preston to raise hell about the unreliability of one of the nurses. Edie Carson, nowhere to be found, Amanda lying comatose and untended in an empty house. Preston made profuse apologies and promised to have her replaced by the next day, and if he had any say about it, Edie would never work in Oklahoma City again.

A regular prophet, that Irv.

The day had ended as smoothly as could be expected, the lies and the coverups seamlessly intact. And the longer the day wore on, it seemed reasonable to assume that if the photographer were going to cause trouble, he would already have done so. Nobody waits until tomorrow to report witnessing a murder. Likely, this stranger had had something illegal up his own sleeve—a little blackmail, perhaps—and had gotten ice-cold feet after realizing what he was letting himself in for. The longer Gabe thought about it, the more this made sense.

Yet the question remained, having occurred to him a full day after the killing: *Why did I do it in the first place?*

Quite frankly, there had been no need.

Paul, that elusive object of worldwide search, had already been located. And if his identity as one of the four Scapegoats had yet to be ascertained, it was but a formality, Gabe had seen the man's ability with his own eyes, *had been on the receiving end of that awesome power.* For Gabe, maintaining a cover with Dawson Ministries was no longer vital.

I was confused. Who I was. What I was . . .

Where my loyalty lay.

Staring into the mirror, all those eyes staring back. He was Gabe. He was legion.

I need . . . help.

No. No. No. No. Too late for regrets now, too late for doubt. He had covered his tracks well, every act that of a logical, thinking man, precisely what he had needed to be in those moments. It would be his secret, with no need to inform Gavin. Gavin would worry needlessly. A thoughtful son protects his father from needless worry, and father is as father does.

Gabe pulled on a crisp shirt, tucked it in. And waited for that knock at the door.

It came, at last, and he answered.

Gavin.

He stepped in from the hallway, and Gabe flicked on the room light, and for a moment they stared. Five years had been a long time, but time and distance melted with those welcoming smiles and the fierce embrace. Backs were slapped. Gabe had missed this man, guiding light that he had been. A voice on the phone was simply not enough.

Gavin Bainbridge had changed little. Tall, still slender until his shoulders flared wide and blocky. His long face held a few more creases, perhaps, and his lank hair more gray. But time had been kind, and tonight his eyes twinkled.

Gabe glanced at the door. "No one else?"

Gavin shook his head. "I made the trip alone. It was just to observe, mind you. I need no help for that. Good *heavens,* whatever happened to your face?"

Gabe touched the scabbed furrows, four in a row, a moment's indiscretion in the sickroom of Amanda Dawson. "I had a bad dream. I tend to thrash when I have bad dreams."

Gavin chuckled like a naughty uncle. "It *looks* as though you've had a tiff with some lass."

Gabe took his jacket, hung it in the room closet, then ushered him to a chair, sit, sit. A half-hour earlier, he had had room service send up a bottle of brandy, and poured. Celebration. There was no need for a toast. A toast would have trivialized their find.

"Were you in the audience tonight?" Gabe asked. "I looked for you on the monitors but I couldn't find you."

"I was there."

"So you saw him. Paul Handler."

"I did indeed." Gavin smiled gently. Wisdom. "Rather an anticlimactic moment, after waiting twenty-eight years. But I believe we have our man."

Gabe, beaming, "His background checks?"

"Perfectly." Gavin leaned back, sipped the brandy, shut his eyes. Opened. "Paul Handler was born on Friday, November twenty-second, 1963. The same day your president Kennedy was shot. Also the same afternoon Albert Meerschaum died in front of me on that elevated train platform in Chicago. The records show that he was born about two weeks premature in a very sudden labor. His mother didn't even make it to the hospital in time. And it happened just blocks away from where Albert died." Gavin shook his head, the story still amazing to him. "I don't suppose we'll ever know what happened, precisely. But I suspect Albert Meerschaum passed the torch to Paul while he was still in utero. Clever, I'll give him that. I should've expected once Albert knew the truth he would become . . . rebellious."

Water under the bridge, though, all of it. They had done The Quorum proud. Much had ridden on Gavin Bainbridge's shoulders the last twenty-eight years, having lost track of one Scapegoat's lineage, but they had made up for it now. They had done the near-impossible, found a needle in a haystack the size of the world.

It had happened but rarely throughout Quorum history, a Scapegoat slipping his watchers. But when it did, the search would then be on, worldwide. All possible leads followed up, all avenues investigated regardless of how remote their corner of the globe. The Quorum had agents dispatched on every continent. And for more than twenty years after the loss of Albert Meerschaum, Scapegoat of Pestilence, the search had been fruitless. The proliferation of global mass media made the task handier in terms of centralization, but what a chore to follow them all.

Then, in 1986, a glimmer of hope. A tale of an unexplainable healing had wended its way out of rural Alabama. It had never been written up, this incident more than six years old, had never made the news. But people talk, stories get passed on, and word eventually reached Quorum ears in Atlanta. A field investigator was sent in the guise of a reporter to interview possible witnesses of the healing of a retarded boy crushed by a tractor. There had been sufficient validation to warrant an infiltration in the life of the supposed healer: one Donald Dawson, now doing big business as a television evangelist.

By that time, Gabe's training in Scotland had been completed by two years. His cover had been established as a ruthless stock trader in Chicago, and he was selected for the task. Infiltration of Dawson Ministries had been shamefully easy, simple manipulation of emotions and presenting himself as someone whose experience could benefit Donny. But Gabe could find nothing to indicate that Dawson had anything more up his sleeve than routine sleight of hand and powers of suggestion. Nevertheless, the assignment had come through from Gavin Bainbridge, now Quorum director: Stay with Dawson and keep your eyes open, potential value may yet come of this.

For five years, nothing. Then a media flurry in St. Louis, the spontaneous recovery of eight victims of a hit-and-run. The Quorum had analyzed it—computer hackers tapping into hospital records—but had been unable to determine any common links. One thing was clear, though: Something unexplainable and unprecedented was going on in St. Louis. Someone, somewhere, with a unique ability he or she may have only the barest understanding of. Given its more lethal aspects, the assimilation of such a talent could not be an easy process.

The directive had gone out from Gavin Bainbridge to Gabriel Matthews. Of all Quorum operatives, Gabe was in the best position to move on this. Maneuver Donny Dawson into a high position of visibility in the St. Louis area, and maybe, just maybe, it might smoke out the true Scapegoat.

Wonder of wonders. It appeared to have worked. He had arrived on their doorstep like a lost babe, this last Scapegoat. His brothers and sisters scattered the world over—one in Sicily, one in Ethiopia, one in Argentina.

With the absentee right here in Topeka.

"How do you want me to proceed with Paul?" Gabe said.

"Just get him to trust you, so you don't have to worry about being surprised by what he might do." Gavin shook his head sadly. "You can rarely level with these people as to who and what they truly are. They feel freakish enough as it is. I found that out twenty-eight years ago with Meerschaum. They're tragic enough without adding to their burdens any sooner than you have to."

Gabe, reeling within, quietly pinched himself until the pain flared red, *Worthy and pure, must be worthy and pure.* "You mean to let him continue what he's doing? As I've understood it, this'll make the first time his kind has done so much healing on such an—an accelerated level. Are you sure that's wise?"

Gavin spread his hands, palms up. "I don't see as you have much choice. You can't force him out of it if this is something he wishes to do. Decisions like that must come from him." His voice became grave. "But remember. There's a duality to be maintained here. It will *not* merely consist of healings. You say he's admitted already having had experiences with the other half. There will be more. I think it best to let him discover that on his own, as much as you find prudent. But Gabe . . . ?

"Whatever you do—*don't get in his way at those times.*"

Gabe shook his head, his understanding total, with pity and respect and fear and above all, the awe. Ye gods, how many men who had walked this earth got a chance to touch living infinity? And of them, how few were put in charge of it? *Nergal, lord of healing, lord of pestilence, I love you most of all.*

"You'll have to play this out as you see fit, Gabe, but here is what I suggest: If you need any manner of leverage within the ministry, you should wield that leverage over Dawson himself. In that way, you can still control Paul, indirectly. Do you think you can come up with a way of doing this?"

Several moments of thought, then, "I believe I can. Yes."

Gavin smiled broadly, with twinkling eyes. "Splendid."

They continued to talk for another hour, sitting across from each other at the round table while the brandy slowly went down. Such civility amid discussions of spiritual balance in the world, the precarious responsibility that was theirs alone. Gavin waxed mournful about the secrecy, their life of manipulating other lives, freaks—Scapegoats—who knew only that they were different, generally learning why only at sanity's end, when The Quorum thought it time for them to pass the torch to another, then live and die as any mortal. Such betrayal, not by stabbing them in the back, but by sins of omission: the withholding of heritage. Gabe empathized, putting it in terms he was more familiar with. Given his upbringing in state homes in Michigan, he had known plenty of adopted kids who never stopped hungering to know their roots. How much greater must it be magnified when, so far as you know, you are utterly alone in the world in your abilities? *There* was Hell.

*But no, Paul, you're not alone because I'm with you, and I'll guide
you as much as I can, and if you ask me to worship you, I'll drop to
my knees and do that too. Because I have seen you.*

The flurry of activity around Paul was considerable at the moment, given the pace of the tour, but Gabe knew the long-term
risks. In ten days or so they would be returning to Oklahoma City,
and Paul would eventually shed the innocence from his eyes. See
what was going on behind his back, under his nose. Right now he
was blinding himself, albeit willingly, to the fact that he was being
used. That Donny was as much as sticking a tap in him and draining
off what was needed. Someday he would see this, for while he may
have been naive, he was not stupid.

And I'll be there when it happens. I wouldn't miss it.

Gabe had wondered how to deal with a possibility that, thankfully, had not arisen this late night. What if Gavin had ordered him
to pull the plug on Dawson Ministries, or to let someone else take
over the task of overseeing now that Paul had been identified?
Which would not have been fair, Gabe had worked for this, had
earned the right to see it through. The answer, of course, had been
quick in presenting itself. . . .

This hotel was tall. This room had a balcony. *Come on out here,
Gavin, it's far too nice a night to sit inside. Have some brandy.* The
man was nearing sixty, likely Gabe could put him over the railing
before he knew what was happening, it would only be fair. What a
tremendous relief that it had not been necessary. So few people left
in this world could he say he truly loved.

"I must be going now. I've a flight back to catch, and I've not
slept in"—Gavin checked his watch—"nearly thirty hours."

Gabe helped him on with his jacket, fretting, then ushered him to
the door. To say good-bye now, well, who knew when they would
see each other again? Very firmly they clasped hands.

Gavin, looking into his deep-set eyes, "I was just two years
younger than you are now when I lost track of my charge. My rise
in The Quorum did not suffer for it. But *I* did." Hands, squeezing.
"Thank you, Gabe. You returned my pride. *Thank you.*"

He was brimming inside, and wanted to weep, so overjoyed this
mentor had not proved an obstacle. "Have I made you proud?"

And Gavin nodded, yes, yes, of course, proud.

Hands locked, "Then call me your son."

Gavin drew back a fraction, rising straighter, and Gabe pressed
hands tighter still while Gavin said, "We've gone over this before,

we are friends and we share a bond of duty like none other. But Gabe . . . we're not related."

He felt throat tightening, mouth drying, say it isn't so, and he trembled. "You gave my life meaning!" He needed to make the cut that would help him focus, attach the clamp that would calm his soul. Vital control, slipping through his fingers, no telling what he might do then. He breathed steadily, calm, focus, calm, then eased himself back from the brink with the sublime realization that frenzy was not the role he needed to play in this moment.

Ah, better.

And when he looked back to Gavin's wise old eyes, he saw reconsideration, a faint smile on those lips. "But inasmuch as you have proven yourself these years? Gabe? I could be no more proud if you *were* my son."

Gabe lowered to knees, kissed the back of one strong hand. It was all he needed to hear, and would suffice.

For now.

24

 Before leaving his room this evening, Paul barely recognized himself in the mirror. He had taken up residence in one of Dawson Ministries' dorms a few days before. And was greeting the weekend with the face of a familiar stranger.

His hair had been shorn; it barely reached the back of his neck now. His fingernails had been manicured, his teeth cleaned and polished. Every rough edge had been honed down into a smooth mellow gleam. He had been fitted for hand-stitched suits by the same tailor who stocked Donny's closet with white ones, and they fit like second skins.

Conformity. Paul never thought he would see the day when he wore it so comfortably, so willingly. The outer man alone, however. For nonconformity, he would match insides with anyone.

At the moment, though, his old autumn uniform of jeans and a clean sweatshirt was still the rule. A welcome link to a past that had been yanked from beneath him like a rug. Out for a walk tonight, old habits hard to break.

There was no pavement here, as he had trod in U City. No traffic lights, no blare of horns, no sirens. Neither bars, nor restaurants, nor hole-in-the-wall shops with secret treasures just past their doors. Very little discernible life at all out here on the compound. Pastoral. Grass and trees, with lights burning here and there in buildings, to ward off the night. An evening breeze ruffled his hair, or what remained of it, and he breathed it in. These were the final days of September, and while the days were still warm, night brought cool new delights. Summer had fallen.

The final leg of Donny's crusade tour, those five revivals in which Paul had taken part, could not have gone more successfully. Cataracts disappeared. Cancer cells died, to be voided with the rest of bodily wastes. Asthmatics were assured of a lifetime of easy breathing. Clubfeet were reformed. Sufferers of scoliosis felt their spines painlessly straightened. The Donny Dawson miracle machine had boldly gone where it had never gone before, and not one person was kept away from the stage if that was what they had come for.

A lot was getting accomplished onstage that Paul knew he would be credited for if his were the only hands on the one being healed. This required innovation, a new twist for whenever the ailment was noticeably physical. The prayer circle, eight hands latching onto the wreck of a body: Donny's, Paul's, and those of Ricky and Robby. Misdirection, a classic magician's trick. Paul could live with it; healing was the only thing to justify his existence. Sole redemption for the harm he had already caused.

Five revivals, averaging one every other night. Living out of a suitcase, *on tour*, a very rock and roll phrase, he liked the sound of it. Hellhounds on my trail, but I can outrun them, and it had all been very agreeable.

Yet over and done with all too quickly. He was settled again, and would those hellhounds think to sniff around here? Dear God, please let them pass on by.

Home was on the second—and top—floor of a long, narrow building with two wings. They called it a dormitory, but it was more upscale than that. Private rooms, carpeted, well-apportioned, and every three shared a bathroom with shower. In some ways, it was a throwback to the preapartment days of college, warehoused with a few dozen other rowdies who swapped skin magazines and smoked dope and smuggled in cases of beer and triggered seismic wars with their stereos and boasted of impossible sexual exploits. Except, in this place, there was none of that. These residents were generally polite, quiet, studious. The little rock and roll they did listen to was cheerily upbeat, blandly wholesome. Music for lobotomies, and Paul realized he would be spending a lot of time wearing headphones.

He had no problem with his room itself, nearly twice the size of standard dorm rooms he had seen, and no roommate with whom to halve things up. Plenty of room for his stereo and TV and books. A small alcove hung off one side, a tiny kitchenette with a half-size fridge and sink and two-burner hotplate. Enough to scrounge together a meal when he didn't feel like the cafeteria. To personalize the place, he slapped up a few posters that nobody could condemn as being too objectionable, and it helped, but not enough.

He sat in their midst, and they surrounded him, avatars of other days. Tear them down? He couldn't bring himself to do so, it would be the final admission that he could never live like a normal man again. Nearly twenty-eight years old, and he was having a tough enough time getting used to the idea as it was.

Sanctuary. Gilded prison of his own construction, enter at your own risk, and beware of wild mood swings.

But on the plus side, there had been no sudden deaths, no sproutings of ghastly disease beneath his hands. Time would restore balance to even the shakiest objectivity. He would grow used to it here, hopefully before he grew old.

He strolled onward, the moon fresh and chilly looking as it rose and gazed upon him like a forlorn eye. Dorms behind him, main offices and production studios ahead. The broad sidewalk in between, a solid creek, all tributaries branched from here. Paul saw someone walking it, a dark silhouette some twenty yards ahead, and he shifted himself so their paths would not cross. Call it shyness, call it antisocial, call it honest.

"Don't worry. I won't bite."

Had his game plan been that obvious? Gabe Matthews's voice, out of the evening gloom. Matters could be worse. At least with Gabe, there was no fear of some uncomfortable buddy-buddy routine being thrust upon you.

"Where are you headed?" Gabe asked.

Paul drew closer, sidewalk now. "Nowhere. Just walking. Aimless."

"Better not let Donny hear that. He'll think you've strayed from the straight and narrow path." Spoken with a snicker.

And what was this, a joke, out of Gabe? Pretty lame, agreed, but so far, Paul had gotten the feeling that Gabe's sense of humor had been left behind at his last known address. A joke—and at Donny's expense, no less. Closer still, and Paul could see how casually Gabe was dressed, another rarity. Jeans and a light flannel shirt.

"Don't you ever take a break from this place?" Paul said.

"I always mean to, but . . ." Then he hunched his shoulders, palms up, what's a guy to do? "I've got to run by Donny's. Why don't you keep me company? It's a long walk when you're not driving one of the golf carts."

Oh why not, and Paul fell into step beside him, west, toward the darkness of a thousand trees. Enchanted forest.

"Do you live on the grounds, here?" Paul said.

"No, I've got an apartment a couple miles away. It seems like I only use the place to sleep, anymore. I'm hardly ever there."

"A workaholic."

"Yeah, Donny's even used that word to describe me."

Paul shook his head. "He'll never use it to describe *me*. I don't even know what I'm supposed to do around here. I mean, I'll be around for the regular taped services, which takes care of Thursday nights, but all we're talking about there is a six-hour work week. What about the rest of the time?"

A wry smile. "You don't feel you're earning your twenty-five thousand per year, huh?"

"You know my salary?"

"I know just about everything that goes on around here. Sometimes I think I know more of what goes on than Donny does."

"Doesn't he resent that?"

Gabe shook his head. "No. It's what he pays me for. To free his mind so he can concentrate on other things. Higher things."

Paul nodded, scuffed alongside Gabe in several moments of contemplative silence, chew on that last one awhile. What Gabe had said made perfect sense, but it seemed so distinctly *worldly* to have to delegate so many responsibilities to another. As if, within the ministry that bore his name, Donny Dawson were merely a ceremonial head of state. Celestial royalty.

"You know, Paul," Gabe seeming to sense his thoughts, "if you understand one thing from the beginning, I think you'll find everything else a lot more agreeable here."

Paul turned, looked at him in profile: set face, tight jaw. "What's that?"

"This *is* a business." Gabe turned as well, measuring Paul with his eyes, then went on, smooth sailing. "It's a calling we all share, of course. We genuinely want to work good in peoples' lives, that should go without saying. But the ministry has no choice but to exist within twentieth-century American economics. We employ a lot of people, most of whom have families depending on them. We have to run things as efficiently as possible, and if we don't, then it all could break down and *nothing* would get done. That's where I fit in, making sure things run efficiently. For the good of all." A faint smile, almost with apology. "I hope you can understand that. Or at least accept it. And I hope it doesn't make me sound mercenary."

Paul shook his head; perhaps too readily, in retrospect. "No. It doesn't. It's just an eye-opener."

"I'd be a little worried about you if it weren't. But you have to remember: This isn't Camelot."

They walked in silence again, but it was no longer the uncomfortable silence of strangers. The hallmark of true rapport. This was easily the straightest anyone had dealt with him since coming aboard, and it was appreciated. No one enjoyed being kept in the dark regarding attitudes, policies, priorities. Might as well be a circus freak then; do your trick, make it good, then back up with the tarp to hide you from innocent eyes.

"Are you okay on this?" Gabe asked, and Paul said yes, he was. Then, "How are you liking it in the dorm so far?"

The hesitation must have given him away, and Paul knew he would have to remember one thing: Gabe was undoubtedly one sharp guy, skilled in the art of reading every nonverbal nuance. Unease turned to relief when Gabe broke into rich laughter.

"Be honest, now," Gabe was teasing. "Thou shalt not lie, and all that."

Paul never knew he could squirm and walk so well at the same time. "It's not quite what I thought it would be."

"Now *there's* diplomacy in action." Another chuckle. "I don't blame you. Between the two of us? I think there are more anal-retentives back there than Freud saw in his entire career. But you didn't hear that from *me*, all right?"

Paul laughed, quite loudly, and oh how good it felt. To cut loose like that, unexpectedly, surrendering to the grand guffaw. Laughter, the best medicine, he had needed this badly.

They passed beneath a shadow canopy of overhanging branches. The trees were getting thicker this far back, dark and hulking, guardians of sylvan secrets with the patience of generations. Spears of moonlight lanced through, dappled by trembling leaves. The enchanted forest indeed. But if you believed in enchantment, it mandated a belief in the darker corners of the world, from that there was no escape. The two must, by necessity, coexist.

As without, so within, and why ruin this perfectly pleasant walk with such introspection, anyway? He had a lifetime to fret over his own personal yin and yang.

"Back at the dorms?" Paul said. "I've been wondering, where did they all come from? They can't all be like me, I know that. And it's not like they're going to classes."

Gabe shook his head. He stooped to pick up a Styrofoam coffee cup, flattened on the sidewalk. Spotless place, this was certain.

"They all have their own stories, and they all work for us in some capacity. A lot of them, both men and women, are ushers. Some work in the cafeteria, a few in the mailroom. Some in the production studios or with the camera crews, or they just work on the grounds themselves, custodial staff. A lot goes into keeping this place running, and they're a big part of it. As far as why they're here, instead of on their own someplace, well—again, they each have their own reasons, I'm sure. Some have come from unstable homes . . . mostly the younger ones. A few are into some communal living ideal, and this is the closest they've found that agrees with their religious values. Some of the older ones, maybe around your age, have had trouble adjusting to full-fledged adult responsibilities. They're easing themselves into it."

"You think I belong in that category?" Paul asked.

Gabe stopped for this one, peering at Paul through the gloom. Leaves whispered above, beside, behind. "Not at all," a firm shake of his head. "Besides. Your circumstances are more than a little extraordinary."

Paul grinned crookedly. "Just checking."

"And some of them," Gabe said, continuing, "came entirely because of Donny himself. You've met the Durbin brothers over there by now, Dougie and Terry?"

"Oh yeah, those two." Paul grinned, shaking his head. The Durbin brothers were blond hulks, from hill country someplace east. Living endorsements for prenatal care and amniocentesis, here's what happens if you ignore them. Not the brightest of lads.

"Dougie's a cable puller for one of the cameras, and Terry works in the mailroom—but they are *fanatics* on the subject of Donny Dawson."

And as long as they were on the subject, denizens of Dawson Ministries, why not, go ahead: "Can I ask you about someone else, in specific?"

A cocked eyebrow. "Who?"

"Laurel Pryce. Why is she here?"

"Aaaaah, Laurel. Our Laurel." Gabe teased out the name, and he sounded light enough, but had he stiffened for just an instant?

Maybe. Maybe he had. Designs on her himself, or something else? "She went through some personal tragedies a little over a year ago. She's very committed to her music. We're what she needs right now, and we'll help her however we can, she's extremely talented. Beyond that—maybe you should ask her yourself. It's not really my place to talk. Why? Are you interested?"

Paul grinned, full of mystery. "Just checking, again."

Gabe nodded, said nothing; sort of a tacit approval in Paul's estimation. Ministry grounds or not, hormones would be as active here as anywhere, though not necessarily acted *upon* quite as frequently. Paul saw nothing wrong with upholding his quota, so long as intentions were reasonably honorable.

He walked with Gabe until the back of Donny's house came into unobstructed view. And by the time they split to go their separate ways and Paul began to backtrack, he was feeling that perhaps he had severely misjudged Gabriel Matthews. First impressions may be lasting, but it doesn't mean they are always correct. Gabe's initial impression had been one of aloof excellence, steeled by self-confidence and no need for humor.

He still wasn't the loosest of guys, but neither was he so tight-assed he squeaked. Probably just very guarded, one of those people who had to be known awhile before they would relax and open up a little. And while he obviously took his duties here seriously, it appeared, surprise, that he regarded the whole situation with just a sprinkling of irreverence.

Which would keep one, more often than not, from developing an accelerated case of megalomania.

This isn't Camelot.

No. It was not, and exactly what it was, Paul could not begin to say. But whatever it may turn out to be, it was good to have finally found a friend.

25

After he left Paul, Gabe continued on toward Donny's house. Paul's footsteps faded into the background, his silhouette quickly consumed by path, trees, darkness.

Twenty minutes, had it been, since running into each other back there? Twenty, maybe twenty-five. Gavin would have been proud of the speed with which he had operated. Successfully. Gabe knew it, could see inside Paul's head, that revision of opinion that made all the difference in the world. *He trusts me now. He'd come to* me *with a problem before he would Donny.*

Gabe had spent the days contemplating Paul, studying him from afar, this fellow who was anything but typical Dawson Ministries material. Paul may very well have been moral, spiritual in his own way, but his spirituality seemed far less restrictively conservative. Which meant he did not quite fit in with the atmosphere of the dorm. Square peg, round hole, and while the square pegs generally will not have it any other way, a little acceptance now and then is still needed to soothe their souls.

And when someone hovers in that lonely realm of self, it's not difficult to draw him in. Level with him in a way no one else does. Make a joke or two at the expense of the nearest sacred cow. Nurture a few laughs with conspiratorial overtones. And he will look upon you as a kindred soul.

Yes, it had been manipulative, but it had not been unkind. This had been no charade, no painted smile given to someone Gabe could only despise. It had merely been a shortcut. Paul had no idea what he needed, and someday Paul would thank him. Profusely.

From the dogpen beyond the swimming pool, Adam and Eve yapped their fool heads off at Gabe's approach. They had always hated him. An essentially stupid breed, the Irish setter, but they were fundamentally brighter than their master. *You see through me, don't you? Donny never has. You see the person, not the role he plays.* And yet if he were to throw them steaks, tenderized with a rubdown of strychnine, they would eat. He could never do it, of course, too much respect for their insight. What good fortune they could not speak.

Gabe keyed the lock of Donny's back door, just off the porch, and let himself in. In the kitchen he found the waste can, tossed the flat Styrofoam cup picked up earlier, and then tracked Donny to the TV room. Charlton Heston on the six-foot Sony, forever young and righteous while leading the children of Israel out of Pharoah's bondage. *The Ten Commandments*, predictably, one of Donny's favorite tapes. Gabe saw it as an interesting curiosity. His own tastes ran to *Beauty and the Beast*. Sympathy for the outcast, now there was escapism. Major heartbreak when CBS had taken that show off, but immortality was guaranteed through syndication.

Before entering, drawing Donny's attention, Gabe touched the small envelope in his shirt pocket. A few tiny lumps met his fingertips, nothing more. It would never be noticed.

Donny cut the sound by half when Gabe entered—he was expected, had called a while ago. Gabe sat. Small talk, minor daily trivialities, most ministry-related. Donny spoke of Juliette Sullivan, the replacement nurse Irv Preston had hired to take over for Edie Carson, missing in action. Donny couldn't figure this one out, so strange, so unexpected. Alice Ward had assured them that the girl had relieved her that Wednesday a couple weeks back, eight o'clock, as usual. What had transpired later would probably remain a mystery. Maybe, Donny mused, she was not nearly as reliable as she had appeared and had cleared out for greener pastures. At least she had stolen nothing but trust.

Frankly, this was uncomfortable, and Gabe forged ahead. He was pumped, primed, get this moving while resolve was strong.

"Guess who I walked over here with," he said.

Slumped into the sofa, Donny wasted little thought. "Who?"

"Paul."

Immediate attention. "Is anything wrong?"

Oh sure, worry about this latest acquisition only as he pertains to the ministry, a commodity, no idea he's the most miraculous human being you will ever hope to meet. The anger rippled, and Gabe held it in with a gentle smile.

"No. Nothing. He was just lonely, I think." Gabe thoughtfully touched a finger to one corner of his mouth. "My guess is he's feeling some culture shock in being here. And it's not helped by the fact that he has so little to keep him busy."

"Well. That makes sense, doesn't it?" Donny grabbed a glass from his end table, tipped it to his lips for a trickle of melted ice. "We'll just have to find something for him, then. I suppose I should spend a little more time with him, too, now that we're home again."

"I think he'd appreciate that," Gabe, watching Donny suck on ice, oh please, just for once in your life see beyond the surface. But no, no, better for your sake if you don't. "When are you planning to approach him about Mandy?"

"Early next week, I guess." Donny drew a shaky breath, lots of apprehension. "But we've *got* to make sure his loyalty is with us first. We've got to be certain. This is a lot touchier than having him work the crowds, you know."

Gabe nodded, wanting to scream, *Then spend some* time *with him, you idiot!* Holding it in with admirable restraint, focusing instead on the rattle of Donny's glass, the clink of ice cubes; such persistence in trying to drain an empty vessel.

"You've made me thirsty." Gabe rose from his chair. "Can I get you a refill?"

Donny smiled, flattered, and pressed the squat glass into Gabe's outstretched hand. "Thank you. Ginger ale."

"Coming right up." Gabe left for the kitchen, and behind him, the TV volume boosted back to where it had been. Donny and his remote control. Every bit as wondrous as his onstage miracles.

Gabe set the glass on the counter, brought one down from the cabinet for himself. Appearance's sake only. He fed a few ice cubes into each, splashed in ginger ale from the bottle.

He then pulled the tiny envelope from his shirt pocket and shook its contents into one palm. Five transluscent green capsules, each about the size of a chili bean and containing 500 milligrams of the sleeping aid chloral hydrate. Standard hypnotic adult dosage was one or two capsules taken thirty minutes before bedtime. Donny was six-foot-one, and since it would not do to have him rousing prematurely tonight, five caps didn't seem to be pushing it to a dangerous extreme.

They had come by way of Irv Preston. A phoned complaint about insomnia, and his pharmacy of choice promptly had them ready. Irv was good about that. He would have prescribed morphine for Elvis.

The last item from the envelope was a new X-acto blade, sheathed in plastic. One by one, he lanced a quick slit into each capsule, squeezed the liquid into Donny's drink, dropped the flattened caps into the garbage disposal to dissolve. He swirled the drink to mix. Behold, the notorious Mickey Finn. More or less.

Gabe served it with a smile, the obedient valet. Donny emptied it cooperatively while the two of them watched the movie in silence, and his head gradually began to dip toward his chest. Two valiant efforts to shake it off, one muttered complaint about being sleepy—though he did not sound worried—and that was that. By the time Moses brought the stone tablets down from the mountain and discovered the Israelites indulging in hedonism, Donny had gone down for the count. Breathing slow, deep, steady as clockwork.

Gabe took their empty glasses to the kitchen, thoroughly rinsed Donny's with hot water, then slipped them both into the dishwasher. You could never take too many precautions. Back in the TV room, he gazed sorrowfully at Donny's unconscious form. Pity. Donny had never missed the end of this movie. Gabe snatched up the remote controls, sent Moses and company winging to video heaven.

He jogged up to the third floor, two and three steps at a time, and satisfied himself that nurse Sally Pruett would not be coming down for coffee or anything else in the next few minutes. Then back to Donny, latching on, arms around chest as he lugged him through the hallways and the kitchen. The man was boneless, as maneuverable as a hundred-and-eighty-pound scarecrow. Heels digging small tracks in the carpet nap, head wobbling about his shoulders. Onward, juggling him through the inner and outer doors, and finally outside. Across the porch and to Donny's personal golf cart. Gabe propped him up on the passenger side, slumped as if weary from a long day of honest labor. Dream on.

Gabe puttered back to the compound, the only movement under the watchful indifference of stars and moon and sky. He kept one hand on Donny's shoulder, couldn't have him tumbling out like a common drunk. He steered off the main sidewalk onto a branch leading to the office and studio building. Friday night, no one would be working this late, no foreseen interruptions. As far as discretion was concerned, the unbreached privacy of Donny's house could not be beaten, but the presence of a nurse ruined all that. And suggesting Sally Pruett take off the last two hours of her shift would arouse too much suspicion, too much a break in established routine.

Gabe wheeled around to the north entrance, the back of the building, unseen from the rest of the compound. He stopped the cart half-inside the overhanging alcove and heaved Donny across his shoulders in a fireman's carry. Dead weight. Up to the second floor and into Donny's private office, dumping him into an undignified heap atop the leather sofa. He drew the drapes before switching on the light. Ceiling-recessed fluorescents, glowing warmly within this home of multimillion-dollar decisions, schemes and ideas masquerading as cathode ray salvation. It was rich in earthtones, from the rust carpet to the walnut shelves and paneling, an antique globe perched atop a floor stand—and the room was undeniably Donny Dawson.

How perfectly appropriate that tonight's assignation take place here. This was better than the house after all.

Gabe locked him inside, left him slumbering alone for the next thirty minutes while he carted over to retrieve his trunk from cold storage in the cafeteria kitchens. As expected, no one had touched it, they would not dare. Dead weight again, this time more literally, and *damn*, but this was hot, sweaty work, scuffing the thing along floors and sidewalks. The trunk was so very cumbersome, and he drove it back to the offices, dragged it up the stairs to the second floor, then paused at the top. Panting for breath. Leaning for minutes atop this makeshift mausoleum, and she inside, cold and silent. Were her stilled bones locked into place, did her eyes yet watch from some distant realm? And did they comprehend the most total of darknesses?

A part of him wanted to learn right now, first hand, *What really does wait for us? I want to know.* But. Duty first.

Gabe wiped sweat from his forehead and dragged the trunk the rest of the way into Donny's office. Ducked out and down the hall for a moment to his own office—considerably smaller, always an irritation—then brought back the camera he had left waiting. Back in Donny's office, he locked the door, you could never be too careful. Three's company, four's a crowd.

Gabe squatted beside the trunk, rested his head against it, *I have to go through with this, it's what's needed,* and he opened the padlock, then unpacked the girl within. He stripped her out of her clothes and tossed them aside. Edie Carson had most assuredly seen better days, but she was still photogenic, in a morbid way. Her face sunken and slack, her skin a fascinating blue-gray, particularly her nipples. In her lower regions the flesh was mottled a deeper hue where the blood had pooled and settled. Swollen feet, almost black. She wore the bruise of her broken neck like a scarf around her throat. The smell was not as bad as he had anticipated.

But the sight alone, oh, the sight, too many memories. The years compressing within seconds, taking him back too far. Half a life ago, nearly, not distant enough for his own needs, and Gabe fell beside her, tenderly holding one chilly hand, *I'm so sorry for what I took from you*, and wasn't it just the same as before, always too late with an apology.

Remembering: Seventeen years old, summertime in Michigan, and it doesn't matter if you've spent the last thirteen as a ward of the state, when it's summer you still feel alive and vital and immortal. Adolescent Gabe, hungry for experience, thirsty for sensation, in a borrowed car with three bottles of wine, and a ripe new wrinkle, Kate. Kate Quinn, fellow child with Michigan for parents, sixteen years old and built like twenty, and while girls frequently steer clear of Gabe, Kate tells him he has animal magnetism. He's hard as a rock. Born to be wild, these two, if only for one perfect night, and the ambrosial wine pours sweet and easy, and they drive to some nearby lake in this land of plenty. Falling and stumbling and laughing, he's never felt this good in his entire life, wet sloppy kisses beneath a summer moon, and the entanglement of sweaty limbs, no Eden could have been any more perfect than this. *Let's swim*, she says, *I want to swim!* and he can only laugh with incredulous delight as she peels away her clothes, there, his first live sight of the nude female form, and she cavorts like some drunken moon goddess, perfect in its glow. He would kill for her, die for her. *Let's swim*, that entreaty again, and he tells her he has a head-start, but she doesn't get it, the joke does not translate. Gabe watches her splash in while he tries to finish undressing, his head swimming, the entire world swimming, Kate must surely be a more experienced drinker than he. And he falls, laughing at himself while she calls from the water, arms aloft and waving, *Come on, come on!* and even at this distance she is still perfection beneath a summer moon. His spirit willing, the flesh weak, the flesh incompetent, the flesh getting sick. He vomits explosively, the reek of cheap wine and a groaning in his ears he recognizes as his own, *I'm blowing it, I'm ruining everything.* He tries to answer, *Be there in a minute, in a minute, in . . . a . . . minute,* and consciousness is the next casualty while somewhere, far away, he hears the flailing of limbs, the splashing of water, the cry of panic and pain. Crazy Kate, what's she up to now? Time stands still, and he sleeps, and it is not peaceful, fevered Dionysian dreams gone the way of sour wine, and when he awakens it is light. Shivering in the dawn, alone, soaked with dew and swollen-headed, his hangover as virulent as a plague, and then he sees her. Kate, cold and pale and adrift, wrapped in the fishing line stretched between two floating milk jugs, and all those hooks she must have fought against, and the most grotesque of all, the one hooked fish pinned against her shoulder while it still struggles feebly with fins and tail and gasping mouth, and all he can do is wail aloud to a vanished moon and hurl empty bottles to a hungry lake. Neither offering acceptable.

Edie. The more things change, the more they stay the same. He wanted to weep in her arms, but tears were a puny apology, anybody could cry. "I owe you more than that," and he drew a breath of resolve and opened his shirt, exposed the pastiche of scar tissue. And beneath the lights, before the sleeping Donny Dawson, Gabe maneuvered his chest to her mouth. Pried it open and fed his male nipple between the cold, cold lips, then slammed her jaws together. The click of teeth, the warmth of blood, and in this way he fed her. If not the pound of flesh that was her due, it was at least a start.

And he could focus again, the clarity almost shocking.

He plucked a tissue from Donny's desk, wiped Edie's chin free of his blood, then dabbed his own not-inconsiderable wound. He drew several more tissues and rummaged in the desk until he found a tape dispenser, then fashioned a crude bandage and left his shirt hanging open.

Donny's turn now, and Gabe helped him out of his clothes as well. The man's sleeping penis was limp and flaccid, too bad, Gabe had been hoping for a dream-induced erection. No such luck.

He dragged Edie to the sofa and positioned her head in Donny's lap, setting his arms and hands so that they looked as if he were holding her head in place. A good one, for starters.

Gabe fetched his camera, attached the flash on top, tested it once, and all was well, batteries charged and full. Off with the lens cap and he focused in, snapped two angles of this first compromising position, and oh, the degeneracy of it all.

To the camera lens, Donny's eyes appeared closed in sheer bliss. What next, what next, well, turnabout *was* fair play. Gabe switched their positions, and this time Donny was doing the oral honors, head wedged into the chilly juncture between Edie's thighs, enough of his face visible for error-free identification.

Next he stretched Donny out atop the sofa, then draped Edie over him like an obedient love doll. Donny's hands appeared to be gripping the livid roll of her bottom, and what a cooperative pair these two made. Game for anything, no request too kinky.

His gorge rose only once, memories near and distant, the snap of a neck and the sound of water in a choking throat, and he battled them down. Focus on the task at hand, *control,* and he put Donny and Edie through position after position. Giant toys, he had to regard them as such, rag dolls of flesh and bone and blood, yes, he could play with them every night of the week and not grow bored.

A one-night stand, however. Much later tonight, Edie would have to be buried, deep in the woods bordering Donny's property. He had already purchased the shovel, and the lime to speed along decomposition. He would offer prayers for her soul.

Focus: Even through the viewfinder, it was obvious that Donny's partner was no hot-blooded tigress, that she was . . . well, *dead.* Which was the least of all worries. An advantage, in fact.

After all, in the wake of indiscretions by Jim Bakker and Jimmy Swaggart, mere adultery was quite passé. But necrophilia, now there was a juicy tidbit, a new moral low, and like it or not, Gabe found his imagination to be boundless.

Position and click, position and click . . .

Every last negative on the two thirty-six shot rolls he had brought for the occasion.

26

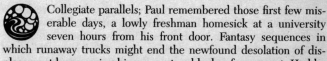 Collegiate parallels; Paul remembered those first few miserable days, a lowly freshman homesick at a university seven hours from his front door. Fantasy sequences in which runaway trucks might end the newfound desolation of displacement by smearing him across two blocks of pavement. Had he learned nothing in the decade since? He had forgotten that eventually a day would come when he would awaken to find things acceptable, maybe even palatable. Familiarity breeds comfort. With some help from a restored sense of purpose, a reason for awakening at all.

The day after Paul's unexpectedly pleasant stroll with Gabe Matthews, Donny took out a good chunk of Saturday to show him around the compound in greater detail. More time-consuming than it might ordinarily have been, for Donny was more than lethargic, the man was physically wiped out. Said he was feeling a bit out of sorts, and if Paul didn't know better, he might have guessed Donny had dropped a couple of 'ludes.

By Monday, Donny was back to his usual self, enthusiastic about their future association, and he charged Paul with a new mission, one that should dovetail nicely with his former training.

"With all the emphasis on our television ministry," Donny said, "we've kind of gotten away from radio. Gabe and I have come to the conclusion that we can fill a lot of coverage gaps across the country by syndicating radio airtime. Mainly into places where it's not feasible for us to buy into TV. Say, rural areas where they don't have cable access or a satellite dish." Then his salesman's smile. "With your background in radio production, I think you'd be perfect to edit the tapes for us."

Finally, something to give a sense of accomplishment. Just waiting for show night to roll around once a week had left him feeling mercenary, a hired gun.

Donny took him down into the studios and turned him loose in a sound booth, a regular toyland equipped with two reel-to-reel Teacs, a mixing board, speakers on either side of his skull, outboard effects gear, and much much more. Including the most comfortable and noiseless chair from which he had ever had the pleasure of reigning.

His first order of business was to produce a sample program, show them what he was capable of. And see if their notions of the end product were compatible. Paul culled the audio track off one of the tapes from the final week of the crusade tour. The sermon alone was seventy-eight minutes, punctuated with interminable stretches of Donny-led chanting that may have breezed by had you been there and participating, but would drag on like a stuck album groove if all you could do was listen. These were the first things he edited out. Next were the pregnant pauses following rhetorical questions, during which distant audience voices would invariably shout an *amen* or some other burst of agreement. He left a couple in for variety, but a few went a long way. Shooting for a one-hour total format, Paul ran and reran segments, timing various stretches, eventually whittling the sermon down to an evangelical lightning bolt. He worked up an intro that could be used each week, gospel music and a voiceover lead-in, and tucked that before the sermon. He left a bit of free time after the sermon on the assumption that Donny would like to tape a studio message with which to cap the broadcast. An appeal for contributions, please, keep us on the air.

The time-honored cash grab, cornerstone of a free economy. *And this time I'm a direct party to it,* a stray thought once he had wrapped the production work. He tried not to dwell on it. After all, *just doing my job,* the world's most popular rationalization. Ten thousand death-camp Nazis couldn't have been wrong, could they?

The unveiling came at midday on Wednesday, when Donny came down from the offices upstairs into the studios. Paul cued up the reel-to-reel master of his sample as Donny parked himself in a corner chair. Without comment, they listened to passion and promises. Paul tuned in for any hint of production glitch, or an obvious edit that had escaped earlier scrutiny. While Donny had ears only for himself . . .

And loved it. He was all smiles, all clasping hands that, strangely enough, felt clammy with sweat. Donny was full of enthusiastic praise, giving his mandate to do a radio version of each week's show while Paul beamed with the bone-deep satisfaction of a job well done, and then Donny's sunshine face began to eclipse into crumbling concern.

Because he had one more job for Paul this day, perhaps the most important so far. . . .

Dawson household, Paul's first trip inside the hallowed walls, and he was duly impressed. Third floor, one of the house's many bedrooms, bright with early October sunshine and decorated in a blatant contrast of styles. Nouveau-country chic meets chronic ward. Curtains wavered in a breeze that bore the subtle contentment of a virgin autumn, the smell of earth in transition. A world turning toward hibernation.

While on the bed, there lay a woman who had beaten the world to it. *She doesn't look much like the woman in the pictures. Not anymore.*

Amanda Dawson, meet Paul Handler. Paul? Mandy. Pardon her if she doesn't get up.

"She was brought home a couple of nights ago, very late. Apparently—" Donny's voice choked off, and he dabbed a finger at a bright drop in the corner of one eye. "Apparently she came down with some kind of fever three weeks ago. And she's been like this ever since. They flew her back from El Salvador on Monday. In case . . . just in case . . ." Donny shook his head, turning away, and Paul decided, no, he did not want to stare at the tremors spasming across Donny's back.

Paul, silently damning himself for his smug pride in the studio an hour ago, oblivious to the man's pain. And while he knew there had to be a good reason, he asked the obvious question anyway: "Why isn't she in a hospital?"

Donny wiped his eyes, red-rimmed. "I thought she might respond, somehow, maybe—to being back home. That she might realize she was back. And it would help her snap out of it. I guess that must seem awfully naive." His voice was a ragged whisper, and he looked six inches shorter, in no way the same man who could mesmerize an audience of thousands. "Plus, I thought I might be able to—to help her. But . . ." Shaking his head, staring at the wasted image of his wife. Half a man.

"But you can't." Paul spoke bluntly, though not harshly. Even if Donny had not leveled with him about his own shortcomings, Paul could never speak harshly to someone so distressed out of love for another. Would that *he* had someone about whom he could feel that passionately.

"It's like I told you when we first met in St. Louis. It doesn't always work for me." Donny cleared his throat, smoothed his mussed hair. Drew together his composure and faced Paul straight-on. "It's a test, Paul. The Lord's testing me in this, my faith. My faith in bringing you on with us. I think it's His way of saying this is where you belong. Because I have faith in *you*, Paul, I have faith that you can *bring her out of this*."

Paul did some quick pacing, ran a hand through his hair, oh man, oh man, what if he blew this one now that the pressure to perform was truly on. He was glad that the three of them were alone up here. Gabe was downstairs, as was some nurse who had apparently been summoned to look after Amanda. Details about this were a bit sketchy; he wasn't even sure he wanted to know.

But. Whatever transpired in this room would remain a secret. Something private, never intended for the camera eye.

"A coma," Paul muttered, moving for the bed. "This'll be a first."

Staring down at her, this latest weight to shoulder and make his own. Different this time, for while they had never truly met, it was indeed personal. He felt the expectant eyes upon his back. Time folded back by months, to the day when he had stood at the bedside of a woman-child named Stacy Donnelly, bounced off a sidewalk, through a window, and into the hospital by a lunatic with a twisted mission and a car. So easy to ruin a life.

Why me? he wondered, not for the first time. *What makes* me *the end of their suffering?*

It had never made sense. But when you can accept on face value, explanations often become unnecessary. And sometimes even get in the way.

Open up and let me come in, and he took Amanda Dawson's hands in both of his own. They felt small, cool, delicate as china.

Within himself, Paul began falling, falling, sealed off from the outer world by an internal universe made vast by a complete lack of boundaries. There was light here, but may as well have been none, for there was nothing to see. Only sensation, a fathomless span of existence muted by the inability to act, react, interact. A huge barrier built with bricks of frustration. This was different from all the rest, no disease, no invader alien to the body. No simple injury, for which time and care and pills would suffice. No. This was all-encompassing, a way of life—or lack of it—entirely unto itself. The closest thing to death he knew he was likely to experience in advance of his own, and in a strange way, it killed some of the suspense of life, solved part of the grand mystery. He knew what death must feel like. And whenever it came riding up to claim him, he would meet it without fear.

Amanda. Yes, she was here, and was ready to come out.

Paul opened his eyes, released her hand, stepped backward. For better or for worse, it was done. The reaction was very slow this time, for whatever reasons peculiar to her condition. This was no lifting of a cataract, or dissolution of a tumor, or repair of a limb. This was a deliverance from the brink, and to know that it could be done at all nearly sent him to his knees, what strange beings we are, mysteries within mysteries.

Twenty seconds after Paul reopened his eyes, Amanda did likewise. Eyelids fluttering sluggishly, a painful readjustment to the light of day. Her gaze roved about the ceiling in search of something on which to focus, and when Donny went rushing to her side, she sought him out, those eyes the first spark of animation in a face that had seemed barren of life.

"Mandy? Hon?" Donny's voice, barely more than a whisper. *"Mandy?"*

Her mouth opened, drooping a bit to the right. She uttered a mewling croak; another. Fingers twitched spastically, clawing weakly at the sheet beneath her. Breath quickened, became ragged with further attempts to speak. Eyes alternating from Donny to Paul to Donny again, awareness deepening with life renewed, with frustration. Amanda's shoulders trembled as she tried to roll onto her side, one of the fiercest struggles Paul had ever witnessed, and despite Donny's plaintive coaching, she gave up a minute later. Sinking back in surrender, tears leaking from both eyes.

When Donny turned around, his movements were thick as syrup, as if the sluggish efforts of his wife had been contagious. His eyes belonged to a shell-shocked veteran of too many battles, witness to too much carnage. But his hands, now *they* were strong, and clamped to Paul's shoulders in desperate rage.

"What have you done to her?" Donny said through clenched

teeth, past a jaw that refused to budge. *"What have you done to my wife?"*

But in the end—or the beginning, depending on perspective—it was Donny's face wearing the metaphysical egg, and not Paul's. Once the professionals were consulted, truths became evident. First from the nurse downstairs, then Irv Preston, who paid a visit and verified everything the nurse had said, and at last Donny's mind was set at ease. Such as it was.

Nobody, *nobody,* awakens from a coma feeling refreshed and ready to bound out of bed. The process is gradual, the first signs subtle: small movements, blinking eyes, attempts at speech. While thinking may be clear, mind-body coordination is fractured; hence a great deal of frustration. Eventually, broader movements are brought under control. And despite Donny's shattered expectations, Amanda appeared to be making remarkable progress in shaking it off, for which Paul felt no small degree of vindictive pride.

In Paul's absence, Preston explained some hard facts to Donny. Several hours of regained consciousness were not enough to undo Mandy's past few months. Her brain had suffered trauma; connections would be misfiring in her head, which was normal under the circumstances. Processes most people daily take for granted would have to be relearned. Her body, despite the range-of-motion exercises performed upon it, had sustained prolonged inactivity. She would need physical therapy, occupational therapy, possibly speech therapy.

Donny was absolutely crushed. He looked like an old man, rambling about his house while its rafters tumbled about his head.

"It was different this time," Paul tried to explain in the privacy of the first-floor library. "Please understand that."

"How? *How?* You tell me how, Paul." Donny, declining into a pitiful self-caricature, rumpled clothing, disheveled hair, eyes red and glazed. Pacing the hardwood floor as if it were his final stage, Paul his final audience, with no idea the man had been treading this close to the breaking point. Obsessive love, but for whom: wife, or self? "Different? *Different?* She was sick. She needed help. I asked you to give it to her. Nothing more than was expected by the hundreds of people you've already helped. And just look at her up there! Look at the state of her!"

Paul, feeling that stoking of temper, "She's out of her coma, right? So fire me, why don't you? Maybe you don't feel like you got your money's worth out of me on this one." Petty bickering, this was what it had degenerated to, but he couldn't help himself. "How about I just reimburse you for that last paycheck and we call it even?"

Donny stalked across the floor, which might have once glowed with a mellow coat of wax, but now seemed dull with accumulated dust. He stood before the inverted, sharp-angled U formed by the window curtains. Night had fallen a couple hours before, and the panes of glass were blacker than a chalkboard. Erase your life and rewrite it upon the night.

Donny's fist clenched upon the window sill. "I wanted her well. I wanted her *whole*!"

"Yeah? Then why couldn't you just do the job yourself, hotshot?" Paul was two breaths from turning around, walking out, heading for his room. Let the night slip away, and wait for a new dawn to set him on a different path. Close, so very close, and the ingratitude of this asshole, like to stick a hand down his—

And then he was telling himself, *Whoa, back off, back down.* Temper, temper. This had been so smoothly deceptive, the first time since joining the ministry that anger had become a factor. And with it the possibility of darker tendrils gaining the upper hand. He would not have it, not that, no more.

Above all, he would not come close to touching Donny.

"If you're looking for explanations, I'm the last guy in the world to give them." Paul spoke with forced calm, getting better at this. Hook him to a biofeedback machine and he could probably tone it down to a beat a minute. "That's why I showed up on your doorstep in the first place, remember?"

Donny slowly turned from the window, nodded, oh yeah; right. "I guess, at least in your wife's case, I can't just turn back time. I don't know what she picked up down in Central America, but that didn't seem to be the problem anymore. The coma was the problem. And I took care of that. But it could be I can't make like it never happened to her. It's not a disease I could cure, or an injury I could close up. She hasn't been using her body, or her mind. And I guess those are things I can't give back to her. Because she's got to get them back for herself."

Donny stood on unsteady feet, swaying ever so slightly. Who knew what he was listening to inside his head? Mulling it all over as anger dwindled to dying embers. With the passion spent, all he had left was a countenance that appeared a decade older than it had this afternoon. Makeup, please.

"Okay," softly, all he said. He met Paul's gaze, his own empty, cored-out. He walked past and opened the door into the hall, destination unknown. As he passed by, managing to whisper, "Sorry."

Yeah, so am I, and Paul was alone in the library, and glad of it. Surrounded by thousands of books, new and old, spines of paper, spines of cloth, spines of leather. Gold-leaf titles gleamed in the light, just blurs. So many questions, so few answers, these books merely educated speculation. They couldn't even agree among themselves, and what fate for the sincere layman?

A more immediate question surfaced, directed out the library door, the last glimpse of Donny Dawson: *Are you even for real at all?*

He left, and carried it with him.

He tried to settle into his room for the night, and it took no more than five minutes to realize it wasn't going to work. Maybe he had been too hasty leaving St. Louis in the first place; nice going, trashing his job, the one thing in life that could always be counted on to vent a spleen full of rage.

Which was not to say he couldn't at least pretend at it here. So he grabbed a couple of cassette tapes and stuffed them into a jacket pocket, then headed out across the compound. He had been given a key to the office and studio building along with his radio production assignment, and let himself in. Well into Wednesday night, he should have the place to himself, and he affected a purposeful stride through the hallways of this subground floor. A few lights on, but no noise, nobody moving, just the way he wanted it tonight.

The production booth was sepulchral in its silence, and he hit the lights and slammed the door. The fluorescents buzzed overhead, a tiny sound, like a gnat, and Paul dumped himself into the chair. Hard to believe, seven hours ago in this room he had actually liked it here, liked this place overall. He turned to the cassette player, popped in one of the tapes he had brought. Hit the master power on the mixing board, flicked a few switches to route the player through the system, and punched it to life.

The music came through and he pushed it to the limits of endurance. The guitars were righteous and vengeful, the stance purely aggressive. A crystal sledgehammer, sending a primal jolt through him, just like the old days, and he added the microphone into this therapeutic configuration.

"This is Paul Handler, back on the air after hiatus," he bitched into the mike, feeling like a fool only in that initial moment; this was just too immediately cleansing to stop. "Sorry about the down time, we had a transmitter loss. I guess the hamster fell off its fucking wheel." Damn the pain, he cranked the master volume higher, feel it in the bones. "It may not be KGRM, in fact I don't know quite *what* to call it around here, but you may recognize our first soothing selection tonight as a tasty slice of aggression from Iggy Pop. The godfather of punk, the Igster!" He had never babbled this much over the music before; letting the music speak for itself had been an immutable code of ethics. Audience of self, now, though, and he was on a needed roll. "You trivia experts out there may recall Mister Pop's shows of old. Genuine family entertainment, he used to roll shirtless in broken glass. Onstage! I shit you not! When somebody bleeds for you, you *know* they have your best interests at heart, which leads us to the inevitable question: Would Donny Dawson roll in broken glass for us? Why yes, I sincerely believe he would, the only issue being what would motivate him. Would he do it for love? Would he do it for money? Would he do it for Amanda? Would he do it for God? Phone lines are open and operators are standing by." He dove for an imaginary phone receiver. "Say hey, we have a winner already! The correct answer is: *None of the above!* It was a trick question! Donny Dawson would do it *only for himself!* And what's our lucky caller won? Mmmm *boy,* a year's supply of sour milk from a sacred cow!" He seized the microphone, rocked back and forth in his seat to the primal rhythm. "You may ask, what motivates *me?* The truth is, I don't fucking know, sometimes I *really* think I'm starting to scare myself. About all I can tell you is, it's a dog-eat-dog world out there, and these days, I've just been eating too many damn dogs."

Oh, and it was good, so very very good, ranting to the left, raving to the right, a stream-of-consciousness tirade to purge his soul of every hypocritical ill it had suffered. Iggy Pop would approve. At last, a discernible ebb in the tide of bile, and he pushed back in exultation to whirl in the chair, feet drawn up off the floor with arms jammed aloft.

One complete revolution, a sweeping glance of the window, oh *great,* this just could not be, did his eyes deceive? He'd dropped his arms by the time he made a second pass, and dragged his feet as brakes. *Stop.* Wobbling in the chair, staring out the window over-looking the narrow hall.

'Audience of self and self alone?

Well—not exactly.

He was quite sure his face displayed never-before-seen shades of red. For several moments, he didn't even register the music. He recognized her at once, though he had never seen her this close up before. He grinned sheepishly, caught with his pants down.

Laurel Pryce was smiling uncertainly at him through the win-dow, as if she had just heard a joke she was only eighty percent convinced she had understood. Arms folded across herself, she looked at the booth door and pointed, arching her thick eyebrows, can I come in? He waved her onward, slumped with his head low-ered to one waiting hand, man with a migraine. Why couldn't the earth open up and swallow him this very instant?

She leaned against the doorjamb. "You do that very well. The Wolfman Jack thing, I mean."

His shoulders quivered, mirth in spite of himself, where's that earthquake? He potted the music down to background level. "When I was thirteen, my mom walked into my bedroom and caught me playing air guitar to a Kiss record. I'd forgotten what that felt like. So thank you, you've just wiped out fifteen years of my life." He straightened up and groaned. "I suppose this is the part where I tell you I'm not really as stupid as I must appear."

She flipped her head with a shrug. "Don't go to any trouble on my account." *Touché,* but it was a pleasant sort of sting.

Introductions came next, Laurel Pryce, glad to meet you, Paul Handler, oh sure, you're the new guy that joined on in Topeka. He was flattered; their entourage was not small, and with her vocal solo spot, she maintained a far higher profile than did he. And of all the moments he would liked to have met her, this was *not* it.

"How much of that did you, um . . . hear? Actually."

"Enough to get the general idea." Laurel had a coffee mug with her, a vat of a mug, and drank from it. She smiled at him over the rim. "I *knew* you were a rebel. And just look at you, masquerading like such a conformist. How come you cut your hair after those first couple of weeks?"

Paul shrugged it off. He could see a faint reflection in the booth window, his own transparent image, I can see through myself. He was hating it more and more, but time was on his side. Ah, but if only his hands were, always a catch.

"If you really want the truth"—and why was he so ready and willing to surrender it, at least in part? Why, easy; she had asked, of all the crazy things—"I think I just wanted to disappear into somebody else for a while."

Laurel nodded sagely. "A lot of people here are disappearing from one thing or another." Speaking from experience? Believe Gabe—why should he not?—and she probably was. Though he dared not ask so bluntly; he was already one up in the moron-of-the-year sweepstakes. Two in one night would not advance the cause.

The cause? Oh yes. Self-honesty could be brutal; he was more than intrigued, and had been for two weeks minimum. The months of celibacy had taken their toll, though he took inane pride in, one, the fact that he still regarded his intentions as honorable, and two, his standards had not slipped. Laurel Pryce had a distinct edge, yet his mom would like her. And here he was, seven hundred miles and years from home, still trying to play both ends against the middle. Pleasing all of the people all of the time.

From his chair, Paul studied her, see how proximity compared with the video image. Not surprising, he liked live better. Conservative dresses were fine, but there was something inherently far more sensual about her faded jeans with the knees worn out and the peach sweater. She wore them more easily on a body that was tall, slender, hinting of athletic grace. Her dark blond hair was loose, pooled past her shoulders in exquisite disarray. Smoke gray eyes, very smart, in an oval face. Low cheekbones, no exotica *here*, but they worked just fine.

"So how did you come to be here tonight?" He sincerely wanted to know, and the idea that others may yet have been lurking just out of sight had only now entered his mind. "Catching me in my finest hour here, this had to have been an afterthought."

"I was down in the music studio." She flipped a glossy fingernail along the hallway, then dug into a pocket for some hastily folded pages. She unfolded them, and he saw they were music staff paper, with the notes and lyrics handwritten. "I was working on a song earlier, on the piano, and I got tired and stretched out on the floor. It's peaceful here this time of night." A cocked eyebrow toward his own sound arsenal. "Usually."

He pointed at the pages. "Something you'll be singing on the show?"

She shook her head. "Oh—hardly. This is just for me, for now. I mean—I have nothing against gospel . . . but there's a certain, um, *sameness* to it all." She strolled closer, hitting from the mug again, and knelt long enough to peer into the cassette player window. "Iggy Pop, that's what I thought. Obviously, you feel the same way."

"The well-rounded listener is a healthy listener." Sounded good, at least.

"I probably owe you one, since I caught you in mid-misgiving like this. My main musical heroine?" She exaggeratedly glanced over her shoulder at the door, beware of lurkers, then gazed at him with shocked eyes, her voice an awed whisper: "Patti Smith."

He laughed, delighted. "You *are* on the fringes, aren't you?" If the Igster had been the New York scene's godfather of punk, then Patti Smith had been its mother superior. This encounter was boding hope for his tenure at Dawson Ministries, perhaps not to be truncated quite as soon as he had thought thirty minutes ago. "I would've bet no one around here had even heard of her."

Laurel folded her arms around herself and rocked in bliss. "Mmmm. Anybody who can sound that passionate *and* insane *and* spiritual at the same time, they have my devotion."

Paul had to wonder, how had *he* sounded ten minutes ago as she had stood unannounced in the hall? Surely he had been firing on at least two of those three cylinders, maybe all of them.

Laurel frowned into her mug, bitter heartbreak. "This is *cold* and I hate it now. Would you, umm, want to come along while I go on a coffee run? There's this place I like in the city, it serves cappuccino that could fuel a rocket. It keeps me going for hours, and I really want to work on this song later."

Paul was already gathering his toys. "Can I get food there? I haven't eaten since"—just when *had* it been, anyway?—"forever."

"Oh sure. If you don't mind health food. The place is called Bran Central Station."

He cocked his head in puzzlement while flicking off the lights, shutting the booth door. "Health food *and* caffeine?"

Laurel led the way along the hall, wired to the gills. Like she really needed another dosage. "Yeah, it does seem rather contradictory, doesn't it? I like to think of it as a health food deli for hypocrites." She laughed, quite the merciless tease. "You should fit right in."

"The rebel."

She nodded, and oh, that hair, it was magnificent. "You'd better watch it, though. If you call *yourself* a rebel, it just defeats the whole purpose."

"Don't worry," practically striding to keep up with her. He patted his chest, heart, soul. "Rebel without a clue."

And she liked that one a lot, too.

27

Donny was at first terrified to see Mandy go to sleep again. Lapse back into a regular cycle, so soon? Hadn't she gotten her fill these past four months? He was apprehensive enough to eat his own fingernails; what if she just kept on sleeping all over again? All of which was irrational in the extreme, Irv had tried to get him over this one too. A coma did not behave like the common cold, succumb to knockout, only to resurface in a mutated viral guise.

No, no relapse, he had to keep waving that flag of faith. If faith could move mountains, then surely it could keep Mandy moving under her own power.

It was Friday, two days after her deliverance, and already she was in daily therapy. Irv Preston had arranged for a physical therapist, and had been prompt about it. First session yesterday, laying out an easy regimen for her first week of consciousness. She would sit up, she would stand, she would turn. None of which sounded like a tough order to fill.

Until you watched her try to accomplish it.

He had watched with a potent mingling of admiration and anguish. *Recuperation* had sounded so pleasant and relaxed. It was, instead, harsh and loud and painful and sometimes quite ugly.

Her anger, her denial, her unconscious rage, all had come to full boil yesterday during the first session. No doubt accelerated by the unique way in which she had emerged from the coma in the first place. That had to have made a difference, because it was so distinctly *un*natural.

Paul. Miracle worker, content to operate behind the scenes, just their little secret. Who did as asked, without complaint, and this made his brief outburst two nights ago all the more surprising. A harsh tongue in that man's mouth. Although, quite possibly, bringing Amanda back from near death may have entailed a far greater emotional impact than he was used to. This had been no run-of-the-mill healing; this time it had mattered on a personal level, a ministry level. And bore with it a new twist: an aftermath that would have to be witnessed.

And . . . admittedly, he *had* been a bit rough on Paul immediately afterward, that first malignant moment when results had not been up to par with conjugal hopes. He would have to remember to make it up to him, and soon. But it wasn't like he didn't care about Paul's happiness, and deeply. He *had* given him the radio show production to keep him busy and content. And was going to great pains to keep Paul from finding out that, in reality, the tapes were not actually being used. Instead of syndication to radio stations, they were collecting dust in a locked cabinet. Radio time would be a wasted investment at their level of game-playing.

White lies were excusable, when happiness was at stake.

Paul would keep, he would be fine. For now, Donny's sole attention was demanded by Amanda. Her efforts and struggles, sorrows and frustrations. All of which were on display at the moment as she sat upright in bed, propped against a barricade of pillows like an egg in a carton. A contraption called a Bobath splint—not much more than a thick rectangular pad wedged into her armpit and a couple straps with Velcro fasteners—held her right shoulder in place. With a left-brain injury, she would need the majority of attention focused on the right side of her body, given the crossover of most cranial functions.

Donny dragged a chair beside her bed, sat with elbows on knees, hands steepled beneath his chin. Love had been renewed, somehow, that fresh excitement of getting to know her all over again. He would try to avoid the same mistakes this go-around. He would listen more.

"There's been so much I've wanted to say to you the past couple of days. Wednesday night, yesterday." He reached out to hold her right hand, in its splint. Her left remained on the bed as she regarded him with eyes that seemed terribly huge within the winnowed-down sculpture of her face. "But it never seemed right. You were in so much—so much pain."

Mandy nodded, her head a tremendous weight to be supported by that fragile stalk of neck. "Mmm hmm." She was getting by, as much as possible, with phrases like that. Her speech, assuming it was regained on its own, would take roughly another week. For now, it was characterized by the round, muted texture often heard in the deaf who have recently learned to talk. The sharp angles of pronunciation blunted by lack of practice and the odd cranial mishap or two. For example, when she said *what*, it was more apt to come out sounding like *wad*.

"I've missed you, I can't tell you how much." He didn't mean to cry, but there it was, the tremble of his lip and the rapture of brimming eyes. "I'd come in and talk to you every day. And when I couldn't be here, I had the nurses play some tapes I made for you. Do you remember any of that? Irv says that even inside a coma, people sometimes hear what's going on around them."

Mandy's gaze lowered to her lap, and she looked up again with a crisp nod. "I . . . *tink* so," spoken slowly, with great care and concentration, striving for normality. "I 'member your voice. Close to my ear." Her eyes darkened then, looking not at him, but off to one side. "Know what else I 'member?"

When she looked at him again and he saw just how truly harsh that stare was, his heart clutched. The tears felt to drain back into his skull, where they would burn, corrosive.

"I 'member . . ." Her eyes closed, and she rattled a fist in defiance of thwarted effort. A word was eluding her, *expressive aphasia*, the therapist had called it. "Shit!" she cried, and Donny winced.

That was another thing he had been warned about. Typically, coma patients wake up behaving like children who have known too little discipline. Gratification is a concern of the great and mighty *now*, and there exist no such things as inhibitions. They speak things no one would ever have suspected of crossing their minds at all. Saintly little old women, exploding into fits of language that would make a longshoreman blush. Kindly little old men, spewing forth lecherous propositions to any nurse in earshot. Couple that with the likelihood of emotional lability—severe instability and inappropriateness—and they were all geared up for more than their fair share of soulful torment.

He had hoped she would prove an exception.

"Falling!" Amanda shouted, following with a triumphant, "Hah!"

Savage ecstasy on her face, she'd pulled it from memory, and what was he supposed to do, toss her a treat for reward? Then, just as suddenly, her face grew sullen again. "I 'member falling. An' fighting. *Why* we were fighting."

Of all the things she had left inside herself, why couldn't that have been one of them? *Dear God, why couldn't You have blotted that from her memory?*

Tired of living out lies, wasn't that her phrase for it? Sure it was, famous last words for nearly four months. He had replayed them thousands of times over in his head since their irrevocable moment of utterance.

"But so much has changed since then." He was pleading with his hands. "So much has happened with the ministry."

"But I haven't changed *my* mind. It's still . . . yesterday . . . to me. An' I don't tink it's right anymore." She frowned at the way the words lurched out. Especially those last two, sounding like *wight anymwah.* Her frown curled into a brittle frightmask of self-loathing, and she burst into fresh tears, and couldn't they give her sedatives? "Oh hell, I hate the way I sound! Hate it hate it hate it! I sound like Elmer Fudd!"

Donny possessed options aplenty. He could laugh, he could cry tears of grief, he could run screaming from this room and try setting foot in it later. Or he could sit in numb distress over the realization that she was a complete stranger to him, *not* the same woman he had been married to in early June. How dare she change on him while she was in there.

The self-loathing proved contagious, for none of these were the acts of a strong and loving husband, and perhaps worst of all was his sudden second realization—maybe he was not the same man who had proposed to her. Change being a two-way street and all.

He dove in, salvage something, anything, leap into this fray, and he wouldn't have to contend with himself. "Mandy, listen, listen to me. Let's stick together through this thing, I promise you we'll get through it and you'll be yourself again, I just know it. . . ." Rambling, on and on and on, years of expertise in pulpit motormouth behind him, with none of the eloquence. He leaned forward to hold her. She struggled against his touch at first, then succumbed and fell still within his arms, frail shoulders twitching with the occasional sob. It was like holding a captive bird, and still he rambled on. No idea as to who he was trying to convince of this fantasyland happily ever after.

"There's something you need to know," he said after a few moments of calm embrace. "I know you were having some problems with—with the ethics of what we were doing. But it's for real now. We've healed so many in the past few weeks, we've lost track, and do you know why?"

With her face buried against his shoulder, now damp, she shook her head.

"Because I've met a young man who can do it, really *do* it. Every time out. Do you think the Lord would've led him to me if he wasn't supposed to be here?"

Amanda pulled back, eyes widening in surprise. Wariness?

"He's the one that brought you out of your coma. You saw him there with me when you first woke up. He restored you."

Settling back against her pillows, she tilted her head at him, quizzical. Red eyes and damp cheeks were the only evidence of distress now. She had forgotten to cry.

"He's from St. Louis," and Donny was already feeling that warm glow rekindled, everything would be fine. Paul healing by the mere thought of him alone. "He's been such a blessing."

Mandy sat up, blinking, rather owlish. "I thought that was a dream . . . something." Nodding to herself. "I 'member him." Then back to Donny, nailing him with another crucifying gaze. "What are you doing with him here?"

Donny cocked his head. "What do you mean? He *works* for us."

She beat on the mattress with a loose fist, shook her head with a heavy sigh. "I mean whose idea was it?"

Donny turned palms up, innocent, nothing to hide here. "I suggested it, but only after he came looking for me. For guidance. He'd had some severe personal problems with it." Better for now to withhold what those had been, and when he got no reaction, Donny plowed ahead. Anything was better than the newly torturous silence between them. "It's important you be careful what you say to him, I need to warn you about that. He thinks you came down with a fever while doing missions work in El Salvador, that's what, ummm, everybody believes, almost, except for Gabe, and Irv, and the nurses, and . . . and . . ."

And Donny had sufficient presence of mind to shut his run-on mouth before this got any worse. In fact, he should have shut it long ago, as he now found himself sucking on both feet at once, while a brand-new front of anger was storming into view across Amanda's face. Awesome to behold, *Shouldn't have told her this, I really shouldn't have, but—but I thought she'd have wanted us to do it that way—*

"You lied to everybody we care about?"

—for the sake of the ministry—

"You LIED?"

—for the sake of our lives—

"You hid me away here the whole time with a—a—a cover story?"

—but—

"You were ASHAMED OF ME?"

—she's not the same now as she was then.

"You're STILL ashamed of me, aren't you? Aren't you? That's why you want to have all the therapy equipmen' built into that other room!" Amanda's eyes, flaring wildly, huge and glazed with intensity. Accusation. Tiny droplets of spittle flew from her mouth, and moments after she finished shouting, she exploded into rich laughter. "Hide and seek! I been the best hider of all, huh?" She laughed herself hoarse, laughed until she was crying again.

His existence had once been so ordered, so meaningful, and for the life of him, Donny couldn't recall precisely when and where the slippage had begun. For now there was only damage assessment. The map-room charting all the familiar territory of their relationship had just been leveled to rubble, taken out by a direct hit. A cruise missile, fired from the top of the stairs.

He reached for her, to caress that quivering shoulder, *She figured it out,* a dull monotone thought, *only she didn't figure it the same way I did.*

Reaching . . .

Contact.

She reacted as if he had jabbed her with a branding iron, jerking up and twisting from his touch. She swung a wild and oddly clenched left fist and managed to tag him solidly on the shoulder. He rocked back, more from surprise than impact.

"Don' you touch me! Don'. You. Touch me." Her breath came in hoarse gulps, long limp hair spilling darkly across her face. She made a couple of spastic attempts to push it back, succeeded. A smear of snot glistened under one nostril, and for all the afflictions, Amanda was somehow exhibiting more—to put it crudely and in sexist vernacular—*balls* than he had ever seen. The demure peacekeeper, the gentle helpmate . . . gone, buried beneath a crumbled wall of inhibitions.

He had to wonder: Could that wall ever be rebuilt? Or was the damage too extensive, eternal? And speaking of eternity, how much of their future had been wrecked, as well? The glimpse he had of their relationship was that of dry ruins, half buried and parched beneath a lifetime of desert suns.

To hold her, to draw together in a fortified stand, these suddenly seemed dead icons. More than a decade past, when the ministry was but a stumbling patchwork dream and nights were sometimes spent hungry, they could hold each other and generate more strength and hope together than was the sum of their parts. God had seemed to smile upon them then, even through clouds and rain.

A lifetime or two ago.

Anger and energy spent, Amanda slumped into the bed, the pillows. Nightgown twisted, though she did not notice, or care. She resembled a carelessly dressed, heedlessly flung toy. The Amazing Mandy Doll. She sleeps, and sleeps, and sleeps—and just when you think things are going smoothly again, she awakens into a cranky stranger.

She rolled her head up to stare at him instead of into her lap. A softer gaze now, the most welcome of changes, oh thank you, thank you.

"Donny? What have we done to ourselves here? What have we done?"

No ready answers, only the sound of his heart ripping loose.

Love is a many-splintered thing.

28

Love had its own peculiar mercies, and if this was not yet love, it was at least a case of the mutual irresistibles. Paul felt comfortable with it happening, hence the mercy: If you've been through it once, you're already broken in, because most all relationships leave the starting gate in remarkably similar fashion. Regardless of where they are headed.

Finding out where, now *that* was the fun part.

Bran Central Station was the arena in which it got its start, and Paul liked the place just fine. Down a flight of stairs from street level, follow the wrought-iron rail. The tables were a fifty-fifty split between round and square, never rectangular, always tiny, always intimate. Large groups need not apply. Walls of aged brick, low-raftered ceiling of oaken timbers, and the Elysian aroma of a whole-bean roast coffee market. Laurel pointed out the minuscule stage at one end their first night there, told him that folk singers sometimes played from tall stools. Ambient tapes played the rest of the time, everything from vintage sixties to digitally recorded whales. Liberal old intellectuals would come here to die.

Over the week following that first night—the first Wednesday of October—they seemed to make it by on an average of every other night. Neutral ground away from Dawson Ministries, and they had the time to spare. Laurel had her music, which she worked on primarily according to the whims of her own schedule, and the weekly radio show's production hardly kept Paul busy with a full-time job. Only Thursday nights were spoken for, when they both cleaned up and went before the cameras to strut their respective stuff.

Except she had no idea what he was really doing there, which seemed regrettably one-sided to Paul. *She* sang, and enthralled the crowd. While inasmuch as could be demonstrated, all *he* accomplished was making sure no one tripped over their own suffering feet. A noble endeavor, though hardly aesthetically pleasing. If only she knew. Secrets already. It *was* a bother.

Over cappuccino and successive nights, their backgrounds unfolded before each other like a miniseries. Laurel told him she was originally from Eugene, Oregon, a nice laid-back town. Lots of relics there, throwbacks, flower children come from wherever to settle and go to seed. She found it quaint.

Blue-collar family all the way, her father a trucker who spent road time for the logging companies, then compensated for his frequent parental absence by ruling like a tyrant whenever he was home. Mom kept a clean house—no wife of *his* would ever work outside the home—and deferred to his omnipotent authority over Laurel and her brother, two sisters. Father knows best. With punishment to match for the nonbeliever.

"It was classic love-hate, all the way," and she spoke as if it were someone else's life, perhaps that of a good friend from long ago, whose life has been made fair game by time and distance. "I loved him and wanted him to be proud of me. But I hated him, too, because he would never, ever, loosen up enough to act like a friend to me. Not even just for an evening at home, not even an hour. It was like—like living with your school principal. You remember when you were a kid, how the principal never seemed like a human being?"

Paul said he did. The principal, demigod of education. Corporal punishment had been allowed freely in those days. Horrors.

"That was home," Laurel said plainly. "Here were the rules, here were the forbidden zones, and woe be unto you if you crossed either one."

"He's still alive, though, isn't he?"

She nodded with an obligatory smile. "Oh sure. He's not quite even fifty, yet. And *now* he's proud, all the neighbors get to hear about what I'm doing here. He calls me his little choirgirl—and I suppose it makes me a terrible daughter, but I *really* hate that. It's like he's trying to make me a kid again and make up for all that lost time. But too little, too late."

"At least you have a father that's around. At least you *know*. Some of us, all we can do is imagine. And wonder." He had already apprised her of his own loss of innocence, that first vicarious trip through Hell, pushed by the hands of the Big C. See Dad, see Dad rot.

Laurel had not taken it lightly then, nor did she now, reaching across the table to shield the back of his hand with her own. "It depends a lot on what you were left to remember. Did your father touch you?"

Paul smiled, an attack of precancerous nostalgia. His father had been the first to teach him of the therapeutic bliss of the backrub. Even little kids got sore muscle kinks. "Yeah. He did."

"Mine didn't, except to spank. He never hugged me that I can remember. And even the spankings, the touching there was almost by remote control. He always used a yardstick, or the back of a hairbrush. Anything like that, to keep the distance."

A postpuberty father, what a concept. They said you couldn't miss what you never had; they were wrong. But debating this topic was no good at all. Their frames of reference were too wildly dysfunctional to get much beyond agreeing that the other at least had a valid point. Leave it.

Gratification and validation of true worth had come from elsewhere as Laurel grew older. Music became salvation, as she had been gifted with a voice that easily covered a four-octave range and could run a stylistic gamut from ethereal lilt to saccharine to down-and-dirty grunge. She preferred the latter; it was most rebellious, and during college, she put it to work in a band called Cain's Mutiny. One of those typical half-assed we'll-play-for-beer attempts at its inception that accumulated importance as they actually began to land paying gigs after a year. Typical bar band, but with proficiency to spare, they were no slouches. Boyfriend/guitarist named Jax, and she the only female, upfront chick to provide a visual anchor. Yeah, well, so long as people listened. They wrote their own music on the side, and sometimes nobody even griped when an unfamiliar piece slipped through.

Eventually, college could wait for completion. Dad had been volatile, but she was no longer living under his roof, and Laurel allowed herself plenty of petty satisfaction over his tirades.

The band eventually fell apart, though, one more rock and roll casualty of ego and disillusion. She and guitarist/boyfriend Jax parted company, gone the way of couples who wake up to discover divergent roads are being trod. In the telling, Laurel breezed through it all in a hurry, no wasted breath. No big deal, she said, just one of those things growing up entails.

It hurt her, Paul decided. *It hurt her more than she'll ever let on.* But he still had an inside track, didn't he? Gabe's nonspecific admission that she had suffered trauma.

"That was around fourteen months ago," Laurel said. "And I didn't know what I wanted to do next. I was twenty-four, almost broke, I had no job, no prospects, and only about five-eighths of a liberal arts degree. And I was way too stubborn to go back home." She wiggled those heavy eyebrows. "My prospects were *not* good."

She told him she went bumming up to visit a girlfriend in Seattle. A weekend turned into two months, uncertainty nosedived into depression, and her hundred and fifteen pounds swelled to one-forty. Life, as a rule, sucked rocks. She happened across an ad for a Donny Dawson revival one night and, with nothing better to do, decided to go for laughs, who knew, maybe he could touch her and make her thin again, ha ha.

But something happened that night. One lost and hurting soul cast adrift in a sea of others, everyone else swept away by passion and music and theater, she found it hard not to be moved. A fallen-away Catholic, that was Laurel. Still considering herself as a part of the faith, but only marginally. There are no ex-Catholics, she told Paul she had heard said, only recovering Catholics. She was used to solemn ritual, and the happy freewheeling bustle of the Dawson service took her by barnstorming surprise. By the end of the night, she had shanghaied an usherette and was begging to audition for the choir.

The rest, of course, being history.

Exchange of bios was mostly completed by early in the week following their initial meeting, just in time for first kisses. They had caught a movie at an art house, crumbling, with all the charm that suburban mall cineplex clones could never even aspire to. The seats squeaked beneath them as they watched a revival of *Dr. Strangelove,* roving hands seeking one another in the dark, then interlocking, not two minutes after lights out.

Touching, sitting there safe and content, actually leaving his killer's hand in the care of another with no dire consequences unless he counted his happily stricken heart. No worries, only giddy relief. In weeks past he had felt truly loathsome, not even entirely human, with precious little rebuttal from any quarter on his behalf. Now, finally, here it was, and she probably didn't even realize how much it truly meant. She stroked her thumb along his own, and he knew that whatever this was between them, it was at least real.

Later that night they closed down Bran Central and endured its rousing cry of *last brew,* then drove back to the compound to walk among its trees beneath a hazy moon. A cool October night, and beneath its passive watch their lips met for the first time. And again, and again.

"Nice," she murmured into his throat, and they went another round while the heat burned hotter and the passion smoldered, while the bodily grinding grew more fevered. First kisses were like fuses, some duds, some slow-burn, others so short as to be suicidal. They were falling just shy of the latter extreme, which was fine, given present locale; any more, and the clothes would begin soaring.

As her lips grazed along his throat again, Paul tilted his head back, eyes open to the sky. He could swear the moon had visibly moved since they had stopped here, and how insanely wonderful, he was actually feeling short of breath. He cupped Laurel's face, and they smiled at each other through moonlight.

"You keep at this," he said, "and I won't want to let you go to your own room tonight."

"Ooo, danger, danger." Laurel was mischief personified, then, inexplicably, more serious. "So, um, you don't think that would be wrong." Statement, not question, spoken with such neutrality he could not discern her own leanings.

"What? Are you kidding?"

"Well," and she shrugged easily, locking her arm in his. Starting to walk again, time for a little stroll, and *damn it,* he hoped he had not blown it by saying too much too soon. He found it easy to forget where they were. And the remark had been half in jest, anyway. Half. "Not that I necessarily go along with every consensus, but what do you think the average dormie over there thinks of shacking up?"

"Oh. I see your point." Paul breathed easier; perhaps he had not stomped on such thin ice after all.

There was the men's dorm, and the women's dorm, and yes, they were connected where the wings met in a right angle. And no, the doors were not locked, and no resident advisers stalked the halls in search of anyone of improper gender and intentions. It was really more like an apartment complex in that respect. But the moral imperative seemed unspoken: *Fornicators shall die horrible never-ending deaths by fire.* How cheery.

How manipulative. Be good cattle.

"You've lived around here a lot longer than I have," Paul said. "What *does* go on under that roof?"

"Very very little, I think. We're all brainwashed to hide our bodies." Then she leaned in close to him, pressing tight a moment. "I'm sorry, you must think I'm a tease all of a sudden. It's that lingering Catholic guilt, I can never get rid of it."

He decided the topic of sex could use a respite, until circumstances were more conducive. A segue was in order. Opt for religion, of all things, no powder keg *there*.

"I've been curious the past few days," he said. "Why *did* you leave the Church? And become a"—what was her phrase for it?—"a recovering Catholic?"

"This is just me, you understand? If it works for someone else, that's great, more power to them." Laurel walked silently for several seconds, putting thoughts in order. "It just got to the place where it didn't really *fit* anymore. It didn't apply to whatever I felt I needed. There was all this ritual, and all this pageantry, I guess you'd call it . . . and once I got old enough to really start questioning things and wanting understanding, all of it seemed so hollow to me. Religion by numbers, you could walk through it in your sleep. The whole idea of having to confess your sins to your priest instead of God, like you need a lawyer to plead your case for you. And then, the acts of contrition he gives you. Magic words, and everything's okay."

"Let me play the devil's advocate for a minute," and they laughed, what timing for *that* particular phrase. "What would you say to someone who told you, hey, you get out of it what you bring to it? If you feel it's hollow, it's only because your heart and soul are empty."

"Mmm, you *are* tough, aren't you?" She thought for a few steps. "I guess I'd say that's true for most things. But when it comes to matters spiritual, I can't buy it. It should *be* there to help carry us through when we're too tired to go on. It wasn't that I was going to Mass feeling empty. I was going with a real desire to keep getting some meaning out of it—and it was letting me down."

Paul nodded, squeezed her arm. "Well spoken."

"Votive candles," she said softly. "I *still* like lighting votive candles. Somehow that still has meaning for me." She laughed in spite
of herself and shook her head, here walks a hypocrite. Then, "Guess
what I used to wish."

"I have no idea."

"I used to wish I was black. At least on Sundays. Have you ever
seen some black services? Oh, Paul, all that singing and dancing
and *joy*, like they really *feel* it inside. All that celebration. Yes,
there's a time and a place for being solemn. But I have no use
anymore for any denomination that wants me to be dour all the
time. You know? And I don't want to be judged by people for who I
am. And I want to feel excitement that there's something out there
so much huger than I am, and loves me. That's all." She sighed,
mighty heavy out here tonight. "Anyway. *Your* thoughts? Arguments? Rebuttals?"

Again, that deep-seated wish to share what he knew of the body-
spirit connection. Not that there was much understanding, but boy,
it would sure illuminate *something*.

"I don't think any one faith has all the answers, to be honest.
Some come closer than others. And some of the more cult-oriented
faiths, I think they miss the point entirely. But I don't think you
could jump from one to another, like a smorgasbord, and pick and
choose and put it all together and still come up with the whole
picture, either. Our minds are just too small. Everybody's just trying to make sense out of it the best they know how. And if they
need a bunch of little guidelines and rituals to tell them who God
really is, if that's what gives their lives meaning and makes them
feel secure—then where's the harm? As long as they don't kill anyone in the name of God."

Walking, silent and dark, trees stirring mildly overhead. From a
distant branch, an owl hooted of some mundane mystery.

"That excitement," Paul said. "Did you find it here?"

"It was a start," and in her voice he could read that not all her
answers could be found on these grounds, and she knew it, and
would make no apologies. "I can build on it. That was all I needed
when I came here. That, and some time."

He smiled, knowing she could never see it, but then it was not
really for her at all. Ironic. Laurel had come here to build and grow
and make things more complex. He had come here to simplify.
Both under the wing of Donny Dawson, along with the others.
Children, in a sense, one and all, and he their focal point of heaven

on earth. A poor choice, perhaps, but Donny was, after all, mortal. As were they. Children of an ill-chosen god.

They walked, they talked, they grew sleepy. Even Laurel's caffeine load flamed out in time. She rubbed her stomach and complained of upset—a burning, maybe too many spices—and good-bye kisses came sweet and long in the dorm lobby. They had it to themselves, and when they broke for separate ways, he wondered if she was anywhere near as frustrated as he.

Soon, he thought. *Soon enough.*

The next night, late, lying alone in his bed and staring up at the ceiling. Blue skies earlier, but come evening they had given way to a constant rain, occasional rolls of thunder. Hours long, a marathon of a downpour, thirty-nine days to go and too late for an ark. If he smoked, that's exactly what he would have been doing at the moment.

He had flashed on something earlier, nothing overwhelming, but too often the little things were what crawled under the skin and burrowed until you had to scratch or go mad. Subversive little thoughts, they could pass virtually unnoticed, until they grew fat and surly.

Once upon a time, Lorraine. Now, Laurel. Both blondes, both with the power to wrap their hands around his heart. Naturally, an introspective soul was forced to wonder: Was he merely substituting the latter for the former? Go figure, Paul wasn't even sure he would care were that the undeniable truth. It felt too good.

Hardly fair to the singer if he was, though.

Enough. Away, away. He was thinking far too much. Let a couple of superficial similarities spring to mind, and he was off and running to question motives. One was supposed to lead with the heart, not with the head, and heart said go with it.

And never mind what role the hands played in it all.

Late at night, and waiting, and when the small tapping knock came he rose to answer. Laurel on the other side of the door, and he let her in and shut the barricade. Leave the prudery and the frigidity out in the hall, for what lay on this side of the door he counted as his own domain.

"Nobody even saw, I don't think," and then she smiled and arced a featherweight slap across her own cheek in mild chastisement. "Oh, who cares?"

He would have taken her coat had she worn one, but the trip had been indoor all the way. Can I take your clothes, instead? It seemed a bit pushy, but within minutes of initial issue-skirting small talk they were all over each other. Peeling clothes from themselves and each other with frantic urgency, get down to the altogether. Bodies by flickering lightning, and it was heaven, beneath the flash there exist no such things as flaws. Laurel. She was long and she was limber, no trace of whatever weight gain she had contended with fourteen months ago, and he admired the hell out of her for telling him at all. The honesty and forthrightness that had taken, particularly in a culture where the cult of body worship ruled millions strong.

He worshipped only hers this night, reveled in it, and she in his. Her breath panted across his receptive skin from thighs to forehead, and he knew it had been a very long time for her, as well. Laurel took it all from him in a rolling lock of fevered limbs, months of buildup. Since Lorraine, he had not even turned his own crank.

It was sweet and it was tender, Laurel beneath him with arms drawn around his shoulders, then his neck, eyes shut tight in the lock of good vibrations, tiny little cooing noises escaping as she crested each rise and fall. And if it was less than technically perfect, plagued by the falterings of unfamiliar rhythms, it bothered him not at all, for the welding of emotions more than compensated. They were here *for* each other, not to work *on* each other.

They spooned together in the afterglow, Paul fitting around her comfortably, encircling her with his arms across her breasts, and Laurel reaching back to drape one arm over his bare hip, her hand on his rump. He took absurd pride in that he was different from the norm in such moments as this, at least if all the women's polls were to be believed: he rarely dropped right off to sleep. Hark, what gallantry.

"Do you think I'm a good singer?" Asked after untold minutes of lazy stroking.

"I think you're a wonderful singer." He leaned in to peck her ear, exposed in a bawdy swirl of hair.

"You're not just telling me that?"

"Hey, I already got laid, I don't need to lie now," and he couldn't help himself, it was out before he could bar the smartass at the door, and he laughed as she feigned a huff and tagged her elbow down onto his ribs. Ow. Then, "No, I'm *not* just telling you that. Why?"

She still faced away in the gloom, her voice distant. "Oh . . .

people do. People lie. They tell you what they think you want to hear, never mind what they really think. I used to love the compliments. Then I got suspicious of them, I was always wondering what this person wanted from me."

He said nothing, probably the wrong move, but his brain was in slow gear, downphased by that most pleasant of hangovers, the sexual variety. He roused only mildly when she rolled over and straddled him, sitting on his stomach, hands clamped down onto his shoulders. Captive, while outside, rain streamed shapeshifters down the window, dim light projecting them hugely onto the walls.

"What do *you* want from me, Paul?" she whispered. Leaning down toward his face, and was she serious in this? Her face was so difficult to read. He saw it break into a Cheshire smile floating above, and even that offered little reassurance. "What do you want from me?"

"Everything," he whispered back, and in that moment it was wholly true. Good or bad, he wanted it all. The bout of pleasant but uninspired lovemaking had confirmed one thing for sure: He was tired of shielding himself from feeling.

"Good answer, you win the prize," and she eased off to roll back beside him. Facing him this time, new breakthrough. "I lied to you the other night."

He pushed up to one elbow, a little elevation for the revelation. He waited, patient, proceed at your own risk.

"Jax, the guitarist I was with for those years?" Her eyes tracked his own, not blinking. "We didn't exactly . . . break up. He shot himself one night. In front of me, Paul. Right in front of me," and out it came, a tale distilled to high potency, of a night of morbid anxiety and floundered dreams and too much Wild Turkey. *I figure our chances of making it are one in six, at the very best, babe,* Laurel said he had slurred from a sagging couch. *Probably not even that— but that's all the room I have,* and he showed her the .38, cylinder flipped open to reveal five full, one empty. One in six, Russian Roulette for the truly hardcore, and she had screamed and jumped to thwart his prophet's demonstration of odds while he had snuggled the muzzle to his ear.

Losers both, and if his brain wasn't working so well by that final hour of life, in the end he at least cast a good portion of it aside. If thine eye offends thee, pluck it out.

The story hit Paul like a club, all her pain still boiling beneath the surface, and he could feel its heat. Trying to imagine what it must have been like. He had witnessed death up close and personal, violent wretched death, and there had been nothing pretty about it at all. Ugly business indeed, and the fact that its most recent visits had befallen those he had not liked didn't even begin to lessen their impact. How much greater the devastation, then, to watch one you love extend the invitation to the reaper, willingly, catch me if you can.

Paul was at a loss over how to react, so he led with his heart, reaching for her. She wanted more, though, and gripped him fiercely, both arms and both hands, and one strong leg curling around his own. Something was different this time, something else entirely churning beneath surface niceties, and damned if it didn't stoke his own ardor.

She was off the bed in a flash, dumping out the contents of her purse. They hit the floor with a clatter, a jumble by night light, and she knelt amid it all, seeking . . . something. She drew a harsh breath, tossed her hair back over her shoulders, and he could see the sheen of sweat. Fresh outbreak or earlier residue, he did not know, did not care. She was back on the bed with the same demented speed, pressing something into his hand.

Her hairbrush. The back was wide, flat. Smooth and sturdy.

"Use it," a plea without pleading, and the first thing to pop into his hopelessly naive mind was the conventional route. But no. Oh no, somewhere when he wasn't looking, this little assignation had gone round an entirely different bend, and after a moment's assimilation he surprised himself by realizing he liked it.

Consenting adults, after all.

"Use it," firmer this time, her voice huskier, and she rolled face down and hinged in the middle, her behind rising before him like some kind of altar, poised and waiting. Laurel murmuring into the pillow, "I don't want you to pretend to be my father, or tell me I've been a bad girl, I'm not into that, I just like the *feel* of it. So use it on me and be yourself. *Use it.*"

He swung one halfhearted swipe, tag-you're-it, and she told him harder, and he complied. The crack was loud and shocking, and she expelled a sharp breath and he knew he'd done right. Harder, and he was there for that, too, dimly watching this unexpected kink from outside himself. Paul, performing like a dazed automaton, raise and swing, raise and swing, and as he broke his own sweat and could admit to himself that he was totally into this, he converged body and soul.

Laurel was biting the pillow in delight, her rump swaying gently, rolling and rising up to meet each fall of the brush, the sounds from her throat nothing at all like those of earlier orgasm and tremors. Deeper now, throatier, huskier, coming from someplace infinitely farther inside. The rain washed across glass, and he could feel her heat baking him as he knelt beside her, and she had to be glowing a cherry red back there by now.

He was flailing with an arm gone wild, every smack of brush on bum a sensory taste he had never dreamed he would like. The wielding of the power, however tyrannical, however instigated by her, it made no difference. Oh, she had read him well; bonded to him once with the tender sweetness, then turned and shown him the other side, the brazen underbelly.

So that he could see himself reflected.

They were two of a kind, really.

Paul was hard as a diamond by the time she snatched the hairbrush from his grasp and pitched it to the floor. Still maintaining her position—who was master now and who was slave?—she gripped him by one thigh and pulled him behind her, and his passage was assuredly easy.

No problems finding rhythm now, they were in sync, they were fundamental, they were primal, and he felt the red-hot stinging glow before him, on hands and hips. As he melted into it, its captive.

Death by fire.

The fears of the prudes had not been unfounded after all.

Laurel woke him in the morning, not much after dawn, by the looks of the light at the window. Still wet, still speckled, the rain must not have ended all that long ago.

She was dressed already, and sat at bedside stroking his touseled hair. He lay facedown—unconscious dream emulation of her?—and her fingernail traced a chill up the furrow of his back. Laurel smiled down at him, and the previous night might have been a bizarre dream, were it not for one thing. The look of intimacy in her eyes was new and undeniable. They had exchanged more than bodily fluids, they had exchanged pieces of themselves.

"I have to go," she said, and it never ended, did it? The curse of random sexual collisions in these hectic times, eat and run. "I better get to my own room before anyone else is up and moving around."

He smacked his mouth; it felt pasted together. "I thought you didn't care."

"You know what I mean." She planted a kiss at center back. "I'll see you later. Okay?"

He nodded and sleepily murmured yes, and she was gone in tiny footfalls and a soft latching of the door. No voices from the hall expressing shock, dismay, or jealousy. Coast clear.

Paul turned onto his back, arms behind his head. Watching the ceiling again, same as before her arrival. Oh, the difference a few hours could make, another layer of innocence peeled away. He ran a hand down himself—all parts present and accounted for. His pubic hair was crusted, felt like steel wool. He returned his hand behind his head. Sighed.

Laughed to himself, new morn exhaustion. He really should think about taking up smoking.

29

 If unemployment was the tree, then time for loopy contemplation and its attendant humiliation were certainly the bitter fruit. Simple revelations, profound in their truth, hit different men at different times. Rusty Sykes was morosely drunk, and never had the world looked clearer. In revelatory terms, pay dirt had been richly struck.

Barston, Oklahoma, on a Friday afternoon. A town of over forty thousand, some fifteen miles to the south of Oklahoma City.

Thirty-six years old, a roustabout for an Oklahoma petroleum company called Alamo Gas and Oil, and all it had taken was the flick of a managerial pen to pack him off to the land of the shitcanned.

Something was *not* right somewhere in this world.

Rusty had fallen victim to the late-twentieth-century equivalent of the witch-hunts that had provided so much jocular entertainment for medieval purveyors of moral standards. Urinalysis for drug use. Rusty, of the scraggly blond hair and untrimmed beard, knew he was no angel, no one was ever going to mistake him as such. But he did not foul his own nest by indulging in controlled substances while on the job. Sure, he might tip a beer or two out in the oilfields, but who didn't? Under that bitch of a sun, you were sweating it out almost as soon as it hit your belly.

Extracurricular fun was the culprit here, residual leftovers after a weekend bag of Popacatepetl Purple. Marijuana by any other name would smoke as sweet. But all bags were *not* created equal.

He lumbered through his house like an unsteady bear, in the kitchen upsetting a stack of grubby dishes. Countertop to floor in one easy move. The crash induced headaches, and he found the plates had been a condominium for a growing family of roaches. Eviction was fast and furious, and Rusty stomped as many into oblivion as he could, decorating the linoleum with a haphazard new design. Frame it and sell it, he could use the cash.

In the living room, Rusty slumped into his mortally wounded couch. TV time, it had been blasting since morning, when he had awakened here. Company only, agreeable voices, he'd had no idea what was playing. Oprah now, he recognized her, oh yeah, she was the one with the weight problem, up and down like a yo-yo. Her voice sounded warbly, and it was neither her fault nor the TV's. He broke wind in salute, and it burned, flaming methane. Three-thirty in the P.M., and breakfast had been consumed a mere hour before, two slices of dry toast and a bottle of Mexican tequila. Half gone and counting.

Too much fucking time on his hands. He supposed he could ring up Ned, erstwhile brother-in-law; fishing would go down easy about now. But Ned would know something was up if he called this time of day. Rusty had barely left the house in a week; a man does not admit to failure or drag anyone else into his problems. Period.

So what's a man to do, then? Rusty knew the answer to this one, like he knew the scars on the back of his hand. A man doesn't take being fucked with by sitting on his ass, he takes a stand, and if no-balls pricks in business suits are the cause of all misery in the known world, then they are to be held accountable. They robbed the poor, they looted the savings and loans, they dropped trou and waved their fat white untouchable asses at the little guy whose sweat has built their palaces.

A man—the real article—looks Fate in the eye and spits in it until it closes. And he puts his convictions to the acid test of action. Remaining forever true to his personal vision of divine retribution.

Rusty shoved himself vertical, wavered a moment, let the room flow back into shape beneath his boots. Steady . . . He left the tequila by the front door, can't forget that on the way out. He clomped into the kitchen for a tiny bottle, half filled with a clear and heavy-looking liquid. He uncapped it, held it beneath one nostril while pinching the other shut and deep-sniffing, then switched

nostrils. Amyl nitrate, quite a rush. No counterbalance for the tequila, but at least a welcome change of pace. For several timeless
moments, his entire face felt as if it were sliding off his skull. One
more mess to scrape from the linoleum.

But whatever the vantage point, the world was looking better and
better.

In the bedroom, he kicked clothes and underwear around until
car keys surfaced. From the hall closet, out of which rolled a swarm
of dustballs, he lugged his fishing tackle box. He and Ned had not
been for a month or more, but it was time to recall it back into
active duty.

Ready, set, go. With one steel-toed boot tip, he turned off the
tube by kicking a televised face into a million shards of smoking
glass.

Tequila bottle in one hand, tackle box in the other, car keys in his
teeth, Rusty sauntered outside to his car. Parked on an ugly bare
patch of front lawn, and while the house may have been leaning
toward condemnation, the car was finer than a thousand-dollar
whore. Late model Trans-Am, charcoal gray, gleaming from a loving
bimonthly coat of wax, her engine a seductive proposition to his
ear.

West, then, just past the fringes of town, toward a site built along
the Canadian River. The gaudiest shrine to Alamo Gas and Oil. Two
blocks from his house, before his exiting dust cloud had even settled, he began to laugh. Could not shut down, all this clarity, how
deliriously funny it all seemed now. His former employers, all
eunuchs and geldings saddled with terminal cases of wishful thinking. *Alamo* Gas and Oil, ah give us all a break. He entertained a
vision of Alamo's top CEOs in their OK City headquarters, pretending to be Texas wildcatters, snakeskin boots and ten-gallon hats
to a man.

He knew just how to catch their attention: give them a hard swift
kick in the wallet.

Westward, a pleasant afternoon drive, plenty of time for deep
thought. Dipping into the reservoir of news of national tragedy, a
random item from a few years back. The fine details were hazy, but
the grand picture was crystal. Some pink-slipped flight attendant
who had taken a Magnum aboard a plane owned by his former
employer. Scratch one passenger airliner from the schedules, gone
to kiss the ground in fireballs and screaming metal. Now *there* was a
man worthy of respect.

Rusty wasn't sure when the cop picked up his tail, didn't even realize he was blowing traffic signals. Sometimes they hung back to torture you, make you squirm, but the laugh was on him. Rusty only became aware when the roof lights lit up and the siren whooped to life. Police escort to the promised land. Rusty braked the car, pulling over to curbside. One eye on the tackle box, the other on the mirror while one of Barston, Oklahoma's finest made the macho stroll from his cruiser.

Time to spare. Rusty slugged from the tequila bottle, felt the guave worm slide past his lips. Ancient wisdom, eat the worm and see a vision. Cause and effect. He unlatched and opened the tackle box, hefting out one item and setting it alongside his thigh, no way could the bacon see it from the window. Not the most typical of fishing gear, a .357, but in places remote, no telling what crazies lurked about. Readiness is everything.

Footsteps outside his window, well-pressed uniform, mirrored shades and the smoothly officious voice of courtesy: "Sir, would you mind stepping out of th—"

Instinct ruled. Rusty swung the .357 up from his thigh and stared straight through the windshield as he jammed the gun out the window. He squeezed the trigger, two amazingly well-placed shots reducing the top of the cop's head into flying wet rubble.

"Asshole." Rusty spat on the leaking scarecrow splayed wide in the street and had become quite the center of screaming attention from everyone else out this fine day. He noticed none of it. "You don't bother a man just trying to do his job."

Point well made, he slammed the car into gear and continued on his merry way. West, and he could smell it even before he saw it, the lifeblood of the nation, the world. Black gold, Texas tea.

Oil, that is.

With the highway on one side, the river on the other, the refinery looked like a city unto itself. A city with its entrails yanked inside-out. At the end nearest Rusty's hammerdown approach, a row of enormous white storage tanks sat like huge vats. Beyond the tanks stood the oil distillation towers, hydrotreaters, catalytic crackers, and more—the spires of some cathedral erected to pay homage to Detroit and the deities of motorized transportation. Linking all was an incomprehensible network of pipes and pumps, furnaces and industrial blenders, with ladders and catwalks the only mode of access to more remote reaches.

Oklahoma crude, flowing through at fifty thousand barrels per day. No great shakes when compared with some of the majors that could handle ten times that, but when most of your days are spent looking at a few humble pumpers chugging away in the middle of a lonely field, this sight was still mighty impressive. This was the true heart of the country, from where the blood was pumped. This was where the crude became something useful, instead of the earth's excrement. No different from smelting gold from ore, or shaping a diamond from the rough.

He wheeled off the highway onto a frontage road, then onto the refinery's parking lot, fancying he could hear the distant bray of sirens. More than one. Yeah, well, they would soon be joined by a whole shitload of others, bank on that one.

Rusty vacated the Trans-Am with the tackle box clenched in one hand, ready to go fishing for paybacks. He slapped a grimy hardhat on his head, all the better to blend in with the rest of the drones servicing this petroleum queen. They paid him little mind as he passed, and he knew the drill. Too much to look forward to this weekend, a coming paycheck to carry them through. Rusty was anonymous, one more slave of the corporate fat cats, in dirty clothes and hardhat, with a toolbox on its way to fix some minor problem.

Rusty wound his way into the middle of a row of four storage tanks, dwarfed beneath them, the only thing bigger the sky. He stood between the center two, snugged himself at the base of one, an arbitrary choice. It would not matter.

All were about to turn into the biggest dominoes in Oklahoma.

Rusty opened the tackle box. So many memories, all those fishing trips when he and Ned got too drunk or too lazy to bait hooks or rig lures. Improvisation; they would instead chuck in the occasional stick of dynamite. Detonation, and a belch of water like some unexpected geyser, and after several moments you had a king's bounty of belly-up fish to choose from and net up. Good old Ned, a construction worker with ties to demolition experts. Ned appreciated a sporting edge.

Kneeling by his tackle box, Rusty fixed the blasting caps into place. Reached into a utility tray for a butane lighter.

He stood. Set two trails of sudden sparks to life. Two hands, two sticks, two caps, two fuses. Simplicity breeds success. He leaned back against the base of the monster tank, arms extended in cruciform fashion.

Rusty Sykes, once more the focus of attention. There was a lot of screaming. A lot of running. A lot of hysterical prayers that would not be answered in the affirmative.

"Well what's a man to do?" he bawled.

One consolation, however minor: No one would remember seeing him crying in public.

Two seconds later, Rusty was vapor and flying gristle at the center of twin blasts. Chain reaction. And all at once, the concept of *hell on earth* took on graphic new dimensions of reality.

30

Laurel was a jogger, as Paul had learned, and since he had a light sweatsuit of his own, it seemed only right that he at least try joining her. She made it look too easy, in her canary yellow togs and her hair pulled back into a ponytail. Running circuits around the compound grounds, she seemed to float, ever graceful. He slogged. Hell, this was hard work. He felt awful about himself beside her, needing only a curly tail and a snout, all the better for rooting truffles.

"You're not concentrating, you're not focusing," Laurel looking over to him—prompted by the sound of a wheeze, no doubt—and speaking with such cardiovascular ease.

"I'm focused," he panted. "On *dying*."

She veered in another foot and nudged him playfully with her elbow. Why did he get the feeling she was holding back and could run rings around him?

"Mind and body, mind and body, they have to work together."

He scowled. She was so abominably *cheerful* about this, that was the worst. Like those vacant cheerleader types on video workout shows. Surely that was not a healthy attitude. Let her spring a surprise S&M spanking fetish on him, he could adapt to that just fine. This would take harder work. Perplexing, no? Perhaps because he found administering swats so much easier to accomplish. And did he have a hidden proclivity for it, as well? The benign sadist in him, maybe, with no evidence of a masochist, benign or otherwise, that would warm to this jogging business.

He paced her as she aimed them for the sprawl of greenery before the dorms' entrance. Eyes surreptitiously straining right, call it sexist, but he found jolly incentive in watching the jouncing of her breasts beneath her top. The carrot at the end of the stick. They slowed to walk the last sixty yards or so, keep the muscles from cramping from sudden stop. When they were before the dorms, she halted and did a few deep-knee bends. Paul collapsed into the grass.

"You're killing me," he said. "Aerobicide."

Even her eye makeup still looked fresh, *damn* her. "It's just your first day. I promise, it'll be easier tomorrow."

He half groaned, half wailed. Tomorrow. This was Friday. He had hoped she took weekends off, but apparently not. No rest for the insane.

Laurel plopped down beside him, and he managed to sit up for her, lean into her. Support. A quick kiss, and it wasn't just pity, he took heart in that. She ran a hand through his hair. It was as far as she'd take it. Decorum held that public affection between couples here was okay; public passion was not.

"Baby," she teased. "You don't see *me* acting like a baby."

He rolled his eyes. "You could run a marathon. What have *you* got to act like a baby about?"

Silence, as her gaze dropped groundward, and while she didn't look unduly concerned, the moment sharpened. Paul could feel it like the sheen of a blade, and he straightened the rest of the way, oh man, what secret had she withheld this time?

"It's my own fault." Laurel frowned, as if she needed to slap herself sensible. "I, uh—I have an ulcer." The wry shameful grin of the truly embarrassed.

He let this settle. An ulcer. Well, nothing life-threatening, and it was not of the venereal nature, though he imagined it was certainly unpleasant enough. This fit, actually, in retrospect. More than once had she looked pained about the gastric regions, passing it off as indigestion. Like a few nights ago, the night of first kisses. Poor Laurel, thinking she had to maintain secrecy about this. Then, realization:

"And you *still* drink coffee the way you do?"

"I know, I know. We're all gluttons for our doom." She knew what a big Indigo Girls fan he was; no mistaking the lyrical reference. "Please don't yell at me, I get enough of that from Doctor Preston."

Hmm, a common denominator, the same doctor as had been summoned when Amanda emerged from deep cover last week.

"What, is he like the usual case M.D. for people here?" Paul asked.

"I think so."

Of course he had to ask the obvious. "What about Donny? Have you seen him about it?"

Laurel looked at him, firm and gentle at once. The look of a young mother preparing to explain the truth about Santa Claus. "What do *you* think?"

Oh, diplomacy, where are you now? Paul stroked his chin, the great statesman. Although why bother? She obviously had some misgivings of her own about the man.

"I think," he slowly said, "I've seen Donny do some genuine good with people . . . and that you're probably still better off going to a doctor." There. Kissinger couldn't have handled it better.

She nodded. "Except I still have the ulcer."

You don't have to for long, and he crept his hand toward hers. A simple ulcer would present no problem at all, he could mend that gastrointestinal hole and not even break sweat. A far cry easier than, say, keeping pace with her as she ran laps around the compound.

But she would deserve an explanation—*all* of it, no omission or sugarcoating of the unlovely flip side—and that would be infinitely more difficult than the healing itself. Whatever the two of them were destined for, this would forever affect it. Was he ready? Was she? Would she find it too mind-blowing to contend with, once the truth sank in, think him loathsome, inhuman?

Wasn't quite like Superman explaining the lowdown on himself and Clark Kent to Lois Lane, now, was it?

Oh, just do it, and he reached for her hand, let the consequences take care of themselves—

"There you are. I've been looking all over for you."

Abort, abort. Gabe Matthews at three o'clock, flanking them from within the dorm. Paul let his hand fall short of intention, and merely held hers. Smiled up at Gabe as he left the sidewalk and approached. Casual Gabe, at the moment, as opposed to dress-for-success Gabe. Wonders never ceased.

"Ready for a shock?" He sounded pleasant enough.

"I'm sitting down," Paul said.

"I've been reduced to playing messenger boy." Self-effacing shrug.

Paul slapped a clawed hand over his heart, oh say it ain't so. "Must be a good one."

Gabe nodded crisply, and only now acknowledged Laurel's presence with a tight belated smile. Intentionally rude, or merely preoccupied? Give him the benefit of the doubt.

"I'm hoping you have some free time now. Amanda would very much like to meet you at their house."

A summons from the cloistered queen of Dawson Ministries, this was most unexpected. He glanced across to Laurel.

"Sure, sure, go," she told him, nodding. Ponytail bobbing. "I was about ready to go catch a shower anyway." She grinned wickedly, shook his knee with one hand. "Jim Thorpe."

"Great." Gabe motioned him to follow. "I've got a cart over at the offices, I'll drive you over."

Paul tugged at the material of his sweatsuit. "Can't I shower too? Or at least change? I look cruddy."

Over her shoulder, Laurel gave him her teasing laugh as she mounted the steps toward the dorm, while Gabe waved his worry aside. "You look fine, you're fine. You'll set her at ease like this."

They hoofed it for the office building and boarded the cart. With a jerk just shy of whiplash, Gabe set off on the western path for Donny's house. Wind in their hair, as if Paul hadn't felt that enough for one afternoon.

"So I assume you'll be staying here after all?" Gabe said.

"Excuse me?"

"Staying," spoken almost cheerfully. "As in, not leaving. Last week, after you brought Amanda back around. I was afraid you were about to leave Donny high and dry."

This made sense now. Paul wondered, though, if Donny had set him up to it. A friendly Q&A session, report back when prudent. It was almost funny, the influence he suddenly held over the man. The goose that laid the golden eggs, who could fly anytime.

"I cooled down. I got it out of my system."

Gabe was nodding. "From what I hear, to be honest, I don't think Donny handled it well at all. I think his treatment of you was inexcusable. But—he's been under a lot of stress lately. I don't mean that as a defense. Just an explanation."

"He made me feel like a pawn that night."

Cresting a small asphalt rise, top speed. Whee.

"You are," Gabe said.

Nothing like a little painful honesty to take the wind out of your sails. "Well. Thank you for being blunt."

"I'm a pawn too. And so is Donny. We're all pawns to something greater than ourselves. That's why we're all here, because we've chosen to be pawns for the same thing."

More compound rhetoric, which Gabe had generally seemed to be free of. Paul nodded, sheer reflex.

"It takes a smart, secure person, though," Gabe went on, "to know he's a pawn, and not mind it at all. Because he realizes he's still vital. I hope you're not overlooking that."

Paul nodded again. "We're square here. We're fine. If Donny's worried, tell him not to be. I'm not going anywhere."

Gabe turned to look him in the eye for several beats, wind blowing his hair back to the right. Eyes off the road, driving by instinct and memory. "I was curious for myself, Paul. You don't think *I'm* concerned about your welfare too?"

Oddly enough, Paul believed him. The guy was so serious. Then he lightened, as if the possibility of hard feelings had been safely shunted aside.

"I take it that you and Laurel hit it off." Light, okay, but very neutral.

"So far, so good. We've got enough in common, I think." Buzzing along in the cart, windblown and free. Like holy golf fanatics. And he thought of her, realizing it had come, the delicate ache within, they were apart at the moment and he wished it were otherwise. He would leave himself open for such beloved pain, trivial yet profound. Gladly.

"She told me."

Gabe turned again, curious. Cocked head.

"About the guitar player. Shooting himself. She told me."

Gabe nodded. No frown, no smile, no nothing. "Congratulations," in that same flat neutrality.

You are one odd *fucker, aren't you?* And Paul decided he wouldn't volunteer another word on it. Speak only when spoken to.

The compound fell in their wake and the Dawson house loomed nearer. Sanctuary, haven, prison. And speaking of pawns, Paul had to fleetingly wonder which Donny was more of a pawn to: God, or house payments? Petty, petty.

He and Gabe entered through the back, porch to mud closet to kitchen to hallways to staircases to third floor. So many doors up here, so many rooms. So much space assigned to nothing.

And Amanda Dawson, surrounded by it. Paul's first glimpse of her was heart-tugging, if anything. Poised in a chair by the windows of her room, staring out with a quietly desperate longing. The gaze of a wheelchair-confined child watching a park swarming with playmates running themselves into happy exhaustion. She wore some sort of one-piece lounging outfit, velour perhaps, nearly shapeless around her, body lost within it. Her right arm was tucked absently against her side, drawn up like a chicken wing. Her skin appeared bleached of color in the fading light of day, but at least more lifelike than before. And her hair, though limp, was clean and shiny.

On the mend, yes, but if only he could have restored spirit along with body.

Gabe softly cleared his throat, and she turned toward them with a start. Frowning briefly, ready to snap at unexpected intruders, and then her brow smoothed. A warm smile, a beckoning invitation. They entered and she looked down at her clenched arm, made a conscious effort at letting it hang more naturally.

"Thank you, Gabe." Spoken carefully, as if practiced. A considerably more pleasant voice than the raspy gargle with which she had awakened. "For bringing him, I mean."

"Happy to do it." Gabe checked his watch. "If it's all the same to you, I'll be shoving off, let you two get acquainted on your own. I've got an in-basket in my office I wouldn't wish on an enemy."

He stepped forward, cordially touched Amanda's hand, squeezed Paul's shoulder with a smile of confidence and assurance, glad you're still with us. Then gone, just like that, and Paul stood awkwardly, feeling vaguely abandoned. Never realizing until now that you *could* feel awkward in a sweatsuit. Circumstances no doubt played a part in this. It was the first opportunity he had had to hang around and see how someone he had healed fared in the aftermath. TV news recaps did not count, real life distilled into twenty seconds. Here, it went on and on.

"I thought we should meet formally." Amanda glanced down at herself, then at Paul's sweats, and barked a tiny laugh. "Well, this is hardly what I'd call formal. You poor thing, I didn't mean for Gabe to drag you over here, come as you are."

"He's persistent."

"Sit. Please." She nodded toward the edge of the bed, and he did so. Gracious enough manner, nonimposing, she had been obliquely quick about setting him at ease.

"I was wondering how you've been getting along."

"Day by day. It's not been a damn bit easy." She winced when she saw the flicker in Paul's eyes. "I'm sorry. Ever since I . . . woke up . . . sometimes words like that just pop out. The therapists say it's normal."

He shrugged it off. "I've said worse."

"So have I." She smiled at him, head tilted lightly to one side. A look of affection, warmth, thank you for making this easy on me. "It's just been this past day or two that my voice really started sounding like itself again. I sounded awfully strange those first few days."

"You'd been through a lot."

"But I'm bouncing back. I'll be up and trying to walk between the parallel bars in another day or two. Oh, it'll be just *wonderful*," her face and eyes hardening with abrupt sarcasm. "I'll have a brace on my leg, and a belt around my waist so my therapist can catch me when I start to fall on my butt. It'll be so much fun, I don't think I can stand it." Brooding by the window, unease condensing afresh in the room, and then she softened. Shook her head and apologized.

"It really did a job on you, didn't it? That fever."

"The fever," she echoed dully, eyes slowly averting. "Right."

In the moment, she reminded him of Lorraine, certain small mannerisms. Back at KGRM during his final days of tenure, so many things walled behind Lorraine's eyes, so much she had wanted to say but would not turn loose of. Because of nameless fears.

Change of subject, too sudden. "You've made quite an impression on Donny. I haven't seen him this excited about much of anything for years." She seemed to share little of that enthusiasm at present. Although it would be difficult to jump for joy when your body wouldn't even allow it. "You really can do it," little more than a whisper, "can't you?"

He nodded, wondering why the awe? She *had* seen Donny pull off similar wonders. Hadn't she? "Yeah. I can."

Her eyes were bright and moist, harbor of secrets swimming for release and finding only clear walls. Where they peered out, in envy. In anguish. Had she been a close friend instead of a new acquaintance, he would have begged her to spill it, all of it, hold nothing back until all was purged.

"Then use it wisely," she said. "And watch out for yourself, too."

Paul nodded, assured her that he would, unsure just what dangers she foresaw for him. Perhaps her mood swings were augmented by mild paranoia, as well. And perhaps not. No further explanation, however, and she announced she'd grown quite tired. He took the cue. His audience with the melancholy queen of Dawson Ministries was about to end.

So he made his good-byes, rose from the bed. As he gently reached down to shake one fragile hand, she told him to come back and visit again. He said he would, knowing he meant it.

She isn't what I thought she'd be, he thought on his way out of the house. Once outside, the fresh air cleansed nose and mind of an underlying reek, so subtly lingering in her room. As if it had soaked into the walls themselves. The room stank of more than illness in retreat, it stank of despair. Her soul was sicker than her body had ever been.

With everything he had heard about her, the pictures seen in ministry literature, the film clips aired on the show, he had expected her to be, despite the coma, all sweetness and sunshine. Undaunted by obstacles, forever focused ahead with the determination of a bulldozer and the grace of a swan.

But no. God bless her, she was human after all.

And he liked her this way far better.

Some truths are painfully self-evident: Paul Handler was not much as she had envisioned. Good news, bad news. On the one hand, such relief that he was not some velvet-tongued huckster out to make a fast buck in the cash machine Donny's ministry had degenerated into. On the downside, though, this genuine aspect of his character inspired all manner of worry over what would happen to him. For she was in no position to keep watch and make sure the machine did not eat him alive.

Or worse, turn him into one more self-deluding cog.

It had all run out of control. Dawson Ministries, assuming an ugly life of its own, somehow, over bygone years when she hadn't been looking. Or perhaps she had seen it all along and had refused to let it register. Little humble girl from Arkansas, grown up to play in the big leagues. It didn't matter now; the cause of blindness is irrelevant when compared with the results.

But in the hours preceding her early-summer header down the stairs, the veil had begun to lift from her eyes. Thinking of Christ, taking whip in hand to drive the money changers from the temple, you have turned my Father's house into a den of thieves. In two thousand years they had learned nothing, only how to raise the ante, and she could still feel the lashes.

Now? Now her eyes were clearer than they had been in years. It was the twist of a cruel knife to realize that she did not much like what she had seen this past week-plus. Too many priorities had turned around or been turned away from entirely.

She wondered how long it would take until she could walk on her own, strong and unassisted. Because if some things did not change around here, she just might feel like doing some walking away from the whole of it.

And Donny, may God help you if you take Paul and drag him down to the same level you're at now.

Worry? Oh my yes, she would, wishing for a remote pair of eyes with which to observe the two of them together. What was said, the guidance given. Donny could no longer be trusted to give a wholly accurate account. And knowing Gabe's loyalty, there was little use in trusting him, either. Although something deeper nagged about Gabe, amorphous and vague, like a dream submerged into the silt of the subconscious.

In the light of the dying afternoon, Amanda let her head sag against the chair, for now as confining as a cage.

I want to walk. I want to run. I want to play the piano. But mostly . . .

I just want out.

The walk back to the dorms was long and tiring, and that in itself ticked him off. Finish that fiasco of a run with Laurel, and before he can even regain a resting heart rate, who should come along but Gabe, scooping him up and ferrying him away. Not even sticking long enough to leave him with a way back.

And why the rush in the first place? Amanda wasn't going anywhere. But no, had to be Gabe's way, according to his schedule, not even time for a shower. And there was the other thing, too: Absolutely unspoken, but read between lines of mannerisms and attitude. If Paul didn't know better—and he wasn't at all sure he did—he would be tempted to say Gabe had been jealous of Laurel.

Things around here were definitely skewed.

Like that dark smudge in the southern sky, now what the hell was that?

When Paul got to his room, he found a note slipped beneath his door. Laurel's handwriting, mood swing complete, all is well again. She suggested they forget about cafeteria food tonight, trek north into the city for something a little more upscale. No problem, he could go for that.

He stowed the note in his desk—her first to him, a historic keeper—then clicked on his TV. Flipped the dial once around, see about catching some news while he readied for the showers.

Local news, and he stood immediately riveted, hand frozen as he prepared to tug off his sweatshirt. The innocent wisp in the sky took on tragic meaning. A young anchorwoman stood well-distant before a background conflagration, Dante's Inferno festering up through a pustule in the earth. A caption supered across the bottom of the screen identified the location as the Alamo Gas and Oil Refinery, Barston, Oklahoma.

". . . untold scores dead and injured here at what officials are already calling the state's worst petroleum industry disaster . . ."

She was bright and perky, appropriately grave of demeanor and utterly nerveless. A real pro, had to be turning cartwheels in her head about now, but no, couldn't let the public see she realized she was on the story of her career, a stroke of luck she could parlay into a quasar of a future if she handled it right. Paul knew how the game worked. A potential star in the making, but whatever personal drama was in the foreground, it was eclipsed by the background. This was no mere blaze, this was a firestorm. Nagasaki in miniature, for the viewing pleasure of central Oklahoma, and they cut to shaky footage of a paramedic crew bearing a stretcher.

Paul could swear it was steaming.

He recalled informational bits and pieces, gleaned from sources as diverse as *Hippocrates* magazine and Richard Pryor, talking about when he'd accidentally toasted himself. The tales of burn therapy were as vivid as they were varied. Paul's skin crawled every time he contemplated it, there but for the grace of God, etc. Few injuries could match a severe burn's potential for suffering.

Scores dead and injured, the news had said, and while he could do nothing for the former, maybe a few of the latter he could spare some disfiguring agony. No way could he sit and isolate himself through the buffer zone of television, vicarious concern, oh isn't that dreadful.

He dug from a dresser drawer his road atlas, unused since coming off the close of Donny's tour. He found that Barston was a straight shot down I-35 from Oklahoma City; he could be there in under half an hour. And while he had no idea where Alamo Gas and Oil was located, once motorized, it would be no hindrance.

Where there's smoke, there's fire.

He had seen nothing like it since war coverage, and nothing short of combat experience could have adequately prepared him. Smoke and fire, chaos and death. Twilight sky eclipsed by stinking black clouds, then lit hellishly from below. And always, the roar.

The interstate was shut down well over a mile before the nearest reaches of the refinery, with traffic backed up at least another two miles, bumper to bumper and awaiting a confused rerouting through Barston. A double-line used car lot, inching along while the voyeurs of calamity made sure they got an eyeful.

This would take forever, hell with it, and Paul cut a sharp right to wheel onto the shoulder. He goosed the accelerator and arrowed past the others awaiting their turn. And was halfway to the blockade and its guardians before realizing that he had been so intent on getting here, he'd not even considered that he had no authorization to get any closer. Sometimes he really took his own near-omnipotence for granted.

Think fast, dipping into the reservoir of instinct that had allowed him to wing it on radio so many successful times. No turning back for battle plans now, and if the grim frustration on the state troopers' faces ahead said anything, it was that they were in no mood to play nursemaid to some ghoul wanting a closer peek.

A trooper who looked to have a bullshit tolerance of zero stepped into his path along the shoulder, one hand dropping to his hip, the holstered pistol riding there. Paul was glad dusk had set, eliminating the need for the mirrored shades they always seemed to wear. It seemed very important to see this man's eyes. Paul slowed, coasting to a stop a dozen feet before him while the lines of motorists veered a creeping left along the barricade of state police cruisers. Five seconds later, and the trooper was fuming at his door.

"Turn your ass around and get back in line!" The usual toneless courtesy these guys spoke with had gone up with the smoke. He was all furrowed brow and clenched teeth, tight jaws and sweat. *"No one's* getting past this point, now *move* it."

Looking him straight in the eye, his own soft as a doe's and aching like a martyr's. "I'm a priest." For the first time he was actually glad of his conservative haircut. "I thought I might at least administer some last rites—*please?*"

The trooper's shoulders lost some squaring. A human being now, instead of an obstacle. "You don't—don't look much like a priest."

Paul conjured the most benevolent smile he could, both hands resting calmly on the steering wheel. "We all start young," and then he looked down at his sweats. "I was in the parish gym when I heard the news. Please?"

The man's head sagged, tongue wetting dry lips. He nodded with weary resignation, motioning Paul ahead with a single flick of one finger. "Just watch yourself in there, okay, Father? Don't park up too close, and for crying out loud, don't get in anybody's way."

Paul nodded solemnly and eased his foot off the brake. Once past the traffic jam and the blockade and most of the road signs, he gained an unobstructed view of the tableau ahead. Firestorm as centerpiece, solid burning pillars trying to bake the new stars from the sky. Circling them was a ragtag army fighting what looked like a losing battle. Fire trucks sprayed arcs of water and chemicals. Helicopters circled overhead in hurricanes of propwash and turbines. Firefighters in shiny anodized suits ventured toward the malignant oven the refinery had become, while others without suits were as close as the heat would allow.

He parked on the highway's shoulder, three hundred yards from the frontage road and the parking lot it accessed. Which looked to have become a center of operations. Paul jogged the rest of the way, sweating rivers by the time he made it into the thick of things. The priestly ruse remaining on his lips in case his presence was challenged.

He consulted a paramedic at momentary rest, gulping water and scrubbing filthy sweat from his face, and got directions to one stretch of the lot serving as a triage zone. Both shouting at each other to be heard.

Paul jogged over, arrived at triage in the wake of a departing ambulance, gone in a scream of siren. He stood in the middle of confusion and babble, ignored for being whole of body, and here was the only place where people were lying down on the job. For they had no choice.

Eleven of them, at the moment, on blankets spread to cushion them on the asphalt, puny comfort. A couple of medics frantically worked on one down the line. Few of these casualties had much of their clothing left intact, and even when they did, it was not always easy to distinguish burnt fabric from burnt flesh. Even gender was guesswork on some of them, ragged and blackened. A few screamed agonies toward sky and smoke, purgatorial voices whose misery Dante would have been hard pressed to convey. And yet the lives of all had been spared. Those less fortunate were farther away, crisp dark lumps beneath a tarp.

Although once he had gotten a better look at the living, Paul wasn't sure they were the lucky ones after all.

He knelt beside the nearest casualty, a man grilled from the knees up, awash in the sweet stink of an overdone steak. Burned bald, he was a breathing, moaning roast. With eyes.

Paul lifted his hand over the man and formed the sign of the cross. In part to maintain his assumed identity, the rest because it simply felt right to do so. Head to beltline, shoulder to shoulder, a quiet strength in the movements, comfort even in this most catastrophic of moments. A center, God's mercy beseeched.

Please help me keep my stomach down, and he lay both hands on the blackened wasteland of flesh. So hot beneath palms and fingers, like a raging fever. Brittle and scabrous, so unlike flesh it was almost like touching something insectile. A carapace, and he then took the flashfire of anguish as the man's burden backwashed into him. Holding tight to his delivery, purpose . . .

Hanging in through to the end, when flesh and muscle and nerve began to regenerate beneath their crusted forerunners, forming in layers from bone outward. Broiled hide, displaced by the fresh tissue beneath, flaking away with oozing white blood cells fighting massive infection. Onward, inward, outward, the restoration was total. And while the man looked no better, still grimed with soot and draped in the tatters of charred coveralls and dead skin, scrub it all away and he would be a new man. But inside his head, with the suffering of whatever trauma the ordeal had branded upon him, he would surely have to fight another battle. Of an entirely different nature, with someone else's help.

When it was finished, Paul nearly keeled over onto his own back. Wrung out, his sweats heavy and sticky, soaked through. Brain baking within skull, thoughts slippery as eels, his insides on slow cook. Something was different this time, as if he had dived too deep, absorbed too much.

Paul shook his head. Swirling, kaleidoscope hell, everything in twos. Balance was shaky at best, and his head began to pound, like a spike driven through his forehead. After another moment vision stabilized, and he cursed himself, no time to flake out now. The night's work had just begun; these screaming voices around him, rescuers and rescued, all sounded in far too much pain. Night's work just begun, he clung to that, no matter how covert the work may be, and he wiped greasy ashen crust from his hands onto his sweatshirt.

The middle of flaming chaos, lives and livelihoods reduced to smoking wreckage amid the birth of new heroes. While Paul moved on. And on. And on.

Until he could scarcely move at all.

31

It was the cheapest renovation ever worked inside the Dawson house. The thought made Donny snort once with impacted laughter; if he could still see humor, however bleak, then maybe he was not too far gone. The second floor, once upon a time, had been merely that. So much more now, though, a neutral territory poised between two others in a cold war. Ground floor his own, Amanda's domain on number three.

He had been up there only once today, midafternoon, sneaking over from the offices and venturing a quick peek into the therapy room. Amanda lay in the center of the sort of mat he had seen gymnasts train on, therapist coaching her as she floundered about and tried rolling from side to side. Their focus was such that neither had noticed him, and for this he was grateful. Standing there, professional charlatan, while his wife looked like a giant infant, lacking even basic motor control. He had spun from the doorway to lean against the hallway wall, ashamed of her and ashamed of himself. Plenty to go around for everyone.

Black Friday.

He was putting off the inevitable, this was no secret from himself. He would have to deal with her sometime, and deeply, no superficial level with good cheer and confidence tacked onto his face like rigid greasepaint. He would have to really *talk* with her, *care* for her, *live* with her again. None of which he had to do right now. For while she had passed back into the land of the living, he was still retaining the services of the nurses for her nontherapy hours. Whatever her needs were—bathroom, mealtime, cleanup—they could handle it. Their shoulders, figuratively speaking, were far broader than his.

Mandy blamed him, he could read it in every fiber of the woman. Her home had become her asylum, and she held him responsible. Which once he might have been able to deal with, if it had been his wife—but this woman he didn't even know.

Was it possible to still love a stranger?

Donny had been thinking terrible things in unguarded moments. Like maybe it would have been better had she died in that coma, or even at the foot of the stairs. So that the memories and her persona would have been preserved, always fresh, always pleasant. There would be guilt and grief, too, of course, but these would scab over in time, and heal. But with present circumstances, every day was an open wound. A weeping lesion.

Such thoughts were brief, but the fact of their presence at all sent him to his knees for prayers he could not formulate.

If only she were as easy to deal with on a personal level as she had been on a ministerial. The latest story being that Amanda was back from Central America and was taking some time off to rest up from the aftermath of a tropical fever.

I've got a problem, there, he had admitted it, and given that admitting a problem was half the battle, surely that was enough for tonight. He could take no more. Diversions, anything to keep his mind occupied. He had already eaten, it was too early for sleep, masturbation was shameful and too brief anyway. Looked like it was TV.

In the TV room, Donny knelt before a cabinet adjacent to the monster Sony. He scanned videocassette titles, something was bound to seize his fancy. He had all his own *Arm of the Apostle* shows, of course. Biblical dramas, Disney features, some Hitchcock, more. Whatever held maximum escapist potential would be tonight's entrée.

He heard a faint noise, behind him, across the room, and turned. Expecting the nurse. Nearly suffering a coronary when he saw just how wrong he was.

"*Paul!*" he screamed. Or he thought he did, nothing was clear anymore, and it had just gotten unbelievably worse.

Paul was shuffling in, reeking of vile smoke even at this distance. His shapeless sweatsuit was stained with ghastly handprints: blood, soot, ash, worse. He bent over, clutching his belly as if suffering severe cramps. He took one look at Donny with eyes that did not even seem to be focused upon this world, and promptly tumbled into the floor.

"PAUL!" And now he was certain he called the man's name, but no answer, Paul was obviously far beyond that. Donny weathered the emotional hurricane that chilled his insides, then scuttled over to kneel at Paul's side. Donny shook him, pleaded for awareness, got only gibberish. Protests muttered in a dream.

A body in his arms, and this all felt as if the hammer of déjà vu had come cracking down upon his head. He lifted the sweatshirt and determined that Paul was at least not physically harmed.

Perhaps the greatest relief of all, *Because I couldn't do a thing about it if he was, could I?* Times such as this were the very worst, when the suffering was real and personal and borne by someone with a familiar face. He could not relieve it, and what cosmic jest or blunder at the dawn of the previous decade had set him to thinking he could? Why the one, and no more?

So think, *think*. Some kind of illness? Perhaps. But this did not account for the condition of his clothes, and the smell. Paul had clearly spent some time around mortal injuries. An accident somewhere on the compound? Not likely; word would have reached him by now.

Somewhere else, then, and what had he *done*, tried to heal so much he nearly planted himself in an early grave? For who was to say that the healings did not extract some sort of physical toll on his body after all? Some cumulative aftereffect.

Gabe. Gabe would know what to do now, could lay his finger on exactly what—

No, he'd not seen Gabe for hours, not since he had left the office for his apartment. Only a few miles away, but still too far when time was crucial, and *damn it*, he couldn't always be relying on Gabe when reality got hinky and the pressure redlined into the danger zone. What if there *were* no Gabe? It could always happen.

This one would have to be a solo flight.

Donny charged up the stairs, three at a time, and got the nurse to hurry down and monitor Paul, make sure his vital signs didn't poop out while he spent some phone time. The phone he had first ignored when Mandy had taken her header down the stairs. The breeze from his passage through the entry hall set the delicate crystals of the chandelier tinkling like wind chimes.

And God smiled, Irv Preston was at home.

A minute later, Donny scooped up Paul's limp form and toted him out to one of the Cadillacs in the garage, then set a course for a rendezvous at the hospital. . . .

Which was one jumping place this Friday night. Overflow from the disaster down at Barston, and once Donny caught the lowdown on what had happened there, and given that petroleum stench of Paul's clothing, the pieces fit together. Adequately, if not enough to give him a precise account of what had happened.

In the emergency room, Paul was cleaned up and over the next seventy-five minutes was given the routine checking out that anyone in his condition would receive. Vital signs were measured, revealing a slightly elevated blood pressure and pulse rate. A panel of lab tests was ordered. A complete blood count checked for infections, low platelets, dehydration, hemoglobin abnormalities; a differential looked at drawn samples of red and white blood cells. Chemical tests measured his electrolytes to ascertain no imbalances, and a blood sugar looked for high or low glucose. It all checked out okay.

But he was suffering from obvious abdominal pain. They ran an obstructive series on him, flat and standing X-rays to look for odd fluid and air levels that might be the culprit. Again he stymied them. At least he was remaining consistent as an oddity.

The only thing of note, and it *was* significant, was the rebound tenderness experienced when the ER doctor manually probed Paul's abdomen. Lower left quadrant, and the educated guess was possible appendicitis, but they didn't have enough to go on to say for sure.

Standard textbook procedure said to admit the patient for observation and let the disease or condition declare itself. Both Preston and the attending ER physician were in complete agreement on this. More tests would be run in the morning, when a radiologist would be on duty.

Because something in there didn't feel at all right. Something in that lower left quadrant was displacing organs.

Irv reassured Donny that Paul would be fine, fine, they'd get to the bottom of things the next day. Let Paul sleep the night here in a private room in the care of their capable hands.

Capable hands, now *that* prickled.

But as he wheeled the Cadillac home, alone, windows open to air the oil smoke stench from the upholstery, it wasn't all knuckle-wringing worry.

Donny felt *good,* in a strange way.

For a while there, earlier, he had actually taken charge.

Dreamtime, despite sedation. Jarring fragments, a whole new world unfurling across the mental landscape, Paul traveling it naked, and by its very air knowing it to be a much younger world. Himself but not himself, two minds in one body, looking at arms and legs and muscular torso, deeply bronzed, and knowing them to be someone else's. The other's name insignificant, no names needed here in the primal desert.

Neither for himself, nor his three compatriots, burning under red desert sun, wind scouring them with dust and grit as the baking plains stretched before them, and they were running—

Glance behind to see the city walls and the angry throng, *Why do you hate me so?,* blood streaming from where a thrown earthen brick impacted with his head, and who were they all, these screaming masses intent on driving the four from their midst? What crime had this quartet committed? *I bring healing to you—*

I bring restoration—

Bricks raining down and hateful jeers lashing at backs like the whip, the abyss opened behind his eyes, other eyes staring from the darkness, the extended hand of invitation, lord of healing and lord of—

But I bring HEALING . . .

NO, let it not be so, that I also bring the other—

Saturday, jerking upright in the predawn, sudden swirling plunge of disorientation of an unfamiliar room, unfamiliar walls, unfamiliar bed. Across this dark room, a TV set hovered from the wall like a frozen ghost. *Hospital,* it made sense. Not the least of which was the exposed vulnerability he felt beneath the sheets, their idea of très chic hospital wear. His rump was hanging out. Paul eased down into the bed again with a groan, the last painful traces of bodily mutiny scraping through head and abdomen.

For the past several hours, dreams had been far more vivid than reality. Fleeing the hellfire of Alamo Gas and Oil; everything since then was gone or, at best, a half-remembered snippet. Interstate at night, blurry and resounding with the blaring horns of other cars with which he had somehow avoided collision. Staggering into

Donny's home, last-ditch effort at some sort of relief. Lying on a hard, cool table as hands probed freely and blinding lights burned from above—*Am I dying?* but nothing else lived in that light, it was barren and sterile. The rest? Blackout, a casualty of his own traitor senses.

This is getting weirder.

And the dreams, now what were these *new* confusions all about? Desert and city, panic and pain, the loss of home and the hatred of the known world. It had been so real, he could feel the sting of each windblown grain of sand. So dimensional and total that it felt less the arcane symbolism of a dream, and more like stepping into someone else's soul and trying his memories on for size.

Maybe there really was such a thing as genetically inherited memory, and this morning's feature had been some sort of random access. But with relevance. An interesting theory no one could disprove. But. Something else had been in that dream—memory?—with him, he was sure of it. Something that watched the potential for sowing seeds of pain and death through the benevolent guise of healing. And it minded not at all.

Maybe it was his own subconscious. The benign sadist, the part that thrived on Laurel's games—perhaps not so benign after all.

I'll fight you, and how ludicrous it seemed. Fighting the good fight—while at war with himself. Winner and loser, both in one neat easy package.

A house divided against itself cannot stand; Lincoln had said it best. Such homespun wisdom.

Yeah. Look how *he'd* ended up.

The nurses woke him bright and early, we're going downstairs for some tests in a few minutes. *We* this, *we* that, why don't *we* just drop the chummy bullshit and *we* should get along fine. He held it in. Getting *awfully* good at this retention routine, it seemed he could hold just about anything in. Except disaster.

Tests. Why submit to these indignities at all? The pains were nothing new, always temporary, and he was feeling better. Just needed a little *sleep* was all, but apparently they couldn't rack up every possible premium charge for that. Tests it was.

The day brightened considerably when they brought him back upstairs to his room. A visitor awaited, and Paul modestly held closed the rearward gap in his johnny while climbing back into bed. Although Laurel had most definitely seen it and more.

"You had me worried as hell," she said when they were alone. Her eyes weary, a little red, short on sleep. He could sympathize.

"I'm sorry," smiling from his pillows. "How'd you know where to find me?"

"When you stood me up for dinner and I couldn't find you anywhere, I called Amanda. As far as I knew, she was the last person to see you around. That was early evening. Later she called me and said her nurse took care of you for a few minutes before Donny brought you here."

Hmm. No recollection there. The blackout must have been deep.

"I think Amanda was as worried as I was."

Paul nodded. "I like her. She seems very level."

Laurel, leaning toward him, no levity, "Paul? Where *were* you?"

"I went down to the refinery fire." His voice sounded flat and worn to his ears. No tread left. "I thought I could help."

Laurel shut her eyes. She was sitting uncharacteristically prim in fashion. Knees drawn together, stiff-backed, arms crossed before her while each hand cupped the opposite elbow.

"How'd things end up there?" he asked. "I don't even know, I didn't even feel like asking anybody here."

"The fire's out. They got it put out around dawn." Laurel didn't seem to appreciate question-and-answer reversal at this stage. "What could you have *done* there? You could have been killed. Paul, I don't even know what happened to you, why you're here, you could have been half burned up for all I knew."

He felt an easy smile crack open and pointed toward her stomach. "Gluttons for our doom. Didn't somebody say that once?"

"This isn't the *same*." Frowning, hell, he knew that look all too intimately. He'd seen it on more than one face those final days at KGRM, people with too many unanswered questions they didn't even know how to ask. Better get used to it, it would follow him wherever he went.

"It's close enough," he said.

Deep breaths, fidgeting in her chair. "Is there anyone I should call for you? Family? What about your mother, shouldn't I let her know something?"

Shaking his head, a little more energy cooked up now, isn't *that* significant? "No, don't. Don't. Don't worry her for nothing. I don't know what you could tell her that'd make much sense."

Had to bring up Mom, didn't she? Though it could hardly be construed as a deliberate act of cruelty. Quite thoughtful, actually, in and of itself. Chew on this awhile, though. *Mom.* October now, and he hadn't seen her since Christmas. Contact had been limited to the infrequent phone call, the even more infrequent letter. Communiqués of convenience, really, obligations sparked as much by guilt as need. He had not even informed her of his radical career departure and change of address until a week into Donny's tour. She had sounded mystified, had said little, whatever you think best, dear.

It had not been intentional, this gulf of mutual negligence. But he could pinpoint its origins, right down to month, date, and year. All corresponding with the day of paternal loss. Funny. Losing Dad lo those many years ago should have driven them closer to each other, but it seemed to have had the opposite effect, and in short order. Withdrawal as self-defense, as if the effects of future mortality and loss could be lessened by beating them to the punch.

As sons went, Paul figured he was pretty much bargain-basement material. Cheap and ill-fitting.

Laurel gripped the low railing of his bed, uncertain worry clouding those gray eyes. The heavy eyebrows, how he liked them; they were very natural. She'd told him plucking was too tiresome and had seemed so pointlessly vain. But that she still shaved pits and legs. More self-hypocrisy; they had laughed at the time.

"*Talk* to me, you," she said. "There's too much here that doesn't make sense to me. Like, why did Amanda want to meet you yesterday? The only reason I know her is because we've sung duets together. She just doesn't up and invite the ushers over. And Donny and Gabe seem to give *you* a lot more deference than anybody else outside their own little circle of directors. And why are you here in the hospital? You've got more sense than to go to an oilfield fire thinking you can just show up and they'll put you to work."

"How's the ulcer feel this morning?"

Her face cracked, exasperation and nerves. "*What?*"

"Your ulcer. How is it?"

"How do you think it is? I've been worried about you, and *that* hasn't helped it." She sighed, then made a visible effort at backing down from the offensive; humor the daffy patient. "I ate oats for breakfast and drank milk and *didn't* drink coffee. So it's not bothering me as much. Now what—"

"Give me your hand." He uncurled his own, waiting. "Come on, just give me your hand."

Flesh on flesh, a reluctant surrender, and he held tight.

"Can you keep a secret?" He really did feel sorry for her at the moment; she was looking at him as if he were insane, and she were doubting her own mental wrappings for going along with him. A nod. "You don't need that ulcer. Let's get rid of it."

Calm focus, letting his eyes drift shut, only took a moment. Sending a portion of himself arrowing up her arm, detouring through body and into abdomen, smooth muscle walls of her stomach. He pictured the hole shrinking closed the way her pupil would contract under a spotlight. Into nonexistence. It was a trifle, did not even cause a ripple in the empathy that grew so weighty at times.

But she had felt it, oh yes, something new and different and furlongs distant from *any* point of reference. Her eyes hung wide and blank, her lips parted as if she had been about to say something and forgot her mother tongue entirely. At last her hand slid from his, and she lay it flat over her belly's left side.

"*What* . . . did you . . . *do?*"

"Feel better?"

"*Paul?*" Such warring disbelief written all across her face, conflicts and incongruities aplenty. A lottery winner thinking, *No, no, there's got to be a catch here somewhere.*

He took her hand again and found that he was still primed to bare his soul. He had been on the verge yesterday when Gabe had shown up, confession interruptus, and despite all that had happened since then, the tale still wanted to be told. Without restraint, without shame, without censure. The experience was cathartic, and he felt as if he were shedding unwanted pounds; let somebody who cares shoulder this, if only for an hour. A minute.

Paul was a hollow man when finished. Good thing the windows were shut; one solid breeze would sweep him from the bed, send him kiting along hallways, and he would lay wherever it dropped him. He wept, and while Laurel did not, she was there in all the other right ways. Holding him with quiet strength, keeping silent of judgment and inane questions, and above all, he supposed, simply believing.

Hollow wasn't so bad. It at least left room for growth.

32

It took an exceptionally powerful reason to bring Irv Preston into his office to log desk time late on a Saturday afternoon. Saturdays were his own. Morning hospital rounds only, quick and breezy, *always* done by eleven. At his private practice offices and examining rooms, let the younger associates handle the caseload. Textbook medicine only, on a Saturday, banal and routine. Mostly the marginally ill scheduling health time around careers, waiting for the weekend. Fine. They *deserved* younger doctors with less experience and more idealism.

Saturdays were routine.

Which made the test results strewn across his desk all the more stunning.

In physiological terms alone, these were by far the most freakish he had ever seen. If they were correct, then Paul Handler was the most unique human being on the face of God's green earth.

When Preston checked up on Paul this morning at the hospital, the abdominal pain had diminished; scratch suspected appendicitis from the list, and this kid was getting to be one bugger of a conundrum indeed. Paul had been lucid by then, alert enough to tell Preston that he had also endured—and still was, though it was waning—a cluster bomb of a headache. Upon further probing, Preston had discovered that this episode had not been the first of its kind. Two or three others dated back to midsummer, lasting for several hours, then tapering off into well-being.

Since Paul had hurdled last night's preliminary tests, it was time to advance to secondary. A radiologist was now on duty, so they ran a CAT scan and took fourteen shots of his brain, serving it up into individual slices. They did an MRI—magnetic resonance imaging—during which an extremely powerful electromagnet is slowly passed over the patient's body; healthy tissue cells resultantly line up in a north-south pole in the field, their images transmitted to a TV screen for a painless peek at all the organs. Another series of fifteen shots was taken of the results.

When Preston first saw them, he'd hit the proverbial roof.

"These can't be right!" he had roared. Imbeciles; either the machine had screwed up, or the tech, or some combination of both. He had ordered them redone and the results had come back identical. Before a third series could be run on Paul, two other patients were tested in the interim and checked out as expected. Human and machine error looked less likely, then the third take on Paul yielded the same screwy results.

"Keep your mouth buttoned on this," Preston had told the radiologist. "For now, this is strictly between you and me, do you understand?"

The radiologist had said she did. It would be an effort. Ordinarily, word of such anomalies would have spread throughout the hospital like a brushfire before high winds.

Paul Handler was growing additional organs in his body. Not duplicates of existing organs, which was, while unusual, not unknown. Preston recalled one example, a few years ago, the case of a South African guitarist who had ruptured his spleen in a swimming pool accident while on tour. The subsequent operation had revealed him to have three additional spleens. Tame, though, in comparison with the Handler case.

These organs were brand new. Never before seen, without precedents.

The MRI showed a mass that had grown among his intestines in the lower left quadrant. Approximately ten centimeters wide by seven tall, and eighteen millimeters thick. It looked as if he had tucked a wallet inside his belly. What looked to be a bundle of nerve fibers branched from its posterior wall and ran toward his spine. Linking somehow with the spinal cord? Preston could have understood tumor, easily. Hell, would have preferred it. But had this been cancerous or otherwise diseased, it would have shown up fuzzy and indistinct, for the magnetic polarity of sick cells is ruined.

But no. By all indications, *this was healthy tissue.*

And the surprises kept on coming. In Paul's brain, a vaguely spike-shaped growth was extending toward his forehead from the corpus callosum, the bridge of nerve fibers connecting left and right hemispheres and allowing them to communicate. Good lord, no wonder the kid was in pain. Preston surmised that these tumors— for lack of a better label—would experience periodic bursts of growth, then plateau into quietude until a later flare-up.

A subsequent EEG showed that Paul was putting out an extra pattern of brainwaves. Had they been charted mechanically instead of on an oscilloscope screen, they might have blown the stylus off the paper. Whereas fully alert people exhibit a pattern of eight to thirteen waves, Paul was pumping out no less than eighteen. The extras, with such an intense amplitude, did not remotely resemble alpha, beta, *or* delta waves.

In letting his prognostication run uncharacteristically wild, Preston ventured that the new cranial organ looked like some sort of tiny antenna. And that Paul was . . .

Transmitting.

Yet despite it all, an unaware Paul had said he felt fine by late afternoon and wanted to leave. That girlfriend of his, no little incentive there. Preston had performed a verbal softshoe over and around the request, hoping to distract them from the gravity of the situation. Until they could figure out just where the hell to proceed from here.

First off, his family should be notified, but since he had none here, then those who had taken responsibility for him. And had brought him in for treatment in the first place.

With the fading Saturday sunshine waning at his window, Preston's desktop lamp pooled a small oasis of light across the papers. He took one last weary look over them, flipped through his Rolodex, and reached for the phone to peck out Donny Dawson's private home number.

He was slipping. Once upon a time, Gabe had had all the angles covered; never had a situation arisen that he had not considered, with a contingency plan at the ready.

Paul's hospitalization, though, was a new wrinkle he had never foreseen. So far as he knew, it had never happened to any of the Scapegoats of Paul's breed. Gabe had been taught that, so long as balance was maintained, they enjoyed splendid health and physical well-being. But expecting the status quo was not good enough, he now realized. Speculation and conjecture were everything; *he should have planned for this.* Paul had been holding in the flip side of his burden for far too long. Which could not be safe, like too much steam—he could blow.

Oh, but to witness that, now *there* would be a once-in-a-lifetime miracle, wouldn't it? Such grand spectacle.

The scrotal clamp rode high and hidden, and all looked clearer now. Probably should leave it on for the next few hours, at the very least. Perhaps days. It left no choice but to focus.

Donny had failed to phone him with news of Paul's collapse until this morning. Ignorant bastard, the man had no idea, did he? After sending fresh-brewed tea across his own living room in fury, Gabe had hurriedly dressed and driven to the hospital. He had peeked in on Paul only to find the room empty, and suppressed the urge to ravage himself for failure until he ascertained from a nurse that there was no cause for alarm. Paul had only been taken downstairs for tests. Gabe had gotten a chance to speak with Preston for a few moments during the doctor's rounds. No reason to stick close, it would be a while before results were up, and the kid seemed in no danger now. And take it easy, Gabe, you look worse than Paul this morning.

Gabe had located the nearest bathroom after hearing that. Leaned with fists on the sink and counter, staring at a reflection he trusted did not lie. Eye to eye, glazed and shining within dark circles in a pale face. He was sweating too much. And this visage was ample incentive to spend some time repeating the belief that had gotten him this far in life: *I am whatever I need to be in the moment I need it. I am all resources I will ever need . . .*

He showed up at Donny's front door a half-hour later, all warmth and optimistic concern. Perhaps they should pray and await word on Paul's condition together, and Donny thought the idea a fine one.

Gabe spent the hours after prayer reading in Donny's front parlor. David Hume's *An Enquiry Concerning Human Understanding;* Hume was a comfort, a focal center, and if the philosopher had closed his mind to the existence of a world of spirit beyond mind and matter, he had at least provided a framework for precision in thought. Gabe found his own mind expanding even as he read passages he had read a dozen times before. . . .

While we cannot give a satisfactory reason why we believe, after a thousand experiments, that a stone will fall, or fire burn; can we ever satisfy ourselves concerning any determination, which we may form, with regard to the origin of worlds, and the situation of nature, from, and to eternity?

How long had it been since he had truly felt the thrill of new discovery? Gabe no longer remembered. And while he once might have thought it something akin to heresy to deny that The Quorum had all the answers, Gabe felt confident enough to admit it now. The key was in Paul, of course. *They* may have seen him, *they* may have overseen his kind for centuries, but did that necessitate they truly understood him?

A revelation: Nay, *they did not.*

But I do.

He had no idea how much time had passed until the phone rang, but when it did, the jangling hit him like a cattle prod. So far as he knew, Donny was still on the third floor, probably trying to make nice with the queen bee around here. Salvage the shambles that her newly awakened sensibilities were making of their marriage. Gabe could see that one coming a mile away, and he was not without pity. In over their heads, those two.

He answered in the middle of the second ring, finding it to be the dutiful doctor. *Yes.* A successful interception, and all the saints be praised.

"I'm sorry, Irv, but Donny's out of the house for the moment. Is it Paul's results? Is he all right?"

"He's still doing fine, but . . ." A sigh of weary bones, and this did *not* sound promising. "There's something very unusual that's come up. It's not the type of thing I like to discuss over the phone."

Gabe murmured total understanding. "Tell you what. Why don't I meet with you and see what the problem is. If I can locate Donny I'll bring him along. If not, I'll give him the rundown later tonight. How's that sound?"

"Fine. I'm at my private offices now. Do you know where they are?"

"I do," said Gabe, and when he hung up, he glanced over his shoulder. Still alone, but moments later he heard footsteps treading down the stairs. He had cut this call just short enough.

"Who was that?" Donny asked. For the first time, Gabe noticed he had actually lost weight. Body, face; a leaner, more harried look. Not an altogether unappealing change.

"Irv." Gabe spread his hands, and his groin throbbed with subjective truths. "Paul's fine. But they're going to be running more tests. We should know more tomorrow."

And Donny bought it. Just as Gabe had bought an entire night in which to operate. Only the hours of darkness, but nights were longer now, and oh, so much could be accomplished before morning.

He put in his appearance, a Gabriel Matthews of pure dichotomy. Outer Gabe apologetic over Donny's unavailability, but Amanda's fragile state of mind demanded some hard decisions of priority. Outer Gabe listening to Irv Preston as he summarized the test results, looking sympathetically distraught when the doctor got to the real meat of things. Expressing brotherly compassion . . .

While inner Gabe fell to his knees over his spiritual proximity to Paul, victim of a body that had become a runaway train of misbegotten physiology.

Ye gods, what a miracle this ancient child was.

Nothing could have prepared him for *this;* Gabe was curious if anyone had ever cut a Scapegoat open before. He had heard their wounds were self-healing, but had of course never witnessed this. Perhaps they really were treading new ground here. Unknown territories, with Gabe a pioneer of iconoclasm like none other.

As Preston enumerated pertinent facts, Gabe tried sorting them, matching them with what he knew of Paul's wild talents. Here, at least, he was several jumps ahead of Preston. Growths in Paul's brain and belly, linked via spinal cord—they *had* to have concrete functions. It was theory only, and he would never know if he was correct, but Gabe began to see the abdominal organ as a kind of evolutionary modification for absorbing the essences and physiological configurations of every disease and injury with which he came in contact. A data bank, of sorts—*imagine*—where it all could take root and grow and flourish. Until he could just as easily turn around and project the physical and biochemical information into another human body. Aided, perhaps, by the brain tumor, to use Irv's vernacular.

Truly a man of miracles, and Gabe considered himself wholly blessed to be alive to play his own part.

So Gabe nodded his concern to the puzzled Irv Preston, told him that Donny would be given a full briefing tonight, tomorrow, whenever it seemed prudent given the situation with Amanda. Gabe ascertained that Preston—long respected by Donny for the virtue of discretion—was the only one who knew of these test results, apart from the radiologist, and had all the documentation. A lid would of course be kept on things.

Gabe smiled with worry and loss as he squeezed Preston's shoulder before leaving the office. All the while, making a mental note as to where Preston had filed Paul's results. Exact cabinet and drawer.

In this case, short-term memory would be sufficient.

Back at home, he planned well and hard and quickly. And above all, efficiently. With a certain amount of justifiable optimism that the unerring *rightness* of his mission would push him through to success. Failure was not an option because, quite frankly, failure no longer fit into his worldview.

Six hours ahead in Scotland, but the time difference was no longer a relevant factor. He possessed the mandate and called, had Gavin awakened. No, no emergency had arisen.

Gabe sat naked on his hardwood floor. Lights out, meditations by moonlight with thin stripes of blood cooling to a crust across his inner thighs. Walls of white traced with the morning's tea, dark and dried and sticky, like painted runes. He carefully modulated his voice to betray nothing but calm reason.

"I wanted to warn you," Gabe said, "you may have called to your attention a few news items with the word *miracle* kicked around. Paul did some more high-profile healing last night, at an oil refinery fire." Listen to the questions, talk talk talk; he had anticipated all. "Paul was in and out before anyone spotted anything unusual. His profile will stay low, don't worry there." More talk, and this man was getting tiresome in the extreme. "I was *there*. We were together when we first learned of the explosion and fire, so I went along with him. There was no stopping him, Gavin, it was go along for the ride and keep an eye on him, or nothing." Gabe could feel his skin crawling, could see it ripple under the light of a moon of benediction. He hooked fingers and let the poisons of self-doubt concentrate in the one arm, let it quake with tremors worthy of Richter scales while his voice held steady. "He's doing fine today, he's in no pain. We went to a movie this afternoon, in fact. And yes, the balance *is* being maintained. I know that for a fact. . . .

"I'm quite sure he let it out into one or two of the mortally wounded casualties last night. For certain a fellow with two severed legs, Paul knew he couldn't heal him without attracting attention, so

—he put the man to sleep, if you will. I'm sure it was quite the ac
of mercy. . . .

"Yes, he did them both a favor, I'm sure that's how Paul looks a
it, too. . . ."

And when Gabe was quite certain that all this had been taken to
heart, he let Gavin return to bed. For the sleep of the innocent, and
the dreams of duty performed. What he did not know would no
trouble him.

Too much knowledge could indeed be a dangerous thing.

Gabe was hoping to catch him asleep in bed, but Preston appar
ently kept the hours of a night owl. To watch from the yard unti
lights-out was no good at all, for the night would by necessity be a
long one. Schedules were best adhered to rather than bent for con
venience.

Preston lived in a neighborhood of solidly upper-middle-clas
virtues, as one-track as it was secure. The ranch-style was a sur
prise, though; Gabe had him figured for Cape Cod, or some othe
quaint two-story affair. Either way, the house was a lot for a mal
who lived in solitary domesticity. The good doctor's marriage ha
crashed on the reefs of estrangement four years ago; no divorce ha
made it official, though, they remained permanently separated. On
of the few times Donny had been of spiritual service to the man.

Great thing about the upper income brackets, they love thei
shade trees and evergreens, their shrubs and bushes. That hunge
for privacy leading them to erect a living screen around their home
that could shield a prowler as much as protect them from pryin
neighborly eyes.

Dressed in black stretch material, skintight gloves, Gabe felt ri
diculously like some wannabe commando, but submerged all doub
as soon as he chose the proper outer window. No lights on at thi
end of the house; he layered several thicknesses of white medica
cloth tape over one of the glass panes. Tapped it from center-out
ward with the barrel of his automatic pistol, gently, *gently*, as i
cracking the shell of a boiled egg, until it gave under pressure. He
peeled the taped glass from the frame and fed in one hand to re
lease the lock. Up with the lower half of the window, the pressur
steady and even, no sudden squeals of wood.

One last precaution; he pulled a nylon stocking over his head
Not to worry if Irv saw him, but it *would* help keep him from
leaving foolish remnants behind. Hair, skin, whatever evidence

forensics team could sweep up from a microscopic floor. Genetic fingerprints could destroy the careless.

And with poise that would do a gymnast proud, he was in.

Crouched on the carpet, window overhung with curtains behind him, Gabe took stock by moonlight. Bed, dresser, nightstand. Guest room, most likely. It had that smell of nonuse, of frozen preparation for company that never came. He could almost feel sorry for the man, what a lonely life he must lead. Dweller and intruder were kindred souls under this roof. Gabe knew what it was like to live entirely alone, with only lies for company, and no, *no*, these were not the thoughts he should be entertaining tonight. They served no one but hesitancy and indecision.

Forward, then, footfalls as light and silent as feathers. Rubber soles, just like a hospital nurse, an irony Irv would never live to appreciate. Dim light beckoned to guide him through the halls, toward prey, and he kept the pistol before him to lead the advance.

He was armed with a Jericho 941 nine-millimeter, Israeli-made, and officially this firearm did not exist within U.S. borders. He'd had it ever since getting his assignment from The Quorum to infiltrate Dawson Ministries. Handguns were issued upon assignment, to be used only as a last resort for worst-case scenarios; Gabe's had been locked away in a strongbox for years. As sidearms were culled only from underground sources, there was no such thing as standard Quorum issue. Gabe's had been smuggled transatlantic five years ago, its last official register in Ulster years before in 1982, confiscated sidearm of a fallen IRA gunman. Lost forever within British bureaucracy.

Beneath the black stretch, Gabe could feel a soft glaze of sweat. Not even fifty degrees out, and he was perspiring. Think of it as lubrication, oiling his joints into smooth hinges, all the better to creep with, my dear. More than human now, less than corporeal, he was spirit, and above all, he did not want to be here to do this to this man—

Focus! Strength and tenacity to purpose, he was serving a god of his own choosing, *I am whatever I need to be in the moment I need it. I am all resources I will ever need.* Gabe had applied this distillation of David Hume's ethic philosophies to his own life for years. If he needed to play the part of a businessman, he had brains and cunning aplenty. Should he have need to convince Donny of pious fundamentalism in religious matters, the persona was there. If he had cause to act as blackmailer, the criminal mentality separating victim from victimizer rose to the surface.

Behavior as a conscienceless assassin should prove no different He had been schooled in these matters too. . . .

And was quite cool of head by the time he stalked Irv Preston to the other end of the house. Warm room, family room if he still had a family, and Irv sat in slippers and a maroon velvet robe, reading in a plush chair set before the fire. Wood tones glowing even warmer in the orange light as flames danced and embers pulsed, alive with omens and images born in one instant, long dead the next. The picture of soft intellectual comfort. All Irv needed was a pipe, and Gabe found it easy to hate him in this moment. Living so much finer a life of Epicurean contentment, he did not understand the harsh joys of discipline and monastic dedication to a higher calling

This man had lost his way.

Gabe crept up from behind, never betraying his own presence until he swung around the chair and pushed the Jericho into Irv' face. Irv gasped, jerked in the chair a second, his book flying, and no no no, don't you die on me, don't you dare suffer a coronary—

"Don't talk, don't talk," he said flatly.

Irv's eyes widened hugely, seeing past nylon, seeing through the voice, identity made: *"Gabe?"*

"Don't talk!" Leaning in and letting him know he was wholly real, and could trust the sight of this gun inches from his eyes. He capped the tip of Irv's nose with the cold muzzle, stroked it along both sides of the walrus moustache, soft as a lover's finger, almost a tickle, and watched without feeling as Irv's eyes squeezed shut into plump folds of skin.

Irv was trembling. Rigid. Fingers curled into the chair's arms like griffin's feet.

Gabe knelt, held up the dropped book in one gloved hand "Judith Krantz?" he read the author's name aloud. "Why are you wasting your time with *this* pablum? Don't you know your mind is a temple?" He could not have this travesty around and pitched the book into the fireplace. The flames fed well, with satisfying brightness.

"Don't talk," again, though Irv was doing well just to breathe. He jabbed the muzzle against Irv's mouth until those eyes widened further, and yes, message received, *open wide*. Lips parting, smacking once with cotton dryness, and Gabe jammed the barrel inside two and a half inches. It would not choke him; Gabe had tried out the depth in his own mouth earlier. Preston made a frightened animal whining deep in his throat, and Gabe produced his roll of cloth tape from a slash pocket in his tights.

"Don't flinch, either," and he hurriedly unwound a strip from the tape roll and slapped it onto Preston's puffing cheek. Big boys don't cry. Preston had shoved himself back into the chair as far as he could fit, and Gabe leaned with one knee on his lap while bearing in, unspooling coil after coil of tape to circle gun barrel and cheeks, chin and mouth. Muzzle to muzzle, and Gabe's own breath panted harder, the inside of the nylon stocking beginning to feel very wet and slick against his own mouth.

When the gun was taped solidly in place, Gabe drew back, left hand holding the grip. He had left Irv's nose clear for breathing, and his breath whistled through rapid and shallow. The pistol was not airtight, he could draw breath through there, as well, but Gabe knew from his own tests that it was unpleasant, smelling and tasting of steel and gun oil.

"Open your eyes, Irv," and several seconds later, when he did, Gabe thumbed back the Jericho's hammer. It brought trembling anew, no sound like that in the entire world, and dear God forgive him, but what horrid manipulation this was. "I need to ask you some questions. Simple questions. Then you need to get me a thing or two. These won't be hard, I promise you. This tape and this gun, they're just . . . just"—shit, he had the word a minute ago, what the fuck was wrong?—"safeguards." There, better, focused again. "Do you understand? You can nod if you do."

A very slight bobbing to the gun.

"We need a pad of paper and something for you to write with," Gabe said. "Otherwise, we can't communicate. Do you have anything like that in here?"

Another frantic little bobble, and Irv slowly lifted his arm to point across the room to an antique rolltop desk.

"Then let's go."

He was in no rush now, letting Irv set the pace as he slowly rose from his chair. Siamese twins of a mutant bent, joined arm to mouth via gun, the movement of each dependent on the other. Irv's legs looked as though they could barely support his weight. Knees sagging, and then Gabe smelled it from the man's pajamas. A stench of piss and fear, acid that set to work on those callous walls separating him from feelings, and down went one brick, two bricks, *no no no,* couldn't let a little thing like loss of sphincter control throw him off track now.

Irv settled into the small chair at his rolltop desk, and over the tape and gun, his eyes begged assurance that this was okay. Gabe nodded and searched drawers until he came up with a notepad, a ballpoint pen. He clicked it, pressed it into Irv's trembling hand.

"Ready?"

Irv nodded. Little whispered whines sounding in his throat. Like words trying to form down there, *please please don't kill me anything you want,* there would be no surprises were Gabe to strip the tape away.

"I want the name of the radiologist that ran the tests on Paul Handler this morning."

A frown of confused realization, questions answered with as many or more newly posed, only he wasn't writing, this would never do, you couldn't let him shirk obligations, and Gabe leaned in hard and fast to push the gun so that the front sight scraped the roof of Irv's mouth.

"The name!" he screamed, and Irv began scribbling. Trying it in cursive, then scratching it out with a palsied hand and printing careful block letters. A child learning penmanship. *Jennilee Philberts,* he had written.

"Is she in the phone book?"

Don't know, Irv wrote.

Well, he could check that later, although if she wasn't, it could present problems. Then an idea: "Do you have a private directory of hospital personnel?"

At office

Splendid. "I'm going to have to ask for your office keys, now, Irv. To get into the place, and for the cabinet where you filed Paul's test results. Where are they?"

Preston began to point.

Gabe jabbed him impatiently with the barrel, little tolerance for this lapse of communication. "Write it *down.*"

Bedroom dresser

Gabe pulled him to his feet, like reeling in a heavy fish. Irv's eyes crossing as he looked down to check if the finger was still on the trigger. They began to move with feet shuffling in small steps of moderation, and Gabe switched off the lamp to put them entirely at the disposal of moonlight. Curtains were drawn back here, no fear of being seen through windows by neighbors or passing motorists. But move beyond this room, there were no guarantees.

Irv would know his way around.

His bedroom turned out to be across the hall from Gabe's point of entry, and Gabe pulled down a window blind before flipping on the light. Lots of mauve in here, from the carpet to the fixtures to one of the patterns in the wallpaper. Frilly dust ruffle around the bed. It showed a woman's touch, and obviously Irv had been unwilling or unable to change the decor during these years of separation. To cling to the past was not a healthy thing.

Gabe shut his eyes, could not feel pity, could not *allow* pity to be a part of tonight's vocabulary, and with his free hand he clawed his fingers and dug into the side of one thigh, *Get myself straight, he's distracting me—*

"I want those keys!" he cried, and nearly staggered as Irv led him to the dresser. Preston pulled them from a top drawer, hands jingling them loose of scattered coins and a roll of breath mints. Keys, pressed into Gabe's free hand like an offering, or a bribe, over a dozen on a Volvo chain, and Gabe made him sort them. Picking out building key, inner office key, file cabinet key. Repeat, again, just to make sure Irv wasn't trying to run a scam of confusion on him, the desperate will do that if you give them half a chance.

And the pity was returning, watching Irv Preston, healer, sag down onto the bed his wife had bought, cowering with the gun thrusting from his mouth like some terrible form of oral cancer bursting through bandages and tape. Gabe knowing he'd done this to the man, achingly aware that you never *push* another human being this low, you *pull* them down to join you. Irv, lifting his hands as if to pray, face sauna-steam greasy with the unhealthy miasma of fear and urine rolling off him in unpleasant waves. He knew, *he knew*, even before Gabe did that there was nothing more to be accomplished. The vision of those near death can be remarkably clear.

And Gabe did not want to be seen by him in these final moments. Clothing and flesh made no difference, Irv would see beyond them. Gabe felt vulnerably naked before him, bereft of all armor, the corruption of rot and decay within as visible as if he had sliced himself open and peeled his own incision apart. Preston would recognize his unworthiness.

"I'm sorry," he whispered, and Preston began to shake his head back and forth, tiny little arcs, *no no no*. And Gabe knew he could

never go through with this if he saw the doctor for what he was, a
frightened overweight man in advanced middle years whose own
urine was growing cold on his groin. No, he had to see this man as
the enemy, and his voice had become a roar before he even knew it,
"You want Paul to yourself and he's mine, *he . . . is . . . MINE!*
You don't even understand what he is, I *know* what you've been
planning and I *won't* let you do it, I WILL NOT LET YOU EX-
POSE HIM TO THE WORLD AND TURN HIM INTO A MED-
ICAL FREAK SHOW!"

Gabe bulldozed ahead, legs wide and pushing like a sumo wres-
tler's, and he and Irv tumbled onto the bed together. The man was
beginning to fight now, and Gabe saw him not for the reality, but
for the worst of all possible futures. Irv Preston, Nobel Prize winner
for medicine for his discovery of a new breed of human mutation.
World renowned, articles in all the medical journals, and Paul, innocent victim of crucifixion by media and experimentation—

And Gabe could truly hate now, screaming inside himself, then
outside, the tears no longer letting him see to work as he groped
while Irv fought with strength born of mortality. Gabe pulled a
pillow free from beneath the bedspread and maneuvered it around
Preston's bloodred face, and he sobbed while folding it together
into a thick makeshift silencer, and the bedroom filled with the
fetor of emptied bowels while Irv floundered with spastic legs and
Gabe screamed from the core of his soul, what a terrible terrible
place of gothic torment it was to dwell, a prison of his own construction, and he fired the gun through the back of Irv's skull, *one
shot* and Irv went rigid, *two shots* and the taped seal blew apart
entirely, *three shots* and the man's head had become sodden fragments, *four shots* and Irv was boneless, and Gabe was no longer
screaming.

Enough.

The silence was thunder and damnation, and triumph. He had
done it. The Church of Lead and Cordite, conversion by muzzle
velocity. To kill was holy sanction.

Gabe breathed deeply, coughed; the air was rank with the spoor
of the kill. He groaned and rolled off Irv's body, left the Jericho
sunk into the cratered ruins of mouth and skull. It would provide no
clues.

And with tonight a double-header, it would be better to work up
a different MO.

Blades had definite potential.

33

Hospitals and maximum security prisons, Paul saw few differences by late Sunday morning. Equivalent food, and in both places there was a real danger of someone creeping up from behind to stick metal into you. Parole came late Sunday morning, with Gabe showing up to chauffeur him back to the compound. No policy of a hundred bucks and a cheap new suit, but he could live with that, and after this confinement, Dawson Ministries would look quite inviting after all.

Paul's first inkling that something was amiss came when his discharge was cleared by another doctor, a stranger, and she looked too frazzled to press for explanations. Hospital halls and staff lounges were abuzz with rumor and innuendo. Dead doctor, shot in his home; dead radiologist, stabbed in bed along with her husband. *Very* strange, these two, and the police were not publicly speculating if they felt them to be related murders. The shooting looked like an execution of sorts, certainly not a robbery, not with cash on the bedroom dresser ten feet from the victim. The stabbings looked more like crimes of twisted passion; the woman had been violated postmortem with a candle holder.

Paul caught only the barest skeleton of fact and fancy by eavesdropping on hospital conversations. Gabe filled in the rest of what was public knowledge on the drive home. Not all that long ago, Paul's reaction would have been a gently sinking woe, token sorrow for any brutal misfortune striking the most casual of new acquaintances, unknown thirty hours before. How truly awful, then perhaps a moment of melancholy contemplation, and life goes on, we can ill afford grieving for every stranger.

Now, though, unease squirmed. Irrational, but it would not be denied its due. However briefly, yesterday he had touched them both. Maybe they had taken that touch home with them, a magnet for mortality, and just stop it, he had nothing to base this on at all. Volunteering for guilt, getting to be quite the martyr.

"He was a fine man," Gabe said from behind the wheel, grim and pale. "He'll be missed by a lot of people."

"Does Donny know yet?"

"I doubt it. But he will soon enough." Shaking his head, tight precise movements, fist tapping lightly on the wheel. "I imagine Donny will have to perform the funeral." Biting his lower lip. "It's the kind of thing that really shakes your faith, isn't it?"

A mile of silence, homage to the fallen, Paul supposed. Dear departed doctor, and Paul did not want to hurt this morning. It was too sunny, traffic was too light, they were strangers. Any superficial reason is as good as another when the taint of death has been following like a stubborn cloud and has worn out its welcome.

"We need to talk about an idea I've been having," Gabe said. A hopeful smile, and what a surprise, he looked so young all at once. Almost vulnerable. "Do you . . . consider me a friend?"

Paul shrugged easily. "Yeah." Though not terribly close, for he and Gabe were cut from wholly different swatches of cloth, virgin wool versus stone-washed denim, but a bond *was* there, wasn't it? "I do."

Relief. "Then humor the ravings of a friend, okay? And keep an open mind, this really will sound off the wall. But I have this idea in my head—and I really want to know what you think."

Definitely intrigued, Paul held up three fingers. "I won't laugh. Scout's honor."

"Nobody is supposed to know about this yet," Gabe began, "but at the beginning of next month, we'll be switching to a live show format for Sunday mornings. It's a revolutionary move. No evangelist has ever done his regular show this way before."

"Donny's never said a word."

"Oh, he'll approve, it's all but official. You know how it is, announcements are never made until everything's in writing. But you should know, *you're* different, you're entitled to an extra privilege now and then. Especially with the involvement I hope you'll agree to try."

Scoring flattery points, but Paul did not mind.

"Here's the loony part, so get ready," Gabe warned. "Have you ever heard comedians doing routines about TV evangelists, and healers, and they'll say something about touching the TV so you'll be healed?"

Paul nodded and stuttered with light laughter, and then what was really going on here hit him like a bad joke, *He wants to try something like that with ME.* The mirth caught in his throat, tight as a swallowed bone.

"I think it might actually work," Gabe said, and Paul was trying not to look at him with as much surprise and *disappointment* as he felt, for up until now Gabe had possessed one of the leveler heads at the ministry. "Listen to the reasoning behind it, first, fair enough? I told you you'd have to humor a friend's ravings."

Okay, true, he had been warned.

"First off, do you know what the human body is, really? One big complex machine running on bioelectrical impulses. At the head of it all is the brain and the nervous system, and the brain is essentially a bioelectrical computer. More specifically, a microwave transmitter and receiver. A weak one, sure, but *everybody* transmits. You don't have to cut into someone's skull to chart brain waves, a few painless electrodes do just fine. Do you have any argument with this so far?"

Paul said he did not. There Gabe went again, confusing him with hard fact.

"I admit it—I don't have any way of knowing if I'm right or wrong, but in your case I'm guessing that you actually transmit something into people when you heal them. You activate their own capacity to heal themselves, you speed it up, you strengthen it, whatever. Because whatever's inside you, it's far more advanced than what the average person has. Even more advanced than what's enabled Donny to heal on a lesser scale." He frowned in thought. "What I'm getting at, there's more than a spiritual side to your gifts. There are mechanisms behind them. They work because of properties unique to your brain and body. With me so far?"

Paul nodded. The logic was nearly frightening. In truth, he *had* failed to look much beyond the mystic wonder in what he was able to do, but it had to work some way. What a lot of people seemed inclined to overlook, especially fundamentalists always ready for literal interpretations, was that God Himself had the greatest scientific mind of all. Because He had established the principles by which life operated. Biology, chemistry, physics, physiology—there was a pattern of order to the miracle.

Creation versus evolution, a battle that would rage as long as people of free will could choose sides. Yet Paul had never viewed the two camps as being mutually exclusive. How great the wonder of a God, to Whom geological aeons were mere ticks of a clock, Who could set such a process into motion.

A proposition that challenged, and ultimately frightened, a lot of narrow little minds. Static preconceptions were safer.

"So once you grasp the basic principle," Gabe said, "what's to prevent you from reaching people through the airwaves?"

Paul huffed with uncertainty. "Oh come on, even if that's what I'm doing, there's a world of difference between working one on one, and doing what you're talking about. You're talking about broadcasting brain waves!"

"Paul," Gabe's voice that of a patient teacher, "it's been done."

He perked up, shut up. Well now, wasn't this sobering, and perhaps his college radio and TV classes had not been as complete as he had thought.

"No lie?"

"No lie." Deep breath, long story ahead. "Back in the sixties, some communications experts in Army Signal Intelligence chanced across some odd signals coming in on a radio. They thought it was random interference at first, but realized it was on a steady sweep, not just at a fixed frequency. Up and down a high frequency range of ten to thirty megahertz, steady as a clock, up and down. Constant. So they recorded it and then slowed it down and ran it through an oscilloscope to look at individual wave forms. Found little blips on the waves."

"Telemetering, sure," Paul said. "The waves were carrying data."

"Mmm hmm. Ultimately, they were able to analyze them enough to determine that what they had were brain waves, loud and clear."

"So where were they coming from?"

"It took some cloak-and-dagger coincidences before all the pieces fell into place. But they were coming from the Soviet Union. There was a scientist named Kokolov working for the KGB, and when he had a meeting with some westerner the KGB wanted dead, they gave him a gun that looked like a cigarette pack and orders to kill. The meeting went off as planned, but Kokolov, he was no killer. He lost his nerve and slid the gun across the table and spilled the whole story. Told his contact he was supposed to kill him, and now he wanted to defect. A Soviet scientist? You'd better believe they made it easy for him. Now he's a professor in California. UC-Berkeley, I think."

"And he was in on the brain-wave deal?"

"Right. He filled in the gaps in what the army knew. What the Soviets were doing was bombarding the entire country with the brainwaves of Russian psychics. They were broadcasting from a couple of installations in the Ukraine."

"What were they trying to do?"

"Oh, who can say, for certain? Trying to undermine American society in some way. The psychics were projecting definite thoughts along those lines. It went on for years. From the sixties into the early eighties." Gabe chuckled. "I find it ironic that they abandoned the project not too long after Reagan went into the White House. Obviously they didn't swing public thinking *too* far to the left."

Paul was trying to pick his way through to a reasonable conclusion. "I suppose it bombed because even though they had pretty sophisticated broadcasting technology, nobody over here was receiving like they'd intended."

"Probably not. But I wonder if it might not have been successful in at least a few cases. On individuals."

"Oh yeah? How's that?"

Gabe hunched his shoulders. "I'm just letting my mind run away with me. But imagine a few people here and there, and maybe they're more receptive psychically. Maybe they *did* pick up something but didn't understand it. Just voices in their heads, telling them to do things. It could have been enough to drive some people insane."

Paul wrinkled his nose. Sympathetic to the few rarities who might have been affected, alone in their own crumbling worlds of paranoia. "Look at the jump in mass murder rates in those years. Lots of them talked about voices in their heads." He shook his own. "Scary to think what we're capable of doing to each other."

"It is, isn't it? But—but don't you find it exhilarating to think how something like brain-wave transmission might be used for *benevolent* reasons?"

Behold, the skeptic returns. "Obviously it flopped on a large-scale basis. Any success they had is pure conjecture. What makes you think I could do any better?"

"I don't know, Paul, *I don't know.* I'm just hoping. But for one thing, you're not a psychic, you wouldn't be broadcasting thoughts. You'd be sending out something a lot more powerful, and you *know* it's been received by people who need it." A smile of dauntless reassurance, bright and happy. "It wouldn't be hard at all to patch you into a satellite uplink. A few electrodes, an amplifier to boost your signal. In theory it's simple, at least in comparison with the technology to get on the air in the first place."

Paul closed his eyes, sunk low in the seat. Couldn't believe this discussion was taking place at all. Like it was no more than a few cable connections to make bad music with some cheesy garage band. The day was young and already his head was tired; let the drone of tires on pavement lull him onto ground less threatening.

"Think about it. Just think about it. For a friend?" Gabe took his eyes off the road for a long, imploring look. He looked ready to weep. Not from sadness . . . something else. Ambition? No, he looked close to—rapture? That was it.

And did Paul like it, in some secret fold of the mind? Some pocket of lonely isolation? *I shouldn't . . . but I DO.*

"Maybe I'm wrong, maybe it'd be a big flop." Gabe, shaking his head in bright-eyed awe, "But if it did, think of the potential. *Think of what you could accomplish.*"

This was folly and flattery, and he knew he was beginning to nibble. But why not? If this off-beat idea worked, he could potentially reach more people in one telecast than in years of interpersonal contact. And if it did not, the loss was negligible, a red face for all concerned.

The voice of caution—*What of backfires, what of Popeye and Mrs. DeWitt, what of them?*—merited little attention. Doom-crier. Circumstances around Dawson Ministries were about as controlled as anyplace he had seen. Especially during the shows. It would not go wrong.

"Paul, it's time you moved up in the world. Donny knows it, and to be honest, I think you've got him a little scared. But not me. Because I see you for the miracle you are. I acknowledge that." Gabe dropped one hand to his forearm, squeezed. Like a vise. "But it's no reason why you and Donny can't continue to work together for now. More as . . . equals? You *have* earned that right, just by the nature of who and what you are."

Paul squirmed in the seat. Blushing. Bashful Paul. He had never taken compliments with utmost grace.

But he supposed he could learn.

Tuesday morning blues, the latest trend. When Monday just isn't enough. Used to be, the trials of the world did not penetrate Donny's office door. Like a one-way valve, but no more, no more. Had he been mistaken all along, or had the rules changed? Now they never seemed to leave.

Dear Irv. Theirs had been a relationship of mutual benefits, financial mostly, later medical, and later still, spiritual. But one thing could not be ignored; Donny had looked upon him and called him friend and had meant it in the highest sense of the word. And had never even told him.

Life was brutal as of late; looking out upon the faces of all those who had known and loved Irv Preston would be but one more bruising blow. The funeral was this afternoon. A lot of people would be looking to him for comfort, to stand tall in the pulpit and weave order like a loom; comfort from chaos, God's will out of murder. A lot of them would surely be leaving empty of heart and hand.

What hunger to escape it all, walls on every side. Here the death of a friend, there the loss of the wife he had always known and cherished. Back at the house now, venomously applying herself to therapy. With her leg strapped inside a full-length brace, she was now managing a few shuffling footsteps between parallel bars. One giant step for Amanda . . . farther from his life.

And now the crown jewel of bad timing. Donny gazed down with muddled dread at the report at center-desk. Neat and clean and free of typos, crisply produced on the laser printer in Gabe's office, tidily bound in a clear blue folder. So very felicitous, yet easily the silliest proposal Gabriel Matthews had ever come up with. What kind of rationale was he working with these days, anyway, and at a time when stoic support was sorely needed?

For once, bad news was going to be a joy to dispense.

He summoned Gabe via intercom.

"Please, sit down." Donny poked a finger toward a chair before the desk, and Gabe settled. "It's about this proposal for switching to a live satellite broadcast."

His face betrayed nothing. "You've read it already?"

"I didn't have to." Donny flexed fingers, steepling them. "Because it's out of the question."

One single twitch of an eye, then total control. "*I have worked hard* on this over the past few days."

"Don't think I don't appreciate that, but—"

Then the most peculiar thing happened. Gabe's head took over independently, began to shake endlessly back and forth. Talking all the while. "In fact, I've already got this under way." Enumerating points finger by finger. "I've written a mailer to go out this week announcing it. Started negotiating for satellite time. I think I know how we can minimize reconstruction on the chapel—"

"I said *no*, Gabe."

"—and I've outlined a plan for revamping our camera and technical crews." Four fingers and holding, head still shaking.

When does he SLEEP? Donny wondered. *Or DOES he? He hasn't heard a word I've said.*

"And this means nothing to you?" Finally, *finally*, stilling that nervous shake.

Donny sighed and groped for his coffee mug to wet his throat. He had hoped this would be painless. "If you went to that much trouble, then you exceeded your authority by far. And to be perfectly honest, I'm disappointed by your presumptuousness."

"Oh no, oh no," whispering, drumming fingers on his armrest. Then, quite bold: "I was hoping you wouldn't make this difficult."

"You had no right to go ahead with any of these plans. You had *no right* to bypass my approval, or that of the Board of Directors." Donny could feel the hot flush creeping into his face, his scalp. "This is not some minor marketing ploy. Now call it off today. *I run this show, in case you've forgotten!*"

Gabe slid to the edge of his chair, grinning slyly, and good lord, the man was actually enjoying this, as if it were a game. A debate. "Give me one good reason why we shouldn't switch to live."

Donny popped with sweat from crown to soles, and huffed exasperation. "One good reason?" He yanked the proposal's pages free of their binder and tossed them into the air, let them spill haphazardly to the desk. "The cost, for starters, how about *the cost!* The uplink dish alone would run well over a million, and that's just the beginning. Renovations, extra salaries for people who *won't* come cheap. There's satellite time to rent each and every week, tons more equipment apart from the dish. And what's more, there's not one indication that a format change like this would generate *any* increase in donations. Is that good enough for you?"

A tiny smile hooked one corner of Gabe's mouth. "The cost."

"Yes! The cost!" He pushed back for some deep breathing. Had to calm down, his heart was thumping as if he had done ten laps in the pool. He forced an even voice. "There's no way I can justify that kind of expenditure."

Gabe lifted a single finger, cool as ice and twice as brittle, stepping for the door. "I'll be right back. I just want to get something from my office."

Donny rolled his eyes with a grimace, shoved his coffee away. Just how valuable *was* Gabe these days? High efficiency could justify putting up with only so much arrogance. And if Gabe was trying to assume undue control around here, then the time had come to consider letting him go. With poor references, to boot, thou shalt not lie.

Gabe returned with a nine-by-twelve envelope in one hand, and he shut the door. Face like a stone icon as he slapped the envelope onto the spill of loose papers, smack. He did not sit.

Donny laboriously unfastened the clasp, whatever it was would change nothing, then slid the contents into a waiting hand, and—

And he feared his heart would burst.

"You can't justify the cost?" Gabe said. "Then let's see you try to justify *these*."

The room was pulsing in time with a sudden ferocious headache as all the bile and coffee in his stomach coagulated into a lump like a tumor. The beads of body sweat became chilly quagmires, fetid with panic. His only movement purely involuntary, shaking hands. No coherent thought, just the paralysis of an animal trapped in headlights, watching the oncoming judgment.

His hands were the first to free, as he flipped from one glossy color photo to the next. How, when . . . ? No trouble identifying his own nude body, but it wasn't until the fourth picture that he saw enough of the woman's face to identify her.

"That's Edie Carson," he whispered hoarsely.

Two more, then they slipped from his hands, and he was barely into the stack. It was not bad enough that they depicted him rolling about with a small naked woman he had once covertly employed—the woman was obviously dead. He wanted to gag, the crawling sense of revulsion, sensing beneath his clothes where warm and cold flesh had pressed in intimate contact. What he was doing in those pictures was not merely depraved, it was unholy.

Awareness expanded beyond self. Edie, so oddly disappeared, was dead. And from the look of her neck—*twisted so sharply cold dry mouth at his own say cheese*—she had not died of natural causes. Which meant her murderer was probably standing . . .

In. This. Room.

Donny looked up, and Gabe towered above like an executioner.

"I," said Gabe, drawing it out forever, "have had a vision that has changed the course of my life. I . . . have come to touch something that has validated my entire existence. And you . . . are in the way. So there are going to be some changes around here. . . .

"I don't care what things look like from the outside, you can play king of the ministry and stomp your feet across the stage all you want to. But don't ever ever ever forget, behind the scenes, you are *not* the one in charge anymore. And you *will* give me blank checks to finance whatever I need to around here. Are you following me so far?"

Photographic reprints in news magazines and lurid tabloids flipped on rapid strobe through his mind. While home and ministry and compound and years of colossal effort (*and the fortune don't forget the money THE MONEY*) went swirling down a toilet of scandal and legal nightmares. He saw his marriage fracture beyond all hope of patchwork.

He nodded to Gabe. Novocaine numb.

"And you *will* stay away from Paul Handler until I have what I want from him. And then? You can have this place back, all of it. Just like before I came along."

Donny found his voice inside a sour breath. "Money. I have money, I can pay you now. I can give you money."

Gabe shook his head. "I don't want your money. I want my own salvation. I want to be free, finally. I want to touch . . . stars."

Donny understood none of it, understood only hard grim reality, which was more than enough. He sat. Feet of clay, ass of lead. He heard the sound of a zipper, of all things, and looked over to find Gabe unfastening his own slacks. . . .

"Look what you make me do to myself."

Donny was not a man given to gasping, but when Gabe tugged down his underwear to expose himself, the sight was so painfully ghastly, Donny couldn't prevent it. Gabe's scrotum, swollen the purple of bruises upon bruises, pinched together with some kind of metallic contraption.

Gabe looked at him, tears beginning to unfurl down his cheeks as he bared himself in shameful display, like unworthy meat. "I was sent here to investigate you. And God help me, a part of me came to love you, because you didn't judge me and you accepted me. But you turned yourself into a whore. And you tore me apart inside. So *look at me*. You're only now getting to see the truth." He sucked in a sharp breath, choked down a little cry as he zipped himself up again. "We've both been living lies."

Donny could only utter a sick and hurtful croak.

Gabe lingered at the door, hand on knob, and straightened. Put on a new face, blend in, make no ripples in the outer world. Keep it all buried in this office, a mausoleum of dirty secrets.

"And please, Donny, get yourself together," his voice changing abruptly, a different person, the executive assistant of old. The facade, the illusion. "You've got a funeral to do."

Gone.

Funeral, Donny thought. Reduced to single words again. As the enormity of this morning's hostile takeover sent his head onto the desk, to spill tears upon the weapon of his downfall. A bittersalt dew.

And while he knew he would be unable to ever draw sufficient courage for the act, he nevertheless wondered just how big a sin suicide actually was.

1982–1984/Scotland

In the heart of desolation, The Quorum made renaissance men and women. An organization born in a different world, it had survived centuries of war, monarchs good and bad, and the decline of Roman Catholicism as the predominant guiding force of the western world.

Entrenched in secrecy and built on a foundation of ancient myth and history, it had survived when the other orders born of the Crusades—the Knights Templars, the Knights of St. John, the Teutonic Knights—had not. And for one fundamental reason—purpose still existed. Scapegoats lived. This spiritual lineage of men and women who had but the merest inkling of what called their bodies home and demanded appeasement through them.

The Quorum outlived its founders—Baron Walter of Kent and the Abbot Baldwin of Huntingdon's Widdershaw Abbey—in a manner neither of them could have foreseen. Established by papal dispensation, it was nevertheless unbeholden to the Church to the point of disavowal, and was more the creation of those in charge of it at the time.

The Protestant Reformation of the sixteenth century proved the first true nail in the coffin of its leanings as a religious order. As well, society itself had been evolving in fits and starts toward a more enlightened age. The advent of a more secular world brought about a divestiture of church from state. A new breed of thinker was addressing the eternal questions of life and purpose, mortality and morality, and humanity's place in each. Philosophy, once the hand-maiden of Church theology in the Middle Ages, now lived and thrived for its own sake . . .

While The Quorum made welcome room for more freedom of thought than its founders had ever intended.

Based out of English castles and abbeys for better than its first half-millennium—a century here, two centuries there—The Quo-rum finally came to rest in the western Scottish Highlands in 1709. Two years before, centuries of strife between the two nations came to an abrupt end when the parliaments of both Scotland and En-gland agreed to the Act of Union, and merged. Thus was born the Kingdom of Great Britain.

In a more crowded world, where isolation was one of their great-est allies, those of The Quorum found it more to their liking to the north. The Highlands had always been of sparse population. A suit-able castle was acquired along Loch Nevis and restored to livability for those who would call it their home, those who trained there, and those who needed respite and retreat from their clandestine duties elsewhere. It was here The Quorum marked passage into the twen-tieth century, and life in the Highlands remained little altered by time, especially when compared with the speed of change farther south, and abroad.

The Highlands, wild as ever, as picturesque an untamed land as it had been when barbaric clans battled for supremacy. Carved with lochs, narrow ribbons of lake, and in late summer the land's lower slopes were robed with purple heather. Most Highlanders were farmers, tending their crofts with frugal care, growing oats and po-tatoes and barley from this rugged land, raising hardy sheep and long-horned cattle. The Highlands were one vast pasture.

And here The Quorum learned to cloak its identity to better blend with the twentieth century. Contemporary tourists and na-tives ostensibly believed the place itself to be a retreat for the employees of some London-based corporation. Why else the shoot-ing range, why else the formidable gate, why else the landscaping undertaken to construct a nine-hole golf course?

Ownership of the estate became secreted within a labyrinth of dummy corporations and holding companies—benefits of more worldly influence and skills acquired over the centuries. Financial holdings were vast and self-perpetuating, stemming as far back as a mere decade after The Quorum's inception. The Fourth Crusade had been a grievous perversion of Pope Urban II's original pious call to arms, holy aims now corrupted by political and commercial greed. The avaricious knights of Christendom never even made it to the Holy Land, instead serving as mercenaries of Venice and seizing Constantinople in July 1203—despite its being a Christian city. The expedition was the single greatest destruction and plunder of cultural treasures during the entire Middle Ages—and no small amount filled the coffers of The Order of The Quorum.

By the midtwentieth century, The Quorum owed as much of its operational nature to military and intelligence networks as to the spiritual leanings of its origins. But, after all, it *was* a far different world. Train and automobile and airplane had given the whole of modern humanity a mobility heretofore undreamed of—and the four Scapegoats in existence at any one time were no exception. If anything, they tended to travel more, miserable human beings—spiritual fulcrums frequently out of balance—trying with desperation to outrun something grafted to their own souls. They needed to be watched constantly, and over the most recent decades, watching from afar had often given way to an operative or two insinuating him- or herself into the Scapegoat's life as a sorely needed friend. For no matter where the ancient deities took root—the world over—the fundamental human need for friendship and acceptance was a constant.

Broadsword and battle-ax of medieval vintage had given way to firearms, for though the modern world was more civilized as a whole, pockets of violence thrived as turbulent as ever. A proficiency here was needed still, and training in the more lethal arts now came largely from former British SAS troops—most of whom believed they were being hired and well-paid for training periodic batches of bodyguards, executive protectors, and the like.

Its selective influx of membership became far less a matter of obligation handed down from father to son, as in the days when chivalry fostered such legacies, than a matter of highly personal recruitment and grooming. With the emergence of psychology as a viable science in the late nineteenth century, a distinct personality profile began to emerge: conscientious and self-disciplined; primarily a rational thinker; nonconformist tendency to avoid acceptance of status quo beliefs; drawn to abstraction and speculation; strong personal independence, yet needful of a forum for unconventional beliefs; a quest for spiritual truths regardless of whether they adhered to the tenets of any given religious denomination. A significant portion of them had suffered some great loss during childhood —usually one or both parents—which had truncated their sense of belonging and set them on a lifelong search for that lost person and a sense of wholeness. They were unfailingly loyal, though loyalty was neither easily won nor blindly given. Quorum recruiters found their most fertile supply of possibles in university philosophy departments and theology school dropouts.

Once recruits were indoctrinated into The Quorum, however, scholarly pursuits continued. By the late twentieth century, a two-year sojourn in the Highlands prepared the novices. A great deal of history was to be learned, and The Quorum had recorded its own quite well. Such was firm tradition; at the time of the order's founding, the power of knowledge belonged to the clerics alone. The monastic life bred impeccable record-keeping.

Ironically, though, it was not until the twentieth century that those of The Quorum *could* fully understand where they had come from, and why, and what function they held in matters of ancient spiritism. The civilization of Sumer had long remained a secret buried by sand and time. Lost to the later world because its architecture provided no lasting ruins. Unlike Egyptian stone, Sumerian mudbrick was leveled by annual rains and floods and shifting sands; once-proud towers and palaces became shapeless mounds indistinguishable from the desert.

But in 1869, a French scholar attempting to decipher some inscribed clay tablets from the Near East decoded a passage that called this ancient land by name. Finally, Sumer was rediscovered by the world.

Found on bricks and tablets, various cuneiform alphabets of different dynasties had already been a subject of study for a number of decades, though blindly, without knowledge of their origins. The Sumerian language began to be decoded when scholars worked backward using bilingual inscriptions—Old Persian led to an understanding of Akkadian, Akkadian unlocked Sumerian.

Archaeologists began unearthing the cities from the desert in earnest during the late nineteenth century. Treasure troves of cuneiform tablets found their way into academic study. Of some ten thousand known Sumerian tablets, thirty-five hundred alone went home with the archaeologists of Pennsylvania State University. And they provided an unprecedented key to understanding the very roots of human civilization whose influence was still felt thousands of years later—from technological advancements to law, from government to art, from the measurement of time to literature—

And religion.

Mesopotamian culture had a profound impact on Jewish liturgy and, later, Christian tradition. Most was assimilated when the Mesopotamian King Nebuchadrezzar of Babylon destroyed Jerusalem in 586 B.C. and carried its people—the Hebrews—into captivity. Biblical Old Testament accounts of creation, paradise in Eden, the rivalry of Cain and Abel, the great flood, and the babel of tongues all had direct antecedents in Mesopotamian literature. Stylistic antecedents predated such books of the Bible as Lamentations, Proverbs, and the Song of Solomon, while many of the Psalms were reminiscent of Mesopotamian cultic hymns.

Where Judeo-Christianity differed in substance from its original borrowed stylings were in matters of ethics and morality; these had no earlier counterparts. Nor did the notion of the bond of love felt by one God for the whole of Its Creation. Almost as if lowly humankind were inching ever closer toward ultimate truths.

But The Quorum withheld secrets from the world, a few tablets that had been in its possession since the Third Crusade. At last its scholars could unlock the original mysteries set down almost forty-five hundred years past by a scribe who gave his name as Annemardu. At last the details of the bargain struck with their gods were known, as well as warnings about the Scapegoats, on which Quorum scholars could never quite agree regarding validity. Were they actually revelation, or were they added later, as human commentary?

Certainly, admonishings to keep the Scapegoat of Famine from their own crops, and the Scapegoat of War from their leaders seemed like nothing so much as common sense. The mandate that the Scapegoat of Pestilence be kept from a barren woman seemed more in the line of superstition. Especially since primitive peoples often developed entire cults around woman as fertility object, carving stone icons with prominent breasts and swollen bellies.

Quorum scholars and theorists took unbridled delight in analyzing the whole of world religion, looking for influences that might have stemmed from that sacrifice in Uruk. Human legacy was charted in the rise and fall of countless belief systems over the ages. Generations and nationalities and individuals of vision, appropriating the past and shaping it into their present to best define their own lives. Their own search for meaning.

Perhaps the quartet of Scapegoats of Sumerian antiquity were reinterpreted by Christian theology as the Four Horsemen of the Apocalypse. Perhaps the persona of the shunned outsider filtered into Welsh heritage with its concept of the sin-eater. The renewal of the spirit into person after person might have been incorporated by the Hindu as reincarnation.

Seeds of belief, sown by need. Who was to say that whispers of that day in Sumer had not insinuated themselves into the very recesses of the human mind and soul? Becoming a part of memory that transcended race, and time, into a heritage of the species.

But no one could ever be certain. Speculations only.

In a sense, the human race was no wiser now than during the dawn of philosophy in ancient Greece. Truths could still never be proven—only falsehoods disproven.

Out of which was born that unmitigated need for faith.

All of which, and more, Gabe Matthews learned between 1982 and 1984 during his stay at Loch Nevis.

Death had largely made him what he was by the time he won a full scholarship to the University of Michigan at Ann Arbor. It had made him a ward of the state. Which in turn had introduced him to fellow orphan Kate Quinn, and Gabe was never far from that night of first splendors and wretched helplessness as her lungs drew water. Seventeen years old, and once everyone had gotten over the initial shock, no one blamed him, *That Kate, she was a wild girl anyway,* and after all, Gabe was a model student. *But it was my idea,* he would think. *We were out there because of ME.*

Never so many questions, and never so few to provide answers that made sense. Religious schooling as an orphan had been minimal, prayers by rote, now I lay me down to sleep. But who was he inside? Where was he going? He combed books for wisdom. What of heaven and hell, and did he have a foot in each?

He had been active in high school drama for years, a chance to step into new shoes, other lives. With that wide mouth and strong jaw, Gabe had a face drama teachers loved; a little makeup, and his features projected all the way to the back row. He thought his finest performance those years was a portrayal of the demon Mephistopheles in a pared-down presentation of Marlowe's *Doctor Faustus.* Never forgetting the chill of pathos he felt for this tragic tempter, uttering the line, "Thinkest thou that I, who saw the face of God, and tasted the joys of Heaven, am not tormented by ten thousand Hells in being deprived of everlasting bliss?"

He identified.

College was split between business and philosophy. The former so that he could live in the world, the latter to give him cause to want to. The professor of an ethics class seemed to take special interest in him. Professor Ludlow, nice fellow, kindly, soft British accent—and not the least bit addled, as most people seemed to expect from an old philosophy prof.

He had been particularly impressed with a paper Gabe had done for his class, a melding of earlier theories into something utterly unique. Gabe felt it to be his crowning intellectual achievement to that point. Beginning with Kierkegaard's stance of theistic existentialism—while there is a God, humans have no fixed nature—Gabe grafted to it the dualistic notion of a soul independent of the physical brain, then imposed upon that the ethical relativism of David Hume. Yet in such a way that it applied not to the variable ethics of societies relevant to their own cultures and timeframes, but to individuals. Postulating what Gabe termed "the malleable spirit"—a soul that becomes what the will dictates as being necessary to accomplish a greater good, possibly even the will of God.

Professor Ludlow had been mightily impressed, began to have long discussions with Gabe outside of class. Finally, finally, here was someone taking a serious interest in him because of who he was inside, what he thought, his concerns beyond self.

And in the spring just weeks before graduation, on a campus aswarm with hopeful graduates meeting with corporate recruiters, concerned with starting salaries and chances for advancement and benefit packages, Gabe wondered just what the hell he was doing in such a shallow world. . . .

Until a most unusual offer came his way, and Professor Ludlow began by asking, since he was somewhat a devotee of David Hume, would he like to study in that Scottish philosopher's native land?

New arrivals were assigned a mentor of sorts at the beginning of their two years in Scotland. A friend, a spiritual adviser with whom to discuss problems and fears, history and ethics, whatever. Cabbages and kings. It put Gabe in mind of academic guidance counselors, operating on an entirely new realm.

Gabe's was a wiry fellow by the name of Bankim Mukerji, born in India, educated at Cambridge. He had to have been nearing sixty—

he spoke of studying during blackouts in England during World War II—but his brown face was nearly unlined, his hair still jet black, his body as thin and hard as a train rail.

The two of them became fond of strolling the shores of Loch Nevis, sometimes early morning, other times at dusk. Gazing out over the placid water, so dark, so secret, its long narrow channel more reminiscent of a river than a lake.

"This is one of the few things here to make me miss India," Bankim once told Gabe. "It reminds me of the Ganges."

"The holy river." That was about it for Gabe's knowledge of Hindu dogma.

"The dying often make a final pilgrimage to a sacred place in the city of Benares. There they die, and their bodies are burned on the shore . . . and the ashes are cast into the river for the gods." He smiled, eyes utterly black and unreadable, but his twist of mouth suggested winsome longing. "When I die, I should like that to be done for me here."

They gazed over the water, rippling beneath evening winds from the west, staring forever. Gabe silently promising that, were death to take Bankim while he was around, this cremation would take place. He would see to it like a dutiful son.

Then, "Do you think time changes them? Spirits, lesser gods? Whatever you want to call them." Gabe had been wondering this for the better part of his first year here.

"Is the immaterial world subject to evolution the same as the material?" Bankim rephrased. "Why should it not be? Is one not the shadow of the other?"

He went on, speaking of philosophical logic with which Gabe was already familiar, but somehow it sounded new and different when spoken in the clipped music of Bankim's voice. Speaking of change as a process, kineology; nothing living could ever be seen as static, only as a cross-section lifted from its ongoing evolution. The evolution set into motion by a prime mover—some called it God—since inanimate matter could not move itself. Change then continuing with the established momentum.

"So do you think it follows, then," said Gabe, "that the Scapegoats are different now? Shouldn't they change with time?"

Bankim chuckled. "In theory."

"It's a more brutal world now than then, I think," Gabe said. "In some ways. We're more advanced, sure, but that brutality—I think it's more inside our heads now. Everyone's more isolated. And there's so much less . . . *wonder* about it all. Less respect." He shrugged, didn't know where this was leading. "Shouldn't the Scapegoats reflect that? Shouldn't they be stronger? Shouldn't their abilities have gotten more powerful? You know, you flex a muscle, even if it *is* spirit, for forty-five hundred years, it has to get stronger."

Bankim chewed on this for fifty, sixty yards of grassy shore. "That I could not say. I've not even looked one of them in the face, in the eye. But someday, perhaps, you may—and then you will know."

Talk about temptation, Gabe thought at the time. *It'd almost be worth it to push one and see how far it could go.*

But of course, that would be against their code. . . .

Kind of like that of Hippocrates: First, do no harm.

Gabe had thought he understood the self-infliction of pain long before arriving in Scotland. Evenings of discomfort, senses heightened by fasting, flogging himself across the back with a supple stick whacked down over one shoulder, then the other, back and forth until he felt he had given the memory of Kate Quinn her due.

Bankim Mukerji proved him amateur, though—for Bankim was a master in the art, as a facet of his heritage. And while he had turned his back on many aspects of the Hindu faith—its four stages by which a man's life unfolded, for one—redemption and purification through pain was something he retained.

Finally trusting Gabe after his fourteenth month in Scotland, Bankim showed him the contraption he had rigged in his chamber: ropes and pulleys, counterweights and cuffs for wrists and ankles. He would suspend himself horizontally above the floor, limbs drawn out from his body with such tension, it was a wonder they were not torn from their sockets. Brown body rigid as he wore only the traditional waistcloth, the *dhoti*, muscles as taut as the ropes.

Bankim's gaze journeyed elsewhere while undergoing the ritual, and at the time Gabe could not follow. Could only imagine, in envy. A spiritual voyage while sinews strained, while sweat pattered in great drops, dark upon the stone floor. Gabe would watch him in awe, this holy man, this new messiah who was living proof that bodily pain was more than justified punishment, it could be bridged to the soul.

But why not; mortification of one's own flesh had a long and meaningful heritage. Hermits scraping themselves with sharp stones; Carthusian monks wearing hair shirts. And while he believed there to be greater mysteries than the Church acknowledged, he nevertheless thought of its saints in their death throes and considered them fondly. Flayed alive, or crucified, or burnt at a stake. Or Thomas Becket, archbishop of Canterbury, butchered in his own church by knights of his king. Men of spirit, pushed by that ultimate pain into the moment of ultimate transcendence.

Oh, to be a martyr.

And Gabe had to smile in spite of himself.

Such a romantic idealist at heart.

IV
Fall from Grace

If man had never been corrupt, he would enjoy in his innocence both truth and happiness with assurance; and if man had always been corrupt, he would have no idea of truth or bliss. But, wretched as we are, and more so than if there were no greatness in our condition, we have an idea of happiness, and cannot reach it.

—Blaise Pascal

34

It had been a month, give or take, since Mike Lancer had turned his lower leg into splinters of kindling. Home convalescence, he wouldn't wish this on an enemy. All these people he'd heard in his life, trudging to jobs like it was a daily trip to the gallows, wishing for extended sick time just to score another paid vacation—boneheads, every one of them. Take it from one who's been there.

He had his computer and phone modem, he could work. But after a month of staring at the same walls, he had the attention span of a gnat.

A possible return to the office next week, if the doctor said okay. Mike contemplated bribery.

When the phone rang, he went for it like a lifeline—human contact with the outer world—notching crutches beneath arms and swinging into motion far more fluid than when the cast had been new. Out of boredom Mike had set up a low-budget obstacle course of junk food delivery containers and empty bottles. A pylon course of the unused mates of shoes he'd worn lately.

Answered by the seventh ring, call the Olympic Committee.

"Hey babe. How's my favorite cripple?"

"Ramon! You're a slag and a weasel, you know that? You haven't visited me once this week." Mike lowered himself into a large rattan chair, grateful for long phone cords. He stared at a panoramic vista of dirty dishes growing from his kitchen sink, then turned away. "Shit. I'm so bored I'm about to start calling up 900-numbers."

"Sorry, Mikey, I been a selfish putz. Make it up to you tonight though, take you dancing. How's that sound?"

"Suck my cast."

"Ooooo, fussy today, aren't we?" And he laughed, ah, the sparring never ended. "Nah, listen, man, I got a piece of mail for you. Dawson Ministries. You know, you said watch your desk, see what comes in."

Mike's belly tightened. So, the holy world of treachery, greed, and avarice was about to rear its head. "Did you open it? I mean, it could just be the latest cash plea. If that's all it is, just deep-six the thing. Better yet, run it through the shredder."

"I opened it. It's, uh—it's something else, Mike."

"You want to run it by? Anytime? Now?" He shut up, sounded like he was starting to beg.

"I'll be by after work," Ramon said, and Mike nodded when they hung up. The gods of homebound recovery were smiling upon him. This month had been like childhood rainy days, a whole summer of them strung together, and he, hound dog gloomy in the window.

After the call, he found he couldn't work. Concentration had flown, winging him back to Oklahoma City, that final day, and there it roosted. Tight focus on murder and broken bones, everything he'd had no idea he would find.

He pondered all from the couch, holding the Smith and Wesson ten-millimeter for company. Not that he worried much for his own safety anymore. Were trouble to follow him south in the aftermath, likely it would already have come knocking. He popped the pistol's clip out and in, chambering the first round, then ejecting it, replacing it in the clip. Over and over. Could do this in the dark now without fear of mishap.

I'm sorry, Edie, a spectral apology spoken almost daily, offered up like a prayer. No closer to conjecturing a sensible reason for her death than on the day she had fallen. She had died for nothing, that ultimate sacrifice, for no more than his own misguided, well-meant ambitions.

The television offered no clues. Since returning, Mike had reluctantly become a regular viewer of Dawson's *Arm of the Apostle* show. Got to feel unclean for an hour, watching the man, all slick charm and manufactured drama. Guy could sell condoms to Mother Teresa. And it just didn't figure. Dawson was so superficial, it seemed the unlikeliest of conclusions that his was a heart of darkness; he didn't seem to have a heart at all.

Gabe Matthews was a different bet altogether. One truly et-up motherfucker. Sociopath? Psychotic? Murderous for sure. But his profile was so low, he was impossible to chart via a public eye.

Mike had noticed a few subtle variations in the show from the handful of times he had watched it before. No Amanda, of course, her solo vocal spots given over to another throat, younger and probably more talented, to be honest.

As well, Donny was bypassing the solo laying on of hands these days, in favor of an entire cluster of them onstage, holy gang bang. Spiritual strength in numbers was Dawson's reasoning, which stank of misdirection. Among the cluster was a new face, some guy mid- to late-twenties. Nondescript in appearance, but he at least looked to have a fully developed soul inside, something in his eyes crying out that Dawson's stage was the last place he belonged. He looked out of place according to size criteria, too. Nowhere near as big as the two goons Dawson had employed as stage ushers ever since Mike could recall.

New faces, new routines, Amanda's continued coverup . . . in a milieu where maintaining the status quo was prime directive, too much was going on at once for all to be unrelated. But from the distant outside, it was one fat convoluted soap opera.

With a body count.

Ramon showed up three hours later, wearing a sleeveless blue sweatshirt, his earring *du jour* a ruby. Somebody really needed to take him out and explain there were more styles of dress than street meat. He plopped into the couch while waiting for Mike to wrangle himself into comfort at the other end.

Grinning, Ramon reached down to the pleated flap hanging along the front of the couch, tugged at something barely protruding from beneath. Sharp eyes. He came up with a sheer nylon stocking, gave it a quick appreciative sniff.

"I knew you'd get back in the saddle again," he said.

Mike snatched it away and tied it to the handgrip of one crutch like a banner. "Angels of mercy, what can I say?"

Ramon leaned forward, gave it a playful flip. "Nice wings." Then he rapped the colorful shellscape of Mike's cast. "How do you manage with this thing on?"

"You can only hit the highlights. I'm thinking about writing a how-to manual. *Reader's Digest* Condensed Sex."

Ramon was nodding, patting the cast. "That's good, Mikey, that's *real* good. I hear sex is good for old peoples' circulation."

Mike jabbed him in the gut with a crutch tip and demanded the letter. Ramon was still laughing when he pulled it from a back pocket and handed it over.

Mike unfolded the letter, on the typical Dawson Ministries stationery he had seen so many times before. Usually the same basic message, too, dig deep and send more cash. The text was printed within a crisp inner border, topped at upper left by a cross emanating beams of light from a centered pair of staggered D's. Very subtle, Donny, what exalted company you keep.

Mike began to read:

Dear Friend in Jesus,

As I write this to YOU, it is with a continued heavy responsibility for YOUR well-being. Especially since I, like the voice of John The Baptist echoing in the wilderness, take delight in bringing you news that forever blesses your LIFE.

Yes, friend, the Lord indeed looks after His children through the good works of His servants. The news I share with you is inspired by hours spent in the company of our Lord, and having a new burden laid by Him upon my heart.

It is with great joy that I announce TO YOU that we are changing our Sunday morning *Arm of the Apostle Hour* from a previously taped format to a show that will come directly to you LIVE as it happens! The transition will first be made on Sunday, November 3rd. I pray that you will be watching as we make television history. Please consult your programming guide for our time in your time zone.

Rest assured that Donny Dawson Ministries will continue to work miracles in YOUR LIFE. And I hope you will join us in spiritual unity on that very special Sunday.

Your eternal partner,
Donny Dawson

Mike finished reading, skimmed it again with a frown of irritable confusion. He tossed it aside, working his tongue inside one cheek.

"Dawson didn't write that."

"Mmm?" Ramon said.

"He didn't write it, and I bet he didn't even authorize it, either. You read it, right? You know what it says."

"Yeah, so?"

Mike plucked the letter back from his table and snapped a fingernail against it. "Okay, you're a beginner, you haven't seen as many of these things as I have. There's one thing missing, one thing that shows up on every single one of them."

A frown, then a ventured guess. "He didn't ask for money."

"Exactly," Mike said, then gave the letter another once-over. Waved it in the air in frustration, this thing was so innocuous at first glance, but the more he thought about it, the less sense it made even in the twisted televangelism cosmos. "And this live-format business, what the fuck *is* this? Live TV, there's no *reason* for it. These bozos like to keep their costs down, and we're talking millions to make that changeover. And the slopeheads who watch him, it won't even *matter* to them."

Ramon grinned crookedly. "Hey, watch it, *I'm* one of those slopeheads."

Mike looked at him, blank as an IQ of forty. Then laughed. "Oh man, not you too."

"Well, you know, ever since you came back, I was curious. . . ." He sagged down a few pegs, into himself. Fists beginning to clench and unclench at his sides. "Mikey, I do *not* like that guy, he's not right, he's not right at all. I mean—I'm not the world's best Catholic, I'm not the holiest guy around, okay? But man, I got some respect, you know? I've read the Bible, it doesn't say diddly about some of the stuff he's trying to push onto people. He's twisting God around into whatever he wants Him to be. Like, sometimes He's a rich uncle or something, and sometimes He's a bouncer that's going to throw you out of Heaven you take the tiniest wrong step." Ramon wet his lips, shook his head. "Guys like Dawson, they got fear tactics down pat."

"He makes you nervous too, huh?"

Ramon's eyes went wide. "Oh man, you want to talk fringe element, there you go. It's like some kind of cult, only he uses the mail and the airwaves, keeps himself cleaner that way." He shook a warning finger. "I tell you something. Scariest guy I've ever heard about? Jim Jones. He's the one."

Jim Jones. The name went beyond blandness into invisibility, while the deeds were so bizarre, their memories were eternal. Jim Jones, self-ordained deity of a jungle kingdom, communion of Kool-Aid and cyanide. Before 1978, had anyone believed human beings akin to suicidal lemmings? Probably not.

They both decided they had bad tastes in their mouths, and Ramon unwound from the couch to pull bartender duty. From the kitchen drifted the gentle clinking of ice in glasses, of bottles in use, soothing as wind chimes to an alcoholic's ear.

"What do you think makes people that desperate?" Ramon asked, unseen. "Follow a guy like that."

"Fear, I guess." It was the best answer Mike had been able to tell himself. "They're scared to death of life. They don't want to take charge of their own lives and their own search for God. So they let somebody like Dawson do it for them. No more responsibility then. They're . . . absolved."

"Easy answers guaranteed." Ramon paced carefully around the corner, a drink in each hand. "Whether they're right or not."

Mike nodded, right, and promises came as cheap as the rest of the talk, from health to wealth, life and love and happiness. A reason for waking up alive. Dawson and his fraudulent brethren would promise anybody anything, anytime.

Relief from diabetes, for one. Always a good trick.

"My specialty," Ramon said, and handed him a glass. "Enjoy."

Mike drank, then held it high for inspection. "Scotch and water? No one can screw that up."

Ramon grinned, eyes merry. "I've known people who could."

He wandered with his own drink to the window, stood with his back to the apartment. Statue, freeze tag. Dusk was dying out there, blue-pink blood smeared across the sky. Palm trees swaying gently in silhouette. South Florida, once the last true eastern American frontier, and now the land had been beaten into submission like anywhere else.

Sometimes human beings could be such a plague.

"So you don't think Dawson did that letter, huh?" Ramon said to the glass, the screen.

"No."

"Think it was that guy tried to kill you?"

"Maybe. Probably."

"Think he's got some kind of goofy scheme in his head?"

Mike hunched shoulders, for his own benefit. Ramon was still staring outside. Distant sirens spoke of some dire calamity in a stranger's life, better him than me, amen and good night.

"What other kind *would* he have?" Mike finally said.

"Good point," and Ramon turned, mouth twisted wryly. "Sunday,

November third. Your cast'll be off by then." A knowing gaze. "You're going back there then, aren't you?"

"I thought I might."

Ramon's head at a slant, nodding. Like he was readying to send a brother off to war, write me, keep your butt low.

"Hell," he said, "I knew that before I even called today."

35

The weeks of October saw no small number of changes in the workings at Dawson Ministries.

A forty-foot C-band satellite uplink dish was purchased for one and a quarter million dollars, delivered and set up behind the chapel. Tons more hardware were brought into the chapel, which had undergone some quick remodeling to accommodate it— a pair of second floor classrooms cannibalized, their adjoining wall knocked out, the newly enlarged area converted to a master control room. It was jam-packed with video and audio equipment, receiving a direct feed from the auditorium's four cameras and numerous microphones. A monitor console showed the input from each camera, previously taped segments cued for play, preview for standby, the character generator for credits and bottomscreen message crawls, and the outgoing master mix as seen by viewers. Directorial commands were handled at a mixing board chock full of sliders and rotary pots, routers and switchers.

The new equipment wouldn't run itself, so new crew members were hired to baby-sit it all, technicians and various directors and managers. Experienced, of course, official Dawson Ministries policy being that cost was no object. All were given a crash course in the particulars of ministry expectations.

Satellite time was booked with a company headquartered in Houston. Gabe saw to it that one of their orbiting birds had an available transponder during a preferred Sunday morning time slot.

Unheard of, throwing together a live telecast with such an anorexic buffer zone of time to get the kinks ironed out, and they didn't know how they could possibly help him, seeing as how all transponders had been booked for months—until Gabe handled the situation with definite diplomatic aplomb. Took a meeting with the company president and showed up with an attaché case choked with a neat array of greenbacks. Under the table with a wink and a nod, just to pave the way for harmonious working relationships in the future. Another televangelist with credit problems was bumped for delinquent payments, casualty of the almighty contract loophole.

It was the best they could do. Sunday mornings, eight A.M. to nine A.M., here in the central time zone. This late, it would have been a logistical jungle to try rearranging the schedule with every independent station across the country with whom Dawson Ministries syndicated, to assure the show was live on all fronts. But a scan of the schedules showed that, across all time zones, this slot was already occupied in 45 percent of the stations airing their taped format. Surely, as was explained to Gabe, Dawson Ministries could accept 45 percent live and 55 percent taped delay. For starters.

Yes. He just thought they might.

Live it would be. For Gabe suspected that no technology could record the intricacies of Paul's brain for later playback. Preparations for the switch steamed ahead on schedule, and from a distant insider's vantage point, it all appeared smooth as polished gold.

Paul looked.

And saw that it was good.

It felt like new air, and he breathed it with new lungs. A new spring to his step, a new sharpness in his eye, everything feeling vital again.

Something's different in me now, Paul thought. *But that's okay.* The old Paul had only been working at partial efficiency anyway. Boosted confidence levels, or something, finally settling into some semblance of comfort with the magic hands. Giving them their weekly workout, funneling the bodily misfortunes out of others, pocketing them within himself under the hot glare.

And he watched them, this pathetic parade, wringing their own hands while hoping for a taste of the divine. Getting it, then having eyes of gratitude only for Donny. Kissing *his* hands, bleating their thanks, weeping their tears, while he soaked it all up like a money-grubbing sponge.

Lately, it was the only time Paul really saw him come alive, and it was annoyingly hard to begrudge him this one joy in life. After all, the guy *had* given him his opportunity here. Now he walked around with shattered stature, or remained sequestered in his office, like a deposed monarch kept on the throne for figurehead purposes. A ceremonial head of state to please the rabble.

Or so he looked. Who knew? Paul did not.

But Gabe's words that Sunday while whisking him home from the hospital came back with striking clarity. *It's time you moved up in the world. Donny knows it, and to be honest, I think you've got him a little scared.* He had given it little thought at the time—more flattery from Gabe, eternal diplomat—but the words possessed unsuspected staying power. Growing tendrils and roots.

Suppose Donny *was* on the way out. Not to dwell upon reasons, which could be myriad, which were secondary anyway. Would Dawson Ministries survive without him? It had, in a sense, developed a life of its own quite apart from him. Creations such as this were often built to outlast their creators. Empires of power and money, influence and charity, continuing unimpeded long after their founders have been put out to pasture.

Or sent to the glue factory.

While worthy successors rose from within the hierarchy. Gabe would know that better than anybody, wouldn't he? Sure he would, he was just that kind of guy. And he was the kind of guy more than happy to shun the spotlight and leave it to others. No charisma to speak of, just a weirdly unqualifiable magnetism of ideas and faith and willpower. He got his rocks off behind the scenes.

Which leaves me, Paul thought. *There is nobody else. I'm the one he sees taking over whenever Donny bows out.* It probably would not come right away, but Gabe obviously sensed its inevitability. And planned accordingly. Perhaps he was just as unhappy with certain facets of the current sovereign as Paul was.

Now is the autumn of our discontent. Pray tell what winter might bring.

The subject weighed heavily on his mind one night in mid-October, he and Laurel coiled together in the dark of his room. Late night, crazy late, netherhours of sweat and passion, cooling under a pleasant throb. Her bottom, his arm, both libidos. Together they burned, and it was dizzying, terrifying, wonderful. She could empty him dry, and he could send her rolling through furious red waves. Sucking each other's breath away. A master-and-pupil relationship wherein each role was up for grabs, the delineations blurred beyond hope. They had mapped each other well, and in short time. Each learning how best to feed from the other.

Yet, didn't he love her? He supposed he did, though he had yet to declare it, nor had she. But this was no one-note relationship, the evidence was there. They shared, they trusted, they nurtured bonds. And both had rocky track records; perhaps deep within, they also shared a fear that present declarations might somehow jinx the future.

Two ships that crash in the night.

"Hey." His hand coaxed her hip. "You awake?"

"Mmmmm . . ." Into his shoulder, sleepy. She fought it before his eyes, won for now. "Mmm hmmm."

"Do you think . . . on our level . . . that ambition has any place? Is it wrong? Does it belong here at all?"

Laurel yawned, stretching with feline power. Marbled under moonlight, shadows light and dark, woman of mysteries. "What *time* is it . . . ?"

"I asked first, fair is fair."

She offered a sleepy smile, resigned herself to staying awake, floating between the two worlds, open to both. "Ambition? Well yeah, I have it, sure. When Amanda went away, I *jumped* at the chance to fill that slot. It bothered me at first, a little. Like I was taking advantage of somebody. But I don't care. What bothers me more is the way some of the other girls treat me. In case you haven't noticed, I'm *not* Miss Popularity on the other side of the dorm."

Paul waved it off. "People do that sometimes. Make like they really support your ambitions, but it's only as long as you aspire to mediocrity. If you're better than that, then sometimes you scare them. Or it makes them feel like shit about themselves, and all of a sudden you're a jerk because you've succeeded. You see that a lot in radio."

"Anyway," she said. "I thought you came here to get away from stress like that."

"Can't hide forever. Things come up." How much to divulge? Oh, why not the whole wad? "I think I'm being groomed for something. Like—in the event of Donny's retirement."

"Oh yeah? Congratulations, champ." She grinned again and loosely snatched his hand, dragging it aloft like a referee. Shaking. "You got the touch."

He scowled in partial darkness. "I'm serious."

"Well so am I." And she was. He'd thought she was kidding, humoring a swollen ego, then realized sometimes people took the unexpected more readily when half asleep. Major news having an easier time slipping past disbelief. Just like drunks, ready to believe anything.

And she had already accepted more news of the weird than anybody should rightfully expect to have to deal with. In retrospect, it was probably that afternoon in the hospital that had cemented them for better or for worse. Holding her hand and corking that one-centimeter hole in her stomach. Laurel had gone through the stages right there in the hospital room: Disbelief to dumbstruck amazement to wary unease to acceptance. The latter accompanied with a certain amount of heat. Admit it or not, everyone gets off on the idea of a lover different from all others. That animal passion for the exotic that few actually seek, much less find.

"However well-intentioned, it's still show biz, Paul. You've had your taste of it, even before you came here."

"Yeah. You're right," musing this over, the loss of KGRM, the lonely hollow where the station had been. All the stations, Lethal Rock Radio and progenitors. "I *do* miss it. I mean, I'm *out* there, but I might as well be furniture."

She rubbed a cool hand up and down his inner thigh, smoothing the hair down one way, scruffing it the other. Up and down. "It's a good feeling out there, under the lights, I won't lie about that. I like an audience." She kissed him, perhaps pity for what he had lost. "So who's grooming you for this? It can't be Donny, I can't see him being this farsighted."

"Gabe." Staring up at the ceiling, still trying to fathom the sense of it all. "He seems to have taken a real interest in me. Kind of taking over from Donny, since *he's* been ignoring me."

"Gabe," a dead echo, hard to read. Guarded neutrality. "I think he's jealous of my place in your life. I've gotten frostbite from him a few times."

"Naah, he's okay with it, I really think he is. I wondered but . . . I don't know." Leave it there, he decided. How could he tell her that Gabe's approval *had* been demonstrated in a strange way?

Despite early cautions, their sex life had not gone unnoticed. Close quarters, he supposed it was unavoidable, someone would see something, hear something. Last week, one of the guys in the neighboring rooms that shared the same bathroom had cornered him on it, telling him it wasn't right, wasn't right at all. Okay, opinion duly noted, he was certainly entitled to it, but like some fourth-grader, the guy had threatened to tattle. Irked, Paul had told him go ahead, take it to the top. The guy said he would, he'd see Gabe and just do something about it.

Now he was gone. Quietly. Efficiently. Empty room for rent.

Lordy, lordy.

Perks like that really set Paul to wondering, just how much weight *did* he swing here? It was sobering. And intoxicating at the same time.

Today, resident brain-deficients Dougie and Terry Durbin had come to his door. Industrial gloom from Ministry had been grinding loudly from his speakers, and they thought it their duty to inform him that that wasn't proper music here, just wasn't right.

Perhaps he could make Dougie and Terry disappear too.

"I can't see myself as a preacher, though," he finally said. Carnal nature at odds with the preacher's existence he still persisted in seeing as a life of near-celibate denial. Even within marriage, a strict diet of missionary position only. "I just can't."

"Little Richard became a preacher. Sort of." She giggled into the pillow. "*You* couldn't be any weirder."

Paul laughed, leaned into her. "Stylistically, *he* can get away with it. Black gospel tradition, all that."

"Oh come on. You've never heard of white-boy soul?"

It was good for chuckles, but he ran it through the serious filters, as well. Deejay . . . evangelist? Not so fast. Public speaking, he could handle that, could remold himself into a creature of live theater as surely as he had mastered the hidden airwaves of radio, of this he was confident. Telling Laurel off the top of his head that his would be a different message, he would not condemn, he would beseech people to believe in themselves and a God who loved them despite flaws, rather than a God who held a headsman's ax, its fall dependent on the size of their offering check.

"Well if you're serious here, it won't matter *what* you say. They'll listen. They'll listen to you. Because of *these.*" She drew her hands around his own, squeeze. Snuggled herself so they rested eye to eye. "And if you go public with it—your life'll *never* be the same again."

She drew his hands to her mouth, kissed them, kissed every fingertip, pressed her lips to each palm. And he tried to think of the awesome responsibilities ahead, really tried, but she swept him closer and closer to the here and now. Future did not exist, all was Laurel, Laurel's mouth, soft moist lips and her scent and her mounting breath, lips skimming fingers and thumbs and tip of her tongue tracing lifeline and loveline, oral palmistry.

Taking control of his hands as if they were her own, pressing them now to her body, running them over every curve, settling them onto each mound and into every crevice of heightened sensitivity. She began to writhe before his surrender, Laurel knows best, as his own stirrings grew maddening under the flesh, under the soul. Paul wanting her so very badly, yet not knowing quite *how* he wanted to take her . . .

Laurel then breathing into his ear, four-octave voice slipping out of control as she moaned and murmured, pressing his hands spread wide to her ribs, "Let it into me, *let it hurt me*," and he knew what she meant, this was no dirty pillowtalk of organs and manhood, this was something much much deeper, and far more worrisome, "Let it hurt me and then take it away again, *do it*," and he tried to tell her no, he couldn't, just couldn't, these were dangerous games—

But he wanted it too, the raging erection gave it away, and he became omnipotence made flesh as he rolled atop her, rose to his knees. Hadn't they been headed for this moment ever since he had opened his innermost secrets to her in the hospital, hadn't he known it would lead to this? She would want more than superficial paddlings, Laurel would want him inside where fibers meshed, where cells became sensation. And so help him, he wanted to crawl in there and make it happen.

Feeling her hands grip him below even as he slapped her cheek, moderately, yet laying it wide open to teeth and bone, and she gasped wetly, blood dewing the pillow before his other hand followed over, sealing the laceration in its wake, *gone without scars*, and he did it again, again, again. Digging deeper now, her hands stroking furiously, female and male, yin and yang, sickness and health, and his hands encircled her waist as he took something from deep inside himself and *pushed* and she cried out. Malignancy, something dreadful, massive and coiled inside her pelvic cradle, and he panted and flexed, *gone*, Laurel free and whole again.

She wanted more, and he had it stored inside, oh my yes, a cornucopia of ills and ails. Raising welts and lesions across the pristine fleshscape, watching them bubble by moonlight, trickling their infections to the sheets before he cast them away, only to be replaced by more. Such an incinerating ebb and flow between them, light years beyond genitalia, her hands feverishly bringing him to the edge and over, more fluids to mingle with her own, and he knew it all, the power and the majesty, and the ghastly shame. Nice girls don't do this, nice boys don't help them, but oh, wasn't this just *the* most unearthly ride, stirring it all up inside himself as he relieved that pressure building since his last misfire into Janet DeWitt, lifetimes ago. Letting somebody else take these foul parcels of genetics and biochemistry and wear them like rotten garments, if only for brief moments—

And when she cried rapture to roof and sky, he collapsed atop her, no more, *no more*, this was *just too bizarre.* He trembled and focused on her beneath him—still breathing, count your blessings.

Taking great comfort in the simple gift of her still being alive.

Donny Dawson Ministries . . .

A funny thing happened on the way to hell: Legitimacy dropped into its lap like a falling star.

It became one of those hot topics of news that occasionally burns like a flashfire comet from shore to shore. And did so for all the right reasons.

Such national prominence had humble origins on Thursday, October third. The Dawson camp still settling back into homebound routines after the recently ended tour. Paul still uneasy on this new turf, buoyed by recent developments with Laurel, their forays as brave strangers. Nobody recalled anything unusual during that Thursday night taping. People had been healed, people had wept for joy, business as usual.

But it had been just as much the who as the what.

The night's service had been attended by a Boston financial entrepreneur named Clarence Hurstborn. More wealth than he could spend in three lifetimes, within the top forty percent of the Forbes 500 list, yet for all his millions, bone cancer had been on the march, steady as termites. Turning his pelvis into rotten balsa wood, malignant eyes on his spine. On his orders, two skeptical aides took him incognito to the October third service in Oklahoma City, last-ditch desperation by a doomed man.

By then, even patients genuinely confined to wheelchairs were allowed onto Donny's stage, come one, come all. Stripped of the $3,500 suits that distinguished him in the boardroom, Clarence Hurstborn blended in perfectly, one more believer in the sad parade. Rolled onto the stage by his two aides, Hurstborn walked off unassisted.

The healing was a publicity agent's wet dream.

The legions of faith healers preying on the nation's hopeful had always been eager to claim a thorough catalog of miracle cures. While claiming was simple, providing documented proof was far more problematic. Countless cures could easily be dismissed as psychosomatic illnesses beaten by the power of the mind, or hysterically induced symptoms vanquished because they were never truly present. Others could be explained away as the results of traditional medical therapy concurrent with the faith healing. In other instances, disease might have gone into remission, saving itself for later.

In the case of Clarence Hurstborn, some of the nation's finest oncologists and orthopedic surgeons possessed reams of X rays documenting gradual bone loss and degeneration of his pelvis. Unanimously agreeing that their richest patient had a problem of colossal dimensions.

Equally unanimous was their surprise when, back in Boston on the fourth of October, he walked in free of his wheelchair, and new X rays showed a pelvis as strong and sturdy as that of a seventeen-year-old track star. Two sets of X rays taken a mere thirty hours apart showed what appeared to be two very different men.

There had been other cures of equal magnitude that Paul had brought about, with Donny taking the credit. But upon people leading quiet, unremarkable lives, their impact on the world minuscule when compared to that of Clarence Hurstborn. And if these humble souls returned to their doctors devoid of conditions from which they had long suffered, perhaps gloating, then their doctors may have been puzzled, even awed—but the newsworthiness of the events somehow managed to slip through the cracks. Faith healing was competition, pure hokum—and wasn't supposed to *work*.

But a Clarence Hurstborn is an altogether different affair. Wealth and power, high visibility, and above all, credibility. Plus the documentation amassed by doctors whose reputations were beyond reproach.

Donny Dawson was publicly credited with performing a bona fide miracle healing. After years of puncturing the same tired fraudulent claims of an entire dubious industry, couched in terms that faith was needed to verify the cure, even skeptics could not refute the evidence. And no one was going to publicly accuse Hurstborn of being a liar.

His case broke the dam, and other patients and doctors began coming forward to corroborate his testimony with accounts of their own. The story was rushed into print in *Time* and *Newsweek* and *The Wall Street Journal*. *60 Minutes* was first to secure a tape of the October third service, and isolated the segment in which Hurstborn and his wheelchair were converged upon by a gang of four. After which he rose for his first unassisted steps in more than a year. Over the next week, it became the most frequently aired newsreel in the nation, ranking up there with such historical curiosities as assassinations and Los Angeles police brutality. Geraldo Rivera immediately announced plans for a two-hour ABC prime-time special on faith healers, even securing Clarence Hurstborn's cooperation in giving his own in-depth testimony.

The Arm of the Apostle Hour skyrocketed in the ratings game, full boosters on. Both A. C. Nielson and the ARB showed that it easily outdistanced all competitors past and present for the religious viewer. Jimmy Swaggart had been king of the hill in his prime, reaching around two million in the United States. Dawson shot from around a half-million to more than five. No way around it, the man was one hot commodity.

Inexplicably, what he was *not* was public. Which befuddled skeptics and hoax-mongers to no end, all expecting to see him turning up everywhere from magazine exclusives to the *Tonight* show. Or announcing sudden political intentions, a revival of the Moral Majority, get into office and lay a finger on the pulse of decent people the land over, heal this great nation of her ills.

But not a word from him. Only some grainy film shot outdoors and in secret, long distance. Donny puttering to his office in a golf cart. Donny sitting without motion or emotion beside a pen holding two Irish setters.

The ministry did stage a staggeringly well-attended press conference, conducted by top assistant Gabriel Matthews. Pale and solemn, the quiet, professional tightly pontificating upon Dawson Ministries' commitment to world illness. And while all in attendance agreed that Gabriel Matthews was enlightening, he was no Man of Miracles.

So where was Donny these days? For even the last two shows had been reruns. Gabe's answer was short and direct and left no room for second-guessing: Donny was in fasting and prayer and meditation over their upcoming format change. In spiritual preparation for a bestowment of miracles such as the modern world had never seen. Believe it or not.

Some did. Some couched their skepticism in quiet snorts of laughter, behold the rationalists, keeping their heads while all about, others were willingly losing theirs.

Regardless, it made great copy. The press ate it up with a spoon. And Donny Dawson became the most unseen, unheard, reclusive superstar since the self-imposed exile of Greta Garbo.

But that's what truly fuels the mystique of legend.

A weeknight, October's decline and fall, Paul deduced that much, as weekends were more crowded in midcity. Weeknight, without obligations back at the compound; if he had any, surely someone would have told him. Gabe. Gabe would let him know. Gabe kept on top of everything, no worries. . . .

Leaving him free to walk the streets wherever his feet had whim and will. Breezy autumn night under a starry velvet sky, dry as disinterred bones. No rain lately, he realized, and the winds bore dust.

Paul had driven up here an hour ago, the area surrounding the city university, younger in spirit and soul than the rest. Walking concrete paths covered many times before with Laurel, everything new again, in all the wrong ways, tilted and off-center, familiar sights and sounds and smells made *un*familiar by going them solo. Here was slippage.

Down the stairs to Bran Central Station, his the only footfalls slapping gently from the stairwell off the street. The same soft squeal of a door that needed oiling, now a banshee wail, and he was inside. Standing just past the doorway, checking the scene with eyes sunken into darkened hollows, hair touseled and flecked with airborne grit. A clientele of perhaps one-quarter capacity, piss-poor turnout for the folk duo at the other end, male and female, guitar and mandolin. Hands flashing, and how could they stand it, he wondered, nimble fingers on tight strings, pickpick*picking*, like scraping raw nerves.

He found a seat, table for none, and let the place fill his head. It could be no worse than what was already there.

Limbo of the confused, lost in the smoke hovering above a table near the stage. Clouds, would that he could fly there, wings of an angel, or a devil trying really hard, overachiever.

"Where's the girl you're always with?"

Paul snapped to, found a waitress beside him, *Don't DO that*, and he blinked. College for sure, sophomore, maybe junior, in boots and a vest pinned with Greenpeace buttons, have you hugged your whale today?

"What?" he said.

"That blonde, she's so pretty, you're always in here together," and then the waitress rolled her head back. "I really stuck my foot in it, didn't I, I'm sorry." Maybe she was only now getting a good look at him.

"It's okay." Paul's finger traced doodles in moisture, the wipedown after the table's previous tenants. "She found out she had an ulcer."

He ordered cappuccino steamed with Frangelica liqueur, maybe it would settle warmly and help mellow him out inside, and the waitress told him to tell his friend she hoped she got better soon. Paul said he would, thanks, and promptly forgot about it.

Laurel would be fine, always be fine, so long as he was around, a live-in—sort of—health insurance policy. No premiums, but then the benefit payoffs were a bit screwy, as well.

Smut letters in dirty magazines, always a laugh, sexual exploits of Olympian stature, and every bit as fanciful as tales of those ancient mountain gods. Here's how I fucked my way through a chorus line. Dream on. Paul supposed he could write in too, guaranteed they would never have heard of *anything* like what was going on in his bedroom these nights.

What had happened to his life, anyway? Really. Everything had made more sense when he *hadn't* been quite this good at the ebb and flow. Breakdown and buildup of this bag of meat and bones everyone walked around in.

The coffee came, and he nursed it listlessly, feeling it scalding his tongue and not caring. The sensation never lasted long. Only the cramps did, and how they capered tonight.

Hanging over his mug, watching his sweat plink to the tabletop. Making a pattern of droplets, perhaps he could read his future. And there it was, clear as lightning: *More of the same.* People on all sides, taking, taking, taking. Draining his soul one sip at a time, breaking his body down by individual slivers. Never satisfied, like vampires who didn't give a shit if it was night *or* day, there they would be, lined up, give me health, make me whole, and the worst of it, these pathetic wrecks with their sob stories didn't even know it was him they were lining up for.

Then there were Laurel and Gabe. Takers of a more cunning breed, although they gave in return, in their own ways. Laurel her passion, Gabe his adoration, this perverse worship coming from them both, for body and soul respectively. The pedestal syndrome. He no longer felt their equals; they would not let him stay that low.

It got a bit much at times.

He would adapt.

Paul left money on the table, coffee and tip and then some, and drew himself together. Threw it all out the door into the night, stalking sidewalks in search of something, not even he knew. Peering into window after window, this gauntlet of business so dependent on the local institution of higher learning, feeding on those who quested for knowledge. Selling them shoes and toothpaste, books and beer, music and sweatsuits. Outfitting them like little soldiers of free thought, hah, as if their thoughts were really their own. They had been programmed from cradle on.

He was seeing remarkably more clearly now than he had at such a tender age. And as time's veteran, he was entitled to despise a lot of what he saw anymore.

He was, after all, the great white hope of TV ministries. Televangelism's enfant terrible, infused with the power to cope with a dark new age, behave or I could come down upon you like the wrath of Judgment Day. Psycho-body surgery, cleaving a bladeless incision beneath the ribs, to reach up into the chest cavity like an Aztec priest, enact a little change of heart.

Laurel had found it interesting last night.

My my my, but his frontiers were expanding daily.

He laughed, and it filled the hollow streets. Now, if only he could just fill a hollow heart.

On a shady side street, less traveled, Paul stopped before a bookstore, independent, locally owned in fierce defiance of massive chains. He admired that. Pausing, looking through the darkened windows, after hours, a skeleton crew of lights burning, illuminating the new, the different. Books, magazines, cassettes.

Magazines.

And what was this, a familiar face, the brand-new weekly edition of *People,* resting on a table against a display easel. Cover splashed with a recent promo photo of none other than Donny Dawson, local boy makes good. Trademark white suit and sweep of golden-brown hair. TV'S OWN MAN OF MIRACLES? the headline read, and inset into one corner was a grainy shot lifted from the Hurstborn taping. Wow, Donny doing cover billing along with Julia Roberts, and Paul stared for minutes, nose to glass like a child at a pet shop window, *That could've been me,* and then he doubled around the block to the alley and found a heavy garbage can and dragged it around front and heaved it through the window. Plate glass imploding, like a bomb blast, a razor crystal shower over books and floor and displays.

He stepped one foot over the glass-toothed sill, shoe crunching glass, and he grabbed the magazine and was gone. Just because no alarm had sounded didn't mean the local bacon wasn't on its way.

Paul zigged a block one way, zagged two another, until he felt the sirens were distant enough to relax and he could do some quick page-flipping. Sitting near a street corner and its towering lamp, beneath the colorshock branches of a sprawling oak, the subtle spice of leaves in dry rot. He felt safe here.

People magazine, all the latest celebrity flavors of the week, and Paul flipped hard and fast. Found the article beginning on page thirty-eight. Next page, the supreme pinnacle of tackiness, a reproduction of Clarence Hurstborn's X rays, before and after. Reprinted by permission, of course, and probably remuneration, the filthy rich bastard was really milking this for all it was worth, another allotment of those Andy Warhol fifteen minutes. Made Paul sorry he'd set hands on the guy in the first place, and there they were all together, page forty-two, caption listing Hurstborn and Donny and "three unidentified Dawson associates."

Paul shredded the magazine into furious tatters he left in his wake, and *damn* him, Donny Dawson, the greedy son of a bitch. A fucking *cover story* in *People,* and all Paul was was an unidentified associate. Just how long was Donny going to let this charade go on, how long would his conscience permit it? Hah, *what* conscience, he thought a moment later.

Of course, Paul *had* let Donny set the precedent of taking advantage of him. But he'd been vulnerable then, you'd think things would change now that he'd gotten himself back under control.

He fumed his way along the sidewalks, and did Donny care about the pain he was in, the cramps that would periodically seize him up? Of course not. Let him suffer, all the worse now with this latest discovery of misplaced adulation. Everything inside him cooking, steaming, trembling under the pressure of holding it in. Laurel provided minor relief, giving her those transient tastes of mortality, but he always held back and had to reclaim what he left inside, and quickly. The ills came back home to roost, as surely as the swallows to Capistrano.

No fair.

No fucking fair at *all.*

A half-block later, Paul caught sight of movement in bushes, something low, something brown and white. Furry and four-legged. He stopped, and it did not. A moment later it snuffled out to him, friendly tail wagging. A collared dog, some family's mongrel pet.

He stared at it for a solid minute while it stood before him like a sacrificial lamb, sniffing experimentally around his knees, its witless way of making acquaintance.

Relief, blessed release. He needed this dumb beast far more than did any family. The tears of children dried quickly. They would forget soon enough.

Paul knelt and scratched the dog behind its floppy ears. Attention finally returned, it doubled its affections, lapping at his hand with an eager tongue. While Paul bit his lip in sorrow at the monstrousness within that was leading him to this, to conjure up the foulest malignancies held at bay inside, then hold tight to the dog with splayed hands, then *project* while that tail wagged incessantly. An accusation of betrayal, and Paul began to sweat again even in the chill night air . . .

And it wasn't working.

Whichever was greater—his relief or his disappointment—he could not say. Obviously, whatever it was that rode him within differentiated one flesh from another, one soul from another. It was no acceptor of just *any* meat and bones delivered to it, only human would suffice. What of ravaging corpses, he wondered briefly? But no; surely, if a living beast was not acceptable, a dead human would not be either.

No fucking fairness *anywhere* in this world.

Paul found his way to a street walked only once or twice with Laurel, a path less traveled, perhaps less savory to more gentle tastes. He liked it just fine. There was a club along here, a place he had thought looked interesting, but Laurel had turned up her nose. A Bran Central gal all the way. He located it easily enough, just follow the people in black.

It was built into a regular storefront, glass walled off from the inside except for a narrow crack through which to peek. A hangout for fringe types, artistic nihilists, the unstable and those on their way. The deliberately sloppy lettering painted above the doorway read J. P. SARTRE'S. Nice touch.

He stepped through into sonic assault, oppressive battery. Reign-of-terror decor from wall to wall, gallons of black paint slapped overhead alone, useless rusty pipes and the choking refuse of an industrial age gone insane. Part opium den, part asylum.

It spoke to his condition.

In a former life, his first stop would have been the bar, far in the back and ringed by red neon. Grab a beer and lurk on the edges for a while, wait until he felt at home before venturing closer to the heart. Not tonight, though, tonight he was immediately a cog in the machine.

The dancing was brutal, no grace, all aggression. Slamdancers aplenty, colliding with neither hate nor mercy, too much energy and not enough outlets. A mosh pit, all sweaty human stew and tangled hair. He threw himself into the savage cotillion, let it buffet him in improvised choreography of random violence, and he gave as good as he got.

Once a deejay, always a deejay, that capacity to let the song take over. The music was new, dark, terrifying. Punk gothic, born of rage and disillusion, suckled on paranoia, and smoking with a forlorn whiff of genocide. He reveled in it, vicious strobing of black light nightmares smeared in his face. Blinding his eyes.

Dancing became a medieval purge, beat the demons out, flogging himself not with bundles of sticks but the bodies of others, so willing. So bony. His ground-glass joints, the scrape of tendons and the rasp of muscle. He could cry if he let himself. No holy martyr had ever bled from deeper within; no accused witch bound to a fiery stake had been more wrongfully condemned.

He belonged nowhere, neither earth nor heaven nor hell. Yet he had been conceived in all three.

He was spread *awfully* thin these days.

He whirled. He thudded. Was shoved and shoved back, nothing personal guy, and this was never going to work. He could dance until his body was one vast bruise, and it would never begin to ease those deeper pains.

Locked into frenzy, spittle flying, leaking from the corner of his mouth, dusty hair soaked with sweat, not all of it his own. He opened his eyes wide, amazed at the new lucidity, showing him true reality peeking through from beneath surface veneers during each flash of black light strobe. The hidden faces of the bad sorts coming out in unwitting display. Gargoyles of a cold harsh world, twisted and gray, and out here he could separate sheep from goats. Knowing he should be terrified, exposed and surrounded by aberrations, but knowing too they could never touch him. Impunity.

And release.

Paul set his eyes on the biggest one, the ugliest, the hairiest. He fought his way over and hurled himself into the guy, like colliding with brick and blubber. Its mutant face sneering, the proportions all wrong, *all* wrong, distorted by infections of genetics and soul.

He rushed in again, a boxer's clinch, slid one hand up beneath a leather vest and felt slick hairy belly, and shoved until fat and organs alike were displaced, and Paul twitched, obscene ecstasy as it came pouring out of him in snarled torrents. All the pressure, all the dark steam, *blowout,* the world would be a far better place without this wretched creature he was dispatching, and he had mandate to judge.

Dancing spasmolytics in convulsive beauty, as a thin stringer of blood came spewing from one malformed nostril. Bulging eyes and open mouth, tongue squirming within like a parasite. The guy's face darkening as he bellowed, a roar lost to the sound system and the music of tribal fervor.

Paul let him go then, dead on his feet and staggering back toward a wall festooned with rusty metal. Striking moistly, splat, staring with sagging jaw at an arm strewn with weeping boils, and no telling what he looked like on the inside, amen, good riddance, and good night.

Paul weaved from the dance floor in the opposite direction, and no one had noticed the dead thing yet, hey, it was just that kind of place, one more sick drunk spat back by a crowd he couldn't hack.

Paul felt light, flightworthy. Free from anchors of body, shackles of spirit. Dizzy relief, and he laughed with joy, no more pain, no more cramps, so let the unworthy fall where they may.

Then . . .

The veil, lifting, old awareness returning as if through time and mist, tentative and sluggish, while with it came fractured wisdom.

Dear God forgive me . . . I just killed *someone . . .*

It had been . . .

Well, unique.

36

Donny decided that he liked doctors, in general. Liked them very much. He had had little use for them for the past decade-plus-change, these healers reminding him of his shortcomings. Medical science often succeeding where his own brand of manufactured faith tended to fail.

Irv Preston had been different, because Irv did not judge, became a friend, even a partner of sorts. Gone now, never forgotten, but by necessity he had to be replaced. Donny had hooked up with one of Irv's colleagues, a younger doctor from Irv's private clinic, a fine fellow who understood the rigors and pressures of running your own empire and who prescribed tranquilizers accordingly.

You could meet the most interesting people at a funeral.

Within six hours of Gabe's hostile takeover, and four hours of bidding public farewell to the earthly remains of Irv Preston, Donny had embarked upon a crash course in the joys of ten-milligram Valium tablets. Five, six times a day. Powder blue wonders, down enough of them and consciousness slips and slides into a whole new realm of soft focus, slow motion wonder, and the sheathing of frayed nerves.

Watching the world go by.

And what an interesting world it looked to be, too, all kinds of attention directed his way. TV, magazines, newspapers, all clamoring for comments when he had none. Yes, Gabe had seen to that, all right, made sure the secretaries and lower echelon peons steered all seekers away disappointed. A human screen, sifting out whatever might intrude and sully this perfect inner world of complete nothingness in which he now lived.

One lifeline: Gabe had said he would soon turn it all back over, and be gone.

Maybe it wouldn't be so bad, by then. Maybe interest would still be there. Maybe he could dust off his mantle of command and step smartly back into place and let the world come to him, and he would receive it graciously. After all, Gabe was still keeping him up on matters, feeding him written reports, old habits hard to break. And they were richer than ever. Contributions pouring in, the weekly volume of letters more than doubled. Gabe had brought him a few, all the same. Pray for me. Heal me. Long distance, I know *you* can do it, I saw you on the TV news and believe you're a true healer, not like the rest. Here's some money and I'll send more when it's done, if I can, when things are better.

Donny burned the letters in his fireplace. Supposing the checks had already been deposited.

He had visited the mailroom a couple of times. Ordinarily, he found it a depressing place. Few of its staff aspiring to much more than minimum wage, hired on for hustle rather than religious convictions. Naive visitors were often surprised to find the place reeking of Marlboro clouds and resounding with off-color jokes, racial slurs. But lately, visiting had cheered him up better than a surprise party, all those bulging postal sacks. People out there loved him, they really loved him.

God bless Valium.

It even made the trips upstairs to visit Amanda go down smoother. Fewer and further between anymore, such a chore trudging up the stairs to the third floor, his legs heavier by the day.

Today he had made the effort, though he wondered why he'd bothered. Sitting in her bedroom with her, rested up from therapy but her cheeks still flushed. Lots of silence between the spurts of words, and while he supposed this was better than her first tart-tongued week of consciousness, he wasn't quite sure. Have to think on that.

"Donny, you look awful," she told him. What a thing to say. Across the room in her sweatsuit, lips curled inward, together, as she bit down on them with shiny eyes. "You're taking something, aren't you?"

"It's just to help me relax. I need it. I'm entitled. It's been a long time since we had a vacation, and I just think I'd rather take one here as anywhere in the world."

"The past five *years* have been a vacation. We haven't done any work. We've just been playing games." Her hands took in the room. "Up here? *This* is the hardest work I've ever done."

She really was making progress, could now ambulate around with minimal assistance. She still needed a cane, but had weaned herself down from a hemi-cane to a large-base quad, then a small-base quad, and would switch to a single-point before long. He knew that her nurses' hours had been cut even more. The return of normal body functioning had been radiating outward, from trunk to shoulders and hips, then out along her limbs. Just amazing.

"This therapy? It's the first time I've felt really good about myself in—in—" Breaking off, shaking her head, knocking a fist down against the chair arm. "And do you know why?"

He shook his head no.

"Because it's *mine*. Mine alone. It's something you can't touch and make *yours*." Mandy angrily swiped at her nose, starting to sound a bit stuffy. "I shouldn't feel that way about things, about you —but I do. And I won't keep it down inside me anymore, not for you, not for anybody."

Valium walls, doing their duty. He could not believe she meant this. "You're just having a bad day, hon, it'll look better."

"A bad day," and she barked a laugh, tossed her head back with a flip of hair. Settling then into the saddest little smile on her dear face that he had ever seen. "A bad day. I remember . . . when all a bad day meant was running short on gas money to get from one church to the next." Looking up then, watery eyed. Shaky voiced. "I think . . . we have reached a stage . . . where we have *very* different ideas about what makes a bad day."

Donny gave this some thought, and it prickled. Well, maybe they did not see things with identical eyes lately, but he could certainly give her a lesson or two about bad days. Blackmailed by a murderous pervert with dirty pictures, forced to hand over the keys to the kingdom, now *there* was a real stinker, wasn't there?

But he had told her nothing, would continue to tell her nothing. Amanda did not need it heaped onto her shoulders, they were already carrying burdens enough as it was.

Such an ache, keeping that one inside, balled into a cold hard knot. Even Valium couldn't warm that one up, make it fuzzy.

"A bad day," he finally said, stirring dregs of memory for some of the free-form eloquence he'd once used to great effect from the stage, "is missing you. Waking up and seeing you're not there in the same bed. Going into my office, and knowing . . . you won't be coming by. *That's* a bad day."

"You don't miss me," she said.

Donny felt his face droop, his eyes burn. "Don't you tell me what I'm feeling. . . ."

"I'M *HERE!*" she screamed through clenched teeth, rearing forward in the chair. Then back down. "I'm here. I've been here all along, *you* saw to that, and it's not *me* you miss. It's the memory of what we both thought I was. But you know what?"

"No," he croaked, groping for an argument for this and coming up without weapons, "what . . . ?"

"I don't miss her half as much as you do."

Paul made the long slow climb to morning light, like crawling on skinned knees, broken elbows. Running the past hours through memory, the best he could. Twenty-four hours, thirty-six, forty-eight? Everything a jumble, puzzle pieces in a box, how did it all fit together?

J. P. Sartre's, that had been night before last. No. The night before that. He remembered quaking beneath blankets for a good twenty-four hours afterward. Ignoring Laurel at the door, her knocks, grateful she had no key. Passing the hours in solitude, dawn to noon to dusk to dawn. Paul, rolling in twisted covers, sometimes sleeping, sometimes not, sometimes dreaming himself awake with untrustworthy memories, *killed him I killed him I didn't mean to but it hurt hurt so bad he didn't look human at first*

Things blurred the nearer to today he drew. Last night, what of last night, and he threw back the covers with molten eyes and tried not to cry out. Different clothes than he last recalled wearing, he'd worn the same ones for two days, and when had he changed?

If you couldn't trust your memory, you could trust nothing.

Fragments, nothing more, *did this happen last night?*, driving under the influence of heat and fear downtown again blocks from the scene of the original crime hands his hands looking for someplace to rest alley cloudy silver moon crescent like pendulum frozen among stars alley and bricks dumpster overflowing a vagrant's bounty of botulin nutrition his hands alley bedtime beneath newspapers under a doorway human refuse in stocking cap and scraggly beard the reek of budget wine waking only halfway while hands finding rest to bring a heart thick yellow burden and everlasting stop—

Last night.

It could have been a dream, or a fantasy. Fevers of the imagination, a bad trip. Like morning-after hangovers with bitter crumbs to fill a void of hours. Knowing that however shameful your memories of behavior beyond control, there was always the distinct possibility of something worse, blacked out forever.

He had done it again. Done it again and barely remembered. Proving hardcore wisdom, understood by soldiers and murderers for hire: The first kill is always the hardest; after that they get easier.

Just how easy would it be to kill by the end? An errant thought, and perhaps the first time that the notion of an ending to this had crossed his mind.

Paul crawled from the bed, dragged himself over to the room's mirror centered on a closet door. See what manner of spectacle he had become, if the lives he had taken had made him taller, more robust, more godlike. No, none of it. Three days of beard had grown when he hadn't been looking, days he had apparently not eaten and hadn't missed it, his face gaunter than he seemed to recall. Wearing jeans and a gray pullover sweater; work clothes, robes of a divine executioner. Fallen angel of death.

He gazed into the reflection, openmouthed. Like staring at a twin, long-lost, presumed dead. No hope. He pointed one finger at the mirror-Paul, gun-fashion, thumb cocked back for the hammer.

Let it fall, bang, I'm dead.

Or he could take his hands and remove them, hack one off with the other—but of course, that would still leave one, unable to turn on itself. Consort with the deities of power tools, then, find a table saw and raise the blade to a height greater than his wrists. Feed each one across like so much excess plywood, let them tumble to a sawdust-strewn floor like dead white spiders, bleeding their venom. Then stomp them until the fingers were mangled beyond repair, kick them toward the trash in hopes that some brave soul might pick them up and finish the job, sensing their worthlessness.

Options were few.

As he sought out shoes, put them on, he thought of peers. How truly dreadful and lonely your existence when you have none. Contemporaries, acquaintances, yes. But none who could be called an equal. Only equals can empathize with the pain that is your lot in life, for they have experienced it too, or know they soon will.

He had none.

But across the compound, however contrived, was the closest thing.

Weary pilgrims of hope, some people climbed mountains to find their god, or traveled halfway around the world. Gabe's walked in through the office door and called him by name. Undoubtedly he was held in high favor.

"Where's—where's Donny?" Paul asked.

"At home, probably," Gabe said. "He keeps an erratic schedule these days." Eyes softening, inner and outer Gabes contending for control of the moment. Deciding the time was improper for worship, his god would not accept it at the moment. "You seem to be doing the same."

"I need to talk to him," a desperate plea, sliding by fingertips down a cliff face. Paul lingered in Donny's office doorway, hand on knob, a stabilizer. He shut it softly, leaning back against it, and slid to the floor. ". . . anyone . . ."

Not all were prepared to bear the weight of so heavy a crown. But Gabe was not the least bit disappointed. Sought out in Paul's moment of weakness, this only confirmed that Gabe was worthy to look upon his face and speak his own mind. To give counsel? This would be divine.

The confusion on Paul's face was understandable, climbing the stairs to this sanctified aerie, barging past secretaries, intent on speaking with Donny, but finding another in the seat of the charlatan, the pretender. Gabe had spent most of his hours the past two weeks commanding the ministry from here. A surrogate on an assumed mandate from Donny. The underlings, easily led, asking few questions. Sheep.

Gavin had been trickier, calling from Scotland, worried about the increasingly high profile in the aftermath of the Hurstborn healing, all that publicity, that authentication. Gabe had soothed him, told him he was trying to steer Paul out of the ministry, but hang on, patience, this was going to take some time. Gavin had hung up, sounding little reassured, but the faith in his protégé still bedrock.

While Gabe, with as free a rein as he could hope for, made preparations to meet his god without barriers of pretense in the way. On terms as pure and holy as he could engineer.

Gabe smiled. "I knew you'd be up here. Knew you'd come."

Paul stared, saying nothing, expecting tricks, or his own demise. "You've taken lives again, haven't you?" What a comfort it was to have occasion to say this. The restoration of balance.

And now Paul began to cry, folding into himself at the bottom of the doorway, head on knees, still every bit the creature of magnificence. Questions in those streaming eyes, *How, how?*

Gabe held a newspaper up from the desk, slapped it with his free hand. "I read, Paul. I *see* things others don't, because I *know* things they don't. Back-page news, those two you've left behind you this week. But they've confused some people. I'm the only one here who can recognize your footprints."

Talk of mysterious deaths, representatives consulted from the Centers for Disease Control in Atlanta. Miracles of a lower order, but Gabe beheld them as no less wondrous than water to wine. For surely, even greater would follow, and soon.

"I'm doing terrible things," Paul whispered. "I don't want this anymore, this is tearing me to pieces, I don't know where to go. . . ."

"And you thought Donny could tell you?"

Shaking his head, wordless broken whispers, *I don't know, I don't know.* . . .

The anguish was palpable all the way across the office. This citadel, shown to be nothing but vain ambition in the purity of such tears. Gabe would gladly have taken these agonies of rebirth and transition upon himself had he been able, but they were Paul's alone. Growing pains, and pain indeed had its virtues.

"They were mistakes. Just mistakes." Soothing his troubled brow, for while the time would come for Paul to know his heritage, this was not it. Great power was often characterized by the fragility of its vessel. "Years ago, I had a job working under a woman who told me one of the wisest things I've ever heard. She told me if I wasn't making any mistakes in my work, I wasn't doing nearly *enough* work. Mistakes can be costly—but they can usually be corrected."

"You didn't *kill* anybody on the job, did you?"

"No."

"Then don't even fucking try to compare this, okay? *Okay?*"

Gabe shook his head. "Elder statesmen once wrote all men are created equal, but . . . no. No. I don't believe that, because the world doesn't work that way. Some men are greater than others, we see that all the time. *You* . . . are a great man. And great men should be allowed to make greater mistakes."

Paul's hands in trembling fists, "But I've killed. I've *killed.*"

"You've healed."

Shaking his head, no, no, "That's supposed to balance it out somehow?"

Gabe's eyes slid closed; this was closer to the truth than Paul realized. "You've healed hundreds. Many of whom would have died, you know we're not turning away terminal patients." Gabe, face alight, the wonder rising, let him shine on me and my death and I can go fulfilled. "You have eclipsed every other healer on earth, living *or* dead. And it's *still* not enough for you?"

"It's not worth it if I have to hurt people."

"Worth it to *who*? If you're talking about your own conscience—then that's a little selfish. Four dead, a tragedy, I'll admit that. But hundreds saved."

Gabe stood up at the desk, not even blinking for fear he might miss some nuance, subtle evidence of any change in Paul's heart. And it was there: equations in his eyes, ratios, the lives of many outweighing the lives of few. Paul might not admit it, might not even be aware—*but it was there.*

Onward, this entire dialogue prepared and rehearsed for precisely a moment of crisis such as this, and he came out from around the desk. "That you've made mistakes doesn't mean you should turn your back on everything you are. And it doesn't lessen what you are when you fail. The Old Testament's full of great failures. Jonah? God asked him to go to Nineveh, and he ran the opposite direction to try and avoid it. It didn't work. King David? He wanted Bathsheba so badly, he sent her husband off to die in battle just so he could have her—yet here was a man after God's own heart, we're told." And Gabe was there. Kneeling beside Paul in this darkest of hours. "Would you elevate yourself above them?"

Paul looking up at him, "No," scarcely a whisper.

Gabe trembled, to touch this magnificence. His deliverer. Hand to shoulder, tentative for a moment, doubting his worth, then thinking of all the pain withstood. Scourge and clamp and blade, he had prepared as fully as he knew how. To feel no shame, then, as he tried his best to allay the weight of Paul's worlds.

Paul sobbed, nearly flattening to the floor as he threw one arm around Gabe's leg, the other around his waist. Baptism by tears.

So very long since he had been close enough to anyone to give comfort. Smiling sadly down upon a trembling shoulder beneath his hand, it was just as well Gabe did not plan on being alive after this coming weekend. For all the years to follow would be but anticlimax. How terrible, with so much of life yet to be lived, to have peaked, and know it.

But he considered it a privilege.

"I wanted," Gabe said, beginning to choke up as well, "to take what's inside you . . . and send it out into the world."

"Can't," Paul mumbled into his knee, "I just can't."

"You can, if you believe. And if you're believed *in*." No more objections, just tight muscles beneath his palms, a good sign. Paul would see his wisdom. "It's easy to be a holy man on a mountaintop. The hard part's carrying it out into the world. . . .

"Take it from one who found out the hard way."

37

Just a couple of guys from Florida, on the road to Oklahoma City; like some goofy homegrown twist on Hope and Crosby. The nonstop jaunt from Delray Beach took nearly thirty hours, Mike and Ramon switching off so one drove while the other caught lousy shuteye. Six states, back to back: Florida, Alabama, Mississippi, Louisiana, Texas, and finally the promised land.

It was a whole new climate of confusion up here, Donny Dawson now part of a national consciousness. The man could *not* turn out to be legitimate after all, please, anything but that. Mike decided to play this as if Clarence Hurstborn had never existed.

Late Thursday night, they rolled into a motel down the street from the one Mike had stayed in before. Staying in the same place didn't seem wise. Maybe they would remember him there, hadn't forgiven him for puking in his room floor. Mike paid cash for one room, two beds, and they wandered in glazed and dazed. Grimy, cranky, sore of butt and red of eyes. Thirty hours of highway humming through their veins.

It would have been easier to fly, but riskier. Packing two guns—Mike's new Smith and Wesson, and an identical gift to Ramon from his brother. No telling what would happen up here, so best to travel without leaving electronic footprints back to their doors.

After check-in, they put up with five minutes of room claustrophobia and wandering attention spans before deciding to head for the nearest bar. A block and a half away; Mike decided he could use the walk, work out the stiff aches in his leg. The cast had come off a week ago. Strength and flexibility were not what they once were, and he'd left behind one pissed-off physical therapist for discontinuing services indefinitely. He'd also left behind a job with a real question mark hanging over it.

Ramon was in better shape, had vacation time coming and never a day of sick leave. Comptroller's pet, that's what he was. Mike still felt gratified in him coming along. Stand-up didn't go *near* far enough in describing him. Brother's keeper, shrugging it off by saying he'd held Mike's hand through this much of it, might as well see it through, make sure he didn't get stomped again.

It was greatly appreciated. Wordlessly so.

The bar was brimming when they walked in, all kinds of mutant clientele in this seedy lounge. Would-be soldiers and witches, an astronaut and a Viking princess, bogus doctors in scrubs and cheerleaders old enough to worry about stretch marks. This was too weird, and they shouldered their way to the bar for boilermakers, take the raw edge from their nerves.

They'd been there a minute or two when the dark-haired girl beside Mike looked at him with a smile. Black lace all over, pale face and bright rouge on her cheeks, red lips. Vampire.

"Where's *your* costumes?" she said.

Mike lowered a few degrees into her face, arched his brows for her, bulging those bloodshot orbs. "These look like real eyes to you?"

Ramon laughed and shook his head. "Fucking Halloween," he said, and laughed again, with a groan. "This's so perfect I can't stand it."

They slept the sleep of terminal exhaustion that night, and early the next morning shaved and showered, long luxurious hot-water rinses. Turning themselves into near-replicas of the men who had left Florida. Breakfast came from a Hardees drive-through, and they ate in the car while Mike drove for South Squire Road. The routine was no different from the old days, leave the car in the same carpet and tile outlet's lot, hoof it through the woods.

"Shit, Mikey, it's *cold* up here."

"It's fifty degrees, quit whining." Thirty steps from the car and Ramon was already complaining, this was rich. "Is it my fault you don't own anything with sleeves?"

Ramon nudged him defensively. "*You* haven't seen me in my suit I brought."

"Maybe if I get married, maybe then?"

Tramping along, Mike began to regret the season. Autumn was poor timing for this. Not because of the chill, Ramon and his briskly rubbing arms aside, but for the changes of fall. Every step, a symphony in crunching leaves. A billion more on the trees, hanging deathly and brittle, just waiting to drop. The lush foliage of early September was gone, along with its ample cover. They might as well be marching up banging a drum and cymbals.

They did the best they could, found a suitable spot to set up camp and keep an eye on Dawson's house. A fallen log, eaten into by little shelves of fungus, served as their bench, and they spread out their gear. Thermos of coffee, two walkie-talkies, a sack with several surplus breakfast biscuits. The pistols they set aside in close reach.

"So what's the plan?" Ramon said.

"Hell, I don't know." Mike checked his watch, seven-forty. "I figure maybe we'll just wait here awhile, see what happens."

Ramon nodded, eyeing the house. "Brilliant."

Mike was halfway into another steak and egg biscuit when something about the front of the house caught his eye. Conspicuous by its absence.

"No cars on that cul-de-sac," he said. "I just noticed that."

"So maybe they're all in the garage. Look at the size of that thing."

"I mean nurses' cars." He lifted the binoculars slung around his neck to scan windows, could discern no movement. He lingered uneasily on the one through which he had come bursting, as if to see someone else on the same trajectory. Or himself, the ghosts of misery. The curtains were drawn, placid. "When I was here before, they were staying with Amanda around the clock."

"Meaning . . ."

"She either died or got a lot better."

Two and a half hours snailed by before movement finally caught their attention. A golf cart was leaving from behind the house, periodic glimpses weaving through the intervening trees. Maybe seventy yards away, aimed for the compound, and from here it looked like Dawson, the dressed-down variety. A late start on his day at the office, nice work if you can get it. Mike watched until Donny had sailed out of sight over a slight rise, then swept his binoculars back over the front of the house. Sometime in the past few minutes, someone had parted those third-floor curtains.

"Somebody's home," in singsong voice, then he lowered the binocs. Flexed fingers and rubbed his leg, wincing. "I wonder how my breaking and entering skills have held up."

"Oh man. Oh man. You're not going in there—are you?"

"Well, yeah—unless you'd rather just sit out here all day and pray for Indian summer. Me, I'm getting bored." Mike pulled the binoculars off from around his neck and handed them over, then grabbed a walkie-talkie for himself. "If anybody shows up, punch the code key. It'll be quieter than your voice, and if I can talk, I will." He wedged his pistol down into his back waistband.

"Oh man, I'm driving home alone, I just know it," Ramon, shaking his head and muttering. "What'll you say to her if she's in there and catches you, huh?"

Mike flashed a rogue's smile, devilish eyes atwinkle. "I'll ask if she's out of bed for the day, or what?"

"Oh would you *be serious*," then more weary head-shaking. "I'll do your eulogy back home, all right? I'll do a good job, poor Mike, we knew him well, we all knew his pecker'd get him killed *one* way or another."

"I love it," Mike grinned, and took off. That Ramon, really, he was better than a mother sometimes.

He kept to the trees, flanking right until he could emerge on the blind far side of the house. He held a crouch while sprinting for the house with a noticeable limp, finally straightening when reaching the wall, pressed flat. Leg aching already, every pulse nudging bone marrow. Mike eased back around toward the front door, ducking low and crab-walking beneath ground-floor windows.

The front door. He was almost expecting the disappointment of finding it locked, of course, couldn't be *that* easy.

He backtracked around the side, kept going until he reached the rear of the house. Pausing at the corner of the foundation, kneeling and taking time to spot trouble, potential or overt. Gardens, weedy and ill-tended. A tarped-over swimming pool. Farther out, a dog pen; hell, lucky he wasn't made already. Then again, most people regarded their own barking dogs with about as much concern as a pack-a-day smoker tuning out the surgeon general. Present company included. He would risk it.

Mike got to the back porch and ascended its steps, slipping through the outer screen door, and not a peep from the mutts.

Maybe Donny wasn't paying them enough. Pressed against the house, Mike wrapped a hand around the doorknob, gave a gentle twist. Success. Either Donny was getting lax these days, or forgetful, or just didn't worry anymore. Now watch eighteen alarms go blaring. He inched the door open just enough to squeeze through sideways, then shut it.

He was in a short narrow passage, mud closet or something. One lonely pair of rubber boots atop layers of yellowed newspapers. Shelves with cleaning supplies—Spic and Span, rags, furniture polish, the usual. At the far end, Mike gritted his teeth and opened the inner door a crack, let us peek, no idea what lived on the door side. Gabriel Matthews and his collection of axes and cutlery came to mind.

Easing the door open by fractions, an ever-widening slice of what was proving to be a large kitchen. One of the many reaches of this house he'd thought he would have time to explore last visit. In the center stood a huge butcher block work station. Its top ringed with pegs, pots and pans and skillets hanging like piñatas. One wall held a spice rack big enough to rival a supermarket's.

Beyond the kitchen, a small nook overlooked the backyard, table for one this morning, and he stared. A woman in a robe, making noisy and clumsy attempts at feeding herself a bowl of cereal. Grazing her cheek with one spoonful before finding her mouth, and as she ate, she stared longingly out the window. Nerve rush; outside, he had crept directly beneath her line of vision.

So Amanda Dawson had come through it alive, good for her. She didn't look much more formidable now than in midcoma. He kept his face pressed into the few inches of open door and stared. Captivated, in an odd sense, feeling less a voyeur than someone privileged to witness a unique metamorphosis, Amanda emerging unsteadily but surely from the chrysalis.

He was content to study as eating occupied her concentration. Her spoon's handle was nearly as thick as a broomstick, clamped in her fist like a child first learning table manners. One side of her bowl curled over into a lip at the top, easier for her to scoop against.

What drive she must have possessed within, she'd had to start all over again. Relearning the intricacies of daily life.

He knew what had to be done next, and it would prove a stroke of genius or sheer catastrophe. Options were few, however. At least he could wait until her breakfast was finished, save her the embarrassment of interruption in midslurp.

Five more minutes, and she let the spoon clatter against the bowl with a weary resignation.

Now, time for panic. Anybody else in the house? No Donny, no cars out front. Gabe? It was a calculated risk. Mike squelched down the dry ball of nerves bunched in his throat, took a breath, and walked on in. Hands out of pockets in plain sight, where she could see them; as if that took away all the worry of a perfect stranger wandering in after breakfast.

Amanda jumped as if given an electric jolt. Backpedaling with her left leg, scooting the chair around and away from the table and toward the far wall. Fumbling at the same time with both hands to bring up a stainless steel cane, four stubby legs at its base. She held it like a spear ready for the thrust, her eyes those of a cornered animal. Frightened, yes, but not like a deer's. A deer would not fight. Mike had a feeling she would, and do a right furious job of it, too. He stopped.

"Welcome back among the living," he said, and smiled.

It caught her good and hard. Clearly she understood at once that he wasn't some random perpetrator ignorant of her well-kept secret. She kept a solid grip on the cane, all the same.

"Who . . . ?" No threats, no cries for help. "What do you want?"

Mike told her his name, confessed that he worked for a Florida newspaper. Assured her that he meant no harm. None of which brought a response either way, fine, move to Plan B and dazzle her with just how much he was privy to.

"On Thursday, June twentieth, you took a tumble down your staircase and hit your head on the banister and went into a coma. Instead of risking public embarrassment, your husband arranged, through a Doctor Irv Preston, for a private nursing staff to treat you around the clock. He spun a pretty good cover story to get you out of the country to alibi your absence as long as it was needed." He sounded ridiculous to his own ear, like Jack Webb, here's the facts, ma'am. "How am I doing so far?"

Amanda's pale face bleached even paler, and she lowered the cane several degrees. "How do you *know* all this?"

He took a seat on the kitchen floor, the least threatening pose he could come up with. The Smith and Wesson shifted, and he repositioned it as if massaging a back spasm. She never knew.

"One of your nurses got a guilty conscience over the fraud she was helping to pull off. And I never believed you were in El Salvador to begin with, so she helped validate it. I was here just over a month and a half ago, I can prove that." He slapped a jacket pocket. "I took pictures."

Visible surprise, what a break from morning routine. "Could I . . . see them? Just to be sure? Slide them across the floor."

Mike produced the envelope, nineteen shots taken before the interruption that turned fatal. He set it down on the tiled floor, gave it a flick, and it skittered to a halt before her slippered feet. Finally easing down the cane, she bent to retrieve the pictures with her left hand.

Confrontation, shock therapy from her own wasted visage, and he was quite the crusader, wasn't he? Muckraker, yellow journalist, dragging her back through everything she was trying to surmount. When she dropped them aside after looking at the fourth one, it was three too many, and he felt only relief.

"I don't want to see those," her voice low and wavering with disgust. "*Why* did you take those pictures?"

How much honesty could she withstand this morning? The situation cried for tender loving care from all sides. "I'd thought I'd do an exposé on whatever was really going on here. But for what it's worth—I kind of lost heart once I got up there and actually . . . saw you."

Close to angry tears. "Oh sure. You're a real humanitarian."

"I deserve that."

Amanda wiped at her nose and eyes, sitting there careworn, contemplating life out of control—and somehow managing to do it with the utmost dignity. This Mike knew: She may have aided and abetted Donny in his scams, but he still did not deserve her. Or she, at least, deserved better.

"Does my husband know you're aware of all this?"

Mike shook his head. "Not a clue."

"I believe *that*." She gestured toward the chair across the table from her. "You might as well sit a little closer."

He accepted, getting his first good close look at her face. Smoothly translucent, her eyes faintly ringed with dark circles. Clearly taking this as it came, as best she could, how to play this bizarre new hand fate had just dealt. And just as much a hit-and-run victim of this ministry speeding beyond control as anyone.

"So what is it you *want*?" she repeated.

"Well, now that's the tricky part, anymore." There was no finesse in blurting out the truth as he saw it, which just might alienate her.

Downgrade Donny, she could very well rise up in his defense, reflex action. Schoolyard honor; you can bad-mouth your mom all you want, but let some other kid try it and he eats knuckles. So. Let her bury Donny on her own, if it was to be done at all. "Are you happy with the way Donny handled your injury?"

Amanda took her time with that one, resistance flaking away a bit at a time. Saying little, actually, not much beyond an admission that she had never been made to feel more in anyone's way in her life. But the vital nerve had been struck, all the quirks of voice and face and posture cueing him in that this woman was perched atop a powder keg of resentment, and her own husband had struck the fuse. He'd seen it before, and would have bet it dated back earlier than her fall.

"I just want to know what's going on here, behind the scenes," Mike said, finally approaching her question. "Something really shook the ministry up this summer, I think. I don't know what, but I don't think it's in a—a very positive direction."

Like what was important enough to kill for? Couldn't club her with too much at once, though. TLC, still.

"Donny, he's . . ." Her voice dwindled, searching. "I know he's been preoccupied, with . . . something. But we just don't communicate anymore. We may as well be on two different planets now."

"How much do you trust Gabriel Matthews?"

A tiny flash, eyes narrowing for an instant. "I have no reason not to . . . but . . ."

"But you don't."

"No. Not much."

Yet she was trusting him, an intruder, even more. Perhaps recognizing an ally against a common enemy, an enemy she may not have consciously admitted she had. Or perhaps she was hideously lonely, walled away from her world with no one left to confide in. When storms are rough, sometimes any port will do. This he knew from experience, no longer proud of it, having ingratiated himself to too many women in pain, for too short a time.

A real humanitarian.

"Something's wrong around here," Amanda said quietly. "And I think it might be revolving around this new employee Donny hired. But he's an innocent in all this, he's not . . ." She shook her head. "I've spoken with him a few times, he *can't* be involved the way they are. Don't ask me how I know, just believe me."

New guy; Mike remembered the fresh face on the show. Gut feelings said one and the same.

"I don't want to see anything happen to him," she went on. "Paul. His name's Paul. He's got a girlfriend here, one of the singers. I tried calling her about him a couple days ago, and she said she was worried too, she hadn't seen him, his room was always locked."

Mike watched wars of conflicting loyalty rage across her face, within her eyes. At war with self, what a doomed prospect, always the loser, never the victor. He was wondering how to steer her away from this rocky ground when she pulled the plug on it all.

"My life and my marriage are falling apart and *I don't know WHY*," imploding rage, it could wither a soul or warp an outlook for life if left unchecked. Then her voice softened as she looked up at him. "Leave. Please leave. Would you?"

Mike nodded, could gain no more, not now, not like this. He stood, gave her shoulder a pat and thought it a triumph that she did not fight it. The revelation about Gabe would have to come later, if ever. Something like that would push her toward overload.

He fished a scrap of paper from one pocket, already neatly printed with the name of their motel, phone and room numbers. He set it beside her hand.

"I'm sorry to put you through this, I really am. But . . . I don't want to see anyone else getting hurt." There, subtlety, let her wonder about that one. He started backing toward the mud closet door, pointing to his note. "You can reach me there if you need to. Do you think we can talk again?"

I don't know, she mouthed.

He didn't press the issue, merely thanked her, said good-bye. At least she took the note, folding instead of tearing it. Slipping it into her robe's pocket.

Use it, he thought. *Please.*

If not for his sake, for her own.

38

"I think this denotes our caste here better than anything else," Paul told Laurel. Pointing none too discreetly at cameras and microphones and the dozens of live people both before and behind them. And the directors fretting over the positions of all. "We're pins on a map." He chuckled. "Pinheads."

All had gathered in the chapel for a Saturday morning run-through, the live TV debut twenty-four hours away. Mandatory rehearsals of everything going out over the airwaves tomorrow, so the floor director and his stopwatch could chart precise timings, facilitate camera switches. Donny was here, plodding around like a zombie with a script in his hand, a sermon pared down to sixteen minutes, how would he ever stand it? He delivered it with all the warmth of a dead fish, none of his usual live service enthusiasm, however Vegas-style, anywhere in sight.

So here it was, behind the scenes, on a grand scale. The search for God reduced to a daily grind with the promise of a paycheck. He wondered if any of these TV techs would get time-and-a-half union scale for weekend work.

They weren't bothering to rehearse healings, because there was no one to heal. The only true improvisational part of tomorrow's telecast, they would get into it forty or forty-five minutes into the show and let it fill the rest of the hour. A handy margin for error with everything else.

As a result, Paul felt essentially useless here, without purpose.

Everyone else getting bossed around, while he was left alone. Hell, even Dougie Durbin had his purpose, cable puller for camera two; probably taxing his mental faculties to the limits.

Paul watched from center auditorium, in a movie house sprawl with legs draped over the seat before him. Laurel at his right, joining him after singing her song instead of slipping back up into the choir. One of the few, the privileged, One Who Knows Paul. Even though the choir was running through a postsermon number, to lead into the healings. Soundtrack for an influx of bacteria, malignancy, and disabilities.

"Let's—" he said, so abruptly he surprised even himself. "Let's leave here next week." Shaking his head, look at things, look at us, what we are, how we live. "This place. This place. If we stay here . . . it's going to eat us, you know that."

Laurel's hand found his along the armrest. He held it without fear, sometimes a touch is just a touch. "I'm a lot stronger now than when I came here. So . . . okay."

"Let's find you a band to sing in, and live in poverty. Nobody'll know us, or want anything from us, and we can bitch to some scummy landlord about all the roaches. Please?"

She let her head roll against his shoulder, laughed softly.

"I miss . . . the real world out there." Even surrounded by the trappings of their current lives, Paul felt cast adrift from it all, an island, just himself and the one linked to his hand.

This was the first genuine time he had spent with her in days, having avoided her at all costs, afraid of something—what she might want of him, what he would do to her. Finally come to a head earlier this morning, Laurel beating on his door before he awoke, demanding to see him, that he *talk* to her, she wouldn't go away until he unlocked the damn door. Then Paul, on his floor, begging her not to have him do those things to her anymore, it wasn't right, wasn't a thing a healthy mind could tolerate for long, and she had held him and said okay. Just like that, okay, and despite its ease, he had felt no relief. Let them fall between the sheets, play the beast with two backs, stoke the passion and *then* see how easy it would be to keep sex from slipping into the morbid, the insane.

"A couple nights ago?" he said. "It's the first time I can remember that I didn't do anything for Halloween."

Laurel squeezed his hand, as if sensing a need for nostalgia, connection with a past that was safer. "What'd you do last year?"

"Just went barhopping with some people I worked with." Smile, shutting his eyes, leaning his head back over the seat. "I won a costume contest at one place. I had on a black and white robe, and this furry Mongol-type cap, and rosary beads, and I carried this fake scimitar. Put on a Fu Manchu moustache. Guess who I was."

"I have no idea."

"Attila the Nun." Shoulders quivering in silent laughter, but sad, those days are gone forever. He felt the brim of tears, the wet tracks as the first spilled quietly free. He could talk forever, cry forever. "That's the real world to me."

"We'll go," she whispered. "We'll go find it somewhere."

He stared up at the blurred ceiling, wanting to believe her, for this to be anything but a hopeful lie told out of pity. Easy words, make them come true, then he shook his head. "No we won't. We'll just look. You'll be okay, you'll fit—

"*I won't.*"

And then Laurel had him by the shoulders, dragging him up and pulling his head around to face her, look at me, *look at me.* Fingers tight, digging into his arms, and he was glad of it, it was sensation, he was feeling something.

"That was you this week, wasn't it?" Laurel kept her face right in his, steady and solid. Desperate. "On the news, those two guys they found different nights, don't lie to me, it was you."

So quiet he barely heard himself: "Yes."

"And you never would have told me on your own?"

"No."

"And that's what this is all about? Leaving, and you not seeing me for days, not talking, the way your eyes look anymore?"

"It's everything, Laurel, it's *everything.*" His breath in hitches. "Sometimes I look around and it's, like, this place is such a sham it's everything hypocritical I ever hated, and now I'm part of it. And other times I *want* to be here, I think of what I could do with it if it was mine, like Gabe seems to want." Hyperventilation couldn't be far away. "I can't trust myself to know what's right anymore, and do you know what that's like inside?"

Paul watched her draw back a few inches, submerging into thought, perhaps her own part in the soft ricochet of his mind.

"Then we'll get you someplace where the only voice you have to listen to—telling you what to do—is your own."

As if that would help. "I don't trust it much more than the others."

Then she told him she loved him, first time for everything. He looked for salvation in the words and found none, even when he returned them, meaning it, but supposing some things were even too great for love to save you from. Love could not save you from yourself. Especially when you were hellbound.

The notion of hell was particularly frightening these days. He was so well-qualified to go.

"Aren't you afraid of me?" he said. "What I might do?"

"A little," spoken with somber honesty. "Yeah. I am. But I don't think I could ever really love somebody I wasn't a little afraid of."

She was smart, he decided. Everybody was that way. She was just astute enough to admit it.

Maybe it would keep her alive.

Paul began the afternoon in isolation, alone in his room. TV on, mindlessly so, background noise for company. Staring at the ceiling from his bed, these solid walls like the reverse polarity of a bomb shelter. Containing from within, rather than shielding from without.

He could explode in here, coat the ceiling with his fluids, litter the floor with his fibers. They could clean him up after he had dried, and the room would be ready for the next sojourner coming to Dawson in hopes of answers.

Why not leave now? he wondered. *Today. This afternoon. Why not?* The answer was simple, quite possibly selfish. Leave now, and it was forever on the coattails of failure; more than failure, murder. One tap and it's all over but the burial. Go through with tomorrow, though, one more round of healing in the blessed name of Donny Dawson, and whether or not Gabe's freak idea of brain-wave transmission worked, there was still a chance of walking away feeling redemption was possible. Proving himself the master of his body, his spirit, and all the intricacies in which they had decided to operate, to his persistent ignorance.

All the sick, the hurting, *I need you more than you need me.*

He was nearly asleep when a light rapping sounded at his door. Not Laurel, he knew that immediately, her knock was louder, livelier. Paul answered and found Gabe in the hall. Stiff and suited, Gabriel Matthews and his transcendent eyes. Bringing with them Paul's temptation to let that look elevate him once more, give us this day our daily fix of homage.

"I need to tell you something." Gabe strolled heel-to-toe over to the TV and clicked it off without asking. They stared across the room at each other, Paul knowing he should not listen to what this man of misguided devotion had to say. Knowing, too, that the pull was too great.

"Do you have any idea what you are?" Gabe asked.

Paul said no, feeling stomach, bowels, everything, clench and freeze solid. Gabe had said this as if he truly knew the answer.

"I came here five years ago in hopes of finding something," he said, "and it wasn't here—until we crossed paths with *you*."

And Gabe went on, at length, for quite some time, with the most astounding tale of myth and legend, history, and the holy hush of ancient sacrifice.

Amanda had come to define her days, and categorize them, entirely according to the schedules of others. She at their whim and mercy, they at her beck and call, her phalanx of therapists. They alone breaking up the cycle of monotony endured in her home, until even they too had become a part of it.

How strange to think, this Saturday afternoon, that a welcome ripple in routine had come in the form of a stranger breaking in after breakfast. Yesterday morning's bizarre visit, Mike Lancer knowing more about her life than she did.

Given the lies told by her, about her, it seemed trust should be the last thing she would freely dispense. Yet she believed him, trusted him to have more on his mind than sensationalism, and could come up with no good reason why. True, she'd had little choice; she couldn't have run or fought well, and cries for help to an empty house would have done no good. But clearly he had wanted to establish that he meant no harm to her.

Donny was another matter.

Mike's visit was her secret, still. In years past, anyone who had come gunning for Donny she would have received as a maniac wielding a straight razor. But she could play his coconspirator and martyr no longer.

Trust . . . *why?* Maybe there had been something familiar about Mike Lancer. Well within bounds of possibility. Before his demise, Irv had told her she might expect to recall things that had gone on around her, that a coma did not negate all awareness. Perhaps she remembered his voice, subconsciously, from her impromptu photo session. Had sensed his compassion that first day, without threat.

But going so far as to help him? She couldn't even leave the house without help, and had she been able, her first priority would have been Paul Handler.

After Gabe had first brought him by, and she had extended the invitation to visit again, he had taken her up on it. Once, twice a week over the next three weeks. At first on the pretext of seeing how she was faring, a few minutes spent with the detached warmth of a doctor's bedside manner, as if he had such miraculous patients all over the compound and was making rounds. The visits growing gradually longer, long enough for her to learn where he was from, how his father had died; why he had come here, those flukes of death brought by a touch in anger.

Amanda had neither feared nor judged, just felt the ache in his heart as if it had throbbed in her own. He was as alone in his world as she was in hers, and why such empathy when she could no longer work up much pity for her husband and the walls he had fabricated around himself? Maybe because Paul had climbed inside her body and mind, taken her by the hand, and led her back out of herself like a shepherd.

But this week he hadn't been by. If the shepherd had lost his own way, she wasn't even sure she would know whom to blame.

Amanda maneuvered with her cane to rise from the chair, easing herself with care to stand by the window. Arm and leg surrendering day by day to her will, a triumph of vast personal magnitude, a toddler's first steps to a parent's arms.

Her window. Autumn lived out there, breathed its breath of winsome sorrow, and she sensed the ache in its hollow bones. A day without sunshine, with winds of bluff and bluster, tears of rain. Trees shedding leaves as if weary of their burdens, letting the ground have its way with them, where they rolled, rested, clustered. Small mounds of the dead. Waiting for the worms.

Paul could heal. Paul could harm. Paul was obviously being exploited for the glory of another, too close to home. And now this unaccountable switch to live telecasts, and the bizarre scheme to send Paul's brain waves out with the satellite feed, it was madness around here, pronounced and infectious.

God, I need some help *down here,* an urgent upward plea. *I don't understand this, not* any *of it.*

Waiting, waiting, and no flash of revealing light came from above or within. She abandoned the window when her leg grew testy from the weight, wandering about the room to keep it flexing, mind me you piece of meat. She didn't stop until her eyes lit on a photo

Donny had brought up a week after her awakening, had rested on the dresser. A much younger and more innocent couple smiled at her from within the frame, on their most humble of wedding days.

Donny's motive in bringing this up was painfully obvious, one more heartstring tugged in order to salvage what might be better off lying wrecked and forgotten. She touched fingertips to it, the glass over the picture like the sixteen years between then and now. Can't get there from here. So many wrong turns taken since that tiny pauper's wedding.

A stringent urge to see him came storming in out of nowhere, if only they could have fifteen minutes of talk, honest and open and free. Renewal. And then she had to laugh, gallows humor, if only he too could spend a few months comatose and wake up to see his wrongs.

But at the moment, he was likely spinning more webs of deceit. Some emergency meeting of the Board of Directors—of which she was a member, his staff was nothing if not handpicked—trying to soothe some outraged tempers over the amount of money spent in converting to a live show.

With the real thing unavailable, video seemed the next best alternative. For convalescence purposes—just like a real hospital room, oh, thanks—he had brought up a small TV, plus a VCR and an assortment of tapes. She turned on the hardware and picked a tape of *Arm of the Apostle* shows from last year, take me away to a simpler time of self-delusion.

Amanda settled into her chair, watched herself filmed with innocence still intact. Fraud, who, me? But with opened eyes, even these old shows had to be viewed in a new light, and a harsh, ugly one at that. Twenty minutes in, she was willing to concede this had been a mistake, like rubbing a dog's nose in the residue of its crime against the rug. Except she and Donny didn't even smell *that* good.

She was working herself up to leave the chair and shut off the tape when Donny's words seized every nerve.

"'Who, then, is a wise and faithful servant?'" said the video-Donny, reciting from the Book of Matthew, the phrase suddenly pulling triggers of memory, everything Irv Preston had told her validated in one terrible brainstorm.

"'Who, then, is a wise and faithful servant?'" *Gabe's disembodied voice in high frantic run-on. Amanda in paralysis and fearing such a loss of control in one from whom she has seen nothing but cool professionalism.*

"He is the one whom the master has placed in charge of the other servants," Donny continued from the screen. Amanda gripping the arms of her chair while memory grew as potent as a whiff of ammonia.

"*'How happy is that servant if his master finds him doing this when he comes home,'*" Gabe's toneless babble, and she cries soundlessly, tearlessly, leaden in a world into which sound sometimes ventures but she is powerless to react, unable to tell these two, Mike and Edie, to run, fight, something.

". . . that servant's master shall one day return when the servant does not expect him," Donny intoned. Amanda hugging herself against the chill of spoiled suspense, she knew exactly what was to come, the memory and sound-pictures rending their way up through floorboards from subconscious to conscious.

"*'And the master will cut him into pieces.'* I'M SORRY I'M SORRY!" Gabe screaming by now. Unseeing, Amanda lies still, tracking his sudden movement by sound alone, flinching inwardly at the horrid wet crunch and subsequent thud, a sound of broken bones and sudden death. She swims in overwhelming gray, the frustration of a body refusing to obey eating her alive, and then her spirits buoy with faint hope for a survivor when she hears the brittle shattering of her prison's window, liberation. A tirade of high quavering cries from this trusted employee turned killer, and he rushes from the room, and she wants no more to do with this place. She would walk away if her legs would hold her, but the only defense is retreat, and a deeper gray beckons, swirling to black like a whirlpool, and she lets it suck her down, beyond even the most fevered reach of husband, traitor, thought.

Over, finally. Remembered, relived, while she hugged herself, meager comfort from childhood, when nightmares woke her and she was too frightened to call out from midnight to her parents, for fear that that nameless thing in the dark would know where she was.

And was *this* God's answer to a prayer for understanding? Let her select the proper cue so she knew only that a killer had touched her life and home, family and friends? She hoped it had been no strain up there.

No longer able to walk, not with the weak shakes wracking her body, Amanda crawled across the floor like a paraplegic to shut off the TV and VCR. Lay beneath them until the worst of the tremors passed. And when she was able, she crawled to the closet and yanked her robe free of its hanger, let it bunch without shape atop shoes. She plunged her hand into a pocket and came out with a scrap of paper.

He had held back yesterday, that reporter, probably to spare her more turmoil. For which she both thanked him and cursed him.

At least he printed legibly.

Even for a workaholic like Gabe, rare was the occasion that brought him into the office late on a Saturday afternoon. Today was different. Today was final. And here he was, grand master of the judgment before which he would stand tomorrow. Hours before, leaving Paul alone with a brand-new heritage to contemplate.

It made one humble.

It made one take desperate measures to insure the overall scheme of things suffered as few setbacks as possible. Paul was now teetering on that brink of breakdown, needing only the final nudge. Gabe would supply it, with finesse, with awe, with love.

Such subtleties of devotion to the inevitable were lost on his two guests. *Thick* was the one word that came to mind whenever he dealt with Dougie and Terry Durbin. Thick of nose, thick of fingers, thick of head. They sat before his desk at hunkered attention, inbred bookends. They would have been the sort of children charitably described as husky, turned by puberty into hulking monsters with heads a bit too small for their bodies. Identical blond hair that looked as if they had used the same cracked bowl for the cut. Dougie and Terry were not twins, but the assumption was natural. Born in West Virginia just nine and a half months apart, some nineteen years past. Their family was vast and rife with odd conjugations, and Gabe never wanted to meet them.

"You understand," Gabe told them, "that evil is a very real force in this world, and sometimes it takes human form."

They nodded, solemn, all business.

"We been looking for it all our lives," Dougie said. The brains of the duo, dear lord, save us. "We don't put up with it when we find it."

"Uh huh, that's right," said Terry. Eager to contribute. "That's how come they come to send us here."

Which had transpired seven months back. Gabe had accumulated files on these two even before their arrival by Greyhound. High school transcripts—before they had come of age and surrendered—and counselors' evaluations. Even as children they had bred mischief like swamps breed parasites. The usual thievery and vandalism, and dead pets could more often than not be traced back to their door. They thumped heads for lunch money and spent it first on comics, later on beer. Everyone knew they were headed for prison someday, or perhaps some economy-minded deputy would do taxpayers a service and just shoot them during the commission of a crime to be named later.

Then the unexpected happened when Dougie was fourteen and Terry thirteen: They got religion. An older sister had died giving birth to their nephew (and if their own theory of relativity ended there, Gabe would have been surprised), and the fire-and-brimstone sermon delivered at her funeral convinced them they would never see her again unless they mended their wayward souls. They decided that very same day to redirect all their natural exuberance to new ends, and become sin-stompers. Wherever sin was to be found, they would wade in with their size twelves and put whatever stop to it they deemed necessary. Leaving bruises aplenty in their wake.

How they had settled on the idea that Donny Dawson had been placed on earth to herald the second coming was a mystery of arcane dimensions, and beyond their articulation. But believe it they did, and for Dougie and Terry Durbin, that settled it.

"I won't kid with you," Gabe said. "There's a threat to this ministry from within, and with your help, I'd like to take care of it. You know what I mean when I say take care of it—don't you?"

Terry nudged Dougie with his elbow and they grinned happily at each other. Only brothers could smile that knowingly, born miscreants.

"But I need warriors on my side. Not cowards. I need a pair of strong backs and stout hearts on my side. Not weaklings."

"They don't come much stronger than us," said Dougie.

"That's right," said Terry.

"Men like Mr. Dawson," Gabe said, switching gears, "are like the generals in our army of believers. And everybody knows that generals are too valuable to do the real fighting. Right?"

They nodded, oh, right, right, everybody knows that. Gabe smiled. Feebs liked military analogies, easy to grasp.

"Men like me—and you—and you—we're the true soldiers. We're the ones who have to fight sin and evil in all its forms, and sometimes we're the ones who are called to sacrifice for it."

"Do we get paid extra for this?" asked Terry.

"Oh yes, I'll see to that, don't you worry," Gabe assured, and they both looked as proud as champion boxers. Keep it moving, keep their attention. "Now just as we fight enemies of good and right in their different forms, our weapons are different too. Sometimes our weapons are faith and prayer. And sometimes . . . we have to use something a little louder."

Gabe unlocked a lower desk drawer and brought out the firepower he had picked up earlier this week. Another pistol for himself, and identical weapons for the Durbins, a TEC-9 for each of them. Wicked little things, barely over a foot in length, each with a magazine of thirty-two rounds. Semiautomatic fire only, which was why they were legal. Cheap, too, he'd talked the dealer into letting them go for two hundred fifty dollars apiece.

"Holy Moses," said Dougie.

"And hallelujah," said Terry. "These is for *us?*"

Gabe stood up behind his desk and contemplated the morning to come, the light of transcendence beaming from his face. They were helpless before it. He could feel it spreading like an infection.

"Tomorrow morning I'm giving you the chance to let the whole world see how strong and brave you really are. And I'm about to tell you the most important secrets that Donny Dawson Ministries has ever learned."

"I got the same initials as him, D.D.," and Gabe indulged the interruption with minor worry, what if they were too unstable to depend on? "Dougie Durbin, that's me."

"Mr. Dawson knows that, and it makes him very happy," Gabe smoothed along, the sooner these lumpen boobs were away from him, the better. "Just like he knows what it says in the Good Book: that even the devil can transform himself into an angel of light."

This settled them down, and they quieted with an intensity of focus that was truly frightening. Those wide-spaced eyes, wary and intent on whatever was asked of them. Sin-stompers about to receive a promotion.

"Like I told you, there's a threat to this ministry, and to Donny, and to all that's good and right. Even though it looks just like a normal person. So tomorrow morning I want us to stand in its way, and *show* the world what it really looks like with its mask off."

He had them now, they were as malleable as wet clay. And he, the master sculptor, the man next in line below their prophet, their idol. Dougie and Terry wanted to know who it was, and he teased them with it for a while, until they could stand it no longer. And when he gave them the name, they were surprised, but yeah, yeah, they'd *known* all along something funny was going on there. They were ready to charge out and do murder then and there.

But Gabe quieted them. Convinced them to wait until the whole world was watching.

That's right.

For a while there, he had almost done it. Paul had almost had himself believing this week could be turned around, the darkness could be left behind. Naive fool, an innocent of the worst kind, believing in such fancies as self-control. The long dark night of the soul so thick now, he couldn't have found his way to climb out with a ladder and a map, and light of dawn had gone the way of collapsing suns.

It'll always be this way.

Since Gabe had left his room, the temperature had dropped outside, wind had picked up, clouds had spat fitful bursts of rain to mourn a dusk that lasted for hours. All unnoticed by him, Paul not budging from one small spot on his floor. Barefoot, in jeans and a sweatshirt, hair an unruly tangle as he hugged knees to chest with chin notched atop them. His only movement a slow and gentle rocking, side to side, a schizophrenic's silent lullaby while blank slate eyes stared into the floor.

His legacy . . .

Scapegoat, latest in a lineage begun four and a half millennia ago. Toxic waste dump for the world's ills, fulcrum of a spiritual balance and medium for sacrifice. With him since the day of his birth, same day as a president's death, a random choice the exact particulars of which he would never know. Therein lay the madness, just the toss of a roulette ball made by his predecessor, a man of whom nothing had been left but gristle and rage and sorrow. Damn him to the same hell he had passed along, and Paul had to suspect that it had been this man who had given his father the cancer. In the shake of a hand, perhaps, a brush of shoulders; somehow. Of course he had done it, just to insure that their mutual progeny grew up understanding the implacable demands of disease. As only a son without a father can.

He wanted to deny it all. Dismiss it as nonsensical ravings from Gabe Matthews, dismiss him as a lunatic believing himself to be some twisted form of undercover agent. But Paul couldn't, he knew better. Recalling the dreams, especially those in the hospital, vivid as shared memories . . . staggering across a blinding desert propelled by the hatred of a mob. His ancient kinsman.

Paul, forced to wonder, *Am I even worse?* The venoms distilled over the years. Victim of a fluke at birth, maybe something afoot in the world that day, and whether the Dallas assassination was the trigger or a by-product, no one could say.

But look at the state of the world since then, that unholy decade of change, ushering in a bleak new age of turmoil and dissolution. The dream was dead, Camelot had crumbled. An assassination captured live for mass consumption, instant replay, slow motion dissection of flying bits of skull. With too many secrets and loose ends to put it comfortably behind as the act of a lone madman, then forge ahead in optimism.

The ultimate sacrifice, made on the altar of media, and the magic had been dismal.

As was his own.

He would never gain true control of it, for there was none to be had. *It* had *him.* The thing they had named Nergal, with its breath of desert winds, it would always demand more. Another life, another offering. And what would the ratio be, how many deaths for how many healings? Or *was* there any pattern to it, would he find it as fickle as a spoiled child?

Life became too clear. Never truly trusting himself from this day on. Living a life with a risk like alcoholic blackout, *Did I kill last night?* The drunk who faces morning and his car without memory, fresh specks of blood and hair on his bumper the only clues to the previous night.

Donny Dawson Ministries. Why leave here after all? Here was as good a place as any to keep the balance. Might as well see where tomorrow leads, how long it would take to grind the ministry into the dust. Donny wanted him? Donny *had* him.

Of course, he could pass this torch along, just as it had been forced upon him in utero. Expel it in hopes of living a normal life, but no, he had taken it too far already. He would always bear the guilt of what he had done thus far; why add the singular damnation of inflicting this hell upon an innocent? He could not spend a normal life living with that knowledge.

Unless . . . he did not live at all.

The coward's option, but maybe somewhere, wherever, he would find understanding.

For the first time in hours, Paul unwound. Joints, stiffened from hours of rigidity, protesting as he moved to his closet. Dug through a box of junk unneeded here at the ministry, but which he had been unable to part with. Mementos, mostly, from the radio days.

He found what he wanted near the bottom, a small boxed kit. A plastic base molded with two shallow trenches into which audiotape would fit, diagonal cutting guides bisecting the trenches. He did not care about this editing block so much as its primary tool. Four of which were rattling inside an old matchbox. He chose the one that looked the most pristine.

A heavy, single-edged razor blade.

Paul locked his door. Took one final look out at the hateful world, wrapped in rags of dusk, then looked down at his wrists. Veins, tendons. Lifeblood. The serious student of suicide cuts lengthwise along the inner arm rather than across. So many more blood vessels to tap that way. He had read that somewhere.

Paul stuck the blade at his left wrist. Eased out his breath. And with an audible hiss, deeply sliced all the way back to his elbow.

39

 For several moments after Mike keyed off the engine, they sat listening to the mesmerizing patter of rain on the car's roof. Its lull suggestive of sleep, a night in bed with someone warm he could care about and forget about tomorrow, let the rain wash their hearts clean and new.

Instead he was here, the place misery calls home. Beyond the windshield, beyond the parking lot, the ministry compound was a scattered array of buildings, barely seen. Lights floating in the dark.

Ramon made sure the safety was engaged on his pistol after carefully chambering the first round, then stashed it beneath his jacket. "If that Gabriel Matthews guy pops up around a corner, I'm not sure I'd even recognize him."

"Don't worry. I'll panic enough for both of us."

"What happens if he shows up?"

"I guess it depends on how frisky he's feeling."

"I'm not hot on the idea of having to shoot anybody, Mikey."

Mike said he wasn't either, but was that entirely honest? Hadn't there been a few vengeance-based fantasies since first coming face to face with him? Acting on Edie's behalf, an eye for an eye. The most Mike could assure himself was that he hoped it would not have to happen tonight.

They worked up nerve to leave the car after their breath began to condense on the glass. Mere shapes in the dark, cloaked by rain, their identities well-guarded, yet it still felt skittishly like stepping onto a stage. This was the closest he had openly come to the compound. Hunching inside their jackets, they headed for the dorm.

The call from Amanda Dawson had been a godsend, as he had been tapped out of ideas beyond waiting until Sunday morning and blending in with the congregation during the telecast, seeing what developed. At least she trusted him now, and more important, knew how dangerous Gabe was.

On the other hand, she had had some peculiar things to relate about Donny's newest employee. A genuine healer, no wonder Donny was pulling the gang-healing routine these days. Misdirection, a classic ploy of any magician worth his top hat.

Raindrops needled their faces, eyes. As they skirted around the chapel, to their right sat a huge satellite dish, pale in the gloom. Tilted toward the heavens, looking like a vast platter. Awaiting the feast of all saints.

In the dorm lobby, they shook off excess water and tried to look like they belonged, every right to be there. Above suspicion. A few people loitered ahead in the lounge area. Some tall skinny kid with a prominent Adam's apple peered curiously at them, then resumed a battle of wits with a stubborn candy machine. A trio of young women watched a console TV. Mike and Ramon ascended to the second floor of the men's wing. Footsteps soft on a dense carpet, they paced down the hallway of numbered doors, from behind which music and voices floated. Mike stopped before one.

"Amanda thinks this is the one," he whispered.

"She doesn't know for sure?"

"Hey, she doesn't get out much."

A steady breath, then Mike knocked. Waited. Knocked again. A faint rustling stirred beyond the door, a slow shifting—

"What? *What?* What is it?" A fierce grumble.

He could say nothing of sense to a closed door, so he knocked again, with urgency. Finally, a lock clicked and the door was yanked open. The room was dark, but the hall light showed more of its resident than Mike was ready to see.

Clothing, hair, state of mind, they all looked as if this guy had lived through a plane crash. Barefoot, he wavered in the doorway while glaring at them with dark-ringed eyes. A crust of dried blood streaking his inner arm, from wrist to elbow.

"What?" A wild-eyed demand. "I'm busy."

"Are you Paul?" Mike said.

He looked into the floor, as if identity could be found there. Then up again, "Uh huh."

"Can we come in a minute? We're friends of Mrs. Dawson." He gave Paul their names.

Paul's contemplation was long and taxing, and he finally lurched away from the door, back into the room. Mike followed, swatting at the wall in search of a light switch. He and Ramon stopped at the sight of a few more spatters of blood dried on the floor. When it had still been wet, Paul had stepped in it, left random footprints across the floor. At the moment, he slouched on his bed, a razor blade loosely held in his fingers. This did *not* paint a comforting picture.

"You doing okay in here?" Ramon asked. "You don't look so good."

"I'm okay." Paul said it too hurriedly, all one word, *Imokay*. "Fine, just fucking fine."

Mike took a couple uneasy steps toward him. Like approaching a big dog that neither growled nor wagged its tail; make a fast friend or lose body parts.

"Amanda's kind of worried about you. She tried to call earlier and couldn't get through."

"I pulled the cord. Out of the wall." He gestured over a shoulder, and sure enough, there sat his phone on a desk, with a severed umbilical of frayed wires.

"She wanted us to give you a message from her, since she couldn't make it over here herself. She was wondering if, maybe, you might want to consider backing out of your part in the show tomorrow. She's worried that something might go wrong for you, or happen to you."

Paul sat on the edge of his bed, held his face in taut hands. Rubbing one over his eyes, through his hair. Dried blood even flaked from his hair, maroon dandruff. He laughed with a sound like tearing cloth.

"I dated this girl in college, see," he said. "And for a whole month I thought I wanted to break up with her. But just before I was ready to do it, the bitch beat me to it. Oh man. I wanted her back like I never wanted anything. Just because I couldn't have her."

Mike waited for further explanations, where's the relevance, but none seemed forthcoming. "I think I'm missing something here."

Paul groaned, looked wearily up at him, as one who did not suffer a fool gladly. "I was to the point where, show up tomorrow or miss it, I didn't care either way. But now that somebody tells me I shouldn't do it, I can't have it, well I'm so so sorry, but I *really* want to *do* this show!" Shaking his head, popping his fists together at the knuckles. "What does everybody think I am around here? Some kind of checker, some kind of pawn, stick me here or there or wherever the hell you feel like? I'm a human being, I have feelings, *feelings,* so just fuck all of you. Fuck! You! All!"

Mike held his hands palms-out, telling him easy, take it easy, a sinking feeling within, here he stood witnessing a personal disintegration live as it happened. He looked at Ramon, who hunched his shoulders, at equal loss. He saw that Paul had let the razor blade fall to the floor, now defanged, and felt safer scooting in, kneeling closer.

"Amanda told us a few things about you. And if they're true, don't you think maybe you should give tomorrow a little more thought?"

Paul's head turning slowly, so slowly, eyes on cold burn, and he knew he had said something terribly wrong.

"If they're true?" Paul whispered. "*If* they're true? What, she told you about me and you don't believe it?"

Mike, feeling as if he were suddenly pleading for his life and doing a right rotten job of it, "No, I didn't mean it like that, I—"

"*Well* then, I guess a little demonstration is in order for *you,*" and when Paul grinned it was the most chilling thing Mike had ever seen. This to a man who, a few years ago, had sat in a courtroom and seen a public freakshow starring the aberration dubbed the Miami Hacker. A true human monster.

This was worse.

Paul swiped up the razor blade and even as Mike was falling backward he knew he had not been fast enough, that he was still in reach when the blade came shearing forward. Vicious swipe, and it caught him on the jawbone to cleave open a flap of skin and grate upon bone, a slice of cold pain even as the hot spill warmed the side of his throat.

"No! No! Don't you run! Don't you dare run away from me!" Paul cried as he dove after him, and then Mike saw the blade was airborne, glittering red and silver across the room, and still Paul was coming, and Ramon was all huge eyes, backing out of the way and reaching inside his jacket to draw the pistol, clicking the safety off and steadying it with two very shaky hands—

"Ramon! Don't!" Mike thrashing his head no, no, spraying drops of his blood, and then Paul had clambered atop him with one hand slapping over the three-inch incision, clamping tight, and Mike could feel a faint tingling inside his jaw, an itch—

And it was finished.

Paul rolling off him, Ramon staring at him. The gun lowering. Mike reached up to feel for himself. Beneath the slick film of blood, his skin was unbroken. Not even so much as a ridge of scar.

Paul got up from the floor. "See? I'm in control." Chuckling without mirth while walking a few steps over to Ramon, who didn't know whether to stay or run. Paul looking down at the gun, "That's very rude, that's bad manners," then snatching it from Ramon's hand.

"Put the gun down, Paul," Mike said, the voice of reason, *We're going to die,* "just put it down and we'll talk, we'll leave, we'll do anything you want, just—"

"I don't think anyone here *truly* appreciates the enormity of what's been going on inside me the past few months." Paul shuffled toward the other side of the room, speaking slowly, choosing words with great care. A demented lecturer holding his class hostage. "I don't think anyone here realizes I tried to kill myself tonight. And couldn't. I mean, could *not* get it to work. Something, somewhere, doesn't want me to die."

He had been speaking to walls, ceiling, floor, turning to them only when he was through. Facing them dead-on as he lifted the Smith and Wesson and snugged it straight into the side of his skull.

"Check it out," he said, and fired.

The gunshot numbed eardrums, the slug burrowed a devastating path through Paul's head and blew out the opposite side. Blood and brains showered while the impact knocked him off his feet and onto the bed, where he bounced as limply as a sack of grain. The gun twirled from nerveless fingers and bounced on the floor.

Mike groaned sickly, at once very chilled, and Ramon crossed himself with a shaking hand, lapsing into a rapid whisper of Spanish. Mike scooted backward to sit against the wall, as far away as possible. Holding head between knees, breathing deeply while fighting to keep his rising gorge down, give it a minute and he would be out of this place so fast—

And Paul sat up.

"Isn't that *intense*?" he said, with a twitch and a fitful burst of laughter. Head coated with gore, its inner and outer workings undergoing some impossible sort of spontaneous regeneration. He never took his eyes from either of them while retrieving the gun and hobbling closer. "I need to take that routine onto *David Letterman,* next time they do Stupid Human Tricks. Bet you nobody could top that one."

Mike wasn't believing he was witnessing any of this, no way, the guy's craziness had infected them all with hallucinations of horrifying intensity, but then he wiped at his jaw again and came away with truth, wet and red and sticky, and then somebody was pounding at the door, oh blessed interruption, a jolt to reality.

"Paul? You okay in there?" came a voice from the hallway. "I heard something, sounded like—"

"I had my TV on too loud!" Paul screamed. "Is that a crime? Leave me the fuck alone!" Gritting his teeth and shaking his head at the patter of footsteps in retreat, it's just been that kind of day, and he continued across the room. He slapped the gun back into Ramon's hand and helped yank Mike up to his feet. My work here is done, and he sat on the edge of his bed as if having done nothing more spectacular than open a window.

"So—you got the idea now?" Paul absently stroking his inner arm, flaking off more blood. The last of earlier loathing. "I—I cut it —and it sealed up again a few seconds later. Just the weirdest thing. And now this." He tapped his head, newly solid, intact. "So —I guess you can tell Amanda that she doesn't have to worry. Nobody can do anything to me. The damage—it's already been done."

He crawled around on the bed, nose wrinkling in disgust as he scooped up a glob of gray matter and slung it onto the floor. "What a mess. What a mess. I gotta get my head on straight," laughing weakly at his little joke. "I'm in control." Sinking into the covers as his eyes lost their dementia, until he looked merely paralytically terrified. Caught in something's jaws and resigned to being swallowed. "Thanks for coming by, I really do feel better now. . . ."

To think they could be of any use in this room was a fool's quest. And when Mike and Ramon quietly bowed out, Paul was muttering away as if he were not even aware of them leaving.

By the time Amanda called later that night, Mike and Ramon had wordlessly gone through most of a bottle of sour mash. The TV played quietly, any distraction from thought. Ramon sat on his bed, huddled within a blanket pulled tight in front. Very possibly they were both in mild shock.

"He's very . . ." Mike paused, grasping for the proper word. *Psychotic* was close to the mark, and probably too blunt for Amanda at the moment. ". . . distraught. There wasn't much good in trying to talk him out of appearing tomorrow. It's almost like he's wanting to prove something to himself. And—I don't know why—but I got the feeling that somebody might have been there earlier, left him upset."

"There aren't that many people around here he's very close to, that could have much of an impact on him." Her voice weighty with apprehension. "Laurel? Or Gabe, he trusts Gabe. I should call Laurel, I didn't want to bring her into this, she's too close, but . . ."

"So we're back to square one." Mike shook the last cigarette from his only pack, chained it off the butt of its predecessor. Wasn't like him to blaze through a pack in two hours. Wasn't like him to watch faulty suicides, either. "What next?"

"They go on the air at eight o'clock tomorrow morning," she said. "That leaves less than ten hours to think of something. Will you . . . be here?"

"Oh yeah," he said. "Wouldn't miss it for the world."

He should have known the night would bring more pounding at his door, pilgrims of abuse, he would receive all. If they could take this savage communion, certainly he could do no less than offer it.

Paul answered, peered through a tiny slit of doorway, and she was there, my love, my leech.

Turning from the door, going for his bed, "Come on in," and when he heard Laurel entering, saw that fan of light sweep from the hallway across the floor, he said, "Leave the lights off. I don't want the lights on tonight."

Sitting on the bed to receive her, Paul watched her walk slowly forward, trepidation. Same sort of walk as Amanda's friends earlier, what was with everybody tonight, treating him like he was wired to blow. Laurel, a silhouette of gray, faint light from the window skimming off planes of worry . . . her face.

"I—I got to wondering . . . how you were . . . feeling, and . . ."

And she was a terrible liar, this night, at least. No chance visit, this, someone had tipped her off, *Go see him, time for his ten-thirty status check.* Never mind who, it didn't matter anymore, he was fodder for this entire dynasty of deceit.

"What happened in here?" she whispered. Sniffing. "It smells like . . . Oh, Paul . . ."

She would know that smell, wouldn't she? The rank stink of a gun fired in a closed room would be forever fixed in memory, no mistaking that one. Having watched a boyfriend commit .38-caliber neurosurgery, she would be initiated for life. Laurel would know the residual odor in those lingering grains of gunpowder, and perhaps, if she were very observant, the underlying whiffs of blood, and worse.

"Don't ask me questions you don't *really* want answered," he said, and held out one hand.

Paul watched her tense and look at his extended hand as if he had asked her to grasp a live wire. Smiling at her through the dark, very calm at the moment, turbulent seas of self placid in the eye of the hurricane. He could lean over, switch on a nearby lamp, grin at her with the runic traces of blood down his temples, his cheeks, his jaw. *Look familiar, remember this? But you've come up in the world, because it's something I can handle.*

"Don't you trust me?"

She faltered, one step forward, stop. "I . . . *want* to," but she did not sound terribly convinced she could, and he supposed she couldn't be blamed for that.

"It's okay," he murmured, "I really want us to do this tonight, just like always. I need to know there's somebody who loves me for *me.*" His breath quickened with the desire to feel her beneath him, surrendering within and without to his touch, and she came the rest of the way. Their hands met halfway, fingertips, then palms, and he closed his eyes, shuddered, felt the outflow as she gasped, pop goes the melanoma.

He rose and kissed her, Laurel's lips wet and tender and hesitant against his own. Her limbs stiff, even as he stripped away her clothes, and she began to weep. Paul licked a tear from each cheek. No sweet tears of rapture, not this time, he could taste the difference, the bitter fear. So familiar with her body and its essences, he could analyze her by scent and taste alone.

Paul shed his own clothes and fed her to the conjugal bed. Watching as she squirmed uneasily after reclining, "Paul, there's something *under* me, what's this in the bed?" And how would it feel to her, how wet, how sticky, how cold? Remains of his earlier cranial indiscretion. Had she felt such tissues before?

"No questions," he reminded, kneeling between her parted legs, running his hands along smooth thighs, what a shame he'd had no access to leprosy. "No questions."

He could reach beneath her, draw one morsel out, slip it between her lips, *Take, eat, this was my body.* A ritual to bind them further, and would she taste the madness of earlier thoughts?

"You're scaring me," her voice pious with the hush of sanctitude.

"Then it must be love."

He worked his magic of hands and virulence, and Laurel writhed.

How far could he take this, the question had always been in the back of his mind. Dislodged to forefront by whatever means. *If I kill her . . . could I bring her back again?*

Such fevered temptation.

40

Sudden death, Sunday morning suffocation, abrupt airless dreams of being a fish out of water, and Donny awakened only when his lungs began hitching with spasms. Awareness, the waking world, he could not breathe . . . a hand in his face, fingers pinching shut both nose and mouth. He thrashed his head with a frightened moan, and the fingers were withdrawn. He blinked in the darkness, dawn a mere hope of things to come. A moment later the bedside lamp was switched on, and he stared up into the face of Gabe Matthews.

"Rise and shine," said Gabe. "Big morning ahead."

His brain had gone to sludge, his body filled with more of the same. Morning mouth, dead tongue in a jar of teeth and paste, with the taste of sour bile. "Sleep," he croaked. "Need more sleep."

Gabe shook his head. "No time for that. We've got to get you up and get the Valium worked out. We can't have you making a fool of yourself on live TV. Can we?"

A spark of purpose flared, one candle in a darkened stadium. The show, there would always be the show, his audience. The only true loyalty shown him anymore, and he dared not disappoint.

Gabe produced a pair of capsules, popping them between Donny's rubbery lips. Before he could spit them out, a glass of water was in his face, rim at his mouth, tilt, water cascading down chin and throat. He swallowed without intending to, eyes bulging in fear. Poison? No, that would make no sense.

"Diet pills," Gabe said. "To get you up and running."

He lay back a moment, letting his eyes get used to the light. His body accustomed to awakening. Trying to squeeze out a few coherent thoughts, powers of the mind all but fogbound. Mandy's voice, just before the fall that forever changed their lives, protesting the living of lies. How prophetic she had been, touching the infinite before mind and body robbed her of months. And what had those months been but the conception of one lie nourished on the afterbirth of another?

This had all been some sort of grand punishment, watching helplessly as his own creation whirled around, sprouted coils of its own, and tried to choke him.

Had Gabe slept here last night? Very possibly he had. Donny peered up at him as he stood in pale blue pajamas decorated with some red pattern. Nothing left inside himself, Donny realized, not even sufficient residual emotion left to hate Gabe for what he had done. Numb curiosity, more than anything.

"This is Hell, isn't it?" Donny said.

"It's whatever you want it to be." Gabe looking down with tender regret, one of those rare moments in which his demeanor of killer instinct had cracked like a mask. Letting out the look of desperate hope, dead dreams. What goals had Gabe had long ago, Donny wondered, before encountering whatever had warped him into this sad creature who manipulated the world to the dictates of some hidden agenda? "Aren't you supposed to suffer in Hell?"

"Yes . . ."

"I don't see the point of it by then," and Gabe began to slowly unbutton his pajama top, hand descending as Donny noticed the irregularity of the material's red pattern, and then he was slipping the shirt off and Donny shut his eyes hoping he wasn't seeing this, what do you know, something could have an effect on him this morning after all.

Circling Gabe's torso, so tightly they sometimes bit into already scarred flesh, were loops of new barbed wire. Most of the barbs half buried, sitting in thickened clots, and as Donny reopened his eyes he knew he had never even come close to knowing Gabe as he thought he had. He had known a mask. And entrusted it with his entire life.

"Suffering pain leads to redemption. The Hindus believe that, that pain purifies. That's their contribution to a higher truth." Shaking his head in frowning wonder. "I really feel that I've gone as far with it as I can. Almost. This morning will finish it."

"You—you need help," Donny stammered. "You need guidance . . . you need prayers . . ."

"Today *is* my answer to prayers." He lowered his head for a moment, letting it droop, world-weary. Then he looked up with a quivering lower lip, and dear lord, his face looked for all the world as if he were about to make his last good-bye. "You may hate me. You may think I'm wretched. You may think I'm a sham. And maybe you're right. But whatever I've done around here lately, I *didn't* do it for money. I did it to find out the truth. I'm no fraud in that sense. And that puts me way ahead of you."

Donny turtled halfway up in bed, sitting among rumpled covers. His honor smarting as if he had been slapped across the face with the gauntlet of challenge.

"I didn't fake it that first time in Alabama. I healed that boy for real. *I did it for real!* Jimmy McPherson, everybody saw me, I—" Donny bit his lip, would not cry. Voice pinching into a cracked whisper, "You have to believe me—it was *real.*"

"Then that one fluke was the worst thing that ever happened to you," Gabe said with terrible wisdom. "Didn't you once, ever, think of some other possible explanation? *Ever?*" When Donny didn't answer, he went on. "Even the most brilliant among us doesn't use more than twenty percent of the brain. Who knows what abilities were lost inside that other eighty, eighty-five percent? Who knows what gifts we were given once, and lost, because we turned our backs on them. Because our faith went into other things instead of wherever the gift came from."

It forced him to think, to at least entertain this notion. A dormant ability, tapped in an instant of pure crisis; in that moment, his faith in a higher power pure and unmuddied; then lost forever in the labyrinth. Yes, perhaps he had remembered how to bestow the gift of healing. And simple Jimmy McPherson, in that childlike faith of the retarded, had remembered how to accept it.

He thought of stories of young mothers, impelled by love and terror to lift cars from the ground to free their pinned children. Did they expect to repeat the act at will? No; they did not.

For they were wise enough to know better.

"I have lots to show for my life," Donny said, faltering.

"Name one."

The clock ticked, excruciatingly loud. Filling the house, all three floors, a hollow echo. Like a pendulum, heavy, heavy, hangs over thy head. Gabe turned to leave, and no, Donny didn't want to think anymore, let him worry and sort this through later.

Gabe turned, poised in the doorway. "Be on time. *Don't* make me come looking for you." Then, like a guardian who would not hold himself responsible for the consequences of stupidity, "Follow the script, and you'll be okay."

Gone, almost forever, and in some ghastly way his absence now left a kind of void. In prison, even the voice of a jailer is preferable to isolation.

Donny sat in bed for several minutes, and after the stimulants began to seep into his system, he set about the safe routine of making himself presentable for the day. A shave. A chilly shower. Breakfast. Wrapping himself in the trademark white suit, his armor . . . rusted. Energy to burn by now, great. If this was what diet pills did for you, he should get a prescription for them, as well.

When it came time to leave for the chapel, Donny stood at the foot of those fateful stairs, gazed upward. Feeling a pull from the third floor, strong as the sirens' song in the ears of Odysseus. He got three stairs up before deciding against it. There would be no facing her, not this morning. Why, this morning was the biggest jewel of all in his crown of hypocrisy. And while he knew that he could easily ignore it, Mandy no longer could.

So he left, wondering if a reconciliation of differences was even possible once day was done, Gabe was gone, and life and destiny were restored to his own hands.

Probably not, to be perfectly honest.

Because it was *his* show, it had always been so. As it would always be. And regardless, the show must go on.

Paul and Laurel had slept in fitful starts and stops. She left well before dawn, not kissing him, merely sitting on the edge of the bed after putting her clothes on. Stiff, knees pressed together, one intrepid hand resting lightly on his chest. Holding him down? Symbolically, at least. In practice, he could rot the hand away. Oh, she was courageous. Or trusting. Or maybe she just enjoyed a good dare.

"See you at the chapel," she said, voice listless.

"Mm hmm." He watched her leave, wondering vaguely how much more she could stand, knowing she would one day awaken to realize she had met someone who could take her too far, too easily. And was probably too willing to do it.

A day of hideous loneliness loomed on the horizon, and Paul welcomed it as much as he hated the thought of it.

He locked himself into the bathroom shared with the other two, showering before anyone else arose. Tiles and steam, and at his feet the water swirled pink with reconstituted blood. The scabrous crusts on either side of his head took the longest to dissolve. The water was as hot as he could stand, and beneath its fierce spray he tried to cleanse himself of the toxins of heart and mind, send them wafting to the exhaust fan with the steam.

Too little, too late. Swaying over the chasm of breakdown, fingernails alone arresting the plummet.

Paul dressed in his finest gray suit, blue shirt, solid yellow tie. Black shoes buffed to a mellow gleam. Staring at himself in the mirror, this outer man so normal, placid. Shatter the mirror or peel back the veneer, the result would be the same: broken fragments with sharp edges, do not touch.

He made it to the chapel just after six-thirty, reporting through the back entrance. Surprise of surprises, he could no longer just waltz in as if he owned the place. The backstage door was locked, manned by a uniformed guard. Rent-a-cop, no doubt more of Gabe's doing, really carrying precautions too far, wasn't he? Cocky young stud with a belly of authority, he opened up when seeing Paul through the glass, checked his name off a clipboard of admitted personnel. No others need apply, presumably.

Backstage, Paul threaded his way among those who would be before the cameras and those behind them. The corridors were already a beehive, smelling of nerves and hairspray. Soundchecks on the microphones echoed out front. He watched as an usher fretted with a carnation boutonniere, finally rescued by one of the sopranos, her blue robe open over her dress as she positioned it in place. Cheek kisses were exchanged, and they parted, eyes radiant for one another, and weren't they just the most adorable things.

Paul tasted jealousy all the way to the makeup room.

"Uh-oh, we've got some dark circles under those eyes today," said the makeup artist, and she went to work on him with cremes and powders. Fingers strong and cool and pleasant on his face. "You're going to have to quit burning the candle at both ends."

"I haven't even started to burn yet," he said.

She smiled, nodded, blissfully unaware. "That's the spirit."

Gabe was there to meet him when he stepped from the chair, and ushered him into the hallway with one hand at Paul's elbow, this way, please, this way.

"You're really wanting to go ahead with this today," Paul said.

Gabe nodded briskly. "Why not? The equipment's already been bought, it's in place. It's not even that complicated."

"But *I am*," and there was strange comfort to be found in someone who knew what he was, did not care, who could take charge and fearlessly point him in the proper direction.

Paul had actively hated him yesterday afternoon, letting it smolder and smoke until even the hatred burned itself out. Gabe was, after all, telling truths. Hatred was like killing the messenger in times of antiquity for bringing bad news.

"It can't be just our secret anymore. This morning you've got to be bringing in more people," Paul said. "What are you telling *them*?"

"That it's something we're thinking of trying out on Donny—and we're testing it out on you, first, just to see if we get any brain-wave readings. That you volunteered because of your radio background and understood the technology involved."

Paul could say nothing. This guy, he was just fucking incredible, an answer for everything. The truth if it wouldn't hurt, a lie if it was more convenient. Either one interchangeable, equally adept at both. *He could've been lying to me all along, and I would never have known. . . .*

Gabe showed him into one of the dressing rooms that was used only infrequently, where waited a single tech. A tall fellow, blond hair, balding pate, who brandished electrodes and wires from one hand. He was the only one with much to say, another of Gabe's misguided rubes, saying now he'd seen everything, brain waves, what will they think of next. Delicately picking apart Paul's hair, he fit and attached electrodes to scalp with spirit gum. Two near Paul's temples, two near the base of his skull. His hair had grown out a bit since that right-wing cut he'd gotten after first arriving, and it helped conceal both electrodes and wires. The tech arranged endlessly, misting hairspray to hold things in place. The wires converged into a single braid at the center back of Paul's head, trailed down inside his shirt, then fed back out at his waist to connect with a wireless remote unit clipped to his belt beneath his suitcoat. The same principle as used by guitarists who want more onstage freedom than cumbersome cords allow for.

A real piece of work, as he watched in the mirror. All but invisible to close scrutiny. After the thorough spray job, his hair felt like a helmet.

"Okey-doke," said the tech, stepping back to admire his handiwork. "Now we've got to soundcheck you, too. So to speak."

They paced the hallways, out onto the platform, focal point of every seat in the house. Paul standing at center stage, looking over the wedge-shaped sections of empty seats radiating from this hub. Acres of gold carpet, intricate stained glass patterned with scenes of redemption, resurrection, ascension, which all seemed so far beyond him now. Such high hopes for this gift within, and now look at him, a sham even unto himself. Knowing its true nature and still pretending to be some angel of light.

And he'd thought Donny was a fraud.

The tech had Paul switch his belt unit on, then shot a thumbs-up into camera two, which would be seen on the monitor console in the master control room.

"How will they know?" Paul asked.

"Think good thoughts."

So he did, staring straight into the eye of camera two, ignoring its operator, and cable puller Dougie Durbin, who was peering at him as if he were a freak on display. Mutant idiot child, that Dougie, *I don't even think I could fix you.*

Word came down that his signal was being received, brain waves actually being relayed to a receiver, channeled through an amplifier, modulated onto a carrier frequency in the outgoing mix. It boggled the mind, yet Paul found that he no longer cared. Just one more gimmick in Donny Dawson's trick bag.

They parted, Gabe his way, the tech his own, Paul wandering backstage again. All these performers and crew, no idea what walked in their midst. Until he met gray eyes that looked deeper, saw beneath his surface. Laurel glanced up from a folder of sheet music, one hand holding a paper cup. Lemon juice, probably; she maintained it was good for the throat.

Nothing but eye contact for the longest time, as she fought to remain the calm professional, submerging every fear and doubt beneath the exterior shell. Her makeup perfect; hair drawn gently back, then twining past shoulders in loose curls. Her body lost in the shimmering blue robe, elevated by black high heels.

Love and fear, such strange bedfellows.

"You look healthy," he said, thought it faintly amusing. Of course he was good for her; in sucking back the carnal illnesses and injuries, he was likely sifting out all other impurities. Distilling her health into peak form. She could last forever.

"Last night," said Laurel, eyes glassy with the trauma of remembrance, "you made me feel like—like I had *no* control anymore . . . like what I wanted didn't count at all. . . ."

"Oh, I see," Paul staring at her as if for the first time, "you only like surrendering control when it's just fucking pretend, is that it?" Shaking his head in disappointment. "And I thought you were as real as I am."

Laurel shaking her head too, eyes wet with bitterness, no, no, it wasn't that at all, it—

"How'd you like to wake up and know you'll never really have control ever again? How'd you like to walk through the day with *that* on your mind? How'd you like to stand in front of the cameras and know that?" And he could make it happen for her, too, couldn't he? Pass his hand over her face and ravage it with grotesqueries of one breed or another, leave it that way, see how she'd like to clutch that microphone and preen for the masses *then*. . . .

And then he saw with clearer mind what he was doing to her, the dissolution and the crumbling of walls, knowing that his new strain of cruelty was gaining the upper hand again, damn him, and if she was to be spared, then distance was imperative. At least until he could sort it all through once more in the light of yesterday's revelations, and he turned to flee her side—

Welcome to my world.

At forty minutes to showtime, Gabe—clutching a nylon gym bag retrieved from his office—linked up again with Terry Durbin. He had already met with the brothers once this morning, listening with satisfaction to their recitation of all goals explicitly spelled out last night. That, and a weapons check.

Gabe led him into the second-floor master control room, introduced him around to the newer members of the Dawson technical staff. Told him who held what function: director, technical and assistant directors, audio engineer, character generator, lesser engineers. All of which went soaring out of short-term memory in moments, but appearance was everything this morning.

"We're taking Terry around," Gabe said, "showing him how things work behind the scenes. His brother's a cable puller, we're looking to move Terry over here out of the mailroom. I hope nobody objects if he sits in and watches this morning."

General grumbles, no, no objections, even from those who knew precisely how limited his resources were. The assistant director looked to be a woman of some pity and took him under her wing, explaining the functions of the more prominent features on the consoles.

Let her try, bless her heart. Imparting knowledge to him was like trying to fill a silo with a teacup. Gabe used the occasion to duck out and quickstep to the nearest second-floor bathroom, along a string of Sunday school classrooms.

He flipped on the light, locked the door. A room of polished tan tile, smelling of cleansers. He shed his jacket, hung it from a wall peg near the toilet, unzipped the gym bag. Reached in . . .

And fastened snug around his throat a barber shop apron. He reached into the bag for the electric shears, plugged them in beside the sink. Clicked them on and began at his front hairline, buzzing back from his forehead in steady, even strokes. On around his ears, denuding the sides, then buzzing down in back from the crown of his skull. Leaving sink and floor littered with mounting piles of short thick locks.

Gabe looked at himself once he was done, his head a field of brown stubble, as shorn as a Marine recruit. He then wet his head and lathered it with shaving cream, using a twin-track blade to bare it the rest of the way. Rinsed it, patted it dry with a towel, welcoming this new stranger in the mirror with his old face, and that pale shiny skull.

Crowning glory, now gone, it was better this way. To stand before judgment under false pretenses, with vanity, would be a grave risk. He unsnapped the apron, let it fall to the floor.

Shears and razor, shaving cream and hair, he left them littering the bathroom while slipping back into his jacket. No regrets this morning, he had lived life as best he knew how, *I do love you, Paul, and I hope you can see that this morning.*

There could be no greater love than that of one for his deliverer. And where there was no greater love, there could be no greater pain. He would meet it gladly, in grand spectacle, as the instrument of its full release. Gabe had planned well . . .

And was so very very tired.

There was the gratitude, he the one chosen by fate or circumstance, it no longer mattered which, if it ever had. But he wondered why Paul had lain dormant for some twenty-eight years before coming to flower. Reasons could be legion, he supposed. Nergal measuring time differently. Paul's abilities needing time to grow out of infancy, just as he had. Or perhaps he had already delivered victims and never known.

I just want it to be over.

He snatched up the nylon bag and left, a minute later turning all heads when he walked back into the master control room. Doubletakes, eyes wide in puzzled apprehension, a few sputters of startled laughter, what's wrong with this picture? To do him credit, Terry Durbin seemed the least surprised, or perhaps he did not really notice.

"Just a simple object lesson," Gabe said. "We're live this morning, so be alert for surprises."

The right thing to say at the right time, met with laughter of release, and the moment of tension abated. Everybody turning back to their own foci of specialty as Gabe picked up a private line headset and slipped it on. Featherweight headphones, a tiny microphone on a stalk at one side of his mouth. One earpiece carrying all conversation among the crew, the other the program audio. Cueing a vox switch riding his belt let him contribute his own comments to the crew.

"Two minutes," the director said over the PL, and as Gabe looked at monitor four, he eased into a huge smile of gratitude. Camera four was trained on the congregation, and he had never seen such a capacity crowd in the chapel.

He amended earlier thought, there was one regret after all: There would be no way to explain to them all that he had never meant them harm.

Early morning sprint through a woodland purgatory. Mike's leg thumped to its own painful rhythm every step of the way. Leaves slickened from yesterday's rain shifted continually beneath his feet, while stray branches slapped at his face. He tried to light a cigarette on the run, couldn't, and spat the thing out. He held his pistol and walkie-talkie, one in each hand, after finding they jostled too much riding in his waistband.

Breath burned in his chest as he paused for a moment at the edge of the woods, checking Amanda's third-floor window. Curtains wide open, her suggested signal for all clear, so he hobbled across the asphalt drive up to the house. Flung open the front door and nearly fell while crossing the threshold, damn this weak leg anyway. He looked up, saw Amanda sitting on the stairway with her cane, wearing a yellow sweatsuit, hair in a loose ponytail.

"Sorry I'm late," he wheezed. Either cigarettes or running was going to have to go. "But traffic—it's backed up on that road like you wouldn't believe."

She pushed up to stand. "Where's Ramon?"

"We abandoned the car, he went on to the chapel." Mike cleared his throat and limped closer to her. Teeth gritting, he really did need a pain pill but feared it would dull whatever sharpness he had left. "He's going in like part of the audience, it doesn't matter who sees him, nobody knows who he is anyway."

For whatever good it would do, because at this eleventh-hour stage, he still had no idea how to play it out. What a fool's quest he had come on. Then he looked into Amanda's face. Firm and resolute as she stood there, looking calmly into his eyes without blinking, calm confidence. Give it time, that look just might heal his leg; the wrong one in the family had gotten the reputation.

"I know what to do now," then she told him she would explain on the way. No time now, Amanda grabbing his arm, leading him toward the kitchen, out of the house. Her gait was slow, worse than his. Mike and Amanda, the fun couple voted most likely to fall down.

"Couldn't we take one of your cars?" he asked.

"We could if I could find the keys," and he felt the rage in her fingers, that fierce grip. "Donny doesn't *trust* me enough to leave my own car keys where I could get to them, oh, he really wants to make sure I stay a prisoner here."

They were easing each other down the back porch steps when Mike noticed the dogs, the Irish setters poised in their pen like wolves on a moonlit hill. Heads tilted skyward as they howled of mournful desolation, some portent only they could feel. Mike remembered tales of animals behaving strangely before earthquakes, hurricanes, other calamities. The eerie sound prickled the hairs along his arms. Thinking, *People are going to die this morning,* and here was one for the books, suppose Donny wasn't such a callous ass after all, suppose he had left Amanda stranded here for her own safety?

They were on the path leading toward the compound before she spoke again. Trees reaching overhead with gnarled arms.

"It's a live broadcast, no delay. Because Paul knew, Donny had to let everybody here know I was back, he couldn't keep it a secret any longer. But on the show, and the ministry mailers—I think he just ended up ignoring me. I guess he'd keep that up until I was as good as new. So there's a whole audience out there that doesn't even know I'm in this country."

Mike was beginning to catch her drift.

"I don't know what they're planning over there, or even *if* they are," she said, turning to him and smiling with tight sorrow. Perhaps even vindictiveness. "But if I was to walk out onstage and start speaking my mind, you can bet the whole show, the whole *live* show, would come to a standstill."

Master control room, taut with expectations and cool focus, while the machine ground into high gear.

Eight o'clock, straight up.

"Roll intro tape," said the director, and a button was pressed, master monitor filling with a swirling aerial montage of the Dawson chapel to a brassy musical accompaniment of "The Hallelujah Chorus."

"All cameras stand by, twenty-five seconds."

Stopwatch, ticking . . .

"Camera three, hold long shot on the choir. . . . Five, four, three, two, we're live, people."

And Donny Dawson's *Arm of the Apostle Hour* hit the airwaves. For the very last time.

41

Ramon found the designation *chapel* something of a mis-
nomer. The word implied small, intimate. Tiny sanctuaries
for Vegas weddings, barely enough room for required witnesses.

But the congregation in the Dawson chapel, oh man, it had to be
at least four thousand strong. Filling every seat, even bulging into
the aisles, and from where Ramon sat, general frame of mind ran
that Donny Dawson could do no wrong. His one fervent wish, that
once this service was over, his only complaint would be that it had
been time wasted. You could always hope.

Ramon was seated between some vast-waisted grandmotherly
sort and a late-twentyish guy, blown-dry hair and a neat beard. The
grandmother sneaked quick sideways peeks at him, trying to scoot
farther away, but there was only so much of herself she could com-
press into the seat. Lips pursed in probable mistrust of him, this
unfamiliar Latin with combed-back hair and earring and Italian-cut
suit. *Such* open-minded people here in the heartland. Just once he
wanted to waggle a lewd wet tongue at her, see how she would
react. On occasion, stereotypes could be *so* much fun to exploit.

Nerves nibbled at him, manifested in a full bladder. Hell, he was
no good under this kind of pressure anyway. Uncertain waiting,
torture of the worst kind. Sitting rigid throughout the blue-robed
choir's opening, voices ringing sweetly over grand piano and syn-
thesized strings, while Ramon fingered the objects beneath his

jacket and hoped they remained hidden. Automatic pistols and walkie-talkies, hardly standard worship sacraments.

Come on, Mikey, where are you?

Tumultuous applause greeted the choir's final notes as they raised eyes and hands to Heaven. Over the heads of the audience, Ramon saw cameras and operators shifting positions, cable pullers in tow behind them, heading off the potential disaster of a snagged cord. A few beats after the song ended and the choir director bowed aside, Donny Dawson came striding out from a stage entrance by the choir loft. White suit, golden-brown hair, angels walk among us.

"Thank you! Thank you so much!" he called from the pulpit, voice pouring like honey from speakers mounted on walls and high ceiling. "God bless you for coming to His house this morning." More applause, through which he smiled while waiting to continue. "This is truly a landmark day for Dawson Ministries, and it's *your* prayers and *your* love and *your* contributions that have made it happen. . . ."

He prattled on at a nervous clip, and Ramon had seen game-show emcees with more sincerity than this bozo. Dawson's voice tight, arms moving with marionette jerks, *This guy's wired up on something,* and as Ramon glanced about, it became obvious that not a one of these folks noticed. Or if they did, they didn't care. The selective blindness of conformity, now *that* was scary.

And you get what you pay for.

After another minute, the walkie-talkie beneath his jacket chirped with a soft double-beep. Anyone in earshot would dismiss it as a digital watch alarm marking the hour ten minutes late.

But Mike was in the building somewhere. Now all Ramon had to do was sit cool, play out the entire murky scenario by ear. Total improvisation. Sounded so easy in theory.

The organ whispered into a hymn as Donny bowed his head for prayer, congregation following suit. The voice of Big Brother, and they like four thousand condemned wretches lowering their necks onto the chopping block. Ramon peered furtively about, prompted by the cracking of Donny's voice, three times, and even from this far back his cascade of facial sweat was apparent. The blind would think it passion.

Ramon was feeling like a heretic for all the right reasons, surrounded by a suicidal tide who would carry him off the cliff along with them, all these people hooked body and soul on Dawson, getting their Sunday morning fix. Junkies planted in their seats and swaying with transcendence, mouthing hushed mantras along with Donny's brittle prayer. Ramon knew what holiness felt like, and this was not it, this was hero worship, pure and simple. They would live for him, die for him, and God had been left out of the pact entirely.

Alone on a ship of fools.

Reaching the backstage doors of the chapel, an accomplishment of epic proportions. Mike's leg, victim of violation by exertion, bone stress, marrow deep. Amanda badly winded, leaning heavily on her cane. They paused on the back walkway for a moment's rest in the vast shadow of the satellite dish.

"Hanging in there okay?"

Amanda nodded, gulping air. The gentlemanly thing to do, Mike reached to open the door, one of two with glass set in the top halves. View looking in on a wide hallway, deserted and ending in a T-intersection. Neither door would budge.

"They're *never* locked during a service," she said. "Never."

Precautions upon secrets, and if they had one thing on their side, that would be ignorance. Mike frowned, inspecting one door's outer lock, circular keyport a foot above the handle. Then he felt the material of the rawhide jacket he wore. Thick enough. "No problem," he said, turning around and jabbing back with his elbow. Once, again, harder, punching out a corner of the window; glass tinkled inside. He slipped his arm through the hole, groping for the large wingnut-like bolt release. A moment later, they were in.

Mike unclipped the walkie-talkie from his belt, switched it on. Thumbed the code key twice for Ramon's benefit, oh Lucy, I'm home.

"The quickest way to the stage is left," Amanda said. "But there's still a lot of hallways to cover between here and there."

Mike nodded, said fine, watching her out of the corner of his eye as she began to take the lead. Reducing her world to legs and cane, with some distant goal at the end of tenacious vision.

"Can I tell you something personal?" he said.

"Sure."

"I'm admiring the hell out of you right about now," and he thought it odd: all the women back home he had never been able to say that to. The only two had been residents of Oklahoma City, knotted up by the delusions of a self-ordained demigod, trying to free themselves after it was too late. He had already let one pay with her life.

Amanda smiled hesitantly, though obviously pleased, clearly something she needed more of these days, and Mike found himself wanting in some capacity to provide it. Weren't they more alike than he would have thought before meeting her? Both sad visionaries, well-intentioned whores who had hoped to accomplish good through the most sullied of avenues.

She might have been about to say something. Train of thought derailed, however, as they neared the intersecting hallway. For if the uniformed man stepping out in front of them had his way, they would get no farther.

Eyes going from Mike and Amanda to the broken glass, back and forth, he was the very picture of authority Mike hated most. The kind with a job to do, and no amount of reason would penetrate that head.

"Where the *hell* do you think you're going?" he said, hand dropping to a nightstick, and Mike felt grateful this rented dupe's belt held no holster.

"I don't know you," Amanda said firmly, and you had to love her, she was holding her ground. "I'm Mrs. Dawson—"

"Uh huh," he said, too flat to tell whether he was convinced or not. "Even if you *were* on my list, I still wouldn't like that broken window," and he reached out like a traffic cop to shove a halting hand against her chest. Mike didn't like the move at all, put his hand without thinking on the guard's wrist, *wrong move*, because next he was taking a step back to draw the baton while Amanda fell.

Mike had to let her, knew he would be the first target, deemed the aggressor, and tried to beat him to the draw, smashing the walkie-talkie against the guard's ear. Taking a numbing whack in the shoulder while plastic cracked, and Mike swung again, and now plastic fragmented, and the guard was staggered and Mike knocked his hand and sent the club flying.

Mike charged like a linebacker, driving the guard against the corridor wall, how frightfully quick this degeneration from talk to brutality. Desperate realization, this guy was just doing his job as he saw it, and the gun in Mike's waistband was a fearful reminder he would have to force the issue.

The guard went groping in his own pocket, then the hand came out and Mike heard the unmistakable click of a switchblade. Quick glance downward, six-inch stiletto jutting from handle, locked into killing mode, and surely *this* wasn't regulation equipment. The guard floundered his arm around and Mike cried out more in surprise than pain when the blade jabbed deeply into the back of his left upper thigh. Warm wet flow, and the son of a bitch could carve on him all day in this position.

Downswing number two sliced near the same place when Mike backed off just enough to worm his hand between their bodies. Fingers closing on the grip of the Smith and Wesson, flipping his wrist to reverse the barrel's direction before he even knew what he was doing, arms race escalation into madness, not believing his thumb was flicking off the safety or that he was leaning in hard again so their bodies would act as a silencer, jamming muzzle into soft gut just below breastbone, finger twitching once twice, *God forgive me I killed him and I don't know why,* the recoil of the pistol's slide like taking a ball bat in the ribs as the slugs tore the guard's heart from its moorings and exited from his upper back to spray a dripping red fan onto the wall.

Across the corridor, Amanda choked and turned her head away, and a moment later, all three of them were on the floor.

What had this taken, four seconds, five? Watching his moral life change in the twitch of a finger, watching another life extinguish entirely, those dead eyes still staring with such surprise. He groaned and disentangled himself from the guard, crawling back to Amanda and leaving smears on the tiles. Knowing he was old, ancient, remembering a time of a mere broken leg, how by nostalgic comparison its pain seemed positively minor.

"Oh look at you, look at you," Amanda said. By the tone of her voice it was the last advice he wanted to follow. She had him roll onto his stomach so she could get a better look at the pair of back-door stab wounds. His pantleg was soaked down to the knee.

She used her cane to hook the fallen knife, dragged it back within reach. Used it to clumsily slice into her sweatshirt at the shoulder, then ripping away the entire sleeve. She looped it around and over his wounds, and he felt pain as a result of her diminished dexterity.

"*Damn* it! I can't tie a knot!"

"I'll do it." Mike rolled onto his back, reaching toward the sodden mess. She had at least done the hard part; he finished the job.

Once it was tied off, they could only look at each other, silent bewilderment, they scarcely knew whom to trust under this roof. Knowing that someone considered them hindrances, to be dealt with as expendable. That they shared in the death of a security guard, accomplices, and soon, second-guessing could become a way of life. What if they had given talk ten more seconds to work? What if . . . ?

Worst-case scenario. Now they were bad guys too.

"Can you walk?" Amanda asked.

"I think." He began to wrestle himself up, getting his legs beneath him, and the going was easier when Amanda gave him her cane. Satisfied he wouldn't take the gravity express back to the floor, he tucked the warm pistol into his waist again.

Her arm went around his waist and his around her shoulders, leaning together to steady the other, and the first step was a clumsy excuse for anguish. The next few little better. The few after that became tolerable.

Close enough.

Paul found he could coast through the services by rote now, sitting with his mind a world of hurt away. Tuning Donny out, the man's words heard too many times already, most consigned to audio trash, a few cues filed away for snapping back to the here and now.

Paul Handler, welcome to the machine.

Hollow as it happened around him, automatically bowing his head for Donny's prayer, neither hearing nor feeling it. Sitting at stage left from the pulpit, with fellow ushers Ricky and Robby, and a handful of other ministry dignitaries. Suited and pious and so respectable in their tiny little pews before the masses.

If he made himself sick, could he cure it? Or hadn't he tried that route before, somewhere, some day long past—and failed?

Paul shut his eyes beneath his cap of sprayed hair and thin wires, trying not to listen as Donny introduced Laurel Pryce, solo vocalist. She came forward and the music began while Donny took his seat mere feet away, and Paul could smell his acrid sweat as a dog smells fear. Donny's one leg jittering three, maybe four times quicker than the music's tempo.

Her voice captivated all present, thousands of them, perhaps millions more at home, and helpless, Paul raised his head to watch her across at stage right. Blue robe and blond hair and microphone, surely the cameras loved her too. Her song of hope, where there was no greater love, there could be no greater gift.

How could she do it? He remembered that last look in her eyes backstage, like he was ripping her heart out and holding it up before her dimming eyes, daring her to lash back in morbid futility.

Not a sign of it now, though, the consummate schizoid, burying pain beyond sight to show another face entirely.

All for good. For there could be no deceit in music when it came from the heart. He had spent a career listening to the proof.

How could she do that, and make it look so effortless? Maybe, soon, she could teach him.

If only first she would forgive him.

In the control room, Gabe watched the console and licked his lips. Laurel filling the screens of the master monitor and those of cameras two and three. Yes, there was some sort of purity there, it was obvious if you had but eyes to see, and in another life, he might have wanted to better understand it. Stand beside it, let it save him from himself.

No wonder Paul had been drawn. And silently, Gabe thanked her, damned her, for giving him that final yoke of control. She had done this to them all. Quite the unholy ménage à trois they had made.

Gabe checked an oscilloscope above the audio console, sole link to the labyrinths of a Scapegoat's mind. The wonders of a god broken down and digitized into readout, coming through clear as a church bell on a country winter day, how soulless—yet technology *was* the magic of the twentieth century.

Brain waves. Twelve cycles per second, what he liked to think of as the omega wave.

Another regret: He would liked to have had a chance to tell Laurel how truly sorry he was. Even her, and his hand went for the vox switch at his belt as he rose and steadied himself for the final genesis of judgment and deliverance—

And then the script began to deviate in all the wrong ways.

The commotion was first born in the choir loft, for they were the closest to recognize who had just entered. Heads turning, voices buzzing. Amanda's presence alone was enough of a surprise. That one arm was bare and blood-smeared and that she was with a limping man in even worse condition was positively damning, and tongues did wag. The audience lost no time getting in on the act.

"Oh no, oh no," Gabe whispered, wide-eyed, at Mike's monitor image, "not this guy again," and he was not even aware of the violent trembling in his left hand.

The video world, live as it happens, Donny plainly deflating in his chair, going a white the hue of spoiled cheese as his wife walked past him toward the pulpit. The music sputtered to a halt of lurching chords and clunking notes, and Laurel turned at the waist, lowering the microphone from her mouth in deference to its rightful heir. Eight thousand eyes on Amanda and her escort, and even the babble of surprise dried to a hush of nervous expectation as she took the pulpit.

"This is what happens," she said, "when people start believing their own lies," and her voice rang as loud as the peal of doom.

"KILL THE PULPIT MIKE!" Gabe screamed, lunging for the console, no time for the cleansing focus of pain. "KILL THAT PULPIT MIKE!"

The audio man was in a red-faced fluster, hands wavering over microphone sliders while craning his fat neck to see what had happened on the monitors. "Mr. Matthews, I—this—*that's Mrs. Dawson!*"

Gabe's hand had gone into his nylon bag of wonders, coming out anything but empty, and he blew a large chunk out of the audio man's throat. Terry Durbin gave a whoop of excitement—good lord, he'd almost forgotten that imbecile—and Gabe took over the mixing board as the tech keeled out of his seat, if you wanted something done right, you had to do it yourself. He knocked the mike out of commission, but by then, the rest of the staff had fostered grave doubts about the workplace. Gabe waved his own gun, dug out the TEC-9, and tossed it to Terry Durbin in his corner. No mutiny on this ship.

"DON'T YOU EVEN *THINK* ABOUT MOVING!" he cried to the rest, and Terry nodded, that's right. "YOU DO YOUR JOBS OR YOU DIE RIGHT WHERE YOU ARE!"

Omega wave, twenty-six cycles per second, and Gabe whirled for another glance at the monitor, Amanda in the middle of silent confusion over her loss of voice, and this could still be salvaged after all, Gabe ordering at gunpoint a master image from camera one, medium shot on Laurel, and then he cued his vox switch, a message intended solely for one very special ear down below:

"Make us all proud of you, Dougie, your brother and I are watching *now DO IT, and while you're at it kill Mrs. Dawson and that demon she's with.*"

Maybe thirty-five feet from one of the cameras, and Mike saw it coming. This morning was just one surprise after another, overzealous guards and immediate sound loss and now this, some blond gargantuan brute emerging from behind a camera operator after clubbing him unconscious with a gun, his face bright with mad righteous zeal.

The gun was up and pointed elsewhere, and Mike heard it chatter, saw the flash. Identification was quick, a TEC-9, a drug dealer's weapon. He'd seen them before, the manufacturer was headquartered in Miami, supply and demand, the things fired as quickly as you could wiggle your finger, and this line of fire was aimed— where the hell . . . ?

The singer. *The singer.*

She came apart.

His reflexes too slow, or maybe numbed by shock, Mike could do little as the gunner pivoted, spraying wild, now homing in on the pulpit, and Mike felt himself knocked off his feet to go down hard, *I don't believe this, the same fucking leg,* oddly calm in that instant, nothing like a dose of reality to bring you back. He grabbed for Amanda's arm, missed, and they both went to the floor as a sweep of nine-millimeters chewed up the lectern. Splinters raining over them, Mike fumbling for his own pistol. Hearing the groundswell of screaming in the audience, and then it was as if they no longer existed, for the people who now mattered could be counted on one hand.

"Are you okay, are you okay?" he said in Amanda's ear. She nodded, and he understood none of this, knowing only it should stop, but had snowballed beyond all control.

People were diving for cover, people were shrieking, feet had gone to stampede and voices to prayer. This entire chapel stewed into a caldron of pandemonium and panic. Mike reached out from the protection of the pulpit to fire down at the approaching man with the TEC-9, missed of course, felt his tattered heart further shred when he saw that he had hit someone in the congregation.

Paralysis by guilt, he had no business here, a hopeless amateur drowning over his head, and they were going to die. . . .

More gunfire joining the fray, sure why not, the more the merrier, and Mike peered down the length of the chapel's main aisle to see Ramon bulling his way against the current.

"The fuck out of my way!" Ramon yelled, voice very high, and he loosed another shot into the ceiling, and no one argued with him. Even in panic, true believers could convert under fire, and the sound stopped the blond assassin where he stood. Divided attention was more than he looked capable of handling, and then Mike's

Cuban savior was lost amid a swarming knot of people who had no idea which way to flee.

On elbows and knees, Donny crawled behind the pulpit, curled himself over Mandy's prone form, while Mike fought a vertigo plunge of blood loss and swirling consciousness. Donny and Mike looking wordlessly at one another, *He doesn't even know who I am,* and if sweat and facial tics and glassy eyes were any indication, the final frayed strands of this guy's mind were about to pop.

Behind his own pulpit, now there was irony.

Gimme shelter.

Even before the shooting began, Gabe tried to blank all else from concentration. Preparation, meditation; distractions could not be allowed to widen scope from its narrow one-on-one focus.

He paid the monitors a cursory glance. Events below had gone too far for directorial commands. Camera operators going into this, thinking it to be just another show, how blissful those uninitiated lives must be, to live in ignorance. Monitor three was blank. Number four showed an unchanging tilted shoelace-level view across the stage. Camera one roved in wild circles, a swirling carousel close-up of ruination.

But camera two? Static, hold on Laurel Pryce, sprawled across the stage. Red, blond, and blue.

"Go to two and hold," Gabe said softly, jabbing with the gun for emphasis. "And leave it there."

He stripped the headset from his bare scalp, tossed it onto the audio console as the shaking engineer locked camera two's image into the outgoing mix. Rising from his chair, the focus of all eyes, directors and techs over whom he held illimitable dominion, and it meant nothing. They understood nothing.

Terry Durbin stood at open-mouthed, wide-eyed ready, TEC-9 swiveling like a weathervane in high winds. Continually shifting his weight from one foot to the other and back.

"Stay with them," Gabe told him. "Don't let them change a thing."

"That's right, that's right, that's right—"

Lingering in the doorway then, he would never see this room again. The monitors, camera one finally at rest, abandoned, long side view across from stage right, Laurel in foreground and Paul treading slowly across the stage for her, gunshots sounding like nothing so much as innocent little pops, omega wave forty-three cycles per second, Gabe stripping away his suit jacket while on the run and unbuttoning his shirt—

And the time had come to go downstairs.

Holy rolling gunfight at the O.K. Corral, there had been no time for anything but reaction, and Ramon found mercy in that. Swamped, wading upstream against a sea of Dawson devotees. Time only for the burn of adrenaline and the controlled panic that gave an all-crucial edge. Fear breeds survival.

But now he wanted to cry. He really did.

Struggling in the aisle, his travails like trying to walk up the down escalator, clumsy serpentine arms and legs making every step gained the effort of ten, and he could only watch as the blond gunner resumed his terrible mission. Treading steps to the stage, stancing wide over the body of that beautiful singer he had felled . . .

And continuing to fire down into her.

It was slaughter, it was obscene, it was rape of the dead. Rolling crack of gunshots in steady cadence, such cold methodical brutality, and with every single one her body gave another jerk. An arm, a leg, a shoulder, a hip, *twitch* of bludgeoned nerves.

A greater madness still to come, inexplicably, this hulking killer turning back toward an abandoned camera, staring into its lens as if that would provide all the answers that were sorely lacking in a life of impossible questions. Thick-featured face wrenched with confusion and utter incomprehension.

"Her face didn't change!" he bawled in vague accusation. A white trash accent Ramon couldn't help but associate with genetic inferiority. "Her face didn't change a *lick!*"

Ramon lost it entirely, could tolerate this no more, and with no one behind the bloodthirsty imbecile and his bottomless well of bullets, so what if Ramon missed with his first shot, or the second, firing two-handed as people around him cried out anew and shell casings pinged off heads, and by the third shot he had a bead on this asshole, who didn't do a half-bad job of twitching and bleeding himself.

The guy fell hard, and heavy, and with finality. And Ramon rolled his head back with a sob, as the crowd swept him like a tidal wave.

* * *

She was his one way beyond this, the last tenuous grasp on something good and pure in a life gone to bleak despair, Laurel Pryce, dear gift from God . . .

And Paul watched her disintegrate in the passage of a moment.

Eruption of chaos, everything happening so quickly, his mind still trying to assimilate the appearance of Amanda and that guy from last night. Her friend, what kind of friend, was this guy fucking her or what, and then the gunfire and Paul knew himself to be screaming, slumping boneless into the pew while greater cowards around him went on full-alert scramble.

Seeing nothing but Laurel bleeding on the stage, hearing the snowballing avalanche of chaos only secondhand as he slid to the floor, legs gone to rubber as he tried to cross the distance, *Heal her I can heal her,* knowing even as he floundered with punctured equilibrium that he could do no good. She had been dead before she hit the stage and hadn't even had time to look his way for the final glance with dimming eyes.

They had both been robbed.

Knocked back to the floor by a random wild shot from Dougie Durbin, the bullet through his chest like a hammer blow, *ow,* no worry, it would self-correct. Watching from the floor in shock as Dougie stood over her and it *would not end,* this violation, why, WHY? *Oh don't do that to her, it's only more I'll have to fix,* trying to puzzle out motives, then Dougie was screaming nonsense to the camera the control room the world, and then Dougie was dead and Paul could feel no vindication, only disappointment that he had been unable to do the job himself.

Crawling past the pulpit with its pathetic trio, he barely was aware of them—*nasty bleeder, that leg*—and the sudden lack of gunfire became loudly conspicuous by its absence. Plenty of shrieking to fill the gap, though, and he knelt over her.

Laurel.

The Lord giveth, and the Lord taketh away.

But no, Paul couldn't accept that. A God of love would never so savagely take away one so lovely while she was so compellingly singing His praises. Which left only human hands, human hearts, and whatever moved them.

Laurel, so still, so inanimate. He held her hand, and if there had been moments near the end when he had hated her, it was only because he had given her cause to feel the same way. Looking at her bare feet, pantyhose only, blown right out of her shoes. Such small, delicate feet for a woman her height. Holding tight to one hand, with his other trying to plug all the holes, prolific and warm and wet beneath his fingers, remembering last night's twisted fantasy, *If I kill her, could I bring her back again?* He had the answer now, oh yes, and it was just as he had feared.

Paul's soul weeping from a thousand prior cuts, bleeding anew from a thousand more this morning. Bursting like a brain embolism under pressure. And he knew, as very few had been either so privileged or cursed to know, what it was like to fear so much and hurt so much that you emerge through the tunnel of anguish on the other side—to find complete apathy.

Which the old Paul might have found the most frightening thing of all, that he didn't even care about the world anymore.

Within his body, rebellion, a throbbing of lower abdomen, as if flesh and bone, nerve and gristle had begun to run themselves. He doubted he could shut down even if he wanted to. Oscilloscope in the control room going berserk, amplitude and frequency of what Gabe had coined the omega waves nearly blanking out the entire screen. Brain and belly, white-hot burn, and any previous backfire of infliction had been mere prelude to this moment of moments.

Before the eyes of four thousand and the scrutiny of millions at home, he had evolved.

Paul, rising on newly strengthened legs to stand before these minions of weakness and deception, and just look at them all. They had come to see him? They had come to witness miracles? Then miracles they would have. And how he hated them all now, *they* had brought this blasphemy on, with insatiable appetites, heal me, teach me, feed me—parasites and leeches all. Such scorn for these sheep in search of the nearest shepherd of demagoguery. They needed a leader? Then here he was, he would lead them into the grave. He would stand before them and wear a crown of thorns, and sit before them upon a throne of nails.

Exits choked with the fallen and trampled, the sanctuary still held a crowd some twenty-five hundred strong. The first to feel the brunt, because of sheer physical proximity. Wall to wall, front to back, a noticeable wave rippling through the crowd. Men and women and children, stricken where they stood, where they had fallen, where they struggled. No pattern, no reason, this unbiased death skirling through their ranks. Some untouched while neighbors succumbed, immunities and susceptibilities as randomly distributed as ancient memories.

Righteous and unrighteous alike, falling to seats or the floor, feeling the stirring of something vast and dark, which above all *did not belong*. Their hands clawing frantically at clothing while flesh fell victim to decay and ruin. The vicious caress of malignancies, the self-betrayal of somatic breakdowns.

He would teach these to all who hungered for his truth.

Outside, a continent of suffering was made even worse in minuscule increments, a hot spot here, hot spot there, triggered by a flickering pulse of brain wave that found soft tissue and gave it rupture. Green Bay, a woman running in tears from her TV with a sudden case of viral meningitis. Chicago suburb, a jogger brought down like a stag by a pack of neighborhood dogs and torn apart in the middle of his own driveway. New Jersey teenager dripping rabid foam, slaughtering his family at the breakfast table. Toronto zoo animals hurling themselves into glass partitions and cage bars to get at the day's first visitors. Tucson, a man developing emphysema as easily as a cold virus . . .

And Donny Dawson's own back yard, beloved pets, two Irish setters whirling into a snapping frenzy, until each was but a twitching heap of ginger fur.

Lying on the stage over his wife, a final moment of sad pride restored. Becoming Amanda's shield, without hesitation—but too little, too late.

Donny felt the same nauseous stirrings within as did so many of his congregation. The gunfire had ebbed, no danger to her now, so he pushed away from Mandy, rose to his knees beside his pulpit and gazed out over the chapel. A moaning, weeping sickbed of true believers.

His empire was in ashes, this he knew. No amount of verbal footwork and histrionics could fix things now.

Such a damned relief, in its own way, and perhaps, if he was charmed, he might yet reel his discount-price soul back from its destined abyss. It was, after all, the only thing he had left.

He began to feebly shake the nearest shoulder, this stranger whom Amanda had kept from him. Questions and recriminations abounded, who *was* he, but there would be time for that later. Or maybe not. But he was now, at the end of all things trivial and profound, an ally.

* * *

The pain, above all, roused Mike from stupor. Some weak hand jostling his shoulder, same spot the guard had swatted with the billy club, tag you're it, kill me if you can.

Mike's eyes focused from the blur of insensibility, found Donny. The man's face nearly as white as his suit, speaking some babble to him, and Mike pushed his hand aside. No more from this whore of deceit, get the fuck away, and Mike left Amanda to him long enough to look out upon the congregation.

What the . . . ? So many of them out there, suffering from something he could not comprehend, no obvious cause. Malaise of unknown origins, and Ramon was out there, where was Ramon—

Mike spotted him midway up from the back, coming up a right side aisle this time, a path of lesser resistance. Only now his feet trod upon a carpet of the dead, the dying, and what was *happening* in this place? Insanity of the highest caliber—

Paul.

Paul. Standing near the edge of the stage, now lowering to one foot and one knee, to cradle the murdered singer as he might a lost child. A moment of private anguish made public, and somehow this ravaged backdrop of pestilence had to be laid at his feet, it was the only explanation.

Mike felt the weight of the gun in his hand, considered it, lights out for Paul, and then maybe it would not be too late for some. Wishful thinking, though, as he recalled last night, seeing Paul take a head shot and come up laughing. He wanted nothing to do with this guy, this freak, because above all, Mike still wanted to live.

His gaze fell upon something hanging out of Paul's collar, wiring of some sort. Flash, Amanda's sketchy information about Gabe's lunatic plan, patching the guy's head into the outgoing satellite transmission.

Dear God, if it really worked, and who was to say what could and couldn't anymore . . .

He couldn't think it through, such devastation was too huge to comprehend.

"Ramon!" Mike shouted, dragging himself farther out to see if his friend could hear him. *"Ramon!"*

No good, too much distance, too much pandemonium, too little lung power. Mike peered up at the pulpit microphone, dismissed it. The thing had cut out after Amanda's first words. His roving eye lit upon the lavalier microphone clipped to Donny's lapel, and he stumped over and snatched it away with a rip of material.

"RAMON!" he shouted into it, voice rolling from a dozen speakers with razor treble. "KNOCK OUT THE SATELLITE DISH!"

Mike swatted Donny's beseeching hands away once more, crawling back right again to watch as Ramon came running, hundred-yard dash through hell. He looked as if to stop, aid and comfort for that horrid mangle of agony Mike laughably called a leg, and Mike instead waved him on, back, that way, the satellite, I'd do it myself, but look how I've spent *my* morning, and Ramon nodded with the dismal understanding only a friend can share and disappeared through a doorway near the choir loft.

Fresh gunfire, fucking hell, what now? Mike had to see, had to witness everything this morning was throwing at him.

The dead live again, or so it seemed at first glance. Some monstrous impertinence who looked to be a duplicate of the first gunner, coming up from the rear firing blindly, screaming the name *Dougie, Dougie, Dougie*, good lord, how many of these clones *were* there? Such determination about him, eyes front as he stormed for the choir loft, and somehow this guy *knew* who had killed the first assassin, and was taking it very very personally.

Mike fumbled with the Smith and Wesson, dexterity gone with the slippage of his own blood, and then he saw that the thing's slide was locked full open, oh shit oh shit empty clip, and he was groping in his jacket pocket for another one when the sound of heavy feet clomping close closer closest rumbled across the stage and this blond twin with Ramon's scent in his nose gave Mike a swift kick in the head with one booted foot, "I'll be back for you," and was past like a speeding train—

and Mike rolled

and he bled

and then Donny was reaching across to seize him by the collar and point at Amanda. Saying, with breath that stank of the grave, "Please—get her out of here."

Corridors, too many corridors—if he lived through this, Ramon really wanted to find the dickhead who designed the place and give him a rap in the nuts. Running as frantically as a starving rat in a maze, *How the hell do you get OUT of here?*

He rounded one corner while cramming a new clip into his pistol. Caught sight of a choirgirl on the run, moussed hair and blue silken robe billowing as she sprinted down an intersecting hallway. When in doubt, follow the leader.

She galloped along the corridor, around a corner at its end, and Ramon was gaining on her when he realized that footsteps were approaching from behind. Had to be that sporadic gunfire on his tail. Pouring on speed, nearly overtaking the girl as she skidded around another corner into a wider hallway with floor and wall decorated with the blood of some uniformed body lying in the rubble of what must have been one intense little fight.

And at this new corridor's end, twin doors and morning light.

The heavy footsteps from behind were closing fast, and he and the choirgirl were neck and neck when Ramon knew by pure instinct that their pursuer had reached the same hall. He and this girl still ten feet from the double doors, might as well have been a mile, and damned if he would let another of these innocents fall victim.

Ramon spun, veering left to crash into her from behind. One of her high heels snapped and she buckled toward the floor, and he raised his pistol, meet this asshole on his own terms, and *this couldn't be,* he'd already killed this guy once, and that element of surprise was all bozo needed. The TEC-9 opened up while the guy was still on the run.

Bullets missed the choirgirl by a good yard's margin, and she cried out, and Ramon was trying to stagger back to balance when he was hit. Three seconds, four, and his chest and gut were so full of holes he may as well have been a strainer. Impact blowing him off his feet and into the crash bars, doors bursting open as he flew out in a blizzard of flying glass. Misted blood wheezed from the holes in his chest when he slammed backfirst onto the sidewalk, this world at once grown too fuzzy, too red.

Lifting the pistol while rebounding from concrete in a torturous skid, aiming by instinct and hope and faith and the uncanny heightened senses that sometimes descend on those who know they are going to die.

One chance to make this right, one shot. Atonement for a life of too many hesitations? Maybe, and he let it go, his killer's face imploded a second after appearing in the doorway. Never repeat that one even if he'd had thirty years for practice.

As it was, he figured he had maybe thirty seconds.

And it wasn't so bad, really.

Ramon shut off the chaos of the outer world; it no longer applied. Concentrating solely on the enormous looming disk of the satellite uplink, rolling onto his belly, whoa, mistake, wounds and hands and knees alike crunching fragments of glass. *Stained* glass, newly so.

He crawled. And crawled. And crawled. Until he lay gulping down the occasional swallow of his own blood beneath the dish, then rolling onto his back, raising the Smith and Wesson in two shaky hands. Every shot pounding the spikes of numbing torment just that much deeper.

The first ones missed, sailing harmlessly into the sky. He zeroed in by the fifth, and did not let up. Multiple bull's-eyes, emptying the clip into the feed horn, the cylindrical unit suspended by braces before the dish. It sparked, its housing cracked, the thing finally disintegrating into a clatter of metal and plastic that rained down into the dish.

He tossed the gun aside with a weak flip of an aching wrist.

Clouds and sky, and then a face, she was standing over him and looking down. Choirgirl, kneeling beside him as one hand touched his cheek. It seemed only fair that she had a tear to share for him. *It's okay*, he wanted to tell her, but could not, he needed air and had none.

I'm scared, he mouthed. Lips still working. For now.

"It's okay," she said, angel with messy hair.

He'd never shared a moment of intimacy with a woman without knowing her name, without her knowing his. Proud of that.

What a time to start.

The dead and the dying, the whole and the fleeing, they had woven themselves into a shifting tapestry of suffering such as Gabe had never seen. Such mortal terror in those cries, a fear he could never share, for the rapture was his alone.

He traversed over them slowly, without impediment. Forsaking the tidal unpredictability of an aisle passage, instead beginning at the back row and crabbing toward front over a horizontal ladder of seatbacks. Quite the spectacle of painful oddity.

Gabe had shed his clothes on the way down from the master control room. A trail of vest and jacket, slacks and shirt, shoes and socks and underwear, strewn along like a reminder to find his way back upstairs. He had no more need of clothes than of hair; the pubic growth he had shaved away last night. Wearing only his body of scars, still circled by the loops of barbed wire and streaked with the crusted residue of striving for purity.

Inner man, outer man, finally able to merge as one on this day of days. Shedding years of armor and repression with every row that passed beneath him. A crooked path, perhaps, bypassing those who had fallen back to their seats to suffer, or die, he would disturb them not, they at least deserved that much in this hour of communion with inevitability. To mingle with the miasma of their decay was intrusion enough.

But little by little, his progress came to its end, at the front of a sanctuary where he had stood a thousand times before. Standing in the middle, pausing for a moment as he gazed off to one side, toward Paul, that elusive object of desire so far gone into his own realms, he didn't even know Gabe was present.

Such a rare gift to observe him in this unguarded moment, and Gabe bowed his shaven head in adoration.

Raising, then, opening his eyes . . .

And inadvertently turning his head directly into a metallic blow that rattled his teeth to their roots.

Please—get her out of here, Donny's one request, Mike thinking sure, right, maybe he could even stand while he was at it. Still seeing motes of light throbbing after that boot in the head, one eye swelling into a slit mushroom, and when he tried to suggest to Donny they do it together, the guy wasn't there.

Best trick of all.

And then Mike saw: Donny had taken Amanda's quad cane and gone walloping for someone, some*thing,* down before the stage. He stared, one long moment of morbid fascination despite all else, this was too grotesque to be ignored. There was something fundamentally familiar about this mutant naked man . . . a slow dawn, *it was Gabe Matthews,* seen as never before. Mike remembered a Gabe of anal-retentive precision and implosive-explosive dichotomies. But this was a Gabe of raw breakdown, a Gabe of shaved head and lacerations, a Gabe of barbed-wire hair shirt raptures.

Donny's first roundhouse swing of the cane connected neatly with Gabe's jaw, sent him to the floor. Somewhere deep inside Mike, flickers of pity for both of these dismally broken human beings, their own worst enemies. At the same time, he felt the tiniest bit of relief in realizing that Donny Dawson may truly have been ignorant of a lot of things going on around here.

He hauled himself up along the bullet-splintered pulpit as Donny treated Gabe to a second taste of the cane. No longer under fire, now safety in standing—if it could be called that. Amanda struggling up alongside him, symbiotically linked hand to wrist as he pulled, and looked out over seats, aisles, doorways.

God's mercy. This was a holocaust.

Mike was telling her they should get moving, and she was adamant, what of Donny, what of Paul? Mike telling her they were sure to follow soon, and then he buckled with surprised eyes, his leg gone traitor. He and Amanda pressed their sides tightly together, wrapping an arm around each other like a pair of picnic gamers in three-legged relay. Moving for the exit backstage.

Wisdom said don't look back, but he had to when she did not. Final glimpses, images to burn themselves into brain and soul: Gabe taking a tumble down the stage tiers, front and center, Donny staggering in pursuit. And Paul, still holding rag-doll Laurel Pryce as if she were the last link to a sanity long-gone.

It seemed to him she was the luckiest of the four.

Mike and Amanda retraced their path to the exit, hobbling along in a tandem drunken stumble. Sometimes they fell. Sometimes they careened from wall to wall. Sometimes he thought one more step would snap his leg off at the bone, leave it behind, wreckage. Get her out of here? What a laugh, it was the other way around. Amanda, saving the only one who apparently wanted to be saved, and had he not lived to this point, Mike wasn't so sure she wouldn't have stuck around to go down with the ship.

If he was getting her out, it was only by virtue of his own helplessness. Whatever works.

Exit beckoning, doors and daylight, and they crossed the threshold into a new realm of suffering. Ramon. Ramon. Mike stared down a moment, then tried to drop to him, check for pulse, for breath, any sign—but no. There could be no way.

He should stay, this Mike knew. Stay beside the body of his friend and they could rot together, brotherhood of bones, there could be no more fitting punishment for involving him in all this.

But Amanda was there, hanging on to him, and her reserves must have been without limit. Pulling him along sidewalk, then green lawn, words of encouragement and purpose, making sense despite this cocoon of torments and vexation. Guiding them for the nearest building, offices, and production studios.

A walk of a thousand miles.

But they made it into the lobby.

Just as the greatest of all hells broke loose at the chapel.

Lost in a virgin wilderness where ancient meets contemporary and sacrifice meets submission. At one with a lineage whose age defies comprehension, already counting years by the millennia when an infant Christ stretched tiny arms beneath a star.

And somewhere in this soul's vast wasteland of decay, Paul could sense himself trailing out through wires, circuits, airwaves. The empathy, again—once a thing they'd called an air personality, ever sensitive to his audience. Now at one with the suffering masses, the connection a two-way exchange, how bitter this harvest. And he opened his eyes, the here and now.

Donny Dawson Ministries. Last exit for the lost.

Paul took his right arm from around Laurel, strengthened the remaining cradle of his left. Twining fingers through his hair, deeper, penetrating the crust of misted spray, down to wires. And he yanked, ripping out tufts of hair along with electrodes. The wires pulled taut along his spine, and another brutal yank tore them free of the belt unit. He cast them aside like a well-used scourge.

A battered Donny was climbing on hands and knees up the front of the stage, white suit speckled red, face bearing wounds that no amount of makeup could hide. When he drew close, wheezing through gelid lungs, Paul smelled dank breath. A malodor of all things brown and gray; once lush, now withered. His father had smelled much the same during those final weeks.

Donny swayed, then fell smack on his ass, sitting down hard. Shades of their first meeting, some other distant stage. Eyes of glass, he looked at the burden in Paul's arms, while Paul looked into her face. No peace of death there, only a lost surprise struggle against being cheated.

"I'll help you," Donny mumbled. "Carry her. Out."

Stiff-neck slow, Paul shook his head. "Don't you touch her."

And he supposed he should have been more gracious, Donny only wanted to help, to atone. Pathetic futility. Then again, Paul supposed he should have warned the man, too—but with breath like that, to what purpose?

The newest Gabe, the last of all Gabes, coming up behind Donny. Battered under the hands of his former master, shuffling forward and raising arms on high, to bring down the detached head from camera three onto Donny's skull. The single sledgehammer blow so tremendous that both shattered. Donny's body spasmed for a moment with a nervous system gone frenetic, hands clawing carpet, then falling still . . .

Prostrate before the fall of the kingdom.

* * *

Engineer of his own vision of apocalypse, Gabe struggled to his feet, shuffling forward to the lip of the stage's top tier. Where deliverance awaited.

Smiling, and how it hurt to do so, thank you Donny, and this was as it should be. The body, the hateful flesh, heavy with woe. The spirit light, fleet of foot and dancing to its muse of righteous suffering.

There was something imminently liberating in placing the ax in the hands of the headsman.

Gabe stopped. Dropped to knees and kissed that right hand.

Weeping.

Behold.

His maker.

Paul had risen to stand once more, heir apparent to all that still festered in this sanctuary. Having released Laurel, and she lay boneless at his feet like an offering. And he supposed, in a sense, she was.

One of multitudes from this sycophant who knelt before him. Head bared like an ancient priest before his god of savagery. Body scoured of all traces of beauty, replaced with a lonely pastiche of gnarled scars, and adorned with wire. His genitals black and purple, like bruised fruit. And the eyes of a doe, soft tears of trembling supplication.

Paul had never known just how deep Gabe's needs must have gone. Nor how deep his own.

The knowledge was an awakening.

"This was for me," Paul whispered, not quite a question. Vast disbelief shining just over the horizon.

"And . . . for me," said Gabe.

Paul wondered how far back this had gone, when had peers under the tutelage of a charlatan gone the way of deity and disciple? He no longer remembered, the transition so gradual. Or perhaps it had been apparent all along, had he only opened his eyes, blinded so willingly by seduction.

He knew what Gabe wanted. It was written all over his body. It was woven from every life that had been forfeit this morning to push Paul to this brink and beyond. To give him the power, the majesty, the rage and the desire.

He knew what Gabe wanted. Same as they all wanted, one more

piece of him to enrich their own lives, give them meaning, make them complete. . . .

Far be it from him to disappoint.

Paul reached down to wrap one hand around a loop of barbed wire, hauled upward and brought Gabe to his feet. Eye to eye now, one pair narrow, one pair wide. Feeling the burn inside as he placed hands on Gabe's slippery shoulders, if this man hated his own flesh so much, then grant him no more cause to worry, and Gabe began to scream, a high note going up up up, loud, louder, as the outer man began to peel away and hurl aside. Wet red ribbons from limbs, great broad slabs from chest and back, airborne, coiling in flight, dropping to slap the floor like discarded wrappings, or catching along the barbed wire. His scream endless, barely sucking air, going to mad brittle laughter in the end, guttural as throat and head stripped into tatters, and finally Paul let him go, to tumble down the tiers and thud onto the lower floor.

Wet and sticky, entirely red, a man of impressive musculature on display, we are all the same under the skin. Twitching, with rasping breath, still alive; Paul had been very careful about that.

Let *him* know, for a time, at least, what it was like to be cheated.

Paul paced a slow tread down the tiers, leaving Laurel behind and gazing out over his handiwork. Listening to their pitiful sounds, these followers to whom he had laid waste. Thoughts of hell no longer had yesterday's power. Hell? Why, here am I in the midst of it, and I created it in my own image. Surely no God of love could forgive him now.

The masses here had fallen still, no more frantic escape. For all who could get out apparently had.

So much work here to be done.

They were, after all, still his responsibility.

He could walk among them, row after row, along every aisle. Kneeling to each in turn, gathering it all back into himself. He could try, at least. But when would the balance tip, turning benevolence to resentment once more? He would not have it.

Death was not always the cruelest option. Sometimes it was the most merciful thing to be done for someone—because it *was* just another kind of beginning.

Paul considered the mechanisms of healing . . . soaking it in, storing it up. Recalling another locale of mass annihilation, remember the Alamo, healing whom he could as oil tanks raged in a background inferno. *Soaking in, storing up.*

Oh, he still had reserves yet untapped, that he did.

Perhaps death was the highest form of love he could show those in this chapel. He had always believed in euthanasia, another legacy from his father. He had just never considered it in a mass format.

He needed a conduit, of course, and knelt to receive Gabe in one last demonstration of mercy. Gently raising him at the waist as Gabe's lidless eyes roved in mad ecstasy, and Paul hugged him close. Feeling one skinned arm weakly slap along his back, the embrace returned.

Paul, digging deep to find the proper tools inside, *soaking in, storing up, the tanks burning night sky*. The thought of his shadowed mentor coming to mind, something an ancient people had named Nergal. Surely it would have no qualms with him for a while, not with the bounty he was about to deliver.

But its price, oh what a price.

"Choke on them," he whispered, prayer of defiance.

And pulled every trigger.

Gabe went to particle vapor, and the devastation beyond was instantaneous and enormous. Standing at its epicenter, Paul was the eye of the hurricane, and like Samson in the temple, he would bring it all down upon his own head.

The explosion was far too much for the chapel to contain, and the entire building disintegrated into a firestorm of rubble, out of which rose one last great cry of martyrdom, more than one thousand shackled souls losing their chains. Walls crumbled out, great slabs of roof came crashing down in boiling gushers of flame. Debris rocketed outward in all directions and showered down over better than a quarter-mile. The nearest cars in the parking lot went tumbling like toys, gas tanks erupting in sympathetic chain reaction, no sympathy for the stragglers, and every window in every building facing the chapel across the compound imploded in its frame.

The destruction seemed endless.

But, after eternal moments, it too passed, as do wars and famines, plagues and funerals. Until the only sound on this early November morning was the crackle of fire, the only movement the slowly twisting columns of smoke rising from wreckage.

And from the office building's lobby, Mike and Amanda crawled from beneath stray chunks of glass and rubble. Little the worse for their latest wear. Beyond tears, beyond words, beyond thought. But not beyond the simple desperate comfort of holding hands while leaning on each other's shoulders.

So they sat on the steps, and scarcely blinked though their eyes burned with far more than smoke . . . waiting for whomever might arrive to help pick up what few pieces remained.

42

Near midnight, wind as cold as Arctic breath, sifting ash and freezing thought. A construction laborer named Carl Krost let another paper cup of instant go scalding down his throat, wearily thanked the woman at the Red Cross table, and returned to work.

God have mercy.

No one could have lived through this. He had seen no messes such as this since Korea, and it was still too soon.

But hope was a battered survivor, reluctant to die, and the volunteers were still out in force, had been working since late morning, now under the glare of banks of floodlights. Just in case one impossible, fluky set of circumstances had protected someone inside. No one had come up empty-handed, but all had so far been disappointed. There were a lot of bodies. A lot of pieces of bodies. A lot of things that might have been pieces of bodies.

The crew had, for hours, suffered frequent turnover. Because a lot of these workers—guys as tough as cast iron in any other respect —could handle no more than small doses. Sifting through the layers, stripping away debris piece by piece like morbid archaeologists, rescuing nothing but human wreckage. Nightmares aplenty for all concerned for weeks to come. Maybe lifetimes.

A charred crater, and the floodlights made hulking shadows flow from blackened mounds. Carl Krost was tossing aside a burnt timber when he heard someone cough. From *beneath* the rubble.

He should have called out. Should have summoned help. Should have raised the cry that would set off weary, needed celebration, their dogged efforts not in vain after all.

But no. He grew roots, with frozen throat, nearly wet himself for the first time since Korea. After twelve hours of finding nothing but dead ruin, there was something frightfully unnerving about seeing charcoal and ash take shape and form beneath your feet. To extract itself the rest of the way from its prison.

It stood without help. Without need of help. Naked, filthy. Hair matted with grime. And amazingly intact from head to toe. It brushed away pebbles and ash that sifted back down to what by all rights should have been its grave. From the soot-blackened mask of its—his—face, a pair of luminous eyes stared with . . . what? Pleading, maybe. But not for help. No, in that respect he appeared quite self-sufficient.

"Keep your mouth shut, okay?" said the young miracle man. "I just want to be left alone."

Carl nodded, oh yes, because this could *not* be natural.

"Can I have your coat?"

Carl gave it over, and he put it on, still bare below the waist. Then he asked if Carl had money, and Carl wordlessly handed over his wallet, but the guy just helped himself to a pair of twenties, gave the rest back, wallet included, and Carl was more than willing to comply. Let bygones be bygones, with more coffee and rest sorely needed medicine at the moment. Definitely.

Images that would linger forever, he had them to spare. But number one on the list was the sight of the young survivor running away, unnoticed, into the nearest shadows, into darkness.

Alone.

Friday, November 22, 1963/Chicago

Miracles.

That golden moment of glories, when through pain and a rush of expelled fluids, one life becomes two.

That this drama had played itself out in the back of a taxi gave no impetus to diminish its power. God had looked down, God had smiled, and that light of life shone through even on this day of gray rain.

The birth had come quickly, with scarcely a warning; the pain intense, though mercifully brief. And through sweat and tears of relief, she laughed, leaning back in happy exhaustion against the car door. Out on the sidewalk, a crowd had of course gathered. If it happened in Chicago, there were those who would watch.

The driver had done the honors. New World Italian, sire of a large family himself, he had told her in reassurance, this process was no mystery to him. He had been the picture of calm fluster while wrapping the newborn in his own jacket, using a clean handkerchief to swab away most of the birthblood. With the smile of a saint, he laid her child upon her breast—still connected by umbilical, which would wait for proper cutting.

So this was the delightful little stranger who kicked in the still of night, who had made mornings dreadful months back. He barely even cried, blinking instead with wide-eyed wonder. She nuzzled the moist eggshell head to her cheek and gave thanks.

The driver had drawn out of the cab, ushering her husband back in—this family should be together—and he knelt in the stained floorboards. From outside came a burst of spattered applause.

He gazed down upon the fruit of their union, then leaned over and they kissed, deeply, quickly, passionately.

"It's a Paul," she said, still short on breath. "Not a Julie." Her eyebrows lifting then, with the maternal smile; these two most important halves of her life belonged together. "Hold him?"

And with coaxing, with the stiff awkward care only a new father can exhibit, he accepted the bundle. Smiling and cooing at his son—

And oh, *such* a change of temperament, the baby didn't like leaving Mom's breast at all, not this soon, and he let out a wail, yet even that sounded like music. One little arm squirming free of the makeshift jacket bunting. Waving with infantile rage.

One tiny hand coming to rest upon his throat.

His eyes widened, her husband, the father of their child . . . and for a moment, without knowing precisely why, intuition said that something beyond knowing had passed between son and father. And in that instant, she knew fear, something that had no place here, not this day, of all days. . . .

Children were such strange creatures.

All that unformed potential. Open to anything.

He gave the baby back.

And rubbed his belly as if it ached.

V
Redemption

Perfection is this: On seeing a leper, you feel such compassion for him that you would rather bear his sufferings yourself, than that he should.

—Saint Bernadino

43

The aftermath of that first Sunday in November followed a pattern tried and true. Saturation news coverage was immediate, on nearly every TV station, front page, and news magazine cover in the nation. The second wave soon followed, editorial columns and reflections on megalomania and unsatisfactory attempts by people who did not understand the situation to make sense of it. And since no one understood, since a definitive explanation was the most elusive component of the entire matter, theories abounded like weeds in springtime.

Some thought it a terrorist attack, though no group or individual came forth to claim credit. Some thought it an aerial bombing, though that did not explain the final images of the telecast before the satellite uplink was terminated. Others thought a rival evangelist may have commissioned an attack out of jealousy over Donny Dawson's newfound, unprecedented fame. While others, making the inevitable Jim Jones/Jonestown Massacre comparison, thought Donny himself to be the mad architect.

Coverage eventually dwindled, shifting out of the spotlight and steadily further from consciousness and conversational mentions, from headline status to a random paragraph at the bottom of page twenty. Until few spoke of it at all, save to shake their heads and say, "Wasn't *that* awful?" It was old news, with fresher catastrophes pressing to fill the void.

There were those, however, who would not so easily dismiss it—had they understood their connection with it at all. Tens of thousands across the country, as surprised as their doctors at a sudden onset of illness. Sometimes treatable, sometimes not, sometimes stubborn in responding to medication. More patients went into the isolation of quarantine than at any time since the early years of the century and its flu epidemics.

But perhaps the strangest—yet most inevitable—final irony was the underground cult of sorts that sprang from the flames. Entrepreneurs managing to scrounge VCR recordings of the final show, before abrupt termination, with grainy dubs bringing huge prices. Human vultures losing no time in descending upon the actual site itself, and shortly thereafter, the appearance of ads in the backs of less savory publications such as *The National Vanguard*, offering for sale holy relics from the devastated chapel. Ashes, wood and masonry chips. Even genuine fragments of bone rumored to have come from the Arm of the Martyred Apostle himself and possess special healing powers.

In truth, all such bodily fragments—and there were many—had been whisked to forensics labs, then cemeteries. But when there's a market, a chunk of beef or pork bone, artfully charred, will do just as well. And true believers will gladly pay for the delusion.

In death, Donny Dawson had become every bit the commodity he had been in life.

All hail the American way.

As a rule, holidays alone sucked, but these days, a lot of former rules were now exceptions.

Personal mail, for one. He used to read it once, then throw it away. But for the third time in as many days since its arrival, Mike slowly read the letter, replaced it in the envelope, saved it for tomorrow. As if it took daily reassurance to believe that, all things considered, Amanda was getting along all right. Or so she let on. He supposed it could be a false front; when it came to deception by mail, she'd had an opportunity to learn from a master. But he believed, for now. And wondered when she would be well enough to come to south Florida and he could judge the success of recuperation for himself.

Thanksgiving, dinner for one, preferring it that way. Tacos and beer, hardly traditional fare—picture Pilgrims and Indians powering *that* down—though he supposed it wasn't so much the food that was eaten, rather the spirit in which it was swallowed. He trusted he had the right idea this year, where it counted.

The football games had been a constant fixture on the TV, for untold hours, but he did not know who was playing, much less who won, who lost. No bets placed this year, another holiday tradition dies without a whimper. Only newer priorities, newer questions.

Why me? Why did I live? Why not Ramon? No closer to answers than the day after the Dawson Ministries Massacre; catchy moniker, and damn whoever coined it, and every callous pair of lips that spoke it with a smug thrill. *And most of all . . . why were we the ones that laid it all on the line to begin with?*

Why? Ramon might have answered. *Know anybody else we could've talked into it?* As good an answer as any; they had been the ones handy, and to think about it in retrospect was pointless.

But the trouble was, when you had little else but time, to think about it became fodder for obsession-compulsion. And time he had plenty of. For he was jobless, had lost a best friend, needed his own recuperation time, and could no longer engage in those meaningless trysts of rampant hormones that had once occupied so much time and energy.

What else was left but thought?

Money, that too was a worry, though ironically by his own choice. In the weeks since the Massacre, the offers had come pouring in to tell of his part in what had happened. All the major tabloids had come sucking around, and plenty of magazines and electronic media types, and would-be co-writers claiming book deals, all sniffing like hungry mongrels and many waving cash promises in hopes of exclusive rights. And some of those amounts looked rather attractive, the more zeroes the merrier.

But it was money he could not have spent with a clear conscience, that would have swelled his miserable bank account like a fat cyst. He told what he had to, what he chose, to the officials of justice who demanded it, and spoke to no others.

Ah. Then there was the other thing the jackals wanted. Word had gotten out, somehow. Word always does. So Mike hobbled into his kitchen. Plunked a metal bowl onto the stovetop, started a small fire in it. On went the exhaust fan, out went the smoke.

And into the flames went the first of nineteen.

In the gratitude of Thanksgiving, he knew that the attention paid him, however unwanted, was already on a rapid wane. Amanda Dawson had been less fortunate, her life and sorrows given microscopic scrutiny on a national level.

Sometimes she was painted as a prima donna, spoiled hopelessly rotten by years of luxury. Other times as a cunning harridan who controlled her husband as a puppet. Still other portrayals depicted a spineless victim, walled into hiding by a husband and tyrant who fashioned himself a demigod.

If she had even once spoken out in self-defense, Mike was unaware of it. But as one who vehemently avoided the press, it did not surprise him. Maybe she knew what he did, that in the end, people would believe exactly what they wanted. No more, no less.

In which he was no different. But he knew her truth better than anyone, and that all those other assholes had gotten it wrong. And that he could hold that truth close to his own heart, where lie could not taint it, where past could not break it.

Two more pictures went into the bowl, curling brown at the edges, then blackening, falling to ash and powder.

Somebody had learned of the photos he had taken of her in midcoma. Princely sums had been offered. And steadfastly refused.

Two more up in smoke, and he had not felt this purely good about a simple act of selflessness in far too long.

It won't set you free, he thought, hoping she could hear, *but at least it breaks one more chain.*

Amanda had come through her fire, and lived to refuse to talk about it with those who did not count. More power to her. So as he watched the pictures burn, one by one and two by two, Mike knew that, at the very least, she had earned the right to be known for what she now was . . .

Not remembered for what somebody thought she had been.

The widow Dawson, it had such an ugly ring to it. She no longer even wanted the name, and pray God she could better cope with a new one.

As the weeks passed, back home with her parents in Little Rock, Arkansas, Amanda wondered if she hadn't already grieved the loss of her husband even before he had died. She had no experience in knowing how becoming a widow should feel—but this could not be it. Not that she didn't hurt. Not that the pain didn't run all the way to the core—all the things she should have said, all the things never done, all the things they had wanted for each other and forgotten or ignored. These would not go away.

But the overall feeling was more that of hearing that an old and dear friend with whom you have lost touch has died. A friend who has lost touch with you and himself at the same time. Which was the more tragic of the two, she did not yet know.

Since release from the hospital and returning to a private life— plagued by intrusion though it was—she had spent a lot of days pondering the triumvirate that had brought about the massacre that bore her name. Donny. Gabe. Paul. Abuse by organized religion and the church had a long, inglorious history, and each of these three seemed to embody a larger truth Amanda had come to despise.

Donny, so wrapped up in his own gain and glory that he used the church for profit and self-deification. The latest in a long line of those who had earnestly longed to illuminate God, and then, after somehow getting the two of them confused, could illuminate only himself. He could not have done it without the aid of his believers, though, and for this she knew she was as much at fault as anyone.

Next, Gabe, revamping the church into his own personal vehicle for self-definition by destruction. Fundamentally no different from the gilded barbarians of the Crusades and the Inquisition. Gabe had merely updated, and turned it inward.

And, lastly, Paul. Coming along with the purest of motives, only to have them subverted by the others. An innocent with no true grasp of his nature, who might have found a path of truth if only his desperate bid for sanctuary had not led him straight into exploitation. Which happened more than she wanted to consider, only the results were rarely so spectacular.

Surely Paul was its ultimate casualty, and she supposed it was for him she grieved as much as anyone.

If he was even dead.

He should have been, by all rights. Imagination still quaked in awe over the magnitude of the explosion that had leveled the chapel. But doubts lingered. . . .

In mid-November, a man back in Oklahoma City, a volunteer rescue worker from that day, had spoken up because he claimed he could keep silent no longer. Dreams and conscience demanded it. Telling anyone who would listen about a young man who had crawled from beneath tons of debris, naked as the day he was born, then stolen his coat and forty dollars, and run off. Unharmed.

General consensus said this rescuer had been suffering too much stress by midnight. Routinely dismissed as confused, deluded, or by those with more cynicism than charity, as a self-serving publicity hound.

But Amanda hungered to believe, wondering how this samaritan would respond to questions she would liked to have asked. *Did he look like he was trying to carry the weight of two worlds on his own?* she would ask. *Did he have these shy eyes of gentle confusion that could still cut through your soul? Did he look like he didn't completely belong in this world?*

Amanda thought she knew what the answers would be. Hoped would be.

But she possessed far more questions, and they shared her daily life, her bed and table and the air she breathed. What of the future, and why could she not feel nearly so confident of its answers? For her parents' home was a temporary solution at best. Someday soon, her life would be her own again. For the first time in many years.

God alone knew how enormously frightening *that* was.

And while Florida may not have all the answers—or any—it would at least be as sensible a place as any to begin looking.

In the heart of desolation, bad news was still quick to arrive. Gavin Bainbridge knew this, it would always find him.

Late November in the Scottish Highlands, and here, winters were wet. Warmer than might be expected, so far north in the world, but so long as those Gulf Stream winds blew in from the southwest, he would have no complaints.

After all, he got a longer golf season out of it.

Damnable game, this golf. He didn't even truly enjoy it, in, say, the same sense as enjoyment was derived from hearth and fire, book and brandy. But the game was so bloody addicting. Always trying to do better, shave off a few strokes.

Gavin played alone, mornings. Standing on the estate's nine-hole course, sometimes pausing between holes to stare off into the distance. Barren rocky summits, sculpted by age, by the rain of aeons, by glaciers that carved this land when humanity was still a new idea, ripe with potential.

One acquired an appreciation for the passage of time in land such as this. The inveterate patience of an earth whose seasons could be neither rushed nor bargained with. They could only be counted upon to occur, with or without you, to them it made no difference. Of man they took no notice.

He found it easy to imagine this land now, the same as it had been centuries ago, when those early Scots had divided themselves into fierce clans for protection against one another, against the land itself. Clans that were no longer needed, because times had so drastically changed.

Yet meanwhile, The Quorum had continued.

Gabriel Matthews. Gavin had to wonder, could they have been so blind a decade ago, not spotting problems with that fellow? Or had all his passion for truth and his potential been genuine—and been twisted by the years of solitude and deceptions designed to maintain secrecy? Warped by those years the same as centuries change the land. Stable at any one glance, the differences visible only when one is able to compare then and now.

The erosion of the soul.

While The Quorum went on.

Gavin had long ago given himself over to Kantian philosophy that ultimate good came out of doing one's duty, and that the recognition of inconsistency served as a basis for knowing that duty. In his experience, it had melded with all things Quorum remarkably well.

How dreadful, this late in life, to be forced to rethink his very reasons for existence. Wondering if perhaps the world no longer needed Scapegoats and Quorum, that these two minuscule factors of humanity continued on as self-perpetuating anachronisms for the amusement of gods who thought them all fools. Because humanity's evolution had rendered obsolete the spiritual bargain made forty-five centuries past.

A Scapegoat of disease was no longer needed when the power of God was now manifest in a different way. In the granting of a human intellect sufficient to understand the complexities of physiology, chemistry, biology, and the rest. God was eternal, but this did not necessitate He could never change His ways.

And what of the others? Of famine? Given the advancement of agriculture, no society need starve. Ethiopia was more a victim of economics and bureaucracy than drought. And what of war? Perhaps war was needed still, given man's refusal to outgrow it. Hegel had speculated that the end of wars would bring about a stagnation far worse than fighting, that only conflict spurred continuing development—and Gavin feared that was right.

And what of death? That most fundamental mystery, with no

more solid answers known now than at the dawn of civilization. Perhaps there would always exist the need to appease death.

The only problem was—death had a tendency to go by *so* many other names.

44

Rush hour, morning drive time it was called by his erst-while profession. Heavy commuter traffic despite the weather, and he the only pedestrian on the eastbound shoulder of I-70. Solitary figure hunching inside a parka against gusting snow and wind that bit to draw blood. Weighed down with a backpack that looked to be holding every bit its limit. His tennis shoes pitifully inadequate for a late February as cranky and vindic-tive as a bear roused too early from hibernation.

One more weak smudge of color against a world gone white and gray, he stopped for a moment to readjust the weight of his pack. Staring at these fringes of the city proper, enough of those suburbs, and still Paul did not feel as if he were really in St. Louis again. This could be anywhere.

He should know. He'd been there.

There had been a lot of cities, a lot of towns, in the near-four months since he had, like Samson, brought the house down atop his head. All running together into one mental megalopolis. Maybe because of the people, all the same, wherever they were.

At least the ones he was looking for.

Paul had not kept track of how many he had healed since leaving Oklahoma City in smoke and dust and ash. Healers don't count, he had decided when this thing felt new even though it wasn't, but by now his tally must have reached into the thousands. He had wan-dered a winter landscape, grimly accepting the fact that he could not end his own life, and with that the case, he could at least commit to atoning for all sins culminating with the first Sunday of November. Seeking out the national refuse and trying to do one little thing that might give the most hopeless a fighting chance against a life as transient as his own. Soup kitchens and free clinics, back alleys and wretched taverns, the dismal clubhouses of people who hurt, who had given up on life, who were waiting only to die— ofttimes hastening the process.

He had touched so many, he had calluses on his hands as well as within his body.

Paul doubled over in sudden spasm, the weight of the backpack tipping him onto the ground. In a flurry of fresh snow, he tumbled to the bottom of a broad depression. On his back, staring into the heart of the snowstorm, listening to traffic in slush, and he lay convulsing for moments until the seizure passed. Then climbed back to the highway. Snow and ice caking eyebrows, hair, beard. He pushed on.

Living this way was easier when its reasons were defined, re- duced to simple cause-and-effect. And he had explained it to him- self so that it made acceptable sense: He was no longer playing this game by its ancient rules even though he knew them now. Throw- ing the balance further out of whack with every healing he per- formed, while refusing to bow to the other side's demands. A life out of balance, and so the fulcrum suffered greatest of all. And while whatever infernal chessmaster who had tagged him with this in the first place could wrack his body with pain, Paul took crazed satisfaction in believing it did so only because it could no longer touch his soul.

True or not, he took comfort like that wherever it could be found.

While the comforts of nostalgia lay still ahead, a city he had once known and loved. Why he had returned, he could not say, only knowing it seemed right, almost instinctual. So he obeyed.

Trudging onward, against snow and ice and wind, leaving I-70 and walking south until he found a Burger King, deciding to go in for a bite of breakfast. He sorted through a fistful of change scrounged here, panhandled there, coming up with enough for an egg and cheese croissant and orange juice. The first hot thing he had eaten in almost a week.

And he enjoyed it fully, a small fleeting gift. Alone and anony- mous, drawing a few stares of disgust from other patrons who saw only one more roadbum, one more transient who had slipped through society's fingers and was a problem to be solved—by someone else. Such granite eyes no longer hurt; he knew what he looked like. The clothes. The hair that had not been cut since September. The untrimmed beard. All of which needed a good washing, perhaps a good burning.

He slapped his total remaining cash worth onto the tabletop. Thirty-eight cents, not a lot could be done with that. So he earmarked the quarter and looked at a clock visible in the kitchen, found there was still time. At a pay phone near the rest rooms he punched in a number he would never forget, hoping the staff at the other end had not changed since he had left town.

"KGRM request line," and yes, the voice was tenor, familiar, a friendly nectar.

"I've still got this question no one's ever answered. Can you play air guitar in a vacuum?"

Silence, eight seconds, a full ten, save for some musical background bleedthrough. Then, *"Paul?"*

"Who else wonders about things like that?"

A cry of jubilation, "Paul! Holy shit! I thought you were dead, I really did," and then Peter Hargrove's voice broke, and he recovered with a cough, a nervously relieved gale of laughter, men don't cry. Cascade of disbelief, pure celebration. Finally, "Where are you, are you in town?"

"Yeah, I'm out in West County, just came in off I-70." Paul gritting his teeth as another spasm wracked him up one side and down the other. For every joy a thorn, it seemed. He gripped the top of the phone carrel, let himself hang against the wall until the tension pulled him through the worst of the cramps. "I'm, uh . . ." Trailing off, tremors still riding his voice as he tasted the sour tang of pain. ". . . just passing through—and—wanted to see how everybody was doing."

"You don't sound so good, are you feeling okay?"

Paul deep-breathed a moment. Sometimes it helped a bit. "I'm okay. Little touch of the flu is all."

" 'Tis the season. Take care of yourself. So when do we get together, huh? Make it by the station today?"

"I wish I could, I doubt it, not today. Maybe . . . tomorrow?" Lies, lies, but he had no courage to say *never*. Not *that* strong inside yet, and to get past it, he prompted that update on KGRM personnel past and present.

So he listened, Peter Hargrove covering one and all, a case-by-case progression. Who had left, who was still there. Latest rumors, who had affected life changes. And Paul listened with an expression that began as a smile, slowly folding inward, a pained grimace as his eyes slid closed and began the silent spill of tears. Clinging in his beard, slowly leaching toward mouth, until he could taste his mourning of the unattainability of these lives, this life-style. The past, glimpsing memories through the glass darkly, never to be touched anew. Wanting so much to be a part of it again that it felt like a physical weight.

But he dared not visit the station, see Peter, any of them. Cross the line, and the temptation to stay would be too great. For he could not subject them to any possible harm, ever. Because the day would eventually come when his guard would drop, when defenses would be slack, when tempers would flare before he knew it. For passion is de rigueur in the pursuit of radio excellence.

Any risk was too great.

Temper was best contained out here in the desolation, living as the wandering hermit toward the end of the life of the devout Hindu. And the solitude had never seemed quite so overwhelming until hearing this voice he loved. It all came home with an impact to crush the heart.

Until he realized that Peter's update was incomplete.

"What about Lorraine?" he said. "You didn't tell me about Lorraine."

"Yeah. Her." Peter was stalling, he could tell. "Well, things have changed a lot for Lorraine. I mean, it's good for *you*, if you've still got those same old feelings."

Paul gripped the phone harder, knowing he should hang up, hang up now, temptation blooming sweet and deadly.

"She's single again. Lorraine and Craig called it a marriage, and that was that. Things weren't that great back when you were here, you know, and they were trying to have a kid. Well—they found out she's sterile, her ovaries don't work right. You believe it, fertile-looking babe like that? So it was the last straw for Craig. The man wants heirs, blood relatives." Peter made a low noise, from the throat. "I'm not the world's most sensitive guy, I've been told that more than once. But I'll tell you, Paul, I really wanted to take that shitheel's head off for what that did to her."

"She's better off," Paul whispered, leaning heavily against the wall. "Where's she living now?"

"Some apartment in the Central West End."

Nodding to himself, while slowly, quietly, a germ of an idea began to form. Origin unclear, like some ancient desert treasure uncovered by a random breath of wind. And maybe, just maybe, here might be a chance for happiness after all.

"What's the address? Maybe I can surprise her with a visit."

"That's the conqueror spirit. Hang on, let me go check the Rolodex on Sherry's desk." A couple minutes of limbo on hold, then Peter returned with the street and number.

Paul said sure, he knew about where that would be, then wiped eyes and nose with the back of his hand. "Do me a favor? Could you keep quiet about me calling, for now? I'd kind of like it to be a surprise when I show up."

"Too late, I already let it slip to Sherry. She squealed, man, she can't wait to see you again, but maybe I can get her to keep it our secret."

Speaking a little longer, and when the time came to say goodbye, Paul knew it. Each word bringing them to the close of this final conversation twisted the knife that much deeper. Barely keeping voice intact, thinking, *Have a great life. Be happy. One of us ought to be.*

Hanging up the phone felt like the slam of a vault that could never be reopened, and what price to make this pain go away?

He abandoned the warm, soulless Burger King for the outside, tears freezing into a glaze across his cheeks. He walked. Walked. Walked. Until his feet felt like blocks of ice, with more to go.

Such a curse, this need for contact with those who had once helped define his life. Any human contact that would last more than a second, a minute, an hour. Why do this to himself, why do it to them? He had been stronger where his mother was concerned. Always stopping well short any of the hundred times he had thought to pick up the phone, hear her voice, surprise her with his own. Maybe, in the end, he loved her most of all, in his own way. She would already have mourned her son, just as she had, with his help more than half his life ago, mourned her husband. Why raise her hopes for scant minutes, only to turn around and give her cause to mourn his exile from the rest of her life?

Let sleeping dogs lie, let dead sons remain cold.

He made it to Lorraine's new home by early afternoon. On a street of many trees, cars lining the curb, some trapped by levees of plowed snow. It was a big old graystone fortress of a building, with gables and heavy balconies, wonderfully personable architecture that was never seen new anymore. Tall windows grew icicle teeth, and caps of snow crowned every nonvertical surface. It looked very warm and inviting, and he found her apartment on the third floor.

When she answered his leaden knock, Lorraine hung in the doorway with paralysis. The long moment searching for identity, the recognition delayed by beard, but there was no mistaking the eyes. And hers went suddenly misty.

"Oh you," she said with cracking voice, and squeezed him, parka, snow, ice, and all. Through the coat's bulky arms he could feel her quivering. "I thought you were *dead.*"

"Reports of my death were greatly exaggerated," he said, and found that, at least for the moment, he could laugh. Until her searching face crackled through the frozen crust of his beard and sought his mouth. Her own so warm, at once so fierce and tender.

"Get in here. You're a Popsicle," seizing him by the wrist to pull him inside, kicking the door shut.

Paul let his backpack slip to the floor, shrugged his coat off atop it, just in time for another spasm to clench into him, and he joined his things on the rug. And Lorraine was calling his name, dropping to knees beside him, "Are you okay, are you okay?"

He coughed it into submission past ribs that felt reduced to tent stakes. "I just slipped." Lying through a forced smile, nothing wrong here. "Feet are cold, I can't feel them too well."

She got him moved into the living room, and he sagged onto the sofa. She had high ceilings, he'd just known she would from out there, and as he gazed upward, the ceiling seemed to go on forever. A flat cathedral, sanctuary for the hopeless wayfarer.

"Are you hungry? Can I fix you something to eat? Something to drink?" She leaned in across to him, one hand on his leg. Its back looked strong, lightly veined, and he patted it with his own hand, as chilly as a corpse.

"I just want to look at you for a minute." And look he did, drinking in every nuance, every subtlety of curve and fold, everything about her he had missed or forgotten, and whose recall served only to endear her deeper the longer he stared. The untamed golden hair. The face that had lost its tan for winter, but looked equally lovely pale, in a more haunting way. The green eyes. And, beneath corduroy slacks and a cableknit sweater, the smoothly graceful body whose comforts he had known but once. And could never know again.

"I suppose you talked to Peter," she said. "That's how you knew?"

He nodded. His hair and beard had begun to thaw, dripping chilly runoff down his face, onto his neck and hands, into his shirt. "He told me everything. I'm sorry. I'm so, so sorry."

"Yeah, well," trying to flip it all aside with a cavalier laugh, painfully faked. Tombstones were reflected in her eyes, carved with the names of children. "I guess some of us weren't cut out to work with the little teeny people of the world." A wobbly smile, ever so much more honest. "Maybe someday I'll quit coming unglued every time a Pampers commercial comes on TV."

He almost said it, *You can always adopt,* but stopped himself. She would have heard it too often, knowing rationally, yes, that option was always there, the wellspring of nurturing love need not dry— but there would always be some itch left unscratched.

Lorraine was doing some staring of her own. Tombstones reflected in his own eyes? "What did they do to you in that church, Paul? Why did they kill that girl? I saw pictures, I saw film from that morning, and it looked like you holding her at the end, and then again it *didn't,* but I knew it had to be you. *What did they do to you to make you look that way?*"

He shook his head, shivering as more water trickled into his clothing. "It doesn't matter anymore. None of it. The only thing that does matter is that it's behind me. That's all."

She leaned over for a hug, but he gently pushed her back for the moment. Now was not the time. Feeling more tears welling up, forcing them down.

"Did you ever regret your whole life?" he asked in a broken voice. "Ever regret you'd even been born at all?" When he got no answer, only an uncomprehending stare, he went on. "That's where I've been living for a long, long time. I didn't want it to be that way, I . . . just wanted to be so . . . so damned *ordinary.* But . . . the luck of the draw, I guess. You know, it's so terrifying to me how little choice we sometimes have in our lives."

No rebuttals, no questions, just her need, and his own. So at last, he allowed the hug. To wait any longer would be to risk yielding to the temptation of deluding himself that he could live normally. It would be so easy to stay, warm and dry himself, wait for her return from work this evening so they could make love all night, and sleep, and wake up tomorrow and repeat the cycle. So easy.

And so out of the question.

That was not why he had come here.

So he allowed the hug, pulling her close to run his warming hands up beneath her sweater, feeling the bra strap beneath his fingers as he splayed his hands across her bare back. He ran them down the tapered sides to her waist, encircling the firmly rounded muscle. All the better for surefire, no-miss policy, even defective ovaries could not hide from him.

Feeling something quietly snap inside him, a deep sense of wrongdoing, like the willful violation of ancient taboo. And he could have wept, but for joy. Because this healing had been a two-way exchange like none other.

Paul drew back from her, kissed her one last, intense time, bless these lips, these eyes, this heart.

"Where's your bathroom?"

Lorraine pointed down a hallway, then got up to show him, eyes in a wary sideways glance, as if intuitively suspecting something was amiss but unable to put her finger on it. Oh, she was sharp, she would make a fine mother.

He lingered in the doorway, hand on knob to hold himself upright, allowing a few moments of final luxury with the sight of her face. Have to make this one good, make it count . . . for it would be the one to sustain him through an eternity.

And then he shut the door.

Barely in time, door latching as he collapsed to the floor, muscle control like an open drain. Sprawled between the vanity and the tub, Paul stretched himself so he was at least less awkward, and let the tears come once her footsteps sounded down the hall.

Smiling faintly, wondering whom she would love someday, and, having consigned herself to the belief that birth control would never be needed, how she would feel upon leaving the gynecologist's office after a pregnancy test with positive results. A revelation he fervently hoped would be regarded as the happiest of accidents.

Wondering what the child would look like. What it would accomplish. If it would discover a cure for cancer. If it would be the nation's first woman president. Or if it would simply live that life of quiet satisfaction he had found so damnably elusive. All were noble pursuits. He just wished he could watch it grow.

But, where he was going, perhaps he could.

Which was hopeful thinking at its idealistic worst, he knew that. For the next several moments were going to be stupefying in the magnitude and terror of their unknown.

He hoped she could someday forgive him for choosing her bathroom for this. But to die before her eyes was unthinkable.

Strange. In all those he had healed, on his own and through the ministry, before and after, he had not once come up against a case of feminine sterility. Which was much less disease or injury than alternative state of existence. In a small, simple way, maybe he had been saving the best for last.

The coup de grace. Violator of taboo, healer of a barren woman. Let this ancient lineage whose spirit he carried at last die out, without successor.

Paul reached forward, fueled by the flames of unfulfilled dreams he would leave to another, and pressed a hand to her bathroom door. As if Lorraine, on the other side, were doing likewise. Two loves separated by a prison of divergent lives.

"I'll leave a light burning for you," he whispered. "But don't hurry."

Strange, too, to think that after the self-inflicted violence by gun and blade, attempted starvation, subzero cold and worse, that the goal he had sought all along would be achieved by the restoration to bring new life.

Bittersweet was a flavor he could live with. Die with.

But its price, oh what a price . . .

He considered it a bargain.

DISCOVER THE TRUE MEANING OF HORROR...  ABYSS

- ☐ **THE CIPHER by Kathe Koja**   20782-7 .... $4.50
- ☐ **NIGHTLIFE by Brian Hodge**   20754-1 .... $4.50
- ☐ **DUSK by Ron Dee**   20709-6 .... $4.50
- ☐ **SPECTERS by J. M. Dillard**   20758-4 .... $4.50
- ☐ **PRODIGAL by Melanie Tem**   20815-7 .... $4.50
- ☐ **OBSESSED by Rick Reed**   20855-6 .... $4.50
- ☐ **TOPLIN by Michael McDowell**   20886-6 .... $4.50
- ☐ **MASTERY by Kelley Wilde**   20727-4 .... $4.50
- ☐ **DESCENT by Ron Dee**   20708-8 .... $4.50
- ☐ **TUNNELVISION**
     by R. Patrick Gates   21090-9 .... $4.50
- ☐ **SHADOW TWIN by Dale Hoover**   21087-9 .... $4.50
- ☐ **POST MORTEM**
     by Paul Olsen & David Silva   20792-4 .... $4.50
- ☐ **THE ORPHEUS PROCESS**
     by Daniel H. Gower   21143-3 .... $4.99
- ☐ **WHIPPING BOY by John Byrne**   21171-9 .... $4.99
- ☐ **BAD BRAINS by Kathe Koja**   21114-X $4.99
- ☐ **LOST FUTURES by Lisa Tuttle**   21201-4 .... $4.99
- ☐ **DEATHGRIP by Brian Hodge**   21112-3 .... $4.99

At your local bookstore or use this handy page for ordering:

DELL READERS SERVICE, DEPT. DAB
2451 South Wolf Road, Des Plaines, IL 60018

Please send me the above title(s). I am enclosing $ _____ .
(Please add $2.50 per order to cover shipping and handling). Send
check or money order—no cash or C.O.D.s please.

Ms./Mrs./Mr. _____

Address _____

City/State _____ Zip _____

DAB–6/92

Prices and availability subject to change without notice. Please allow four to six weeks for delivery.